Praise for Shadowbridge

"A tough-minded novel that confronts some disturbing issues, and that is remarkably efficient in the telling, it also achieves a kind of Florentine grace and balance rare in modern fantasy, interpolating tales within tales, playing ingenious games with point of view, and offering more than a few passages of surpassingly lovely prose...For all its painterly beauty, *Shadowbridge* is a tough-minded novel that confronts some disturbing issues, and that is remarkably efficient in the telling. Frost could be on his way toward a masterpiece."

—Gary K. Wolfe, *Locus Looks at Books*

"Frost (*Fitcher's Brides*) draws richly detailed human characters and em-bellishes his multilayered stories with intriguing creatures—benevolent sea dragons, trickster foxes, death-eating snakes and capricious gods—that make this fantasy a sparkling gem of mythic invention and wonder."

—*Publishers Weekly*

"One of fantasy's most challenging thinkers, who also knows how to tell a top-notch story."

—Karen Traviss, New York Times bestselling author of *City of Pearl*

"The prose has an exotic, even ethereal feel."

—San Diego Union-Tribune

"I particularly enjoyed how the legends and stories of *Shadowbridge*, which are vitally important to the book, weaved together and even overlapped with the plot. Leodora and her small troupe are absolutely wonderful, *Shadowbridge* is fantastic."

—Experiments in Reading review

"*Shadowbridge* is a compelling work...emphatically not for the faint of heart."

—Faren Miller, *Locus*

"One of the best reads of the year."

—Jay Tomio, Fantasy BookSpot

"Leodora's journey is filled with the brilliant details of Frost's masterful world building. . . .[He] has created a world containing all manner of fantastic story and the promise of a fascinating history as Leodora moves into her destiny and the unknown future."

—Regina Schroeder, *Booklist* (starred review)

"[O]ne of the best fantasies of the year."

—Paula Guran, https://www.darkfantasy.org

"Frost immediately pulls the reader into a world of stories within stories with the tale of Leodora."

—BookPage

A *Romantic Times* Reader's Choice Award nominee (2008).

SHADOWBRIDGE

Also by Gregory Frost

From Book View Café

The TÁIN duology:

Táin
Remscela

The Girlfriends of Dorian Gray & Other Stories (originally: *Attack of the Jazz Giants & Other Stories*)

Elsewhere

Fitcher's Brides (Tor)

The RHYMER trilogy (Baen):

Rhymer
Rhymer: Hoode
Rhymer: Hel

Beyond Here Be Monsters (Fairwood Press)
The Secret House (JournalStone)

Shadowbridge

Gregory Frost

BOOK VIEW CAFE

Book View Café

SHADOWBRIDGE

ISBN: 978-1-63632-423-4

Publication history:
Del Rey Books 2007
Book View Café second edition 2026

Book View Café
304 S. Jones Blvd. Suite #2906
Las Vegas NV 89107

www.bookviewcafe.com

Dedication

For every disobedient heroine

Part 1:
Leodora

Chapter 1
Conferring With Gods

The first time Leodora spoke to a god, she had climbed to the top of a bridge tower and she was masked.

It was late in her third day on the span called Vijganar, a broad segment on one of the infinite bridges that uncoil across the oceans of Shadowbridge. She went there before her performance as the mysterious puppeteer known as Jax, to withdraw, to be herself awhile, and to answer to no one.

The towers—there were three supporting Vijganar—were like great flat-topped and frieze-covered behemoths looming above the buildings and creatures on the surface that threaded the distance between them. Leodora climbed up the outside of the western pylon, going up the rungs hand over hand. To either side of her, statues of avatars and demons, monsters and heroes hung out from the corners to stare at each other, so that the climber between them could not help sensing the painted eyes that seemed to watch her hooded figure as it ascended. Most of their identities, along with their stories, were unknown to her. Like any span of Shadowbridge, Vijganar had its own gods and tales, and she hadn't been here long enough to collect many of the stories; but she did recognize some of the elements: the talaria that sprouted from one figure's ankles, the gnarled knobkerrie brandished by another. These things described and adorned gods and heroes she'd heard of, whose tales she knew from elsewhere—some from the three other spans she'd traveled before this. Other objects confounded her, and she hung awhile between sky and sea, trying to guess what purpose they served. One of the figures, in a long coat, leaned around from the back edge and held up a disk as if about to hand it to her. It looked like a shell strung on a necklace that, instead of circling his throat, plugged into his ears. What could that possibly be? And what legend could it be from? The next figure above him didn't help her, either. Painted black, with spiked blue hair, sharp-tipped ears, and red eyes like flames, the figure's identity eluded her, too.

She climbed on.

At the top, she reached up and, finding gouged handholds, curled her fingers into them and pulled herself over the top. Her blue shadow stretched before her. She lay awhile against the cool stone to catch her breath, staring down the length of the walkway that ran to the far side of the tower. Finally, she gathered herself up and knelt on one knee.

On both sides of the walkway stood more statues, figures larger than life, two rows of them hedging it all the way to the far side of the span, where presumably there were other rungs down the opposite pylon. The statues were positioned, as gods should be, overlooking the buildings and beings of Vijganar. She wondered if the gods of enigmatic Edgeworld had cast them when they made this span or if the inhabitants of Vijganar had chiseled them. The nearest ones looked to have been brightly painted once upon a time long ago. The colors had all but faded away.

Leodora got to her feet. The walkway was deserted. Unlike on the span of Phosphoros, where other people frequented the tops of the supporting towers, she was alone here. She pushed back the hood of her tunic and, reaching behind her, undid the ribbons of the domino mask that covered her head to the nose, and drew the mask away. She sighed as if all of her tension had been bound up in the disguise, as perhaps it had. The thick braid of her red hair unfurled from inside her hood.

Turning about, she beheld the world.

The sun hung like a spectacular gong behind thin clouds on the horizon, not quite ready to relinquish the sky to the two deformed moons of Saphon and Gyjio. They were creeping up into the eastern sky behind her like two furtive eyes while the sun's dusking light spread molten gold across the sea and painted every spire and minaret with its fire.

This was the hour when sacrifices were performed and spells cast and oracles consulted; the time when light and darkness split the world down below, and one could seek for glimpses of each in the other.

The dying evening wind plucked at her loose clothes, the breeze sliding up her sleeves and dancing around her torso, billowing her tunic like a sail. It reminded her of a moment in the story of how Death came into the world.

She leaned over and looked down the way she had climbed.

In the ocean below, the shadowy shapes of large fish clustered around the immense pier at the base of the pylon, there to breed in the warm, buoyant water. On many spans fishing off a pierside was a popular pastime, but not on Vijganar, where the people held many fish to be sacred, some by decree. No one's line dangled in among the fish she saw.

The notion of fishing drew forth unpleasant memories. For most of her life Leodora had viewed Shadowbridge only from below one straight and decrepit span, called Ningle; it was somewhere off to the east, over the horizon, part of another bridge. Almost as an act of defiance now, she climbed the tower heights of spans to look upon the world as though it might be something she could possess. As if she reigned with the lined-up avatars in a sky palace somewhere even higher.

In the sun fire, she glowed like a burnished goddess—a goddess of Edgeworld, surveying the whole of Shadowbridge from beyond the moons. She would have climbed through the clouds themselves if there had been a ladder so tall.

She ran a hand over the top of her head, caught the leather strip binding her braid and gave it a tug. Her hair fanned out across her neck and shoulders—hair as copper and shining as the sunlight upon the sea. She shook it, luxuriating in the freedom. Here, at this height, she was unrestrained.

Stepping back, she turned and strolled a ways between the stone figures. There to the right was one that might have been Chilingana, one of whose stories she would be performing tonight. Glancing left, she spied a figure of certain identity—the demigod Shumyzin, recognizable by the tusks protruding from his mouth. He faced west and brandished a shield and short sword to hold off a clawing gorgon whose snarling face promised death. The swollen sun gave color to Shumyzin's terrible pop-eyed and unpainted features. Almost health. She sauntered over to him and ran her hand along the edge of his shield, then crouched on the balls of her feet and peered from beneath it down upon the span itself.

Far below, hundreds of people milled about in the lanes and crooked byroads. She regarded the onion domes of spires finished in gold filigree, the sloping roofs of simple houses cast in darkness beneath them, and colorful tower cupolas, no two the same shade. In one slender nearby minaret, a servant carried a torch from level to level, lighting candles and oil lamps, kindling globes of fairy light in window after window, creating a steadily rising spiral of candescent jewels.

Open fires lit Kalian Esplanade, one of the two main thoroughfares. The first torchbearers had emerged to look for work—for couples and parties they could escort from place to place. There was good money to be made by a well-spoken and knowledgeable torchbearer. Theirs and other lights coruscated the length of the span, all the way to the northernmost support tower of Vijganar. The salmon sunlight also bathed the flat-topped heights of that terminus. She espied the edge of the next span beyond it, curving out from behind that tower and dwindling into the darkness of the northern sea.

A goddess's peace settled upon her as she contemplated her temporary domain. "This is where I belong," she said. And it was true, and she had always known it. Never again would she live beneath the endless spans of the bridge of life, watching but separate and unwelcome. She was going to be forever of the life, immersed.

The breeze whispered across her face, suddenly cool. She glanced up.

The statue of Shumyzin was staring down at her over the rim of the shield with furious eyes. "Hai," said the statue as if in agreement.

Leodora skittered back from beneath him.

The head of the statue tracked her over its shoulder. Shumyzin didn't look like a statue anymore. His skin was bluish beneath the sun's glow. His huge eyes glistened white with pinprick pupils. Around his tusks he was smiling. His golden armor gleamed.

"Who are you?" she asked, the only question she could think to ask.

"You don't know? I thought sure you did." His voice was a growl, as if gravel slid roughly inside his lungs.

"I—" She dared to look away from him. "Statues can't talk."

"But gods can."

"But a statue isn't—" she began, but gave up. Even she recognized her impertinence.

"—isn't a god?" he finished. "And I suppose that a traveling storyteller posturing over a city should be? Especially when that city might eject her if it knew she was a woman." He pointed his bronze sword at her.

She shook her head. Had he somehow read her thoughts? She tried to gauge whether she could get to the end of the tower and reach the rungs before he caught her.

"If you're so certain of your divinity," he said, "show me what you do. Tell me my story."

"Tell?"

"That is what you do, isn't it?" He looked at himself, at his colorless feet where encroaching night had cut off the sunlight. "And you had better be quick, too, or I'll be stone again and it won't count for anything."

She goggled at him, unable to think.

"So, it was just empty talk, then," Shumyzin derided her. "A child's whimsy. A true god would know another god's story. They know all the stories that are."

Her jaw set defiantly. She didn't like being taunted, not by anyone. She knew his tale, all right. Soter had taught it to her five years ago, when she was eleven.

"Well?" challenged the demigod.

Leodora drew a deep breath and recited.

≈ The Tale of Shumyzin ≈

Shumyzin was the great conquering hero of that ancient span of Mankandikha. But if he hadn't learned to conquer fear and anger first, no one today would know his name.

As a child Shumyzin bore many insults. He was an object of scorn from adults as well as other children because of the crooked teeth that jutted from the corners of his mouth. He had no tusks then, only two big deformed and protruding molars. With his round eyes and thrust-out jaw, he looked more amphibian than human. One day the king of Mankandikha spotted him in the main street. He halted his palanquin to get a good look at the boy. A crowd gathered around. They heard the king give Shumyzin a cruel nickname: a nickname that followed him everywhere thereafter.

"Frog," proclaimed the king.

Shumyzin ran home in tears. The name chased him through the narrow streets. It followed him like a tail.

His mother was a mortal. Her name was Yemin. She said to him, "Don't listen to them, little one. They know nothing about you." She stroked his cheek. "Your father, the great god Gopurbh, weathered many insults, too, before he was given charge of all the winds. We have balmy days most of the time because he's so hard to anger. You also are made for greatness if only you can learn to withstand their insults. I know this, because I'm your mother." He let her voice and her promises soothe his troubled soul, and soon he fell asleep in her arms.

Now, everyone else claimed that Shumyzin's father had been a local rich man's son, Cabor the Drunk, who'd climbed into the wrong house one night and cruelly forced himself upon Yemin; afterward—the story went—Cabor's father paid her a tidy sum to keep quiet about his idiot son's indiscretion. Both she and the elder Cabor strenuously denied that such an incident had ever occurred. It was the drunken lout, Cabor himself, who spread the story. One time when the ugly child passed by, Cabor abruptly proclaimed, "That's my bastard there. Look how he turned out!" The story spread quickly. People called Frog's mother a whore. The boy seethed with the desire to kill them for it. But she wouldn't let him. "I can bear their lies," she said, "and so must you."

He didn't look like Cabor. He didn't look like his mother. Or like anyone else in the entire city. Yet people often prefer scandals and gossip to rational thinking, and so the story became fact.

Frog grew up strong and steady. Unflappable. He weathered the worst taunts he could ever hear. The cruel jibes at his mother were the most awful, the hardest to bear. He worked daily for her, pushing a great grinding wheel that crushed grain into flour for bread. Yemin baked and sold the bread. Over time her son's shoulders became striped with muscles, and his back grew wide. As he grew older, his grotesque visage changed, too. His eyes bulged more than ever and his twisted teeth straight-ened, forming two small vicious spikes, as if all his suppressed anger had taken form in the corners of his mouth. He became terrifying to see, and although he did nothing to suggest hostility, the taunting of him stopped.

Then one day the span was invaded by a demon army. Of

all the citizens, Shumyzin alone didn't panic. Nor did he try to flee.

All those who did try to escape were cut down or rounded up to be slain later. The king who'd once made fun of Frog tried to bargain with the demons. They stripped and paraded him before his people to destroy the will of Mankandikha. His money and property were taken from him. The leader of the demonic army rode around in the king's fine palanquin, forcing eight naked women to carry it. They were whipped if the carriage went too slowly; and sometimes they were whipped anyway.

While all of this was happening, the avatar of Gopurbh appeared to Shumyzin in his mother's house, cloaking them both in mist, so that not even Yemin knew he'd appeared. The avatar said, "This is your day, and I am your father. Here are the means to defeat the fiends." The clever god gave his son a fine scimitar and shield, and golden armor.

Once Shumyzin had put the armor on, his father told him, "You can't be harmed today, nor seen in that armor by your enemies."

When the demon soldiers reached the street where Shumyzin and his mother lived, the smell of her bread enticed them. They entered the shop, intending to steal its goods. They saw only Yemin at her oven, unarmed and helpless. They drew their swords to kill her.

Not one of them left the bakery alive.

Like a wave of heat Shumyzin slipped unseen through the enemy's midst, slaughtering them one after the other. With each he killed, his tusks grew larger.

Demons on the streets suddenly clutched at themselves and doubled over, spilling their life into the dust. Their limbs dropped off, their legs were slashed out from under them. The survivors fled in terror from the lethal phantom. They knocked over their leader's stolen palanquin, smashing it as they clambered over the sides, kicking their king in their haste to get away. The whipped maidens scattered before them, shrieking.

When the demon king pushed himself out the window, Shumyzin glided invisibly over and cut off his head. Then he ran through the streets, shaking the gory trophy at the enemy. All they saw was the gaping, dripping head itself floating upon the air. Some of them jumped to their deaths in the sea. Others raced to put a thousand spans between them and that phantom.

They heard a raw voice shout after them: "Tell everyone that Shumyzin, son of Gopurbh and Yemin, guards this place, and will take all your heads if you come back again."

After that, Shumyzin's heroic deeds fell upon the span like drops of monsoon rain. He became a legend, the defender of his city, the slayer of a thousand foes. Grateful for his protection, the citizens rejected their king—the same one who had belittled Shumyzin years earlier—when he tried to take back his office. They placed Shumyzin on the throne in his place. The hero proved to be a generous ruler. He married the maiden, Kyai, daughter of the sun. Although they'd humiliated him for so long, he exacted no penalty from the people . . . save for one episode.

One afternoon he was alerted that Cabor the Drunk was causing trouble. He found Cabor in a narrow side street. The new king's self-proclaimed father was whipping a dwarf with a bamboo rod. Beside him lay a maiden whom he'd beaten unconscious. Shumyzin flung Cabor against a wall hard enough to knock him senseless. He had his soldiers arrest the villain, and for a week exhibited him in a cage hanging outside his own house. He confiscated all of Cabor's property and wealth and gave it to the two people who'd been harmed. When the week was up, Shumyzin cut off Cabor's nose and ears, and threw him out of the city, off the span.

Thus did the hero save Mankandikha and exact retribution on the cruel Cabor.

"And that is the tale of how Shumyzin the Sufferer, once called 'Frog,' gained renown, but not how he and Kyai found bliss, which is another tale altogether." She concluded with the traditional ending, the promise of the next story, spontaneously. She had become so caught up by it that she'd forgotten herself. Her hands were extended, fingers pressing together, as if she'd been maneuvering her puppets. She supposed that she had. Self-consciously, she glanced at the demigod. He had tears on his cheeks.

He said, "I haven't heard my beautiful Kyai mentioned in a very long time."

"It's better with puppets," she responded, and when he growled she thought she'd angered him, but realized after a moment that the gravelly rumble was laughter.

He said, "Ah, Leodora. You tell the world of your genius but you doubt it to yourself."

"You know my name."

"I'm a god, girl. I have to do something to warrant it besides killing a few mouth-breathing Jatos. Add that to your tale when you speak of those demons: Jatos is what they were, straight out of a sewer."

She took note of the name, but was more curious about something else. "You haven't heard your wife's name in a long time? Isn't she with you?" Even as she spoke she sought among the eikons for the figure of Kyai. The goddess was not represented in the statues nearby.

Shumyzin replied, "Death doesn't work like that. You tell the stories—I know you know about Death, Jax." When she looked surprised, he added, "Just as I know the identity you travel under." He made to shake his head, and a look of alarm strained his features. He glanced down at his torso. The shadow of night had reached his collarbone. "Quick now, Leodora, come here. I must tell you something."

She got to her feet and took a reluctant step toward the frightening god.

"Closer!" he snapped.

She edged nearer.

"Listen," said Shumyzin. "I know the one you travel with. We're old acquaintances, he and I."

"Soter?" she asked.

"Pah! Not the lush. The other one. The deathless one. The one who visits you in your sleep."

She stared at him in awe.

The tiny black pupils fixed her. "I know the riddle of your coral friend." The shadows touched his throat, and his voice shrank to a whisper. "And a warning. Jax rattles the darkness where he travels. A piece of it is sure to come calling." His neck was now in shadow. His intense goggle-eyes regarded her in a way that imparted both his regard and his great concern for her. She had to look away from such intensity. He wheezed, "One more thing, and the most important." He fell silent abruptly, and that drew her gaze to him again. Shumyzin's head had turned back into stone. He faced the gorgon, a statue, as she had found him. She realized that a purple cloud now masked the sun.

"The most important thing," she muttered.

For an eternity she stared at the streaks of water on the polished cheeks—the only evidence to convince her that she hadn't dreamt the conversation with him. She waited, hesitant, hopeful, but when the cloud passed and the dying sunlight touched him again, he did not return to life.

The overhead sky, a crepuscular blue, now twinkled with stars as if it were an inverted sea reflecting the lights of Vijganar. Before the dusk disappeared altogether she must make the climb back to the ground. She hastily rebraided her hair, curled the braid around her fist, and then tied it up and stuffed it inside the collar of her tunic. She pulled the hood up on the back of her head. Across the horizon, only a magenta swath remained, as if the sun had bled out upon the sky.

She turned and knelt, placing her fingers in the handholds. With her left foot she felt for the first of the rungs carved in the side of the bridge, then pushed herself over the edge. At the last moment, she gave a final glance up, but Shumyzin remained gray and still.

The way down she took much more slowly and carefully than she had climbing up.

By the time she reached the pier, night owned the sky. All illumination now came from torches and lamps and the crescent of bold Saphon shining over the massive tower. Gyjio still hid behind it.

She easily replaced her mask as she circled the pier and then set off along the street paralleling the tower wall.

People paid her no mind. No one could tell that she among them all had just conversed with a god.

She was going to be late, but she didn't care. She picked an outdoor cafe and sat down, her legs gone weak. The aftershock had caught up with her—the stupefaction of what had happened on the bridge. She tried to dismiss its effect upon her, telling herself that since she hadn't eaten since morning, this was just hunger making her feeble.

She had ample money to pay for a feast, but asked only for a single dish of strongly spiced scallops and vegetables stewed over kelp, and some fermented rice wine to steady her nerves. She sat quietly awhile, watching people pass by, sipping her wine. It tingled in her belly, its sizzle reaching to her fingers. Her awe receded, the way the impact of a dream steadily recedes once one awakens.

Shumyzin had been ready to tell her something important. Maybe she could come back tomorrow . . . although somehow she suspected he would not manifest again, whether the sun fell upon him or not. The rules of things known and unknown were in play, and though she was incognizant of them, she sensed that what he had been about to say fell into the category of things that could not be known until their time.

Her food arrived, and after two mouthfuls she was sniffling merrily from the bite of the spices and washing the fire down with her wine. Though her face flushed with heat from the seasonings, she kept her hood up and her mask on.

On Vijganar it was not uncommon for people to go about masked. The wealthy in particular did so, sometimes in order to conduct liaisons with lovers who, for one reason or another, might have been inappropriate. As a result, masks had attained fashionability. Many were intricate, sequined, edged in gold, scales or feathers. A wide variety of them passed by as she ate; jewels and sequins gleamed in the torchlight. Her mask was far more simple—a tight, shiny black cloth with a diamond pattern in the weave; it covered the top of her head to the tip of her nose. The idea was not to draw attention to herself. She might easily have been a rich young man disguised to go slumming, and no doubt it was this impression that attracted the tattered procurer who slid onto the bench across from her, crooked his pinkie finger to his nose and asked, "*Paidika*, young master?"

Leodora looked up coldly. He still held his pinkie to his nostril. She set down her spoon, then bit the tip of her thumb and flicked it at him.

The grubby man affected a look of indignation. He bowed a hasty apology and moved off to find a willing client. She watched him glide from table to table, and eventually to an elaborately masked couple being led by a hired torchbearer. They discussed his smiling proposition and, to her surprise and disgust, went off with him, dismissing the torchbearer with a coin. It was risky business—the procurer might have been laying a trap to rob and murder them—she noted that both the man and woman wore *khanjarli* daggers across their bellies. They weren't fools, whatever else. However, his skimming the area made it likely that the grubby pimp did in truth represent a *paidika*—a harem of boys. She shuddered at the thought of what such a place, run by such a scabrous creature, must be like.

With the meal finished, she stood on stronger legs. The wine and food in her belly gave her a compact, integrated feeling—a feeling that she could do anything. After all, she was a favorite of the gods. She was a great storyteller. And she was now most definitely late. Soter would be wringing his hands in worry that something horrible had befallen her. He always expected disaster. He courted it.

She hailed a girl with a torch, who could not have been more than twelve, and said huskily, "Lotus Hall." The girl led her down Caritas Avenue. They passed a cluster of other unhired torchbearers, all of them the girl's seniors, and all of them male. They glowered sullenly. Leodora chuckled.

The girl led her to the open doors, there bowing with proper respect. Leodora smiled and handed her three silver coins, where one was sufficient pay. The child's eyes grew wide. Leodora leaned down and said, in her own voice, "There, and don't share any of it with those ruffians we passed." The girl's amazement doubled as she realized she'd been leading a woman, who now slipped into the dark interior of Lotus Hall.

Some nights statues spoke and women dressed as men.

Inside the hall, torches in wall sconces to each side of the doors had been lit, as had the main chandelier. The oil burned brightly, smoking, above a noisy crowd. She didn't see Nuberne, the owner, but his wife, Rolend, stood beside the serving bar. Moonlight trickled through the lancet windows, splashing milky radiance upon the tables. Between tables and wall lay deeper pockets of shadow. Leodora skirted the main crowd, trying to keep in the shadows, trying to avoid Rolend's attention. But it was Rolend's nature to notice everyone who came into her hall, no matter how crowded it was. Before Leodora was halfway down its length, the mistress of the hall had swept out from behind the bar, snaked among tables and revelers, and blocked her path.

"Jax," Rolend said, taking her hand, "I'd begun to worry that you weren't going to perform tonight." She thrust forward her ample bosom as though stabbed from behind, then gave a look of coy embarrassment as both breasts settled on Leodora's arm.

Leodora drew back but bumped up against a chair. She forced a smile while she tried to maneuver around the mistress without making contact again. She replied with Jax's deeper voice, "I always perform."

Rolend's smile grew sly. "I'll bet you do, my Jax."

Leodora's smile never faltered, but in trying to step around the chair, her foot caught behind one of its legs, and it clattered along with her. She couldn't seem to untangle herself. Rolend gripped her fingers tight with one hand and smoothed the other across her palm. "You have such *hard* hands, my dear Jax. So rough for someone of such delicate skill—"

"Ro!" From the kitchen Nuberne's voice cut through the din. "Where's the damned yarrow, damn you?"

Rolend's eyes hardened for an instant. She released her hold and smiled as if she hadn't heard. She said quickly, "After the show I'll bring you some dinner and we can dally a bit. He's already in his cups." Then she called out, "Yarrow's on the bottom pantry shelf . . . dearest!" so shrilly that Leodora's eyes teared.

As the mistress of the house turned away, Leodora sighed, and a voice from the table in front of her said, "She's taken a real shine to you, *lad*."

"Soter!" He had his back to her, his feet up. The bald dome of his head rested below the high back of the chair. She wriggled around the table to sit facing him. "Soter, something strange has happened. I need you to explain—"

Instead of hearing her out, he interrupted, "I'd begun to worry 'bout you. It was my misgivings that top-heavy tart related, not hers. She has none. She merely wants to make certain you'll accommodate her after."

Soter had been tanned by every wind that had ever blown across Shadowbridge. He was lean and dark and dry as leather. His was neither a happy nor a sad face, but one that had encountered some version of every possible eventuality. At the moment it was flushed from an extended encounter with a wine bottle.

"What am I going to do?" she asked.

He puzzled for a moment. "Feign death?"

"What did my father do?"

"Well, generally, he was about the most accommodating

man there ever was." With the two fingers of his that were missing their last joints, he scratched his stubbled chin, and then winced at what he'd said. "That is to say, until your mother performed his reconstruction. I don't believe he's the paradigm you're looking for at the moment. 'Course, he wasn't pretending to be somethin' other than what he was." She glared at him, and he waved his hands in defense. "I didn't say you had a choice, dear heart. Prejudice is the way of the world. A few more spans up the line here, you'll have gathered yourself a reputation to bank on and you can come out of your headgear like a turtle out of her shell—make a big production of it, a spectacle, if that's what you want to do. Not that I'd advise it. And there'll still be some stretches—Malprado for instance—where you might be prohibited . . . where women have no business doing business 'less it's illicit. The mask they'd make you wear there would cover your mouth, too. Be very anonymous there. I doubt we'll go that way. No, somewhere like old Colemaigne'd be better for you. They won't care at all, except about the performance. Most places'll be swayed by the wonder of you, the mysterious masked wonder called Jax. Make you an exhibit, a treasure. 'Course, if you want to remove the mask, I can't stop you." He poked his finger into his chest. "Not me."

Someone in the crowd shouted out, "Jax!" but at the booth, not at her.

"Yes, but what do I do about *tonight*?"

Smiling crookedly, Soter sank back. "Perform, m'girl, perform. Get that idiot musician to play decently for more than five minutes at a time and we'll do all right." He got up, seeking his balance. The small bronze libation bowl in the center of the table rocked, splashing out liquid dark as blood. It was nearly full. How many drinks did it take to fill a libation bowl, when the offering from each drink was but a drop or two?

That lush, the god had called him. It was amusing on a puppet: when Meersh drank himself stupid, people all laughed. Leodora's jaw clenched. She needed advice and he dismissed her with a line he thought amusing: "Perform."

"So, anyway," Soter said, "where in the Great Spiral were you?"

"Talking to a statue," she snapped, then marched off, leaving him staring after her in his befuddlement.

At the far end of the hall from the doors stood her booth. Twice her height, it was three panels of black drapery comprising three sides of a tall box, and open at the top. The ends of the upright poles protruded above the drapery. In the center of the front panel, she lifted a smaller flap of material that acted as a curtain covering a flat featureless white silk screen. As she pinned the curtain up, some of the patrons began whistling and clapping. Without acknowledging them, she circled to the side of the booth, parted the drapes near the rear corner, and stepped into darkness.

Inside, the booth's framework of stout wooden poles, tenoned and pinned into each other, was more obvious, and all the secrets of her skill were revealed.

Behind and above the silk screen—covered on this side by a small curtain of fabric identical to the one she'd pinned up—stood a stanchion on which her lantern hung. Unlike most other lanterns, one side of it was solid brass, dull with age, another had been cut with tiny holes and two crescent moons, and a third had been fitted with a plate of blue glass. Only one side—the one facing the screen—contained anything like a lens, as a normal lantern might.

In the back right-hand corner were stacked two coffin-sized trunks in which the entire show was transported—the bottom one for the poles and drapes; the top one for her puppets—and on top of the trunks, on his back and making a noise somewhere between a snore and a gargle, lay the accompanist. He was a small dark-haired man, unshaven and in clothes that were better suited to mop-buckets. The unwashed smell of him wouldn't have posed a problem on the boulevard, but in the small booth, it could bring tears to her eyes.

Nevertheless, she had to wake him now; but she held her breath as she tapped him on the shoulder. His head rolled. Then he jerked awake. His eyes shifted, found her, and he sat up, drawing back on the case, knees up, almost fearful in his pose.

She had no time to be concerned about his confusion or fears. He wasn't a particularly good musician to begin with, but he was all that they'd been able to find. Soter complained that they needed a *good* accompanist, that they weren't a troupe without one; but thus far they'd had no luck acquiring anyone else whose playing warranted keeping him on. Authoritatively, Leodora said, "Come now, you, we have to begin. Go help

Soter, set up your things beside the screen. They're already getting sour out there."

The musician jumped down, and then slouched out of the booth. She quickly secured the ribbons that tied it closed so that he couldn't get back in.

She unfolded and set up two low trestles, one on each side of the silk screen, then lifted the top from the upper trunk and placed it squarely over the right-hand trestle, forming a table.

Then she set to work. She knew what stories she needed to tell tonight. The necessary pieces for Shumyzin's tale were scattered in different compartments inside the trunk. She would have to root around for those during an intermission. Soter ought to know where most of them lay. Right now she was late, and the audience was hooting.

With the first box prepared, she took off her tunic and mask, and stood wearing only trousers and the wide elastic band that pressed her breasts nearly flat against her ribs. She would have been happier if her breasts had been smaller and easier to conceal. The band was giving her a rash. She peeled it off, then quickly took a towel and patted the perspiration from beneath both breasts. For the show she could be free of the harness, her sex hidden entirely from outside view. The beautiful thing about being a puppeteer was that she remained anonymous. She disappeared into her stories.

Dry, she wrapped herself in the loose, comfortable black shirt that she always wore to perform. She took a deep, calming breath, stood for a moment longer, then undid the ribbons on the booth flap.

From a punt she lit the lantern, rotated it so that the blue glass side faced front. Then she knelt on her padded stool beside the box of puppets and lifted the inner curtain covering the screen. As the curtain came away, the stretched silk glowed a deep, submarine blue. Outside, the musician's flute sounded, and the crowd cheered. There were cries of "Shut up!" and "Sit down!" and "Quick, bring me another *nabidh*!"

From the box she took the first piece: the image of a single stick-legged house. She deftly hooked it upon the silk. Then she lifted by its rods the first puppet, a magnificent construction. She waited.

The audience muttered, settling in. The flute played an introductory trill, slipped a note, but finished, held fairly steady, then faded.

The room fell silent.

Soter's voice filled the quiet. "We bid you welcome all. Tonight, if you've never witnessed it, you will see a rare thing. If you've been here before, then you've come back because you now know that I did not lie when I promised you this the first time.

"Many years ago, I traveled these spans. There was a master puppeteer in those days, to whom people flocked from sometimes two cityspans distant."

She heard the name of Bardsham carried on murmurs as upon waves. "Bastard," she whispered. He'd never done this to her before: However sober he sounded, he was indeed drunk, and she was helpless to shut him up if he went too far. She held the rod puppet at the ready, beneath the screen where the light couldn't throw its shadow onto anything.

"Yes, that's right—Bardsham, a magical name. The greatest of all entertainers, so great that, although he's been gone for near twenty years, we still speak of him in whispers, in awe. Well, I make you a promise that anyone who can recall his skill as I do will be bedazzled by what they see here tonight, for this is as near as . . . no, no, I won't say that. Rather, judge for yourselves. Ladies, gentlemen, princes and paupers, foolish virgins and wicked libertines, lovers of story one and all, please dedicate your attention to the entertainments . . . of *Jax*!"

Applause followed, some cheering, a few whistles that might have been in mockery of the old man. She heard him walk past her on the far side of the drapes, sensed his entry behind her. He stumbled in the constricted darkness, chuckled to himself, then found his seat. By then the crowd had fallen silent and the light filtering in over the top of the booth dimmed—Nuberne had doused the central chandelier.

Leodora went to work.

≈ The Tale of Creation ≈

There is a story that explains Shadowbridge to itself.

At the beginning of the world the first fisherman, Chilingana, caught the first storyfish. No bridges existed then. Even the first dragon beam had yet to appear. Chilingana lived in a stilt house built on rough pillars that climbed straight out of the sea. From Phylos Bar, looking south, you can see the ruin of them still. Chilingana was down among the pilings around one of these pillars when he caught the storyfish. He had never seen one before because they swim so deep, and Chilingana did as he would with any fish on his line—he dropped it in his creel along with the others he'd caught already and went on fishing.

At the end of the day he hooked a line to the creel, then climbed home on the steps that curled up around one of the pillars. When he reached the top and had gathered his breath, he drew up the line to raise his catch. He could smell the fire his wife was preparing.

Behind his house Chilingana had a huge stone on which to clean the fish. From there he could throw their entrails back into the sea, a ritual to feed the kraken that dwelled below the pillars, in this way keeping it appeased as they still do off Phylos Bar, lest it surface and pull down the pylons of their span.

Chilingana reached down into the creel. Its weave was so tight that water would remain in it for a day and a half. His fingers clutched one of the fish. Holding it by its tail, he slapped its head against a stone to stun it.

He split the fish down the middle.

He cleaned it, and threw the guts into the sea.

He made ready the first fillets.

He killed and cleaned each one thereafter until only the big storyfish with its dark blue head and golden eyes remained. He dipped his hand into the creel and hooked his fingers into the fish's gills; this caused a hidden barb inside the gill to pierce the crease of his palm. Chilingana cursed and yanked back his hand.

He stared suspiciously at the trickle of blood veining his wrist, then at the fish watching him from just beneath the surface, only the tip of its snout protruding. He could see its tiny mouth and harmless knobby teeth. He couldn't see the barb and thought maybe he'd foolishly impaled his hand on one of its spines.

With much greater care he started to reach into the container again, but before he could touch the fish, the world began to tip over. Chilingana grabbed the big cutting stone, sure that he was about to tumble right over the edge and into the sea. He tried to cry out but poison in the barb had numbed his lips. His legs trembled and gave, and he fell like the moon rolling across the sky.

When her cooking stone was so hot that it smoked, but the

filets had still not arrived, Lupeka went looking for her husband. He had been gone far too long. And where were the fish?

When she arrived at the gutting stone, she was amazed to find her husband nowhere in sight. A row of pale fillets lay there, all in a straight line, but one of the fish had jumped out of the creel and lay on the ground, barely breathing. Lupeka picked up the fish and dropped it back in. Let Chilingana finish up with these last two when he returned. She told herself that he must have gone back down the steps. His absence disturbed her more than we can imagine, for in those days there was nowhere to hide, nothing but the great house on stilts and the empty sea all around it. No other people but these two.

After looking over the edge for him and seeing nothing but the sea, his wife took the prepared fillets back inside. Wherever he was, he would smell the cooking. Surely that must bring him out of hiding.

Chilingana came to his senses to find himself swimming. Beside him a vast blue island protruded from the dark water, and he supposed that he must have fallen from the house into the ocean, miraculously surviving, and had floated away. He must have floated far, for there were no islands visible from his stilthouse, and the sky was a peculiar dark brown. Despite this, the island looked oddly familiar. It seemed to rise and fall in the water.

All at once he realized it was no island at all. It was the snout of the storyfish. Beside him. And the sky was no sky, but the wicker of the creel. He began to struggle to pull himself out, but he had no *arms*. What had happened to him?

The fish laughed. The sound made the water bubble and roil.

Then the fish spoke to him. "This is how it is for us. We don't have the luxuries of you who've been dreamed into being by greater forces."

It was the first Chilingana had heard about this. "Dreamed?" he asked, and although he didn't think he'd said this out loud, the fish replied, "Yes, dreamed into being. You in turn are capable of dreaming a reply to the creators. Where your dreams meet theirs the world takes shape. Today your fisherman dream met my dream of being a fish, and mine prevailed. So here you are, having fished yourself into my story."

"Is that what happened to me?"

"I put you in my tale before you could take hold of mine."

The fish chuckled.

"Am I a fish forever, then?" The storyfish did not answer and Chilingana grew nervous. The silence likely meant there was no good news for him. His terror broke loose. "I don't want to be a fish!" he cried.

The fish said, "Well, is that right? Too good to be a fish? Very well, then. But before I'll help you, you must grant me three wishes." The island swam nearer.

"What?"

"First, whenever you catch a fish of my kind, you must throw it back."

"Of course. How could I eat you after we've spoken?"

"Second, you must show respect for those fish you do catch, and return to the sea the ones too small to make a meal."

"I would return you to the sea right away. All right, I agree. What else would you have of me?"

"That you tell all other people my rules and make them abide by them."

"All other people? What other people? There is only me and my wife."

"And if I tell you there will be more?"

"Who? Who else is coming?"

"That I cannot see. But they teem like a red tide."

"Where are they?"

"Ah. That's a puzzle, isn't it? Tell me, how did you begin your life?" the fish asked.

"Well, I—" Chilingana stopped, bewildered. He didn't know. He had never thought about it before. He had always simply been. His wife and the world had always been. So, too, the storyfish must always have been.

"You know little of the world," said the fish.

"All right, you're so clever, you tell me how I was begun."

The fish's tail flicked impatiently. "I've said already all I'm going to say until you honor my wishes. I do hope you're a social animal."

The fish's snout loomed over him. Its laughter shook the waters, and Chilingana floundered helplessly.

He awoke with a start to find himself slouched beside the creel. His stung hand was red and swollen. The storyfish floated just below the water level, its huge eyes following him. "Why," he said, "I must have dreamed this."

"You think so?" said the fish. Although it remained

beneath the water, its voice rang clearly in his head. "Honor your promises tonight. Then come and talk to me in the morning before you throw me back into the ocean, and I will tell you the most important thing of all—a thing you will not want to hear. But you must."

"What's that?"

The fish said nothing more.

Chilingana got up. He grabbed a clay pot and hurried down the steps to the water. The smell of frying fish made his stomach grumble but he ran on. At the bottom he filled the pot, then hauled it much more slowly back up.

His wife met him at the top. "So there you are, you foolish man. I looked all over for you, I called to you. Where had you got to?"

"I was right here."

"No, you weren't, I came out and found your fillets but not you," said Lupeka. The discussion would surely have blossomed into an argument, except that she noticed her husband's swollen hand. "How did this happen?"

He first scuttled over to the creel and emptied the pot into it while he spoke. "There, fish. There's some more water for you." Setting down the pot, he said to his wife, "The fish stung me. It's nothing. Nothing at all."

"Nonsense, that needs tending to. It'll have poison in it."

She led him inside. His wife had cooked the fillets beautifully. He stared at them, his mouth flooding with desire, while she bandaged his hand. Finally, she let him sit on the floor and handed him his portion.

He was about to take his first bite, when he hesitated. The food dangled from his spoon. Lupeka asked, "What's wrong?"

"Nothing," replied Chilingana. "I just—" He lowered the spoon. "I just want to give thanks to these fish for letting me catch them. For giving their lives to sustain ours."

"That's an odd thing to say. And why are you bellowing?"

He said, "No, it isn't odd at all. From now on we're going to honor them whenever we eat. We're going to thank them just like this." Then he ate the food.

His wife decided that the poison from his hand had affected his mind, and so she refrained from argument.

After dinner, Chilingana was exhausted. His wife insisted that he go to bed and rest. He complied. She covered him with her body to keep him warm. Into her ear, as he drifted to sleep he muttered, "Tomorrow I shall know *everything*."

In the morning, he awoke to his wife's scream. He sat straight up on his mat and looked around the hut. She wasn't there. He bounded outside, to find her beside the door. She had been carrying a huge fillet, which lay now at her feet. Its skin was blue. It was the storyfish.

"Fish!" cried Chilingana, and he knelt beside it. "Fish, oh no, fish, forgive me. Please forgive me. I would have put you back! Tell me the secret thing. The important thing."

The headless fillet did not answer.

"Where is his head?" he demanded, finally paying attention to his wife. "What have you done with his head?"

She did not seem to see him. Her gaze lay beyond him on a more fearful thing. In a tiny voice, she asked, "Husband, how did you create all of this?"

Chilingana turned where he knelt to see what she meant.

Beyond their small house now a great curving road stretched out across the sea. Where it curved he could see arch upon arch supporting it and immense towers reaching into the sky. The far end vanished into the morning fog. It was an impossible development. He could have worked for years erecting it all and never built anything so grand. He rose to his feet in wonderment. Where had it come from?

He knew the answer. He held the answer in his hand. "The fish wants me to go exploring." He said it low, almost to himself.

"What?" asked his wife.

"I said I wish to go exploring. To see the world."

"You—you've never mentioned it before."

"Well, I don't tell you everything," he replied. And that was the very first wedge ever driven between two people.

"But how was this done? How did you build it?"

Chilingana, holding the glistening meat of the storyfish, could only answer, "I'll never know."

They ate the storyfish. Chilingana said the small prayer over its delectable carcass that the people of Vijganar repeat to this day before eating a fish. He and his wife eventually set out to journey along the new spans. Every night when the fisherman slept, new ones formed, so that each morning was the first morning of a new world. It is a process that may still be occurring somewhere, for who of us can view the world all at once and know what develops everywhere? Some spans are old, and some are young. On some, the gods of the Edgeworld light the Dragon Bowls and send down their gifts; on others, the light no longer falls. Chilingana never learned its secrets, nor has anyone since. Without the storyfish to explain, no one knows the secret ways of Shadowbridge, or whether Chilingana travels and dreams among us still.

" . . . travels and dreams among us still." The words of her epilogue reverberated in the rafters.

With one hand Leodora balanced the puppet figures of Chilingana and his wife on the screen. With her other, she reached up and rotated the lantern so that tiny stars and moons spread across the silk. The two dark figures sank slowly from sight. She unpinned the curtain and let it drop over the screen. The musician played a final note on his flute, and thumped a small drum once.

For a moment there was utter silence. Then the applause exploded. Pottery banged against tables. The audience, depending upon their background, cheered, whistled or belched approval. Her name—the name "Jax"—resounded from all around the hall.

She glanced back at Soter. He grinned in reply, then broke into a yawn. Had he dozed off during the performance? Possibly. It was a story that had required no participation from him. She had narrated where necessary, doing the three voices. It was a story known to everyone in the hall, and they could have followed it even if she'd said nothing at all.

Soter stood, stretching. He picked up his hammered brass bowl and went out through the drapes. He would make the rounds, visit every table, answer questions, accept drinks, tell lies about the background of the mysterious Jax, and collect what she hoped would be a sizable compensation. She had plenty of time to prepare for the next tale, "The Druid's Egg." Altogether, she would perform three stories tonight: the demigod, Shumyzin's, last of all. People loved to go out on tales of heroes.

As she thought of him, she perceived shared features between her encounter and the story she'd just played out. What had happened to Chilingana in the tale had happened to her on the bridge: The most important thing had not been spoken.

She sat back, stretching awhile. Her gaze finally fixed upon the second trunk, and the sounds of the crowd outside faded away; she heard again the words of Shumyzin: "I know the riddle of him." How did he know so much? she asked herself, but the answer was perfectly obvious.

She closed the top case and stood it on end at the back of the booth so that it blocked the access slit in the drapery. She pulled the lid off the bottom case, and lifted out the three inner compartments full of puppets and props. It now appeared to be empty. She slid her fingers along the inner edge of the bottom piece until she touched the loop of black cord. Carefully she pulled up the false bottom, then knelt, holding it up with one hand, ready to drop it if interrupted. Only Soter knew about the false bottom and its contents. He didn't know, however, about the dreams. No one did, except for a statue.

The sounds and smells of the hall faded. A dim glow surrounded her, and a crackling charge tickled her brows and stood the hairs on her arms on end.

There lay her secret companion. Her treasure. The Coral Man.

She reached into the box to touch him. Fearful, awed, excited all at once. Her fingers traced the roughness of him. She could have shredded the tips if she'd pushed hard enough. The shadows cast by the lantern made his face seem more defined than it really was. She withdrew her hand, fingertips now coated with fine and vaguely luminous powder. There was powder in the box, too, a light dusting off it. She sniffed at her fingers, then put her tongue to them and tasted sea salt. Within that flavor lay her whole life before the spans: the cavern called Fishkill, the lagoon where she swam, the tales of her mother, the smell of the breeze entering her tiny garret.

Memories of the backwater island life she had abandoned.

Chapter 2
Bouyan

She was five years old the first time they let her go to Ningle. Ningle-in-the-Clouds, as Soter properly called it. They carried their baskets of fish—her uncle and grandfather—on the path that wound beneath the canopy of trees, with the ever-visible span looming ever closer. Before then she'd only seen it from across the island, a great black stripe of cloud showing through the trees, which never moved, never broke apart, but hung in the sky like an omen. At night, it transformed into a band of fairy lights coruscating in the sky. She wasn't prepared for its true size. Almost an hour's walk from her home, one massive leg of the span anchored somewhere deep in the bedrock of Bouyan beneath them. Steps had been carved into the side of it, each block so big that she had to clamber up with her hands—or would have if her grandfather hadn't hefted her along with his baskets.

Soon he had carried her so high that she closed her eyes and buried her face against his neck, smelling sawdust and varnish, the scents of his workshop, which clung to him even more tightly than she.

At the top he set down his basket and unwound her from his neck and back. Between them they had an old game where he swung her and swung her, and she laughed, screamed, giggled. This time, though, he only swung her once, held her up, her feet resting upon stone. He said, "Now open your eyes, Lea." She did, and was so awed by the view that she forgot to be terrified right away.

The island of Bouyan lay so far below her that wisps of

cloud gauzed the treetops, and she could see clear across to a hint of their rooftops and even all the way to where a chimney of smoke signaled the location of the fishing village of Tenikemac, and farther still—to the sea itself, like a great sheet of glass upon which the whole world was set. She could see that the Adamantine Ocean stretched forever just like the stories said.

That day, standing upon the rail, with her grandfather's hands enclosing her waist, she heard the call for the first time. It was not a voice exactly, not words, not something anyone else could hear. It whispered her name, spoke to her in the silences, invited her to find it, join it, embrace it. All without words. She thought then that it was the ocean calling her. There was nothing else to see.

"Isn't it fine?" her grandfather asked.

She turned her head to look at him, and now she was afraid. The wordless, communicating voice was frightening, and she didn't know whether her grandfather was referring to it or to the view. He saw her fear and took her off the rail, assuring her softly, "It's all right, child, it's all right. I wouldn't let anything happen to you, you know." She knew this to be true, but she wasn't paying attention to him.

The moment he'd touched her, the ocean call had ceased. She listened hard, but it didn't reappear.

She would not hear it again for years, but on that day (she was certain of this now) the caller had located her. It had sought her, knowing she was somewhere. Now it would be able to find her again.

Throughout the next year, Leodora spent nearly every day on the span. It teemed and surged with life, with the noises of excitement, the smells of otherness, newness. Bright costumes and plumed caps dazzled her, and facial adornments from rapier sharp beards to spiky stiffened eyebrows, beauty spots to shaved scalps drifted past to amaze her. One day she saw a man with wide and tightly waxed mustachios, the tips of which burned with blue fire that didn't consume them. And on another evening a raggedy fellow walked the thoroughfare with a box dangling from a lanyard around his neck while he cranked handles on either side of it, which in turn caused two metal hooks facing each other through the top of the box to spark and burn and glow in the space where they didn't quite touch. The ragged man looked lost as he went by and she heard someone say, "from a Dragon Bowl, that one. Ruined him." But when she asked her grandfather about the man, he replied, "Nothing to do with us, Lea, so never you mind it."

Her grandfather did not always accompany them. As often he stayed below, on Bouyan in his workshop, crafting or mending their furniture. Like her uncle Gousier, he was a big man, barrel-chested and powerful.

The buildings on Ningle, all made of stone, were nothing like the structures she knew on the island. Her own house and those of the fishing village were mostly made of wood and woven thatch. Houses on Ningle were dark and roughly finished, and not quite true. Their angles, as her grandfather showed her, were all slightly off the square. He took her to one street not far from the market where the buildings were so crooked that she couldn't understand how they didn't fall over.

The market comprised a stretch of mismatched awnings, boxes, carts and poles. In comparison with many of the others nearby, their own stall was clean and orderly. On three sides of the center, whole fish and cleaned fillets lay in ceramic boxes, atop ice chipped from the depths of Fishkill Cavern. Deep blue awnings kept the stall in shadow and cool.

Gousier usually had someone working for him, someone on Ningle who set up the stall before they arrived, and took it down at night; and someone to help haul the fish and watch that the clientele didn't steal any. She could remember none of these men (for they were always men) during that year. None of them remained for long. The work was too hard. And—she would later learn—descending to the island for work was considered beneath the dignity of most of Ningle's denizens; but there were much more reprehensible acts that were not.

Her uncle seemed to enjoy her company. While they walked and climbed to market each morning, he taught her the names of the fish in his baskets and described how they were caught, what they could be used for. Once the stall was set up, he set her right up front, and when someone came by and inquired about one of the fish, Leodora would proudly repeat what she knew about it. Most of the time after listening to her recitation, a customer would buy the fish, and Gousier would tell her, "Why, you're a fishmonger, child. Look at what you *sold*." He would give her a coin and let her buy something for herself. Eventually he let her parade up and down the boulevard, calling out the names of the fish they were selling, and this led more people to their stand. Her uncle and grandfather treated her like a princess out of a story—like the girl, Reneleka, who emerged from an oyster, coiled around a pearl, and who had created the sea dragons. It was a story they told in Tenikemac. She felt as if she, too, had been magically created.

Then one afternoon when she was sitting to the side of the stand, a woman came over and spoke to her. It seemed the most natural of events, one more person asking her questions. The woman was fidgety and furtive, but Leodora didn't appreciate the meaning of this. She had only known kindness.

The woman invited her for a walk, with a promise of an undisclosed surprise at the end of it. Leodora would have told her grandfather, but he was with a customer on the other side of the stall. She might have told Gousier, but he was haggling with still another person over the price of a halibut. The current assistant had wandered off.

She strolled along beside her new acquaintance for only a few moments before the woman took her hand and drew her suddenly into the nearest crooked little alley, with the promise, "Your treat's up here."

It was the same alley her uncle had shown her, full of tilting buildings, and she marched along bravely into the not unfamiliar gloom. Then a man unfolded from the deeper shadows, and she stopped. Leodora remembered him—he had passed by their stall two or three times and then asked her about the cod; listened with a wolfish grin to what she told him and thanked her for her recitation. He hadn't bought anything. He grinned at her again now. He had very good teeth.

The woman shoved ahead of her and said, "Give me my money." But the man shook his head. "When I've made the delivery, when they're happy with their new arrival." Both of them glanced down at her, and that was the moment she knew something was wrong, but the woman still gripped her wrist. The two began to argue. Leodora pulled with ever increasing urgency to get away. The woman was too busy squabbling to notice. Abruptly, Leodora broke the hold, but it was so sudden and she'd pulled so hard that she spun against the wall. The man was on her before she could get up. "All right, darlin'," he said. The stink of him smothered her. "You come along with me now to get your surprise. No more working in a fish stall for you, not a lovely girl like you. They'll like you where we're going. You'll be the most popular girl they have." Smiling though he was all the while, his sweet words were more ominous than anything she'd ever heard. She twisted, but his grip was much harder than the woman's, and the wall was at her back, offering no way to put distance between them. She started to scream. The man clamped his hand around her face and hissed at her. He ordered the woman to do something to silence her, and they both closed in where there was hardly enough room for one of them alone, and the acrid sweaty stink poured over her like the stench from rotting meat. The woman crouched, cooing, trying to sound tender beneath her jagged, hungry sharpness. Leodora fought for breath beneath a mask of filthy fingers over her nose, her mouth. She grew dizzy.

The grip abruptly lifted from her face, the stench and the man swept away as if by magic. The woman bit back a shriek, grabbed Leodora again and tugged her down the alley and back out onto the boulevard.

A crowd was collecting. They blocked the woman's retreat, so that she cried out, "Someone, someone stop him!" and then, almost as an afterthought, "My child, my baby!" She wrapped herself as if protectively around Leodora, and the crowd obligingly opened a space for the two of them. Even as they lurched into it, the crowd moved with them, stepped back as if to accompany them; but they weren't following the woman. They were fleeing something else. Leodora twisted her head around to see.

Her grandfather.

He caught the woman before she could get past the last of the people choking the boulevard. He tore Leodora from her grasp, and then wedged himself in between them. Dreamily, she looked back and saw her uncle in the alley. He was bent over and seemed to be gesturing fiercely. His fist raised high and held, hovered. It gripped a mallet. The hand and mallet were wet and dark. She had seen her grandfather holding a mallet that way as he drove pegs into holes he'd cut, but Gousier brought it down harder than grandfather ever had.

People began shouting "Kuseks!" and she looked up at their mouths, their fearful eyes. Then the woman toppled beside her, knocking someone aside, skidding on her face upon the paving stones. Their eyes locked, just for a moment, before the woman's expression went slack and the eyes fluttered shut. The crowd turned, roaring, and split in two directions. The space filled almost instantly with a swarm of police—the Kuseks, so named for the striped sashes they wore. They grabbed her grandfather immediately. She saw him struck with a stick, and she screamed.

Her uncle charged from the alley. Blood drenched his face and clothes. He bellowed at the Kuseks to release her grandfather. She watched it all as if from the rail of Ningle, as if it were all transpiring far below, far away from her—the mallet striking once, the police beating her uncle senseless, and beating him even after that. Her grandfather swaying on his knees, blood from his scalp covering his face like a membrane, as he tried in vain to stop them.

Everyone was taken into custody, including the woman. She wasn't dead after all. She portrayed herself as the victim, and the wounds to her face lent her credibility. She claimed the six-year-old girl was her daughter, and kept touching Leodora, running trembling fingers through her hair. Of course she was not Leodora's mother, nor looked anything like her, but the bold assertion smothered her denial with the warped aroma of hope, a possibility that was impossible. It surely would have tripped up no one other than a girl who had no mother, generating an internal conflict that terrified and silenced her when she most needed to speak. Finally the authorities had to send for her auntie Dymphana, hauling her up from Bouyan to prove that this hadn't been something else, a lover's quarrel, a domestic dispute. The moment she saw her aunt she began to wail, and flung her arms about Dymphana's waist, and the Kuseks knew absolutely. They set her grandfather and Gousier free.

The family were escorted back to the market to find their stall a shambles. The fish had been stolen, some of the ceramics were smashed. Apologies from the nearby vendors, who might have intervened but more likely had participated in the plunder, did nothing to mitigate the damage or curb Gousier's anger. His ribs were broken, his face bruised and swollen, and he'd lost a tooth. The police pointed out that he'd been caught in the act of murder and should be thankful he was alive to complain.

For weeks afterward he could hardly walk along beside the laborers he had to hire to cart the fish up the steps. The workers were hardly better than beggars, but no one else wanted the work. Once his bones had knit, he visited the Kuseks and paid them to see that the pathetic kidnapper was banished to a prison isle called Palipon. It was a bare chunk of rock so far out in the ocean that it could not be seen from any of the great spirals of bridges. No one sent to Palipon was ever heard from again. When he announced this over dinner, the whole family stopped moving as if upon a signal. They stared; they paled. Gousier retorted, "It's where all her kind should go." Then he lowered his head and ate as if no one else shared the table with him and his heart was as light as a cloud.

Later, from her bed, she heard the family arguing. Gousier snarled, "Well, what sort of a woman would sell a child into perdition? Or maybe she's an Edgeworld goddess, do you think? It was a better life she was going to give the girl, in a tiny cell, chained in filth to a bedframe, waiting for her next customer? Because that's what was going to happen. These people are worse than anything you know, Dymphana, I don't care if you grew up in the same house with them!" Her aunt said something too quiet for her to hear, but Gousier drowned out the last of it: "Then maybe you'd rather have stayed up there! Maybe the street has more to offer you!" After that it seemed that no one spoke again until after she'd fallen asleep.

Her grandfather, although he'd only been struck the once, seemed unable to recover. He suffered spasms, numbness, and headaches that rendered him helpless. A few months later, he was dead. Her grandmother died of grief less than a month after that. Leodora was no less devastated than anyone by their combined loss. Her world was shrinking, closing in on her. She dreamed of the two of them with her in an alley where the buildings were sliding together to crush them, and both her grandparents were pushing her, trying to get her out before the walls met, but she could see the space narrowing ahead, and she knew she would never reach the avenue in time, never reach it at all, and then the walls did slam together behind her, so loud that it woke her up. The dream proved portentous.

Gousier forbid her ever to set foot on Ningle again.

Over time she would learn that he blamed her for everything that had happened that day, including the deaths of his parents, which became the foundation for unlimited blame thereafter. Gousier remained as bitter as patchroot wine. His retribution was bottomless.

It was during one of his tirades that he inadvertently called her "Leandra." He caught himself, but the realization of what he'd said only fueled his anger, as if she had cleverly diverted him. Provoked him. After that, almost her every error or act of defiance was equated with something Leandra had done, although he never spoke the name except in anger, because he refused to acknowledge that he had ever had a sister except when too angry to help himself.

Leandra. Her mother.

Leodora put one leg in through Soter's window, then had to double over nearly all the way, head to knees, to ease herself over the sill. She felt with her toe for the floor, stretching so much that she slid off-balance. Almost immediately her foot touched the floor, which left her balanced on one leg with the other sticking out the window and raised halfway to her ear. She couldn't get her other foot inside until she had placed her hands on the floor as if about to perform a handstand. Then she carefully folded her leg in through the window, crouched down noiselessly, and looked about.

She was inside his makeshift pantry. She had never seen inside the pantry before: It was larger than its narrow doorway implied. To her left hung a heavy tarp, which hinted at even more space. She stepped into the doorway, parted the curtain and stuck her head into the main room. Almost at once she drew back.

Soter was there. His silhouette perched on a low stool, knees up high, his arms splayed, like some spider creature. He was muttering softly as if to a companion—whispery words that she was unable to catch. She didn't see anyone else. He was not looking in her direction, so she stuck her head further out. He gave a loud, abrupt curse, and she thought he must have seen her. She stepped back behind the curtain, and glanced at the tiny window, certain that she would never get through it fast enough. She scrambled instead behind the tarp and, turning to pull it tight, backed into two black cases. As she stumbled, she twisted about and caught herself on the top case, but her weight made it slide. Something from a shelf farther back fell with an alarming crash.

Soter yelled, "Damn you louse-ridden rodents! How did you get in this time?" He marched into the pantry and flung back the tarp. He had a cleaver in one hand, poised to cut her in half.

She screeched and slid as far back on the cases as she could go. Half a dozen more items bounced and rolled and crashed onto the floor.

Soter closed his eyes and clutched his ears, nearly burying the cleaver in his own head in the process. "Oh, don't squeal, Lea! Don't shift about!" he hissed. He groaned and backed away, dropping the tarp. "Oh, I've got a Glauber's head this morning," she heard him say.

A minute later he returned without the cleaver. "What are you doing in there, anyway? Out, come out here now." He gestured her from the room with one hand and pinched his temples with the other.

She told him about her fight with her uncle over the amount of fish she had cut up, valiantly trying not to cry while she did, and he nodded with care, rubbing his eyes, pulling at his nose. He offered her some biscuits.

"I'm surprised," he said, "that he hasn't come bellowing down upon me like the wind, hammering at my door. Then I might find a place for that cleaver. He doesn't know you're here, does he? Doesn't know, doesn't care. Just chased you off and gathered up his fish and went off to sell them to people who wouldn't have anything to do with him otherwise on behalf of some other people who wouldn't have anything to do with him otherwise." He patted her head and told her, quietly, that she could stay as long as she liked, provided she made no more noise. He retreated to the outer room. She followed, and found him pouring a cup of his latest brew. After a few sips, he sighed. "Rejuvenation."

Leodora nibbled at her biscuit awhile. Then she asked him about the long cases behind the tarp.

"The undaya cases, ah-ha, yes," he answered, very conspiratorially. "Those are a secret kept from your uncle. He doesn't know I have them, or he'd probably want to burn them, and me along with them."

"Why?"

"Because," he replied, and she thought that was all he would tell her. Then he added, "They belonged to your father."

It was a revelation that tore the breath out of her. She set down her biscuit. She had known that she'd had a mother, but no one, not even her aunt, had ever mentioned her father.

Soter, wincing against his headache, shifted his gaze, as if wondering if he'd revealed too much.

"But you said—" she began, much more loudly than he would have liked.

Hissing violently, he raised a hand as if to ward her off. "I know what I said," he whispered. "I know." His gaze held her steady. "I promised your uncle, you see. He can be very insistent when he threatens. Which you know better than I. He did not want you growing up with a lot of dreams and ideas in your head about your father. Did not . . . want you to know.

"I gave in because I wanted to stay here, too, where your grandfather had permitted me. Gousier does have the power to remove me. He could banish me from this island if he didn't find it more satisfying to be able to *tell* me that he can do it. All of this is his property, this dung heap amidst the thorns, and so long as I keep to his path I get to remain." He grinned unevenly, which made him press his palm to the side of his head and close that eye. "I seem to have stepped off today. Wonder how we should handle this? Discretion will be key, I think. No reason he has to know anything about anything—which anyway I've maintained for years."

"But what's in the cases?" she demanded.

"Oh, well, lend me a hand with them and we shall find out together, hmm?" He held up the curtain to let her enter the pantry again.

The two cases were as long as Soter was tall, and brown with dust, spattered darkly where wine or something else had slopped over them. The nub of the leather was worn off in places, too. One case was decidedly heavier than the other. Kneeling, one eye still squeezed shut, Soter fumbled at the hasp on the smaller one. He slipped the pin free, then he pushed and prodded the top up. He didn't remove the lid, but peered secretively underneath.

Then suddenly as if he wanted to drive her back, he shoved a clicking, clattering thing at her. She leaned away but refused to be startled. She stared at what he was holding.

It was a shadow puppet, the first she'd ever seen. The body was articulated: the wrists, elbows, shoulders and knees all revolved on pins, and each segment was fitted with a hinged rod. She pinched one of the loose ones and the puppet's jaws opened in a great leer. She pushed on another, and from behind his legs his penis emerged. It was almost as big as his thigh, and the tip was cut with small swirls that made it seem to have a face of its own. Despite the monstrousness of his anatomy, Leodora had to bite her lip to keep from laughing.

"His name is Meersh," said Soter.

"Meersh," she repeated. She moved his arms and legs, flexed his wrists, marveled at the green tissue-thin skin stretched over his form. She held him up admiringly, and with an ease that surprised her, circled the rods so that the puppet appeared to give a gesture of welcome to Soter. Something stirred within her. She forgot her uncle, the cavern, the hatefulness of the rest of her life. Some shape that had possessed no shape until that moment collected and formed deep inside her, and drew its first breath. She leaned around the lid to look into the case. There in three compartments lay stacks of puppets as deep as her arm, and each puppet unique. She looked up past Meersh to Soter; tears were already forming in her eyes.

Soter gaped in awe or terror at her fingers twirling the rods of the puppet, as if staggered by what he saw. She wanted to speak but only a croak emerged, and she sobbed. Soter looked her in the face and recoiled. He dropped the tarp, escaping the sobs, escaping her, escaping the future that in his drunken cleverness he had just cast. He did not in that moment understand that what he had pried open was her life.

Her life incarnate: The puppets of Bardsham.

It may have been ridiculous ever to have believed that she had no father, but it seemed reasonable at the time. Gousier and the villagers called her mother a witch, and Leodora had simply concluded that the witch had conjured her into being. If nothing else, the explanation allowed her to be magical, and she liked being magical.

Suddenly not only did she have a father, but a father of legendary stature. Even in Tenikemac, isolated from the tumultuous life of the bridges, she'd heard his name—the name of the greatest shadow puppeteer who had ever traveled the myriad spans of Shadowbridge: Bardsham. And there before her, in the care of a grizzled old drunk, lay the puppets Bardsham had used. As it had been with her mother, her father was a revelation.

Soter soon had all the compartments and both cases open. He judiciously selected more puppets and spread them around him. They belonged to a dozen different stories but he assembled them to tell his own. Then he asked her for Meersh.

The grotesque Meersh was going to represent her father. For her mother he picked a sinuous figure he called Orinda.

He began the performance, sometimes looking at her, sometimes squinting as though pained at having to squeeze his memory through the cracks in his hangover.

"Your father," he began, "came from a span far to the south of here, and at least three spirals away. You do know about the spirals, don't you?"

"They're other bridges," she answered uncertainly.

"Other great long, unimaginable arms of bridges, yes, child. And each one, sooner or later, curls up like a nautilus shell, or so it's said, because you can walk a thousand different spans, a thousand different great, wide communities filled with all sorts of people and creatures and not ever reach that curled-up point where the bridge started or maybe ends. Who knows which. But your father, he came out of one of those places, one of those spiral ends. Or so he said. . . ."

≈ Bardsham's Tale ≈

His parents had their own troupe of traveling players, The Mangonel Circus. "Mangonel" was his real name, too. They played in public for money. They juggled and danced on cords strung high above the streets. They performed a skillful whip act with your grandmother holding up things like flowers or torches that your grandfather snipped the heads from or extinguished with a snap of his whip, until finally she held a jeweled ring lightly between two fingers and he snatched it without her fingers even moving—snatched it and with the same movement sent it into the audience, where a fight inevitably broke out over its ownership. It was a cheap ring, but a dazzling trick. The way your father told it, no one had ever seen such skill before Mangonel. There was quite a bit of sleight of hand in among the crowd, too; and which had to be done most carefully if they wanted to avoid any trouble. The boy—that is, Bardsham, your father—he had a natural dexterity. Right from the time he could walk, he could steal coins from between your fingers and you wouldn't feel so much as a breeze—just like his father did with that whip. Plus he was so sly that anyone would have sworn he'd been across the avenue the whole time. He was a child, none too large, and who noticed him down around their hips when people were doing handsprings on a rope way up there?

The family did not overlook his talent. They trained him and trained him until he had the most skillful fingers in the world. His only limit then was how much he could make off with before the weight of his boodle pulled the pants off him.

One night another member of the troupe, a fellow called Peeds, took sick an hour before the performance. Peeds was the Mangonel shadow puppeteer and a great favorite of the boy's as well as of the audience's. Bardsham had heard Peeds' stories hundreds of times, and was always transported by them. He sat through every rehearsal, absorbing all the details like any small child. Like you. When he wasn't outside fleecing the audience, he even sat in the dark booth with Peeds. Mind you, he wasn't supposed to be in the booth at all. His father had a temper to make your uncle look positively unassertive. But the boy took risks. And he and Peeds were friends.

So, Peeds took sick and there was nobody could do his part. Your grandmother sometimes narrated a tale for him, but she knew nothing of the puppetry itself. Nobody else had paid any attention to his old stories—they had their own acts to develop and refine. The family needed an act to link the other acts together—that's what Peeds did with his stories, his puppets. He moved things along from the jugglers to the knife throwers, weaving the distance between the two with some tale that touched both. The boy decided to risk punishment. He confessed to his parents that he'd been studying secretly with Peeds and he could do the act. He swore he knew it by heart. They didn't have time to argue or fight or punish him—not right then. So they capitulated. That was when Bardsham the Great was born.

He'd followed how Peeds used colors to change mood, how he spun the lantern, the different ways he moved figures off the screen. For the rest—what he didn't know—he had the instinct to invent.

His mother came up with the name. She told him, long after, that she had walked out to the end of the dragon beam sticking off the side of the span where they were performing—*every* span has a dragon beam, Lea, not just Ningle. She stepped into the tiled Dragon Bowl at the end of that beam and asked the gods for the name, and it had come to her right then and there. That's what she told him anyway. During his performance, she stood outside the booth, telling the stories where they needed narrating, doing the introductions.

The thing about puppeteers is they're invisible. Never seen. All you see is the handiwork, the skill. So any story she fabricated about Bardsham, it was the real story. Who he was, where he'd come from. Anything she felt like adding. If the story changed from night to night or span to span (as it did), that only added to the mystery of him.

It all began as a single provisional performance, but poor Peeds never recovered. He got sicker and thinner, till he"d grown as thin as a puppet skin himself. On his deathbed he bequeathed young Bardsham all of his puppets, his tools, his stage. His stories.

From then on, the boy spent less time thieving from the audiences and more listening to them tell the stories of their spans, their people, their families. He did something no one else had ever thought of—he started collecting the heritage of Shadowbridge. Diverse elements he folded all together, making something that had never been before. It became a great giant of a story, a spiral of a tale, just like Shadowbridge itself, all linked and spun together into something bigger than any of us can see. Except for Bardsham. And such vision, you know, it makes you a little bit mad.

His father was none too happy about losing his talented little thief permanently. But he was no fool either. The Shadowplays of Bardsham were soon bringing in the largest crowds. Nevertheless, pig-headed creature he was, he insisted that while the other acts went on, the boy must mingle with the crowd. After all, they didn't know who he was. He was a stranger, and still small. And still a skilled pickpocket. But it was a risky and foolish proposition. Anyone could see that sooner or later the child would be caught. What pickpocket hasn't been? And there were spans where the authorities cut off fingers if not a whole hand by way of punishment. The circus would lose far more than their little thief if that happened.

Finally it was his mother who confronted the old man to keep the son out of thieving. His hands were pure gold, she said. If he was caught thieving, the troupe would be ruined. Picking pockets brought in so little. Puppets brought in crowds. She was right, but her husband did not like being shown that he was wrong; as with many a man, it only made him insist on *being* wrong. He refused to listen to her. They argued. He threatened to stop the shadowplays, instead, which would have been sheer folly. He didn't care. He wanted the boy to obey him.

The time came for them to perform their show, with the two of them still arguing and as far apart as could be. They went out with that disagreement hanging unfinished between them.

That night at the end of the whip act, Mangonel missed the ring his wife held up. It had never happened before. The whip snapped against her face instead. He swore it had been an accident, but I don't think even he believed it. After that she had a scar across one cheek. Her husband could not look at her without feeling the twist of guilt in his own breast. The only way he could expiate his crime was to capitulate on Bardsham. He released the boy from the duties of thieving.

Now on every span they came to, the boy disappeared. Wherever they went, he sought out the elders almost immediately, returning only when it was time for his performance. He asked them questions, sometimes describing versions of the stories that he knew, and listened to the oldest tales they knew, hearing endless variations on the ones he told. He brought back no money now when he mingled with the crowds, but his act became more and more refined, precise, taut. He was the lure for the Mangonel Circus. Placards portrayed him as a faceless figure in a swirling purple cape. They announced his imminent arrival before the circus had even set foot upon a span. Audiences whispered his name. He was the mystery puppeteer of a million tales. Bardsham had traveled the whole world. Bardsham had been a librarian in the mythical Great Library. He was an Edgeworld god, because he knew every story on every span and only pretended at mortality—an ingenious argument given substance when an old man in one crowd claimed to have seen Bardsham's performances when just a child. He was a shill for the circus, of course, but the story spread. People watched the troupe arrive, counted their numbers, but failed to find this mystical genius. And that, too, fueled stories of him. By whatever magic, Bardsham could look inside the audience and read the stories in their hearts. Bardsham.

And what was your father's reward for all his work? To vanish.

His father took all the bows, receiving the kudos while the boy stayed hidden in the dark, listening to audiences shout his name, but unable to reveal his identity.

Mangonel may have given in to his wife's demands, but he still had the means to keep the boy in his place. He got to acting as if he had performed the shadowplays, even hiding out during some performances to reinforce the impression.

Meanwhile, the gulf between him and the other two family members deepened. He took performance money and went out on his own after shows, sometimes not coming home until the next day. His wife knew what he was doing but said nothing about it. After he'd scarred her, she had nothing to do with him beyond rehearsals anyway.

The world went on about its business. The Edgeworld gods blessed some spans, showering their Dragon Bowls with gifts, and completely ignored others. Women gave birth. Lovers quarreled and made up. Fish swam and ate smaller fish. The troupe traveled its circuit of spans and spirals. On each one they might play four or five locales before sailing off to another arm of Shadowbridge, and sooner or later back again. It was a small circuit, hardly anything compared to all the possible spans, but enough to keep them moving all year round without returning to any particular span more than once every few years. Bardsham the child developed into Bardsham the young man. As he grew older, he also grew more frustrated. He choked at having to hide in the darkness of the booth while his father accepted his acclaim. He had great skill and he wanted to be recognized. The mysterious phantom Bardsham received letters and money from admirers, invitations to palaces, even proposals of marriage. His identity continued to attract speculation. He was a djinn kept in a bottle. No, he was horribly disfigured. He was deformed. That was why he hid his face.

While not particularly handsome or tall, the real Bardsham was not unattractive either. As he grew older, he became a more conspicuous member of the troupe. Mangonel required him to pretend to be an idiot lest someone suspect him of being Bardsham. Now when he was old enough to be accepted as Bardsham, it had become imperative that the mystery be maintained. The mystery of Bardsham was what filled the benches. He helped set up the acts. He assembled and broke down the platforms. But he had to pretend to be less, always less, than what he was. He was finding other people more and more appealing. Women interested him particularly. After all, they wrote him invitations. But what chance did he have with anyone he took a fancy to when he had to play the gibbering fool? Inevitably, some people taunted him as he set up. They even jeered, "Hoy, *there's* Bardsham!" at him while they pointed and laughed. He was doing twice the work of everyone else in the troupe. He had to be seen working like a lackey and looking like a fool. Secretly, he had to practice, to perform. Even more secretly he had to find ways to gather information on stories without revealing his identity. He donned disguises or masks, when he spoke to the elders on the spans. The whole process was exhausting him.

The critical clash with his father was inevitable—a mere question of when the two tempers would flare in unison. His mother did her best to act as intermediary but she must have known she couldn't do it forever and dreaded the day when the two men clashed.

That day came: Bardsham had shirked some onerous chore in order to lurk about the span and gather up new stories. Mangonel saw him returning and called him. The old man had his whip.

He asked him something like "Where have you been and why haven't you done what I told you to do?" You know the sound of it, your uncle brays the same way—when he tells you to do one thing and then damns you for not doing another. Mangonel knew perfectly well that his son had been out doing his job as Bardsham. But he hadn't shoveled manure or swept off the stage, or cleaned some animal's pen, which were his duties, too.

Now, Bardsham wasn't big, but he performed so much of the troupe's donkey work that he was much stronger than he looked. And right then he'd had enough of trying to placate, of appeasing when it was himself being mistreated and maligned. Instead of apologizing, he walked over and told the old man that he could hire someone else to do the grunt work from now on. Bardsham had more important things to do and he was tired of carrying the burden unnecessarily, just for show. Just—as he saw it—for Mangonel's amusement. "I'm done!" he shouted, and started away.

The old man might have pretended that what he'd done to his wife was an accident, but what happened next was a hot-blooded assault.

His whip tore at Bardsham left and right, striping him with welts and blood, ripping his clothing, driving him back and back against a wall. He fell over some jugglers' props that had been assembled—some braziers and flags and large wooden pins. When he scrambled up against the wall the whip tore his shoulder open. If he'd been a second slower, it would have been his nose. He had nothing to protect him, nothing to hide behind. The old man might have been trying to kill him, too—he snapped the whip at his face, just missing an eye and leaving him afterward with a scar to match his mother's. Maybe it was seeing that scar that made the old man realize he'd never lost control of the whip in his life, not even once, not for a second. Not with anybody.

He raised it again and snapped it, but slow enough that Bardsham caught it and pulled with all his might. Hauled off his feet, the old man flew toward him, and Bardsham, quick as lightning, let go the whip and snatched up one of the juggling pins and swung it all the way around, swung it with his arms stretched out, swung it with all his anger behind it. When it hit, that pin cracked and splintered, and bits of it flew off across the yard. It stove in the side of his father's head.

Bardsham said he stood there afterward for the longest time, feeling a terrible fire in his throat, as if he might cry, but boiled with such hatred that he did nothing for the man who lay twitching and bleeding on the ground in front of him. Of course *he* was bleeding, too. His shoulder and back. His face was a mask of blood from the slash beside his eye. He dropped the broken pin and walked away.

He packed everything he owned, including the puppets left him by Peeds, and disappeared that night. Didn't even say good-bye to his mother, which he regretted the rest of his life. But that was his choice.

Mangonel didn't die, as it happens, but he was never any good for anything after that. He couldn't speak right and he couldn't walk a straight line from one end of a room to the other between one day and the next. The Mangonel Circus is what Bardsham had killed. The Mangonel name.

The puppet that was her grandfather had jerked, stumbled, and fallen over. The figure of Meersh stood alone and somehow wretched.

Leodora had asked, "Did he ever go back?"

Soter shook his head. "He would send money to his mother whenever he had some and remembered it. But never a note, never a word. He was too ashamed to write, to say where he was. There was nothing he could say. He knew he would have killed his father. Happily. Of course, his mother would have understood—you and I can see that, but not Bardsham. She must have known that she could find him, because he was famous, you know. Bardsham only grew in stature once he'd escaped from the circus. She could have found him any time."

"Like my mother."

For a moment he looked alarmed. Then he smiled nervously and said, "Ah, I see what you mean—like your mother ran away from home. Yes. I often thought that his break with his family was the cause of much of his debauch—that is, his excesses. He drank and . . . well, drank more than any human being I've ever known. You could not be friends with him and not drink. He often said that he didn't trust men who didn't imbibe. They were afraid of something. Something inside themselves, and he felt he should be wary of it, too."

"So when did you come to know him?"

Soter set down the last puppet figure. There would be no puppet for him.

With obvious relish, he said, "I came across Bardsham while I was selling nostrums. He needed a reconnaissance man, a vanguard to make arrangements, make sure we had a place to perform and to sleep on every span, wherever we went. Make sure there would be no trouble. Likewise it must be someone with the necessary sophistication to announce him, a person of skill and wit to suss the nature of the place and its inhabitants. A person of reliable character and cunning and . . ." He paused, opened his hands as if tossing something in the air, and bowed slightly. "He had a need that I filled perfectly.

"Without such a person, Bardsham had to handle these things. He had to come out of the booth between each set and announce himself, interrupting the flow of the stories. That made him seem ordinary, and you can't seem ordinary if you want to perform. Besides, he was Bardsham—ordinary wasn't an option. The cloak of mystery was crucial.

"The two of us had been traveling parallel circuits, you might say. Every span's different. Laws are different, permits are different. Sometimes you need one, sometimes you don't. Sometimes you'll get arrested if you set up without bribing the right fellow. Sometimes you get arrested if you try to bribe them. It's half your life keeping on top of such things. A great artist cannot be distracted by such petty matters." He sounded to her as if he were quoting someone. "An artist's head is full of tricks and tales, not the names of who to pay off and how to finesse the obdurate authorities."

His tone was one of longing. They had been young men then, on an adventure together. She could hear it. "The world was all before us," he told her, then fell silent. Warily, she asked, "What about my mother?"

The dreaminess in Soter's expression pinched into a look almost of pain. His eyes darted her way for a second. Not encouraged by his reaction, she pressed her point: "Is what uncle Gousier says about her true?"

He picked up the puppet figure of Orinda. It glided across the case as he spoke. "What your uncle knows of your mother on the spans, he's pieced together like a quilt—a word here, a rumor there. He never spoke to anyone who knew her. That is, other than me; and he'd prefer not to know what I know because it might spoil the picture he's framed. He knows nothing of how she lived or what she did to survive. His account's a fabrication. When I arrived here with you, your existence only confirmed everything he'd invented about her. That she must have been a wanton to produce a child and then abandon it was all too clear to him and he set it like a minaret atop the story he'd already invented. You're the crowning piece whether you wish it or not. Here you are and Leandra nowhere to be seen." He slid the puppet back inside the case.

"But she was dead!"

"Which made no difference to him. That she'd left you in my care, in Bardsham's care, before she went off is what matters, you see. In his mind, she abandoned you. Her death's a mere inconvenience after the fact. An orphan proved what he already believed. She was unfit. Unfit to be his sister. And that's the real issue."

"Was she—" and here she stopped, poised at the brink of asking the critical question that would either vindicate or damn the image she retained, her mind shaping words the specifics of which were beyond her, but the depravity of which she'd inferred from the way her uncle's mouth twisted and his eyes went hard as he uttered the name. "Was she really The Red Witch? Did she have powers?"

"Red Witch?" The name troubled him, she could see. "Where do you"—he tried unpersuasively to sound amused—"where do you get such a name?"

"From you," she answered, and she watched as he

hesitated, tried to recall when he had let this slip.

He squeezed shut his eyes and rubbed his forehead. "Oh. Well. It was just a name, that's all, Leodora. A reputation. The same way that Bardsham was a name." Orinda fell over and lay still on the box. "That's enough now, I'm tired."

But she would not be diverted by his pretense of exhaustion. This was too important. Her world was taking shape. "Was she the Red Witch? Did she lure men to their deaths?"

He stiffened. Slowly his hand uncovered his face. His bilious eyes distorted his haggard face into something inhumanly furious—gaunt and hard and evil. One corner of his mouth curled as he replied: "Ask your father. She lured *him*."

He rose up, gathered the puppets and shoved them back into the cases. Ignoring her as if she were no longer in the room, he carried the cases back to the dark pantry.

After that he tried never to mention Leandra again. If she asked a question, he wouldn't answer with anything concrete or helpful. Mostly he feigned that he remembered too little to be of any use.

She couldn't trust her uncle to tell her anything concrete because he did nothing but call his sister "the witch," much as the villagers did. To ask him was to invite trouble. Her aunt was especially reticent when Gousier was around, but even when he was absent, she professed to have come to the island only after Leandra was gone and so couldn't provide any help. Leodora suspected this wasn't true, but she didn't want to accuse her aunt and lose the sympathy of the only person who ever sided with her.

Beyond Bouyan her mother was nothing but a half-condensed phantom, a legend, a myth. On Bouyan she was a scourge, a harlot, an abomination.

While she couldn't probe him for information, she did induce Soter to teach her about the puppets. He accepted her apprenticeship reluctantly at first, but with increasing devotion as, over time, her dedication and skill emerged. It wasn't just a casual interest in puppetry she displayed. Nor were his first impressions of her dexterity off the mark. Leodora had her father's gifts. Many times during the first years of her training, Soter proclaimed it.

The secret practice sessions gave meaning to her life. They made the indignities suffered at her uncle's hands almost bearable. They gave her a goal to strive for—a means to leave the island, to strike out on her own.

The goal had no date. She didn't know when or how she would leave, and she might not really have gone at all. She really had no idea then what she was inviting—how much effort would really be involved, how much of her life she would devote to practice. She would train and train, while Soter forever reminded her that she wasn't quite ready, that her skills still needed sharpening; that there was a world of detail she didn't know, of subtlety she didn't yet possess. As time passed, she began to think that she might spend her whole life preparing for just one performance.

Life on Bouyan ran along with a tedious sameness.

Each morning she awoke in her small garret atop the boathouse. It was a room she had taken as a sanctuary after discovering it on one of her flights from her uncle. It had a small bed and sparse furnishings in it, suggesting that someone had lived there before her. Her aunt and uncle didn't resist when she asked if she could move into the garret. In truth, she had asked Dymphana, who as always had acted as go-between for her; but she had watched the interchange, had seen her uncle's hooded gaze shift to her with an incomprehensible look of relief, as though he wanted her gone. For once his desires and hers agreed. She was thirteen. Her body was changing and with it her emotional compass: She wanted privacy; she wanted her own places on the island. Her uncle's one stipulation was that she cease all complaining about her assigned tasks.

Once she had arisen, she dressed and went down the beach to Tenikemac to watch the sea dragons surface. The village dotted the whole curve of the bay just over the north ridge. The ridge took half an hour to reach, and as she walked she watched the people already up and working, especially the half-dozen women gathering seaweed in baskets along the beach ahead of her. Soon she had reached them, but for the most part they ignored her, letting her by as if she didn't exist. On the ridge, she stopped and watched.

The men in teams of two carried their rolled-up nets down beside the water, where they unfurled them. Tastion and his father made up one team. He pretended not to see her, so no one was suspicious of the true relationship between them.

Soon four younger boys waded into the water up to their

waists, each carrying a large conch with pierced ends. In unison, they raised the shells to their lips and blew a trumpet call.

Everyone stopped what they were doing and turned to study the surface.

Farther out, the water rippled. Slithers of yellow appeared, darted beneath the grayish waves. Then the heads rose up, one after another, strange, long-snouted, magisterial heads with large, black and protruding eyes. These were the Sea Dragons.

There were sixteen of them in all and she knew every one. She had never ridden them, never touched them. As a female, she wasn't allowed. But she'd given them names. Her favorite was Muvros, the youngest, his head yellow and black, freckled with the red spots of youth, and his snout as thin as a reed. The tiny mouth at the end of it seemed forever puckered, as if sharing a kiss.

The conch boys fed the dragons long strips of the gathered seaweed and would feed them again when they returned. Meanwhile, the fishermen, dragging their nets, moved into the water two by two. The dragons seemed as fascinated by the men as Leodora was with the dragons. They bowed their heads and let their riders clamber over their necks and sit. They seemed not in the least encumbered by the riders.

With a storyteller's inquisitiveness, she wondered when this ritual had begun, and who had tamed the first dragon. Even the village itself didn't seem to know, or else she would have known the story, too. Soter had taught her every one of their tales with the intention of having her perform them for villagers—once he was satisfied that she was skilled enough.

The dragons snaked off into deeper waters, their riders rocking from side to side. Some of the men would return early with full nets. Others stayed out all day, hunting a more difficult catch but one which might earn them more money on Ningle. Tastion and his father were among those who hunted farther away.

She watched until he was gone from sight, then turned and set off into the trees to perform the most hateful task in the world.

Fishkill Cavern lay not terribly deep inside the hill—the entrance was barely out of sight behind her before the passage turned and widened into a broad chamber. Close to the outside or not, no matter what the temperature on the island might be, the cavern remained as cold as an iceberg. Water barely dripped from the stalactites; when she was little, it had been fun to watch and watch until a single drop fell. Now she felt as if her life was measured out in those drops, slow and icy and suspended for eternity.

Halfway between home and the village, nature had created the perfect repository for the village's daily catch. A congeries of fish and mussels and other, articulated creatures surrounded Leodora every morning, laid upon reed mats that covered most of the floor. A large table comprising boulders and one flat slab stood close to one wall. That was where she spent her mornings, gutting, cleaning and filleting; cracking and splitting and deveining. The offal poured, cold and slick, into baskets beside her, most of which would be taken back by the fishermen and thrown into the sea, sometimes as bait for other fish. The product, ready for market, was heaped on other mats and placed inside round wicker panniers with straps.

She didn't clean all, or even most, of the catch—most of it was sold as it was. Even so there was enough work to keep her busy through the morning.

She wore her ragged clothes in layers. They kept her warm even as they became spotted with gore. Her feet were well-wrapped, too. She always made a point of drying them before entering the cavern. If she hadn't, she could have lost her toes, like the fabled trickster Meersh, against the icy cavern floor. Her hands could not be so protected. Her nimble fingers grew chilled and red, and finally numb. Her greatest fear was that she would lose so much feeling in her hands that she would chop off a finger and not notice it until her own blood was mingling with that of the fish. It was a fear grown into a phobia. Outside the cavern she kept a basket of ocean water placed in the sunlight. When her fingers numbed, she ran out and plunged them in the water. The flesh tingled to life and soon felt as if it were ablaze, the ends of her arms boiling. She did this four or five times a morning, preferring discomfort to dismemberment.

At some point her uncle would arrive, sometimes alone, sometimes with whatever vermin he could hire from Ningle to help tote the fish up onto the span, another half an hour's walk from there. Gousier's assistants turned over almost as often as the tide. They tended to ogle her, this young girl whose body was developing its adult shape earlier than some they knew.

While they might have been the lowest of creatures on Ningle, down here on the island they were in a place that they could consider below even their station; and she, being of the island, was a pleb at their disposal. At least, so Soter had warned her. He predicted that, sooner or later, one or both assistants would try to grope her. He told her what to watch for—those subtle, vulpine glances being one of the signs. But so far, no one had harmed her.

When her uncle had taken the panniers full of fish onto the span, then Leodora was freed from servitude.

Sodden with fish blood, she left the cavern and followed a small path south of the house, past Dymphana's garden, and up over a few weedy dunes to the far side of a low promontory there. His claim on the land ended with the dunes, where the grass turned quickly into brush too thorny to cut down and the beach beyond narrowed to a footpath. The brush might have been a wall to fend off invaders from the sea—it was that thick. But if one continued along the strip of beach to the far side of them, the shore made an abrupt hook, creating a natural jetty of rock that doubled back upon the promontory like an index finger almost pressing against a thumb. When the tide was out, finger and thumb did close completely, and the small isolated inlet became a lagoon for a while. Even with the tide up and the waves coming across the hook, it remained free of strong currents and riptides, a hidden stillness. The dunes hid the lagoon from view on Gousier's side, and the rocky hook rose inland like a low wall, as if a failed span had once upon a time attempted to push up out of the island, producing finally nothing but the thorny wildwood. No one had any use for it and no one else ever went there.

On the sheltered strip of beach she peeled off the foul clothes. Underneath, ruddy patches marked her skin where the blood had soaked through. She immersed the clothes in the shallow water, and like coral smoke the blood swirled lazily out of them.

She left them soaking in the shallows and waded past them into the depths of the lagoon. Untied, her red hair fanned all the way to her waist.

Tiny creatures nipped at her toes, and she yelped and dove in, swimming out to the far rim of rocks; locating the gouge in them through which she could slip into the deeper water. She plunged headlong beneath the waves, kicked back up to the surface and broke free with a gasp, in imitation of the sea dragons. She liked to play at being a dragon, at wriggling through the water with her feet together like a tail.

She had been born swimming, she thought.

The lagoon had been her private retreat for over a year. She kept this secret even from Tastion; and, anyway, he was always out fishing or else working the fields on the distant side of the village when she went there, so there was no reason for him to know. She wanted—she needed—something to be hers alone. Even the puppets she had to share with Soter. And with the ghost of her father.

That day as on most days after swimming, she lay sunning herself, warm and muzzy and so nearly asleep that she didn't hear any approaching footsteps. She had the impression of a sharp intake of breath, and then a voice poked through the membrane of dream with a single word: "Witch!" So loud and so near that she didn't think it was real at all until she opened one eye and found him standing right beside her. He stepped up and his shadow blocked the sunlight.

She screeched, and rolled away across the sand, scrambling for her wet clothing, draping the tunic over her budding figure before she turned to confront the intruder.

No one was there.

She roughly brushed the sand from her face, thinking she'd dreamed it all. But in the sand were his footprints, clear and cautious impressions in approach, wild gouges upon retreat. He'd fled past the wildwood and right up the rocks. She ran to them and climbed up high enough to look over the rise and saw him far away, still running in the shallows, not even daring to look back, his arms flailing ahead of him. A moment later he had disappeared around the curve of the beach.

She'd only glimpsed him for an instant—an impression of tangled, matted gray hair and ragged clothes. And that word—that word lined with horror. "Witch."

She dressed in the sandy, sodden clothes then and ran to her uncle's house. Dymphana was outdoors, digging corms from her garden.

Her aunt's features pulled tight with concern at the sight of her. She asked, "What's happened, child?"

Trembling, fidgeting, Leodora told her. A man had

appeared, a stranger. He'd seen her and then run away. She clung to her aunt and cried, "But why *witch*! Why did he call me a witch? Why did he say that?"

Dymphana replied, "Oh, child, it's not you, it's your mother used to swim there, too, and I'm—"

Pressed against her, Leodora felt her aunt stiffen as both of them realized what had been said.

"How do you know that?" She pushed away, no longer frightened. "You said you didn't know anything, that my mother was gone before you came to Bouyan!"

It seemed for a moment that Dymphana might try to bluff her way out of the trap, as if she weighed whether she should compound the denial with another obvious lie. Finally, however, she set down her hoe. "You must promise never to tell your uncle nothing you hear from me. He'd know in a second where you learned it, because Soter doesn't know a thing about Leandra's life on this island. Gousier never told him nothin', neither."

"I promise," she swore.

"You are so like her, you know that. More each day, to my eye. When I promised your uncle never to speak on your mother, it was when you was so tiny, and it seemed right then not to have you burdened with what we knew. Your uncle said he didn't want you growing up like her. That seemed good wisdom then. But you are her daughter—and no one who knew her could ever mistake it.

"Your mother thought the ocean belonged to her, same as you—that lagoon especially, same as you. It was hers. Oh, you didn't think anyone knew?" She smiled with tenderness through her exasperation. "Dear heart, I keep track of you far more'n you realize. I know perfectly well that you lie about nude in the sand over past them dunes. Just like your mother did."

A thrill ran through Leodora at the thought of her mother lying in that very same spot, seeing the same sky. The pleasure was followed a moment later by the realization that her private spot was no longer private. Like everything else, she shared it.

"The man you saw, he'd be an Omelune," said Dymphana, as though that explained everything. "I expect he thought you were your mother."

"Everyone calls her a witch. Everyone in Tenikemac. Uncle Gousier. Even Soter. He calls her 'The Red Witch.'"

"Oh, does he now? To you he says this? That old fool. He has no right to talk on her at all, even if he does know such things as we don't."

"Well, at least he doesn't *lie*," she snapped, and for a moment she thought her aunt was going to weep.

Instead, her expression still pinched, Dymphana explained, "'Red Witch,' is a name from the spans. No one ever called her that here. To be sure, the Omelunes called her worse. I always wondered if she adopted the name on purpose to mock Bouyan. Thumbin' her nose at everything. That'd be like her."

"What are Omelunes?"

Dymphana took her by the hand. "Come here and let me sit." They walked over and sat on a broad stump in the shade. The breeze on her wet clothes quickly chilled Leodora and she scooted off the stump and onto the ground, where she could face her aunt from within a warm patch of sunlight.

"You understand that I was no part of the household in her younger days. I didn't meet your uncle 'til perhaps two years before she'd gone. She would have been a few years older than you are now when I arrived. Whenever I look on you, I can't help seeing her like she's a ghost right inside your skin. I've almost called you by her name more than once. You have so much of her—her body, her face. Your uncle sees it, too. I know he does. Even your stubbornness is your mother's, although I'm inclined to think that being stubborn just runs in your family. For that brief while after I came, it was we two women and your grandmother living together in a small wood house all day long—it was smaller then. Your grandfather extended it three times with them extra rooms. He was a great carpenter, a builder."

"I remember."

"We all thought it would be filling up soon with more . . ." She paused, her face pinched, her eyes casting now toward the woods. Leodora knew that her aunt had given birth three times and that none of the babies had survived beyond a few months. She knew where the graves were, and that the final stillbirth had almost killed Dymphana. Her uncle would have no sons.

"Leandra told me all sorts of stories about herself. She didn't mind telling them on herself, either. Didn't mind looking the fool if it made for a good story. You might not have guessed, listening to her laugh at herself, make fun of herself, how much iron there was in her backbone. I came down from Ningle to live with your uncle, and I had certain airs when I first arrived here: thinking I was above this place, better than it was, and that I was above everyone born here. I needed to pretend that then. My family on Ningle—they're all gone now—they were so poor that this life is much better than I could have hoped for there. I'd have been in a gutter or worse. Gousier was so fine and strong. He used to laugh. You wouldn't know it now. He used to be like your mother that way. Or maybe she let him share some of her joy, so that he seemed happier than he was. All I know is, when she left, she took that joy away with her. I've missed it so long, it's like something I dreamed of once that never really happened.

"It didn't take me long to learn my limits. Your grandmother straightened me out about who I was and what was expected of me. Your mother, though, wasn't about to be straightened out. She challenged everything.

"She used to swim out past your lagoon, where she weren't supposed to—over the rocks and into the deep. One morning she vanished altogether out there. She was missing so long that your grandparents feared she'd drowned. Gousier went out in his esquif, paddling all over, looking everywhere. Even some of Tenikemac came out to hunt for her in sympathy. They'd lost swimmers of their own to the hidden currents and undertows—some was never seen again. And it was no balm to your grandparents' spirits to have their standoffish neighbors come and console them over their loss. That was like the final proof that she was gone.

"It fell dark. Everyone had returned from the sea. Your grandmother was wailing now. They'd all given up. And in walked your mother. She came in stark naked and exhausted, and not a bit ashamed of her deed or her body. Proud, if barely able to stand on her own feet. Worse, in the eyes of Tenikemac especially, she claimed she'd ridden home on the back of a sea dragon. No one gave her much credence. They thought she was saying it to stir them up more. She didn't mean to be evil. She didn't do it to hurt them. She did it to tear down a limit. It was like she had to beat the gods of ocean themselves. She would have been, I think, just as happy if they had destroyed her for the challenge. It would have meant something had happened, she'd gotten the gods' attention at last."

"Did her parents punish her? What did they do?"

"Oh, they forbade her to swim, but you know they never

enforced it. They were happy that she wasn't dead. It's difficult to be angry when you're so elated. And then she collapsed right there in front of them, so mostly they were too busy nursing her well to threaten her much. Her task was gutting fish, same as you. There was no worse punishment they could have inflicted on her, and none that would have done anyone any good. Couldn't keep her from cleaning the fish unless someone else did it, and when you're all covered in blood and guts, well, who's going to forbid you to wash? They don't want the stink of you like that, either."

"So she went back to swimming?" Leodora rather liked the idea that her mother had bested them all.

"Yes, she did, child. In the end, though, that willfulness of hers boxed her in. No islander would have her. The family was even more cut off from Tenikemac then. It's only in the past few years Gousier has opened them up a tiny bit again, at least some of the men. The women are harder. If there had been a chance for Leandra before with them, there wasn't one after that night. Their own men had been out hunting for her, and if she'd drowned, they'd have all mourned her and made sacrifices to the sea in her name, but she weren't drowned nor even in peril, and after that the women shunned her and made their men shun her. If she'd ever gotten into real trouble after that, they would have lifted nary a finger to help, an' probably would have hoped the gods destroyed her."

It was clear from the look her aunt gave her that she was supposed to take instruction from her mother's folly. She said nothing and Dymphana seemed to regard this as acquiescence.

"Leandra had already given up on that village anyway. I don't know exactly when she began to look elsewhere on the island.

"The Weejar people were on the far side of Ningle as they are now, isolated by the legs of that span, and half a day's walking around the beach unless you can find the paths, what I could never do. But back then there was a third group lived down around the southern tip a good three hours away—"

"The Omelunes," guessed Leodora.

"That's right. You're so clever, you got there ahead of me. The Omelunes were a fishing village, the same as Tenikemac, only they didn't have the skill with dragons. They used boats. Some of their people also took their fish up to Ningle, and so Tenikemac would have nothing to do with them. Weejar is more like the Omelunes were—boats for fishing, and rice swamps inland. The rice is the only reason Tenikemac trades with them.

"One day, while the men of Omelune were out fishing or selling fish, Leandra swam all the way around to their village. The women on the beach saw her splashing in the waves, and damn them if they didn't pick up stones, every one of them, and walk to the edge of the water and start flinging them at your mother to keep her from coming in to land. They knew she didn't belong to them. They thought she was one of the merfolk that overturn boats and drown the sailors."

"What merfolk?" asked Leodora, half disbelieving and half curious, wondering if Soter had any figures of merfolk buried in his stacks of puppets.

"Tenikemac knows of them, too, you can ask someone there. It were such a long swim to Omelune, you can well imagine that no one from here had ever tried it before. It's not like somebody was expecting her. What else were the women of Omelune to think?

"Leandra must have been very tired, but she turned back—they left her no choice. The problem was, the women chased her along the beach, throwing rocks wherever they found them. Finally there was this spit of land, a little peninsula sticking out in the water. Leandra wasn't watching ahead—she was keeping her eye on them women and diving down when something looked like it would hit her. So then all of a sudden she found the women coming right at her as if across the water itself. They cut the distance in half before she understood what had happened and leapt to swim away. One of the rocks struck her in the head, and she floundered, and she sank. The women must have thought they'd killed her. They left her alone and went marching back home in triumph. They'd killed a merwoman, and wouldn't that be something to tell the men when the men came back from fishing?

"It was pure instinct kept Leandra afloat. Pretty soon the currents had her. She kicked up her legs when she thought of it. When she was sensible. Blood stung her eyes, and it was about all she could do to keep her head above the surface. She was drifting, she didn't know where.

"The next thing she knew there were hands on her body, and she was being dragged through the water. She said she thought that the gods of the ocean had finally got her for all the times she'd taunted them. She tried to fight, but she had no energy left and fainted dead away. Then she was being pushed up into the air and onto something hard.

"Some young fool—and a brave one, I expect, to chance rescuing a merwoman—saw her floating there and pulled her into his boat. He was from Omelune. He had no idea what had happened, he just saw this naked girl in the water and he dove in after her. When he found out who she was, he paddled her back home. By the time he'd got her back to our beach, your mother had decided he was the one for her."

"And that's the man who called me a witch?" guessed Leodora.

"Hush, now. You want this story, don't try and race around it.

"Afterwards, the two of them met in secret. Even in Fishkill Cavern if your uncle can be believed—which he can't. He thinks the worst of them both, of course, even though he doesn't know anything at all. She didn't tell him half what she told me. She was in love. She wasn't going to tell her brother about that, now, was she?

"Now, the village of Omelune must have had some inkling what was going on, but maybe they didn't know just where he was going. Surely they couldn't have guessed that the red-haired creature they'd fended off was the same one he was visiting regularly.

"Then one night he and Leandra arranged to meet on that ridge of rocks that makes your lagoon. He was such a fool for her that he decided to swim from Omelune to the lagoon just to match her feat. To prove to her or to himself that he was worthy. He didn't tell a soul, just set off.

"Leandra, she waited and waited and he didn't come and his boat never appeared. She could have gotten into Gousier's esquif, but not her. She had to swim off to look for him. I think she was still planning to tease him: She would creep up on his boat just to scare him. That was her intention.

"In the morning, we couldn't find her anywhere. The family looked all over. It hadn't been so long since we'd thought she drowned, so we weren't quite given over to panic this time. She wasn't in the cavern. She wasn't at Tenikemac. We had no idea where she'd got to, so it was late in the day before your grandfather thought to go looking for her in the direction of Omelune. He found her on the beach. Somewhere between here and there, not all that far from home. She was sitting, just sitting, cold and wet and rocking back and forth, with that poor dead boy's head cradled in her lap. He'd drowned trying to match her. You see what happened—her willfulness undid her in the end."

"He died?" Leodora couldn't understand that turn of events. She had already jumped to the end of the story, where her mother ran away with the boy from Omelune, and this turn ruined that story.

"He died, yes, and afterwards nothing was good for your mother on the island. Omelune blamed her for his death. When they saw her, when they realized who she was, the women accused her of being a water witch, a lorelei. A love-struck girl wasn't enough for them. She tried to drown herself, tried to swim to the ends of the ocean and let the gods take her soul; but your grandfather had some sense of this. He was watching her close now, and he went after her, brought her back, locked her in the boathouse with only her grief for a companion, and wouldn't let her out until he was satisfied she'd gotten the idea of drowning herself out of her head. Even I couldn't see her or talk to her that whole time. He let nobody near her. And then, while she was locked up, a terrible storm struck the island. Nets and boats were tossed around and torn apart. Your uncle's esquif was smashed up on some rocks, and that's the hole what's still in its side. Weejar and Tenikemac both suffered, but not like Omelune. That poor cursed village was stamped flat, and so many people died that you couldn't have made a village out of what was left. The survivors blamed your mother for it all. They knew already she was some sort of ocean spirit. Now she was worse: Leandra the Red-haired Witch, the Soul-Drinker. Either they couldn't see her misery or they didn't believe it. Weejar took in some of the survivors—of course, Tenikemac so typically refused to be a haven for those who'd sold fish on Ningle. The Omelune opinion of your mother, though, spread everywhere. Weejar traded with Tenikemac the same as now. Pretty soon your mother had nowhere to go at all. The whole island had set itself against her."

"Why didn't grandfather . . . do something?"

"What could he do? We were already viewed as no better than a necessary evil by Tenikemac. It's a role we've long accepted, because we make a good living by filling that niche. The taint of the spans was bad enough, and her jeopardizing their men worse, but now we harbored something cursed.

"When Leandra insisted on accompanying your grandfather and Gousier onto Ningle, the two of them agreed it was a very good idea. She was seventeen. She was a beauty. She ought to have been married. And it was clear that she could never find a suitable husband here. I think they hoped she would catch someone's eye up there.

"A few times she went up, and I'm sure she must have been learning all she could of the place. Laying her plans. She said nothing to me or anyone. One morning she went up with the men and never came down again. Vanished right out from under their noses. That was the last time anyone in the family ever laid eyes on her."

"She ran away."

"That she did, and alone, too. No one thought she could get far, but they had always underestimated her distance. Gousier went looking for her up and down the span and found nothing, not a trace. She'd taken a full purse from the family coffers—we had as much then as now. No one begrudged her that; she would have been given more as a dowry had things gone right. The money meant she could buy herself into the shadows, though. Buy passage to some other great long stretch of spans, leaving no trail to follow, no way to guess which way she'd gone.

"The day Soter came down those steps, carrying you as proof of his tale of her, of her death, was the first we'd heard of her in years.

"Your uncle cried like a baby himself. I know that's hard for you to imagine, but it's true. So long as he had no idea of his sister's fate, he could make up whatever he liked, and even if it was awful and cruel and defamed her with every word, it was comforting somehow. Like he kept her alive by inventing a world of failures for her. The truth wiped it all away. It broke him. It went much worse on him than on either of your grandparents. They'd come to accept her choice. Gousier took to drink. What he made in the stall of a day he spent in the pursuit of his own undoing. Trying to erase her, hiding from her. I couldn't talk to him, almost like he couldn't see me. One time he fell partway down the steps from Ningle, he was so drunk. For a while he wasn't allowed to go up. Soter and I filled in as much as we could. Of course then Gousier accused Soter of trying to usurp his position—Soter, who wanted nothing to do with fish, but felt he owed your grandfather something for letting him stay. Gousier was crazy awhile, and nothing he said during that time is worth recalling. When it went on past all reason, your grandfather locked himself and Gousier in his workshop for the better part of a day. Neither one of them ever told what went on in there, but when they came out, your uncle was bruised, bloody, and sober. And quiet. What-ever his opinions were, he said no more about her. Never mentioned his sister afterward, as if he'd never had one. He went back to work and after a time, he eased up. He was good for a while—you might even remember from when you was little. Then, when your grandfolk died, it all came out again, everything he'd bottled up, and he cursed her for their deaths, too, blamed her all over again, but this time it was different. He bellowed at her as if she was hiding in the woods and could hear everything he said. He told her she'd killed them by breaking their hearts as surely as if she'd murdered them by her own hand."

The idea terrified her. "Is that true? Did she?"

Dymphana leaned forward and took her hand. "Now, you think on it. Years had passed between her going and theirs. She wasn't no more responsible than you was. They were old people. Whichever of them went first, the other was going to follow. Them Kuseks up on Ningle had more to do with your grandfather's going than your mother and you. No. Leodora, your uncle's like the Omelunes—he needs there to be someone responsible for all the bad things. Someone he can point at. I think he was in love with your mother a little bit, and I think part of it is envy. I think there's a part of Gousier that'd like to roam the spans, but the dutiful part tells him he has to stay here and maintain the tradition that his father maintained. An' if he has to, then so does everyone else."

She stared, dumbfounded. Her aunt's story revealed a depth of comprehension and thought that she'd never suspected. How could Dymphana think and see and know so much, and keep it all to herself? Why didn't she feel as Leodora did the need to express her feelings, to fight the restrictions that were placed on her?

Then Leodora's face clouded with another puzzle. "If the boy from Omelune is dead, then who is the man who thought I was my mother?"

"I expect he's one of the other villagers, someone who didn't leave there with the rest. There was a handful, tried to rebuild. I daresay he won't come our way again, not now he believes the witch is still with us."

"But how can he have been there for so many years and not come here before?"

Dymphana shrugged. "Life's full of mysteries. Not all of 'em have answers, Leodora. Why did a storm destroy Omelune when it did? And why not Tenikemac?"

"I don't know."

"Well, and you won't neither. The world has its mysteries. The gods have designs into which we and the world are woven."

"But—" she stopped herself. "But how can anybody know if the things they're doing are part of that plan or not?"

Dymphana smiled. "And aren't you the deep thinker?" She tousled her hair. "Better be careful asking that sort of question aloud, or the archivists of the Library will hear and come take you away to teach them." She laughed at the look of bemused terror on Leodora's face. "Oh, it's just a myth, dear heart. The Library's just a story."

"It is?"

"Of course."

In that case, she wondered, why hadn't Soter taught it to her?

Two years later she did know the story of the Library of Shadowbridge, and far more than that.

By the time she turned fifteen, Soter had given up all his stories, and there were mermen and archivists of the Library in among the tales, along with Meersh, and two brothers who coveted one another's gifts, and brides who drowned their husbands and husbands who beheaded their wives—of course, Bardsham could have spun even more stories, but Soter had attended so many performances that he remembered a great many of them.

Now, instead of teaching her stories, he taught her how to take the elements and mix them together to make new stories. "Not until you can improvise from all you know will you become a true shadowmaster," he told her. "That's where your *father* truly excelled." The way he said it suggested that he didn't anticipate her excelling there ever. Yet she was devoted to the craft. She had every intention of succeeding. The world of the spans was going to be her oyster. She had decided. But while she laid her plans and dreamed of far-spun fame, other forces were conspiring to demolish every dream and keep her a prisoner there forever.

Even before she opened her eyes that morning, she heard the strange murmurous call. It woke her nearly every morning now, no louder—if such could be said of something silent—than when she'd first heard it as her grandfather held her at the railing of the span, ten years before; since she had moved into the boathouse it had become more insistent, urgent, although the urgency gave her no guidance, no advice, no real idea of what to do in response. She climbed from her bed and crossed the narrow garret to stand in the window, to stare across the water as if this morning she might spy the source. It—whatever it was—might suddenly top the horizon to reveal its shape, and in appearing explain why it called to her and no one else. What did it want of her? It wasn't calling her to come to it, but by the same token it was not going to let her forget its existence.

The curtains flapped in the breeze. The light coming off the ocean was gray and vaporous. It smelled of rain, though there was nothing of rain in the sky.

Melancholy joined her then, a late-awaking twin. Leodora leaned out the window like a figurehead on the prow of a ship, and stared along the shore to the north, out across the point and past, where the call was strongest, like a smell on the breeze or a gull's cry wrapped in the wind; loud in its silence, bright in its subtility, overwhelming in its absence—the source of her soul's unease. One day it would surely appear and she would have her answers. She had learned to accept the frustration of not knowing when. The call remained, but she let it recede into the sizzle of the surf, and withdrew from the window.

It took her a few minutes to dress in the ragged and stained clothes for Fishkill Cavern. She climbed down the steps into the boathouse, where her uncle's small esquif lay on supports, the hole in its side aimed at her like an empty socket. He was never going to repair it—she understood that now. It was linked to her mother and now to her, because she lived here.

She walked barefoot across the planks and picked up a wicker basket as she pushed open the wide double doors. She jumped down the stone launching ramp then padded across the beach toward the water. Streamers of seaweed were scattered all along the shore, and she collected each one, and shook the sand and debris and little perturbed creatures out before placing it in the basket.

The sand was soft and sodden between her toes. She jumped when an irate sandcrab nipped her foot before digging in deeper. Most of the little crabs scattered and scuttled and burrowed before she reached them. Later, when the tide had withdrawn, the shore would teem with gulls, squawking and fighting over the same scurrying snacks. Yet there would be new ones tomorrow, just one more of life's mysteries.

After walking awhile, she climbed to the top of the ridge and surveyed the village, concentrating on the figures there, forcing the ocean's call out of her head.

Moving her way were the usual group of women collecting seaweed. She spotted Kusahema and headed down the slope to their beach. Kusahema was married now, and pregnant.

When they were face to face, Kusahema smiled and held out her basket, and Leodora took all the strands of seaweed she'd collected and gave them to her.

"I liked your shadows the other night," said Kusahema. "They were very funny."

Leodora closed her eyes and bowed her head in thanks. Then she reached out and placed her hand on Kusahema's protruding belly. "Will it be today, do you think?"

"Only the ocean can know," came the ritual reply. Both the touch and the interchange were considered propitious. They grinned at one another, but then Kusahema's smile faltered and she took her basket and moved on.

As recently as two years ago, they had been close friends, sometimes swimming together. But as Kusahema became nubile, her family had forced her to withdraw her affection and cease meeting her friend.

Only Tastion remained close now. And that, as she had suspected for some time, was due to motives of a different sort; and even he was betrothed, soon to be married. He still told her that he would run away with her, a plan they'd hatched when they were seven, but she knew it for an empty promise.

Soon her only connection to the village would be the shadowplays that she and Soter performed for them, and which by their very nature connected her with the spans—even though most of the tales they performed for Tenikemac were its own myths and legends.

She stood alone and watched Tastion and his father, the two of them looking like two versions of the same man. They unfurled their net and moved into the water. They even moved the same way. Tastion of course pretended not to see her, which he must, just as she could not stare directly at him for any length of time. She pretended to watch the crowd further up the beach, and so happened to be staring at Koombrun when he suddenly lurched away from the crowd and grabbed hold of one of the nets. He was trying to help, desperate to take part in the ritual, to accompany the other men. Before he'd taken two steps, he'd put his foot through the weave and tripped himself. He sprawled onto his back and turned to get up. By then his mother had come forward, and she slapped him with a series of blows that had him cowering, ducking, crawling across the sand, his foot still stuck in the net. One of the other fishermen, Lemros, came to his rescue. The crowd was laughing, but Lemros calmly unsnagged the poor brute, then wedging himself between Koombrun and his mother, helped him to his feet.

Koombrun was a year older than Tastion, which meant he should have been riding dragons long ago. He was large and strong enough, but mentally feeble. He had always been. Even as a child, he hadn't been able to keep up with Leodora and her playmates, and none of them had treated him very kindly, something she regretted as she watched his mother attacking him. His deficiency would have been no more than a tragic burden upon the family, except that his father had drowned three years earlier. In any other family, the son would have stepped in to do the father's work; but Koombrun couldn't be allowed to fish. She often heard him in the audience during shadowplays, his nasal bleating laughter drowning out other voices. He laughed at the obvious jokes, and sometimes added his voice to everyone else's, as if he thought it wise to pretend to understand. As if they would accept him if he did.

The village made sure that he and his mother were looked after, of course, but this came with a price for her—always to be humbled, humiliated, dependent upon others. No one else had come forward to marry her. No one would. No one wanted Koombrun in their family, and his mother would never have another child. So she punished him for all the things he couldn't control or comprehend. For being different. Leodora sympathized with his plight. It wasn't that much different from her own.

She stood on the beach and watched until Tastion was gone from sight. He would likely be out all day, for he and his father fished farther out than many of the others. Where they went and how they found their way back on the vast and featureless sea was a mystery to her, and even though Tastion had tried to explain it to her, she didn't understand. All she knew for certain about fishing was that she was forbidden to do it.

Later that afternoon, after dressing in clothes uncontaminated by blood, she emerged from the boathouse to find Soter awaiting her outside.

He observed her sternly, his expression grave, although she couldn't think of anything she had done to warrant it. Maybe, she thought, he was unhappy that he was sober. Then he turned sharply, commanding her: "Follow."

She smiled to herself as she obeyed. The imperious stride was all too familiar. Today, Soter was acting the sage, the teacher, the wise old man whose pupil was a source of constant disappointment. She knew his roles: They had little to do with her, everything to do with him.

Where most people she knew were recognizably constant, Soter comprised a collection of posturings, guises, a composite of masks, so many that she had no idea if any one of them had ever been the true Soter, or if there had never been anything but masks.

He marched her across the island to his hut. They passed Gousier's asymmetrical house and outbuildings, where the smell of Dymphana's white root pie filled the air. Where the path split, they went right, away from the cavern, away from the trail to Ningle.

Soter made a show of sidestepping a large tree root that snaked out of the ground in the middle of the path. His dodging it reminded her of the night he'd fallen over it: less than a year ago, after he'd performed for the villagers without her, and gotten roaring drunk as well. She had heard him yelling and careering through the woods with the two undaya cases and stole out to see what he was doing. He had tripped across that root and crashed to the ground, the cases landing atop him. She arrived in time to see two village elders, fairly pickled themselves, drag him to his feet. He was weeping, blubbering incoherently, and not at the two men, but as if he were alone. The villagers took him by the arms and carried him and the cases the rest of the way to his hut. His behavior was so peculiar that she had followed along behind them. As the elders returned, she had ducked into the shadows. Passing close by, one of them told the other, "He's ashamed to be alive."

She glanced now at the scaly back of his head and wondered if that were true. Why had he fallen to weeping that night? Ashamed to be found so drunk? But he was drunk so often. It wasn't something she could ask him about.

His hut stood hidden among an overgrown mass of vines and weeds so thick that only the glinting hexagons of the windows hinted at its presence. The roof had been rethatched not so long ago, and thick, new windows added, bought from a Ningle glazier; but an ancient smell of charred, smoked fish remained. Even the fermenting vats behind the hut couldn't obliterate it entirely.

He'd set up the booth against the back wall. Because of the smallness of the hut, it was only half as deep as a real booth. There was no room for an accompanist.

Within the curtains, on top of the undaya cases, Soter had laid out six puppet figures for her. He pushed into the confines behind her, moving to the side to watch as she considered the puppets. Leodora knew every story Soter knew. His tests now probed whether or not she could formulate what specific tale or tales he expected her to perform, based solely on which figures he'd selected. He was adamant that she be able to carry every single story and all of its nuances in her head; that she be able to take any elements and weave a performance from them.

"There are only a handful of true stories," he said so often that she could parrot his exact emphasis. "The rest are simply embellishments, or reconstructions. Variations, my girl. When you walk the spans you'll hear a thousand versions of the same story. Some are dark and others light. Tales get rewritten to suit people and place. What's beheld as divine wisdom on one span will be mythic farce on another, with nary a word dividing the two. All depends on what is believed. I've seen stories revised from top to bottom, too, after the gods have sent something down to a Dragon Bowl. That one about the girl made of wood who receives a magic visit from an Edgeworld god who sends her off to find a prince and her wedding—well, it was once someone much lower than a god who granted her wishes, some local spirit somewhere. After a while, that local spirit wasn't recollected anymore and got replaced. Stories, you see, are alive, or else not worth the telling."

As to which tales might be originals, she didn't know. Perhaps everything was embellishment. Was the simplest the more fundamental? Or just a true tale stripped of true meaning? In the end she had stopped fretting over it. It was no more important than knowing on which span the story had begun. She was expected to know every one of them, regardless of their origin.

Upon the case now she considered the figures Soter had laid out for her: the orange figure that was sometimes a beggar but most often a thief, a pair of winged dragons, a maiden, an emperor, an assortment of tiny weapons, two guards, a young man and an old man. Soter had fit a straight wand in the old man's hand. From that she knew he was a wizard. Last of all was the resplendent figure of the handsome suitor.

The key object was missing, however. He had withheld it on purpose to challenge her. She smiled to herself for having recognized this, too. "It's the tale of the Druid's egg," she announced authoritatively.

Soter rocked on his heels. "You are positive?"

"Yes," she replied, concealing the doubt his question let in. "But you have the title element." She boldly held out her hand.

Soter's gaze fastened on hers. "How did you identify the tale if I have the key?"

"The thief figure is also the beggar figure, so his limbs are detachable. In the Druid's Egg tale, the thief isn't swift enough to steal the egg without being bitten by one of the twin serpents who hold the egg aloft, and he loses an arm to its venom. The old man is the wizard with the magic wand. He transforms himself into the handsome suitor to capture the heart of the princess, who is the true love of the thief. She's the reason he stole the egg in the first place—to have her for a wife. The wizard wants her because he wants to rule the kingdom. He wants power. The thief fears she won't want him with one arm, and so—"

"Enough! Here!" He handed her the prop of the translucent gold egg. "Show. Don't tell." Then he collected the figures of the guards and the emperor.

"Wait! I need them. How can I tell it right?"

As if the question were superfluous, he answered, "Improvise." He pushed apart the drapery and left the booth.

The lantern was already lighted. She had only to rotate it to cast its beam upon the taut white silk screen. Beneath the screen was a narrow shelf. A groove ran the length of it.

She brought the figure of the wizard to the screen. Normally the trappings of a set would have been hooked in place around the puppet. But Soter forced her to rely on storytelling alone to convey situations.

It was theater without a stage.

She picked up her story: "The wizard disguised himself as a physician, and gained admittance to the palace in that form, taking a small room that overlooked the city. There he performed his dark arts. He used his powers to discover every suitor the princess had, worthy or not. He saw the thief's passion for her. That was why the wizard, in the guise of the good doctor, had sent him on the impossible quest for the Druid's egg—with that prize and his knowledge of how to unlock it, the wizard would gain remarkable powers, and as a reward would give the girl to the thief, after first stealing her love for himself.

"Other, more suitable if simple-minded suitors, he plagued with easy magics so that they would never arrive in the city at all. Some lost their bearings and wandered into other spans. Some fell in love with barmaids, hags, or even their animals."

By rotating the puppet's arm she made the wizard's shadow sweep the wand above his head. At the same time she spun the lantern, and its light flashed and flickered, white and red, as the different lenses splashed the silk.

"Now he was unopposed for her hand. There remained only a final act to secure her. He must hide his true unwholesome nature."

She caught the lamp. It stopped with its red lens glowing upon the screen.

"With a blast of magic he transformed himself."

She gave the lantern a gentle twist. The red light slowly slid to the right, replaced by darkness—the blank side of the lamp. Then the dark, too, was pushed aside by the light of the clear lens. But in the instant that darkness covered the screen, she deftly swapped the old wizard's figure for the young suitor, carefully fiddling the rods to keep the suitor's arms in the same position as the wizard's.

"He became the handsomest man in the world."

She heard Soter's grunt of approval. It was her embellishment of the text to make him not merely handsome, but the handsomest.

"Transformed, he paused to consider himself in a mirror." The suitor touched his face, ran his hands down his sides, then held them up to look at them. "He was pleased with his handiwork. His power remained undiminished. No one could refuse him!"

The next scene she could not fully perform without the puppets Soter had withheld.

"He went before the emperor as if just arrived from another span. He bowed with a deep respect that he felt not at all, and then asked to be considered as a son-in-law."

The suitor knelt on one knee, bowed low, and finally lay prostrate, with his hands outstretched as if to plead with someone off-screen.

"His clever disguise protected him from an emperor who would have killed him for all the evil he had created in that kingdom and others.

"The emperor sent the new suitor to his daughter. She knew already that he was in the palace—word of him had reached her through her servants. Now, with her chaperone behind the nearest curtain, she met the suitor. His face did take her breath away. He was smooth in every nuance. Calculated in every implied invitation."

The princess, dressed in a purple gown, extended a hand and he kissed her, bowing. His gestures were graceful, and each one ended with the slightest pull, drawing the girl slowly across the screen, nearer with each flourish until she almost touched him. Then he reached out behind her and his hand wove magic knots in the air.

"Soon the princess was caught in his spell. With a flick of the wrist, he put the chaperone to sleep behind her drapery. Then he was alone with his victory."

The suitor stepped back. He touched the princess's shoulder and swept her clothing away. The diaphanous purple gown caught on the puppet's sharp fingertip, and lifted off the tiny pin that had held it in place on her figure. It dropped from the screen onto the small shelf below.

Leodora thought she heard Soter stifle a gasp, even though he knew that Bardsham's princess was designed for this shocking moment. The stripping and the presentation of the rape of the princess were Bardsham's embellishments. No one else had ever performed it this way. No one else had never constructed a puppet whose clothing could be torn away.

She stood revealed in all her translucent nakedness. The sharp nipples of her breasts, even the dark thatch in the meeting of her thighs, were plainly visible. In a full rendition of the story, the audience had heard her speak by now and had come to know her with affection, and often a cry of alarm accompanied the moment, protests of outrage rang out as though a real girl had been stripped bare by the fiend.

The suitor glided up against her and pushed her roughly down. She vanished below the screen. The suitor lay on top of her. The top of him became the bottom line of the screen. Slowly his body began to move back and forth, telling the story in agonizing silence. The figures sank from sight, while the red of the lantern passed harsh judgment upon the scene.

"What has happened to the poor thief meanwhile? Sent out by the wizard, he has lost his left arm and very nearly his life to the dragon's venom. More than this, he has lost his hope. What princess will have a poor man consigned now to a life of begging?—for no other fate can await him. The egg is just an egg. He can find no power there. The thief's quest is ended. He has no power to win the affections of so beautiful a creature as the princess; the kindly doctor who sent him will dismiss the trophy, claim that he took it from some huge bird, a roc perhaps, but not from the deadly serpents. He sees now that his dream has been pure folly. He would only want her if she wanted him; and whatever made him believe she would?

"He will, he decides, complete his task and afterward climb all the way to the top of the highest minaret and throw himself to his death.

"Outside the palace, he stands for a long time beneath the window of his beloved. He sets his resolve to see her one last time, that her image might be with him when he dies."

The thief began his climb. But the same vines that had carried him before were not so navigable with only one arm. He lumbered clumsily up to the balcony of his beloved, but saw nothing from the ledge. She was not there. The puppet hung his head.

"Fate was cruel today, he thought."

He continued with less enthusiasm on toward the higher apartment of the doctor, to bid him farewell. Whatever else, he was honorable, and he would leave the egg there as he'd promised.

As she moved the puppet's limbs with one hand, Leodora steadily lowered the vertical cutout of the vines beside him to create the illusion that he was climbing ever higher. The cutout folded in places so that it stacked neatly on the shelf as she drew it down.

He hadn't climbed far when his hand slipped for a moment and he twisted and grabbed a branch to save himself; but the violent movement caused the magic egg to fall from his pouch. Certain it would shatter, he dove to catch it before it struck the tiles on the princess's balcony below. If he'd had both hands, he might have reached it, but with only the one he couldn't. His fingers just brushed their target, and the egg hit the floor. The thief tucked his head and rolled as best he could to protect himself. It was not a long fall but without his other arm to absorb the blow he struck the floor hard, bounced, and then lay there dazed.

"He sat up, horrified to be on this of all balconies. But it seemed that no one had heard him fall. The curtains remained drawn.

"He turned to snatch the egg and found it beside him, split in two. A fiery glow emerged from within each half."

Leodora nimbly separated the two rods controlling the prop egg she had.

"The glow poured over him and through him. He felt as though he were the sun, burning."

She took hold of the lanyard that secured the lantern and lowered it until its red lens was aimed straight through the translucent puppet. The skeletal structure etched lightly into the taut skins caught the light, gaining emphasis. His body seemed to have become glass. She pulled on the lanyard, raising the lantern again. The thief stood up. And now—for all eyes would follow the light as it moved—he had two arms again. The new one she had hooked into place as she pulled the rope past the screen and secured it below. The thief stood and marveled at his two hands, then danced a little jig of joy.

"He looked to the skies and thanked the gods for his good

fortune. No one had seen him yet, so he fit the two halves of the egg back together and prepared to leave. But at the moment he heard a noise, a terrible moan, emerge from beyond the curtains that closed off the balcony. His curiosity and his desire held him there. He crept across and ever so carefully parted the curtains.

He beheld a horrible sight. His princess, the jewel of his life, lay naked and ravished. A handsome figure climbing off her turned to close its robes, faced him, and started as their eyes met. That moment seemed to last an eternity."

The handsome suitor edged back from the princess. Her figure lay just visible, propped in place at the bottom of the screen by its rods, secured in the groove of the shelf below. The suitor suddenly sprang off-screen.

"'Guards! Guards!' the magician cried. 'Come quickly—a thief has broken in and attacked the princess!' Never for a second did he imagine that the thief had succeeded in carrying out his mission. No one had ever met the twin dragons and lived. The wizard assumed that the thief had never really gone at all or had given up, as anyone else would have done. As he would have done. The plan fixed itself even as he cried out. The unconscious chaperone behind the curtain—the thief had struck her and hidden himself there. As for the girl, the wizard would magnanimously offer to marry her, thus securing her father's eternal debt. The rape would remain a secret between them. The thief would be executed before day's end, the shamed girl reduced to his docile slave. It was all too perfect, even better than his original plan."

Leodora had no guards to bring onto the scene. But she did have their pikes among the weapons Soter had given her. The suitor's figure she locked in place for a moment by setting its control rods in the grooved shelf. Then she picked up two pikes and leaned them in from the side, one above the other.

"The guards entered. The suitor thrust a finger at the thief. "There he is. Look at what he's done!"

She drew the suitor's figure back slightly from the screen, so that his shadow swelled in size, while the thief leapt into motion.

"'No!' cried the young thief. 'I didn't do this—he did. I was climbing up the vines outside to fulfill my pact with the good physician who dwells higher up, but I fell onto the balcony trying to catch this!'"

He lifted into view the golden Druid's egg. Leodora

swung down the lantern again, and spun it red at the same moment that, with her pinkie finger, she coaxed apart the rods of the egg, splitting it open.

"'Aiiieeee, I'm undone!' cried the suitor. He tried to grab the egg, but the thief hopped back. The wizard stood trapped between the thief and the guards he had called. He quailed at the power of the egg. Its power would defeat any enemy—and most certainly he was the enemy of this thief. Even if the thief didn't realize it, the egg knew."

She gave the lantern a spin so that light became stars became red became darkness; and in that precise instant of darkness, she switched the suitor with the sharp-featured wizard.

"Helpless, the wizard watched himself transform, and in terror he ran to escape the deadly influence of the egg, ran blindly for the door—his only thought to get away from that hellish glow. But the guards reacted as guards should and lowered their pikes. They impaled the evil man."

The pikes slid behind the wizard's torso. She brought her middle finger to her thumb, and the figure doubled over. The pikes lifted him into the air.

"The thief knelt beside his beloved. The Druid's egg shone upon her. She stirred, awakened, to find herself clothed in light. A total stranger was at her side and her wicked seducer was dead upon the pikes of her guards."

The princess got to her feet, her body trembling. The young thief rose also.

"'Who are you?' she asked."

The thief lowered his head.

"'I'm no one. Just a common thief.'

"'How can you say that when you have saved me?' she replied.

"'I saved one for whom I would willingly perish.'

"'Don't say such things. How could you feel that way for me when we have never met?'

"'I could. I do. I can't help it. But I must go now before your father finds me here. I don't belong here.'

"'Then take me with you.'

"'How can I?'

"'If you go, then I no longer belong here, either.'

"'Oh,' said he. 'In that case how can I not?'"

The princess reached to him and he took her hand. The

two shadow figures embraced in a long, lingering kiss. The egg slipped from the thief's other hand and cracked open at his feet. The screen turned red with its light, and then, as Leodora unlooped and let slide the lanyard, the red light sank like an evening sun, taking all shadows with it. When it was below the silk screen, she blew out the light.

Outside the booth the room might have been empty, it was so quiet. She set down the figures, stood and stretched, then stepped through the curtain.

Soter seemed to gape at her, as if she were something he had never seen before. She swelled with triumph before he regained himself: His look clouded, became critical, and he said, "That's not the way the tale ends. The emperor arrives, discovers what has happened, and gives the boy everything—the keys to his kingdom, his daughter, wealth."

Leodora smarted at the criticism. She would not be robbed of her glory. "'Improvise', someone said to me. Tales get rewritten—who told me that not an hour past? Who stole the figure of the king?"

Soter waved his hand, dismissing each point, but finding no way to contradict her. He gave a nervous laugh, and tried to shift the discussion away from her objections. "Now, no matter, you did a truly fine job. A most worthy attempt in fact—"

"Attempt! Confess it, I took your breath away!"

"No, no, I'm sorry, never happened. You're certainly getting there, but you are still a little clumsy with one thing or another—not very much, you understand, but there is always room for improvement. Those vines, not smooth enough. You are . . . coming along quite nicely, Leodora."

"I'm ready," she said with iron.

"Well, my girl, of course you *want* to be ready. You entertain me well enough, and the native islanders. But who are they? A far distant and less discerning cousin to the audiences on the spans. You cannot trust their simple approbation. No, no. Not reliable."

She glared at him.

"Oh, I think, another year, perhaps. Possibly two?" He smiled like an uncle full of deep concern for her well-being—it was exactly the smile her own uncle had been giving her the past few days. It was not a look she trusted. It masked something else, something that did not have her well-being at heart.

Enraged by his false kindness, she kicked aside a stool and stormed across the hut.

"Now, Leodora," Soter called. The voice of appeasement, another mask. She would have exited without a word if he hadn't spoken.

She whirled about. "You pull off the role of the forgetful fool much better when you're in your cups, old man. In fact, if you're so stupid as to say, 'Oh, just two more years, my girl,' you'd best be drunk. At least you'll have an excuse for lying. Go ahead, pretend you can't see! But I know. Understand? *I* know. I'm better than you say. I'm better than you can do yourself. I'm better than Bardsham!"

She flung his door out of her way.

Soter sagged in the chair where he had watched her performance. He sighed once, long and deep, as if he might expel all the air in his lungs. He hunched forward and picked up the puppet king. After staring it in the face for a long still moment, he began to roll the main rod loosely between his thumb and fingers. The puppet gyred to and fro, unable to settle on a direction. Its clattering arms swung loosely, embracing nothing.

"Back then she was only a child," he said, as if responding to someone else in the empty room. "Of course I didn't worry where it would lead. Why should I? Who knew what skills she had—or that she would even *care*." He glanced up with a sickly grin, eyes focused on a point in front of him. "That's right. Berate me for it now. You didn't step in then, did you? You could have manifested, objected. 'Don't set her on this path, Soter,' you could have said. Did you? No."

He dropped the puppet and picked up a clay jug from the floor beside the overturned stool. He took a long anxious drink, but even before he'd finished, his worried eyes opened, focused again upon something before him and began tracking it. Whatever he followed, it was invisible to Leodora from her position outside his window. She'd come back with the intention of apologizing, provided that she could make him confess the truth about her abilities. She'd only meant to watch for the most propitious moment to make an entrance, and instead here he was engaged in a conversation.

Except that no one else was there.

Soter's hands trembled as he put down the jug. "Look," he said, wiping his palm across his mouth, "I saved the child, didn't I? Brought her back here. That ought to have been enough for you. After all, you owned my life, didn't you? Had me in thrall, didn't you? Used me any way that suited the moment. You think just because I was in the thick of it that I didn't know the situation. Think I would have left her to the mercies of the spans if I'd known? You don't understand devotion and never did—and you all moon-eyed and weepy with it yourself. For all that you could bedazzle your innumerable lovers, you never expected that hollow heart of yours might fill up, did you?"

He paused, head tilted, as if listening, then abruptly shook his head. "Ridden by your own demons? Oh, and so many of them, too, love. You could wrap anyone around your nimble fingers. And still you don't ken how you can be enslaved and not be able to do anything but submit. Can't imagine being on that end of it, even now and it's over and you're dead. But you were. You were. Don't try to deny it to me. I was there!"

He flashed his teeth, shook his head, then seemed to perceive something else.

"Oh, I meant nothing. I was *convenient*. Just part of the troupe, easy to replace. 'Get rid of Soter, he's becoming a nuisance, I don't like the way he looks at me.' Think I didn't overhear that speech? Oh, the calumny I bore. Don't you come floating in here this late with your demands, either. You've no claims on me. I protected your daughter from the darkness, you poxy . . ." He swung up the jug, swiped at the air. The jug, encountering nothing, spun him about. "Away! Away all dead plagues. You unrepentant ghosts—go back to the dark spans and the seabeds where you belong! I banish you! Begone!" As though sensing someone now at his back, he swung around, wielding the jug like a club. "I rescued her!" It was a broken cry, terrifying to hear.

He turned again, shoulders hunched, his head twisting with a canny look. Instinctively, Leodora drew back into the shadows. When she peered at him again, he had righted the overturned stool and sat down. The jug dangled from his hand. "No," he said, "You're wrong. That's all I'm doing, it is. I'm keeping her from that danger. She's safe down here on Bouyan. We're all safe down *here*. No one comes looking nor ever will. A little lie keeps her safe, and when did the truth ever help us, heh? We were liars for a living. No. Better to be safe . . . down here on Bouyan."

His head sank on his chest. He wasn't asleep, nor could he be this easily drunk. It was more the position of someone dreading to see anything other than the floor before him. The boasting, besotted Soter had withered before her eyes into a spindly, tremulous thing. Rickety with age. An old man.

Leodora squatted awhile longer beside the window, her brain full of portentous imaginings. Had he been railing at her mother? He had been in love with her mother, and her mother, jealous of him, had tried to get rid of him—that was how it sounded. She couldn't accept that there were real ghosts here. If her mother's spirit truly roamed abroad on this isle, she would know it, wouldn't she? She would have encountered it herself in all the places she shared with her mother's past. Her mother could not come back without appearing to her. But then, could guilt and shame become so manifest as this—that Soter would punish himself with terrible visions and memories? Could guilt take such form?

He had rescued her, he said, but from what? Why were they—all of them, he'd said—in hiding?

She thought that he was spent, and she started to slide carefully away through the tangle of branches, when suddenly he spoke one last time, in a tone of abject defeat: "All right, all right. If the time comes, I swear. I promise. Yes. But not now. Please, not yet. Ask me later, can't you? Let me get used to the idea awhile."

She waited, crouching, holding her breath, straining as if she might hear the phantom answer. There was nothing but a final sobbing breath from Soter.

He sat on the floor, head bowed, his arms wrapped around the jug protectively. When he said nothing further, she withdrew.

Most days, by the time Leodora had finished her session with Soter, Tastion had returned and was waiting for her.

He and his father usually had good luck in their fishing. Sometimes she even passed them on the path to Fishkill as she was returning to the boathouse—either hauling their catch or returning with the net rolled up between them. Tastion would pretend to disregard her, as his father did. Later he would sneak into the boathouse to meet her. Where his family thought he had gone, she didn't know. His work was done for the day, so perhaps no one was watching, no one noticing his absence. He risked a great deal to meet her, but not as much as he pretended. The risks had limits. Any punishment meted out would affect her more than him.

His marriage had been arranged years earlier, to a girl named Vosilana. If he'd been found alone in the boathouse with Leodora, the marriage arrangement might have been nullified, and his family would be humiliated by the revelation. He would certainly be whipped, and most likely banished from his home for a time. But he was strong, handsome, and his family one of the most powerful on the island. Punishments would be temporary, and if reparations could not be made with the bride's family, some other girl would be happy to take Vosilana's place. Leodora could not replace her, even had she wanted to. Tenikemac's response to her in that event would, by comparison, make their bare tolerance of her now seem tender and loving. It would be she who had led him astray, she who had corrupted him. Gousier would have a new witch in his household. And her uncle . . . well, the whipping Tastion got would be far preferable to anything Gousier would do.

Given all that, she could not quite explain even to herself why she continued to see Tastion, except that she had done so for so long. It could not be that she loved him, for she was just as sure he didn't love her, that his concept of love was something physically propelled—something he wanted that she wouldn't part with. Not love then, but desire. A very particular desire.

There was kissing, of course—she could hardly have denied her own lips their sweet fulfillment. Kissing scorched them both, but when the heat of passion consumed him, and although she had loved Tastion forever, a small whisper of reason stopped her from relinquishing control. In his importuning, she thought she heard a tone that said once satisfied, he would go off in search of other fruit. Because she loved him she did not deny him some familiarity, and sometimes she became dizzy with him. Because she knew her place in his world, she stopped short of drowning in pleasure—which served only to frustrate and further incite her would-be lover. To his credit, he had never sworn falsely to marry her—that is, if one discounted that the two of them had been promising to run off together since they were children. Tastion never claimed that he could defy his parents, his village, or the assignment of his bride. He never pledged to give it all up, only to find ways around the rules. She wouldn't have believed him if he had.

Today, angry and frustrated, she entered the boathouse with an urgent need for Tastion that had nothing to do with passion. She needed to ask questions if only to hear herself ask them so that she would know what her questions were. She needed him, but Tastion wasn't there, and her spirits plunged further. She sat on her bed, took off her boot and rubbed her toes that she'd bruised when she kicked the stool.

The force of her rage caught up with her, exhausted her. The warmth of the room added to her torpor. She leaned back on her elbows, and finally lay back to stare at the beam over her head. She saw in the grain of the wood weird faces and creatures she'd identified years before, when she was tiny; once recognized, they could never be random patterns again. One of them she'd decided was her father's face. Another was the torso of her mother, twisting out of strings of seaweed like a mermaid. A weight like that of gathering tears filled her head with a kind of forlorn pressure but without enough weight for the drops to fall. The thick air hung about her, pressing down upon her, and she drifted to sleep.

When she awoke it was dark in the room. The sky outside was purple, streaked with the last glory of sunset at the very edge of the sea. Her head ached when she sat up. She knew that she was hungry, and that the evening meal must be ready soon. Hunger at least was easy to think about.

She got up and drew on her boots. She left the trap door to her room open in case Tastion turned up.

The sea rice in its broth was salty. Leodora chewed and tried not to make eye contact with Dymphana, which was facilitated by Dymphana's preoccupation with the empty stool where Gousier usually sat. While Leodora wondered about Soter's ghosts, so her aunt appeared preoccupied with where her uncle might be. Their unease they shared as if it were a condiment; but neither could speak of it.

Finally, when they were halfway through their portions, Gousier arrived. The smell of sweat fermented in fish and liquor accompanied him like a homunculus. Had they missed the liquor's stink, neither of them missed the looseness in his stride and the flush to his face as if he'd run home from Ningle. Gousier drunk was too familiar a sight—it was the timing of it that was peculiar.

Dymphana stopped eating to watch him. She was watching, Leodora knew, to see how he reacted to their having begun without him. If his day had gone poorly, he could explode without warning, angered by meaningless things. More than one dinner had been brought to a halt by his unprompted anger, and drunkenness did not necessarily augur well.

This night he fairly beamed at them, however. In particular, when he looked Leodora's way, his eyes grew sly. It was clear he would not lose his temper; but the cagey, slow smile with which he considered her twisted knots in her stomach.

He took his place at the head of the table, and Dymphana spooned a serving into his bowl. While he waited for her to finish, he remarked, "What a grand day I've had. Just grand."

"The fish sold well?"

"Yes, yes they did. We hardly had to throw any away."

"But you had to stay late up there?"

"Late? Ah, no." Another darting glance at his niece. "No, we come down about sunset as usual. I don't like to navigate those steps in the dark, you know that. No, I been back awhile." He considered Leodora again with hooded eyes. "I went over to settle up first."

In a voice from which she couldn't mask suspicion, Dymphana said, "They invited you to drink with them?"

He smiled. "They did that, yes. One of them in particular wanted to toast with me. A widow, she is."

This last piece of information seemed so entirely superfluous that the two women exchanged glances to see if either of them understood the reference.

Obviously enjoying their perplexity, Gousier offered up another clue. "The poor creature has a terrible burden to bear. Her husband is dead."

"Is there a different kind of widow than that?" Dymphana asked in a distinctly icy tone.

"I didn't finish. Dear." A hint of his true nature punctuated the syllable. "Alone, she's burdened with a son. Her only child. A man must fish to provide for his family here. This one, though, can't fish. Can't be trusted with a net. Why, he'd be pulled right off any dragon and drowned."

"You're speaking of that poor imbecile, Koombrun."

"Right you are."

"And why should his circumstance matter to us now? Are you going to put him to work? Is he going to haul your fish?"

Gousier chose that moment to begin eating. He chewed the rice as if he had years to finish. Then he drank some water, cleared his throat. "Tenikemac would never allow such a thing. Why, that would only alienate the poor woman further. She'd be a pariah if anyone in her family went onto the spans."

"So, he's to help me in the cavern, then, uncle," Leodora guessed.

"Oh, I do hope so, after his fashion. As best he can, being what he is. You'll have to teach him. Once you're married, of course, I expect you'll have to teach him everything from gutting fish to where to stick his—"

"Once I'm married? To Koombrun? To an idiot?"

"Just because he is mentally deficient don't mean your children must be. Probably, they'll all be normal. I'm sure they will and so's his mother." He beamed at her with affected bonhomie, beneath which an edge of malice glittered.

Her first instinct was to throw her bowl at him, but she grabbed the table instead and tried to maintain control over her terror and hate. "I'm not marrying anyone," she said.

"Oh, but you are, Leodora, my little niece. You're in my house, and my keeping. And I'm telling you that your only hope on Bouyan is to marry into that village. The normal ones there would never even consider you. You've been up on the spans yourself and the fact that you were a toddler, not aware of the rules, the choices, that cuts no fish with them. This widow—she needs providing for, she's a burden on her neighbors, and you can fix that with your share of the takings every morning. The three of you'll live in the boathouse for a time, till we can build something more substantial. Or better, maybe I can toss that old bastard Soter out and you can have his shack. That's roomier." He turned to his wife. "Yes, that's what we'll do. We'll get rid of him in the bargain, won't we?"

When neither woman said anything, he gave a shrug, took another bite of his food and, with his mouth half-full, added, "This is the opportunity for our family finally to join the village. This imbecile—call him what you want—your children will be their children. You'll have to guide him in that, too, won't you?

But he's equipped." He smiled and chewed. "You ask him and he'll show you. Happy he is to show you." He laughed and shook his head.

Softly, almost kindly, Dymphana rebutted, "They won't see it your way in Tenikemac. They won't bring us in."

"Of course they will. They'll have to."

"How long have you been working at this, uncle? All the little things you've said, the funny little looks—you've been winding up this woman's hopes for weeks now. This didn't just happen tonight."

His eyes narrowed although his smile remained. "I don't know that I care to be accused, my girl. Especially with all I've done for your future. You'd see that if you—"

"Liar," she snapped. She rose to her feet, and now her control deserted her. She heaved the bowl of rice into his face.

Gousier erupted from his seat with a howl of anguish. "My eyes!" His hands swiped at the rice stuck to his cheeks. He shook his head, pressing palms into eye sockets, and lunged all at once across the table, knocking over a pitcher and a bowl, which shattered, spreading more rice underfoot. But his hands closed on nothing.

Leodora's place was empty.

He blinked and squinted. "I'll kill you, you ungrateful bitch, I will!" His words burst the walls, sped through the night, pursuing her like a maleficent spirit. "Get done with your petulance, girl—the ceremony's in two nights and I'll deliver you to it if I have to carry you there in a net like one of their catches! Two nights hence!" Then she heard his laugh, and she knew she'd been right to run. There'd been a knife right in front of her on the table. If he'd hit her, she would have stuck it through his eye.

She fled to the boathouse but not to her garret. If he followed, Gousier would have her all but trapped up there. She went halfway up the steps instead, ready to jump if the door opened. She stuck her head into the room above and called, "Tastion?" The silence of emptiness answered her.

She took a seat on the lowest steps, with the boat close by. If Gousier came in, she could squeeze through the rotten hull of the esquif before he even saw her.

She stared through the hole in its side. She and the boat

were identical. Both helpless, trapped here at her uncle's whim. Kept from the life they were meant to live. The boat was meant to be on the ocean, it should have been on the ocean. The boat had no recourse; but she did. She must.

Again she wondered where Tastion was. Twice today she'd needed to talk with him and he'd failed her. Now she had to concern herself with the prospect of bidding him farewell. Whatever had bound her to Bouyan before, whether it was the thing that called from across the sea or the impossible hope that she and Tastion might find a life together, it couldn't hold her any longer. Tastion would marry his chosen wife just the way he was supposed to and the dark, slithering call would have to find a new listener. There was—

The boathouse door swung open.

Leodora slipped from the step and through the hole in the boat. Footsteps skittered past—too quick to belong to her uncle. Then she heard her name called, her name sharp with excitement. Had he heard about the arranged marriage?

He came back down.

"I'm here, Tastion," she said through the hole.

He jumped back against the stairs. "Zarya's teeth! That's a mean trick to play. What are you doing in there?"

"Hiding from Gousier."

"Oh. What have you done this time?"

"Thank you for your confidence."

"I didn't mean—I meant that he always blames you for everything. The bastard looks for excuses to beat you."

"I know that's what you meant."

"Right now you have to come with me," he insisted.

"Why? Where have you been all evening? Did you stay out all this time?"

"We had a—it will be easier if I show you. Come on." He held out his hand. "Come on. What I found can even make you forget about your uncle."

She extended her hand but said, "I don't think so."

He found her fingers in the dark and drew her out of the boat. "Just wait."

She shushed him then. They both stood listening, hardly breathing. She decided that she hadn't heard anything after all.

Tastion, unable to keep still, began whispering to her. "We found it this afternoon. The net got caught the way it does sometimes. It wouldn't come loose and I had to dive down to it." He pulled her out of the boathouse while he babbled softly. "But it wasn't caught. I swam all the way to the bottom, and there was this thing in the net. We'd been dragging it along, just like . . . like I'm going to drag you if you don't speed your step."

She looked around, back toward the house. There was no one there. Absently, she asked him, "What was it?"

"That's where I'm taking you. You'll see."

Soon she knew they were going to the cavern. The entrance was dark. Leodora complained that they'd brought no lamp.

"You won't need one," he told her, and tugged her into the cave. She thought he meant they would be kissing in the dark. But as her eyes adjusted, she realized that the deeper cavern was lit by a feeble bluish glow. "We put it in here," Tastion explained, "to keep it from drying out too much. It seemed only right that it should stay with the fish. It took four of us with two nets to lift it from the bottom, and all the afternoon for our dragons to haul it back."

They rounded the bend. The whole chamber was visible. The stone table where she cut fish was outlined in a blue halo. The source of the light lay hidden behind it.

She tugged free. Tastion released her hand and she strode boldly to the edge of the stone. What she discovered made her inhale sharply and step back. She bumped against him. He was looking over her shoulder.

A body lay on the cavern floor.

It was not a normal—not a living—body. Its luminescence she had seen before: the color of the ocean at night when tiny sea creatures clustered, darting and swaying. The color of their radiance. It seemed to emerge from within the shell, the husk that had condensed, making the features into shadows, not unlike the puppets on their sticks when the lantern shone through them; but this body wasn't hammered fish bladder. It was a crust—a coral grown into a human shape.

A coral man.

A lump defined the nose, and shallow cavities the eye sockets. Water pooled in them, creating an illusion of wet and shiny eyes, rolled back in its head. The mouth might have been invisible were it not for a darker vein through the coral there. Swirls and ridges of accretion created the illusion of clothing, too. Maybe, she thought, beneath the crust there lay a statue, and the coral had merely built up and up over that original form, so that with each new layer, the unknown sculptor's work became less defined. Maybe . . . But it had no discernable feet, as if it was still growing.

When Tastion spoke again, she flinched.

"It weighed as much as if the whole of Shadowbridge had been poured inside it. I tugged at the net but it wouldn't budge with just me pulling. Finally I had to swim up for air, and told my father what it was. We found Lemros and Sel on their dragons, and Sel and I dove down with their net and looped it beneath our own, and then the four of us hauled it. The dragons never worked so hard. Then in the shallows we four stood on the beach, and others came and helped, and we pulled it up out of the water. We unfolded the nets to see it, and then we just marveled. No one knew what they were looking at any more than you do. But here's something more peculiar, as if the look of it weren't enough. After it had lain on the beach awhile, when we went to pick it up—" He stepped around her and cupped his hands under the figure's head— "it weighed hardly anything at all." And so saying, he lifted it upright as if it were a stick of driftwood. "It must have been the water that weighed it, in all the little holes."

He prattled on about their being afraid of it, and who had argued for taking it back into the ocean and who was for keeping it; but Leodora barely listened. Gingerly, she raised one finger to its cheek, straight across from her own. On contact a current flowed up her arm. Sparks spun from where her finger touched. They circled her arm, danced upon her shoulder and up her neck, around her head—sparks that only she could see, for Tastion, though he stood just beside her, kept right on babbling about bringing the figure here. The sparks dazzled her. Penetrated her as if she were coral, too.

Tastion's hands gripped her, and she recoiled, only to find herself incongruously dangling from his arms, as though she'd fallen.

"What happened to you? What made you swoon?"

"Did I?" she asked. Her mind was a vacant beach. She let herself be drawn upright, held onto.

"You just tipped over like you'd fallen asleep. Am I that boring?" A joke to disguise his worry.

She could only shake her head. Tastion drew her away from the upright figure, and stepped between them. Now the glow surrounded him. In his shadow she blinked as if she'd been asleep. Where were her thoughts?

Tastion turned her, led her out of the icy chamber, away from the figure. She went passively, too confused to contest his judgment, although she muttered, "I'm fine," to reassure him. She glanced back at the figure.

Out of the cave, he guided her down the path toward Ningle, and then beneath a stand of fir trees, a spot they had come to more than once to be alone. No one traveled the path to Ningle at night, and couldn't have seen them sitting on their bed of needles in any case.

He said, "You aren't taking care of yourself, my girl," and brushed her hair back. "You shouldn't fight with your uncle until after you've eaten something."

"But I—"

"You need to have someone look after you." He kissed her neck. "Someone to care for you." He kissed her cheek. "Someone to provide everything." He turned her chin and leaned forward to kiss her.

Leodora pulled away. His shadowy face seemed to wear a smile of mild exasperation, as if he were saying to her, "Well, I had to try."

"Someone to provide everything for me? Why, Tastion, how thoughtful. Who has been assigned the task?"

"Don't mock me."

"Why? You can't fulfill any such role yourself, if I asked, which I haven't and won't. We both of us know to whom you're already tied."

"That's just ritual. I have to pledge to her when she comes of age, but my heart, Lea—"

"Your heart. Your heart is not the part that throbs for me, Tastion. What am I to be? Your whore in the garret?"

"What is the matter with you all of a sudden? We've kissed like this, made these promises—I haven't said a thing I haven't said before, and you liked it before."

"I wasn't the bartered bride of Koombrun before."

"What's that supposed to mean?"

"It means that in two nights my uncle will have me married to the one creature in your village wretched enough to accept the tainted daughter of a witch." She felt the heat of tears flooding her eyes, and swung her head sharply to fling them back. She would not cry over this.

"He has no right!"

"He has every right. I'm his ward. His property. He can sell me the same as any fish in his basket."

"Well, then we'll just . . ." He hesitated, finally grunted in defeat. There was no idea he could come up with that she hadn't visited already in the boathouse. So long as both parties wished to see the union through, she would be married. Unless the village interceded. Which it wouldn't. "Fine, then," Tastion said. "It'll be perfect. You can live with Koombrun and still meet me. No one will be the wiser—certainly not Koombrun. It's the perfect camouflage, even better than the boathouse—"

She got to her feet. "I'm really nothing to you, am I? Just convenient. If I'd given in to you before, you wouldn't even be here now. You'd have had your ride and finished with me and passed me on to your friends. Lemros and Sel could have a turn. I could carry your child and there'd be no consequences for you. Oh, maybe a rebuke from the elders, a retreat until you came to your senses, were purged of my *spell*, hmm? I'm not of the people. What happens to me can be kept outside the village. It won't embarrass anybody, will it? Outside. You can't be made to marry me. You can't share with me what you can share with any other woman on this island."

"That's not so, Leodora."

"It is so. We've pretended for so long that something would simply appear when we needed it to change everything. We made our pact as children, Tastion, and we're still trying to be children. But we're feeling things beyond what children feel, and almost doing them. Sooner or later we're going to do them, because we *want* to. There never has been a solution. Not on Bouyan. The whole world here would have to change for us."

"Where, then?" His uneasy question.

She turned, pointed through the trees to lights no brighter than stars. "Up there."

"Lea, you know I can't go up there."

"I can."

Tastion seemed lost then, as if he'd never before considered the real limits imposed upon her and upon him, as if for him things were always going to roll along, allowing him the freedom to glide through the imposed rules. She was sorry for what she had said because of what could not, as a result, happen between them, but what she'd said was the truth, and they both had to acknowledge it now. She had. Tastion was not prepared to, and he left her.

She called to him but he didn't stop. The darkness swallowed him up.

Leodora returned to the path and followed it to Soter's hut.

He didn't seem to be home. She entered anyway, going straight to the back of the hut. In the doorway to the back room, she lingered, regarding the two stretched undaya cases lying in the recesses. She'd always had a plan of sorts, unformed but lurking at the edges of her life. Now she must shape it. She needed Soter's help to do that.

She left the hut and continued on the path to Tenikemac.

The long house lay at the center of the village. All the other abodes were built along paths radiating from it. It had a low, nearly flat roof containing smoke holes for three different fires. Off the side facing the ocean, a huge carved merwoman figure reached with both arms as if she had been transformed in the midst of jumping through the wall, though her presence there, Leodora knew, was supposed to represent the bestowing of her blessing upon the whole village. Meetings, ceremonies and entertainments took place in that house, and the goddess's name was never spoken except inside it. Leodora had performed there numerous times. In two nights she was to be married there.

Soter brought his fermented product to the long house to sell. Often, after he'd bartered the liquor for food, clothing, or utensils, he would linger to drink with the men. "Absorbing my expenses," he called it.

Tonight he seemed to have absorbed rather a lot. She walked in on him regaling half a dozen others with a rude story about a hermaphroditic mermaid. Leodora entered at the far end of the long house, and had passed the first two, untended fires before anyone noticed her.

Two of the men turned at once. One of them was Agmeon. His eyes were bloodshot. They went wide as he recognized her. He jumped up, barring her way. She nodded, making the requisite shallow, respectful bow, but when she looked up again anger still burned in Agmeon's eyes, and he still blocked her way. "What are you doing here?" he demanded.

Soter had stopped talking. He gazed at her, bleary and

unfocused.

"I came to get him. I need to talk to him."

"Have you no decency, girl?"

She looked at herself as if expecting to find she'd forgotten to wear clothes. She shook her head. "I don't understand. I come here all the time. I was here only a few nights past, performing for you. You saw me."

"That was before. Now you're betrothed to Koombrun. You do know you're betrothed?"

"Yes."

"It's unseemly to be found in one man's house with him, even worse to be here. It's the behavior of a mispel. You leave now." He thrust a finger past her, and spoke with such vehemence that she started to turn, to leave; but her will overrode her instinct and she stopped. She had never been a part of their world, nor governed by any of their rules. Now suddenly she was required to, even though she would gain the respect of no one for it. Their women had to ask permission to enter the long house. She had seen it enough times to know. After the shadow-plays the men stayed and the women left. She wondered if they would even consent to her using the puppets afterward. To consort with Soter. He was a man, too, however besotted, and to practice, she must enter his house. They would brand her a mispel for that, most certainly. No, they would never allow it, maybe not even if Koombrun accompanied her. She could imagine the pleasure Agmeon would take in controlling her, the same as Gousier. There wasn't a soul on the island that wasn't allied against her.

She stood considering long enough that Agmeon circled her. "What's the matter with you? Leave!"

"Not without him."

Agmeon looked as if he would strike her then. Soter suddenly lurched upright and stumbled in between them, slurring his words: "What's all this nonsense, you two? Agmeon, this is Leodora, you know who she is. Lea, what *is* so urgent?" He hung there like a great tortoise, with his head pushed out and swinging back and forth. When he received no reply from either of them, and the two continued to stare one another down, he waved his hands loosely and said, "All right, all right, I've had too much hospitality anyway. I'd get lost on the way home without a guide. Come on, child, help me with my goods and let's go."

Agmeon's glance flicked between them. He seemed to weigh the matter. She could almost hear him thinking that at least with Soter she would be gone. He released an exasperated sigh and sharply withdrew, allowing the two of them collect Soter's payment. She gathered up loaves of bread, dried seaweed, and a shirt, stuffing them into his net bag along with a few empty jugs. He shuffled up beside her carrying his own jug and nothing else. For once she didn't mind being his drudge. He kept turning and bidding everyone goodnight the whole length of the house.

Outside, they had barely gone a dozen steps when he spoke quite soberly, "Now, what was all that business about, Agmeon not letting you in? What did he mean, you're betrothed?"

By the time they reached his hut, she'd told him the whole story and he had launched into his own verbal assault upon Gousier: "The utter fool, does he truly believe the village will warm to him for this? Or to you? Link with his family? They can't possibly have told him that. He's made it up from what they didn't tell him."

He stumbled approaching his hut, quickly caught himself, then stopped and stared at his own feet for a moment. "Some of us are foolish," he said, "you from youth and I from drink. And we try to compensate for our weaknesses when we're not giving in to them. But your uncle, Lea, is the worst kind of fool—the cocksure fool. Malicious and proud in his certainty. No one can tell him anything, and the more he stands on his points, the more wrong he is. And the more vicious."

He entered the hut, then spun around to face her, his arms flung wide. The jug in his hand tugged him sideways. "Look at your mother!"

Not following his train of thought, she glanced about. "Where?"

"On the spans, of course!" He set down the jug. "Your uncle chased all over trying to locate her. Would not be dis . . . dis . . . wouldn't be put off from it. Never once did he consider she might not wish to be found, and that he could've better used his time selling his damned fish. Idiot. Idiot." He collapsed on a stool, and repeated the word now almost as if chiding himself.

She put down the net full of crockery. "Soter," she asked,

drawing closer.

"Mmm?"

"You have to tell me now, no more dodging. No more maneuvers."

"What?" He looked up. Though she was right in front of him, he seemed to have to search for her.

"You have to tell me now, am I any good."

He said, "Dunno what you mean."

Apprehension colored his attempt to fall back upon being drunk as an escape. His eyes glistened with such fear that she found herself glancing around, expecting to discover the ghosts of his conscience condensing behind her. Those ghosts, whether she saw them or not, would keep him in check unless she rattled his world enough to dissolve them. She said, "I have to know, Soter, because no matter what the answer, I'm leaving the island. Now. Tonight. I don't have a choice anymore."

"There's always a choice."

"You know there isn't. I won't marry Koombrun, but I have to marry Koombrun. What choice does my uncle leave? If I stay, he and the village control my life forever. I will never be allowed to come here and train, to work the puppets, to learn. So I'm taking the puppets with me. All of them. They're mine—you said so—and I'm taking them. But I have to know now: Am . . . I . . . any . . . good?"

She watched the fear drain out of him as he assessed what she'd said. She had broken the wishful bubble in which he lived—the lie he perpetuated to keep things as they were, which he'd admitted to her mother's specter. He was no different than Tastion. Or Gousier, for that matter. The three men dwelt in fantasies of their own devising, with never a thought for her as anything other than an object within the frame. One after the other, she was showing them that she neither shared nor accepted their worlds.

When Soter answered her, it was in the quiet, attentive voice of a man focused upon a single, critical issue; one who had reasoned out his course of action before this night.

"Where do you intend to go? Ningle?"

"Of course."

"How will you hide from your uncle? He knows many people up there. How will you know who you can trust?"

"I—I don't know. I won't trust anyone."

"And you'll carry both cases by yourself? You couldn't

carry them both from here to Tenikemac much less up that stairway. Do you know how long a span is?"

"No." Worry warped the syllable.

"Will you head north or south? Which is better?"

"I don't know."

"It's good, then, that you've thought this through, worked out the details." He spoke without a trace of sarcasm. He didn't need any to make his point. "Lea, dear, you can't be a performer by yourself up there, either. Proper shadowplay needs three or four. I've told you this, I wasn't making it up. Who's going to play your music for you? We'll have to find someone. Can't be a girl puppeteer up there—the way they treated you in the long house just now will be nothing to how you'd be derided on most of the spans near here. How you go about by day's no issue. But on stage . . ." He reached up and pushed his fingers into her long hair. You'll have to give this up. We have to disguise you. Do as your father did, starting out."

"We have to do it? *We*?"

"You and me."

"Soter, I don't want anybody—"

"It doesn't much matter if you do. Haven't you been listening, or must I ask you the questions all over again? I'm coming along."

"But why? Why do you want to?"

He pulled at his nose. "Well, first, because, as I said, you can't do this on your own, no matter what you think. Second, because Gousier will make me pay in your absence once he's done beating your aunt, and I don't care to take your punishment when the whip comes down, thank you very much. Third, there's no one better'n me at arranging these things. I've told you that."

"Yes, but—"

"I'm not finished," he said testily. "Fourth, I'm coming along because, Leodora, you have in you the skill to be the greatest shadowteller that the whole endless spiral of Shadowbridge has ever seen. With my guidance you might achieve such recognition as no one has ever had. As for if you're good" —he smiled slyly— "let us just see how you perform when the audience isn't an inbred village of sea urchins."

She wanted to cry and laugh at the same time. She forgave him his need to dramatize the answer. She wanted to run and embrace him, thank him, but she did not let herself. She grinned but kept her passion in check. She had, after all, known she was great all along.

He drummed his fingers on the seat of the stool and said, "Now, when are we leaving?"

It was not a simple question, but a test. He wanted her to think about all she had to do. "Tomorrow night?" she ventured.

"He will come after us, same as he did your mother before you. You'll have humiliated him in front of the village. He'll be worse off than he was before he dreamed up this scheme. We must be careful how we go initially." He relaxed, as if something had been decided. "Now you ought to get your sleep. He expects you to be at work in the morning and you don't want to give him a reason to suspect anything. He's already angry with you. Don't provoke him, however much you want to. Let him lord over you. Let him gloat. He doesn't know what's coming, which is how you want it to stay. I'll make some arrangements meantime. Go on now."

She shuffled her feet, made a lopsided bow, feeling idiotically in his debt for something she'd forced upon him. She withdrew before she could embarrass herself in some other way.

The boathouse was strange to her then. She lay in her bed, conscious that it would be her final night here, curling her toes against the coarse blanket as if she'd never felt it before, listening to the surf outside crackle and hiss upon the sand.

Sleep took forever to arrive. It had to catch her unawares.

The restive night delivered her to the morning tired, dreamy and distracted. She saw everything as if through a mirror, all of it real but lacking its former substance—as if an interloping spirit had taken residence in her head. Her preoccupation blinded her, until she was climbing down the stairs, to the silence. She stopped.

Nothing called to her from across the sea.

She strained to listen. Gulls screeched. Waves spread upon the shore. Her curtains flapped. The sound beneath the sound was gone.

She was still listening for it as she wandered down the beach toward the village, not really aware of her surroundings until she saw Kusahema on the ridge. Quickly gathering a few strands of seaweed, she carried them to the pregnant girl. Kusahema refused to meet her eyes, and held her basket out shyly.

Perplexed but wishing to follow Soter's admonition, Leodora asked, "How are you this morning?" and reached to place her hand on her friend's belly. Kusahema jumped back, wild-eyed, shoving the basket between them. With her head tilted, she looked as if she were cringing from an attack.

"What's wrong? What is it?"

The girl made no reply. She shook her head, shrank away, backing into the surf in order to get around Leodora. Then she hurried up the beach, a desperate waddle, while casting backward glances to make sure Leodora wasn't pursuing her.

"Yesterday's blessing is today's curse," she muttered—a line from a shadowplay that suddenly made sense to her. Gousier's arrangement had altered her relationship to the whole village, even more than she had imagined. Who knew how many proscriptions now weighed against her?

She walked over the ridge but refrained from approaching too close to the fishing party gathering their nets on the beach. She'd come to bid the dragons farewell, not the people.

Tastion had promised many times to take her with him to fish, but it had been another child's promise made first in ignorance and later in mock-defiance. He would never have dared, not really.

The men unfurled their nets and waded into the choppy sea. Tastion glanced her way nervously, then kept his back to her. The women stared straight at her, a gazed barrier.

She saw Koombrun. He could only bring himself to look at her askance, shy now, maybe even fearful. His mother saw her and began slapping him, driving him away. He ducked and clutched his head and shrank back with the speed of someone who'd been beaten many times before. She regretted the misery she was bringing to him. None of this was his fault. When I'm gone, she thought, they'll punish him for that, too. She'll be more humiliated by that than by the union itself. The island's no more your friend than mine, Koombrun. I'm sorry.

The other women watched him driven away. A few looked back at her as if to say, "See what you've done?" There was no point in remaining. All she was doing was defying some other rule that she was about to abandon anyway.

She glanced out at the dragons again. To her

astonishment, the creatures had all turned and were facing her. Their riders, nonplused, were gesturing helplessly. The dragons beneath them just floated in place. For a moment they seemed to acknowledge her estrangement. Then the moment passed, the creatures swung about as one and headed out to sea. The women's stare after that was furious. Leodora turned her back on them and set off for Fishkill Cavern.

The coral man stood upright in the back of the cave. The glow seemed to have left him altogether. The cold had probably killed all the tiny creatures living within him. His dullness should have made him less imposing, but she found that she could not work with her back to him. Despite the fact that he had no eyes, the sensation of being watched overpowered her. She couldn't help looking to be sure he hadn't come to life and edged nearer. When she couldn't trust that he hadn't, she went over and scratched a line on the floor in front of him. Even that corroboration failed to satisfy her in the end, and so she moved around the stone table and worked on the other side. It was inconvenient, because the cavern wall jutted out there, forcing her to hunch over her work as she beheaded and sliced and gutted each corpse. It put the mats on the wrong side, beyond her reach, and instead of placing each cleaned fillet in the basket, she had to let them pile up and then walk all the way around the stone to lay them in the baskets.

Being able to see him didn't improve her situation either. Her attention kept flicking to him, as if he were moving in her periphery; but it wasn't movement. It was more, she thought, as if he were singing to her, whispering at a level she couldn't hear but feel.

And all at once she stopped and set down the knife and stared. She knew well the sensation she had just described. It had been absent in the boathouse but it was back now. Only the call no longer from across the sea.

It came from across the room.

By the time Gousier and his fool assistants arrived, she was ready to bolt. Her uncle took in the coral figure as if he'd seen it there every day of his life. Obviously someone had told him about it. He looked it up and down once—he towered over it—

and then turned his attention directly to the business of the day.

She had cleaned perhaps two thirds of the fish she should have prepared, and he saw that immediately. She anticipated a beating, and for a moment as he scowled she knew it was coming. But then he looked at her and the scowl spread into a knowing smile and a narrow-eyed glance that said, "Go ahead, enjoy your final act of defiance." The coral man loomed behind him in the shadows, and the two of them combined was more than she could stand. She put down the knives and turned, knocking one of the fools aside as she marched and then ran out of the cave. She heard her uncle's savage laugh, heard him say, "She's nervous before the event," and heard the fools join in the laughter, but for all she reacted they might have been discussing someone else.

On any other day if she had walked out on him, Gousier would have dragged her back by the hair, cursed her, slapped her, whipped her. None of that was necessary now.

She washed and warmed her hands, then hurried away from the cavern before her uncle and his fools emerged. "Don't provoke him," Soter had said. For her that meant being elsewhere, and she went to her beach.

The tide was in, and the inlet lay open to the sea. She sat on the spit of sand, knees drawn up, the salty breeze ruffling her hair. Despite her impending escape, she felt as if a huge weight were tied to her. She could barely contemplate stripping off the bloody clothes and going for a swim for fear that the weight would pull her down and drown her.

It wasn't Gousier. She wouldn't miss him nor the fish guts and the cold cavern to which he consigned her any more than she would miss the marriage he'd arranged. She would miss Dymphana terribly, though. Her aunt would grieve when she'd gone, and weep for the girl who hadn't even said good-bye. She didn't dare, because Dymphana would stop her, even if such betrayal condemned her to marry an imbecile. However much her aunt loved her, she must follow Gousier's way, having long ago succumbed to his governance.

This is what it was like for my mother before me, she thought. Who I hurt and whether I care—those are my choices.

The rest of her burden the coral man provided. She knew that effigy would call her back to Bouyan, plague her with its siren song, and in that moment she made a leap of intuition, a guess. It had come from the sea, the same as the dragons. Like her they had heard its call. That was how a dragon had brought Tastion to it, and that was what the dragons had been staring at. Not her. She'd been standing in direct line between them and the cavern. Magic thrived in that figure to which they and she were attuned because . . . and here her surmise failed her outright. Dymphana had told her that not all mysteries were explained; but on the cusp of one, she resented that she couldn't find its final panacea.

She almost got up then, to go off and prepare whatever needed preparing. Then, looking across the inlet, she thought, This is the last time I'll ever be here. Her mother must have thought that once upon a time, too, looking out from this spot to this ocean. It seemed important to acknowledge.

She pulled off her small boots, drew off her bloody clothing, then ceremoniously walked into the water.

She swam across to the far side of the inlet, where she pulled herself up on a rock and perched like a sea otter. Like the evil mermaid of Omelune.

A cloud rolled across the sun, and the wind riding the water turned chilly. She shivered with gooseflesh and slid back into the inlet, splashing, diving down in the crystal-clear water to the bottom, where she grabbed a handful of weeds and sand, and offered a prayer of farewell to whatever could hear her thoughts. It was what Tastion said the fishermen did on their final outing.

When she kicked off from the bottom she found herself face to face with a sea dragon. She darted back in surprise. The dragon moved with her. Its protruding black eyes swiveled, studying her. She surfaced and drew a deep breath, ready to dive back down; but before she could, the dragon's yellow head popped up beside her.

It wasn't full grown. An adult sea dragon could never have fit through the narrow mouth of the inlet even at high tide. But it wasn't a baby, either. Its body was mottled the way an adult's was. Close up, she could see small soft spikes protruding from its ribs—features not visible from the beach. Features that only fishermen ever saw. A feathery ruff surrounded its neck, as thin as a dragonfly wing.

The plumes off the back of its head ended in purplish fans—one at the top of the head and one lower on the back of the neck, that seemed to rest on the water. Below the surface, its gills fluttered daintily. A puffy reddish mound, speckled like the torso, encompassed each eye. Tiny needle-like teeth encircled the crumpled mouth at the end of the reedy, tapered snout. The mouth flexed, wheezed, and blew spray at her. She thought of Muvros, the smaller dragon Tastion rode, and how it looked as if it were forever puckering for a kiss. This one was like that, too. She couldn't help but smile.

"Hello," she said to it.

The dragon glanced aside as if considering if it should answer.

"What are you doing here?" she asked herself as much as the dragon. It exhaled another small jet of water.

One of its paddle-shaped feet slapped against her side, and she flinched before realizing what had touched her.

The dragon turned its head to face her straight on, its eyes swiveling to find her. With its snout it nudged her, and its whuffling breath sprayed her face.

Abruptly it turned as if to go, but remained, paddling in place. Its tail snaked across her belly. She dared to touch it now, expecting the creature to dive, to flee from her. Its skin was slightly rough. The mottling across its back was bumpy. Far down its back a third plume lay folded along its spine—another feature not visible from land. Now she understood how the riders could perch in place: they fitted against the base of the plume and held onto the lowest fan on its neck.

The dragon glanced around at her, clearly impatient. The third plume fluttered in invitation. She swam up beside the dragon and pulled herself onto its back. The rough and oily skin chafed her belly and then the insides of her thighs as she sat upright. She bent her legs and clutched its sides with her knees. They fit in between the larger ribs quite naturally. Whoever had first climbed upon a sea dragon would have thought the creature had been designed for them—as she did now. The dragon seemed to think so too.

She leaned against the rear plume and held onto its neck. Neither her weight nor hold seemed to inconvenience the dragon. She was thinking, "Well, this is nice," when it suddenly dove. The surface slapped her chin, closing her mouth. Water jetted up her nose, but she held on.

The dragon made a swift circuit of the inlet, lunging forward with each oarlike sweep of its paddle fins. She leaned close to its back, hoping it wouldn't stay under too long. And as if aware of her need for air, it immediately surfaced. Leodora flexed forward like a branch that had been pulled back and then released. She clung to the dragon's neck, spitting, coughing, gasping. And then laughing.

She laughed with a joy as naked as she. The dragon craned its neck and observed her with one solemnly inquisitive black eye. Then with a flick of its tail it scooted straight out of the inlet.

The rocks to either side scraped against her legs. Another month, she thought, and the little dragon would be too big to fit through that opening. Another hour and there wouldn't have been enough water to clear it.

"How did you know about this?" she asked, as if the creature might suddenly explain itself. The transparent ruff fluttered, no communication she could understand. She had never seen any dragon in or near the inlet before, and she swam there nearly every day. When had it discovered the opening? Had it heard her farewell prayer? No, it would have had to be there already. Then she recalled that Dymphana had said a sea dragon had brought her mother home the night everyone thought she had drowned. This surely couldn't be the same one—it was too young. But how did it know to find her? "How did one know to find my mother?" she wondered aloud. "Oh, I wish you could talk to me."

Soon she had adjusted to the dragon's thrusting motion through the water and sat with her knees bent, her heels clutching its sides, riding erect, the way the fishermen did as they left in the morning. Proud.

They journeyed well beyond the safe haven of her inlet, and further out, around the point that divided Gousier's land from the village. She watched her boathouse go by, stared through the open window as if she might glimpse herself watching herself. The dragon seemed to have an objective, a purpose. It carried her steadily within view of Tenikemac. "This is not a good idea, dragon," she cautioned, but it didn't heed her. She could have jumped off at any time, but the dragon's purpose fixed her in place. The idea of the violation tempted and excited her. She was a girl out of their own stories. She was Reneleka and she was riding a sea dragon.

The first villager to see her was a woman on the beach, whose distant shout of alarm reached her ears even as others appeared in doorways and started down the beach. The woman flailed at the air and pointed. Shortly a dozen other women stood at the water's edge.

Only then did she remember that she was naked. She was violating practically every taboo imaginable. Public nudity on a dragon. It almost made her laugh. She still might have dived into the water, hidden from view behind the creature. Maybe they wouldn't have recognized her. But she stayed.

Then the dragon began circling away from the shore.

When it had turned to face out to sea, she saw coming straight at her another dragon. On its back sat Agmeon. He had the ropes of a net wrapped around his wrists as he held onto his dragon's plume. Agmeon's son on a second dragon held the other end of the net. They were returning early with their catch. The son's gaze traveled down her body and then up again, meeting her eyes with a look both of arousal and embarrassment.

Agmeon's furious, bloodshot glare held her rigid. She couldn't shrink away now, and his anger passed to her, fueling her defiance; pride and self-esteem mixing with resentment of all the rules he embodied—how arbitrarily her position changed when he chose it. Let them banish her. They were too late. She had already banished herself.

Agmeon's mount swam past hers. From his look as he went by, she knew if he'd had a weapon and could have dropped his net he would have killed her on the spot. His son passed more closely, but could only look at her from the side of his eyes. No one spoke. Only the dragons moved. Hers swam on as if it had encountered nothing. Nor had the other two seemed to notice it.

The dragon took her around the point again and back to her inlet. She rode proud and straight the whole way, despite a trembling in her limbs she couldn't control even though there was no one to see her now.

"You meant to do this to me, didn't you, clever little dragon?" she asked as they arrived. "You tricked me."

The creature didn't acknowledge that it had heard her.

"I think I'll call you Meersh, how would you like that?"

The sea dragon drew up beside the opening to the inlet and paddled in place. It looked back at her expectantly. The tide had begun to ebb, and the dragon could not swim into the inlet any longer. It seemed to know this.

Everything that had just happened, she thought, had to have happened exactly when and as it did.

She slid off and swam to the submerged shelf of rock. The

dragon hesitated, watching her. "Go on, Meersh," she said. "Go back to the story you came from. You've done your work. There can't be any marriage with Koombrun after this. I'd have to leave the island now even if I didn't want to."

The dragon extended its neck. Its puckered mouth whuffled in her face as though in reply, spraying her with gentle tears. Then it swung away and dove from sight. The sea immediately erased even the ripples of its going. She looked out across the water for a long time. The sea dragon did not resurface.

Finally, Leodora swam back to her clothes. She wrung the blood out of them and put them on. Then, with one last look across the inlet to the unbroken sea, she started up the beach to her garret. The only proof that she hadn't imagined her voyage was the red chafing inside her thighs from the dragon's skin. She knew, however, that Agmeon would provide all the proof necessary for everyone else.

She spent the rest of the afternoon out of sight in the boathouse.

At dinner she gauged Gousier's mood before appearing, but he was ebullient and carefree. He didn't know yet. "What a perfect day this was. Business was never better," he said, adding, "I could have sold twice the fish I had"—which was as close as he came to upbraiding Leodora for what he perceived as her dereliction that morning. He rambled on about the stall, a wealthy family throwing a party, who had taken every shellfish he had. He used the idea of a family to lead into his delight with the village and how exciting it was going to be when they were united with Tenikemac in a "great, big family." Obviously, he hadn't visited before coming to dinner, and with luck he wouldn't have reason to before tomorrow. One more day was all she needed.

While her uncle ate and grunted and babbled this way and that, Leodora experienced once again the recognition that she was doing something for the last time. With a focused inner quiet, she gazed around the room, burning each detail in her mind—the horizontal lines of the reeds that composed the walls; the rough plankings underfoot; the blue-dyed, frayed mat by the door; the fish oil lamps with their curlicue handles of carved bone. And, beside her, Dymphana. She saw her aunt detailed in guilt: brittle, thinning hair shot through everywhere with strands of gray; a face wrecked and ravaged time and again by a useless sagacity she wasn't allowed to express against Gousier's pig-headed presumptions and temper. She was tied to him forever and she had no idea that Leodora might not be. It was their lot; escape was unimaginable—and wasn't that implicit even in the way Dymphana told her of her mother? Leandra, who escaped to nothing. To doom. It had been a cautionary tale as much as anything else. Gousier imposed the limits and the women must do the best they could within those limits. Defiance destroyed you.

Eventually Dymphana sensed her stare. While Gousier babbled, their gazes met, and for a heartbeat Leodora thought her aunt must see her plans as if painted upon her face the way wedding blessings would have been this time tomorrow. But Dymphana read something else in the look, smiled a worried, empathetic smile, and then pretended again to be attentive to Gousier's chatter.

Later the two women carried the wooden bowls and utensils down to the water's edge to rinse them. The moons were up and bright. The sea was calm. To the north the bridge spans glittered distantly their bejeweled solicitation. Emotion boiled up in Leodora. She found herself hugging her aunt and saying what she had fought not to say: "I love you, Dymphana. I'm sorry I have to go." Horrified by her own confession, she could only wait for her aunt to destroy her.

Dymphana stroked her hair and said, "My sweet girl, it's all right. You won't be far. We'll still have time together. And maybe . . . maybe it won't be so bad." In the midst of her reassurances she began to cry. Soon it was both of them in the throes of miscommunicated despair. Leodora couldn't stand the lie—this was worse than the confession. Another moment and the truth would explode out of her. She broke away and ran before she could confess everything she intended.

Outside the boathouse she wept awhile longer. The tears now were for the future, for the pain Dymphana would endure. Gousier would take out his anger on her just as Soter had said. There would be no one else left to hurt.

Finally she wiped her eyes and, snuffling, went inside, climbing the stairs. In her grief she failed to appreciate that a candle was already burning in her garret. She was almost at the top before she realized, and by then she could see him lying on her bed as if with eternal patience.

Tastion. Naked.

When he saw her face, however, his smile of feigned nonchalance went flat. He sat up, covering himself. "Gods, he spoke to Agmeon. He's beat you, hasn't he?"

She shook her head, unable to communicate the events in any sensible way. He held out his hand. She didn't take it. Remained where she was.

Finally, as if she had asked a question, he said, "I came here to see you because . . . To tell you that the ceremony's off. They're proscribing any contact with you."

She was hardly surprised.

"Do you understand that I won't be able to come here again for awhile? Maybe a long time? Not until things settle down. Why did you do that—ride a dragon? You could have done almost anything else and it would have been better. Parading naked through the long house is nowhere near as bad, and it's bad enough. How in the ocean did you get a dragon to take you?"

Unable to explain, she didn't try. She said, "I won't marry Koombrun."

He smiled. "I knew that. And whatever happens, you'll still be mine."

"Yours?" After the emotional turmoil she had just put aside, his presumption was more than she could tolerate. "When have I ever *been* yours? When could I ever *be* yours? If I'm yours, Tastion, let's go now and tell the village. Your father. Come with me, right now." She offered her hand. "Come. Come on. Let's see Agmeon for his blessing. You can go just as you are. It'll be perfect."

It was his turn not to move. "Didn't you hear what I just said? Just being seen with you right now would be punishable by drowning. And still, here I am. But why do you want to reject what we do have? What we've had all along. You act as if it's all been just me. But it hasn't been just me. It hasn't only been what I want. Or were you not there?"

"It's too late for this argument."

He leaned forward and tried to reach her, but she shifted back. He would have had to stand up to touch her. "How can it be too late? You're not marrying him. This will blow over in time. They'll forget, or at least they'll get used to—"

"I'm leaving."

"You keep saying that, and I don't believe you."

"I'm leaving Bouyan, Tastion."

He snorted as if this were an impossibility. "Going to ride off on a sea dragon? Agmeon can't talk about anything else. And no one knows the dragon you were on—no one's ever seen it before. Or since."

"It was almost a baby, not grown up."

Tastion shook his head. "There aren't any babies in our herd this season. So you don't know where it came from either. How can you expect it to come back and take you where you want to go. Believe me—dragons are headstrong. As moody as people."

"Tastion—"

"Look, Lea, everything will return to normal for us in a few months, at most a year. You won't ever have to marry Koombrun, you'll stay where you are and we'll meet in secret like always."

She shook her head. How could he be so obstinate, so blind? He was no different than Gousier: his mind was made up regardless of the facts. "You should get dressed."

For a moment he sat in contemplation. Then he pulled his clothes from beneath the bed. He got up, standing brazenly in front of her in a state of half-arousal. He sorted through the clothes as if unable to identify his trousers, offering her one last opportunity to have him. She held her position. When it became obvious that she couldn't be coerced or enticed, Tastion shrugged as if to say it didn't matter, and began to dress.

She saw as if for the first time his true nature. Although she had always desired to ride Tastion as fearlessly as she had the dragon, she would not succumb. She would have left it at that and let him go; but then, in a way that all but dared her to disagree, he muttered again, "You'll still be mine." His shirt was half over his head. Leodora grabbed his hand and yanked him to the steps.

"Wait, I don't have my shirt on, Lea!"

She ignored his complaint, hauled him stumbling down the steps and through the dark below. "Lea!" he said again, but laughingly this time. He thought he had won.

Outside, on a path she could have found even on a moonless night, she led him into the deeper jungle. But she kept going, passing by their hidden spot, dragging him on. He was silent now, and even his hand in hers betrayed his tension behind her.

When she stopped, the tower of Ningle loomed overhead. Lights sprinkled on either side of it, a coruscation on the night sky, a glow suggesting lines and forms, solidity out of nothingness.

Leodora began to climb the stone steps. She still had hold of him, and he stumbled up onto the first step after her. "What are you doing? Stop it."

She paused and looked down at him. "Climb up with me."

His eyes traveled beyond and then back to her. He craned his neck to see if they'd been followed. "Do you want me to be banished? I can't do this. You know I can't—"

"It's forbidden. Proscribed. Like me. Coming to my room and offering yourself to me naked is a crime, but you can do *that*. Why can't you do this?"

"That's different."

"Because you want to do it. I want you to do this, but this you can't—because you don't want to." She climbed another step and he tore free of her grasp. She let him go.

He slid back down a step. "Stop."

"This is where I'm going."

He looked at the tower, at the sky. He tried to laugh at her. "Don't be stupid. You don't know any more about up there than I do. You don't know anything except stories."

"It's all I need to know. I can be whoever I want. You already are who you'll always be. When my life moves forward, you won't be part of it any longer."

"But, Lea," he tried desperately, "you don't have to go now. Don't you see? The marriage is finished. You've destroyed it."

"Ah, and you don't want to give up until you've had me completely. What you really want to say is that you'd have me remain on Bouyan for your pleasure."

"And is that so awful?"

"Not for you. For you it's idyllic. Just what you want. You ride out every morning, come back in the evening, drink and laugh with your friends, and then creep off to your kept whore. Of course you won't be beaten to death on the morrow, either, or drowned if caught." She climbed down past him and started back along the path. She heard him come crashing through the underbrush after her.

"It was what you wanted, too."

She stiffened. Then she nodded. "Yes, you're right, Tastion. It was what I once wanted, too. But it's not what I want anymore." She set off again. Soon he closed the gap between them again.

"I'll tell them. I'll tell them and they'll keep you from leaving."

She stopped so fast that he ran into her. She turned. In the shadows he might have been simpering, showing her how clever he was, she couldn't be certain. She didn't have to see his face. He had just told her what she had meant to him. They had both been teasing arousal from each other for so long, but the difference she saw now was that she might actually have loved him.

"Tell them, then," she said. "Tell Agmeon, tell the elders. Be sure and tell them the means by which you learned it, and how many other nights we've spent together. Tell them everything we've nearly done and everything you want to do. All you'll do is bring the stars down upon your head, as well."

Quickly, he changed tack. "I'll tell Gousier."

Fear knifed her belly. Everything she had ever felt for or shared with Tastion evaporated. She took a step and he moved to block her. She kept coming nevertheless, impelling him backward by force of will until his heel caught against a root and he fell. He tried to grab her as he toppled but she dodged his fingers and kept going. She expected to hear him shout his threat again, but there was silence behind her.

Where the paths branched, she turned left and went to Soter's.

Oil lamps burned brightly within his hut. She stopped in the doorway.

One of the puppet cases stood open in the center of the room. All the puppets lay in a heap beside it, a congeries of articulated limbs and rods. At the rear, Soter emerged, his eyes sparkling in the oil light, a smile on his lips at the sight of her. He looked uncommonly sober.

"Come see," he urged. She crossed the room. "You see how the case is made?" He leaned over it and found a small black ribbon in its depths, which he ceremoniously pulled. What appeared to be the bottom of the case rose up like the trap door to her garret room.

"Extra compartments," he said. "We put our belongings in

this one, beneath the puppets. The other's bigger, deeper. Your father used it for whatever came along. If pockets were picked and the boodle found its way to us, in it went. The moneys collected during performances, too. It pays to be careful on the spans. He was doing very well, and thieves lurked everywhere, in the most unexpected guises. That's something to remember about the spans and spirals: You can be as intimate as you like with someone and the next thing, they turn on you."

"Yes, they do, don't they?" Through her fresh bitterness her thoughts were already leaping ahead, in another direction. "The other case is a little larger."

"It is, yes. Like a coffin, big enough almost. Bardsham managed to fill it, though. We once carried a young . . . never mind."

She hadn't heard him. She was regarding the larger undaya case. "Do you believe in coincidence, Soter? Or do you think that some things just happen to take place at the right moment?"

He stared at her in perplexity.

"We need to take everything out of the case," she told him, "all the puppets. I need it."

"But I just packed it."

She started past him, and he hurried after her, around her, muttering, "All right, all right." He took hold of the case before she could and dragged it out of the small back room. Unfastening the lid, he carefully began removing the puppets. "They're in proper order, be careful," he advised when she reached in, too. Piled on the floor, there were so many, she couldn't believe she had tried every one. Soter lifted the false bottom. "You don't want to put anything heavy in here, you know. These cases will wear you down. In the morning they're hardly an inconvenience, but you haul one along till sunset, and you won't think you'll ever stand up straight again."

"It isn't heavy, what I have in mind. It's light as air."

He dropped the bottom back into place. "Well, I hope it's important. We can't have anything frivolous on this escapade." She closed the case and carried it out, leaving him bewildered between the puppet piles.

She didn't dare light a lamp. She had to feel her way through the cavern.

Around the bend, the coral man was glowing, but now no brighter than the farthest star. Just as well for her—she didn't think she could have touched him again if he were brightly lit. This way, she could pretend that he was dull and harmless.

She stood the case up beside him to compare. As she had thought, he was smaller than the case, just as she was. Once it was open, she had to pat around in its depths to find the black ribbon. As she pulled up the false bottom, from the corner of her eye she thought she saw the coral man lean toward her. She jumped and looked straight at him. He hadn't moved of course. It was, she insisted, her steaming breath in the air that had caused the illusion. "Why in the world am I doing this?" she muttered, and answered herself: because he wants me to.

She had to summon every reserve of courage to touch him. She lifted him by the shoulders, and just as Tastion had said he felt as light as a handful of sand. She stood him in the case. It might indeed have been his coffin. She closed the false bottom and it fitted perfectly over him. As she started to close the lid, she paused. The cave seemed to tilt, her stomach to flip. In the midst of the moment's vertigo she experienced a premonition that this had been pre-ordained, that no accident had provided the perfect coffin for her enigma, just as no random sea dragon had swum into her lagoon. From her mother to her, from the sea to this empty figure, forces were at work, conspiring, aligning. She was supposed to go. She was certain of it now. Nothing was going to stand in her way, she couldn't be stopped.

The moment passed but her fingers trembled as she fitted and snapped shut the lid. She tipped, lifted the case, almost expecting the thing inside it to rap on the bottom and kill her with terror. But it did nothing. It weighed nothing. The case might have been empty.

In utter darkness she shuffled back the way she'd come, traveling by instinct this last time through the uterine cave and out the narrow cleft.

Soter asked where she had been, but she said nothing to him as she handed over the case. He held it in puzzlement, and she imagined that he was trying to feel the weight of whatever she'd added, and couldn't. He set the case down beside the puppets, opened it. Before she could stop him, he pulled up the bottom. A small sound emerged from him—the word "What?"

He dropped the false bottom back into place and immediately began replacing the puppets. After a moment he said, "Later you'll tell me what that is and where it came from and why it's going with us. Right now you'd better hurry. We don't want to arrive on Ningle too late, or no one will take us in. Get your belongings and hurry back quick as you can." He flicked his fingers at her. "Go!"

Obediently, she hurried out and along the dark path.

In the boathouse, she saw that the light in her garret was lit, then chided herself for having left it burning. She hoped Tastion hadn't come back.

She crept up the stairs, but it was impossible to be silent in that building. Every step creaked or groaned. She sensed rather than saw movement behind her, but before she could turn something caught the braid of her hair and yanked so hard that she was lifted off her feet. Her scalp blazed with pain. She dangled, swung like a bell once, and flew the length of the room. She slammed into the wall beside the windows. An arm's length to the left and she would have plunged through it to her almost certain death. The wall didn't kill her but it knocked her half-senseless.

She didn't have to see or hear him to know it was Gousier. She tried to react. Her mind screamed; her body refused to respond.

Gousier lurched across the garret, caught her hair again, dragged her across the floor to the post beside the stairs. He hauled her up again and, with his hand on her throat, crushed her hard against it.

His face was all but inhuman, and his sweat stank of liquor as well as fish, but he wasn't drunk. Drunk, he might have been escapable. "Well, my girl, you've done me up good, haven't you? Bare-tit riding their dragons? I'm lucky they haven't just come and cut my head off and burned my house down. They've condemned you. No wedding. No anything. And worse. They say they'll find someone else to haul their fish up to market. Unless—" He winced as if saying this hurt, and his head swiveled as if the room were moving around him; he let go of her throat, let go as though forgetting she was there; she sucked in a desperate breath, but before she could act, he struck her so hard across the mouth that the back of her skull hitting the post exploded lightning in her head. Colors, lights, blackness spun together, shattered.

The floor scraped her chin. A splinter stung her awake. She tasted dirt, but couldn't focus on it. She wasn't even sure how she'd fallen—the memory had been knocked out of her. She heard her uncle raving. He smashed the bed frame, tore the bedding into shreds. She ought to get up, but still couldn't find the means to drive her muscles to act. Not in time.

Gousier came back to work on her. He curled her braid around his hand, and jerked her upright, where she dangled at his eye level. She screamed at the pain.

"I can save myself. They want me to give you up. And I'm going to. I'm going to give you to Tenikemac. Agmeon says they haven't had to use the purging ritual you'll endure in over three generations. No female's been so stupid as you. Not even . . . not even her." While he spoke, he tore the clothes off her, pushing her to tug and rip them down, and finally dropping her again. He used the shreds of her bedding to gag her and tie her hands. He recited all the while. "First they carry you out into the water and hold you under as a purification, see, appeasing the dragons' spirits, penance for your outrage. He says most people pretty much evacuate out every orifice before they're finished, cleans out everything. But then they stop. They want you alive, see, at the end. From water to fire, that's how it has to go. They burn you next. In the long house. Over the center fire. They cook you slow on a spit shoved right up your arse and down your spine. You go crazy from the roasting, the pain, the fire. But you don't die then, either. You're still alive when they cut you up into pieces. The flesh is still alive and singing with agony. And they sprinkle you out across the water to make amends for the way you've violated the honor of the sea. You become part of the sea and the world goes back to how it was. Fish don't disappear, storms don't come to smash them. No one else has to suffer. Oh, my, yes, I'll do that, my dearest little Leandra, yes I will. But first, first I'm going to have you right here, the way everyone else did. Everyone on the spans, everyone . . . you gave yourself to everyone and not even a thought for me. I'm going to ride you till you've got splinters in your back, and you'll be asking for the fire at the end of your night, little bitch. You show yourself to them that pays, you'll show it to me, too."

He dropped her and untied his own belt. His face was contorted and he whined in the back of his throat, as if even in madness he couldn't hide from himself what he was about to do.

Leodora felt blood spreading like the chill of death through her hair. If she lay here he would rape her and everything he promised would follow. Without knowing quite how, she made herself get up on one knee and started to climb to her feet. Gousier saw it and, though his pants were half off, he kicked out savagely.

She dodged his foot and threw herself with all her strength against him, struck his hip but tripped against another support post, which knocked her back against him again. Gousier's foot was still in the air. He nearly caught his balance from the first blow, but was no more ready than she for the rebound. She knocked him sideways.

He twisted and swung his descending foot to catch himself, but it slipped off the floorboard and into the stairwell. He made a desperate grab for the nearest post, shredding the skin on his fingers as he tipped through the opening and fell down the steps.

Leodora pressed herself against the post as if it were consciousness. Blood was in her face, stinging her eyes. Inside her head, the world burned bright, and she lost the sense of where she was, or why she'd been tied. When she opened her eyes again, the room held steady, and she tried standing on her own. She worked her hands to get free of the bedding, but it was so tight that her fingers had gone numb. She thought that her wrist was moving but there might have been no skin left on it for all she knew.

The steps creaked, and she whirled about to see Gousier, his face filthy with dirt and blood, come rising up out of the hole. He looked for her, turned and saw her, and he grinned the most terrible, feral grin. "Leandra," he growled, the name an emblem of all that he intended. Now he would do everything he'd promised and worse. He put his hands on the floor and continued up.

Leodora threw herself against the raised trapdoor. It snapped off its pin and slammed down onto her uncle's head. His fingers slipped and he fell partway, and the door, with her riding it, hammered into his head a second time and then banged shut. She heard his body tumble down the stairs. She lay on her side, dust erupting out of the boards.

Silence followed while the dust settled. Streaked with dirt, sweat and blood, choking on her gag, she strained to hear if he was coming back, praying to any gods that would listen not to let him. She was finished if he did now.

She might have lain there forever before she heard the stairs creak once more. She rolled over and tried to sit up, but her arm beneath her had fallen asleep. She lay back across the door, knowing that her weight would not deter him if he could still use his arms. If he got into the garret this time he would win.

The trap door thumped once. Twice, trying to rise. A pause.

A muffled voice called, "Lea?" It was Tastion.

She whined a ragged breath and rolled off the door. He pushed it open. The moment he saw her, he scrambled the rest of the way up the stairs.

"Oh, Lea, Lea, are you all right? Oh, what a stupid question, of course you aren't. Is he coming back?" He untied her hands and helped her sit.

"He's not . . . not on the stairs?"

"No." He wiped his palm across her forehead, smearing away some of the blood that covered her entire face in a crimson mask.

"Close the trap, Tastion. Close and lock it."

She leaned back against the wall and flexed her hands, rubbing her wrists together. Her head throbbed. Her jaw ached. She rested a moment and Tastion, to his credit, didn't bombard her with questions. He observed calmly, "The door won't latch. You've broken it." Then after another moment had passed, he added quietly but defensively, "I didn't tell him."

"No." Her fingers tingled now. She tried to get up, pushing against the wall. Tastion closed his hands around her waist and drew her to her feet. "Help me down to the water please."

Saying nothing, he opened the trap door, then preceded her down the steps, but Gousier did not strike. At the bottom, she said, "Wait." The light from above revealed the shape of a leg behind the steps. She edged to it, bent down. Sparks jittered across her vision for an instant.

Gousier had careened off the stairs before reaching the bottom and somehow ended up halfway beneath them. He lay with his head tucked under one arm as if hiding from the light. Leodora nudged the arm, and a groan escaped him but he didn't move. She backed away.

"He's not dead?"

"Not yet." She limped away from him, out of the boathouse and down the beach. The quiet sea was warmer than the air, and she entered the water, wading in until it reached her waist, then sat with it up to her neck. She lay back, letting the water wash her hair and clean her wounds. The salt burned, and though it made her hiss, she was glad of it. Glad to be alive to feel it. The inside of her mouth was cut. Her cheek felt stiff and puffy. She submerged her head, and listened to the sound of blood in her ears, her heartbeat thundering; her head and mouth stinging.

Coming up again she was dizzy. Tastion had to help her out of the surf. She shivered in the chill air; her naked skin prickled with goose bumps. She began to cry.

Tastion let her cling to him. After a while, he turned her, then guided her back to the boathouse.

The wound in her scalp was superficial—not from the pulling of her hair but from striking something as she fell. It had stopped bleeding and would be only a bruise and a headache on the morrow. She discarded the clothes her uncle had torn off her. She couldn't wear them now, even if they weren't a ruin. She thought, *Just one less item I have to bring*. She'd finished crying. It was time to act.

She put on other clothes, whatever was hanging on the pegs—she hardly noticed what, even as she was pulling them on. Wiping her eyes, she began picking up items from around the room: a pair of boots that she'd made herself; a few combs of bone, one of which Tastion had given her; sandals; a shell that she'd found on the beach many years earlier, which was nothing extraordinary but all the more precious to her for that and because it, like she, had survived her uncle's assault. Everything she gathered into the center of a cloak, and tied that into a bundle. There was her whole life, weighing practically nothing. "Light as air," she said, thinking of the coral effigy, which she was stealing from them. She would not tell Tastion. Then he wouldn't have to lie. He watched her with eyes full of worry.

With the bundle slung over her shoulder, she leaned forward and kissed him. Her mouth twinged.

On the second step, she paused to look around the garret, to make it a space in her mind, her memory. Tastion followed her down.

At the bottom, she set aside the bundle. In her hand she carried strips of cloth, the same ones he'd used on her; she went to Gousier and rolled him onto his face. This time he didn't make a sound. His head lolled. She tied his hands over his head as hard as she could, then gagged him so tightly that his back teeth showed. She attempted to haul him by the arms. One of them was twisted the wrong way and she knew it was broken. He was too heavy. Tastion grabbed his legs then, and they picked him up and clumsily slung him over the lip of his rotted boat. He landed with a sharp report of snapping boards. The boat shook as if it might split. It tipped toward them, and Gousier's naked buttocks abruptly protruded out the rotted hole in its side.

"Well, uncle," she said without humor, "you finally plugged her leak." She had to lean against a post while sparks spun away in the darkness. Tastion touched her shoulder. "No," she said, "I'm all right. Soter's waiting, I can rest afterward."

As they came through his door, Soter started to bellow at Tastion until he moved aside and Soter saw Leodora. He stared accusingly at Tastion, who shook his head and mouthed, "Gousier."

Soter nodded. "In that case, it's good you're here, boy."

And so, despite her protests, the two men carried the cases and Leodora followed stiffly with only her small bundle of belongings. When they reached the steps, Tastion never hesitated, but climbed straight up. She called his name tenderly, knowing that he must be petrified, but he was deaf to argument. On the landing at the top, he placed the puppet case on the wall that edged the span. He gazed out over the island. Leodora came up beside him. She looked where he looked—at the lights of Tenikemac and the beautiful ocean beyond.

"You shouldn't be here," she told him.

He turned his head, surveyed the crumbling stone building on the other side of the wall. "So, this is Ningle. Doesn't look monstrous, does it? Just kind of seedy and rundown, and it smells like something rotten. I think it could use some mortar at the very least, don't you ag—"

She touched his shoulder and he stopped talking. He faced her.

"I love you, Lea," he said. "Everything I said before was because I couldn't stand letting you go. You've always been here. There was never a time when you weren't here with me." He grimaced. "I wish I could take it all back. I wish you hadn't heard any of it."

She slid her arms around his waist and drew him against her.

When Soter finally reached the landing, they were still embracing. "Would have been damned nice if someone had come back down and helped me with my burden once he'd flown up the steps." He dropped the case dramatically, but they still didn't move. He wheezed at them, refusing to grant them any solace, and glowered as they kissed.

Then Tastion pushed himself back from Leodora. "It's time you found . . . time you went." His voice broke, and he lurched around Soter and hurried down the steps. Tears trailed silently down Leodora's cheeks.

Gently, Soter patted her hair. He inadvertently touched the cut in her scalp and she flinched. He withdrew his hand. "Your uncle?"

Snuffling, she wiped at her nose and replied, "I don't know. He might be dead."

"I wouldn't grieve. I won't so much as pour a drop of libation in *his* memory ever." He picked up his case. "You're following in your father's footsteps in almost every detail. You do see that, don't you? We'll have to find a new name for you . . . on the next spiral. Come on now, grab your burden and bring it along. I know you'll hurt all over come morning, but one thing's certain: If he is still breathing, he'll come looking. We need to be tucked away before the sun's up." He went through the gate.

Leodora remained standing there until Tastion had vanished into the darkness of the trees. "Reneleka, take care of Dymphana," she said softly. She picked up the case and followed. Her final view was of the whole dark half of Bouyan, her home.

She was never to see it again.

PART 2:
DIVERUS

Chapter 3
Paidika

This is the way, when someone asked, that Leodora told his tale:

There was once a silent boy who lived beneath the bridge. He lived neither on an island nor on land, nor even upon the water, but within the frame of a span itself. Chiseled supports and struts formed the foundation, beams and crossties created an intricate latticework of layers between them, and upon these platforms were laid surfaces on which huts and fortifications were erected, all at different heights and lengths because no one who built there required the permission of anyone else, and few there were who sought others' opinions. Mad geometries were the result.

As a baby the boy had sat outside his tiny hovel and looked without understanding upon the random sections of this sub rosa city. From his platform a ladder ran to the next, which was suspended at a slightly higher level and broad enough that three dwellings had been erected across it. Another ladder, of rope, declined to a level below theirs on the opposite side.

Houses beneath the bridge had few roofs because there were no elements to protect anyone from (save the prying eyes of those situated above). The thick stalactitic surface of the span provided all necessary protection, and just acquiring the materials to erect walls was hard enough. In most cases, divers, who lived on the lower levels, brought up the stone from the sea bottom, especially from around the piers, where rocky ocean floor had been crushed and heaped as far down as anyone could see. It cost money to pay the divers, and more to have the stones hauled up on ropes and pulleys from layer to layer through the underspan hierarchy. Everyone knew that a stone was going to disappear here and another there as the pile of rock ascended, and if you were lucky and the pullers not too greedy, perhaps half of the original pile made the journey. It was the way of the underspan and no use railing at its unfairness; it had been thus for centuries and would be thus for centuries more. What it meant, however, was that walls were not built very high, but more like boundary markers than sides of a house. Most were not even as tall as the inhabitants themselves. There would be one entrance, and only the one great room. Privacy was at best an untested notion. There was always someone on a level above yours. You learned quickly which corners of your home offered sanctuary or at least deep shadows, and you conducted your intimacy there.

The boy often spent his time looking down at other people, whose behavior was as alien to him as the life of insects. Like insects, they seemed to live in patterns. The patterns he could make out, though not their meaning.

All of this may seem uncommon and strange, but on almost every span of Shadowbridge we know, substructural societies flourish below the main boulevards. Many forms of life thrive in caverns, and more in shadows, in the dark. Some of them can't stand the light at all.

By the time he turned twelve, the boy had no family.

His mother died of a wasting disease, and her body was ejected into the sea with little ceremony; his father, a man of scant talent and less ambition, had only remained with her because she managed to bring in money by begging upon the surface of the span. She used the boy for this. Even as a baby he was clearly, visibly deficient. The impoverished mother clutching her damaged child while reaching one claw of a hand toward passersby tugged at all but the hardest hearts, and she did very well for herself, for her husband. When she died, the father unraveled. He knew he couldn't care for a child, never mind one who was practically an idiot. He was the sort of man who preferred to be blown from place to place by the winds of fortune. Wherever he went he'd always found someone to take care of him, exactly as the boy's mother had done. He had pretended to go off in search of work every morning, and she must have known he wasn't really doing anything more than finding someplace to drink up her coin, but she never said anything to him, because he was handsome and solicitous, always showing her kindness, always promising to do better the next time although he never did. He was handsome enough still to think he could find such a situation again, provided he didn't bring any baggage along. He was looking over the wall of his house at his son as he thought this.

The silent boy sat near the edge of the platform with his feet dangling as he stared across the underside of the bridge, down and down to the water. He focused upon the spot where his mother's body had vanished. He could remember every detail of how her form, wrapped in a sheet, had been carried three platforms away, where the inhabitant had assembled a chute for the disposal of the deceased; how his father had paid the inhabitant a few coins and then carried her to the edge of the chute and callously slid her off.

In his interior world, the boy imagined that she had turned into a merwoman or a siren, or even a fish. He assumed that this was the natural order of things and that one day the same would happen to him, although he didn't like the idea of becoming a fish and being caught and eaten by someone living up here, which is what happened to fish every day—he might even be caught and brought up to be eaten by himself after all, who could say with certainty that the flow of time didn't allow such things to happen? Who could be certain time didn't fold over upon itself or weave back and forth like an Ondiont snake on the surface of the ocean? Certainly not he with his swirled thoughts. He didn't want to eat his mother, and so he made up his mind that she was not a fish, but a sea creature, definitely a merwoman living now in a city on the bottom of the ocean. It was a city that looked like the one where his mother had taken him to beg, up above. It had towers and spires of stone and glazed tile, bright pennants and lamps, and happy people—of course, they would all have fish bodies.

Time passed, and he lay down under the weight of this dream and dozed.

All the while he dreamed of his mother's transformed life, his father was busy gathering up a few belongings from the house. He paused to watch the boy sleeping, curled up at the edge of the platform. If he felt anything at all for his child, perhaps he felt it then; but it wasn't strong enough to move him to action—at least not to action in the boy's favor.

The poles of a ladder clacked against the side of the platform from a level below, directing the father's attention toward the group who appeared one after the other at the top—a father and mother and two daughters. They were better dressed than he, in clothes that might have been cast offs from the richer people on the surface. They approached him, and he welcomed them, let them inspect the house, turn over the pallets, stir the ashes in the tiny hearth. There were pots, a skillet. He was leaving all that behind. Close up, the family stank the way fish did after floating for a few days. If they noticed the sleeping boy out at the far edge of the platform, they said nothing, and finally gave the father his money, enough to keep him lubricated until he had left this span far behind. He clasped hands with the father, then threw his pack over his shoulder and climbed up the ladder to the next level, and on from there, until the gloom of the place swallowed him up as if he'd never been.

The new family spent the day carrying belongings up from the water's edge where they'd been living, and where everything smelled like brine and rot. They carried the smell with them but it would go away, now they had moved up to better accommodations. Here they would have to live with nothing worse than cooking smells. Much higher and the air would have been smoky all the time. This was better, they thought—a perfect balance between the green swirling ocean and the dark heights beneath the span.

A black bird swooped in through the tangle of habitations and landed beside the boy. It tilted its head one way and then the other, and finally hopped over and cawed at him. He woke to shining beady eyes just inches from his own. The bird plucked at his hand as if he had food hidden there. The boy sat up and the bird squawked and flew off. He rubbed his eyes, and looked around. The sun was sinking. The whole underside of the span burned orange in the light and each spar and beam threw off stretching shadows cut out of the air. Down below, fishing boats had tied up around the piers. His eyes moved to the one important spot in the ocean again, but there was nothing to see. He stood and shuffled back home.

If anything seemed peculiar about his home, he didn't

notice it until he had entered the doorway. A little girl stepped out and barred his way. She wasn't any older than he, but she rose up as if inflating, and ordered him to get out. He couldn't understand what she was doing in his house. Because he'd been asleep, he experienced the odd sensation that he'd dreamt his whole life before now, and it had evaporated forever the moment he awoke. His father was nowhere in the house, and all the scattered clothing and belongings lying about were things he'd never seen before.

Seized by terror, all he could do was wave his arms and wail wordlessly. The two adults rushed from their fire.

They didn't know what to make of him any more than their daughter had, but they were not heartless, and it was clear he thought he lived here. The man who'd bought the platform from his father had indeed noticed him sleeping at the far edge, but because the boy had gone unmentioned, not even looked at, he'd assumed him to be a passing vagrant and nothing to do with the house; now he suspected that the boy *had* lived here and the man who'd sold them this place had known it. But it was too late to do anything about that—he knew that man would be long gone. The couple communicated to him that he could stay the night and in the morning they would solve his problem. He sat by the door, ragged and sullen. The space that had been his was now occupied by the two small girls. The one who had confronted him remained awake after her sister and made faces at him. He might have run off that night, and the man and wife would not have minded if they had awakened in the morning and found him gone, but he lacked the sensibility to forge such a plan, much less set out on his own. He stayed.

In the morning the man took him to a different platform, well across the width of the underspan from his own. A woman lived there with a house full of children. The man and this woman bargained and bickered about him as if he weren't standing beside them. She said, "Look, I've got a full house now, more than I can feed, and half of *them* can't steal for spit despite my best efforts to teach 'em. The rest are all what keeps us above the tide. What you want me to do with another, then? What's he got for me?" She knelt and looked him in the eye. Her breath was foul, her teeth brown and rotten. She clutched his wrists tightly. "What talent do you have, boy?" Her tone implied nothing friendly.

The boy could not think of any talent, and the woman

frightened him. He looked away from her.

"Dumb, is it? He can't even talk? What good is he to me?" She let go his arms and straightened up. "I can't use him."

The man said, "What happened to the girl you put out on the beam?"

"How you know about her? Wasn't one of *your* girls, anyhow, so you've no business asking."

"She bring anything back for you?"

"Nah. Ran off, she did. Someone cut her loose, took her away. Probably felt *sorry* for her. Took her off *my* hands, anyway, and that's good enough. Could have had her for supper for all I care. Nothing would have come of it anyway, that old beam hain't lit in years of waiting."

The man looked down at him. "Still," he said, "it's a position that needs filling."

"Fine, then you take him up there and you look after him while he waits."

"I can't go up there anymore. You know that. If they saw me . . ."

"Yeah, I know all about that, now, don't I? You got two daughters and a wife now what don't know nothin' about your life before. If she knew, would she let you near them girls anymore?" She smirked at his discomfort. "You're gonna tell me you've changed, hain't you? Well, don't bother. Matters nothing to me whether you have or not." She glanced down at the boy, and her fingers curled like vines around his chin. "Your troubles don't make a case for this sad bit of drool."

The man stood awhile in silence, whether in contemplation or anger, the boy couldn't have told; but finally he reached over and drew her hand away from the boy. She hadn't expected his touch and jumped at the contact. The man held her hand from underneath, her fingers still curled as if cupping the boy's chin. He placed his free hand on top of it. The boy saw something shiny slip from the man's fingers into hers; then he let go with both, but her hand remained there, hovering just in front of the boy's eyes. She uncurled her fist and contemplated its fresh contents. "All right, then," she said, and glanced his way askance. "I'll take him to fill a vacancy. But if he's rewarded, his gift is mine. I don't share."

"A fair enough bargain," the man agreed. He didn't expect the mindless boy to do anything other than starve out on that beam, as countless others had done before him and would do again; the important thing was, it would not be *his* problem. He would never have to see it happen, which meant that so far as he was concerned, it never did. A million cruelties occurred each day, but out of sight and out of mind.

He knelt and told the boy, "Now, you stay here with Mother Kestrel and she'll provide for you. Whatever she says, you do it for her, just like she's your own mother. Do that and everything will work out for you."

The boy stared back at him the way a fish might have, and the man doubted that anything he said had penetrated. In fact, the boy was visiting his mother again, under the sea. He had always obeyed *her*, and still she had left him.

The man roughed the boy's hair as he stood again. He gave the woman one more look that might have been a warning or resignation. Then he walked away, climbed down the ladder, and was gone.

"Well, come in, then," said the woman, and she grabbed him by the hair and dragged him beside her.

The woman did feed him that day. More than a dozen children were crammed into her dwelling. They approached him, sniffing around him, trying to figure out what he might be, and whether or not his presence meant trouble for them. He had never been near so many other children before and shied away from them, behavior that only got him into trouble, as it made him an easy target for the bullies in the group. He had no defenses. Soon enough most of the others had allied against him behind the bullies and teased him, plucked at his ragged clothes, called him names, told him he smelled awful, laughed at him. They might as well have taunted a toadstool. He cowered against the wall until the woman came and drove off the attackers. She kept him away from them the rest of the day, even feeding him separately. He got a larger portion than the others and they resented him for that, too, even though their own tyranny was the cause. They swore among themselves that the next day he would be made to pay.

The boy dozed fitfully that night, exhausted by constant fear but on guard against a concerted assault. Some hours before dawn, the woman woke him and led him out of the house. She gave him a crust to gnaw on while they traveled, and a small pack that he was to carry. They went up and down ladders, across makeshift bridges until they reached a ledge carved out of the bridge support itself. They moved by feel alone then, because no light reached the cavernous recesses just below the surface of the span. They had to walk carefully on the ledge. The trapped air hung thick as tepid gruel, and it stank of humans and oily fish and offal. The ledge led them out into the air. One moment all was blackness and the next a sky shot with stars stretched above them. The boy stared up in awe at the sight and nearly stepped off the ledge into the air. Only the woman's grip saved him. She muttered a curse and yanked on his arm to get his attention.

A flight of perilously narrow steps led up to the surface of the span. He remembered the steps. His mother had led him up them every morning and down them every evening. Seeing them, remembering her, he tried to look back again at the sea where she'd slid under the surface, but he couldn't see that spot from here and the woman was hauling him up. They emerged into an alley and from there onto one of the broader cobbled streets.

He had never seen this world after dusk. He stared at everything, glimpsing towers and minarets like shapes cut out of the night. People strolled about, not as many as during the day, but they all seemed to be disguised behind masks and capes, feathers and jewels, and someone brandishing a torch or a lantern led their way. From the street Mother Kestrel turned into another alley. The boy heard voices echo in it, whispers that seemed nearby but came from empty corners. The alley snaked around as if going somewhere but in the end it dumped them back at the edge of the span again. Along the horizon, a thread of reddish glow hinted at the approach of dawn.

Across the road there was a break in the railing as there had been where they emerged, but this time there were no steps down. Instead, a skinny curving walkway projected from the edge of the span out into the void. The woman dragged him out along it indifferently. Over the side he could see all the way to the ocean. It was a long, long way down. Waves shimmered upon the black surface, but not a sound could he hear.

Halfway out, a short wall arose along one side of the beam, while on the other side, pieces of a similar wall showed here and there like rotted teeth, suggesting that the length of the walkway—the beam—had originally been protected, but the inner sections had collapsed sometime in the past. People huddled against the bits of wall, one or two with their knees drawn up, another with his legs stretched in defiance across the width of the walk. The boy could see him watching, eyes shining in the pits of his sockets, as they climbed over his barrier and continued to the end of the beam.

A convex bowl hung off the end. The crumbling wall gave way to a ring of bollards supporting a circular railing. Perhaps twenty people could have sat around the ring at the top of the bowl, but only four were in the bowl at the moment.

The woman chose a spot for the boy and told him to sit. He was paying her no mind, still watching the man they'd had to step over. She had to push on his shoulders to make him sit. When finally he realized what she wanted, he complied at once. She took the pack from him, opened it, and drew out a length of chain. This she threaded between two bollards and back in around one of them, drawing it tight, then securing it with a lock. The loose section of it ended in a cuff. The woman fitted this about the boy's ankle and snapped it shut. He looked in puzzlement at his foot, then at her.

"There's a good lad," she told him. "You've got length enough to move about some, to relieve yourself off the edge as needs be. I'll come back with food for you but you're going to have to make do otherwise. You have to wait and hope and curry the gods' favor. They appear here sometimes," she said, "come to those who wait, who show their true and good hearts. If the gods favor you, then we will be blessed, you and me. You'll have something no one else has. Don't know what it will be, but we'll hope it makes us rich. You hope for that. Think on that. All the time you're here. You want the gods to *understand* what you need if you're to have it."

When she walked away he tried to crawl after her out of the bowl, until the chain snapped tight and he fell on his chin. He made a whining sound but the woman didn't hear. She had gone, back along the beam, back into the alleys, and back into her underworld. What she didn't tell him was that he was the fourth child she'd chained to the dragon beam, that the first two had died—one of starvation, the other by foul play when no one was about—and the third had been set free to disappear, but probably to no good fortune. What she didn't tell him was that everything she believed about the dragon beam, and the gods, and how they chose to appear, was based on gossip and invention and steeped in envy.

The Dragon Bowl became his existence. He didn't starve, because the woman had learned from experience, and returned every couple of days with food for him—not a lot of food but enough to keep him alive. At first no one spoke to him or even acknowledged that he was there. The man who'd watched him being chained up came onto the bowl and sat close by, but pretended not to notice him, and then began to whisper imprecations. Even the feeble-minded boy understood that the man was whispering to imaginary beings, asking questions and hearing silent answers to which he responded. He babbled loudly until someone else ventured into the bowl. When they did, the madman curled up and clutched his belongings, wrapped in a shred of cloth, to his chest, and eyed them accusingly.

People came and went throughout the day. There were young lovers who came for the novelty of it, and described for each other what they would wish for if the gods were to appear. Often this was wealth, but as often it was to be happily in love with their partner forever. There were those who showed themselves to be terrified at the prospect of stepping onto the rim of the bowl, despite the number of people already waiting in it. The boy watched them all.

The first night, the man edged over to him and said, "I know you're stealing my luck. I know you are. You can't have it, you hear me? If you try and take it, I'll throw you over, right into the ocean." He grabbed the chain and yanked at it but he couldn't unwrap it from the bollard any more than the boy could. After a while he seemed to forget what he was doing, took his bundle and moved back onto the dragon beam.

"My luck," he repeated, but no longer to the boy.

Three days later when the sun came up he was gone, and only the bundle remained to mark his place. The boy managed to reach it and drag it into the bowl before anyone else saw it lying there. Inside the cloth lay a broken phial containing nothing, a wooden button, some black polished stones and white polished shells, a heel of bread that had gone green with mold long ago, and fragments of a parchment that had been written upon, but torn into strips. The meaningless contents of the bundle filled him with despair, and he savagely fought with the chain and the shackle until he'd rubbed his ankle raw and bleeding. Another man came along the beam, saw the scattered items at the top of the bowl and scooped them up. He picked at each in turn, disappointed with each find, and finally tossed the whole thing off the side of the beam. "Worthless," he proclaimed.

The boy gestured at the chain attached to him, begging the man to set him free. "You want me to set you *free*?" the man responded incredulously. "Free?" He began swatting at the boy, slapping and beating him, and all the while speaking calmly, "It is your *duty* to *wait* on this *spot* for the *gods* to *honor* you. Your *duty*!" He made one final, ineffectual kick at the boy before moving across the bowl and squatting on the far side of it, where he searched the sky as if for a sign, a reward. Nothing happened, and he finally gave up looking and hunkered down and fell asleep.

From the beating the boy learned one important thing—to be invisible. He remained a huddling shape, his head down, reflecting his defeat in life, expressing that he would take any gift the gods condescended to give him.

The woman came the next day and fed him. She noted the state of his ankle and slapped him on the head, one more bruise to teach him nothing. He was by then too exhausted to fight back or protect himself, though he would have rejoiced if the madman across the Dragon Bowl had jumped up and killed her. Instead, the man snorted as if concurring that the boy was getting his just desserts.

Thus went his days. He sat unprotected in all weather, crouching to hide from the sun, lying flat in the curve of the bowl when the rains came and washed the dirt off all of them into the center of the bowl, where it drained back into the ocean. The floor of the bowl was tiled but he could not understand what the tiles represented, if they represented anything at all, so many of them were missing.

One day a woman stabbed a man to death at the end of the beam and then leapt over the railing to her own death. The man, who had tried to assault her, died hung across the railing, watching his blood trickle into the sea. The next morning he had been pushed off, too.

The boy didn't have any idea how long he remained chained up. His leg festered and healed. The rain seemed to cleanse the wound, but rotted his clothes until they were tatters.

True to her word, the woman continued to bring him food. She seemed surprised by his tenacity. Every time she came now, she said, "I bet this is the last time I see you." But he was always there the next time, emaciated and exhausted.

The food she brought seemed of a better quality then, as if she were so awed by his continuance that she was rewarding him. She touched him each time before she left, gently, almost tenderly. He couldn't understand the look in her eyes.

One afternoon someone jumped off the beam. The boy leaned over the wall to watch the body drop to the ocean. He had only seen the movement of the jumper peripherally; he didn't even know if it was a man, a woman, or a child. He might have jumped then, too, if it would have finished him quick; but he knew he would only have ended up dying slowly upside down, hung from the railing by the chain. It would also have called attention to him, and whoever hauled him back up would surely have beaten him again, or worse.

When the visitation finally came, he was asleep.

It was so silent and swift that he didn't even stir. In his dream, the world flashed white, scalding his eyelids. Something thin and tall spoke to him in a reedy voice, words that were not human language, and yet which he understood after a fashion, the syllables weaving through his brain, knitting together things that had never been united before, bits of thought that had never found a way to coalesce, like a glue bonding the strips of parchment in the madman's bundle.

He awoke to someone babbling nearby. The light of dawn gilded the Dragon Bowl through the spaces between the bollards. It lit the face of the man babbling beside him. He remembered the man from the day before, remembered that he'd been surly and greasy. Now the man stared with wide eyes and his hair had gone white as clouds and sprayed out from his head.

The bowl itself had been transformed. The missing tiles had all been replaced, creating a colorful mosaic. On it lay a host of small objects, all clear like glass but flexible—containers and lids scattered about. The people who'd been sleeping on or near the beam scrambled out onto the bowl and began grabbing up the objects. Lids seemed to be the wrong size for containers, and the people combed through the scatter in a frenzy, tossing one and then another lid aside, shoving each other to get at the next, fighting over a complete container whenever a lid fit. The sealed containers seemed to have an effect on whoever held them, for anyone who made a lid pop into place immediately began to wail more as if they'd lost something than in joy at completion of a task. Some struck those nearest them with the completed containers, while others collapsed and clutched them to their bosoms, rocking back and forth while weeping as if they held a dead child in their arms.

More people traveled along the beam every moment, pouring out, filling the bowl. Citizens of the span had seen the visitation—that was what the boy heard them calling it—and all wanted to share in whatever bounty the gods had left. Word of the event spread quickly, even to the underspan. Within the hour the boy's keeper had pushed her way along the beam to find him. She demanded that he give her whatever the gods had bestowed upon him. He drew a container from behind his back and handed it to her. He'd found a lid to match it and handed that to her. He waited breathlessly to see if she would fit the lid into place. Instead she stared with swelling anger at the two pieces. "This? This is what I've fed you for all these months? The time I've invested in you, and you give me a container for fish scraps?" She backhanded him as if he had lied to her. "I thought—" she paused, shook her head and sighed. "I let myself believe in you, in *this*, how stupid am I? You are useless to me." As she said it, she bent down and snatched another of the small containers that had been overlooked, hiding it in her blouse. "Useless," she repeated, and then as if she'd forgotten about him, she walked around the bowl and back along the beam. Only then did he notice that the beam, like the tiles, had been repaired—that an intact low wall now ran along both sides of the narrow walkway, as must have been the case when it first appeared. The woman stepped off the beam and was accosted immediately, and from what he could see, she began bargaining with citizens too frightened to come out themselves and grab one of the odd containers.

The boy didn't understand any of it—not the woman, not the crazed people about him, not the excitement over an event that seemed to have produced nothing of value. What sort of gods played such tricks on people? They'd repaired the tiles and the beam—that seemed to be the major transformation, but of interest only to him.

He sat against the rail and watched. He had nothing, said nothing, and no one paid him much mind. As people got something, they deserted the beam, but there were many who, now that a visitation had occurred, decided to sit and wait for another. It would all begin again. It *must.*

Because of the "blessed" event, there would for a time be more people on the beam and in the hexagonal bowl on any given day, more abusers of children, more who resented his presence here, never mind that he was a prisoner and would gladly have left if they'd freed him. For a while everyone would anticipate the next visitation, until this one faded into memory and most of the cormorants drifted away, back to whatever routine had filled their days before.

He rocked in place, furiously frustrated by the stupidity of people. After a while, different ones came and took the madman with the white hair by the arms, stood him up and walked him down the beam. One glanced his way and the boy said, "Please, take me, too." The two paused. They contemplated him as if considering whether he was worth the effort; but he didn't notice them any longer because he realized that he had spoken. He had spoken and it had *made sense.* Thoughts inside his head were making sense. He was observing the world around him and it was making sense—or at least the nonsense of it all was suddenly comprehensible to him *as* nonsense. For the first time in his life, he recognized and understood the motives of others.

The madman took notice of him and began to laugh. The two handlers dismissed the boy and hurried on with their charge.

He was aware! He stared up at the sky, at clouds and birds and sun. Whatever the gods had done for everyone else, they had given him the gift of himself.

He was still marveling at his transformation when the woman returned some hours later. She told him, "Well, I've found someone to take you off my hands, and that's what I'm going to do." She unlocked the chain from the bollards but not from his ankle. She let him get to his feet, but then pulled him along, and he had to hop to keep up.

They arrived back on the span. He wanted to run off, he wanted to shout at her for how she had treated him, but he did neither. He pretended to be the idiot she saw. His skinny legs trembled from disuse. It had been so long since he had walked anywhere beyond the length of the chain, and he was starved. He intended to bide his time, to see what she had in mind. While he now had the gift of thought, he still didn't know very much about the world or how it worked.

She led him through twisting alleys and small rough streets, avoiding the main thoroughfares, where his situation might have proved inconvenient for her, and finally came to the very end of the span. The great wall of the tower rose up before them; but instead of taking him into the tower and off the span, she turned and walked down the narrowest of lanes with the tower wall on the left and the fronts of houses on the right, so close that he could have climbed in their windows even on the chain. The lane was a cul de sac, but near the end of it, a dark doorway had been carved out of the tower wall.

The woman banged on the door, and it opened almost immediately. A slender but round-faced man with darting eyes stood there, dressed in an embroidered robe that was belted slackly at his waist, revealing a hairy abdomen above loose trousers. He beamed at the woman. She handed him the chain. He looked the boy up and down. "He ain't much," he said. "Looks like a skellington, he does."

"I told you, Bogrevil, he's been living on the bowl, waiting for the gods."

"I heared they come last night. They talk to you, boy?"

The boy kept his mouth closed and acted as if the question had been directed at Mother Kestrel.

"He's mute?" Bogrevil asked.

"Yes, as I told you, he's an idiot," she replied testily. "You don't want him, that's fine, I'll be on my way." She reached for the chain, but Bogrevil drew it out of her reach, which tugged the boy inside the doorway.

Bogrevil said, "If he's been visited by the gods, then I get whatever he's got. You don't."

The woman looked at the boy, but he stared dumbly at the ground as if unaware of his circumstances. She snorted with laughter. "Oh, I'll agree to that. He's got anything from here on, it's yours to keep, including vermin."

Bogrevil reached out and dropped three coins into her hand then. "Excellent," he said and drew the boy closer to him. "And if you find yourself with any other boys to be rid of, you know where to find me, m'dear. I'm always in need of stock." He reeled the boy through the doorway and shut the door with the kick of one foot.

"There's an end to that," said Bogrevil. Outside the door, the woman was expressing a similar opinion, though with a curious pang of regret. She had foolishly put her faith in that boy simply because he hadn't died. She'd let herself become sentimental. Never again, she swore. Never again.

In the dusty and dimly lit foyer, Bogrevil took him by the shoulders and pressed them back, tilted his chin up, then stepped away from him. "You're skinny as fishbones, but that's from her feeding you on air and dreams. Otherwise, you're well turned out, or will be when you've had somit to eat. Waste of talent, though. None of my clients will want to inhale an idiot. Still, we'll find a use for you. See if you can juggle a tray, hmm?" When the boy did not respond, Bogrevil patted his cheek and released him. "Well, come on, then, follow me." He threw back a curtain, and light from a distant source below him splashed his shadow across the ceiling of the foyer. "We'll get you fed and bathed and into some whole clothes." He started down a steep stairwell. The boy had forgotten about the chain, and nearly stumbled as it snapped tight and pulled him to the edge of the steps.

"I wonder what the gods gave you," Bogrevil said as he descended. "Many's the time I've said the gods are capricious. Sometimes they give us what we need, and sometimes they offers so much that it drives us mad. Sometimes they see the greed inside and they curse us for it. Sometimes the gifts don't mean nothin' at all."

They went down into the belly of the tower.

True to his word, Bogrevil had the boy fed. It was more food than he'd seen in a single serving ever. After the near-starvation on the dragon beam, he couldn't eat half of it. All the while he watched the other boys sizing him up. They seemed envious of the attention being paid him, though it was no more than had been paid to them upon arriving. He kept his eyes on nothing and focused on the meal. The other boys took this to mean that he was harmless and ignored him.

After the meal, Bogrevil had one of the other boys pick the lock on the cuff and removed the chain from his ankle. Two older boys led him to a steamy chamber, stripped him of his clothing and dropped him into a large bathing pool. A dozen others swam in it, a few laughing and squealing but most just floating, withdrawn, it seemed to him. He luxuriated in the warmth. He had no memory of anything like it. Finally, to his shock, a woman waded into the pool. She headed straight for him and took hold of him by one biceps. As naked as the boys, she might have been ten years his senior, but she wasn't much larger than he. However, she proved to be a good deal stronger. She caught hold of him, then scrubbed him with a brush so hard that he thought she was flaying him, but he couldn't squirm out of her grip. A couple of the boys hooted at his predicament but stayed beyond the woman's reach while they did. She poured something into his hair that she worked in. Whatever it was, it burned terribly, and he struggled furiously to get free of her and dunk his head. She must have expected it, for she wrapped her legs around his belly to keep him in place. Finally, when he thought the hair must be sizzling, she shoved his head under water, then hauled him up again. He spluttered and spat, sure that his scalp had been burned away. Without a word, the woman let go of him and stalked one of the jeering boys, who hadn't been far enough away after all. The other squeallers scrambled naked out of the pool for their lives, while the rest watched her and the goings on in the water as if none of it mattered. The boy patted his head and was surprised to find that he still had hair.

Later, the same woman lifted him out by the arm and wrapped him in a great cloth. She was wearing one, too. He saw that she had an odd, dark birthmark on one shoulder. She said, "I hope you have the sense to bathe yourself, because I'm *not* going to do this for you every day."

Bogrevil came in while the other boys were dressing. "How is he, Eskie?" he asked her.

"Clean," she replied, and pushed the end of the cloth through his hair. "I rid him of his lice, though it peeled the skin from my fingertips."

"Good." Again Bogrevil lifted his chin and studied him. "How old you think he is?"

"Old enough, I'm sure. He has hair, hasn't he? But he's been underfed so very long, it could be he is seventeen or more and only looks twelve. He does not know?"

"Not likely. Anyway, doesn't matter, he's not on the menu."

"He has the looks for . . . the menu. Fill him out a little and an attractive enough body will appear."

"Don't need attractive to clean and serve. Can't sell half-wits anyhow. Most clients are superstitious enough to think it's contagious—an idiot's essence will make them the same."

"Mmmm," she replied. "I'm not afraid. Or else it's too late for me." She fluttered a hand in front of her face as if to cool her fevered brow.

Bogrevil chortled. "You think you can get a rise out of him, my Eskie?"

"Is that a request?" She shook her head. "I am only saying that he's a pretty one, though starved." She snatched the drying cloth off him, left him standing naked while she retrieved clothes for him from a table. "Come, then, give us your arm," she said as she drew a white tunic on him. "Come," when she wanted him to raise a foot. Her fingers touched him everywhere, but didn't linger. She buttoned the tunic down his chest. Its stiff collar nearly reached his chin. Her hazel eyes studied him closely. He blushed at the way she looked at him: he couldn't help it. She noticed the color in his cheek, and her careless gaze became curious; but she said nothing. Her fingers brushed his hair from his forehead. "A proper server," she commented and stepped back to let Bogrevil see the boy dressed in white finery, loose silk trousers and a slender jacket.

"He wears the clothes well enough, don't he? Superb, Eskie, superb. Now we must find out if he can balance a tray."

She considered him. "I shall be surprised if he cannot."

Bogrevil turned to leave. "Oh," he said and raised a finger. "We have to give him a name. Can't keep calling him 'boy.' If I were to call out 'come here, boy' whenever I wanted him, I'd be crushed by the onslaught."

"He has no name?"

"I don't know. His former keeper didn't bother to assign him one, and *he* can't tell me, if he even knows."

She put a finger to her lips and tapped them. "Let's call him . . . something like 'divers.'"

"What?"

"Because he is different."

"Diverus," he repeated, mispronouncing what she'd said. "Yes, we got others like that, don't we – Delicatus and Draucus. Like a – what, lineage, yes."

Rather than correct him – never a good idea with Bogrevil – she concurred. "Diverus, then." It was not a bad name in any case.

"Different. Oh, yes, he is. Nice job, Eskie. I can always rely on you an' your upbringing." She bowed her head at the compliment. "You go take him to his room, show him about. Maybe some of it'll stick. We'll try him out tonight if he can balance a tray." He went off to see to the rest of his merchandise.

Eskie had put on a long white robe. Her black hair cascaded down the back of it. She wore bangles on her wrists and a small chain of bells on her ankles, so that her every movement tinkled and chimed as she led him through a warren of rooms and tunnels. Something about the sound created an odd warmth in his belly.

The main parlors of the paidika—there were three—had intricate tapestries hung upon the walls. Two had carpets on the floor, and pillows strewn upon the carpets. The room farthest from the stairs had a square platform in the center, like an enormous trap door cover, and small, backless cushioned chairs ringing the sides of it. Lamps and candles of various sizes and shapes filled every corner, and lanterns dangled from the ceilings. Bowls containing some sort of aromatic herbs floating in liquid stood off to each side of the doorways, so that entering the room swirled an invisible membrane of spice around one. The rooms were not occupied.

Leading from the parlors were narrow halls. The one she led him along opened onto a wider corridor lined with curtained doorways, with leather settees in between them.

Eskie saw him trying to peer into the rooms, and she stepped up to one and drew the curtain back. It was sumptuously decorated, though small and dark. The central feature of the room was an immense sinuous hookah, the cap of which nearly reached the ceiling. Two hoses depended from the side of it and snaked around the bulbous base, mouthpieces resting on pillows as if the smokers had just left the room. In the shadowy recess behind it lay a peculiar lacquered box big enough for someone to lie in. Curving tines of bone like the ribcage of a monster as big as the hookah rose from the side of the box and curled over it toward the center. Symbols painted in the lacquer were meaningless to him. Along the rest of the walls were shelves and niches that held candles, small lamps, and assorted odd objects—tiny silver pill boxes, a few statuettes of fish and other creatures, some carved from wood, others blown from colored glass, and more things he could not identify.

When he'd had a good look, Eskie dropped the curtain again. Owing to the nature of the paidika's business, she said, the boys generally slept the day through. She led him down another hall and a short flight of steps, taking them even farther from the public part of the paidika. At the end of yet another hall, a set of double doors barred their way. She opened one quietly and ushered him in.

The stone walls of the dormitorium bore brown water stains in jagged rills. The smell in the room reminded him of the underspan itself. High up near the ceiling, he saw a grate, no larger than his head, which let in all the light there was, and he imagined that if he could climb up to it, he might find himself looking out upon the very makeshift platforms and hovels from which he'd been removed.

The boys slept on pallets appreciably better than the one he had known at home, most of which were occupied now. A few boys' eyes opened as chiming Eskie led him through the room, and he thought he recognized some from the bath.

She explained softly, "Everybody sleeps here, unless they're purchased for a longer time. Even so, they're carried back here after, to recover . . . but there's no reason for me to explain this to you, is there? You won't be serving in that way. And we'd better determine now if you're capable of serving in other ways, which I hope you are. I would hate to see you cast into the laundry. Whatever you do, you don't want to displease your master. He's nice enough, providing you do as you're told. Like most of his kind." She stared hard into his eyes. "I hope you can understand what I'm telling you. It's a matter of survival here."

He sensed eyes observing him—gazes like those of lizards, watchful and cold.

Eskie took him to the kitchens next. The two connected kitchen chambers were smoky, the walls blackened with years of soot from cooking fires, even though the hearth built into the far wall exhausted into a chimney hole. The place smelled of old, rendered fat. The bald cook looked up at them as they entered, but his hands continued to work, grinding seeds with a pestle in a wide mortar.

Eskie led Diverus to an area full of polished silver trays, utensils and pitchers. She selected a tray with an oddly shaped base and straps hanging off it. She lifted it over him and lowered it upon his head like a crown. His head was small, though, and the tray tipped. Eskie fitted the straps together beneath his chin and cinched them tightly. She tipped the tray with each hand. "Still too loose, we'll have to find you a smaller one."

The third one she tried seemed to fit him well enough that she didn't cinch the straps. She placed a silver cup upon the tray, right at one edge and filled it with liquid. He could feel the weight tipping the tray and tilted his head enough to counterbalance it.

"That's good," she told him. "That is what you want to do." She set down the pitcher and strode across the kitchen. "Now," she said from the far side. "Carry my drink to me."

Diverus started forward. Liquid splashed his arm. He stopped and looked down at it and immediately the rest of the liquid spattered the floor in front of him, soaking his feet, followed by the clang of the cup itself as it bounced across the stones.

Eskie laughed and walked back to him. "You must not get distracted by things if you're serving. You can't go studying your feet without dousing the entire clientele should you be supporting a full tray." She picked up the cup and filled it again. "Let's try once more, see if you can do it." She put the refilled cup on the tray and walked off again. "All right, come to me," she called from across the room. The bald cook stopped to watch. Diverus cautiously walked across to Eskie without spilling the cup. When he reached her, she said, "Now, can you lower yourself so that I can reach the cup more easily?"

He thought about it for a moment before extending his back leg out, widening his stance to lower his torso. She took the cup. "Wonderful, Diverus! You learned that right away, faster than a lot of boys would've done."

The cook said, "Clever lad, i'n it," then went back to grinding.

She replaced the cup on the tray. "Now, let's see how you do with a full tray."

After he had successfully walked the length of the kitchen twice while balancing a tray covered with cups, Eskie had the cook feed him again. She maintained that he was in need of extra nourishment. If Diverus passed out in the middle of the evening, a disaster would ensue. And while *he* might be forgiven, Bogrevil would certainly blame, and punish, her.

Once he'd eaten a cup of the soup that he would have again for dinner, she took him down to the lowest level of the paidika: the laundry.

This proved to be a large room at sea level with a square, shallow pool in its center. There were boys already at work in the laundry. They were different from the boys he'd seen above. A few were cruelly formed, with lumpish backs or twisted limbs, or heads too small for their bodies. Some of them were brutes, too large to be boys except that they were. They had dull faces, childish faces, faces expressing their inability to grasp anything beyond the work they were doing. The rest shuffled about with dirty or wet linens clutched in their arms. They seemed incomplete in some manner, like sleepwalkers, ignoring him and Eskie and everyone else. The ones in the pool plunged bedding and tunics into the water, sponged and squeezed and pounded the cloth, and every bit of their minds must have been focused upon the labor. One of the sleepwalkers noticed Eskie and Diverus, and stopped, gaping. His face looked old and wan; the eyes expressed a veiled panic, as if the source of his fear was inaccessible, and the lips were pulled back in a kind of rictus that drew the skin of his face tight across the bones. Diverus didn't comprehend what the look meant, but he saw in these boys his old life beneath Vijganar, and what Bogrevil intended for him if he failed in his other duties.

Because of Eskie, he *had* other duties.

Across the pool a wide barred gate revealed a view of dark water. He circled the pool and walked up to the gate. His fingers curled around the vertical bars. The padlock securing it was nearly as wide as he was—a giant's padlock stolen from some other world. He pressed his face into the bars to see as much as possible. Where he stood lay at the very bottom of the span, looking out toward the pier of another tower on the far side of it. A boat with a single sail trolled past through the narrow channel, so close that he could make out the weathered features of the single occupant. If he could have gotten outside the gate, he might have jumped from the narrow ledge into the boat. Overhead he could see nothing save for the hint of an arch curving above the far pier. No platforms had been constructed in that space between the spans.

Eskie had come up behind him. He felt her press against him as she put a hand upon his shoulder. "It's the way out in emergencies, this gate. If we're raided. Which has only ever happened once or twice, because some of the magistrates are regular customers and they protect us. They don't think we know—they come in disguise, most clients do—but Bogrevil has an informative network and he knows things he's not supposed to. He takes care of himself, which takes care of us."

He slid his hand down, and fingered the keyhole cover on the padlock . . . a small keyhole for so large a lock.

She must have noticed, for she said, "Far too big for anyone to remove it alone. Some of the boys were street pickers before ending up here, and they surely know their way around locks. That one—even if they can work it, they can't get out without two more boys to help lift it."

He glanced back toward the pool.

She looked at the pool, too, seeing what he implied. "Oh, they're big enough, but they have no wish to leave. The paidika is the only proper home most of them have ever known. Many were horribly treated where they were before. You could never get them to help. In fact, they would probably stop anyone who tried to get out. Some of them sleep down here, in the corners. Like the demon sentinels of Nechron's underworld, they are."

He shifted his gaze, met hers with his brow furled.

"What, you've never heard the name of the god of the underworld? No. I suppose you wouldn't have, would you. Who would have taken the time to educate you? They would have considered it time wasted, but I think you're cleverer than they know, Diverus. You'll learn everything here—especially now as you'll be a server rather than a scrub boy."

He looked out at the water once more before turning away and accompanying Eskie back up to the higher level. The laundry boys watched him leave as though watching him walk out of their memory.

Eskie left him at the dormitorium after assigning him a pad to sleep on. She told him to sleep as long as he could during the day. Once the paidika opened for business, he would be on his feet the rest of the night.

She didn't lie to him: Diverus wandered between the three main rooms throughout that entire first night, weaving between clients and other serving boys, and the boys on display.

Most of the clientele were costumed and masked, as if arriving from a fancy ball somewhere else upon the span. He watched them descend the long, high stairway, dressed in loose pants and sometimes with sweeping capes. Bogrevil was often there to meet them—many, he seemed to know despite (or perhaps because of) their costumes, welcoming them broadly and taking them immediately to one of the three chambers, where he would point out someone in particular. Most of the time, the guest agreed with his selection and allowed himself to be escorted into the narrow halls and the rooms beyond them. A very large boy—practically a giant—stood beside the base of the steps, with folded arms, still as a statue, though his eyes cast from room to room. Diverus he considered with disinterest.

The boys were costumed, too. Some had been painted in extravagant makeup and wore flowing garments, veils and scarves. They could have passed for women. Others wore very little—short trunks or diaphanous robes. Some, especially muscular older boys, sported leather collars, and wide bracelets at their wrists, as if prepared for some combat. One of them strode from room to room, proudly naked beneath green paint. His hair had been spiked about his head like that of a sea sprite.

Those clients not swept up immediately by Bogrevil milled around, appraising the boys as they might have done a bolt of fabric. Their masks made them silent, somber, bestial. Beaks and snouts turned the liquid eyes above into wet stones, as if what lay beneath the mask would prove to be less recognizable even than the caricatured surface.

Whenever his tray was empty, Diverus returned to the kitchen for more. Initially, Bogrevil clasped his shoulders and nudged him to let him know that it was time; but after a few hours, he was able to sense from the weight of it when the tray was almost empty.

The first one he carried held cups of wine, the second, plates of finger-foods. He and the other serving boys walked carefully with measured strides in and out of the rooms, eyeing one another without comment. In the center parlor, a boy sat cross-legged and played lamely at a stringed instrument with a curved neck. Diverus had never seen such an instrument and didn't know what it was called, but he knew from the dissonant notes that the boy was not accustomed to it. The clients all but ignored the performance until one young guest spilled a drink upon him, and the clustered entourage burst into laughter. That brought Bogrevil into the room so fast it seemed he'd anticipated it. The young man smirked as if the matter were not of consequence and made a vague apology, insisting it had been an accident; but the trio who'd accompanied him still sniggered and exchanged glances as he spoke which, even beneath their masks, expressed cruel delight. Bogrevil asked them if they had any particular preference for the evening– "a particular essence you cared to sample." It seemed an innocent question but somehow conveyed the message that they must now either choose or leave. After fidgeting and shrugging between each other, they turned and departed back up the steps, with Bogrevil at their heels. He smiled and waved them along, but when he came back down the steps, his face had gone sharp and humorless. To the giant boy at the bottom, he said, "They never come in again, separately or together. The gate, if they do." The giant nodded slightly, though how he would distinguish them, Diverus couldn't fathom.

To the wine-soaked musician, Bogrevil snarled, "At least tune the damned thing."

The remainder of the evening provided no excitement or diversion, and exhaustion replaced curiosity well before the end of the night. Sent off to bed, he slept so heavily that he likely could have been tossed into the laundry pool and wouldn't have noticed. He neither sensed nor cared who else shared the room, or who was missing.

In the afternoon, when he awoke, he found Eskie seated beside one of the pallets, feeding a boy as though he was ill; and he looked ill, too. He watched Diverus through sunken eyes so asthenic that they couldn't maintain the glance and fell, unfocused upon anything this side of the grave. Eskie wouldn't meet his glance at all.

The nights thereafter were much the same. He learned to identify returning customers well enough that if he was carrying their preferred drink or food, he would meet them at the bottom of the steps—an act that did not go unnoticed by Bogrevil, who reconsidered him, scrutinizing him as if to decide if he'd misjudged Diverus and, granted that he was a superb judge of flesh, been in some manner misled. He commented to the giant, "It's a shame that one's a mute, 'cause it's clear he's much more clever than what appears." The giant, who was *not* more clever than he appeared, stared at Diverus in perplexity.

The later the night wore on, the more the clients came in clusters, and by the second half of the evening there weren't but one or two individuals in any of the three parlors. The rest had retired to the private chambers. On his way to and from the kitchens he noticed some of them in the corridors, lolled on the settees between the private rooms; sometimes they were sleeping, but even the conscious ones appeared exhausted and muddled. Occasionally, they needed assistance to manage the steps up to the span again, which task was assigned to boys who hadn't been picked, or to him and the other servers if no one more suitable was available. These people always smelled mephitic, as if some poison leaked from their pores. Diverus did not focus on what was going on in the paidika, or what it meant that boys who were chosen for a night the next day had to be spoon fed and didn't leave their pallets and often were given a second night off to rest. He didn't want to know. He listened to other servers gossip about it—tales of how boys who pried into the goings on in those chambers disappeared. The boys who entered the chambers with clients refused to tell those who weren't chosen what happened to them.

Exhaustion became his excuse for not pursuing any answers. He slept through most every day and worked through most of the night, with barely enough reserves to find his way back to his bed every morning.

Then one very busy night, very late, one client in a purple cape and wearing a spangled mask arrived in the final minutes and there were no boys left for him. At first Bogrevil tried to talk him out of his desire. "It's so late, sir, you'll hardly have time to enjoy yourself." He gestured to the hourglass in the corner, as if it somehow supported his argument. "Come back tomorrow night—it's an anniversary, a celebration. We'll fete you better than anyone." The client remained adamant, in the manner of a drunk who has made up his mind. He demanded satisfaction, and Bogrevil finally suggested that the man consider one of the servers. He called a coffee-colored boy named Abnevi over. Though unattractively scarred with pockmarks, Abnevi was intelligent and (Bogrevil assured the client) "brimming." The client, with obvious reluctance, accepted the offer, and Abnevi set down his tray to follow. His eyes were round with terror.

When the three of them had left the parlor, the remaining server, named Olk, nudged Diverus. Olk had a deformed, withered arm, and Diverus supposed that as with himself, superstitious clients feared that the deformity was communicable. Grinning sourly, Olk said, "We're lucky, the way we are. You're stupid and they don't want you, neither."

Before he could ask Olk to explain more, Bogrevil came back and dismissed them. As Diverus passed by, Bogrevil grabbed him by the arm and whispered, "Another night, you'll be chosen, don't you worry, son. You're too pretty to go to your death in servitude." Then he strode off.

The paidika closed up for the day, and the boys returned their trays to the kitchen and slunk off to the dormitorium. Diverus hung back until the rest had gone. Before that night he had avoided looking at what it meant to be selected, at what purpose a paidika served, because there was only one purpose for such a place that he could imagine, and one use, finally, for all of them, however kindly Bogrevil pretended to be.

He turned from the hall to the dormitorium and took a different corridor, one that led to the private rooms Eskie had shown him.

Most of them were dark behind drawn curtains, but in a couple, candlelight flickered, and in creeping to the nearest one, he heard a slow, quiet susurration that ebbed and flowed like waves rushing up to a beach.

Edging deeper into the doorway recess, he peeked through the space between the wall and the curtain. He could see the client, the one who had chosen Abnevi, still dressed in his billowy costume and seated upon the tail of his purple cape, cross-legged beside the immense brass water pipe. His glittering mask lay at his side. His blond hair hung over his eyes in an oily fringe, and under it the stripe of a black blindfold circled his head, like a crown fallen low. The rhythmic "whooshing" came as he pulled on the pipe, inhaling and then leaning back to exhale, his mouth open, slack, drool glistening like a snail's path from the corner of it down to his collar. Barely a wisp of bluish smoke emerged from the chimney of his mouth. Abnevi was nowhere in sight on that side of the hookah. Diverus touched a finger to the curtain and drew it back further. The tiered body of the hookah filled the middle of the chamber. A grayish fog emerging out of its top led his eye around the curtain to the far side.

Abnevi lay in the long, inscribed lacquer box, beneath the curious fingers of bone. His eyes were closed so that he would not see what Diverus now looked upon—what neither of the chamber's occupants saw. The fog congealed above Abnevi, into manifest horror. Perched upon the bony tines like a creature of prey, the thing was yet insubstantial—a translucent, ribbed torso that glistened in the candlelight like a grub; it overlooked the sleeping boy. A bluish vapor rose out of Abnevi's face toward it. The skin of his cheeks rippled as if seen through heat, and the body twitched once, twice, as if tugged at from above. Diverus didn't think he made a sound, but the apparition's head drew up abruptly as if alerted. It faced him. Two horrible white orbs fixed upon his position—milky eyes hard as alabaster. The jagged black hole of its mouth spiraled shut, snipping the stream of vapor, which snapped as if sprung, back into Abnevi. He bucked once, more forcefully than before. The creature trembled, fluttered, and with an outraged screech flung itself off the tines and collapsed all in a moment, reeling into the hookah so fast that Diverus wasn't sure if he'd seen it go in or it had simply evaporated.

Oblivious of any change in the situation, the blindfolded stupefied client leaned forward again and inhaled from the hookah. He choked suddenly. Then he dropped the mouthpiece, clutched his throat with one hand, his chest with the other, and fell sideways. He pawed at the blindfold and drew a dagger from his waistband, waving it as if to ward off something in the air above him. He spasmed, gave one final creaking gasp and lay still. A darker, greasy smoke trailed from his mouth.

Diverus dropped the curtain and stepped back—bumping against someone else, who said "Oof" as he struck her.

He spun about, and there stood Eskie, glaring at him. "What do you think you're doing?" she hissed. "Do you want to be drowned in the laundry?" He might have answered, forgetting himself, if she hadn't gone on. "If you interrupt the process, you could kill someone, the boy or the client. Afrits have been known to turn and devour everyone in the room."

"Afrits?" It was a word Bogrevil had used earlier.

"That which resides in the hookah. A dem—but you spoke. You *spoke*!"

He hadn't meant to. Unaccustomed to his own voice, he hadn't realized what he'd done, but Eskie had.

"You've been able to speak all the time, haven't you? You kept this hidden, pretending to be the fool Bogrevil believes of you."

He cleared his throat. Having not spoken for so long, his voice was coarse, barely a whisper. "And idiot is what I was before I arrived here," he replied somewhat defensively. "He sees what he wants. What he was told he'd purchased."

"But you pretend to be mute."

He gestured his head as if to say "What should I have done?" Then he asked, "What is an *afrit*?

"A spirit, a demon. These ones are tied to water, the ones Bogrevil serves. And caverns—they are not accustomed to living in light."

He knitted his brow. "He serves *them*?"

She nodded. "His very survival depends upon his service to their kind. I know nothing of how he came to be so indentured. That is something he never speaks of. But he provides them an essence to which they're addicted, and which in turn produces a vapor the clients crave."

"An essence . . . the boys?"

"Youth is powerful. The afrits thrive upon it."

His eyes widened at the enormity of what she was saying. "Doesn't it kill them?"

"Over time—a long time for most—it . . . alters them. But it's a pleasurable process for them."

"How can you know that?"

She gave him a look as if he *were* a fool. "Because they tell me so. What was I doing in this hallway just now, do you suppose? Did you think I was looking for you? Every morning I come as I do now in finding you. When the client emerges from the room, I go in. With Bogrevil or Kotul—the big one who guards the door—I assist the hired boys to their beds because they can barely walk afterwards, and I serve them food to replenish them, usually soup, a broth, and often they sleep a full day through. It's then almost as if nothing has happened to them, as if they'd been ill with fever and I've nursed them through it. They tell me sometimes of the dreams they've had, which are like fever dreams. Wondrous places they've visited while they slept—it might even be that they journey to Edgeworld." She shook her head as if to dismiss her own observation. "But they do not see the afrit. They only know the dreamlife it gives them, for it sends them to sleep before it emerges. They are, I think, unaware that anything has been lost to them until perhaps toward the end, when their thoughts grow too confused to be unknotted. By then they are as addicted to the dreams as the clients are to the afrit's vapors. They cannot distinguish any longer between this and dreamlife, and the one often seems superimposed upon the other. I think they really don't know which is which."

"The boys in the laundry."

Her face screwed up at their mention, as if she wasn't prepared to think about them. "Some of those. But they don't know it. Nor much of anything else."

"That's my destiny, then. It's what everyone has intended for me. Even you." He looked her in the eye, expecting confirmation but seeing instead her alarm.

"I want nothing like that for you. You mustn't reveal to Bogrevil what you've shown to me, ever—that you speak, that you're aware."

He said, "Tonight he promised me I would find myself in here soon, that somehow it's better than serving."

"Listen to me. You must disguise your cleverness, and continue to play the mute simpleton. Otherwise . . . and for you it would be death because you know the truth and would resist, and if you looked into the afrit's eyes . . . ." She glanced away from him. "If it saw you, it would devour your soul."

"You do this for him, knowing the truth." He tried to sound neutral, but the words accused her.

She burned scarlet. "I live, the same as you. I have the choices you have, maybe fewer. My family—" She stopped, shook her head. "I have nothing beyond the paidika, nothing to go to if I'm thrown out. Bogrevil takes care of me and I take care of the boys. I keep them healthy and alive. If I were to refuse, then they would begin to wither and die the very first time, and perhaps in great misery. You judge from the outside, Diverus, before you even know what you judge."

He had been trying not to judge but to understand. He apologized, secretly thrilled that she had instructed him not to become one of them. However she attempted to mitigate her own role, she nevertheless wanted to keep him from becoming the sort of boy to whom she ministered. He asked, "Do others know?"

"No one knows. Sooner or later most of the boys have been hired for a night, but none would ever dare intrude as you've done. One or two may have done early on—or else Bogrevil invented the tale to scare the others off, of how those interlopers were never seen again. Those who aren't fed to the afrit are too simple to act upon such curiosity, and so must you be. If you had walked into that room, you would have been destroyed."

He recalled suddenly the aftermath of what he'd seen. "The client," he said, and turned back to the curtain. He opened it and heard her gasp behind him, but the afrit, as he knew, had fled into the safe haven of the water pipe.

The client was sprawled upon the floor, and even from the doorway Diverus could tell that he was dead.

Eskie pushed around him and ran to the body. He followed her, though watching Abnevi, who lay in a daze, his eyes darkly ringed, and unfocused as if no thought guided them. His head rolled from side to side. *It will devour your soul,* she'd warned.

"He is dead," Eskie proclaimed of the client. "What has happened?"

Diverus looked down at a face that was swollen as if the man were trying to hold in a lungful of smoke. The blindfold had been pushed up above one eye. Eskie removed it. His eyelids had not quite closed, and he looked as if his own death bored him. The dagger had fallen from his hand, and his open fingers seemed to be reaching for the brass mouthpiece as though he might yet drag it to his purple lips for a final draw.

"I'm the cause of this," Diverus said. He sank down, then explained how the afrit had somehow sensed him and retreated, and how the client unknowingly had continued to draw from the mouthpiece.

"Oh, gods."

"But what happened?"

"The water in the pipe must have become poisonous when it withdrew. He was no longer smoking its vapors; it would have been the angry poison of the demon itself. What are we to tell Bogrevil? This man is dead, and surely someone will come looking for him."

"Surely, *I* will," came the reply from behind them, and they both turned to find Bogrevil holding the curtain up. "What has happened here?" He eyed the hookah, then Abnevi with a distortive repulsion before he entered the room.

Eskie stood and moved aside. As Bogrevil crouched down she gave Diverus a sharp glance and gestured "no" with her head. Then she answered, "I came to retrieve the boy and found this man in this position."

Bogrevil rolled his eyes nervously up at her; his glance flicked again to the brass hookah and back. "The afrit?"

"It had gone."

That seemed to allay his fears, but he pretended not to be concerned for himself. "Lucky for you. You wouldn't be telling me now if you'd met it." Then he acknowledged Diverus. "And what's *he* doing here?"

For a moment she hesitated, then said, "I enlisted him to help me. With the boys. Because he can't say anything. You and Kotul were absent."

He stared at her. It was clear to Diverus that he didn't believe her; but a lewd smile crossed his lips as he contemplated both of them, and he said, "'Enlisted,' is it? Well, it's no matter, and we'll need his help now. Now he *is* enlisted." He fitted the mask back onto the dead man's face, drew the cape out from beneath the lifeless bulk and spread it over his body like a shroud, then stood, with the dead man's dagger in his hand, the tip pointed at Diverus's throat. "Khanjarli," he said. "Good craftsmanship." He tucked it into the back of his belt.

At that moment, Abnevi stumbled out from behind the hookah. He leaned against the brass bowl, his legs trembling, and stared. "Where's my pen?" he asked. "I must write a policy and I've lost my pen. Oh, what's this, is this a different dream?"

"What's he talking about?" Eskie asked.

"An unfortunate accident," said Bogrevil. "The dream owns him." To Abnevi he said, "Your pen isn't here. I think you need to come along with us, now. It's a long descent to the bottom and if anything falls out of this man's pockets, I want you to pick it up, yes? Maybe *he* has your pen."

Abnevi nodded brightly. Diverus felt ill, watching.

Bogrevil took the body by the legs and Eskie and Diverus each took an arm as they carried it down the hall. The cape might have disguised the identity but not the substance of their burden. The body swung between them, the head dragging on the floor. No one was about at this hour, and no one else saw them.

The stairs were difficult to navigate, in part because the head struck every step, and even though the man was dead, the "thock" of each impact made Diverus wince. Behind them, Abnevi muttered, "Are we going to wash him? I want to bathe, too. Reasonable and customary cleanliness is a clause I put in every policy. It's healthful."

At the bottom, everything was dim, although the early morning light cast enough of a glow beneath the span that the checkered pattern of the gate was distinct. They lay the body down and Bogrevil fetched keys from a cord around his neck and unlocked the padlock. Abnevi broke away from them and clambered down into the washing pool.

By then one of the behemoths had awakened and lumbered over to see what was occurring. He was nearly bald, and his head was deformed, as if the skull had developed bulbs beneath the skin. When he saw Bogrevil, he grinned stupidly and grunted. "Yes, yes," Bogrevil said, and patted him on the shoulder. "Good fella. We need to move that lock." The simple giant stepped over the body as though it were a log, and with Bogrevil's help, raised the padlock. The two of them managed to hook it over one of the bars on the gate. The giant then pushed the gate open.

Bogrevil came back and they picked up the body again.

Outside, the position on the ledge afforded a view in both directions. To the right the edge of the bridge pier was close enough that the joints between the blocks of stone were visible. It would have taken only seconds to reach the corner of the pier. Beyond it the surface of the sea shimmered with distant red splashes of dawn. To the left, the ledge dwindled steadily, vanishing at last into the darkness of the span's underbelly. A bright semicircle defined the opening on the far side. Above them the air was filled with only darkness and the flitting brightness of a few passing gulls. No platforms, nor people—the underworld from which he'd emerged would be on the opposite side of the tower. There were no boats near enough to see them.

Bogrevil set his end of the corpse on the ledge. He got down onto his knees and plunged his hand into the water off the side. It took him only a moment to dredge up a large stone. This he dragged to the body, where he threw back the cape and pulled loose the man's trousers and shoved the stone inside them. When he had done this three times, he cinched the belt again. "That's good enough," he said. Getting stiffly to his feet, he gestured his helper to come out onto the ledge.

The lumpish giant shuffled past the gate, round eyes darting from side to side. He made a whining noise.

"It's all right," Bogrevil said. "Nobody's tryin' to make you leave. You two, put down your end and come over here and take a leg with me."

They obeyed. The giant picked up both arms. "Now, we shall swing him three times. Third time we let go. You understand?" He was asking the giant, who nodded, but kept glancing fearfully at the sea, as though something might come out of it at any moment.

"One."

"Two."

"Three."

The body sailed out over the black water farther than Diverus had expected. It hit with surprisingly little sound, and sank immediately. The cape floated for a moment and then disappeared. A stream of bubbles trickled up to the surface. The exotic mask bobbed up, expressionless without eyes behind it; it swiveled about as if looking for something, and then drifted out toward the open water.

"Right, then. Back inside, everybody," Bogrevil ordered.

It wasn't until the gate had closed that Diverus realized he should have run then and there. The ledge would have taken him someplace, and neither the behemoth nor Bogrevil could have caught him. Even had he dived into the sea, it would have carried him away—to a boat, to the pier of the next span—but now it was too late and he was part of the paidika again. Why hadn't he run?

They slid the lock back onto its latch and Bogrevil turned the key before turning to them. "Now, this did not happen. That gentleman, whoever he was, was never here, you never seen him, and you slept the whole morning through. Everyone slept."

Behind them, Abnevi splashed and splashed and tittered in the pool. His head lolled back and his eyes rolled up at the ceiling. "Oh, that's pretty," he slurred, but almost immediately he raised an arm as if to protect himself from something in flight, and dove, crying, "No, no! Get away!" He remained underwater only a moment but when he came up he was laughing.

Eskie said, "What about him?"

"It's done somit to him, hasn't it? Dunno what, don't care. He likes it so down here, I'd prefer he stay. Don't want him babbling—we don't know what he saw, do we? What he might tell if his mind were to come back. Down here, it won't matter. He can tell everybody. They're just like him." He reached out and caught Diverus suddenly, dragged him close.

"It's our paidika's anniversary tonight and we don't want nuffin' to spoil the event, see. Nobody answers no questions.

You want to have a little fun being 'enlisted' in the wee hours, I don't mind, see, 'cause *you* don't take away from no customers. But no mistakes, pretty one, or what happened to Abnevi'll be something you'll wish happened to you."

Diverus shook his head and drew a finger across his mouth to indicate he would say nothing. Bogrevil nodded that he understood. "Oh, yeah," he said, "that's right, you can't say anything about *anything*." He released Diverus then, caught Eskie by the elbow, and started back up the steps with her in tow. "Can't say a thing!" he called out, and vanished up into the dark.

The sound of Abnevi's unmoored laughter followed Diverus up the steps like a curse.

Bogrevil took Eskie with him, so Diverus had no one to speak with, no opportunity to confess the terrible guilt he felt over Abnevi's fate. He returned to the dormitorium, where everyone was asleep, and lay down, certain that he could never fall asleep again. Abnevi's mind was shattered and it was his doing—he had interrupted the afrit at its feeding. He kept reliving the moment when the creature's head turned, severing its connection, the blue tendrils snapping back into the helpless boy: His fault. Those round white eyes seared him with accusation.

The next thing he knew, he was crawling from the depths of sleep and uncertain that the events had been real. Two other boys lay asleep in the room, sunken-eyed and pale. Afrit victims. Everyone else had gone. He got up and hurried past the sleepers to bathe and eat.

When he returned to the dormitorium, Eskie was feeding one of the weak boys. With the spoon she pointed to his pallet. A costume of red crushed velvet and white silk lay there beside a long white band of cloth. He dressed while she finished ministering to the other boy. The sleeves covered his hands, and strings dangled off the cuffs. She came and tied the strings to loops at the shoulders. The sleeves were so full that he could freely move his arms, but they looked like wings. Then she took the cloth and wrapped it around his head, forming a turban, efficiently, as if she did this every day. She tucked the end of the cloth into a seam, then fastened a cheap jewel to the front of it. "That looks very good, you're becoming one of the more attractive boys here," she said.

The comment so appalled him that he stepped back from her. "How can you be so—" he snarled, but got no further, as the façade she had been maintaining collapsed. Her eyes filled with tears. She put her arms around him and whispered in his ear, "Remember what I've told you. Stay out of his way, stay out of sight. Don't do anything to call attention to yourself. He's dressing you for them and tonight he might do anything."

When she drew back and smeared the tears with her palm, he saw that her cheek was bruised and swollen. "He hit you."

"I—" She sniffled. "It was my fault."

If he'd had a knife just then he might have changed all their fates.

The celebration commenced. Corridors and parlors overflowed with guests, more than he'd ever seen. A trio of musicians had been given to Bogrevil as a gift for the evening. They stood back to back in the center of the middle parlor: One played a small drum dangling from a lanyard around his neck, another plucked a lute, and the third fingered a reed instrument called a shawm. The paidika's musician sat on the floor in the corner behind them, watching with envious eyes.

The side parlors had been fitted with long tables of food, artistic displays that were quickly turned into skeletal remains as if by a horde of insects and as quickly replaced.

The other boys like Diverus had been fitted with gaudier costumes than usual—feathers and glittering scales, splashes of color everywhere.

Diverus carried tray after tray of drinks—in his arms for a change instead of on his head. Guests snatched everything off each before he'd even reached the parlors; some on their way to the afrits' chambers (as he now thought of the back rooms). The masked visitors grabbed whatever he carried, as if fearing they might be stranded without sustenance for days.

Bogrevil remained at the bottom of the stairs, dressed in regal violet embroidered robes. He bowed with great flourishes to each individual or group that descended, a sultan welcoming his guests. Initially people escorted their choices to him, but as the evening wore on and the guests came to outnumber the paidika's stable, they came to him with names written on slips of paper, which he wrote down on a small parchment on a podium beside his mammoth guard. They understood that they would have to wait to take their turns. Later arrivals might not have anyone left to choose from at all. He might send in a second client while a boy still lay in the afrit's perch, but not a third. Nobody could recover from three sessions in a row, and it wasn't as if he was going out of business after tonight.

Early in the festivities, one guest clutched Diverus as he was retreating with an empty tray. He looked at the hand on his sleeve, noting the polished nails, and glanced up at coal-black eyes fringed by long lashes behind a gold mask. Dragged before Bogrevil, he listened as the guest said, "I'd have this one." It was a woman, as Bogrevil must have known, too. He expected to be let go.

Bogrevil closed his hand over hers. "He's lovely, you know. Your taste is uncommonly fine." He let this statement hang in the air for a moment—to tease, or to torture Diverus. "He is, however, of diminished capacity, and it might well be catching. Let me assure you, were he not, he wouldn't be serving food. Now, let me offer you something else tasty," and he led her away. Diverus didn't see her again for some hours.

One by one, the boys were purchased and taken off, while others milled about waiting their turn. Each time he watched someone leave the room, he wanted to stop them. Didn't anyone notice Abnevi's absence? Didn't they wonder what had happened? Could they read the guilt in his eyes?

He couldn't help thinking of each of them in their curtained and candlelit chambers, lying beneath insubstantial monstrosities as their life was drained, their souls served up as refreshment. How could Eskie suggest that they desired such a thing?

As the evening wore on, other guests considered him. Their eyes spoke their interest. He wondered what they got from what they inhaled, and why any one boy was more appealing than any other. And why was it only boys—a preference of the afrits or merely less problematic than if the genders mixed? Would there be paidikas full of girls, or was there another word for such places? He knew so little of the world, so little that was of use.

Each time his tray emptied and he escaped to the kitchen, he stalled as long as he could, staying at the back of the line, remaining as invisible as possible, remembering what Eskie had said. Perhaps the fourth time he had done this, the cook placed small brass cups upon the tray as he held it, then filled each with a green distillation. As he filled the ones nearest Diverus's body, he leaned across the tray and said, "Clever boy. Dressed so nice, have you become merchandise now?" At Diverus's look of shock, he laughed. "Can't dodge all night long, you know, no matter how you hang back. It'll be *my* turn to choose eventually, when they've all gone. He's saving you for me."

Diverus flung the tray at him.

Thick green liquid spattered the cook from head to waist, most of it running down his filthy apron. Diverus shoved past those waiting behind him. The cook yelled at him then erupted in the sort of laugh that promised punishment, but he didn't stop. He ran out and into one of the back corridors full of afrit chambers.

A curtain parted and the woman who'd earlier attempted to rent him stumbled out. Her dark eyes were slits, barely open, her features slack. A blindfold hung loosely about her throat on top of her gilded mask. So drunk on the essence she'd inhaled was she that she'd forgotten to put her disguise back on, or even all of her costume. She was barefoot now and bare-shouldered. The cape she'd worn must be in the room still. She kept to the wall to steady herself. As he passed her, she called out, "Pretty boy," reaching limply for him, but then slid down onto the settee as if the gesture had robbed her of all energy.

He eluded her easily and merged into the cramped halls leading to the parlors, wriggling through clusters of guests and boys, realizing that he should have gone the other way, down to the laundry, where at least he might hide until the anniversary was over, even at the risk of never leaving it again.

Instead, he emerged in the foyer before the parlors and ran right into Bogrevil, who was escorting someone from the main stairs. "Well, well, escaped from a harem, have we? Where's your tray?" He seemed to be drunk, but it only increased his malevolence. He turned to the guest behind him and asked, "May I recommend to you this handsome creature? He's very quiet but you can tell just by lookin' that his essence is the stronger for it."

The guest considered him for but a moment, then nodded. "Definitely," he said, a deep, almost sultry, voice.

"Good," Bogrevil replied, and clamped onto Diverus's wrist. "Time spent with an afrit will do you proper, my boy. World of good, take *you* down a peg and remind Eskie who she owes her life to." He started forward as the besotted woman with the gold mask emerged out of one narrow corridor, still lacking half her costume. She pointed at Diverus, the blindfold hanging from her hand. "Pretty boy," she repeated. Bogrevil turned to the client, grinning. "See there, he's very popular." He snatched the blindfold from her and snapped it to get the sentinel's attention. The huge Kotul took the woman by the shoulder and guided her toward the stairs. Bogrevil called out, "Be sure someone retrieves—ah, ne'er mind, I'll do it." Then with an exaggerated wigwag, he led the way down the narrow hall. Boys and clients stepped aside to let him through.

In the afrit corridor Bogrevil directed them to the room the woman had just abandoned. He marched Diverus to the box in the corner and, by twisting his wrist, forced him to his knees. "Get in there. Now." He didn't let go, so Diverus could only crouch beneath the steepled tines and step both feet inside. Bogrevil released him. "If you try to come out of here," he said, "I'll drown you myself. You understand?"

The client, with obvious dismay at the tone of what was occurring, took the blindfold Bogrevil held out to him, and went around to the far side of the water pipe.

Bogrevil swept up the abandoned cape and boots, then as if a signal had been sounded, rushed out into the corridor before anything emerged from the hookah, transparently fearful. He might have been in league with the monstrosities, but clearly he didn't want to encounter them.

The curtain snapped shut.

Diverus lay in the box, watching the flicker of candles, listening to the breathing of the client. He waited, anticipating he didn't know what—Eskie had said that it put the victims to sleep before preying upon them, but how specifically he still didn't know. He didn't want to be awake.

Slowly he became aware of the candles growing dimmer, the light fading away. But the darkening room only made him more alert. Then on the curved ribs above him something slithered. Its grayish fingers ended in black talons, and it pulled itself along the tines as if climbing up a wall rather than dragging along horizontally. He was sure he was supposed to be asleep by now. The glowing orbs of its eyes became visible at the bottom periphery of his sight and he squeezed his eyes closed so as not to see more. Shortly he could feel it directly above him, feel it staring down at him with such a magnetic pull that finally he couldn't help himself.

He looked up.

Gone was the white-eyed monster, gone the tines of bone and the room. Above him on a sharp outcrop of rock sat a beautiful sphinx. Her hair was plaited in a rainbow around her smooth and perfect face. Her full breasts rested upon her paws, and her paws upon a pink marble ledge. She watched him with such tenderness that his chest grew chilly with emotion. He wanted to climb upon the ledge with her, to rest beside her. She smiled to him, reading his thoughts. Then she raised her head, looking past him, and he turned his head to follow her gaze.

On the far side of him a strange black booth had been set up in the sand, with a pale blue screen in its center. The world about them darkened then, and as the screen began to glow, the shadows of two grotesque caricatures of people walked across it as if their joints had been broken, and then began to speak to each other. One looked like Bogrevil. He could hear the shadows speaking, but it was gibberish. Somehow, though, he knew the story being told, knew what they were going to do. He watched, laughed at humor that eluded him, and was stabbed by sadness at tragedy he didn't comprehend. She spoke then, the sphinx, despairing. "You know this story?" He nodded, still watching, though he couldn't think of its name. "I played so small a part," she bemoaned. "But if my role were larger, then we should not have met at all in this place." He couldn't fathom that. "It wants music," she commented. "That will come soon enough, I know." Her voice broke.

He turned back to her, his heart wrenched by the sound of her weeping. Tears flowed to her paws, and dripped off the claws. He cupped his hands until they were full, and her image rippled in the held pool. He couldn't understand how, when everything was dark around her, she continued to glow as if in soft bluish moonlight.

He raised his hands and drank her tears as if he might absorb her grief. When he opened his eyes, she was receding, though neither of them seemed to be moving at all.

"Sleep, my darling," she said, and he knew the voice at last though he hadn't heard it for such a long time: She hadn't become a merwoman at all. She'd changed into this doleful manticore. "Sleep," she said again and though he wanted to run and embrace her and never let her go this time, he could only watch her shrink into the distance, a source of retreating light that filled in with black despair and was soon gone altogether.

He turned back to the play, but the booth was closed now, the screen covered; then the remaining light dimmed and the booth also disappeared. Everything was dark now, and he was alone, floating, a mask on the waves, free of anguish, of pain, of the helplessness of his life, and he released himself to the will of the black water as it carried him away. Out to sea, he hoped.

When he awoke, he didn't at first know where he was. His mind was confused, jumbled. Candles burned nearby, reflected in the white bone of the tusklike tines above him, making them seem to dance as the candleflames flickered. He was in a bed, but the sides of it were higher than he. It was a box, really, a shallow box; not far away stood a towering brass water pipe.

Then he remembered, and he knew what had been done to him, but he was so drained of emotion, of fear, anger, that he didn't react to the knowledge, only contemplated it as if the emotions belonged to some other person.

Eskie should be coming for him soon. She would help him back to the dormitorium, put him to bed and later bring him some broth, something to revive him. That sounded very appealing. He realized that he was ravenously hungry. Now he understood why the boys let themselves be chosen, even fought for the privilege of service. Already he wanted to be with the sphinx again, to hear her voice, his mother's voice; he needed to tell her that he loved her and wouldn't let them throw her into the sea this time. No, he would cling to her as she moved into darkness, wrap his arms around her neck and climb upon her back and ride her so that she couldn't disappear.

He licked his lips. They were dry and licking them made them sticky. He remembered again that he was hungry.

After a while, he crawled from the box on his own. No one remained in the chamber. The blindfold lay curled on the floor beside the pipe as if for the next client. He stood, swaying, and placed his hands on the belly of the pipe to steady himself. It was cold, and when he drew his hand away, his palm was imprinted with the designs etched in the bronze. He rapped his knuckles against it to listen to the sound echo inside. What did that do to the afrit? he wondered. Did it slumber after it had drunk of someone like him? Did it hear him? Know he was out here? He'd have liked to communicate with it, if only in the dream—if it *had* been merely a vivid dream and not real vision of Nechron's world, of some manner of afterlife. What did afrits show every-one else? He closed his eyes and rocked his head. His existence was suddenly compressed, the whole course of a lifetime squeezed inside him. His eyes ached as if they'd seen too much.

He shuffled away from the water pipe, made it to the doorway and then out into the hall. No one was there either. Candles still burned in a few of the chambers, but in most the curtains hung open upon darkened rooms. Perhaps even now Eskie was helping someone else back to the dormitorium.

He shambled along the hallway, looking into the darkened and empty chambers, wondering if everyone else was asleep and he the only one left.

The corridors proved to be confounding this morning. He would turn a corner but almost immediately forget what hallway he'd been in prior to it. In no time at all, he lost his way to the sleeping quarters. Down a corridor that should have returned him to the dormitorium, he found himself at the base of spiraling steps that he'd never seen before. What if they took him up and out of the paidika? Might there be an exit no one had been told about, that only Bogrevil knew? He had to see, because he couldn't imagine he would ever find his way back here again.

He climbed slowly, carefully, using hands and feet, and sometimes knees. He felt like a turtle. Each step took all his effort, and he tried to count them as he climbed but too soon forgot the number. He became aware of a noise, not voices exactly, but cooing and deep groans. He raised his head and saw that the steps ended in an open doorway. Dim light spilled down from it. He crabbed up a few more steps, until his head was high enough to see into the doorway, into what he knew immediately was Bogrevil's private rooms. Neither of them saw him. Bogrevil was too focused on sensation, his eyes closed, mouth drawn back in a feral grin, and foam bubbling on his lips. Eskie lay with her arms out, head back. Her legs were locked around his waist. She moaned once, licked her lips, and turned her head, folding her arms around it in a gesture expressive of pleasure.

Diverus sank down and let his head rest on the cold step. He couldn't drown out the grunting and murmuring. Beyond that what could he do? He could barely crawl. If he intruded, Bogrevil would kill him before he'd dragged himself through the doorway—and for what? Eskie wasn't being harmed, wasn't performing against her will, not like he had done. Then he imagined that he saw the sphinx again, and he forgot his will.

He slid back down the steps, more confused than ever. Eskie had warned him, protected him against Bogrevil yet here she was, his mistress, his lover if love was involved in the repulsive bargain. He wanted to feel betrayed but foundered in prying loose enough emotion. Why did he have to know this? He didn't want to know it. Better that the afrit should wipe away all of his memory and return him to the imbecilic state in which he'd lived his former life. What good was knowing the truth of things?

He stumbled through the maze of halls again, and finally into a dark and unoccupied guest room, into the box and onto his belly. Let the creature come for him, let it steal his soul and send him forever to live with the sphinx. He didn't care.

He fell asleep like that, but no dreams came, and if the afrit perched above him, he never knew. He woke only when one of the boys came to clean the room and found him. Thinking him dead, the cleaner ran out, calling Bogrevil's name and shouting, "Dead! Dead!"

Diverus pushed himself onto hands and knees. His joints ached. He was like someone who has been laid down by a fever and, having come through it, wants to get away from his illness. His legs held him as he plunged across the room. He was almost at the door when Eskie arrived. She'd run from wherever she was, and when she saw him her breath caught. She reached toward his face. "Thank the gods, you aren't dead. I thought . . . I was looking for you, you need—"

He slapped her hand aside. "I don't need anything from you."

"Diverus, what is wrong?"

He replied, "Get out of my way, please. I have to . . . have to eat something." He couldn't even look directly at her, but smoldered, his jaw clenched; yet he didn't move.

She read his inaction, his fury, and understood, though not how or when he'd found out. "Diverus," she said, "You can't be in love with me."

His whole face burned; his eyes scalded. "I'm not," he said.

"He *owns* me. My family sold me to give them enough money to live on. My father was ill, he needed things we couldn't afford. Medicines."

"Shut up."

"They sold me to him. I'm his *slave*. More so than you or any of these boys you live with." She twisted at the waist and pulled back one sleeve of her shirt and rolled her arm so he could see the dark crescent near her shoulder. "This isn't a birthmark. It's his sigil. It doesn't come off. I'm property. That's all I am, all I can ever be." Then she stepped aside and he pushed past her; he was not ready to hear explanations or excuses, least of all hers.

He shoved through the curtain and through a gathering of boys, then took one of the narrow halls that led to the kitchen level.

The cook was chopping turnips as he entered. Glancing up, the cook said, "Well, well, come for your special treat at last, my little harem boy?" He set down his knife, placed both hands on the cutting board, and leaned forward. "Is it my turn finally, hmm?" As he reached across the board and tousled Diverus's hair, he smiled with vulpine connivance.

Diverus snatched the knife and drove it straight through the cook's other hand and into the board.

The cook shrieked to the ceiling. He clutched the handle but it had been driven hard into the board, and he had to rock it to loosen it, which made him squeal and squeal. His blood began to soak into the pale raw turnips. Diverus grabbed another knife and this one he held to the cook's throat. The cook clutched the handle stuck into his hand and whimpered. He quavered, his face pale as dough and glistening with sweat. Diverus said softly, "Never." Then he laid down the knife and walked away. Behind him, the cook shrieked again as he finally freed his hand from the board. His cries rose and fell in waves of agony behind Diverus.

In the tight passage Bogrevil knocked past him, giving him a cursory but suspicious glance before hurrying to the kitchen. More boys followed; a few glared accusingly at him, others with a look more akin to worship. His own cored-out look challenged them all.

He went back to the dormitorium, to his pallet, and lay down. The others in the room were either asleep or too weak to do more than watch him lurch past. Kotul, asleep on his belly on the largest pallet, was sprawled halfway onto the floor.

By the time Diverus had fallen upon his pad he was

shaking and feverish, and he drew his legs up, folding his arms around them, and waited for sleep that wasn't going to come. Strangest of all was that nobody pursued him for his crime. He expected them to pour into the room, Bogrevil and his legion of boys, to drag him against his will down to the laundry pool, there to drown him in the dark and toss his miserable, weighted corpse into the sea just as he had helped dispose of the dead client. Through the vents high up on the wall, he could hear distant noises from the underspan, from the world where he had been a captive to his own helplessness. He'd escaped it only to be a cap-tive here, no higher nor closer to the surface of the world. The difference was that he knew it now, but knowing improved nothing. Knowing was worse than being an idiot. He wished almost that the gods had never made him aware; he'd been better off when nothing stayed with him, when the abuses rolled off, one after the other, and he felt nothing more than the immediate pain, the anguish of the moment, forgotten soon enough. This—this thinking, feeling, knowing—hurt too much, demanded too much of him. He didn't want to die, only to lose himself once more. His brain whirled around the subject, and he closed his eyes to wring it out, to exorcise thinking, like a demon from his mind.

Eventually Eskie entered the hall. She carried a tray through the dormitorium, which she placed on the floor beside his bed. A large bowl and a fist-sized chunk of bread lay on it. She didn't expect him to take it from her. "You need to eat," she said, as if to the whole room. The bowl sat within his line of sight unless he rolled over onto his side, turning his back to it. Steam snaked out of it and his stomach clenched at the smell. His eyes felt as if they would at any moment collapse into his skull, the sockets them-selves throbbed. He had to order his hand to reach for the spoon. Once he had it, he had to concentrate to direct himself to lean up on one elbow, and then he had to drag himself closer to the tray.

The soup was hot and oily and thick. If the cook had made it for him, it must have been before . . . before the accident. Other-wise it would have been full of broken sea shells or something else to kill him. Or maybe Eskie had made it. If only he'd spoken to her, said what he felt, she would have stayed, would have fed him as she did all the other boys. They didn't care that she belonged to Bogrevil, why should he? He was a boy, nobody at all. She wasn't his age. She'd never given him a reason to hope or even believe—no, that wasn't entirely true. She had warned him, had protected him, had in her way made him feel special and different from all the others. He didn't want to be just one more boy in the paidika, his body a source of someone else's pleasure and an afrit's meal until he was nothing but a husk, back where he began, stupid and helpless forever. Why would anyone desire that? But when he closed his eyes, he saw the sphinx again, alive and bright and loving, and he wanted her more than anything. He trembled with desire.

By the time he wiped the crust of bread around the bowl to sop up the last bit of the liquid, he felt newly born. He'd have crawled into a box for another client now—at least, he felt as if he could. It would turn off his mind, set him free from what he knew. Later. Let them ask him later.

He lay back and was soon asleep.

The paidika didn't open for business the following night. The events of the anniversary had taken a toll and required recovery. Some boys had indeed been subjected to the afrits twice that night, which Bogrevil never would have allowed any other time. The ones who weathered the abuse best needed to be carried to their beds; even when fed afterwards, they showed little improvement. Recovery would be slow. One boy, like Abnevi, had gone mad, his mind scrambled. "One more for the laundry," was Bogrevil's glum response. It meant one less money-earner among his brood, for which reason if no other he didn't punish Diverus directly.

The cook, with a hand swollen to twice its normal size, took to his bed, where he intended to remain for days, whining that he must be avenged. Food became a matter of immediate concern, and Eskie had to take over in the kitchen. Without sustenance, the exhausted boys would not recover, and Bogrevil needed them active by the second night. He knew perfectly well how the cook goaded and teased certain boys and that he'd repeatedly tried to have his way with some of them; in Bogrevil's opinion, the bastard was lucky the blade hadn't ended up between his ribs. Nevertheless, Diverus had to be seen to pay for inflicting it. Such an act of rebellion could not be allowed to pass unchallenged, or soon the entire paidika would be out of control, stabbing cooks, snubbing clients, and more importantly, disrupting the afrits. Those monstrosities would not take to being inconvenienced for long, and the price would be Bogrevil's to pay. His servitude to them had another year to run, after which he suspected he would be dispatched or, if lucky, merely forced to find someone to take his place before the ephemeral monsters released him. It wasn't as if he could escape them on his own. Where, in a world of ocean, could he hide from water creatures? He'd been young and insanely foolish, a ship captain's cabin boy emptying the slops over the bow, unaware that their ship had entered a demon-haunted Sargasso, oblivious to the horrors swimming in their wake. And then when he'd befouled them, he'd laughed in their faces. It was a wonder they had let him keep his own face; but afrits did nothing but for a reason. They had wanted something from him. They needed a human agent for their purpose. Oh, to be a ship's mate again, to be free of these infernal tunnels, to breathe sea air and not worry about the likes of these misfortunate boys . . . which thought brought him back to the problem at hand.

The simplest solution seemed to be to rent out Diverus as often as possible from now on.

There is much in life that seems random, events for which no obvious purpose is apparent even though they may compound. In the aftermath only can a pattern be discerned—missteps lead to an inevitable conclusion, an inescapable fate, sometimes doom and sometimes triumph. We curse the one and pretend to be responsible for the other, while neither fortune is true.

The next evening the paidika opened for business again. Only two of the boys were still out of commission, and that was excuse enough for Bogrevil to recommend Diverus to some of the clients. Immediately, this proved unnavigable: he had been too clever. Previously he had talked so many of them *out* of engaging the handsome "damaged mute" that the first time he proffered Diverus like some newfound treasure, he got a look of such intense shock and loathing from the client that he made a great show of laughing nervously and proclaiming the suggestion "just my little joke," before sending the client off with a reliable boy at half the going rate by way of an apology. Then he sat on the steps with a blighted look about the eyes.

He could not recall which or how many of the various strutting peacocks he'd dissuaded from Diverus in the past.

There had been so many. If he didn't refrain from promoting Diverus, he would surely see his reputation suffer—one could not cover such an injudicious suggestion with a bit of laughter or soon the clients would decide for themselves that he was unreli-able, and then he would find himself at the mercy of the afrits' smoke. However he looked at it, promoting Diverus spelled doom.

The result was that Diverus was demoted back to walking about with a tray strapped to his head, and Bogrevil chose the last remaining punishment available when he loudly ordered Diverus to clean the three parlors after everyone had gone. "An' before you retire, too—you don't sleep till these rooms is spotless!" He had to hope that such a bellowed exaction sounded harsh enough. At least until he could think up something else. Meanwhile, he discovered that he had a much more pressing—and annoying—problem: his musician.

After a night of blissful accompaniment provided by the donated trio of players, Bogrevil found the out-of-tune plinking of the household musician no longer tolerable. It was a shortcoming that needed remedy, or else he would assuredly strangle the talentless lad in short order.

The trio had left behind a shawm, bestowing it upon the paidika as a kind of lagniappe, for indeed they had been richly compensated by the lubricious crowd all through the night, more so than at any venue where they'd previously performed. Bogrevil had even petitioned to buy their contract from the guest, who happened to be their owner, but the price proved to be wildly immoderate. Nevertheless, he couldn't—he just couldn't—go back to the discordant torture that had graced the parlors before then. How had he ever tolerated it?

In a moment of brilliance (at least, he thought so), he proposed a contest to all the boys in the house, that whoever was able play the shawm would be relieved of all other cleaning and serving duties and *elevated* to the position of musician, a proposal dependent upon their ignorance of the fact that "musician" was not a title currently deserving of any respect at all, and certainly not something to which one aspired given the verbal abuse their master and his customers had heaped upon the hapless boy and his tuneless lute from the very first night. For those serving, however, the prospect was so much better than their current station that, one after another during that slow night, they took up the shawm and tried to play it—with unsurprising if excruciating results.

If an untuned lute was a pitiful thing to hear, the squeals of a tortured reed proved infinitely worse. Many of the boys could produce noises on it, but no one was able to produce music. For the paidika the only consequent benefit was that arriving clients were quick to pay for and select a boy for the evening and go off to a distant chamber just to escape the teeth-grating cacophony.

Word of the contest spread to the depths of the laundry, and those with enough sense and a desire to escape their fate made the climb up and crowded the hallways. Abnevi was brought along, too, but unhinged as he was, he could neither determine which end of the shawm went into his mouth nor tell when—as it happened, never—he was making music.

Watching each of his peers fail, Diverus found no reason to try it himself. He knew he had never held a musical instrument in his life. Instead, he stayed away from the parlors and out of Bogrevil's way, even hid in the stairwell to Bogrevil's chambers, where he managed to doze awhile.

Finally, late in the night, long after all the boys had tried and failed and retreated dismally to their inescapable duties and from there finally to bed, he entered the empty middle parlor to gather mugs and plates to carry to the kitchen. Some client's grubby hand had smeared a wall with an oily print, and he brought in a bucket from the kitchen and scrubbed at the mark.

Having cleaned the handprint, Diverus wandered over to the pillows where the lute and the shawm lay. For all their efforts, no one had managed to coax a single musical strain out of the shawm. It seemed likely to Diverus that the hapless musician would have his job back tomorrow. Perhaps he would improve, now that his position had been so threatened. Perhaps he would practice.

Diverus picked the shawm up to look at it more closely. The reed mouthpiece had been deformed by teeth biting it too hard, boys clamping and chewing on it in an attempt to accomplish what they could not through blowing. The tubular body was still gaily painted, though the lacquer was worn away around the holes from many fingers over many years. The wider bell had been chipped, but long ago. It now bore Abnevi's teeth marks, too. It had seen a lot of use before arriving here.

The instrument felt odd in his hands, soft and pliable, but

he assumed that was because his arms were tired. His palms seemed to slide around the shawm as if they and it were old friends. Without thinking, he lifted it to his mouth and his lips pressed tightly around the reed. His eyes rolled closed. The sound of blood roared in his ears; then, distantly, he heard a drone that rose and fell and swirled, catching him up. He felt as if he were approaching the place again where the sphinx dwelled—close, he was so close, and the swirl of the music took on added urgency as he strained, and failed, to reach that place. He could almost hear her voice again. "It wants music." The whisper threaded past him in the darkness of his mind.

When he opened his eyes, a client was staring at him. Perhaps the man had been sitting outside one of the private rooms, disheveled and drunk on the essence he'd smoked; he was pressed against the tiled edge of the doorway as though it were the floor and he had fallen there. His hands pressed to his face beneath a look of wonderment, or shock, as if what he'd heard had cut into some private and forgotten piece of his soul.

A few moments later Bogrevil arrived from wherever he had been. The disquiet of his features might have been rage, and Diverus reacted to the look, quickly put down the shawm and stepped away from it. "I'm sorry," he said. Confused by what he'd done—not really certain what he'd done, he spoke the words before he could compose himself. He hadn't meant to speak, but he couldn't take it back, too late.

The master of the paidika then proved himself a master of the obvious. "You spoke," he said, and in those two syllables was an undertone that said he ought to have known all along.

"—" He could think of nothing to say, and his voice sounded as raw and strange as when he'd spoken to Eskie. He cleared his throat, lowered his eyes. In the shadows behind Bogrevil, others were arriving, stumbling, shambling.

"Never mind the words now. Pick that thing up." Bogrevil pointed at the shawm.

Reluctantly, Diverus obeyed. "I meant no harm," he said.

"Put it to your lips again."

He needed no coaxing: Drawn to action by the very touch of the shawm, he tasted the reed again, tasted his own spit, and in an instant the sound emerged. He tried to watch his fingers close over the holes, to watch as a tune settled over him like a cape, coming from he knew not where; but his eyes rolled up of their own accord and he floated away, back into the dream space where she dwelled. His mother the sphinx was there, somewhere, he could feel her like a breeze upon his cheek, and in the distance that pale rectangle of light that he'd seen in his vision, and there, the pink slab of marble . . . Whether the song lasted one minute or ten, he didn't know; but when he returned to his senses, he saw that the client in the front had sunk to his knees and was sobbing. Others—boys who should have been abed, and other clients who emerged from the corridors—gaped at him, struck dumb. Weaving through the paidika, the sound had pulled them here, its magic so powerful that clients had come without their masks and costumes. Two women stood in their midst, having shed their male disguises; one was half undressed, as was the man with her, suggestive of the manner in which they'd been sharing the afrit smoke. And the afrits—had they allowed the people to escape? Did the music affect them, too, the way the flute of a snake-charmer entranced a cobra?

With the tune ended, some of them looked at one another with a shock of recognition, as if they were acquainted outside the brothel and would never have dreamed of finding each other here. At the back, Eskie peered apprehensively between two of the boys.

Bogrevil drew a deep breath. If he'd been angry at first, the wide-eyed look upon his face now wasn't rage at all, but something like ebullience. He entered the parlor and held out his hand. Diverus gave him the shawm.

"Why," he asked gravely, "have you kept this skill, this gift—for it's surely what the gods gave you upon that dragon beam—why have you kept it a secret from us?"

"I didn't know I knew it."

A moment longer Bogrevil stared at him. Then he laughed deep in his throat, once, twice. He turned to look at the assembled clients. "*This* is my anniversary present." He pointed back at Diverus, chuckling as he did. "I'm blessed by the gods themselves, am I not?" He seemed to become aware of the state of his audience, cleared his throat and then to no one in particular stated, "Yes, it is not the policy of this establishment to cater to the female sex. It's not my prejudice, but the law of the span, which I'm sure everyone on the span knows. This being a special night, exceptions will be made . . . still, let's not be *advertising* our violation, hmm?" When no one moved, he added, "He's not going to play no more right now, so get off."

At that, they did disperse, albeit with reluctance, some up the stairs, others to collect their masks and costumes. The boys looked him over with a mix of resentment and reverence. Bogrevil had Kotul help the weeping client up and on his way, then said to Diverus, "I can't let you have this back just yet. Got to get them all out the door and the rest of us to bed, or we'll be standing here all night. You could transfix the sun and hold the night with that reed." He bent down and lifted the untuned lute by its neck from the pillows and handed that to Diverus. "Here. Amuse yourself with this instead."

He strode back to Eskie and presented her the shawm. "For safekeeping. We'll need it later, assuming—" He was interrupted by the strumming of the lute. Still out of tune, it had not kept Diverus from plucking a lilting phrase from it. Bogrevil wheeled about and watched him, amazed.

Diverus held the lute away from himself, and with his free hand turned the pegs one by one as though knowing exactly how much each needed to be adjusted. His eyes were strangely unfocused, as if he was listening to someone tell him how to accomplish this. When he strummed it again, the lute was in tune. The sound of it was as sweet as a zephyr, one that had never blown before through that sunken place.

Clients coming to the steps to leave stopped again and watched.

Bogrevil hurried to Diverus, and covered the strings with a hand. Glazed dark eyes focused on him again, uncertain in their gaze. "Was I . . ." He saw the effect upon everyone and didn't need to finish the question.

A small hourglass drum lay on its side, and Bogrevil picked that up. He snatched the lute away and handed him the drum, nodded at it. For a moment Diverus caressed its shape as if by instinct, as he might have done the body of a lover. Seating himself on the pillows, he began to play an easy, loose beat, and shortly added flourishes, making it complex, intriguing. There was magic in the rhythm beneath his palms and fingers.

"You can play anything?" asked Bogrevil.

Diverus stopped. He didn't realize he had sat. He looked up at his owner. "I don't . . . I don't know where it comes from. I don't know how it happens."

"Well, don't you worry on that, 'cause *I* do," Bogrevil repli-ed, and the look he wore was of a man envisioning great wealth.

Diverus became the celebrity of the paidika. The few who'd heard him that first night came back again the next, accompanied by a few more. While he played, the clients were transported, almost as they would have been by afrit smoke, and for far less investment—at least initially. They stood, leaned, sat, forgot their drinks, their conversation, even their established goal in coming here. One or two wept during a mournful passage he played on the shawm, and even Bogrevil looked stricken by the beauty of it when Diverus finally stopped—but not so stricken that he didn't jump up immediately and take advantage of the now-pliable clientele. It turned out that the music weakened their resistance to Bogrevil's overtures. He easily matched them with boys, now also similarly docile, and sent them all off to the back rooms, even collecting a *higher* fee than he'd previously asked. His instinct for profit assured him that they would pay—he could smell their surrender—and they did, unhesitatingly. Either dazed by the music or magnanimous because of it, they paid his price and went off to smoke the boys.

Almost immediately someone petitioned for Diverus's company; Bogrevil was ready for that with a price that he would never have asked for any boy before. The client looked stricken by the figure, but Bogrevil justified it. "For you to have him to yourself deprives everyone else of his magic—the music stops, you see. The smoke sucks the will out of him this night and likely tomorrow. The cost has to compensate for that much loss. You ain't paying *me*, see, you're paying all of these good people to deprive them of the serenity he provides. But if you're willing to cover it, he's yours, make no mistake." The client hastily declined and chose another; but that was all right. Bogrevil had his sights on other evenings. Word would get out, and someone would come along and pay it simply *because* the price was so exorbitant.

Meantime, word of "the gods' musician" spread across the span.

Weeks passed, with Bogrevil fine-tuning performances, limiting the shawm to a few minutes a night or whenever a fight threatened to break out. Diverus developed a sense of when to pick it up in order to quiet down the customers.

The shawm soon became but one among dozens of instruments: As word of him spread, so did the story that he could play anything given to him. At the end of the first week someone placed a santur before Diverus and handed him two sticks. He set down his lute, accepted the sticks, and with almost no pause, delicately hammered a plangent tune that made people shiver. The next night someone gave him a single-stringed fiddle with a bow, and he made it sing as if with a human voice.

Two nights after that, Kotul at the bottom of the steps called for Bogrevil, who came running from the back, thinking that a great disaster had befallen them. What he found was a line of curiosity seekers that extended all the way up the steps, and each person had brought an instrument and each wanted to make Diverus play it. It was a disaster in the making. The business of the paidika was becoming the performances of Diverus.

Thinking quickly, Bogrevil shouted up the steps, "It's a con-dition of this establishment that if the boy can play your instru-ment, it remains *with* the establishment." The line of turbaned, masked, cloaked men and women roared with indignation, but Bogrevil waved them silent. "Look here, nobody's making you come down here like this—you have two choices. You either rent his time privately, in which case you can use him as you like, or you accept the challenge that he'll play anything you hand him. The boy don't come cheap, but that's how it is. He's blessed, and you pay for that."

The line broke up. Only a few remained to accept the rules and challenge the boy with their obscure instruments. They all went home empty-handed, but in most cases not until Bogrevil had packed them off to one of the rooms in back. Even losing, they were transported by the music.

Disaster was averted, and money flowed copiously. Bogrevil thought that if he could sustain this level of income for even a few months, he would retire from the brothel with enough wealth to flee to some large isle—oh, there were some big enough, he'd heard it from travelers, five or six spans on—where he would live far away from the demons, the ocean, and the children for the rest of his life.

The pile of instruments surrounding Diverus grew steadily, a testament to his magical skill. He would pick up the simplest ocarina and then a small harp, without hesitating, without thinking, and play. Bogrevil luxuriated in the attention as if it were all about him.

Then one evening, moments after they had opened their doors for business, Mother Kestrel arrived. She had with her three youths, and they shoved aside the boy on the door and went down the stairs together in a cluster, a four-headed dreadnought. Above them, the boy at the door stuck two fingers in his mouth and whistled a signal to Kotul at the bottom. They made it halfway down before he stepped into view like a barbican gate dropped in their path. Her boys drew up and eyed her nervously. One complained, "You didn't tell us about *him*."

"I couldn't, now, could I, being as how I've never been down this far."

Bogrevil, sent for the moment the alarm was sounded, appeared beside his behemoth. "Ah, Mother K, *lovely* to see you as always," he said. "Of course, you're not really supposed to be here during business hours, are you? I mean, there *is* a prohibitive policy regarding undisguised female clients. 'Course, maybe you'd be unaware of that, bein' as how you're no client."

She slipped down a few more steps, while her escort hung back. "I'm not makin' a delivery this time."

"Well, there's a pity, because they look strapping strong, your youngsters. I can always use boys with good constitutions. They last so much longer."

"I'm here to talk about the idiot."

Bogrevil glanced around as if to identify the subject. "I'm afraid," he said at last, "I've got no idiot here at this time. My boys are rather more than that." A tune played on a lute floated up the stairwell, as crisp as a chilled wine.

"That's what I'm talking about," she said. "The stories come to me that our lad finally showed his gifts, what he got on the dragon beam."

"*Our* lad? I wasn't aware we'd ever coupled, you and I."

One of the boys sniggered. Mother Kestrel came closer. "You know who I mean," she accused. "Word is, you're taking in a lot of coin on account of his gifts."

"Well, *some*, certainly. But, you know, we struck a bargain, you and I, when I took him in—that all his gifts and the proceeds from those gifts were to be mine alone—"

"I spoke in haste."

"No doubt you did. You were aggrieved to have looked after him and took my recompense for your trouble. I recall that you were paid agreeably and that you discarded him with a great expression of relief."

She stood a moment longer. "So you won't cut me a share in him now that he's valuable."

"No," he replied. "I don't think I will. We concluded our bargain where he is concerned. Now, should you care to fob off another one so blessed by the gods, I'm sure I could be persuaded to pay less up front for what might manifest through divine intervention later on. It is a risk, isn't it?"

"Bastard."

"My dear, that's a given, so you gain nothing by pointing it out." He reached into a pocket and produced a gold coin. "Here." He tossed it up the stairs to her and she caught it as efficiently as a hawk snatching a meal out of the sky. "Never let it be said I'm ungenerous."

She stared at the coin in her palm, then back at him. The coin was gold, but the fact that he could throw such a coin to her so casually, dismissively, spoke volumes about the money he must have taken in on account of that creature she'd tended. For months and months she'd tended him. One coin only made her greedy for another, but she saw well enough that Bogrevil had no need to give her more. If she wanted her share, she would have to make not parting with it too dear for Mr. Bogrevil. She turned and started back up the steps.

"Very nice to see you again, m'dear," he called after her. "Always looking for some good strong boys." Her entourage parted as she pushed through them. One glanced down as if considering Bogrevil's offer, but they all followed after her. The boy on the door was speaking to someone just outside. Mother Kestrel poked a finger toward him and one of her lads dragged him out of the way.

"A short figure in a gray tunic and domino mask stood outside the paidika that night, blocking Mother Kestrel's path," says the narrator. On the screen of the booth then, the puppet figure of the shadowpuppeteer appears, its malachite eyes gleaming, and the audience chuckles as the joke spreads: The puppeteer has become a figure in her own story.

"She was eluding the amorous intentions of her hostess on that span—a woman named Rolend, who'd fallen under the spell of the puppeteer. She had hired a procurer to take her to a place where women were not allowed entry, thinking that this would protect her from pursuit. She, dressed as she always was in those days—as a man—would have no trouble entering the paidika.

"Even as she allowed the crone and her gang of thuggish oafs out, the puppeteer saw, back along the alley, the light of a pole-lantern, proof that she had not escaped her amorous pursuer after all. She paid the procurer and stepped quickly through the doorway of the paidika. The procurer turned his attention immediately to the woman and her gang of boys. He called, 'Madame, good evening to you and your young fellows. If it's further pleasures you're looking for, allow me to guide you to them!' The puppeteer watched him scurry, ratlike, after the woman. Then the door closed and she was safe inside the paidika.

"There was no hint then that she was about to have a life-changing encounter."

Outside, the procurer hung back behind the line of Mother Kestrel's thugs until they had passed the oncoming lantern, which turned out to be a guide and a woman in a hooded cloak. Then he wove around the trio and up behind Mother Kestrel as he tried to reach her before she exited the narrow lane. "Is there somewhere you might wish to see?" he asked, "I know everywhere on the span, the places that would invite you in, not like that exclusive place back there." While he babbled to her, one of the boys glided up and casually snapped a blackjack against the side of his head, relieving him of his purse even as he collapsed. Mother Kestrel stopped and turned back. She sized up the situation. The lad tossed the purse to her and she caught it as she walked back to him. "Good lad, Jemmy, I've taught you so well," she said affectionately, and tousled his hair. To his utter amazement, she then dropped the purse into the lane beside the dazed procurer. "Right now, my dears, we need to be respectable, terribly respectable, which means we can't have the likes of him calling the law down upon us. No, no, no, for once we need those very forces ourselves. So, no more mischief. Not till I solve my little problem with Mr. Bogrevil." She walked on.

The lads stood around their victim in the dark a moment longer and only grudgingly left the purse there as they followed their leader.

Bogrevil made a sweeping bow and said, "Welcome, good sir, to the land where dreams o'ertake your other life. You would like a boy to smoke for the evening?"

The puppeteer hesitated, and glanced from parlor to parlor, uncertain which one was providing the music. "I'll browse?" she suggested in a deep whisper.

Bogrevil stepped back and broadly waved his arm. "By all means." If he suspected she was a woman, he didn't show it. She was disguised, and therefore following the rules. He said, "If I can be of assistance, or when you've chosen, don't hesitate to call upon me."

They made respectful half-bows and she strolled past the lefthand parlor, and drew up before the middle parlor. The icy music of a santur trembled behind the bead curtain there.

Seated cross-legged upon pillows in the middle of the room and surrounded by musical instruments, Diverus did not react as she stepped through the curtain. A boy wearing a tray glided up beside her to offer a drink. She took it, but then turned back, fascinated by the elegance of the tune being played, and contemplating all the instruments lying about him.

The musician himself was under the spell of his music: His eyes remained closed while he played, and his head rolled, snaking back and forth. His fingers flicked the tiny mallets with astonishing speed and accuracy. He never looked at them once. He continued playing for another ten minutes before the piece found an end, and his eyes didn't open until the last tinny note was fading. Then his back arched and he inhaled sharply, suddenly, as if his spirit had plunged back into him from whatever dreamscape it had flown to on the wings of song.

Some of the others arose and made their way past her on unsteady legs. One was propped up by his rented boy. Outside the gauzy curtain, behind her, she heard Bogrevil direct them to various rooms. The beads hissed as he came into the parlor.

He stopped beside her. "Remarkable, ain't he?"

She nodded. "I wondered, how much . . ."

"For an evening? Don't misunderstand me, young sir, but I doubt you could afford him." Then he named the shocking price, almost apologetically. "You see, if I let you have him for the rest of the evening, then I deprive everyone else of his boundless talent. Thus he comes very dear. No help for it, I'm afraid."

"He plays all of these?" she asked.

"Oh, every single one. Nobody's yet brought an instrument to our establishment that he couldn't play, and with skill equal to what you just heard."

"The gods favor him then."

Bogrevil laughed. "Indeed, they do."

Leodora considered for a moment while Diverus rolled aside the santur and took up a teardrop-shaped ud. He seemed to shiver at touching it. She asked, "What if I were to wait until the evening was over? No one would be deprived of their music then."

Bogrevil's brow knitted. Nobody had ever proposed that before. The quoted price for his services usually ended the conversation.

"That's hours from now. I mean, I sup*pose*," he said, formulating, "the price would be a *little* more reasonable under those conditions. He'll be tired, though—don't know that he'll care to accept. And still higher, I'm afraid, than most of the boys since the experience will still drain him and he'll still have to recover, and—truth is—nobody's had him like that. It might drain him too much to play *next* night. There's a lot to think about here. I must ponder it awhile."

Leodora nodded as if she understood everything he'd said. But knowing nothing of what actually went on in this paidika, she couldn't fathom what it was that might drain him. "I shall just listen then—if that's all right."

Bogrevil opened his mouth to object, but she touched his hand and a coin slipped between her fingers into his. He glanced at it, surprised and delighted by what he saw; and he wondered why he hadn't thought to charge for the pleasure of listening to Diverus right from the start.

"Listen to your heart's content," he said. "I'll see that he plays the shawm for you before daybreak."

"That's his best?"

"It stops everything in this place when he does it."

The first few plucked notes of another song began. Bogrevil gestured Leodora to a nearby pillow, then withdrew before the spell from the double strings clutched him as well.

She listened, watching at first, but with eyelids soon falling shut as she was spirited away by the sound. She was imagining the song accompanying a performance; it would be the perfect marriage of music with her art. She could not help but wonder if the procurer hadn't been a god in disguise, who had led her to a destination she didn't even know she was seeking. It was the sort of thing a trickster might do, and wasn't the world full of them?

As the last note hovered and faded like a sunset, she opened her eyes and smiled at the performer. He nodded to her and she back at him. The room emptied out then—the remaining patrons going off either with their evening's choice or in search of one elsewhere. The serving boys pushed through the curtain again with their trays, but she waved them off.

"You have incredible skill," she told him. "You must have begun playing very young."

He tilted his head as if considering this. "Yes, I must have—before I was born, I think."

"And you can play them all?"

"So far." He set down the ud. "Is there one you'd particularly like to hear?"

Before she answered there came a distant shout and a loud whistle that abruptly cut off. Then a voice cried, "Raid!"

Leodora jumped to her feet. She poked her head through the beaded curtain. The clamor came from the top of the long stairwell. The immense guard at the bottom of the steps had taken a position blocking the way. Out of the other two parlors people bolted, most of them in disguise and all heading away from the steps; they fought each other to get into the narrow halls, where Bogrevil gestured them to hurry. His expression was sour.

"What do we do?" she asked the musician.

"Flee, I think," he advised. "This hasn't happened in all the time I've been here, but we've been instructed again and again so that when it happened we would know what to do. You should follow me."

He picked up the ud and some of the other instruments. She reached out to accept one of the lutes and a double reed instrument. "That's a *mijwiz,*" he said. "I'm very fond of it. I'm called Diverus."

"Jax," she replied, and then they were in the foyer and past Bogrevil.

As they entered the narrow passage behind him, someone shouted, "There! Stop them!" It was a woman's voice, and

Leodora craned her head to see. At the bottom of the stairs the woman who'd shoved past her as she was arriving was flailing her arms madly. She had four large uniformed men with her, but they were busy combating the giant of a bouncer behind her, and the woman charged after Diverus without protection. Bogrevil stepped in front of the passage then, blocking the way with his body. Behind his back a gleam of light delineated the double-curved blade of the khanjarli dagger in his hand.

It was Leodora's final view of him and of the events in the foyer. Diverus drew her out of the sloping passage and into a broad hall containing dozens of doorways and more passages leading off it. People were running about everywhere, some half-undressed and many stumbling as if drunk or drugged. One sat on a small divan, head hanging between his knees, unable to rouse himself enough to take flight. She was surprised at the number of women scurrying from the rooms. Clearly, they'd arrived disguised as men and only thrown off the disguises once they'd gained entry to these private rooms. Diverus dodged them all. She glimpsed some of the chambers they passed, each containing a giant water pipe, like a fountain fixture set in the center of the floor. Someone lay sprawled beside one, but most of the rooms were empty, the occupants already fled. In the last one, though, through the slit of the curtain she glimpsed or thought she glimpsed a face inhuman and insubstantial, with fierce marble eyes. She passed it so quickly that she didn't make sense of it, didn't register what she'd seen—a floating form, a ghoulish countenance—except as an after-image, like something you can only see when you close your eyelids.

She and Diverus fell in behind a line of boys who were flooding into one dark doorway in particular. It took them down another flight of steps, easily as long as the stairs from the street. Footsteps and voices below echoed back up oddly as off of water, and sure enough the room they reached contained a broad pool in which a few boys were laughing and playing, as though what was happening in the paidika was a lark, nothing to concern them.

Beyond the pool, an iron gate hung open. Most of the boys and the sensible guests were escaping through it.

Outside, a narrow ledge ran in either direction. They were under the bridge, at ocean level. A few lights shone across the water, where another tower wall loomed, seeming almost close enough to touch in the dark. The water stank of rot.

The ledge was hardly wide enough for the two of them to stand shoulder to shoulder. To the left of the gate, boys had lined up, shivering, pressed to the wall of the bridge pier as if this was as far as they were able to come before terror incapacitated them. Their line trailed into the blackness of the bridge. The clientele on the other hand had all turned to the right and even now reached the end of the ledge and vanished. Diverus hesitated for a second, but turned and pursued the escaping clients. No one tried to stop him. Encumbered by various instruments in his hands and tucked beneath his arms, he could have done nothing to defend himself if they had. From the other direction a woman's voice called out, "Diverus!" and he went rigid. He glanced back then, first at Leodora, and then beyond, into the depths of the darkness beneath the span. His face twisted up as if he was wincing in pain.

Under his breath then, he whispered, "Goodbye, Eskie," and turned away again. Leodora glanced back, but no one had stepped out, and whoever had called couldn't possibly have heard him.

The clients had disappeared where the ledge ended, as if they'd stepped off into the ocean and evaporated, but it was an illusion. The ledge wrapped around the corner, to roughly carved steps, which led right up the side of the pier. To be sure, they were cracked and treacherous, offering barely enough purchase for both feet placed side by side, but the customers from the paidika climbed briskly up them, clustered bodies lambent in the moonlight. The musician and the puppeteer followed them.

Perhaps a third of the way up the side of the pier, the steps reached a landing of sorts. The landing, a broader platform with a rail around it, jutted off the backside of the tower, and the two of them lingered there to catch their breath. No one else was coming up behind them; Leodora gazed off across the ocean, where a single lantern's light glowed distantly. She turned back to find Diverus leaning far over the rail on the inside of the platform. She pressed around his shoulder to see what had so captured his attention, and fell upon an astonishing view: The underworld of the span of Vijganar.

Fires and embers glittered on dozens of levels, as far into the distance as she could see. From the look of it, the place ran the full width of the bridge. The glow from the fires suggested structures—an arch overhead and all manner of struts and supports on the far side of that arch, and even more platforms. She remembered that Ningle, too, had supports beneath it, columns of stone that propped up the great boulevards and buildings. But she had seen no one living beneath that span.

"That used to be my home," Diverus said.

"Where?"

"Somewhere in there. Someone else lives in it now. Or maybe they've moved on, too. That woman who raided the paidika is from here. What do you suppose she told them to get the authorities to act on her behalf? I should have stayed behind and exposed her, shouldn't I?"

"I don't know how you would have done that," she replied. "She was after you?"

"She wanted a cut of the profits I brought. I would have been trapped again if I'd stayed. He wasn't ever going to let me go." He sighed. "Poor Eskie. She *is* trapped." When she didn't ask him what he meant, he let the matter go. "I've never seen it like this, not from here. There'll be another landing above us, one they can step out onto from underneath."

As if to prove his point, a shout burst from above them, then another more like a scream, which grew abruptly louder. A body hurtled past.

Leodora sprang back from the rail. Diverus didn't even flinch. "I wonder," he mused, as if the killing going on above them were a mere inconvenience, "we might want to wait a bit. Let the two sides sort it out." Another body fell past, this one silent. He leaned over the edge, followed it down and then looked up. "The thieves are outnumbered. They couldn't have anticipa-ted so many all at once. They're used to couples sneaking off to hide, or their own sort fleeing from officials up above with what-ever boodle they've snatched. Easy marks." He tilted his head to one side. "I can't even tell you how I come to know that. I couldn't have known it back then, but someone must have said so, I must have heard it even though I was too dull to understand."

Leodora considered that they with their arms full of musical instruments would be "easy marks," too.

After minutes passed in silence, Diverus started up the second tier of steps, and she followed, wondering all the while why she inherently trusted the strange musician.

The second landing when they reached it was occupied

only by a corpse. Though masked, he wasn't one of the paidika's clientele. In the moonlight, a dagger hilt gleamed in his chest. Of the clients there was no sign. A small wooden ladder, nearly horizontal, reached from one of the inner platforms to the edge of the landing. Diverus shoved it away and it dropped, but swung below them from ropes and clattered against a lower level. Someone shouted a complaint.

Without a word, he continued his climb up. By now Leodora's legs ached, and she would have liked to sit and rest for an hour. It hadn't seemed, she thought, anywhere near this great a climb down through the tower. The smell leaking out from the underworld grew more intense as they ascended—a greasy, sour stink it was, too.

As they neared the bottom of the surface level, Diverus paused and pointed to where a makeshift platform butted up along the backside of the tower. They could have stepped right off the narrow stairs and into the underworld from there. "This is where I used to climb from. My mother took me up, many times. And Mother Kestrel, too, when she put me on the dragon beam."

"The dragon beam?"

"In the Bowl—it's where I learned how to play all of these, though I didn't know it at the time." He continued quickly up the steps, as if to be quit of the subject.

"How long ago?" she asked.

Over his shoulder he replied, "I don't know, really. Not years, I think."

Then he rattled up the last steps and through the rail to the surface. She found him waiting for her, alone. The clients had dispersed back into the lanes and streets of the span.

"You must tell me," he said, "why you chose tonight to come to the paidika."

"I was escaping from a situation. I thought, if I went there, I could elude someone."

"You're not addicted to the afrits then."

"Afrits," she repeated, and recalled the vaporous thing she'd glimpsed.

Her ignorance seemed to reassure him. He looked around. People strode past, but in every case led by someone with a lamp. He and Leodora alone stood in the shadows. "I must impose up-on you," he said. "I've nowhere to go, and I know no one up here."

Leodora said, "I can help. In fact, I can offer you employment of a sort that will make use of your talent." A light-bearer approached and she gestured him over. "Lead us to Lotus Hall," she said, and handed him a coin in advance, in good faith for the distance he must cover. He lowered his lantern on its pole to check the coin, then tucked it into his tunic and directed them to follow.

As they walked, Diverus said, "Would it be a good idea for me to play music? They might be looking for me, or at least listening. Word will travel."

She nodded. "Yes, they might. On *this* span anyway."

"We're going to another?" The idea seemed to take him by surprise.

"Between your troubles and mine, probably the sooner the better. Have you never been on another span?"

He shook his head. "And what is it you do, sir, if I may ask, that you have a use for me?"

"I tell stories," she replied, "which seems to have become a far more complicated occupation than I'd ever imagined."

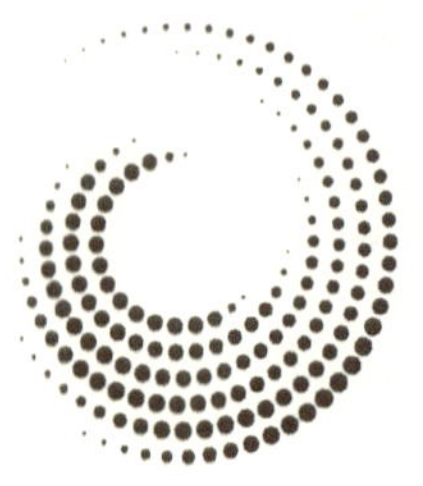

Chapter 4
New Spans For Old

Soter knew that Leodora had eluded Rolend the previous night by escaping from Lotus Hall. And he knew she hadn't yet returned by the time he fell asleep; but he'd no inkling that the booth concealed a new member of the troupe.

Pushing his way through the curtain at the rear, he found a boy asleep upon the undaya cases and concluded that he'd come upon a vagrant who'd chosen the darkness of the unattended booth to sleep off his drunk.

"Of all the damned cheek!" he bellowed, and lunged.

Diverus reacted by sleeper's instinct—he rolled away from the shout and fell off the cases. Soter banged his foot against a lute that hadn't been there the night before and he sprawled across the top case. The only thing he caught was the small nay flute that had been lying beside the boy. In pain and frustration he cursed and clutched his leg.

The commotion brought Leodora running—she had stayed up all morning to keep this very thing from happening. Naturally, Soter had entered the booth the one time she'd gone off to the latrine.

She pierced the entrance. Soter glanced back at her, pointed triumphantly where Diverus had been, and cried, "I caught this little thief pilfering from the puppet cases!"

Diverus stuck his head over the top of the case. "That's not true," he said.

Soter swung back and started to grab at him again.

Leodora said, "He's not a thief. He's a musician."

Soter answered, "Yes, I see that well enough now. But we don't need one."

"Don't need one? Who is it complains to me every night that we won't be a troupe until we have a *real* musician."

Soter recognized that he couldn't win an argument formulated on his own complaints, and changed his tack. "How do you know a scrawny street brat like this is a real musician?"

And so she told him the story of how she had eluded Rolend by escaping into a paidika in the leg of the northern tower of Vijganar. "Their claim to fame was their musician, who could play any instrument ever made."

"Him?" he asked, the word dripping with skepticism.

"That's right. They were raided and I ran with him. We escaped the raid and the paidika both, and I promised him I would hide him. His name's Diverus. You won't find a better musician anywhere in Vijganar. And for that reason I think it would be wise for us to leave Vijganar now, before the paidika's owner hunts us down."

"First of all," Soter replied, "we're not leaving here till I say so. You're drawing bigger crowds every night. Second of all, please don't tell me you believed twaddle of that sort, and from a brothel, no less! It's how they get them in the door, that story. *He's* some sort of magical musician? Lea, I am astonished."

"It's not—" she said, but Soter held out the nay flute and said, "Here, play something. Right now."

Diverus accepted it. He glanced at Leodora. She nodded for him to proceed. He stood up and put the flute to his lips. Even in the shadows of the booth, his transformation was evident. His eyes closed and his face twisted as if some invisible entity slid beneath his skin. Leodora shivered. Soter saw the change, too, and tensed as though against an impending blow. The song started softly, gently. It was so seductive, so lovely, that Soter's eyelids fluttered as if he were about to fall into a trance. Then in horror he identified the tune, and he lunged again at Diverus, crying out in anguish and tore the flute out of the boy's grasp. "What sort of treachery is this?" Betrayal filled his eyes like tears as he looked from Diverus to Leodora. "How do you know that song? You've no right—"

"I don't, sir!" Diverus protested. "I don't know what song it was, nor where it comes from. It just . . . it just comes."

"It's a divine gift," Leodora added. "The music pours

through him. I listened to him last night, I *saw* the effect his music had on the clients in that place. On me."

"Well, *that* song never pours out again, or he finds himself abandoned on the spot, do you understand?" Soter shouted. He made himself calm down, made his hands stop shaking by lowering them to his sides. He gripped the flute tightly. The choice of that song couldn't have been an accident, yet how could the boy have known it? Leodora didn't know. No one left alive knew nor could have found out. It was just a song played in an alley by a wizened and blind old musician. It had no significance to anyone but him. No, they couldn't have known. But something did. Something.

His hand rested against the undaya case, and he snatched it back now as if the leather had grown hot. For a moment he stared at it, his mind peeling back the cover, the layers of puppets, the false bottom, until he saw the chalk white thing lying there. In his vision, it had eyes that opened to stare back at him. The booth suddenly shrank. The sides closed in upon him and the ceiling of the hall was about to squeeze him. He didn't dare look up at it. He slammed the nay flute on the case, turned and dove past Leodora and out of the booth.

In the wide empty hall, he stood with his head back, gasping the air. Sweat soaked his neck, his body. "They don't know, they can't know," he whispered like a chant, one meant to reassure and protect himself.

He circled the booth then, putting distance between himself and the Coral Man most of all. He hardly noticed the cavernous room around him, the empty chairs, the tables, nor did he see the one figure watching him: a squat gnomish shape seated at a table in the second row, and which watched him from under its lowered head until he had almost passed by, then looked up and said, "Stand me a drink for old times, would you?"

Soter stopped in midstep as if time had paused. He came about slowly, warily. Purplish eyes, amused and sharp, met his own. "Grumelpyn?" he said, and drew closer. "By anyone's gods you haven't changed a day—it *is* you!"

"Well, if you'll recall, we age slower than your kind, we do. You've changed, of course, but not so's I wouldn't know you—I just never expected to find you traveling the spans again, old man. Not after—"

"Yes, not after that." He took a seat at the table across from the furtive elf. "Not my choice, really. I'd have been more than happy to stay tucked away forever. You'll remember that. Bardsham's girl, though—she's got his pulse, can't help but wander, and I couldn't very well let her wander off alone. Not after . . ."

"So, then, 'twas a daughter, the baby. Should have let us take her for a changeling, you should've. Your people wouldn't have known the difference, the parents were off the span, and the replacement child would've obeyed your every whim."

"I thought changelings were known to be cantankerous. Ungovernable."

"Lies," sneered the elf. "Lies and rumors put about by people who renege on their bargains."

Soter winced slightly at the criticism embedded in the comment. "Of course," he said, "now let me stand you that drink." He got up and wove his way around the tables and chairs to the kitchen where, conveniently for him, neither Nuberne nor Rolend was present. He filched a bottle from below the serving counter and carried it and two cups back to the table. The closer he got, though, the more he distrusted Grumelpyn's motives. He was not so damaged from drink that he didn't remember how he and the elf had parted. It was no cause for camaraderie.

While he poured, Grumelpyn chattered idly. "So, Bardsham's daughter. You're taking her north, I assume. Yes, of course you are. Came from the south of here and you can't go below that, can't go back that way." He sipped, musing. "She following in the old man's footsteps all the way, is she really?"

"Grumelpyn, she's better'n he was."

"Oh. My, my, you really should've swapped her, then. We like a good storyteller."

"Yes, for *dinner*."

"More lies. We don't eat children. Generally."

"All the same, I didn't swap her, so wishes are air." He raised his tin cup and clinked it against the elf's. "This bottle's on me. All of it." He leaned forward on his elbows. "Truth is, I need your help. I have to keep going north, like you said, but I don't remember the half of it any longer."

"Well, well. You need a map." He grinned with sinister delight, revealing unnaturally pointed teeth. "Fifteen years ago you left me to fend for myself against the Agents, and now you think to buy me with a bottle and get my help in the bargain, you do."

"You know that I couldn't have done a thing for you. You don't think I wanted to leave you? For cat's sake, man, I had to leave Bardsham, too. You think I took *pleasure* in it? I had to look after the child. I'd sworn!"

"Oh, yes, I'd forgotten. You weren't acting to save your own skin at all. You were thinking of Leandra's baby all the time. Dear, sweet Leandra about whom you could never say enough."

Soter nodded vigorously. "I was, absolutely, thinking only of the child. Why do you think I'm with her now? I could have abandoned her to the spans and had done with it, couldn't I?" He waved his hand about as if to wipe the air clean. "Look here, I'll pay you for your trouble."

The elf snorted and set down his cup. "As soon accept coin from a sea slug, I would. I only came here because I had to see for myself if you were connected to this phenomenon called Jax. And now I knows all about it. Wonder who the highest bidder would be for information on Bardsham's offspring. Think there's anyone left who cares, do you?"

"Soter?"

At the sound of Leodora's voice behind him, Soter stiffened. Grumelpyn leaned around him, smiling, to look at her where she stood. "My, my," he said, "I know whose daughter you are. Even with that mask, I'd know. You've red hair beneath your hood, I'm sure."

Leodora responded to his ingratiating overture by warily glancing at Soter's back, but he remained hunched over his drink as if unaware of her. The elf rose and extended a hand that ended in long and curling nails.

"You're an elf," she blurted.

He glanced about himself, at his torso and arms. "Why, so I am. Imagine that. I must have been transformed." He gave Soter a look of scorn. "Why didn't you tell me?"

She blushed. "I'm sorry, that was rude. I didn't mean—I meant only that we haven't encountered any elves before, on the other spans."

He waved away her embarrassment. "I'm surprised not at all. Few of my kind travel this run of spans. Except for your neighbors to the north, Hyakiyako, these spans are not partial to the elvish, they're not. And even Hyakiyako just wants us in their parade." He glanced around the room as if expecting to find some enemies. "If word of your extraordinary performances hadn't got out, why, I'd have never imagined old Soter was on the spans again. I was just saying." He leaned forward for emphasis. "Rumor has it, you're the essence of an accomplished performer. I'm so looking forward to a few performances, myself."

Leodora felt shy, excited and proud all at once, jumbled enough that she stood tongue-tied.

"Yes," Soter said suddenly. "A shame we're not staying longer." He craned his head around until he could see her, then to the elf added, "Tonight's our final performance here. Heading north in the morning, in fact. To your friendly Hyakiyako."

"We are?" she asked.

"My misfortune then," replied the elf, and he gave Soter another sly look. Then he brightened. "At least I'll have the privilege of seeing you once before you go. Do you know any elvish stories, by chance?"

"Some. Soter taught me them."

"Then they'll be corrupted, no doubt." He chuckled. "But still worth seeing, I'm sure, if you would humor an old troll like me and perform one."

"Of course. I'll put one in early." She seemed discomfited, as if the suggestion troubled her.

"And I thankee for it."

Soter could feel her staring at him still. "Is something the matter, Lea?"

"The musician—he really didn't know the song, he wasn't lying to you. I watched him play last night."

"Of course you did."

"So, you'll let him be if I go off to sleep awhile. I won't come out and find him absent."

"Really, Lea. Where do you get such ideas?" He smiled at Grumelpyn, but the elf continued to smirk over what was being revealed in the conversation. "Of course he can stay. Didn't I say we needed a musician?"

"I—" She fell silent.

"What is it, child?" There was something wrong, he knew it.

"I'm—I must be tired, that's all. I dozed awhile after we got back this morning, before you were up, and now it feels to me as if I dreamed this . . . this moment. Only your friend wasn't here. Someone else was."

He turned as far as he could then, to see where her troubled eyes looked; and though she looked where Grumelpyn sat, Soter could almost see what she was seeing. Her expression told him everything. He took small consolation in knowing that he was not the only one pricked by that presence. He wondered if he could get her to cast it back into the ocean.

"I'm going to sleep awhile. I was up all night till now."

The price of mischief, he thought, *no different than her father in that, either.*

"You won't let me oversleep. You'll wake me in time."

He knew that she knew he would. The tension in the questions intimated a fear of sleep. He said, "Of course, dear."

As she left, he watched the elf following her with his gaze. A slow smile spread across Grumelpyn's face. "Remarkable," he said. "Under that tunic, is she built anything like her mother? That would be something. Oh, what a shame no changeling—"

"Enough!" Soter slammed his palm against the table. "You are too bold." Grumelpyn closed his eyes and gave a small laugh. "Hate me all you like," Soter said, "but you leave her out of it. She's the reason things went the way they did, believe it as you like, or don't."

"Better than her father—is she really?"

Soter nodded warily.

The elf leaned back, stretching. "So . . . a map." He grabbed the bottle and poured himself another drink. "You waste your time, Soter, you really do. Even if I draw you a map—which I will do for a price—you won't be able to linger anywhere. Word of her is spreading like blood in water. I wasn't even on this span nor the next and I heard about the shadowplays of Jax. If I hear, then *they* will hear. Sooner or later. They travel everywhere after all. You've already lingered too long on Vijganar for your own good. Or are you perhaps hiding out from more than one party? Someone else looking for her, is there?" He held up a hand as if to ward Soter off. "Please, don't tell me, since you'll lie." He sipped softly a moment. "Tell me instead how you propose to avoid them."

"Let me worry about that. All I want from you is a map. No threads to link you to me, nothing to put you in jeopardy unless you're fool enough to sign it. I couldn't harm you if I wanted to. Now, can you help?"

Grumelpyn tapped his nails against his cup, the sound like a skittering cockroach. "You mentioned you would pay."

Soter glared, but when he placed his hand on the table, trapped beneath it were three gold coins. He slid them forward.

Grumelpyn reached out and patted the hand like a cook testing the plumpness of a chicken. At the touch of his chitinous nails, Soter snatched his hand back, leaving the money. "All right, then," Grumelpyn sighed. "For *her* I will do it. She is sweet despite who raised her, and I wouldn't wish to see her go the way of her mother. By the way, how *did* her mother go? Was she screaming?" His smile widened, eager and repulsive.

Soter lifted his cup and drained it, closing his eyes and then avoiding Grumelpyn's. "I get the map tonight, then."

"That's suitable. After her final performance. I would, perhaps, accompany you north myself, only I'm bound for southern spans. Emeldorra."

Soter blanched at the name of that fateful span. It was where he had last seen Grumelpyn—and Bardsham—fifteen years before. The taunt was too much for him. He pushed back his chair and stood. "Fine," he said. He strode away.

"Don't forget to wake her," called the elf. "Or perhaps I could return one of these coins to you and you'd allow *me* to wake her, hey?" He chuckled.

Soter rounded the booth and pushed inside the back.

Diverus flinched where he lay atop the cases, but Soter waved away his fear. "I'm not here to eject you, so you can relax, boy. For now, anyway."

He moved to the rear corner and sat on the floor. He pressed a hand to his forehead. "Gods and ghosts conspire," he said, but not to Diverus. It was a comment seemingly directed at the floor.

The sordid conniving elf was, regrettably, right—they needed to move on. They couldn't afford to stay more than a night or two anywhere. The money was good, better each night—that was the trouble. He'd gotten greedy, remembering how things had been with Bardsham. He couldn't afford the luxury of staying here anymore. The troupe of Jax needed to catch up with the gossip, pass it by. And he'd thought he was being so careful. . . .

It wasn't until they were standing in front of Vijganar's north tower the next morning that Leodora glimpsed the map for herself. She was played out after a second night of little sleep, following a triumphal performance, and did not at first realize what Soter was doing.

The boulevard ended by dividing into three tall tunnel mouths—three routes for leaving the span. She hadn't imagined there would be more than one. All other verges between spans had served but one course. She could only wonder why this one should be different.

Soter set down the case he carried at the side of the road and walked away, parallel to the three exits as if to get a better view of each. This left Leodora to look after their belongings and Diverus. She had dressed him up in blue robes and a turban incrusted with bright if cheap glass jewels, and darkened his face with a stain made for the puppets. He looked now like a member of a royal household and nothing like the boy who'd only escaped from bondage the day before; nevertheless, by forcing him to stop in front of the lane that led to the very paidika from which he'd escaped, Soter had him all but crawling under the lid of one of the puppet cases. He crouched behind them and placed the knapsack containing his instruments on his lap to obscure himself further. Leodora recognized where they were, too. She considered Soter either ignorant of the location or callously indifferent for this unnecessary pause, and she went after him. Whether or not he wanted Diverus with them, he wasn't going to strand them at the mouth of this particular lane till someone out of the paidika finally recognized their truant musician and dragged him back into that subterranean pit. It was conceivable they might remember her, as well. Although she had revealed her true identity to Diverus after their final performance—it would have been impossible to keep the truth from him without trapping herself in the identity of Jax eternally—she had, at Soter's insistence, set out this morning in Jax's clothes, "just to be safe." He hadn't elaborated on what she would be safe from.

Soter had his back to her and, as she came upon him, she saw he had unfurled a brown parchment with darker brown ink covering it in swirls and lines like veins across a leaf, but also in words, names, a few of which she recognized. Ningle for one.

"Do you not know where we're going?" she asked.

"I—" he swept the document from sight and turned

defiantly to face her. "What do you mean, sneaking up on me like that? Of course I know where we're going."

"At what point did you begin consulting a map, then? You didn't use one before this—you made a great show while in your cups of knowing the way across all spans—so don't pretend otherwise."

It was exactly what he'd intended to claim, and her rebuke left him without a response.

She glanced back at Diverus and the cases. "We have to go now, Soter. He'll run away pretty soon if the paidika's master doesn't come upon him first. Don't you appreciate where you've arrested us?"

"You should never have brought him along," he squawked. The complaint wearied her even more, but she did not want to be drawn into another protracted argument. Instead, she gestured at the three tunnels.

"Which one, Soter? If you don't tell me, I'll pick up my case and take whichever one I want and damn the consequences."

"The first one," he answered. She turned away with a dismissive abruptness, and would have been content with the answer had he not added, "Grumelpyn gave me the map."

She stopped. Without turning back, she asked, "The elf just happened to have a map for you?"

"I paid him for it."

"Why?" She glanced darkly back at him.

Soter drew his arms against his body as if expecting her to assail him with her fists.

"Why?" she asked again more insistently.

"Because," he answered, then hung his head, "I can't remember." He brought the map into view again and smoothed it open. "We played so many spans, your father and I. More than once, some of them many times. I don't know any longer what comes next, whose establishment we performed in, who put us up, even what sort of span it was. It's all jumbled up, you see. Grumelpyn—his elvish span is way to the north, dozens of spans out. So I knew he would be familiar with everything in between, because he's just traveled it. He drew this for me for the price of some drinks, before the performance." He gazed at her with wounded eyes. "You simply don't trust me enough."

"I don't trust you at *all*."

"Leodora—"

"When you complain that we need a musician, and I find

possibly the most remarkable one in the whole world and you say get rid of him; when you make secret appointments with old friends and acquire secret maps; when you argue with the ghost of my mother as if she's in the room with you—what should compel me to trust you?"

He gaped at her. "How did you—"

"I've overheard you. I have my secrets, too, Soter." She continued back to where Diverus cowered and helped him up. Then she lifted her case, and Diverus his satchel, and the two of them entered the first tunnel, leaving the remaining case behind.

Soter folded the map and tucked it into his shirt. Well, she had heard him and there was nothing for it now. But better she should think he was losing his wits than that he tell her the truth. One small lie covered so well the larger and more fearsome ones.

The tunnel had its own seigneur, who lived in a boxlike house in the middle of the passage, from which he controlled the flow of traffic and collected a fee from every traveler. The fees for crossing varied from span to span. More ancient and decrepit spans often had no collectors at all any longer—it was a position that tended to be handed down through families, and families could die out—while on richer spans that considered themselves favored by the gods, the fees might be exorbitant. Soter had dreamed from time to time of being a seigneur. It seemed such an easy life.

Leodora and Diverus waited at the seigneur's booth for Soter to catch up. A few other people passed them without acknowledging, paid their money and kept going, in one direction or another, their footfalls echoing away. The far end was nothing more than a ball of bright light without details, as if the tunnel led straight into the sun.

Soter set his case down beside them and walked up to the booth.

The seigneur—his beaky, chicken-like head protruding from the window on a scrawny neck—named his fee. Soter put a hand to his chest and stepped back. "Outrageous," he grumbled. "That's twice what it used to be to come through here."

Observing this performance, Leodora commented, "I thought you couldn't remember this span."

"I didn't say I didn't remember *everything*," he replied, using umbrage to disguise that he'd been caught out, but he could see that she was skeptical of everything he said. When, he wondered, had she decided not to trust him? And why? If she had heard him talking to Leandra's ghost, that had to have been back on Bouyan, because she hadn't haunted him since they'd left the island. He wasn't sure—he had never been sure—if his ghosts were real or just the manifestation of his darkest moods, his memories, his betrayals; but thus far no ghosts had followed him. Nothing was coming after him. It was what lay ahead that he feared. He couldn't tell Leodora without having to explain why, which he could never do, for she—like her mother—would steer straight for the heart of doom instead of turning away. She would seek out Chaos, and nobody would escape this time. A thousand little lies, a million tiny betrayals were infinitely better than that. As long as he adhered to that goal, perhaps the ghosts would leave him alone, let him be. He was protecting the child as best he could—what he'd sworn to do. If she defied him, finally, what more could be expected of him? He couldn't make her dispense with this musician boy. He couldn't tell her the real reason she shouldn't be adding to the troupe. Certainly, he had said all along that they needed a good musician, but he couldn't have predicted she would find someone like Diverus, someone into whom the gods had fed their magic. Gods' magic was always capricious if not openly treacherous. All the same, she was supposed to be collecting stories on the spans, not *people*. He couldn't have known. Stuck, he was stuck now, trapped by his own words, which hadn't seemed dangerous when he'd uttered them. The performances *did* need a good musician; but that was something for *him* to find, not her. He'd been guiding Leodora, cautiously, carefully. How then had he lost control so easily? It was all the fault of that woman, Rolend, chasing after the great puppeteer, a celebrity she could bed. He'd made light of the pursuit when he should have helped Leodora fend her off. Such an insignificant mistake. He'd been in his cups, she couldn't expect him to be ready to offer advice on *every* little detail of their journey. She was the one who was late, who vanished for hours and hours. But, no, she'd taken refuge in a paidika and found a damned freak, touched by gods. . . .

He glanced up. They were staring at him—both she and the seigneur—and he realized he'd been standing there tangled in thought for an eternity. With a show of resentment, he paid the fee, and then marched ahead, leaving Leodora and Diverus to catch up.

The dank, echoing tunnel smelled of salt and mildew. Whitish crystals grew like veins across the walls.

As he neared the end of the tunnel, he set the case down again, and then sat on the edge of it and waited. There was no point in petulance. He wasn't about to abandon her, however angry he might be. She made him angry because she didn't understand his motives, and that was how it had to be.

Finally she came up beside him and set her own undaya case down beside his.

"This span—"

"Hyakiyako," he named it.

"You do remember being on it?" she asked.

He heard in her voice that she was trying to make temporary peace with him. He replied, "Most certainly. You can't go farther north without traveling through, therefore we played it."

"But you've no memory of it?"

"My dear," he answered with exaggerated patience, "I tried to explain, we played *hundreds* of spans for *thousands* of audiences. They all bleed together after a while, and one is much like any other. You must remember that your father and I didn't start out from Bouyan, we didn't start out anywhere near it."

She kept her own counsel on this point. Her opinion, based upon the four spans she'd seen thus far, was that no two of them were remotely alike, even where their attributes had melted together. The few stories she'd pried from tellers on the previous two spans, while they shared common themes, elements, images, were also as distinct as if the spans had been isolated from one another for centuries. She did not know why this was, but she had already established that the pattern existed. The "Ashgirl" of Merjayzin became the "Dustgirl" of Yorba. While they both wed a prince in the end, the Dustgirl drowned her stepmother first, while the Ashgirl's sisters mutilated their feet in a desperate attempt to displace her.

"Do you know *any*thing about this span at all?"

"I do *know* my job, you know," he replied. She interpreted his irascibility as a reaction to believing she was attacking him. There was no point trying to convince him otherwise, so she let him go on. "I asked Grumelpyn last night. He travels the spans much the way I used to, and he knows the best routes and places to lodge. Of course I thought I would have more time—a few more *nights* to buy him drinks, talk over old days, find out everything."

"Yet you made the choice to leave, after telling me we were staying. What did he tell you?"

He pretended with his answer not to know what she meant. "That there's some kind of parade at night here. Not every night apparently, but he couldn't say why or which nights or what it means that there's a parade, because he was strongly advised to stay inside while it was going on, or else never be seen again."

"A parade." She glanced back at Diverus. He sat with his head down. The bejeweled turban and the tunnel shadows made him look considerably older than he was. With his bag of instruments thrown over one shoulder, he might have been a wandering mystic guiding two travelers away from the fleshpots of Vijganar. It would have convinced *her,* in any case. He caught her look, and shook his head as if to say that he knew nothing of Hyakiyako. Of course, so insular had been his life, he hadn't even known the name of the span he'd been living under.

"I'm afraid that's all I can tell you," Soter insisted. "At least we should have a captive audience—I mean, if they can't go out, then they'll be wanting some entertainment while they're trapped inside. Can't be bad."

"Can't it?" she asked but more to herself than to him. What sort of parade, after all, took place if everyone was dissuaded from participating? If the people all stayed indoors, then who was marching in the parade? Grumelpyn's story made no sense. Whatever the answer, the three of them could not remain inside the tunnel. They had to go on.

She stood, hefted the undaya case by its strap once more, and continued walking.

By the time they reached the end of the tunnel, they were shielding their eyes against the light, like Meersh the trickster upon his return from the land of the dead. And surely, the world had presented no stranger sight to him than the span of Hyakiyako.

Vertical banners hung from poles up and down every street. The symbols painted on them meant nothing to Leodora.

Unlike the spans she'd seen before, there were hardly any tall structures on this one. The buildings were low to the ground, and wide, with double roofs—a smaller one on top of the main one, as if it were necessary for every building to represent itself in miniature above itself. Here and there even odder structures that looked to her like crookedly stacked cups poked up at the sky. Far down the span, probably in the middle, one great gateway dominated. It was a thing of two dark angled pillars and two curving crosspieces that ran the width of the span, the way most of the towers did. It was misty in the distance, impossible to tell what lay beyond the gate; but if that was the halfway point, then Hyakiyako was a very long span indeed. There would be no climbing that gate either.

She glanced to her left and discovered more extraordinary things about the new span: it abutted a hillside. The other two tunnels gave onto separate branches of the span, which ran parallel at first, but slowly curved back toward the main one on which they stood; each of the stems was narrower than this. Where they connected to the broader span lay somewhere in the haze, near or beyond the great gate. However, instead of there being nothing but ocean between the branches, there were hillocks rising above the level of the rails and then dipping down again out of sight.

Beyond the third branch, she could make out the crest of the largest hill and upon it a single tower—another of those crooked cup stacks.

It was the first time she'd seen a span that incorporated a landmass, although she'd heard of such places—Soter had taught her stories that could not have unfolded upon bridges, and thus implied the existence of land; and Bouyan could not have been the only island linked with a span, else it would have been celebrated as a novelty instead of shunned as a backwater that nobody cared to visit.

Soter only commented as if to himself, "The right-hand tunnel is the main thoroughfare. Grumelpyn was absolutely right. We can trust this map of his, I think. Good, good."

Ahead of her on the streets, people milled about, dressed in jackets and robes that seemed finer than those worn on Vijganar. A man who seemed to be acting as gatekeeper on this end of the tunnel bowed to them most formally. He wore a long dark coat, and he said something incomprehensible as he gestured for them to enter the span. Clearly, he wasn't asking for money, but was welcoming them. It was a completely alien gesture. And then, suddenly, it wasn't.

As had happened previously when she stepped onto a span, everything changed for Leodora in a moment. The foreignness of the place evaporated like a sundog. The symbols upon the nearest banner now read, quite obviously, "The Spectre of Nikki Danjo." Behind her, Diverus asked, "What does it mean, do you know?" She glanced back to confirm that he was staring at the same banner.

"It's a story," she told him, and then to Soter added, "You taught me a version of it."

"That's right," Soter agreed. "A ghost story."

"It means we have something to perform tonight," she said. "Assuming we can find a *place* to perform."

"We'll have a place. I will find us a venue." He stared at the sky and with affected injury said, "The child does not trust me."

Leodora set down her case. She decided to tease rather than confront him now that they were here. "The *child*," she said, "has seen you drunk."

At this the one-man welcoming committee roared with laughter. Soter opened his mouth as if to tell the man to be quiet, but seemed to recognize immediately that it was pointless. He hefted the undaya case again and marched into Hyakiyako.

The banner over the door read, "Eat this and have a cup of tea," and beside these words was the drawing of a circle.

Soter reacted to it as if he'd been hunting for the very phrase, and lurched suddenly across the cobbled road to the wide steps up to the porch that appeared to girdle the building. A pedicab for a single passenger ran past, cutting him off from the other two. It slowed as the puller considered Leodora and Diverus, asking a question with his eyes. She shook her head, and the cab trundled on.

At the entrance beside the steps, Soter had left his case and removed his shoes, which sat next to a row of others, giving the impression that a dozen people had been lifted from their footwear and vanished upon the threshold.

Leodora placed her own shoes beside his, set her case beside the one he'd carried, and then sat upon the two of them. She stretched her neck and flexed her knotted shoulders. As her muscles found their limits and her vertebrae cracked, she groaned luxuriously. "We could use one of those pedicabs," she remarked to Diverus. "Put the cases in instead of us, and pull them along. It would have to be easier than these straps."

"We can trade if you like," he suggested. "My instruments aren't nearly so heavy."

Before she could reply, Soter burst onto the porch. "We have lodging!" he proclaimed. "*And* a courtyard in which to perform."

"A courtyard?"

"It's their custom here. The entertainments are held outside but inside." He clambered down the three wide steps, shooed her to her feet, then grabbed his case by its strap.

"Would this have something to do with the parade?" she asked.

"I wouldn't know. I've no memory of the place, though we must have played here. Of *course* we played here." He stood with one foot on the porch, the other on the step, a majestic pose as he looked at the city around him and added, "I think."

"Maybe you went some other way?" she suggested.

"How? There is only this one span linking Vijganar to other places north, and thus it's been since Ningle-in-the-Clouds. Haven't you paid attention to *anything*?"

Her temper lit in response to his hectoring tone, but she capped it before it ignited. "*You* said," she stated with forced calmness, "that you didn't begin at Ningle when you traveled with Bardsham. You began somewhere else, you said. Somewhere—"

"South," he interrupted. "We came from well *below* Ningle, Lea. Traveled for years, you understand? Years before we crossed paths with your mother. Took boats between spans. Years and never the same span twice. That's how big, how vast, this world is. Places down there are most inhospitable. Don't take to storytellers like up north here—never mind what they'd say to a girl in masquerade. Thought we were thieves, stealing part of their lives and like that—telling their stories was taking their souls, keeping them, taking them with us. You didn't *want* to go that way, which is why we didn't go that way. It's why I have a map now. I'm your guide, Lea, you have to trust that I know what I'm doing."

"You know what you're doing but you don't remember what it is." She glared at him, only to find that she could not maintain her anger in the face of his ebullience. "All right," she said with a sigh, and perched again upon her case, flexing her toes, and considered that his justification had inadvertently provided her with more information than he'd given her since leaving Ningle. Why, she wondered, hadn't he told her about the south before, even back on the island? He'd told her so many things about traveling with Bardsham, but she realized now that they were only cursory things, events without details, as if he hadn't wanted her to take an interest in life on the spans. He had specifically avoided telling her stories about her parents. He'd answered questions when confronted, but he had never volunteered anything. How had he manipulated her for so long, teaching her to perform stories without ever telling her the one she most wanted to know?

She had to know about the south. Had they gotten into trouble there? Had her mother been with them then? Had something happened on the southern spans that led to . . . led to—and once again, she didn't know, did she? She didn't know the specifics at all. Soter couldn't be pinned down and her aunt and uncle would not even speak of her mother. He owed her this story. He owed it to her right now.

She would have demanded it, except that Soter had left her musing, entered the building and disappeared into its depths.

Leodora wearily stood, lifted the case and climbed up the steps. The slickly polished floor of the porch like unbroken water reflected the case and herself upside down.

Diverus made no move to follow her inside. He had watched the expressions of frustration and puzzlement cascade across her features, but he remained unmoved by her resolve, as he was ignorant of it. Further, the rows of empty shoes bothered him. "Come on," she said, but in response he only shifted his weight uncertainly from leg to leg. "Diverus," she inveigled. It was clear she would leave him outside if he didn't climb the steps right now. Reluctantly, he slipped off his own shoes, placing them against hers, then climbed up beside her.

"I just play music," he said, as if that explained something.

"Yes. And tonight, it's in here." She lifted her puppet case. Side by side, they went in.

The glossy floors extended all the way into the depths, making the place seem huge, reflectively doubling the height of the translucent wall panels. The light melting through them rendered the interior into a state of permanent, golden dusk. People sat cross-legged on the floor at low tables, eating—at least it was her impression that they were eating—and drinking. They remained no more than shapes, lumps in silk tucked into corners and alcoves of which there seemed to be an impossible number. She wondered how they could see well enough to know what they were eating. Or maybe they didn't care. She couldn't tell if they were watching her, or even whether they noticed her. Perhaps not, if they couldn't identify more about her than she could of them. She might have been nothing more than the scent of barbecued eel, collecting for an instant above the tables.

Then out of the shadows the proprietor emerged, coming right up to them—a small man with crooked teeth and a sloping forehead, not much hair, and bright, eager eyes. Like two smooth white gems in that dusky light, his eyes glittered. "Yes, you come, you come," he said. He plucked at her sleeve, at Diverus. "You both come!" He tugged them still deeper into his establishment.

It hadn't looked all that impressive from the front, but "Eat this and have a cup of tea" proved to incorporate more rooms in its depths than she might have imagined. She soon realized that they were walking around a central area, the source of the wan light beyond the screens, and guessed that it must be Soter's courtyard. At the point she decided she had been led through a complete circuit, the proprietor abruptly turned and pushed back a screen, revealing another room, this one with mats on the floor.

There, seated beneath a low table, Soter twisted around as they entered. He held a small cup in one hand, and a small pitcher in the other, caught in the act of pouring. "About time," he said. "I'm famished."

The meal proved to be sumptuous and exotic. Neither Leodora nor Diverus had ever tasted anything like it, but once sampled, they could not imagine never having it again. When she raised the question of the central space they had seemingly walked around, Soter agreed that it was the courtyard where they would perform. "It is both outdoors and protected from the parade. Oh, yes, Mutsu told me about the parade. It's a horrifying thing, to be avoided at all costs. Your very life could be forfeit."

"Mutsu. You remember his name?"

"Naturally." He sipped his tea under her critical gaze, which exerted a kind of pressure on him. He set down his cup. "The truth is, he came up to me, called out *my* name and said, 'Don't you remember me? I'm Mutsu.' So, there. He remembers *me*. All I remembered was the banner. Satisfied?"

"For once," replied Leodora.

They ate awhile in stiff silence after that, until Diverus asked: "What happens now?"

"Now," said Leodora as she stepped around a cart peddling fruit, "we hunt for stories."

"Soter doesn't come?"

"No. He makes arrangements, asks questions, tries to find out if there are other places on a span we should play, promotes us to the local people."

"He angers you," Diverus stated.

She eyed him askance. They walked through a bazaar of stands, most sporting bright awnings. The smells of fish and confections mixed with more human, bodily smells. It all reminded her of Ningle and her childhood, back when her uncle had been clement. Those memories were intertwined with Soter, too. "He angers me because he lies," she replied. "I don't always catch him out, but the ones that I do only make me assume he's lying the rest of the time, too."

He changed the subject: "How do you hunt for stories, then?"

"Well—" she glanced around— "you look for signs that stories are about."

"Signs," he repeated with evident confusion. The confusion wasn't his alone, either, for in truth she had little experience looking for stories. Prior to arriving on Vijganar Soter had been too nervous to let her go off on her own for very long, and when she could sneak off at all, she'd climbed the bridge towers. Yorba had been the first place she'd asked about a story and been given one, by a group of workers who'd been mortaring a building. That was the Dustgirl's tale.

A palanquin crossed their path. Four men hefted it by two poles, which rested upon their shoulders. A woman's silhouette was just visible behind the gauze curtains.

Leodora tilted her head at the passing vehicle. "There. Like them."

"The palanquin?"

"Not the palanquin itself—but the carriers. If you could spend time with them, there would be stories in it for you."

"Why not the woman hidden behind the curtains?"

"First, she would be reluctant to tell a complete stranger very much. Second, her carriers would tell me all about her because they're paid to transport her but also to be blind and dumb about it. They'll have seen things. They would want to talk because they're not supposed to. They carry her *and* they carry her story."

"I see. That is, I think so."

She grinned. "I'm making this all up." Doubt clouded his expression, and her smile grew wider. "The truth of it is, so far anyway, stories seem to find me."

"The way mine did?"

"Exactly. I didn't attend the paidika in search of a story, but I found an extraordinary one that even has elements in it from other tales I've been taught by Soter. Your life up till now is a story."

"So, he *does* know something."

"Quite a lot," she admitted, and stepped through an open space between two stalls selling various aromatic kernels, the combined smells making her nose twitch as if she might sneeze. "But I think he withholds far more than he tells. When he was training me, that was helpful because he forced me to knit stories together out of scraps. As a test."

Diverus was thoughtful for a while after that, and soon they passed the stalls and the crowd thinned, at which point he asked, "How can you be sure that the tests are over?"

She had no ready answer to that.

Ahead, there lay a park lined with intricately shaped trees and shrubs. Some looked like exotic animals. Others were either abstract or imitations of things she had never seen. In the middle of the park, a group stood clustered beneath one tree, watching two figures in their midst. The two were engaged in a game of some sort, sitting opposite each other across a square board, with the rest ringing them as though they represented the height of excitement.

Diverus followed Leodora through the park. If the group was her ultimate goal, she took the most circuitous route to arrive there—pausing to contemplate the displays of flora, which he had to admit were remarkable: one bush had been sculpted into a flock of pigeons just leaving the ground. The fronds that represented the outstretched wings even seemed to be shaped into feathers. The artist had cleverly linked them so that from any angle some of them looked completely separate from the rest.

Eventually they arrived at the game. Members of the group glanced their way. One nodded in so formal a manner that to Diverus it was the equivalent of a bow. That man had a narrow spear-shaped beard growing off the point of his chin. He turned his attention back to the game immediately but as if his look had been a signal, the people to either side of them edged away to give them space to join in.

The two players hadn't acknowledged any of this. One was a small, thin man with a shaved head save for the wide stripe of red hair that hung from the back of his skull. He would have been the most striking member of the group were it not for the second player, who had the long-snouted head of an animal, completely white, and who sat beneath a strange ball of light. Fist-sized, it floated just above his head. Diverus touched Leodora's shoulder, his eyes wide. She understood his startlement, and whispered to him, "Kitsune. A fox-trickster."

The kitsune gazed intently at the cross-hatched board and the array of small stones dotting it, as if the stones might change position if he looked away. If there was a pattern there, neither Diverus nor Leodora could fathom it.

The stones—some light and some dark—looked as if they'd been polished by the sea, like small stones and shells that washed up on the beaches of Bouyan all the time—in fact some of the white "stones" proved to be small shells. The aggregate of dark and light remained obscure to Leodora even as two more stones were laid, one by each of the players.

With the kitsune's placement of the next dark stone, some of the watchers exchanged knowing glances as if something significant had occurred. The fox-player picked up a group of the lighter stones from the board, placing them in the lid to a small clay pot at his side, and she gleaned that he had surrounded them somehow, and thus won them. Even as he collected the "dead" stones, she noted, his black eyes remained locked on the board, his expression hard and his whiskers bristling. She had the sense that he was not certain he'd made the best move. The excitement wasn't necessarily in his favor.

The other player picked a white shell from his pot and

held it a moment while he pointedly assessed the arrangement of the remaining stones. As if following his thoughts, the fox's seemingly permanent smile fell with resignation. He muttered something that sounded like "shimata." The light stone was placed. The fox nodded. Then he and his opponent eyed each other. The dark-stone kitsune waved a furry hand once—he would not take his turn. The other placed another stone and the fox waved away his turn again. The group relaxed, and began to talk to each other as if picking up from an earlier conversation, which had been suspended by the game.

The two opponents clasped hands across the board.

Diverus leaned forward and asked, "What just happened? I couldn't see why they stopped—there are still lots of open lines."

"I don't know, either. Let's find out." She moved around some of the observers and approached the white fox. He stood now, stretching catlike, his orange-furred arms above his head, the loose sleeves of his gown falling down around his skinny arms to his shoulders. In that position he turned to them as they approached. Leodora repeated Diverus' question to him.

He gestured to the board, where three of the observers were bent over, and discussing, apparently, earlier moves in the game. "I arrived at the point where I could see the outcome. The battle is engaged where I removed his stones, and that and this other are the only two open areas remaining. But the most I will be able to do from this moment forward is expend more stones before he deprives me of them. If this were truly war, what a foolish general I would be to send more and more soldiers into a place where I know in advance they cannot prevail. Those already taken are lost, and I cannot have them back." He reached into his pot and raised a handful of black stones, opened his palm. "Should I not preserve these soldiers for another day and a better game? Only an idiot would do otherwise."

Leodora met his eye and smiled.

Diverus asked, "And you both knew this?"

"We both" —he sprinkled the stones back into his pot—"both concurred." He looked at them critically. "This is your first game, then," he said as he stepped away from the board.

"We've just arrived."

"Then you've made good use of your time. And if you stay for another, you will see how one arrives at such a crossroads."

He gestured behind himself where two other audience members were seating themselves and removing the stones, which they returned to their respective bowls.

"What is your interest here then, young travelers? You don't know *gō*, so is it the park, the sculptures?" He scrutinized Diverus closely. "You need more stain for your skin, perhaps?" Diverus tried to draw in upon himself.

"Stories," said Leodora.

The fox tilted his head and considered her again. "How so?"

"I collect stories," she said. "It's my . . . calling."

"That is a grand calling. But tell me, how do you keep them? Are they in a satchel? Do you have them tied up somewhere? Because the ones I know are disinclined to sit still."

She laughed at that. Behind the fox, the new players eyed her as if warning her not to laugh while they were engaged in play. "It's quite true, they don't sit still and they like to change shape."

"Exactly so," the kitsune agreed, and showed his prominent teeth in a smile.

The player behind him made a shushing sound.

"Ah," said the fox, "we must be polite and move away if we're to talk . . . or would you attend a game from the beginning? It's greatly rewarding."

She glanced at Diverus, to find him leaning around her in order to witness the opening moves. "All right," she told the fox, "one game and then stories."

"Excellent!" the fox replied, then he also turned to watch the game.

Unlike the previous game, the one they watched from the beginning ended with a definitive final move followed by the counting of open squares—or intersections, as the fox explained it—and captured stones. "Shells has won again," he proclaimed. "Next time, I'm going to insist on being shells."

Some of those nearest him laughed and slapped him on the shoulder. "You can't have shells, not with your white fur!"

He told Leodora, "They think I'd cheat. Imagine."

"Yes, ridiculous," she said, but she knew enough about kitsunes to side with the group.

As they were laughing and discussing the game with the

players, the fox waved his arms about and said, "My friends, my friends, these two are itinerant story collectors and would like to add to their collection from our repository. Does anyone have a story they would particularly like to tell?"

The entire group began to babble at once. She heard "ghost" and "tanuki" and "When Oiwa became a lantern!" before the fox waved them to silence once more. "Please, please, we can all tell our tales but not at the same time, if they're to make any sense of it."

"Well," began the one with the sharp beard, "tell her about the emperor who forgot about war. That has one of your kind in it!"

The fox waited to see if anyone objected to this choice. No one did. He asked, "Do you already have that story?" Leodora shook her head. "In that case, I shall tell it, and if there's time we'll pick another—or better, you can tell us one of yours." Everyone nodded enthusiastically and settled down to listen. The fox strode around as he declaimed, and acted the various parts.

≈ The Emperor's Tale ≈

Way over there (said the fox) our span touches land. You can see the hills and the tower that stands high up on the tallest hill. We call that land Kochokana, and legend has it that's because it looks so like the fluttering wings of a butterfly. The truth, however, is that we named it after a legendary empire. We don't know where this original kingdom is now—some say it's sunk beneath the sea, others claim it lies at the farthest end of the eternal bridge. Whatever the truth, at one time in our history, the original land called Kochokana was ruled over by a warlord. As this title suggests, he was a man who came to power by violent acts, and who maintained his power in like manner.

He had been trained in the strategy of war from earliest childhood. This art he had taken to, proving to be the greatest strategist ever seen in Kochokana. With his childhood full of political and martial matters, he had never spent much time with women; and because of his position—because he was being groomed to be, one day, an emperor, only two women in the empire were considered worthy candidates for his affections. It is not overstating things to say he disliked them both intensely. They were spoiled and shrill creatures and he would have nothing to do with them. Had his parents been alive, surely they would have arranged a marriage with one of these harpies regardless of her shortcomings, but as he was in charge of his life—ascending to the position of emperor at fifteen upon his father's death—he simply refused to choose between them, no matter how much members of his court wished to see him produce an heir. He determined not to marry a woman he did not love. And so his life might have been spent—in endless battles—but for an accidental visit he made to the royal gardens.

Now, it's often said by the most scurrilous of folk that we foxes are only out to trick humans. *Not so!* I tell you. We *kitsune* are the victims of jealousy and bad publicity. It's not our fault that we are handsome creatures, and that humans who fall in love with us fall very hard. It's not as if we do anything to cause it.

So was the case here. There was a *kitsune* who worked as a royal gardener. She lived alone in the woods beyond the fortress, but she liked the company of people, and so every morning she assumed human form and came to work in the gardens. In this way she was part of the populace but outside and away from prying eyes, which suited her very well.

And then one morning while she knelt at her task, she sensed someone observing her, and turned to discover the emperor standing there. Recognizing him, she could not move, didn't even dare to breathe. Dirt and sweat covered her, but the emperor saw only a beautiful maiden. Even beneath the dirt, her fox-magic shone.

The emperor knelt beside her in the black dirt. So close, he became transfixed by the beads of perspiration upon her lip, and by the scent of her body. "I've watched you," he told her, "as you wiped your brow, as you dug a hole for this flower and placed it, filled it in. You were so intent upon your work that you didn't even hear me." Then he leaned forward and began to dig the next hole for the next plant, beside her. She sat stupefied. Here was her emperor ruining his silk robes as he clawed in the dirt with her. He held up his hands, admiring the moist dirt attached to them, and began to laugh.

"I did not know," she said, "that our great lord enjoyed gardening."

He sat back on his haunches and replied, "Neither did I.

But that was because I didn't realize what a radiant blossom I would find here."

She blushed and lowered her face, but he put a finger to her chin and lifted her head to meet her eyes again. "Never bow to me," he said.

"But, my emperor—"

"No, no. Not emperor. Husband, rather, if you would allow it."

She stared at this handsome man, saw in his eyes the love he had for her, and fell in love with him in return there and then. She replied, lowering her head, "I would."

Because he was the emperor and she was his choice, they were married, and his advisors, as they wished to keep their heads, kept their opinions to themselves. But soon enough it became obvious to them that this was no ordinary affection. The daily reports delivered to the emperor went unread. When someone tried to read one of them aloud, the emperor, lying on a divan beside his bride, waved him to silence and ordered that those he'd put in charge should solve these matters, not bother *him* with them. The daily reports ceased, and soon only the chambermaids saw the emperor and his bride. They reported back to the advisors that he and his bride saw only each other, utterly moonstruck in their affection.

Now, amongst his advisors lurked two spies from the neighboring province of Maitake. They had infiltrated the court long before in order to look for opportunities for invasion. Delighted by the news that the emperor was completely lost in the fox-woman's charms, they'd no idea that she was a kitsune just as she had no idea that her love could doom a kingdom or rob her lover of his martial skills. The beauty of the situation was that, should anyone suspect them of plotting, they could blame the woman, even accuse her of being the real spy. The attack would appear to coincide with his bewitchment, and the minds of the men would forge the links to her.

When the weather turned warm, and the emperor and his court moved to his summer tower, far from the border with Maitake, the two spies sent word to their king that he must strike fast and furious. The emperor knew nothing of the attack when it came. His generals alone saved the empire from being overrun, and a border siege began.

In the summer tower, the siege was but an abstraction. The emperor's every thought was of his wondrous bride. When the generals petitioned for his advice in the siege, he told them, "Do what you feel is necessary," and then dismissed them. The greatest strategist their people had ever known had deferred to his generals and his advisors. The agents of Maitake gleefully reported that the empire must fall, and recommended more assaults on the borders.

The emperor's advisors held an emergency meeting. "Can we trust the generals?" one advisor asked.

"Their allegiance certainly. Their skill against this formidable foe is . . . untested, though. They've never had to concern themselves with strategy before. We cannot be certain of the outcome."

"We *need* him!" someone cried.

"He won't listen. We've implored, importuned. It means nothing. He moons over his lowly gardener and waves us away. What fools devised this enchantment? Did someone here provide some potion in the hopes of producing an heir? Well, he may well produce one, but shortly there will be nothing to inherit."

No one admitted anything but they all eyed one another distrustfully.

"There's no way to move him," said one. "The empire is surely doomed."

Then a young member of the entourage said, "Wait, there is a way I've just thought of."

"What?" cried the others—the two spies especially.

"If the empress were kidnapped by Maitake, then he would pay attention."

"Brilliant!" they all cheered, until someone said, "But how do we get someone from Maitake to do this?"

"Ha!" cried the young man. "We don't. We convince the empress to pretend to be kidnapped—for the good of our land."

"Brilliant!" they all cried again.

The difficulty was in approaching her, since she was rarely out of his company. Finally the advisors approached her personal bather and explained to the woman what she must say to her mistress. The girl complied, and finally the fox-woman understood the danger she had brought to these people. Yet she could not unmake his devotion any more than she could stop her own heart from adoring him.

She stole from the bath to meet with the advisors, and agreed immediately to go along with their deception.

The two spies, at some risk, hastily returned to Maitake and reported the plot. Seated before their lord and his advisors, they said, "Look at this opportunity! We can put our own men in place and kidnap her for real! Isn't that wonderful?"

The warlord of Maitake leaned forward and said: "Are you both idiots?" The two looked at each other. They didn't *think* so, but this was hardly the response they'd expected. "If we kidnap her," the warlord explained, "then her husband will bring all of his attention to bear upon our invasion and he'll destroy us, just as he will if he *thinks* she's been kidnapped. You fools must do everything in your power to *disrupt* this plot. She must not be taken by anyone!"

"But she's in on it," they complained. "She's going to help."

"Then," growled the warlord, "you have your work cut out for you. We launch our supreme attack in two nights, and he had better not be paying attention if you want to have a home to return to."

The two spies crept back into Kochokana, and debated about what they should do. They knew they couldn't stop the plot from unfolding. The empress would steal away in the middle of the night to the gardener's shed in the royal gardens where the emperor had found her, and his advisors and generals would swear she'd been kidnapped. If they said anything else, their true allegiance would be revealed. "I suppose it could be worse," said one. "How so?" said the other. "Well, the advisors could just have asked her to ask the emperor to destroy Maitake as a favor to her." His partner pulled at his lip. "Let's not mention that to anyone, all right?" he said. "But I do have an idea how we might undermine this without implicating ourselves."

The kidnapping of the empress went off without a hitch. She withdrew to the hut in the gardens of the main fortress. Her disappearance was "discovered" by one of her women and the alarm sounded. The generals importuned the emperor to gather his wits and help them destroy the enemy who had obviously taken her. But before they had even laid out their maps and battle plans, the emperor received a note from his queen, which told him to come to her at once in the gardener's hut, where she was safely awaiting him. "Oh, my heart's delight!" he cried and then raced from the tower, and rode across his land to the royal gardens. Sure enough, he found his wife in her bath and was so overcome immediately with lust for her, that they sent away the servants and made love there and then in the wooden tub. The battle plans remained untouched.

"How did he figure this out?" one advisor asked the group.

"He's too clever for us," replied a spy.

"No, she sent him a note. Didn't you see?"

"Why would she do that?"

"Maybe she's an agent of Maitake," one of the spies suggested.

"Is that possible?"

"What other explanation is there?" the other spy asked. "The spell must have been her own."

"What can we do? The enemy's at the very gates! We need him now."

"Maybe," someone said, "we could have the spell removed."

"We don't know if there's a spell."

"There must be a spell."

"Maybe we could kidnap her again. For real this time."

"We can ask her to visit us. Can't we? And then say she was kidnapped on the way here."

"Will he believe a second kidnap plot?"

"Do we have a choice?"

They couldn't think of an alternative, these clever men, and so they sent a message to the empress. To their dismay, she answered that she would not attend. Instead, she commanded all of them to attend *her* at the gardener's cottage. At least, they thought, they might confront her in the emperor's presence. However, when they arrived, they found her alone.

"Where is the emperor?" they asked.

"I sent him off to war."

"You what?"

"As we were making love, he asked me what I wanted most in the world, and I told him that I wished to see him victorious over his enemies." She unfolded a slip of paper and placed it in front of them. "He has more enemies than he knows. He tells me everything, you see. He keeps no secrets. He's too good a man for secrets. I wish to do likewise, yet I cannot help but keep secrets when such plans as yours are required. Such plans depend upon deception." She raised a hand to stop some of them from protesting. "Please, don't defend the need for subterfuge. The problem with your method is that it's quite easy to hide one deception inside another. This note, for instance. It's a note from me, telling him that I've hidden myself in this cottage in order to have an assignation with him away from all the business of the court, and that the kidnapping was merely a ruse.

"I wrote no such message. I was playing *your* game, gentlemen. By your rules. Therefore, one or more of you must be a traitor."

"Arrogant child! How dare you accuse us!" yelled one of the true traitors.

She stared at him, and the fox emerged from that black stare. The fox snapped its jaws at his throat. He clutched his neck with both hands and fell back a step. His neck was unmarked, but he knew that what he had seen would happen if he said one thing more; pale, trembling, he took his seat again while his partner looked on, fearfully mystified.

The fox woman made some slight gesture and suddenly four armed warriors stepped into the cottage. All of the advisors reacted with fear then; but she watched their expressions carefully for any that were more or less than they should have been. She already had the first traitor. And now the second one gave himself away as his hand slid into the folds of his robe, where his hidden dagger lay. But the soldiers merely blocked the exits. They made no move to attack.

"All of you are under house arrest," she said, "although I do now know the identity of at least two traitors in your midst." She made a point of looking at none of them, although they looked at each other.

"I love your emperor dearly, yet nothing he says to me can I trust, because it's threaded with magic, which is my fault. I told you that I would have no secrets from him, and I don't. He knows what you are about to know." Before their eyes, she transformed then. Her sweet face became that which the traitor had seen. Her hands and bare feet changed shape and grew soft with fur. The advisors gaped; even one of the soldiers drew back. She continued to speak as if none of this had happened. "Because of my negligence, not one word could I be sure came from his true heart. The magic of the fox people is such that we ensorcel you with our glamour whether we wish to or not. Now he knows my nature and when he comes back from this war, I will know his true feelings. In any case, this siege is about to end, and there's no need for further trickery. He will blast the enemy."

"What if, when he returns, he doesn't love you?" asked one of the advisors.

"Then," she replied with bowed head, "I shall be no different than you."

She directed the soldiers to arrest the two spies she had identified. If there were more than that, she knew they would now flee for their lives.

She left the advisors and retired to the tower to await her husband's return and his answer. The execution of spies would come later. The guilt of those men meant far less to the fox-empress than the true heart of her husband.

The kitsune let the image of her in her tower hover in the air a great long time before he drew another breath and relaxed, so that his audience knew the story had ended.

"And what did he say?" asked Diverus. "What did her husband decide?"

The fox glanced at Leodora, who was beaming. "That," she answered, "is another tale."

"Just so," the fox agreed, and bowed his head.

"Beautifully told," she said. "I know no one who could tell it better."

"Ma'am." He bowed still deeper, his mouth curved in that slight smile that foxes wear. "We, all of us, have tales we could share with you if you care to hear them."

"I do," she replied. "Truly. But it's evening now and we were advised not to be out after the sun set."

The fox shared a look with his fellows and they all burst out laughing. But he said to her, "Quite right, you don't want to be caught out." More tittering accompanied the comment, though she couldn't see what they found so amusing. "I think it's best that you allow us to accompany you back to your accommodations, wherever they are. As a precaution."

"That's very kind of you."

"It's nothing. We can't very well sit here playing once the sun goes down, and it's just about to set, as you say."

She stood with the fox, Diverus at her side. The rest of the group folded around them like a shield and they began to walk back through the park. "And what is the name of your abode?"

"I think it's called 'Eat this and have a cup of tea.'"

"Ah, know it well, know it very well." He glanced at some of the others of the group with another meaningful look.

Leodora turned to the man beside her, intending to ask him . . . whatever it was, the question fell from her mind as she saw him. He was changing as they walked, no longer human. He had a great curling nose now, and his chin hung down as a beard might have on someone else. The man behind him was more grotesque still. His head had become part of his shoulders, flat-topped, and his torso funneled down into skinny legs and long taloned feet, as if he were the child of a bird that had mated with a parsnip. He blinked back at her with round, inhuman eyes. The eyes all around her had changed: some bulged, others had turned hard and black. Noses had reshaped, distorted, or vanished altogether. Likewise hair, which had disappeared or else sprouted in odd places, or transformed into feathers, reeds, seaweed. Only the fox, transformed before she'd met him, remained the same, although in the dark and among this company he looked more sinister and rapacious than before.

As they all walked down the seemingly deserted thoroughfare, more shapes emerged from the shadows or rose up through the pavement to double their numbers.

Diverus clutched her arm, all of his terror in his grip. He was staring behind them so intently that she looked back, too. A crowd had amassed, walking behind them, some thin and stalky, others squat, some slick and others furry. Two of the squat creatures held lanterns on long flexible poles, and ran along the edges of the crowd to keep up. Behind the lights, there were even more creatures, but in shadow, only now and then glimpsed between other bodies and in cast light. If anything they looked more grotesque than those nearby. It was a parade of monsters and she and Diverus were their captives. Soter would say it was all her fault for not returning while daylight remained—that is, if he ever saw her again, he would. She wanted to speak to the *kitsune*, but he had drawn ahead to lead the parade. Two more lights on poles bobbed beside him.

Something cold brushed her shoulder, and instinctively she pressed against Diverus, away from the source, as a towering ghost drifted past. His mismatched eyes regarded her with surprise as though he recognized her. He wore odd clothing—a black jacket over a white shirt with another strip of material hanging from his throat. She wasn't sure what manner of pants he wore because his legs faded below the knee into an ill-defined grayness. He floated past and toward the front.

Then all at once the parade came to a stop. Beside Diverus the creatures stepped aside, and there stood the fox. He grinned. "Well," he said, "we've arrived."

Behind him lay the steps up to "Eat this and have a cup of tea." The fox waved them out of the parade. Holding hands, they stepped toward the steps.

"I couldn't persuade you to come with us the rest of the way, could I?" the fox asked.

"Rest of the way?"

"To the end. The parade goes on to the very end."

"Of the span?"

"Of time," he said, as though surprised that she didn't comprehend this already.

"So, we . . . couldn't come back."

"No, quite impossible. But we should love your company. You know so many stories."

Diverus was edging to the steps and tugging her after him. He said, "She can't. She has a performance tonight."

"Really?" the fox said.

"Yes, it's true," she replied.

"Oh, well." He sounded sincerely regretful. "You'd best go on, then. But come again to the park and we'll tell you another story. And you can share one of yours."

"That would be . . . I would like that."

"Goodnight, then, Leodora." He made shooing gestures at them both, then turned and took his place at the front again. The parade moved off behind him. Some of the creatures watched her and Diverus as they passed. Others stared straight ahead as if this world did not exist; those in the very back somehow did both at once.

"He said your name," Diverus noted.

"I'm sure I never told it to him."

"You wouldn't really go to the park again, would you?"

She made no answer, but gesturing toward the steps, she said instead, "We're probably late."

They climbed up and, after removing their shoes, entered the building. The moment the door thudded closed behind them, the noise and bustle of the front room died. Every single person there turned from their meal, their drink, their overtures and conversations, to stare at the new, and unlikely, arrivals.

Diverus and Leodora walked barefoot across the polished wood floor. With wide eyes upon her from every side, she felt as if she were still in the grotesque parade. The eyes tracked her closely as if expecting at any moment that she might transform. One man close by made signs in the air and threw some kind of dust at them that glittered as it sprinkled down and caused Diverus to sneeze violently, which in turn caused the man to dive for safety beneath his table. Pausing, Leodora brushed the dust from her sleeve. When nothing happened, the man poked out his head, tittered nervously, and sat up facing his food, refusing to look at them. Diverus rubbed his nose. The crowd lost interest.

The proprietor entered then. He carried a woven tray full of covered dishes. "Ah-ha," he said, "there you two are. That Soter has taken to drink because he couldn't find you. He was sure you were gobbled up by goblins."

Diverus glanced askance at Leodora, who asked, "Are we late?"

"Not for my needs, no. You can see—they are all still eating. And I am not of nervous disposition."

"I understand. When is it we begin, then?"

"Oh, any time you like, although if you would wait perhaps until those who ordered this food have had their fill, you'll be less likely to play to an empty garden."

"Of course."

"Grand." He hurried off to serve the food, leaving behind lovely smells.

The central courtyard was nearly deserted. Cut off from the street and the front room, the handful of patrons there did not react when they entered, connecting them neither to the parade nor directly with the anticipated performance of puppetry.

At a small table beside the booth, Soter sat alone, his head on his arms. Candlelight floated in a bowl by his head, illuminating his slack expression, telling her everything she needed to know of his condition. He stared at nothing, but then sensed her, and shifted. When he saw her, he closed his eyes, licked his lips, and pushed himself upright, swaying slightly.

"The vagabonds return," he muttered.

"We were collecting stories," she said sharply. "The way I do on every span. You know that."

"The sun set long ago. You were even warned about it."

"Our performance wasn't set to begin before this, and it looks as if it will have to go on without you."

"Nonsense." He bowed his head as if tired of the argument. "What happened to you? You could have been consumed by the monsters that walk these streets at night, the parade—"

"We joined the parade," she interjected.

"What? What happened?"

"They ate us." She had the satisfaction of seeing him dumbfounded. "The good thing that came of it is, I have a story to perform belonging to this span, that we've never heard before, and perhaps more to come. Wasn't that worth it?"

"My girl, my headstrong mad girl. You are your mother's child, and like her you rattle the dark."

She gaped at those words. He had no way of knowing that Shumyzin had said the same, and for an instant she stood in two places, atop the tower on Vijganar and here, as if two moments had merged, folding over the events in between—as if her life going forward would comprise such moments, clues to show her the path she must adhere to, though to what end she had no idea.

"You rattle it long enough," he went on, "and it'll rattle you back."

"So, I shouldn't look for new tales?"

"I'm not saying that. I'm saying, be careful you don't *become* a tale." He poured his cup, but then pushed it at her. "Here, drink for stamina before we go on." She picked it up. "And don't worry about my condition. I could do my part roaring drunk, and you know it."

She sipped the wine and put the cup down. "I know you've tested the notion enough times."

He snorted, smiled. "I have, and even before your time. Now, go get ready, and where's Div—ah, there you are, boy. Get in the booth. I'll go call us up an audience. You apply your skills, the both of you, to this story you risked your lives to get, and tomorrow night they'll be murdering each other to get in. We'll save Nikki Danjo's ghost till then." He drew himself to his feet.

Leodora pushed into the booth with Diverus behind her.

He picked up his lute. "We risked our lives?" he asked.

She shrugged at him. "Maybe a little."

Their performance of "The Emperor's Tale" that night proved so wondrous that it was to the audience as if two demigods had manifested inside the booth to render the story. Diverus plucked a delicate tune underneath Jax's prologue, then switched to a small flute to represent the fox empress, inventing a bittersweet theme for her on the spot. Even Leodora, in the midst of depicting the story, found her throat constricting with emotion. Every note was the perfect complement to the shadow figures on the screen. During an interlude, when she could glance back at him, she saw that his eyes were closed and his head was swaying as he played, as if while his body sat with her, his spirit ventured into some other realm to bring back a music that no one had ever heard, yet knew the instant they heard it that it already lived in their bones, threaded through generations. Wherever he channeled this music from, he was playing music that had formed the moment the story was first told—the music of the story's origin. She knew, even before she took her bow afterward, that they would be weeping as they applauded. She made Diverus come out, too, with his flute, and presented him to them. The ovation doubled. "Kitsune Jax!" someone yelled, and coins rained upon them. If Soter had an opinion of the musician at that moment, he didn't express it, but gestured, redundantly, to them both as if the audience needed instruction in where to direct their acclaim.

The next morning, with a mist hanging over the span, she and Diverus went back to the park, but the kitsune and his brethren weren't there. The benches on which the players had sat the day before were empty. No one played *gō* today. The strangely cut and shaped flora seemed different, too, but Leodora couldn't be sure if it was her imagination or if the topiary had been changed. She didn't remember the one cut like a huge bird with a fan for a tail, nor the one that looked like a giant depiction of her Meersh the Bedeviler puppet—and surely she would have noticed that one if it had been there the previous afternoon. Who was it cut these bushes, anyway?

People strolled through the park in leisurely fashion; some passing nearby stared at her curiously. Diverus noticed this first and pointed it out to her, and the two of them watched people watching her as they passed. Then one woman, rather than just watching, approached her. With her face hidden behind a small fan that she fluttered, the woman asked, "Would you sell me, young woman, some of your hair?"

"My hair?" She self-consciously touched the fall of it at her neck. She was wearing it unbound today, enjoying the freedom of anonymity.

"Enough to make a wig for me. I'll pay you well."

"I'm sorry, but no."

The woman made a slight bow of disappointment, then fluttered away.

Diverus said, "They must never have seen hair like yours."

"But it's just hair!"

"To us. We might want to leave this park, though, before she finds someone who's willing to take it from you."

"Take my hair?" Clearly, she found the idea absurd.

"In the underspan of Vijganar, if someone liked what you had, they took it. If you disagreed with them, there was usually an argument, sometimes a fight. Sometimes a murder."

"You saw this?"

"Not every day, no, but often enough. Own nothing to feed someone's envy and you'll live a good, long time. Otherwise, you have to be willing to fight."

"You had something to steal?" she asked, thinking that he wasn't merely reciting but spoke from personal experience.

"No," he answered. "I had nothing, less than nothing, so I was left alone."

They continued to wander idly through the park, which appeared larger than possible. Beyond the benches and up a few steps, the way was blocked by a stand of bamboo grown so thickly together that when they at last located a meandering path of small stones between the stems, they had to walk single file along it, weaving through an increasingly impeditive forest, so dense that the clogged air hung motionless, while in patulous branches overhead, unseen birds chattered shrilly. The world became green, crepuscular, and claustrophobic.

When it seemed the forest could be compressed no further and be navigable, the bamboo began to thin, until they were catching glimpses of the world beyond it again. Soon only a single, random row of stems stood between them and the world beyond. The path ended at a few steps, leading down a slope to a circular pond. In the center of the pond, water trickled over an odd pile of stones that seemed to have been arranged to produce the most noise possible—the trickling and burbling drowned out even the bird song they'd left behind. Orange fish with large sleepy eyes suggesting a jaded intelligence swam lazily near the edge of the pond and followed them as they walked around it. There were benches at intervals but no one sat. This whole portion of the park stood deserted.

The path led to a broad oval of sand, ringed by rocks. A solitary figure stood in the sand, his face hidden beneath a low conical hat. He held a small rake and, as Leodora and Diverus came upon him, he was carefully creating a series of crosshatches. The sand had been worked elsewhere into swirls and nautiloid patterns. In silence they watched him perform, and Leodora felt as if she were watching the creator himself, making the world. He paused to consider what he'd done, standing idly with one foot on his thigh and his weight upon the rake. He seemed then like a statue, as if she had only imagined his movement. Quietly, she and Diverus crept past him. If he was aware, he didn't show it. He didn't move at all. On the far side and bordered by short conical trees, a few steps led down from this strange plateau and across another area of exotically shaped bushes, and to a set of polished wooden trellises that served as gates. Beyond them, people moved past randomly, as if unaware of this enigmatic park.

Exiting through the gates, the two found themselves on a secondary boulevard that paralleled the one they'd taken upon arriving on the span the day before. Looking back, they found that they had walked beneath the oddly canted central tower without noticing and viewed it now on the far side of where they'd begun, halfway to the end of the span. "Maybe the bamboo forest hid it," suggested Diverus, as if reading her thoughts, but even to himself he sounded unconvinced. He added, "Maybe we want to walk back on the road instead."

"There certainly wasn't anyone to ask for stories," said Leodora.

"I think it won't be the same going back anyway." She looked at him questioningly, and he explained, "I think it'll have become another park."

What struck her as the most odd about his observation was that she both understood and agreed with him.

This entire span seemed to be alive with elusive magic.

They walked along the boulevard toward the center tower, passing other pedestrians, fruit and vegetable stands, pedicabs, and shops. The shops on their right hid the park from view, and when they did catch a glimpse, all they saw was a stone wall.

The two of them had only just entered the shadow under the central tower's crossbeam when a procession cut across their path.

It was nothing like the parade of monsters from the previous night. The people—for they all looked human this time—wore white garments—robes, pants, shirts, all white. Only one woman, near the front, wore color—a bright red scarf upon her head. In the middle, lying upon a board but held up above their heads on a series of poles, lay a body. It, too, was wrapped in white, from head to foot.

Leodora turned and started after them. Diverus followed her reluctantly. "I have to see this," she told him. "I don't know why, but I have to."

The street ran directly to one of the canted uprights supporting the swooping beam overhead. The street widened to circle the upright, and the procession flowed around it like water around a stalk of bamboo. On the far side, the split road opened even wider, into a crescent at the span's edge. The funeral group spread out to fill the crescent. Leodora and Diverus remained on its fringe, slightly separate from the others so as not to intrude. They didn't know how they might be regarded.

The woman with the red scarf began a recitation: "There are two-hundred levels to the universe. The higher we ascend the hotter it becomes. The realm of the spirits would scorch us, and even they cannot reach the level of the fire and water gods, but are connected to it only by rays, as the sun connects to us."

A woman standing beside her and clutching the hands of two children began to wail. The children took their cues from her and added their voices to the anguish.

Diverus, disquieted by their grief, moved off from the clustered group, to the rail at the edge of the span, Leodora trailing behind him. She could still hear the priestess's recitation, but the talk of levels made little sense to her. Ahead, she saw through mist the other wing of the span, still separated from it but close enough that she could just make out the features of people on it. She saw below them the darkness of land, sloping out from under the surface of the span, a hillside. Nearing the rail, she looked down into the valley in between. Houses on stilts stood nearby in the valley. The ones at the very bottom stood in water, in the narrow stream that snaked through it, and she followed the course of the stream back to a waterfall in the gray distance. On each side of the stream, the land had been flooded—a system of small gates and channels allowed water to be diverted from the stream, enough to cover the valley floor. Some sort of crop grew in the spread of water, and people worked there with hoes and other implements, with baskets slung over their shoulders, standing ankle-deep.

The recitation ended and the body, still on its plank, now fastened to ropes, began its descent off the edge of the span. Leodora leaned against the rail now to see straight down.

On this side of the valley lay a huge opening—a grotto—directly beneath the crescent. The sides of it were jagged, and down in its depths lights flickered, like candles, revealing more white-robed figures. They stood awaiting the body, reaching up as if eagerly as it descended toward the open mouth of the hill.

Diverus said suddenly, "My mother died and they dropped her down into the sea." She glanced sidelong at him. He seemed calm, almost entranced. "There was no land under Vijganar. Just water. They wrapped her up like that and then they sent her under the water."

"Diverus—"

"I used to imagine she'd become a mermaid and lived in a city at the bottom of the sea."

She found she could watch the descent of the body by watching his eyes. He tracked it until it was taken by the figures in the hole.

"It's the same, though, isn't it?" he said.

The priestess recited: "After the Storm of Raruro, comes a reuniting, and all spirits join. Shukkon and fukkon will join. Until that day he must remain separated from us—that is the order of things."

"Yes," Leodora answered, "I suppose it is."

He pushed away from the ceremony and through the many figures in white. Leodora followed after him. He didn't go far but sat down against a wall where a cart had been standing earlier—a few cast-off vegetables lay scattered there. He rested his face on his fists. As she came up to him, Leodora thought he looked like a little boy. She knelt, and then sat beside him.

"It's strange," he said immediately. "I can remember it all, but in the way you remember the stories you tell, the way I remember the story that fox told us yesterday. It never happened to me, but I can recall that emperor and his fox-wife now—as if I *was* there."

She said nothing, but considered that a while. Idly she picked up a long-necked gourd and a taro potato and began toying with them, dancing them about. There seemed to be no answer, really. Diverus had been present, and yet from what she gathered, the Diverus seated beside her hadn't existed then. He was a creation of the gods. A Dragon Bowl had made him.

Meanwhile, the funeral procession was returning from the burial. The wails of the two children at the rear of the group reached them well before the children passed by.

Without looking at him, Leodora said, "It isn't as if you could have saved her, Diverus. Any more than I could have saved my parents. They both died before I could talk." She met his angry eyes and held his gaze. "You think she died on your account."

His eyes widened with surprise and betrayal, and she knew that she'd guessed right. She spun the gourd around, then waltzed it to the potato. "There isn't a day when I don't miss my aunt Dymphana. I can't see her again, maybe ever." Her throat tightened and her face flushed. She'd thought she was just saying this for him, not to express her own pain. She wanted to stop but had to go on so that he'd understand. She willed herself not to cry. "It's not my fault I can't see her. I didn't make it this way, my uncle did. He made rules, and what I've done . . . is because of that."

People were walking past now. She lowered her head, unable to look at him or anyone else, knowing that she might burst into tears if she did—and how stupid and pointless that was—but she couldn't help it. She focused on the vegetables, on making them waltz about and pirouette upon the stones.

The crying children came abreast of her but she didn't look up, even when their noise was right on top of her. And then suddenly the crying stopped.

At that Leodora raised her head slowly. The children stood directly before her. They were watching her hands in fascination. They might have been twins, both with black hair and almond eyes. Above, holding their hands, their mother, the widow, met her gaze and made a pitiful attempt at a smile, ruined by grief. Her tears had etched trails in the thick powdery makeup on her cheeks. The thought came to Leodora: "We're all here on account of death."

The rest of the funeral party moved on, but the mother

couldn't work up the energy to order her children away, and so she stood there as if expecting Leodora to read her a future.

Quietly, Diverus suggested, "Tell them a story."

She glanced at him. He seemed to have forgotten his despair. His eyes shifted from her to the children and back again.

She spoke what she'd been thinking. "We're all here on account of death," she said, and she spun the long-necked gourd about, as if it were turning to face the children. "Death is everywhere, but do you know that once upon a time Death didn't exist? No? Then let me tell you how Death came into our world." She raised her eyes to the widow. "I think you should sit down to hear this. It's not a long story, but it isn't short, either."

The mother knelt and her children sat beside her.

"Now, does anyone here know who Chilingana is?" asked Leodora.

One of the twins said, "He dreamed Shadowbridge."

"That's right. He was the original dreamer." She walked the taro potato forward, and hid the gourd from sight, then leaned over and picked up a small cluster of enoki and set it aside. She said, "One day, a different dream came to him."

≈ How Death Came to Shadowbridge ≈

In those times the sun was called Lord Akema. He was a warrior god, terrible to behold, who would blind all those foolish enough to seek for his features. That's why there existed the second—the false mask of Akema—Nocnal, upon which everyone might safely gaze, and whom they could petition when they wanted a favor from the war god. Behind the mask of Nocnal, the warrior would listen and sometimes answer.

It was under Nocnal's aegis that the fisherman Chilingana dreamed the bridges of Shadowbridge into place. Each night, more bridges appeared—covered in structures, in houses and towers, in parks and alleys, but all of them were empty, lifeless and still. Soon his dream stretched far across the world, and Nocnal observed it all as it unfolded.

By day, beneath the burning face of Akema, Chilingana's life persisted as flat as bread. He fished, he ate, and he dwelled with his wife, Lupeka, in his stilt house. Although he could have stepped across the gap onto the first bridge he'd dreamt, he didn't. He talked about going, almost every day, but each time he came to the edge of his own small world, he hesitated, peered down the empty way until his eyes ached, and then gave up. He could not go traveling out upon these spans. To do so would have invited the unknown, and Chilingana, for whom everything had ever been the same, feared the unknown. He didn't understand that the unknown needed no invitation.

One night while he lay upon his seaweed mat, a chill wind called loneliness came floating down the empty spans of the bridges he had dreamt. It swirled about his house. It slipped into the sleeves of his clothing and fluttered the cloth against him. His mouth filled with it and he rose and went out and stared off into the distance, across the near-black sea. He looked for what he knew not.

Chilingana thought his wife was asleep inside, but she lay awake. The wind had filled his house, and she had breathed it in as well as he.

She was aware of him outside, yet did not call him. No distance had ever existed between the woman and the man before he dreamt the bridges. They stretched into infinity like the lives of Chilingana and Lupeka. This new distance touched her with longing. She wondered: When had she come to be, and who had built her house? She assumed Chilingana had done it, but he never said. She had never before thought to ask. The two of them wanted for nothing: All the food of the world swam through the ocean beneath their house. Why, then, create such things as bridges? What purpose could they serve?

Fear gnawed at her then, that her husband wished to travel away from her into an unknown so vast that he might never return. The distance opened like a pit beneath her, and her breath caught in her throat.

The wind of loneliness heard her and was surfeited.

She arose and crept out the back of the house onto the balcony that surrounded it on all sides. She gazed out across the sea away from her husband. Her eyes followed Nocnal's bright stripe upon the swirls and waves until she made out, just above the horizon, the black edge of a bridge's line, and in the middle of it the black spire of a tower, and her fear frothed and foamed. She knew in wordless fashion that these spans connected to some other place, although she knew no other.

Her fearful musings disturbed Lord Akema's rest, prodding the face of Nocnal to call down, "What troubles you, lady?"

"Well," she answered, and then fell silent before the

immensity of what she wanted to say. What was still emerging inside her soul had no words. She had never known anything but herself; how could she express something so much larger? She kept silent. If Nocnal had to ask, then he didn't understand.

Yet he continued asking her till finally she retreated inside where the walls were near, the territory small and safe. When her husband came in later and lay down beside her, she rolled over to clasp him and he held her tight. "I know," he said.

"What?"

"Something is coming."

The certainty in his words terrified her more than her own inexpressible unease. "What is? What's coming? Tell me."

"When it arrives, I'll know it." He couldn't tell her more, and they lay like that, tightly bound in unshared fear, too conflicted even to remember shared desire.

Chilingana tried to forget what he'd told Lupeka. He continued fishing as he had always done, but with uneasy glances over his shoulder, down the length of the adjoining spans, across the ocean to where they vanished over the horizon.

One afternoon the face of Lord Akema was particularly fierce. Chilingana lay on the shadowed side of his house as people still do to escape the god's fury, and he happened to glance up to find a stranger walking up the next span.

The fisherman who had created the world leapt to his feet. Other than his wife, this was the first person he had ever seen. Whatever he'd dreaded for so long, this had to be it.

The stranger was tall and gaunt. He wore robes that we would say belonged to a mystic. They were deep red and glittered with powerful designs woven with silver thread, thick as fishbones. The hood of his robe kept the stranger's features in shadow. All Chilingana could determine was that this traveler was very dark indeed.

The stranger came to the place where the dreamed bridge ended and stepped across the gap onto the balcony encircling the stilt house. The stilts groaned beneath him as if he weighed as much as the world. He walked right up to Chilingana, who huddled shivering in the shadows. It took all the fisherman's reserves not to cry out and flee inside. He stared into a face of sharp cheekbones and high polished brows, looked into bottomless eyes. "Who are you?" he asked.

The traveler replied, "I am Death."

"What sort of name is that?"

Death laughed. "One new to you even though you're the Dreamer. Your bridges have grown to encompass the world, reaching even as far as the land of the dead, which is a barren and uninhabited place I was happy to leave. Your creation invited me to walk the world and I set out directly to find you."

The fisherman raised his shoulders. "You aren't making sense."

"I think you'll see that I am, once you've come inside me." Death opened wide his robes, and Chilingana saw a place so cool and inviting that the harsh rays of Lord Akema couldn't find him there. He must have fallen into those robes, for he had no memory of walking. Once he was inside the cool place his mind tumbled with memories. The robes that had been held open closed, and at the core of the darkness within them lay a red glow of life out of which came discordant noises he'd never known—crackling energies and devices that rang and then spoke, the barking of dogs, the canister rumble of machines as they rolled along an empty boulevard, the clicking of a metal thing that unfurled strips of paper covered in indecipherable symbols, and the voices of people—more people than he could hold in his mind—all speaking at once and shouting through objects in the sky that were nothing like Akema, lifeless creations, but that sprayed chatter out and down like rain in a million different tongues drowning him under their flow. He saw impossible blue-glass buildings across which clouds slid like oil, and lighted things that were not fish but traveled far beneath his perfect sea, and he knew that all of these things, however they were new to him, were also ancient, long gone, dredged up out of a collective silt of memory, from some other time and place before he and his wife had arrived. And he knew torment, for in all his new recollections, his birth was nowhere to be found.

He sank to the stones before the traveler. His head hung, too heavy for his neck to lift. Death spoke. "Now you know mortality. Now you'll live and age and cling to what memories you have, because you will always be falling away from them."

Then Death left the fisherman there and entered his house. Chilingana tried to crawl after him, to shield his wife from this terrible conjurer. Why should she have to know these things? She hadn't done this—she hadn't made the bridges. But she couldn't be spared, else gaze down upon a mortal man whom she no longer would recognize as her husband.

Death did not leave, but when the fisherman dragged himself feebly inside, the traveler had gone, and his wife lay upon the bed, naked and open to him. She had been made fertile, able to bear children. Thus did Death plan to people his realm.

Nearing her, Chilingana recovered his strength, and they folded together and slept, safe so long as they touched.

In the morning, when he awoke, he was alone and certain that he had dreamed the traveler. He stretched, to find that his body ached unfamiliarly.

As he stood, he kicked something from the mat. It clattered across the floor. It was a silver object, small enough to lie in the palm of his hand. Grooves threaded the length of it; at the top was a large single slot. He had brought it back from the realm within Death's cloak.

After he stooped and lifted the thing, Chilingana dropped to his knees with his fist closed, and began to weep because now he could remember his entire life and he recognized that each day would hereafter be different from the last, and farther away than the land of Death itself.

Time upon Shadowbridge had begun. Life had arrived, carried by Death.

Leodora laid down the taro and the enoki. The gourd she'd already hidden in one sleeve, and she let it roll slowly out. It came to rest sitting up, its "head" canted as if toward the children. For them it had become the figure of death; and for their mother, as well. She smiled at her storyteller and now that smile was proof against grief. Her tears had dried and those of her children. "Thank you," she said.

Some members of the funeral procession had stopped when they found the widow missing, and had wandered back. They clustered close enough to hear the story, and complimented Leodora by dipping their heads in an informal bow. The widow turned to her people and then folded the children back in among them, but the two kept glancing over their shoulders at Leodora and the gourds as they were drawn away, and then lost from sight.

She got up, wearily, her legs stiff from all the walking followed by sitting awkwardly while she performed the tale. She saw the expression on Diverus's face. "What is it?" she asked.

"I—I've no words. I stand amazed."

Blushing, she lowered her eyes. "You've no call to be. You have a far more remarkable talent than mine."

"No," he said. "Mine was a gift from the gods."

"How do you know mine isn't?"

"But—" He stopped, thought. "You've never even set foot on a dragon beam—you said as much."

"And is that the only way one is granted gifts?" Her voice teased now.

The question being too enormous in implication, he could only laugh with her. "I don't know. I don't know much of anything, do I?"

A cloud passed over the sun, and the empty street became suddenly dusky and vaguely ominous. At the crescent, where the body had been lowered, nothing had been left to mark the spot. Every building appeared to be deserted. Leodora gathered herself up.

Diverus asked, "How did you know what story to tell them?"

"I had three vegetables. The tale of Death was the first thing I thought of with three characters." She faced him as a look of doubt crossed his face. She let it go. She didn't want to explain herself, didn't want to answer how stories found her or how she'd looked into the faces of those children and their mother and known what they needed to hear. She would have to admit that she didn't understand how it happened, either; she didn't know where his songs came from. "Right now I'm famished. We have a long walk ahead of us still and I wouldn't care to have to join that parade of monsters again—they might not let us go this time."

She offered her hand and drew him to his feet, and they walked off together.

After their performance that second night, Soter informed Leodora and Diverus that they would be journeying on following the third performance. "We need to spread your reputation far and wide, can't be falling into the trap of staying in one place too long, even if the audiences are respectable."

"Respectable?" Leodora all but laughed at the word he'd

chosen. The central garden had been filled. People had crowded into all three entrances to see the performance.

Soter pretended not to hear the sarcasm. He rocked back and forth on his feet the way someone does when they feel the matter they've spoken of is closed. He could not have infuriated Leodora more.

"I understand none of this," she said. "We stayed on in Vijganar even when the mistress of the theater very nearly exposed us by trying to have her way with Jax, even after I complained of this to you. We were going to stay on even when I told you we needed to go. In fact we would be there still if it weren't for your encounter with that elven one."

"Grumelpyn." He said it as if correcting her.

"So tell me what he said to you that has you pushing us along now before we've even set down our belongings and drawn a breath. Even when we thought Uncle Gousier was hunting for us, we didn't flee where we had an audience. In fact you advocated for remaining on Merjayzin. You were willing to risk an encounter with him at the thought of a paying house. We stayed there for two full weeks!"

He'd stopped rocking on his heels by then, and—oddly—focused upon Diverus as if he might appeal to the musician and the two of them outvote her. "Those were early days," he explained. "We needed the reputation to build, to fly ahead, to do the work for us so that by the time we arrived upon the next and the next span, they had already heard the rumors of a magnificent puppeteer, and so welcomed us, and were willing to haggle over a larger percentage of the take for us than if we'd just come in off the street like two vagabonds who hoped to swindle them a bit before climbing out a back window and making off with our loot."

Before Leodora could respond, Diverus asked, slowly and thoughtfully, "So by the time she found me, her reputation had grown enough that now you don't need to worry whether the next span has heard of her, yes?"

"I—" Soter hadn't been prepared for that question. Why couldn't they just do as he asked for once, instead of requiring a more thorough explanation of why he expected them to do as he wished? The little musician was as bad as she was. "Of *course* we need to have her reputation spread. Of course we do." He tried to laugh, to make it all light and unimportant that they might not wonder at the tension that underlay every word he spoke—the tension of fearing that he might have to give up more than he wanted. "But you know, there are infinite spans, infinite peoples and tales and don't you want to see more of them?" He knew, even as he spoke, that he'd taken a wrong turn, because the question itself offered her the power to decide—the very thing he wanted to avoid.

"I do want to see them all," she said, "but I also want to learn every story, and I can't do that if I leave each span so rapidly that I haven't time to find the stories, hear them, add them to what I know. You said my father did the same."

"Yes," replied Soter, knowing there was no other answer, and no way to distract her from what she would say next, which he heard as if it were an echo preceding the sound that made it.

"I want the time to collect stories."

"Lea."

"No, don't grease your words to me. Don't make promises and don't explain my behavior to me when you can't account for your own."

"All right then." He hung his head. It was the only option left him. "How long do we stay?"

"I don't know."

"Yes, and that is because it's not your responsibility," he insisted but carefully.

She shook her head. She could not argue sensibly with him. He was forever pushing the argument into some place where he could control it, where he could maneuver her. He was so transparent.

"Three nights?"

"Longer," she said.

"Five then."

"I don't know."

He sighed. "Once again, Lea, it is my part, my *role*, to ascertain the best venue, and how long we can rely upon the people to attend, and who will pay us the most. This is a job I do well. I'm certainly no puppeteer, but without me, you would have no place to prove that *you* are." When everything else failed, flattery still got the job done.

She leaned forward then and said, "All right. Five nights."

He nodded, and said "Done!" so agreeably that she knew there had been two levels of manipulation at work. By watching the obvious one, she had been directed into choosing exactly what he'd wanted all along. She couldn't see how he'd done it, but she knew he had.

She got up with her hands curled into fists. "I've two hours before the performance. I'm going to *rest*." She stormed out of the courtyard, which seemed to tremble at her passing.

Left behind, Diverus fidgeted, stealing glances at Soter as he commented, "I'm new to human interactions, but I wonder that anybody understands anybody." He, too, took his leave of the garden.

Alone, Soter toasted himself and, after downing the small cup of liquor, said, "We can live with five. For now."

For three days, Leodora set out to collect stories. Each day she checked the park. She did find a group playing *gō* there, but it wasn't the fox and his friends. They did not reappear. "Maybe it takes a long time to go to the end of everything and come back," said Diverus.

"But they invited me to come back the next *day*." Even as she argued, she guessed the explanation, and before Diverus could say it, she countered herself: "Maybe days and nights aren't the same to the demons in that parade."

"That's what I think, too," Diverus replied.

Instead, she roamed the span, roaming onto the split on the far side of the valley she had seen with the funeral party, seeking groups, clusters of people at leisure whom she could chat up and ask for a story. She even found the palanquin bearers she had used in explaining story collecting to Diverus; and as she'd told him, they did indeed serve up a plethora of salacious stories about their mistress. None of these could be performed, but they contained images and ideas and moments she might borrow, retool, and fold into some unrelated telling to make it unique.

She received stories such as the tale of the priest who was so lonely that he created an artificial friend, but got the spell wrong—a story she performed the same night, provoking both laughter and gasps.

The courtyard filled earlier each night. People declined to take dinner until afterwards in order to get close to the booth.

Their final night in Hyakiyako, they concluded their performance with a repeat rendition of "The Ghost of Nikki Danjo." While the puppet of Masaoka pressed against the side of the screen and raised her arm to keep from screaming, her son died in agony of poisoning. She dared not cry out, as the audience knew, else give away that she had discovered the identity of the real villain—Nikki Danjo.

Soter sat to the side of the booth, both to watch Leodora's skillful performance and to mingle with the crowd. Once again, the courtyard was full to overflowing. Mutsu would be deliriously happy, almost as happy as he had been furious when Soter told him that they could not stay beyond five nights.

The crowd booed when the evil regent Nikki Danjo slid onto the screen again. The body language of the puppet implicated him as he crept across the room to advise his lord, and the puppet of Masaoka, behind him, equally betrayed her fear. Soter, though he was used to Leodora's craft, found himself swept up in the tale. The puppets became real people. He could see the room that surrounded them rather than the shadow of doorways, screens and lanterns. He heard not Leodora's voice, but the voices of the overlord and the woman and the evil Danjo. He shook his head as if he'd begun to fall asleep, and blamed the many cups of rice wine he'd consumed. It was powerful stuff and he wasn't used to it. Plus, he conceded (if only to himself), Diverus's music made her voice seem to change, adding weight and depth to the male voices.

He straightened up on his stool and rubbed his eyes. He glanced around himself at the crowd, all so riveted by the performance that not one met his gaze. He found himself similarly drawn back to the pale screen, glowing lightly red now as the story neared an explosive climax. She had learned to increase the colors subtly, slowly, so that the audience hardly noticed that it had gone from white to crimson by the end of the play. Gods, he was proud of her! She had no idea how proud. Why didn't he tell her? Why couldn't he tell her?

As Soter stared at the screen, it seemed to draw him in, growing darker the closer he got.

When he looked up, the courtyard had turned red the color of blood, as if the light from her lantern had become liquid and smeared every surface. Soter dragged the back of his hand across his eyes. He looked first at the starlit sky above to confirm that it was still in place; but when he glanced down again the audience had transformed into puppets—giant, articulated puppets, their profiles translucent, features sharply drawn. He yipped and craned away in his chair, only to find that he was leaning into more puppets. The closest one swiveled its leathery head and gave him a nettled glare. He stared at the booth then, straight at the screen where Leodora performed. He clung to the identifiable shadows, denied the room. The performance continued, the story unfolded. In her fiction lay his truth. Without daring to glance away, he reached to the small table behind him and patted about for his wine cup.

A moist hand closed over his wrist and held it.

He stiffened. He sat paralyzed.

Close behind him a voice said, "So here we are at last." It was Gousier's voice and it was all Soter could do not to leap away screaming. Instead, denying the hive of panic whirling through his belly, he made himself slowly turn around, outwardly calm, his mouth fixed in a ghastly smile. Even that little resolve deserted him the moment he saw the speaker.

Behind and above him stood the Coral Man. It glowered down at him—he knew it though there were no eyes in its head, no distinct features at all. The grip on his wrist was some sort of clammy tentacle extending from beneath the table, as gray as the figure but alive and slick.

"Soter," it said, the voice no longer Gousier's, but distantly familiar—a voice he had heard so long ago that it had detached from its source; a voice from a void deep inside him that he wanted to deny. "Soter, you'll be found. Make no mistake. Found wanting."

He could not bear the force of the scrutiny, which writhed like a living thing. It was as if all the little creatures that had once lived in the pores of that chalky coral had burrowed into his skin and now this mass of flesh-devouring worms feasted their way all around him. Soon he would be nothing but bones, enveloped completely. He had to break away, face the performance, the red screen—he trembled with the effort of dismissing the apparition—turning in time to see the fitting end of Nikki Danjo, a haunting it was, yes, and "remember the story," he urged himself, it was a puppet ghost, but somehow he was in the story now, seated among puppets with a ghost of his own looming in their midst. He stared so hard at the red light and the shadow figures that his eyes burned with tears from not blinking. His arm, so twisted behind him, ached until he moved it, and his hand, clutching his cup, slid freely upon the table. Only then did he blink and glance around, wiped again at his eyes, this time with the meat of his palm; opening one eye while he covered the other, warily peering at his neighbor who, sensing his movement, grinned at him and said, "Very good, yes?" A normal face—bad teeth, certainly, but a normal face, not that of one of her puppets. Soter knew before he'd twisted around on the stool that no Coral Man would be hovering at his back. Everyone wedged into the courtyard looked normal, joyous with recognition of the masterful storytelling they'd just witnessed. They raised their hands and applauded—a burst of noise that made him jump.

He rolled his wrist and saw it then, the one perfect circle, the sucker mark, purple where it had bruised him. Everyone else was clapping and cheering.

The screen had gone dark, the lantern extinguished. Instinct took over and Soter stood, walked forward, clapping his own hands and calling, "Jax, my friends, the artistry of Jax!" while the crowd shouted and pounded their cups on the tables, and someone broke out a flute and began to play a frenetic melody above the din. The cheering flowed to follow and then accompany the flute, becoming a song.

After a minute, Leodora stepped through the side of the booth, her head cowled, her face masked, and the song dissolved into a roar. She had played their stories and won their hearts. This was how it had been with Bardsham. The impeccable skill of a genius had overwhelmed the crowds. The energy of their pleasure flowed right through him to the artist. It was wonderful. Behind her, Diverus came out—it was becoming a routine now—and waved the shamisen he'd been playing; the audience cheered for him, too.

Here was everything they sought and he was making them leave because he was afraid. And the Coral Man had stood right there and told him it would do no good. Run to the next span, he would be found. If you wanted to remain hidden, you could not have great talent. Talent made noise, people would notice you, remember you. Jax—they would be speaking of the master puppeteer from one end of the span to the other tomorrow. A few more days and word would have spread across the next up the line and then the next. This was also how it had been with Bardsham. "You'll be found," he muttered the warning.

Why, he asked the air, why did she have to be brilliant? Why did she have to shine so brightly? Why had she made them leave the damned backwater of that island? He blamed her, knowing full well that she wasn't to blame. He seethed, and smiled to the crowd. Then he realized she wasn't wearing the band that restricted her breasts. She'd forgotten to put it on after the performance. Someone would see, someone would fathom the truth. He thought to move, to face the crowd and step between them and the object of their adoration.

Then Leodora did the unthinkable. She pushed back the cowl and drew her braid free.

Watching the crowd for any sign that they'd recognized her womanliness, he only glimpsed the flash of her hair. "No," he said, more in disbelief than as a warning, but no one heard him over the din of the song they were singing.

He faced her then, crying, "Don't you dare!"

But she'd already reached a hand in front of her face, and she pulled the black mask up and away. The crowd yelled louder. She tugged loose the cord binding her hair, then shook it all free, a shining red fan, a copper waterfall around her. They simply went mad then.

"Jax! Jax! Jax!" It was the only word in the world. Coins flew through the air and rained all around her.

Soter wanted to sear her with a look the way the Coral Man had crushed him with its regard, but her stance defied him, denying him the right to hide her any longer. It was too late, said her pose, you may dictate the dates and the venues and the spans, but you'll not control my identity any longer. He knew this story; he'd told it to her: how had he thought it would have a different ending this time?

Something broke inside him with that realization. He could not oppose her, he had no will any longer, no strength for the battle that preceded every move with her. Chaos was coming after him, bearing down upon them all, and it would find him whether he hid her or not. It was what that hideous coral monster had been saying. There could be no going on to the next span now. No simple passage through a tunnel would help.

She had unleashed herself and now they had to flee.

"What do you mean, 'by boat'?" Leodora asked Soter.

"I mean," he said, leaning upon the undaya case, "we have ourselves taken to another spiral of the span. We abandon this trip north along this arm of the spiral and begin again—"

"—where we're not known! It means everything I just did

is for nothing. I go back to being Jax, a boy, because they won't know anything about what happened here tonight. The story of this will carry up the line, maybe even as far as your elf friend's span."

"Grumelpyn."

"I *know* his wretched name," she snarled, and for a moment he actually feared she would strike him, pick up a cup or a knife and attack him; but her anger, boiling up beyond her control, brought tears to her eyes, and despite her every effort she began to cry. "Daimons damn you, Soter, I won't do it!"

Diverus, standing uncomfortably behind her through it all, raised his hands as if to place them on her shoulders to comfort her, but seemed at the last to lose his nerve; he drew them back against himself like a mantis about to fall upon a victim; Soter saw it, registered the significance—that a bond had grown already between them that he would be foolish to try to sever—and bowed his head, pinching the bridge of his nose. His head hurt. He should have objected to such language from her, but he couldn't work up the false ire. He deserved every invective. Worse, he had no argument to justify this change of plans—he could hardly tell her the truth. In fact in that tense moment he could think of only one story, lame as it was, and only one promise that might convince her.

"You won't have to," he said. "You don't have to pretend to be Jax anymore—or, rather, Jax becomes a woman. We'll sail to a span where they won't mind. Colemaigne. We'll go to Colemaigne." It had been the span of choice anyway. "It's one of the oldest spans, and they have *no* restrictions about . . ."

"About women?" She might have been crying but her voice remained all threat.

"About much of anything. They're the epitome of the debauched."

"Like Vijganar."

"Oh, my dear, Vijganar is positively puritanical. It hides its predilections beneath its surface." He gestured at Diverus as living proof of what he said. "In Colemaigne there's no hypocrisy of that sort. And they'll welcome you. Perform 'Meersh' for them first thing. They always loved him. Positively their favorite. I'll be surprised if they haven't erected a statue to him by now."

"I don't have to pretend?" She was wounded but the anger had drained from her voice.

"No," he assured her. "No pretending. And we'll work our way around, you see, while the story of you spreads from two sources instead of one. By the time we play a dozen spans on that spiral, the tales of you will have closed up, they'll meet with us in the middle. Maybe we'll even sail to a third one before then and spread your reputation farther still. Why, the whole of Shadowbridge will know you. An infinity of places, think of it, every spiral speaking your name. There's simply no reason not to. You *wanted* to see the world, didn't you tell me that?" He waited for her reply, hanging everything on that reminder—the argument he'd fabricated even as he was saying it.

She sniffled and made a weak smile. "All right. That is—" she turned about "— Diverus?"

"Yes?" He seemed surprised that anyone cared to ask his opinion.

"Would you want to go? To sail to another span?" Behind her, Soter observed him coldly with a look that might have implied a threat.

He replied, "I've nothing to compare it to. I've never been on a boat." Then as an afterthought he added, "But if it takes me farther from Vijganar, that's probably good, isn't it?"

She nodded. "All right, Soter. It's settled." He smiled but she didn't meet his gaze, wouldn't look at him as she parted the fabric and stepped out of the booth. He tried to listen to her retreat but she trod silently like a cat.

Then it was just the two of them, with Diverus looking puzzled and uncertain. "You care about her," Soter said. "I saw. Well, so do I. I'm protecting her, though she's unaware of it."

"Protecting her from what?" asked Diverus.

For an instant, he contemplated confiding, but rejected the idea as foolish. "From everything," he replied. He stared at the open case and shivered. The Coral Man lay hidden in the bottom of it. When that figure had invaded Leodora's dreams, he'd dismissed it, or at least pretended to. Now he appreciated what it meant to have something without a mouth, without a face really, speaking to you.

He'd have liked to open the case, haul out the boxed puppets and confront the figure. In his mind's theatre he carried the Coral Man to the edge of the span and tossed it into the ocean where it sank without a trace, for someone else to find. What he said was, "Be sure you secure that case well and then grab yourself some sleep, boy. We'll be up *early* tomorrow for us. Or, rather, today." Then he, like Leodora, stepped out of the booth and left Diverus alone in the dark, lit only by the lantern glow, and that light source all but shrouded.

Diverus secured the lid and then blew out the lantern. He removed his sandals, lay down on top of the case, and let exhaustion consume him.

It hardly took any time at all. If a gray and undefined figure moved through his dreams, he remembered nothing of it when he awoke; and he awoke to find Leodora standing over him. She told him softly, "Time to go now."

From the stern of the ship, she watched Hyakiyako shrink slowly, steadily, rounding upon the horizon until the whole length of it and of the span to come—which they would not know hereafter—lay upon the sea like the body of a great dark snake, with the towers that divided the two spans projecting like horns, but even this image dwindled and soon only the tops of the towers remained, illusively rising and falling, buoyed upon the choppy sea until, finally, they vanished and with them the sense of the continuity of her life. Disconnected, she could not mask the pit of terror this opened in her, that everything had now been abandoned and she was lost in a way she'd never been, even when turned from Bouyan and the haven of home.

When finally she pushed away from the lost view, the tillerman, seated beside her with one arm up and pressed to the rudder bar, looked her up and down as if not sure what he made of her.

She walked unsteadily toward the ship's prow—for all that she'd ridden a sea dragon and lived upon an island that fished for its livelihood, she had never set foot in a boat before, and this one seemed determined to throw her to her knees. It was a shallow-bottomed craft and felt much too small and flimsy to undertake journeys across vast stretches of open water—especially with no one but the tillerman seeming to pay the slightest attention to how it sailed.

In the middle of the deck and butted up to the main mast stood the only shelter the boat afforded, a small shack—at least, that was her opinion of it. The crew called it a "house." Soter had ducked into its dark recesses before they'd even left the span, along with the remaining three crewmen, and he hadn't come out since. He'd been unusually reticent this morning, mostly nodding or shaking his head in response to questions, and more than once as they'd waited to cast off she had caught him looking past her, at the other boats moored along the two quays that projected from the side of the span. She would have preferred to think that he had come to realize how little she wished to hear his opinion on anything, but in truth she knew it had nothing to do with her, at least not directly. He wasn't hiding from her, nor from Diverus, who was sitting in the shadows of the shack, too, with his arms wrapped about his knees, trying very hard not to become ill. Diverus posed no threat, nor did she. All the same, Soter was fearful of *something*.

The two undaya cases were secured to the side of the little shack, surrounded by more crates and baskets of amphorae packed in straw. She steadied herself against them as the ship abruptly lurched. Then she took hold of one of the sail control lines and swooped beneath the woven main sail and toward the second mast. A control line ran from that smaller sail to the side of the boat, and she caught it and swung beneath it with her feet up and was a child again for a moment, free and untethered. She let go and landed beside the mast, almost kicking what she took to be an enormous yellow cable as big around as her waist and encircling the base of it. The cable flinched, and Leodora caught herself against the mast, leaning forward precariously over the cable. In the middle of it an eye opened and a thin reed of a tongue flicked into the air. The cable's color changed then, yellow becoming brown, darkening to viridian. It was not hemp rope at all, but an enormous snake. She backed away from it, then scurried to the prow of the boat, and once there glanced over her shoulder. The snake hadn't moved. Its color was blending with the deck again, until she was looking once more at a coil of rope that had no apparent eyes or tongue. The snake had gone back to sleep. It didn't care about her.

In the "V" of the prow, ahead of the lug sail, a small step boosted her high enough that, gripping the side tightly, she could lean over the stem head of the boat to look down into the water as it parted beneath her. She saw a fragmented reflection in the ripple, a face split into shadowed halves topped by a burnished cowl of hair that flared with the late afternoon light. The water was a deep blue, almost violet. She felt that if she'd leaned down far enough to dip her hand in, it would have come out dyed.

Ahead lay only more ocean, and no hint of any other span. Gulls wheeled around them, probably hoping for some food, and that suggested to her that nothing else lay anywhere near, for surely gulls would find better feeding off a span or even an isle than from a single small boat where no one was eating.

If the world was infinite as Soter claimed, then how far might Colemaigne be? The way he'd described the world when she was small, she'd imagined that one span led to the next, and wherever you were you could look out over the rail and see the nearest spiral just across the way. That was certainly not the truth, however. The world might contain infinite spirals, but they could also be infinitely separated. And so, no longer able to assume that what she assumed was true, she wondered about the truth of Colemaigne. It was a much-celebrated place, the subject of endless fables and tales and, most likely, lies. A locus for hedonistic delights, they said, where wine flowed from a huge central fountain and through a thousand capillaries, so that no matter where you were, you had only to dip your cup to sample it. Streets were paved with a crust of hard candy, and pastry shell houses leaned over them. No one ever went hungry and every pleasure was indulged—no worries, and no desires left unfulfilled. She might have been amazed by such tales once, but now—and especially after rescuing Diverus from the paidika—she understood that for one person's pleasure to be indulged, another must submit to indulging it. Pleasure had its price, even when paid by another.

In any case, the stories were ancient, as old as those of the storyfish and Meersh, according to Soter. What Colemaigne might have been in its past said nothing of what it was now. Look at Ningle, a decrepit, crumbling span that had once been new and glorious and blessed by Edgeworld, and which was surely much younger than their proposed destination.

Colemaigne by implication had to be on an ancient spiral. How else could a span so old exist? Every span linked to it must likewise be old, mustn't it? Or did bridge spans spring up suddenly after long intervals, the way that spans had appeared night upon night in Chilingana's story? Another span, called Valdemir in one of the Meersh tales, had fallen into the sea because it was so old. Would another span have replaced it, then or later, or was there a permanent gap where it had been? She hadn't seen enough of the world to surmise much less know the answers to such questions. Besides, every span on every spiral had its creation story; many were alike, but just as many contradicted the rest. While Chilingana's was nearly universal—at least on her span—it didn't account at all for the unseen gods of Edgeworld, for Dragon Bowls or the myriad creatures and cultures she knew existed. How could one fisherman have dreamt it all? Finally she doubted she knew anything about the truth of the origins of Shadowbridge and suspected nobody else did, either. It didn't bear contemplating. She was part of this world, and the truth of its creation and its being, whatever it was, wouldn't change that. Nevertheless, she wondered if she could ever unravel it. Maybe, someday, if she ever found the mythical Library and it contained all of the works that it was supposed to—maybe *then* she would discover the truth; surely not here, not in the company of a drunken old liar and a boy whose memory barely stretched back beyond a few subterranean months. So she focused her thoughts on their destination and let herself be excited by the notion of setting foot on one of the most ancient spans no matter what shape it was in now, for such a span must know the oldest stories, the earliest versions of all the tales she already knew. With luck Soter would decide they had escaped whatever thing he feared and let them stay awhile on each of these spans, giving her time to hear everything.

She stood at the prow until sea spray showered her, then jumped back, but too late, already drenched. The lug sail slapped against the back of her head.

"The price of curiosity," hissed a low voice.

She crouched and looked beneath the sail. Nobody else stood on the deck; but the snake, against the mast, had raised its head. Although its body was yellow, the head had darkened again to green.

She pushed her dripping hair out of her face and walked halfway to the second mast. "And what's *your* price?" she asked, just to be certain who was speaking to her.

The snake's head rolled from side to side. It said, "That would depend upon what you're purchasing."

"What sort of snake are you, then?"

"Do you mean, am I the sort who would sup on you?"

"It would be useful to know."

"Your drenching hasn't done a thing to curb your curiosity, has it?" He sounded amused.

She walked closer. Her bare feet left wet prints across the

deck. "I'd rather know than not know, if that's what you mean."

His head bobbed back and forth as if he was weighing her answer, then suddenly he stretched toward her. She leaned back but otherwise didn't move. She'd judged that he would have to unwind one coil to reach her; but close, she could see the remarkable blue and yellow facets of his eyes. He opened his mouth wide in a yawn. There were no fangs.

"If you must know, I'm an Ondiont."

"Ondionts are water snakes."

"So, you know something, then, after all. Yes, we are water serpents, my people."

"Then, what are you doing on a boat?"

"Being lazy. Actually, I'm supposed to be a sentry to protect the cargo these creatures shuttle back and forth from one span to another. I've been sentry now for months, and so far I haven't had to do more than stick out my tongue to send off the occasional scavenger. Eventually, I've been assured, they will ferry me home."

"Do Ondionts have a span of their own?"

He snorted. "A span? What would we do with a span? How would we get up the stairs from the sea?"

"I've no idea."

"Nor does anyone else. No, we have an isle, mostly rock, full of caverns, very nice, cool caverns out of the sun to sleep in."

"So, what do you eat?"

"Everything. Same as you." He rubbed the side of his head against the mast, his eyes closing ecstatically. "We squeeze it to death first. If necessary." His narrow pupils settled on her again. "So, what is it you're buying, storyteller?"

"How do you—"

"I listened to all you were saying to each other when you boarded. People will tell you everything if they don't realize you're listening. Stillness is a great skill. I'm sure you know this. I'm sure there are moments when you hold your puppets absolutely rigid to draw in your audience, and then *strike*." She thought if he'd had teeth he would have been grinning at her.

"If you know what I am, then you must know what I'm seeking."

"You would like a tale of the Ondionts, as different from your own people as I am from you." When she nodded, he said, "My price for this is that you must sit beside me."

"So that you can squeeze me to death before you eat me?"

His tongue flicked irritably. "So that you and I have a pact of trust. You must trust that I won't crush you."

She rubbed the bottom of one foot against the other ankle. "That would seem to put all the trust on my side of the bargain. What are you trusting me to do?"

"I am trusting you to honor the story every time you tell it on the spans of men and other creatures, by telling it true. Mine is the greater trust, because if you break it, there's nothing I can do about it."

"There's nothing I can do about it, either, should you choose to crush me."

"That's quite probably true. But you might attract the sailors and your comrades, who are inside, and they could certainly kill me before I could finish my meal. And anyway, they would see. It's not as if you would be easy to hide once I did eat you."

They faced each other in silence then, and if the snake was thinking anything at all, she couldn't tell. Yet she sensed that, like the kitsune who'd led the procession of monsters, the snake meant her no harm.

She walked boldly up beside him and sat down cross-legged on the deck. "What story then pays for my trust?"

The snake opened his mouth wide and hissed. She tensed to flee, until she realized that he was laughing. "You've steel in you, storyteller."

"Maybe not as much as you imagine."

"Oh, the contrary. I'm a judge of such things. But now to your reward. Here is a story you do not know." He lowered his head and, very delicately, laid it upon her lap. His crystalline eyes swiveled to look up at her as he spoke. "There was once a serpent woman who collected souls."

≈ The Story of Missansha ≈

Her name was Missansha, which means "the lonely one" in the Ondiont speech. She was born blind, and this is very rare among my people. Perhaps because of this, she schooled her other senses. We have a strong sense of smell, but hers was superior. She could flick her tongue and tell you what lay beyond the horizon, picking up its scent long before anyone else could.

However, as she came of age, she developed one particular talent that no other of us has—she could sip life itself. When she came near anyone else, she drank from them. She surely didn't know this was unusual. It was how she was. Nor could she control it any more than the living can control the urge to breathe. Inadvertently, like a basilisk, she drained the life from two playmates.

We have elders among us in whom we place our governance, and she was taken before them for this crime; but even as she was escorted into the room, she was draining those guards who accompanied her. One collapsed at her side, the other slithered away for his life. No one, nor especially her family, could come near her. The more she cared, the more absolutely she absorbed.

Now, we do not slay our own, least of all for things they cannot control, and she bore no responsibility for this. She wept for those she destroyed. We could not harm her for it.

The elders chose the only solution they could imagine. They would commission a tower for her, high enough that she would never again come near them. As you can imagine, for snakes such an undertaking was near impossible, and so we sent out messengers to the bridges, to ships, to other islands, asking for assistance. There were few who accepted our very generous offer to come and erect our tower. Serpents have an unsavory reputation among other species, most of which we've done nothing to earn. We're simply distrusted for our appearance and stories concocted about us, our decency dismissed. But I digress.

There were humans who deigned to set foot on our island. They were paid handsomely for their masonry skills, their talent and their labor—we have much gold in our caverns. And there were no unfortunate incidents of the sort that can spoil a relationship . . . that is, until the tower was complete and it was time to place Missansha in it.

Some of us there were who speculated that Missansha's powers might only hold sway over her own kind. The long, ascending rampway that spiraled around the outside of the tower, though it was built for snakes, still posed a burden to us. We asked that these foreigners would escort her to her chambers. None of us wished to be close enough, and we could not have her slither off the edge of the narrow ramp.

We made another generous offer and two of them volunteered. The rest waited alongside us.

Only one of the volunteers returned. The other died as he reached the top. His body became as glass, transparent and stiff. The survivor managed to lock her in before he stumbled back down the spiral to safety. We offered to nurse him back to health—we had much experience by now with the effect of her—but, no, the foreigners did not trust us after that, these alien creatures. They departed our shore and never returned. The tower they'd built was solid, well-constructed for the ages, and we left her there, banished with us but never among us.

Once a week someone carried food to her, leaving it where she could reach it. At least for a long time this was so. Over time, the act of delivering food became a ritual. To be chosen was an honor. Because it was codified as ritual, no one asked if the food was taken, if there was a sign she still survived. She surely had long since died. The ritual continued nonetheless.

And so it was for centuries, the lonely one isolated safely above us. We congratulated ourselves that we had found a benign solution to her existence.

What happened then was that Death paid us a personal visit.

Death as you know looks like anyone. When he is among you humans, he looks like one of you. Among the Ondionts, he was a serpent, and yet dissimilar. Obsidian of eyes and sheathed in bone. Unlike us, he had arms, thin as reeds and supple, down the sides of his body. We knew him the instant he arrived, and he did not dissemble, but came right to the point.

"I want to know," he said, "how it is that you have all stopped coming to me."

The elders, who had been unborn when Missansha was sent away, shuffled meekly up to him. They replied as one, "We don't know what you mean."

"There are rules," he explained. "I for my part must adhere to them as must you. Else what sort of a world would we have? You, for your part, seem to have ceased to die, and I wish to know how you have done this—what magic or art now protects you. I've traveled a long way for the answer and I will not leave without it."

Now, none of them understood Death's accusation. Ondionts had been born and had died as always. Our insignificant island would have become surfeited otherwise and our caverns jammed with wriggling tenants. Death saw this for himself even as they protested their innocence. He noted the tower rising in their midst—something no snakes had built—and his sinister arms pointed at it.

"Why is that erected?" he asked.

Before they had even finished reciting the now-mythic story of Missansha, Death gestured them to silence.

"You think then that by placing a problem out of sight, you resolve it? That is your notion?"

"But how could we punish her?"

"Forgive me, did I suggest you should have punished her?" answered Death. "And yet you are of the opinion that she relishes her imprisonment. That placing her in a tiny room in the sky is not a punishment to her?"

"But . . . but she wasn't put to *death*!" exclaimed one of the elders, who immediately regretted his outburst and shrank away. For a moment, he had forgotten to whom he spoke.

"No," agreed Death, showing his teeth. "She was not. Not to *death*, but surely to madness have you condemned her. You are not people who fare well when isolated, and she began life more isolated than the rest of you." With that, Death passed through the crowd. One by one they lay down before him. At the tower's base, he stared up into the sky, to the very tip of it. He imagined himself there and a moment later he stood at the top, for that was how Death traveled.

His hands pressed that barred door, and it opened to him. Inside, it was dark and cobwebbed. Spiders had busily taken over the space. They dropped from their webs as he passed beneath them.

Deeper into the chamber, Death saw tiny lights burning—an entire wall of them. This struck him as unlikely. The lights sparkled. They were round like the eggs laid by Ondionts. They *were* eggs in fact, and the fire in each was a spark of life. He reached the wall and pried one loose from the mucilage that held it. He held it in his hands and with his needlelike fingers, he cracked it open and let the light escape. Like a flame it leapt up at him, and then through him. He heard it, saw it, experienced its life in a burst, because that is what the soul is—every moment of the life that was known, compressed into a flame of existence. It sang to him as it passed from this plane of being. And from the darkness behind him, a voice unused to speaking croaked, "What was that? How did my little song escape?"

Death turned around and there she was. Impossibly alive, thin and ancient, and yet to him unutterably beautiful.

"I let it go," he said.

Missansha gasped. She uncurled and rose to his height, the height of his voice. She'd learned to do that as a child, as a way of protecting herself. "How did I not hear you enter?"

"No one hears me enter, just as no one can surprise me. And yet, you have just done that impossible thing."

She didn't need eyes to identify him. The sense of him burned her like heat.

"These," he said, and turned back to the wall.

"My songs," she replied. "Long ago they began to come to me here in this chamber, I don't know from where. They entered me, pierced me, and then I birthed each one. So long ago that began, I can hardly remember the time before it."

"Another impossible thing, I think." He could still taste the essence of that soul he'd freed; he understood now how she had lived for so long. The lives entering her had passed to her a little of their being, each one rolling back her age. "Once upon a time, you lost your wits. You had already a power, a great and fearful power that frightened your people, and in the madness of isolation, this gift transformed. It grew. You became as I am."

He drew beside her. His hands embraced her, and for the only time in her life, Missansha felt what it was like for others to stand near *her*. There was no pain, but she was sundering from the world. "Am I dying?" she asked.

Death answered, "No. Something else."

She could not think what to say.

When it was done, her metempsychosis, they opened the eggs together and let Missansha's songs fly. It was orgasmic. The songs swirled and swept through her. She leaned back her head and her tongue flicked at the sky. She moaned and would have swooned but Death caught her. "You're not used to it," he told her. "So many at once is dizzying."

She would have agreed had she been able to speak, but her voice failed her. She looked into his empty eyes and realized that she could see. He, as if apprehending her confusion, said, "Your corporeal eyes could not see; but you no longer have need of them."

Soon the last of the souls had been released from where Missansha had collected them. She had been preserving them—though she hadn't recognized it—as a dowry for her groom.

When, after some days of speculating, the surviving people climbed the tower, they found the room at the top abandoned. No trace remained of Missansha save for her cast-off skin. Her body was missing and the floor covered with shattered eggshells, dry and empty; covered also with the bodies of a hundred spiders, curled and desiccated.

Of Death himself there was no sign either.

"And that," said the snake, raising his head from her lap, "is how my people met Death. In return for providing him with a bride, we were given very long lives. And we've never been sure if that was his blessing or his punishment for how we'd treated her. What do you think?" He leaned over Leodora; the sun had all but set now and the penultimate orange glow glittered in his eyes like hunger.

"Both," she answered without hesitation, and the snake tilted his head thoughtfully and then gave a small nod.

"Ssseeyash," he said and placed his head on her shoulder.

"What does that mean?"

His tongue darted. "It is not translatable, you don't have the concept in your language. It references the shedding of the skin, the death of the old shell and the life manumitted beneath, the balance of the two coexisting being true existence, and so it is a word that expresses ultimate truth."

"That's a very complicated way to say you think something is true."

"Yes, which is why we have a simple word for it."

She reached up and stroked his nose. He sighed and closed his eyes. After a moment he muttered, "You're dangerously brave, Leodora."

"Foolishly so?"

"That has yet to be determined, and won't be by me. You imagine that stories protect you, and that makes you brave. But it doesn't mean it's true."

"Is that a warning?"

"Advice. Nothing more. Death comes looking for everyone eventually."

"I'll try not to invite him."

"I suppose you must take it lightly," he replied. "To do otherwise is to admit your fear."

"If I let it stand in my way, I'll never get off this boat. I wouldn't have gotten on in the first place. I wouldn't have ridden a sea dragon. I'd have married the choice of my uncle."

"All concrete objects of fear, real and tangible," said the snake, and she knew by the way he said it that there was another kind of fear he didn't speak of.

She would have asked him, but at that point one of the crewmembers raced past to the boat's prow, and she turned to look where he did.

Riding the horizon, a black sail protruded against the sun's embers. It was tiny, but clearly a ship.

Soter walked up beside her. She looked up; saw the abject horror on his face. His gaze flicked over the water to where the crewman was looking, then down at her as he said, "You have to come inside now."

"Inside?"

"In the shack, the house, here, now."

"Why?"

"For safety. Please, don't start a fight with me, just come inside till that boat out there is gone."

"What about my friend the snake?" She turned, to find that the snake had retreated, his head down, eyes closed, back around the mast so that he looked like a rope again. His was the perfect disguise.

"Snake? What are you talking about?"

"Nothing," she replied, and got to her feet. He grabbed her arm and drew her along beside him. As they hurried clumsily into the shack, one of the crew came out from it, carrying a large lit lantern. He carried it to the starboard side and hung it off a hook there. It hung out over the water.

"Why not in the bow?" she asked.

"In case someone hostile comes, they'll see the lamp, but from a distance they can't tell if it's fore or aft, or port or starboard, and so can't gauge where to board till they're close upon it. Every ship, every boat, puts the lamp somewhere different, and the only thing you can do is steer a wide berth around 'em."

How, she wondered, did he know so much about the way things worked on board ships? "Hostile?" she asked, but he didn't answer.

By the time the new ship neared, the sun was gone, the sky black, and the breeze had died away. For a while Leodora had watched the ship's inexorable approach. One light split into two—two red glows like mismatched eyes of a behemoth slithering silently toward them. Soon the ship came close enough that she could make it out—at least the places where it glistened. It was black as the night around it. The red running lights were strung upon ropes, one off its nose and one off the stern. As it overtook the tail of their own boat, Soter pulled her back into the blackness of the house. Where he sat behind them, Diverus looked up at the commotion. The nose of the black ship pushed into view.

The ship had a high foredeck that dropped off before the main mast. It was a deep-bottomed craft, and its ropes and tackle creaked as it drew alongside. The red lantern on the prow rocked back and forth.

Soter's grip on her shoulders squeezed tight, and she almost cried out before he released her. She could hear him draw deeper into the darkness, his fear like an oil sprayed upon the air. The forward light glided past, and then the side of the ship hove into view. It seemed to be lined with odd pillars. Then all at once she realized that the pillars were people, figures standing motionless along the side—she counted five of them, their bodies as dark as the ship, edged only in the rolling lantern light; their heads smooth, gleaming, hairless, their eyes seeming to welter in deep sanguine sockets. Their fixed stare like a braided force sliced through the protective shadows. Red lantern light splashed along the deck ahead of her, doubling and bending the shadows, penetrating the depths of the three-sided house, steadily, rhythmically, like a pendulum as the lamp swung. She watched, hypnotized, as color flowed toward her feet and away, cast back again, closer, away and closer, away and closer. Then Soter snatched her into the depths of the shack, and the light splashed across Diverus where he sat staring at it, either unafraid or too ill to move. It lit the room, hooks and gaffs, ropes and tackle, all along the wall where Diverus sat. Soter pressed Leodora against the starboard wall and out of the light completely.

Yet, for all that his dread was palpable, nothing happened. The black ship glided on into the night until the light of the lanterns had merged into a single spot again, an ember that cooled, shrinking, until it went out altogether over the horizon.

"What was that?" she asked without turning to look at him.

"Trouble," was his answer. Then he pushed past her and

strode to the stern, where he appeared to strike up a conversation with the tillerman, but too quiet to be heard.

"Does he mean 'pirates'?" asked Diverus.

"I don't know."

"Would the snake?" He glanced up from where he sat; in the lantern light, his face devoid of anything she might call wry.

"How do you know about the snake?"

"I walked around the house before, while he was speaking to you about a tower. You had the same look you'd had with the fox, and so I knew you didn't want to be interrupted and I came back here to wait."

She thought a moment, then said, "You know about pirates."

"Only from things said in the paidika. There were two boys, and they'd been stolen off a boat by pirates, far from Vijganar, and brought to market there. I know no more than what they said, and so the black boat *could* have been pirates."

"I'm not certain, but I think it's something else."

"What?"

She shook her head. "Something that Soter feared."

Stars smeared the sky overhead. The boat sailed on and Soter stayed beside the tillerman, while Diverus and Leodora hunkered down inside the house. Tension and the motion of the boat worked upon them and they fell asleep against each other.

In the morning, the light of dawn woke them, and they walked stiffly onto the deck, to discover that they were docked below an astonishingly high wall. It must have been twice the height of Hyakiyako. Pennants flew from its top. The wall was rough, the stone uneven, and scattered across its surface were small star-shaped objects, like medallions, that glinted in the early light. Farther along, away from the jetty, the wall opened into a dark and uninviting arch that wouldn't even have accommodated their mast. Any ships wanting to pass to the far side of this spiral would have had to sail on to the next span up or down the line. The rest of the span repeated the pattern of massiveness broken up by low arches. The steps and the jetty appeared to be dead center along its length.

One of the crewmen, red-bearded, came up behind them, carrying a basket on his back. He passed them and, climbing up and over the prow via the step Leodora had used to look into the sea, he walked down the jetty to the wall. A platform attached to ropes lay there, with another of his shipmates standing by, and he set his cargo carefully in the center of it. Then the two of them gave two of the ropes a tug. The ropes snapped tight and the platform lurched slightly and then began to ascend. They steadied it until it was out of reach. High above them but below the top of the wall, beams jutted out, and between the beams, an opening, another arch. The sound of a squeaking pulley echoed distantly down to them.

As the crewman returned, Leodora asked him where Soter had gone.

"Up," he said, and gestured his head at the wall. "First one of us out, he was."

She turned, anger infusing her until she saw that the puppet cases were gone, too, already uplifted. Soter had accompanied them. Behind her, Diverus set down his bundle.

"Time to go, then," she muttered, then looked around for the snake. He was nowhere to be seen. The mast he'd girdled was empty, the sail drawn down and wrapped in loops of rope.

The bearded crewman and another came lumbering around the house now, carrying one of the larger crates. The platform was still ascending, so they set the crate down and watched it from on deck.

"The snake," said Leodora. "Where did he go?"

The two men looked at her, then at each other, then at her again. "Snake?" asked the bearded crewman.

"The snake who guards your cargo. He was wrapped around that mast there last night."

The other one said, "She saw it, too." They remained facing her, their faces tight with worry as if weighing what to do with her, and she thought that perhaps she shouldn't have said anything, that the snake was their secret, and that her life might well be forfeit for revealing what she knew.

Abruptly, the bearded one said, "Then he weren't crazy. He was tellin' the truth."

"And we trussed him up for nothing," said the other. The morning sun glistened off the stubble on his face. "This snake, he speak to you?"

She nodded uncertainly. Behind her, Diverus said, "I saw it, too. Talking to her." They all looked his way then. "Last night. It was telling her a story."

Said one to the other, "But why can't we see it? Why these two and not us?"

"Does it matter? It's real. That's all, that's what matters.

We have us an avatar on board. We're blessed."

An avatar. She'd spoken to an avatar before that no one else had seen . . . and Soter hadn't seen the snake, either. But Diverus *had*.

The bearded sailor grabbed her by the shoulders. Close up, he smelled of sweat and brine. "You've brought us luck, girl, you and your friends. You ever want to venture between spirals again, we're your men. We'll take you."

"Thank . . . Thank you."

He let her go and lifted his end of the crate again. To his partner as they carried it the rest of the way off the boat, he said, "We go back to Merjayzin and get him released, first thing. We've committed a crime here, we have to make it right. Bring that poor sod back on board and let him talk all he likes . . ." They climbed onto the jetty, their words fading.

Diverus asked, "We saw an avatar?"

"Apparently."

"What *is* an avatar?"

"A spirit of the gods. Or a god made flesh."

"Or snakeskin." He smiled a little sheepishly and hefted his bundle of instruments.

"Yes, snakeskin." With a final glance back at the mast, she followed him up and off the boat.

From right below, the stairs looked even more imposing than they had from the boat, impossibly steep. At least, she thought, they were wide.

Responding to the same view, Diverus drew a breath and started up. The sack of instruments rattled on his back.

As she ascended, the two sailors waved to her; they grinned as if the oyster girl, Reneleka, had arisen from the water and handed them her pearl. And, thought Leodora, perhaps she had. Perhaps the snake did indeed herald great good fortune.

Twice on the climb up the steps they had to stop. The second time they stood parallel to the pulleys that lifted the platform, still a dozen steps below the top. By leaning out from the step, they could see arms reach out of the wall, grab the goods and drag them off the platform and into the wall. Clearly some sort of space existed just beneath this span—possibly nothing more than a storage space; but with the memory of Vijganar still fresh, they both could well imagine a more extensive underworld. The semicircle out of which the pulley beams projected was itself an ancient opening, the lip of pinkish stone grooved as from years of ropes cutting into the face of it as cargo was raised, perhaps from a time before beams and pulleys had been applied.

Down below, the sailors had become no bigger than gnats and the boat a toy in a crystalline harbor. Off to one side of the boat, something serpentine floated upon the surface. It might have been only the ridge of a reef—she couldn't tell from this perilous height.

Above them threadbare pennants snapped in a strong breeze, which buffeted them as they came up the final steps.

If, as all the tales claimed, most ancient Colemaigne had once been made of spun sugar and other confections, then centuries of rain and wind had eroded the hard façade of the nearest buildings, exposing more traditional materials underneath—crumbling mortar and stones. These skinny buildings had lost their flat surfaces, their precise edges. Rooftops dipped, and tiles co-existed with thatchwork, while the frameworks leaned askew. One section was worse than those around it, the roofs and the top floors gone completely as far back as could be seen. It was as if a monstrous arm had swung down from the sky and scooped a diagonal swath across the span. The buildings themselves in that patch were chalky ruins, their cracked beams like broken bones. The wounds looked old, yet no one had repaired or rebuilt the houses, which seemed odder still.

The steps opened onto a wide square of broken flagstones, off which half a dozen streets branched. For the supplies being hauled in below, there was no apparent egress.

Small ramps ringed the steps, wedges with their apexes facing in toward the square. At some time in the past, carts would have met travelers here and whisked them away across the span in either direction. She could see them in her mind, the carts backed up to the little ramps, accepting trunks, crates, whatever people brought. She could hear them, too. The excitement of that time crackled up into her through the broken street. The sense of displacement lasted a few minutes, then evaporated as if blown apart by the wind; after that, she was fluent in the language of Colemaigne.

In the center of the square stood a fountain, with figures in the middle of some sort of animals, four of them facing four directions. The waters of the fountain poured darkly from their mouths. Soter was seated upon the edge of it, with the cases beside him. His head was down, arms resting upon his thighs and his hands holding a cup between them. The stones of the street between the ramps and the fountain were pitted and cracked, difficult to walk on.

At their approach Soter glanced up, then lowered his head again, as if they weren't what he'd been waiting for.

The fountain flowed with wine. It looked black, but Leodora knew that it wasn't. She thought, at least one part of the myth was true. Small earthenware cups like the one he held dotted the lip of it.

They flanked him and sat. Without looking up, he said, "It didn't used to be like this. When Bardsham came, they had banners flying. A welcoming crowd. They knew us, they cheered us. This place was *alive*."

His words slurred appreciably. This was not his first cup of wine. She asked, "What's happened then?"

"Blight," he said. He gestured with the cup toward an open stall selling vegetables and fruits. She noticed that his hand was trembling as if the cup was heavy. "I asked there, and they told me," he said. "Chaos came. Had to start somewhere, I suppose, and Colemaigne's as good a place as any for it. Barely touched down here, right here, but the place has never recovered. The richness is gone, washed away. Your father and me, we entered this very square once in triumph, and it was everything I said it was, a confection of a span. Good days, those. Good days."

She didn't understand what he meant—his description of the maelstrom made it sound as if a water spout had descended, shattering one piece of the span then spinning away. He used that word too freely to account for too much. He blamed everything on chaos. "So, where do we go? We're here and we're surely not climbing aboard that boat again and going back."

He jumped when she said that, as if she'd stuck him with a needle. "Gods, no. Not an option, going back. Anyway, it might not be so blighted deeper in. There—there's another square on the far side, mirror to this one. We can look. Things are better over there, they said. The whole span might not be so bad. Depends on how far . . . how deep." He lost himself in some thought then, but came out of it quickly. "And it's early, you know, barely past dawn, so there's not much of a crowd out yet." He twisted about and dipped his cup. "The fountains still run, I'm pleased to say."

For once she was inclined to let him have his fill, although his rambling about the blight upon Colemaigne told her very little. It was a span that had been great but had fallen upon hard times. Between that and the line of small stands selling food, she thought again of Ningle. Someone brought the produce; someone caught the fish. She understood better than anyone the complicated processes that no one saw—and no one cared, so long as what they wanted was available.

"Let's see the other side, then," she suggested. "It's not that far, is it?"

"Not far," he agreed. He stood, an unsteady moment. Prominent veins mapped his left calf and, although she'd noticed them before, it was only now she appreciated that he was an old man, strong and proud and unwilling to bend. Perhaps it was the magic of this span, or the result of meeting with another divine advisor, but she seemed to be experiencing any number of epiphanies today. She found herself feeling affectionate toward him despite everything that pitted them against each other time and again. She got up and kissed his cheek. Diverus could not have looked more shocked, while Soter's bewilderment had to swim through the muddle of his brain.

"All right," she said. "Let's see the rest of Colemaigne. We have to find somewhere to perform."

She hefted one of the cases and ducked under the strap, then started walking.

The two men eyed each other distrustfully a moment. Then Diverus, as though taking a cue from her, offered his lighter bag of instruments to Soter and shouldered the second undaya case. "You can't imagine what this place was like," Soter told him as though he hadn't described it. "It was so magical."

Diverus kept his own counsel on it, but he was pretty certain that magic was still afoot.

The far side did prove to be in better shape. Whatever tumult Soter had described, its effects hadn't blanketed the whole span. Some of the slender houses near the opposite square still maintained their surface coats, which were hard like stone, shiny and carved, like sculptures, with all manner of swirls and motifs. In one narrow lane, Leodora wetted a finger and wiped it across one bright green wall before sticking it in her mouth.

"Sweet," she said around her finger. "It really *is* sugar."

"No one in the world knows how they do it, either," Soter told her. "They've a guild, sworn to secrecy. Can't even catch them working if you try."

More people were gathered in the new square, too, the span now awake for the day. They milled about the shops and stalls. This was exactly like a market day on Ningle, and Leodora felt a chill enclose her breastbone as she recalled her grandparents, her aunt, her ill-starred childhood.

Soter inquired at the shops about places and names familiar to him, and was given directions and information. Eavesdropping, Leodora gathered that, yes, the theatre where Bardsham had performed was still standing, although performances there had been few of late; that the owner had died, but that his offspring had taken over in his place; and that they probably could find a place to lodge a trio of performers.

This news served to brighten his mood, and he strode into the lead, along a seaward lane so narrow that they had to go single file with their luggage and press up against the buildings if someone needed to pass by; he regaled them all the while, in love with his own voice. "Oh, yes, we played here a month. By the time we finished, people were coming from half a dozen spans away to hear, not thinkin' or maybe they just didn't care, that we would be moving on to theirs eventually. 'Course, in the end we didn't, we got on a ship right down there—" he pointed at the quayside below "—and off we went to Remorva, and wasn't *that* an adventure. So, I guess they were right to journey all that way for the great Bardsham, 'cause they wouldn't see his like again in a generation—till now, in fact. So they'd better let us play or they won't know what they're missing."

While Soter babbled away, he strolled along the narrow lane as if without a care. With his load lightened, he failed to notice the distance he was putting between himself and the other two. The dragon beam of Colemaigne was approaching, and he pointed to it and called back, "Look at it. That thing hasn't seen a visitation in your lifetime. . . . What am I saying? In *my* lifetime, which is much more considerable."

He pressed against the buildings to let a woman in a dark purple wrap scuttle past, saying, "Begging your pardon," as she did. She kept her head down and gave barely a sign that she'd heard him. "Not very sociable, are you," he muttered to her back, and returned his attention to the dragon beam.

It did look as ragged as if it had been gouged out of the sky, so thin in the middle, it was a wonder the weight of the Dragon Bowl on the end hadn't caused it to snap off and plunge into the sea.

Diverus and Leodora, meanwhile, had fallen back. The cases incommoded passage along the lane. The corners kept bumping against the uprights in the railing. The woman in purple reached them, and they had to set down the cases and step back to let her by.

Leodora asked, "Was the Bowl on Vijganar as decrepit as this before your transformation?"

Diverus peered at it ahead. "Not this bad, no. But similar. The beam was crumbling. The walls of it had fallen away like this. The Bowl had broken tiles in the bottom, you couldn't even tell what the mosaic had been."

"Do you dare me to go out on one?" she teased.

He turned around. "You've never been on a Dragon Bowl?"

She shook her head. "I've meant to. At first, Soter argued it was too dangerous. Too public. My uncle might see. That was when we worried that he might be following us."

"I thought you said he was dead."

"I said he might be. I don't know for sure. But Soter wouldn't allow me near it. I started climbing the towers instead. Your story is the closest I've gotten."

Diverus slid the strap over his shoulder. "Well, wouldn't dare you, I think. Unless it was the *only* way to get you on one." He gave her a puckish smile and walked off with the undaya case.

She followed, but her attention stayed with the ravaged beam.

Soter passed the beam. Not a single person sat along its length. These people had long since stopped believing in the capricious gods. That woman who'd passed him, she hadn't even looked at it. That they'd let it fall into such ruin . . .

He concentrated on that and his opinions of how far the span had fallen, so that he had gone some distance past the beam before he detected the change in the buildings on his right. He stopped.

The building beside his shoulder was dead. In its windows half the quarrels were missing, others broken. The glossy façade was gone, eroded, and the revealed underlying structure gray and powdery. The higher stories loomed above him as if they might soon tip into the sea. The top floor and roof were missing. This was true of the building next to it and the one next to that. The swath he had seen cutting an angle across the span emerged here. "Tophet," he muttered, "This was no accident." He leaned over the rail and looked down, far down, to where the quay had once been. It was rubble now, boulders sticking out of the water. No jetty at all.

It couldn't be new, this destruction. It hadn't happened recently. This blight had struck sometime after he and Bardsham had played here. After they had sailed from the quay below with Leandra. He could not now help concluding that this had been a punitive act: Colemaigne had allowed them to escape.

Diverus came up, set down his case, and joined Soter in peering over the side. "Is there something to see?"

"Not anymore," answered Soter. He realized unhappily that he was exuding friendship to Diverus, and withdrew from his reverie. "Where is-" he began, looking past the musician. Then, in a voice tight with horror, he said, "Oh, gods, no."

Diverus turned, too.

Leodora had set down her puppet case and walked out the crumbling beam and onto the Dragon Bowl.

She considered the beam's condition made it slightly perilous, but hardly more so than climbing up a tower. She didn't fear the height, she embraced the thrill of it.

What had Diverus felt? What was it like to stand within the hexagonal bowl, waiting for some sign that you were exalted, chosen? A thriving span, covered with people, and only one or two would ever be blessed by the gods in such a way, and no one able to predict who it would be, when it would happen; no one sure it would ever happen again. There must be stories in that—of course there were, like the tale of the two brothers that Soter had taught her years ago. She'd nearly forgotten it.

This Bowl was in worse shape than Diverus had described. There were almost no tiles remaining. If he hadn't said, she wouldn't have thought it had ever been covered with them.

She turned around and looked back along the ragged beam. From the narrow lane Soter was waving and she waved back. The buildings behind him were osseous husks, like the ones on the far side they'd seen. Her attention, however, was drawn to the underside of the span, visible from where she stood, because unlike the opposite side, this one wasn't hidden behind a solid wall. It was more the way Vijganar had been, the night she'd climbed from the paidika with Diverus.

She could see underneath Colemaigne, and what she saw seemed utterly impossible. There were houses in a kind of mirror image of the city above, hanging upside down off the bottom of span. She crossed the bowl and leaned over the lip, astonished.

The wind gusted as it had when she first arrived. It blew back her hood. Soter shouted something but she could not hear him over the wind.

Diverus called to her, too. His words were drowned out by a rumbling in the sky overhead, and she tilted her head back. Above the Dragon Bowl the sky was roiling as if throbbing with heat; the blue had darkened to greenish black as though the substance of the sky itself was scorching. Lightning flicked from this mass like the tongue of the Ondiont snake, transfixing her in fascination. She wasn't even aware that she had stepped back into the center of the bowl. The air crackled. It pulsed with energy that tingled right through her. She spread out her arms as the center of the darkness flared and exploded, and brilliant white lightning struck straight down into the bowl. Where it hit it expanded, swallowing her, the bowl, the beam and everything near it.

Upon a black ship well on its way across the sea to Vijganar, beneath a thick, striped awning, a bony, bald-headed creature saw a bright flash just above the horizon whence they'd sailed and inadvertently said, "Ah?"

At this utterance, another, who might easily have been his gaunt twin, poured from the darkness behind him to see what had elicited a comment, but there was nothing now to behold. The morning sky all the way to the horizon was untroubled by so much as a single blemish. The two stared into each other's sunken eyes and both shrugged together. "Enh," said the first, and the second one reached over and pressed a fingertip to his nose to cover a spot of calcitic gray showing there; and when he withdrew his hand, the spot was gone, the nose pink. He gave a satisfied nod. The other turned to look off into the distance behind them once more. Then he flowed back into the raven recesses of the ship.

Part 3:
The Blight Of Colemaigne

Chapter 5: Advice From a Lion

"Everything has its own vortex," said a deep male voice. Whoever spoke must have been right at her back. Leodora glanced behind herself but saw only a great expanding gyre, a white-scorched tunnel stretching all the way back to the span of Colemaigne – to the hexagonal Dragon Bowl on which she stood . . . still stood, surely. Diverus and Soter must be there even now, and all of this a dream. Someone else's dream that had scooped her up and carried her off. "Wake up," she said, but nothing changed, and she wondered if anyone could hear her.

She had no sense of motion; she hadn't taken a single step, and yet the Dragon Bowl shrank until it was like a pinhole at the far end of the gyre, so she had to be moving, carried, transported . . . somewhere. She looked down at herself – at her legs stretched a thousand wyrths down the tunnel, as long as a full spiral's length from one coiled end to the other, which was farther even than she had traveled with Soter from Bouyan to Colemaigne. She kicked her feet but they were so distant in this dream that she couldn't see them, or her ankles. The view of her impossible legs fascinated her.

The disembodied voice spoke again, solemnly, beside her now. "The Traveler thro' Eternity has passed that first Vortex. She enters another."

She glanced up, facing the source, but once again no one was there.

As if cooling, the tunnel surface lost its white-hot glow as if cooling, and the duller orange glow left in its wake revealed that the walls of the structure: intricately linked geometric shapes in a state of constant flux. She rushed along beside the bright geometries, diminutive satellites whirling in interlocked orbits. "I'm past the world," she said.

"Thus is heaven a vortex passed already," replied the voice.

"I must get back," she told it.

"You haven't *been* anywhere yet," the voice answered her.

"And where is it I'm going?" She thought she sounded remarkably calm to herself.

The voice didn't reply. Behind her now the tunnel appeared to have no end point, unspooling forever. Her legs, however, had come unstuck from the distortion and had returned to their proper proportions. *At least I am myself again,* she thought.

Slowly, a vinegary stink stole upon her, a foulness as of a few unwashed bodies that grew until it was like the stench of a crowd, as if a mob coated in filth pressed in against the glowing tunnel. Her eyes watered, it was so noisome. She put out a hand as though to repel the odor, and her palm penetrated the spinning geometries and brushed something solid, moving. Alive. Another's hand tried to grasp at her fingers, but she snatched them free of the greasy grip. This motion propelled her away from the stink and the unseen thing and through the tunnel wall of spinning stars and globes, triangles and trapezoids, which washed over her body without sensation, passed through her like ghosts—like the bizarre phantoms that had paraded with her across the span of Hyakiyako and toward the end of time, the end of everything.

It had never occurred to her before to wonder what the end of everything might look like, how different it might be from the infinite bridge spirals of Shadowbridge. Perhaps that was where she was now, and this wasn't a dream. Had she, perhaps, died?

Outside the tunnel, separated from it, she stood on solid ground and watched it twist snake-like, as if alive, away from her. The glow of its spinning geometries dimmed like a cooling ember, until it was a golden thread of beaded sparks that finally flickered out, much like the red lamps on the black, silent ship that had passed hers on her way to Colemaigne and so terrified Soter. She must remember to ask him about it, when she returned. Or woke up. Or . . . where exactly was she?

A thick fog swirled out of the blackness to enclose her.

Beneath her bare feet lay an unseen and uneven ground of hard rough stones. It was cold, and she wished that before she'd started walking through Colemaigne she'd put on her boots or the sandals Tastion had given her back on Bouyan.

The putrid stench still hovered near but less intense, blended as it was with an odor of food, something meaty frying with onions. And distantly, or else close but muffled by the fog, she heard a rhythmic knocking noise of something hard upon the stones, getting louder as she focused on it, a *clop*-clop-*clop*-clop that drew her to it, louder and louder every second and behind it, beneath it, a growing roar. The noise swelled, almost on top of her. She raised a defensive hand as a monstrous dark shape erupted out of the fog, giving her not even time to scream as it bore down on her. In that instant something grabbed hold of the hood at her neck and yanked her to one side. The fog roiled where she'd been and a huge creature with a great snout and a black glass eye surged past her so closely that she could see the sheen of its coat. Behind it came a large black carriage with curtained windows and skinny, wiry wheels thundering over the rough ground. Animal and carriage swept by and were swallowed in the fog as quickly as they appeared.

"Do you *want* to be squished?" asked the voice as Leodora's hood was released.

She turned about. The figure stood behind her, but the fog obscured his features. He was tall, and the fog abstracted his features until they were smudges, like the features of the Coral Man that lay in her puppet case back on Colemaigne.

"What *was* that thing?" she asked.

"Your demise if you don't learn to get out of the way. Standing in the middle of the road is never a good idea. You can be knocked down from *both* directions. As for what that was—surely you know."

"A palanquin, yes, but what monster led it?"

"Oh, no monsters here. Then again, *here* is itself monstrous to you. We're quite the world apart."

"This is Edgeworld, then?" Briefly she glimpsed wet gray paving stones under her feet.

"I think it most unusual that you've transported here. That's not how it's done generally. Seems your gift wasn't determined. I can't recall the last time that happened . . . at least, not at *our* particular terminus. Who can say *what's* gone on in Babylon? May-my, that could be a song title."

She tried to steal nearer the speaker. "Do you write songs?"

"I'm thinking about taking it up. 'Oh, what's gone on in Babylon,' late Enkidu inquired. 'For I've been dead,' is what he said, 'and missed . . .' Drat, I have no idea how to complete that rhyme."

"I would offer to help, but I don't know the story."

"Don't *know* it? How Enkidu died and the hero Gilgamesh went into the underworld and brought him back?"

She shook her head, then realized he probably couldn't see the gesture any better than she could see him. "No," she replied.

"Well, there's a wonder. What are they teaching you in . . . where were you just now?"

"Colemaigne."

"Oh. Never mind, then, they don't teach anything there. Others build moments, minutes, hours. Not Colemaigne, not ever. Land of honey and surfeit."

"What happened to it?"

"Hmm? Oh. Not surfeited anymore, is it? Blighted by Tophet, was Colemaigne. Hell, in the guise of Chaos, placed one hand upon the wall of a building, and from his imperishable fingers spread the web of decay. Sum and substance cracked and spilled out bitterness, in shoals of torment."

"Who is Tophet?"

"More like, *what* is Tophet, if you're going to ask. Dispensed with the *who*. For Colemaigne, he was the Destroyer, come from the far side of the world seeking vengeance."

"But he didn't destroy all of it."

"Yes, and lucky the span was, too. He became distracted. Else it would have been a silent place forever."

"What distracted him?"

"Something. Something to do with *you*, it was. Something to do with death."

"Me?" She edged still nearer. "But it happened before I was born."

"True. And false."

She puzzled at that. "*You* know, though, don't you?" she said.

"Goes without saying, dear heart, goes without saying."

"Then why can't you explain it clearly?"

"Why? Because. It's necessary for you to find the answers to the larger puzzles of life yourself. They can't be handed out, providing information that would change the pattern you have to walk. The maze. The labyrinth. It's yours, I can't go about altering its shape just as a *courtesy*. Your mettle is to be tested and no one's to interfere in that. Besides, you won't remember a thing I say."

As he spoke, gesturing with caped arms, she stole ever closer, and before he noticed she'd slipped up beside him. When he looked down, she saw him clearly.

It was Soter's face.

"Taking a peek at eternity, are you?" he asked, amused.

"You're—"

"No, I'm not. This is a false body, an incrustation over my immortal spirit." He winked. "For *your* benefit, I should add."

From deeper in the fog came wailing, as if a chorus stood beyond the limit of her vision, responding to his words, answering or lamenting.

"Terrible time, this, terrible. But then what time isn't, hmm? We all wear the mind-forged manacles in this world to bring forth your own."

"I don't understand at all," she answered.

"Stories—yours and others'—they're the products of disenchantment. Without it, no telling would be necessary. All would be harmony. But it never is, save in memory where the disharmonious is excised as with a scalpel, and 'Oh, for the Golden Days of Old' becomes the Song of Delusion, when no such days ever have been or will be. Joys impregnate. Sorrows bring forth."

Leodora shook her head. His words danced along the edge of comprehension, as if his meaning, like the chorus, lay just outside the wall of fog, attainable if only she could penetrate it. To delve into the fog, however, meant to move away and lose sight of him, which seemed to her a great risk just then.

The chorus sounded again, in doleful harmony with her dilemma. They were nearer, right behind him, as if they or the street were moving, sliding.

The rhythmic clop and clatter of another carriage approached, and this time she drew back as it neared, well before his hand grabbed her, so that this time she pulled him away. The fog parted as though fleeing her, and there stood the chorus in a half circle around a low stone wall upon which perched a large, long-haired cat. The cat's fur ran through a rainbow of colors, as bright as if a beam of sunlight were somehow penetrating the fog bank and striking the creature. One of the members reached out and ran a grubby hand the length of the cat, smoothing its fur. Its mouth opened, and a weird music floated out. The chorus listened to the notes and then as a group repeated them. Their dissonant chants had nothing to do with her songwriter after all.

"Beast knows all the tunes," he said.

She became aware that the latest coach had slowed and come to a halt behind them, and she turned back.

"It's for us," said the songwriter. His hand at her elbow gently impelled her. His gaze—Soter's gaze—was benign.

"Where are we going?"

"That I cannot say. It's *your* journey, and you must tell the carriage where to go, when to stop."

In the mist behind him, the cat lit up in colors and let forth another musical refrain of gliding notes that the crowd tried to emulate immediately, producing a caterwaul of conflicting voices. Had she been any nearer, she would have winced.

"How can I know where to stop when I can't see anything?" she asked him.

"Perhaps," he suggested, "it's not something you do with your eyes?"

"I'm not used to this. I'm not ready."

"No one ever is. Nor will you be here long enough to adapt. Not that you'd want to. The stink of old Londinium would win in the end. Blackened churches, the sighs like blood running down the walls. Not for you." He held open the door of the carriage and reached out, his palm up. "Come into my hand," he said, which she found stranger even than what he'd said previously.

She took his palm and let him lift her forward and up into the carriage, which rocked back and forth as she took her seat. He got in behind her and closed the door. Then, with a walking stick she hadn't noticed previously, he rapped twice on the ceiling.

The carriage lurched, and he said, "Off we go."

She studied him now. In the shadowy confines of the carriage she could make him out more clearly than in the fog. It was Soter's face, all right, but with a thick shock of hair wild about his head, and much less dissolution across the terrain of his cheeks—a Soter who hadn't drowned his every trouble in tuns of wine.

Under her scrutiny, he commented, "The maiden forgets her fear."

She sat back. "How is this my journey?" she asked.

"You walked the pattern, although it wasn't visible any longer. That's an impressive enough feat for almost anyone. You traveled though you never left the spot. Now you choose the thing that returns with you, which might be important, or superfluous—but you do choose it."

"Does everyone?"

"Does everyone choose? May-my, yes, everyone who comes here, though none—including you—remembers. Nothing I've told you will you remember."

"Diverus, then. He chose his gift."

"I assume that is the name of someone who came before you? If so, then yes. I didn't meet him, but what are the odds of two who know each other arriving in my care in my moment? Surely astronomical. Your look tells me that you remain confused, which is as it must be, and no matter, for you'll lose this conversation shortly. The ride, the smells, the caterwauls, the beast that draws us—all will fall away. For now . . . you have but to choose."

"But what am I choosing?"

"What everyone chooses. What your Diverus chose."

Frustrated, she folded her arms. He shifted on the seat and his forehead furrowed, giving her the impression that if he had known more, he *would* have told her, but the larger picture was as obscure to him as it was to her.

She asked, "How do I make the choice?"

"You say *stop*. The carriage stops. You pick your prize, whatever it might be, and this all comes to an end."

Leodora said, "I see," although she didn't. His explanation explained nothing. She was to decide without knowing. How could Diverus have chosen when he had no mind to think with? And yet he had—had chosen the divine gift of music. There really wasn't anything she wanted, except perhaps shoes for her feet, which had almost gone numb on the pavement. If Diverus had taken this same carriage ride, how would he have known when he'd arrived at the thing he wanted? Or had they healed him first? There seemed to be no point in asking if she wasn't going to remember the answers anyway.

She closed her eyes and listened to the carriage, the creak of wood and leather. The roll and jounce traveled through her, the steady rhythm of the hooves of the beast pulling her down into reverie or dream, a senseless state that was neither alertness nor slumber.

Then all at once she cried "Stop!" and the carriage drew to a halt so fast that she lurched out of her seat and back again.

Her companion, his eyes half lidded, remarked, "Excellent choice."

"What?" She *had* said stop. She *had* come alert. But she had no idea what had provoked the response.

"Go," he said, and opened the carriage door. "Quickly now. Once you choose, you've only a brief time to retrieve."

"Don't you—"

"No, I do not," he answered as if he had known the nature of her question before she even spoke. "I give you a golden string, but I await you here."

He gestured with the stick, and she climbed down from the carriage. The humid fog was as thick as before, the bricks of the street slick and fetid. She stepped up onto a raised walk, which proved smoother underfoot. Crossing it, she came upon wide steps going up and, beside them, a smaller set that descended beneath the level of the walk.

Up or down? She'd called out, chosen this spot, but didn't know why nor how to proceed. Up or down? It would matter. It must. Yet how was she to proceed when she didn't know what prompted her, what compelled her now? Up or down?

She stared at the arrangement of the stairs, railings, the wide blank doors just visible at the top of the steps. Uncertainly, she started up, her hand on the cold iron rail. She looked over the side of it. The lower stairwell curved beneath the steps, leading to a doorway that was upside down as she viewed it. The arrangement reminded her of the inverted world she'd glimpsed under Colemaigne and of the underworld of Vijganar. There were secret worlds enfolded in her world. And Diverus was from the secret world, sent to it after he'd stood upon the Dragon Bowl. These thoughts, notions, observations interlaced, although why they should she couldn't say. She had to operate on instinct and nothing more. Instinct instructed her to descend, just as it urged her to hurry.

She ran down the lower steps, which were black and worn as from a thousand years of use. Inset in the wall to her right was a window, its other side framed in lace. She peered in upon a chamber beneath the sidewalk where a rose-red lamp glowed warmly. Farther back in the room were people—a family, two parents and three children. They looked happy, contented, affectionate, oblivious of her presence, though she must have blotted out the light as she pressed to the glass. Tenderness for them consumed her—a longing to be in that room, part of that family, to be so loved. The ache of that desire drove her from the view and down the last two steps.

She stood before a door, surely the door that led to that room, that family. It was green, wet with mist, and embellished with a large brass knocker in the shape of a lion's head that held the knurled ring in its mouth.

Leodora reached up, grabbed the ring, and swung it hard against the door. The sound of it thundered, echoed as along endless hollow corridors. The lion's brass head opened golden eyes and stared down at her.

"The choice is made!" said the voice of her companion, and she jolted upright in her carriage seat, then glanced about herself in disorientation.

Across the carriage, Soter-but-not-Soter leaned toward her and said, "What is now proved was once only imagined." He offered her his walking stick, and the head of it was the lion's head of the door knocker. Had it been thus earlier? She hadn't looked closely enough. But she closed her fingers over it.

"Good-bye, Leodora," said the songwriter, and through her hand, between her fingers, the geometrics she'd stepped through before came swirling. They spun about her, twisted into a cylindrical blur that drew her upright and held her with her arms extended to the side, fingers skimming the patterns as she descended, flowed through the dream, sliding down the golden string, which settled her gently back within the hexagonal bowl. As her toes touched, the bowl reignited with so bright a light that it seemed to burn straight through her as though she were no thicker than the hammered skin of a shadow puppet. She looked at her hands glowing red from the blood within, and then all at once brighter still. In a burst that consumed her, she became light, and as the blaze faded all that remained was the thread of gold, which she followed downward into darkness.

Diverus maintained that he had slept through the visitation of the gods to the Dragon Bowl in which he'd been chained. He'd gone to sleep an idiot and waked a whole and reasoning being with no memory of the event that linked the two, which presumed that the event *had* been a visitation—that gods *had* descended in the night, driving mad all who saw them. Now that he had stared into the milky wasting eyes of soul-drinking afrits and been transported to some other place or time at acute cost to his life, he could well imagine being driven mad at the sight of beings divine and horrible.

Whatever he had envisioned of that missing time, it had been dark and subtle, nothing like a flash of light bright and powerful enough to knock him down in the sea-lane, dazzling him where he sprawled. His senses returned, a moment or an hour later. Along the rail and the bollards beside him a bluish fire scurried, crackling like grinding glass. It edged the building behind him, too, and sparked off Soter, who still lay stretched out in the lane. Rising up, Diverus saw his own hands, arms, and torso defined by the dancing fire, like an illusion, with no hint of sensation. As he got to his feet, this flame flickered and leapt as if willfully to the rail, abandoning him and merging with the glow there as though it shunned anyone conscious. Beam and Dragon Bowl both pulsed with the blue fire. The bowl stood empty. Leodora had vanished.

Now people appeared, out of doorways and from between buildings. People in cloaks and vests and some in careless dishabille looked, saw, came running along the narrow lane. Wherever they brushed the blue glow, it sparked and crackled but seemed to harm no one. They ran to him, to Soter, to the space in the railing where the dragon beam projected.

Soter climbed unsteadily to his feet and had to be held up. His head had a gash, a crooked line of blood over one eye. With a dull expression, he focused on Diverus, and his eyes went wide. "Lea!" he said, and with sudden ferocity he wrestled free of helpful supportive arms and hands while Diverus, already panicked by the sight of the empty bowl, plunged onto the dragon beam ahead of him.

The length of the beam had been repaired. Before the blast of light, the retaining walls had been nothing but crumbling remains. Now they were smooth and waist-high on both sides of a brown-tiled walkway. So, too, the wall around the bowl, sparking with blue fire, had been rebuilt. It shone hard and glossy. People in the lane were crying, "Lookit, lookit!" but only one or two were willing to step onto the beam so long as that blue fire burned.

The beam curved around to the outside of the bowl, entering it, as was the tradition, from seaward. Diverus ran, looking, seeing only an unoccupied bowl. With each step his anxiousness swelled.

The brown tiles continued as a motif into the refurbished bowl, circling it in a pattern that Diverus recognized immediately as a maze. And lying in the depressed center of the maze was Leodora, on her back with her red hair fanned out like blood around her head.

He ran across, unheedful of the maze pattern: He wasn't entering the bowl to capture the gods' goodwill; he didn't care.

He slid to his knees beside her. Her face was flushed or sunburned. He touched her, and she was warm as with a fever. Warm, which meant alive. He rejoiced, at the same time trying to recall if he had been similarly affected, but all he could remember of it was confusion upon awaking.

Behind him at the entrance to the bowl, Soter collapsed—peripherally Diverus saw the old man spiral into a heap like a broken puppet clinging in anguish to the wall. Soter's crust of pomposity fell away and revealed his true concern for Leodora. With a sharp stab of pity, Diverus said to him gently, "She's only sleeping." Soter glanced sharply up. The agony in his expression was slow to allow hope.

"It lit up," he said, "the gods—"

"The gods have favored her," Diverus replied, adding, "At least, if they haven't driven her mad, they have." He recalled that not one of the others who'd been in the Dragon Bowl with him had walked away sane.

"And if they have?" Soter asked, clinging to his misery.

Diverus had no answer for that, saying only, "We should move her off the beam before that crowd comes out here and picks her apart. They will, as soon as the blue fire dies, and they won't be reasonable." Already the strange fire was dwindling.

Soter cast him a peculiar look, and it was only then that he realized he was explaining situations, giving orders. Where the information came from, he had no idea. There had been no blue flame when he'd been in the Dragon Bowl of Vijganar. Why would he possess such authority and foreknowledge? Right now there was no time to ponder it.

Quickly, then, they each took one of her arms and placed it over their shoulders, supporting Leodora between them.

Diverus, as he did this, saw a chain dangling from her loosely closed hand. He tugged gently upon it, and a gold object slipped from between her fingers. In the same instant her eyes opened and gazed blankly at him, closing again almost as fast. Soter could not have seen it. He took a step up the bowl, but Diverus cried, "Wait!"

"What is it?"

"I think we have to walk the pattern out of here."

Soter seemed to consider the maze for the first time. "Did she walk it coming in?"

"I don't know. But I think we have to if we're to take her out, to protect her. The gods embedded it, we have to assume it applies." He glanced toward Colemaigne; the blue glow along the rail was flickering out. "And we'd best hurry."

Supporting Leodora between them, they walked the brown-tiled maze from the center out, around and around the bowl, out to the edge but looping in closer to the center again. Finally, on the fifth tier of lines, they arrived at the lip where the brown tiles led onto the dragon beam. Before they could even step onto the beam, the first and most daring of the citizens blocked their way, not menacing but anxious. "Is anything in the bowl—she have anything on her?"

"No," Diverus lied. "But the pattern has appeared, you see?"

"Then . . . oh, my."

"You should walk it," Soter suggested, but the man wasn't staring into the bowl. He was gaping at the view beyond it, at the span itself. Soter and Diverus craned their heads to follow his gaze, discovering that the row of buildings lining the sea-lane, all of which had been ruins before the blast of light, now stood whole and gleaming, newly formed.

"The gods have come! We're blessed again!" the man cried, and leapt past them into the Dragon Bowl. Disregarding Diverus's advice, he charged into the center of it across the lines of the maze.

Soter and Diverus wasted no more time, but carried their unconscious friend along the curved beam. So narrow was the space that they had to crab sideways with her. As others started out onto the beam, Soter snarled, "Back, back, the lot of you, or I'll stamp you flat!"

Diverus smiled at the effect that threat had on the crowd. They skittered timidly off the beam. Then he happened to glance off to the side of the beam, and he saw in the darkness beneath the span's surface what he took at first to be a reflection of the new buildings above, cast upon still water . . . until a door opened in one of them and a figure walked out upside down, went to the rail, and stared across right at Diverus. Above, upright in the newly recast lane, there was no corresponding figure. The upside-down man, as blue as lapis, lifted one hand, and it seemed that he waved, and Diverus answered with a wave of his free hand, swinging the gold chain and, on the end of it, a medallion in the shape of a broad face.

When he looked up again, the man had turned and gone back inside the impossible upside-down house. They were nearing the end of the beam then, and the edge of the span gradually cut off the vision. One of the citizens, unable to wait, jumped up and perilously walked the retainer wall to get around them. He glowered at Leodora and Diverus as he edged by and then leapt onto the brown tiles and ran, crying out, "Gods, I'm here, your devoted servant is here!" With raised hands, he rushed into the bowl, turning in circles, face to the sky, until the one who'd preceded him struck him down from behind. *It's starting*, Diverus thought, and quickly pocketed the medallion.

They reached the end of the beam, and the people there opened a space, not from courtesy so much as to get them out of the way. The moment Diverus stepped down, the nearest ones knocked him aside in their surge up the curving beam.

Someone asked, "What did she get, what did she see?" and Soter replied, "We don't know, do we? She's unconscious yet." A few eyed her as she was carried past, obviously weighing the desire to wait and find out what had happened to the girl in the bowl against the immediate lure of the Dragon Bowl itself. They all chose the latter. Some slid by. Others touched her reverently as she was carried past. When from one jarring movement her head lolled, someone said, "Why, she's dead," and Soter growled, "No, she's not, you fool. The gods dazzled her, the same as they would have anyone. Same as they will you." That acted as an invitation to the speaker, who bounded toward the beam.

"They were really here? The gods really came?" asked the next man. Behind him a veiled woman with aristocratic poise reached forward and touched his shoulder. She silently directed his attention to the front of the house beside him—to the hard, slick coating that edged it. The man licked a finger and reached across Leodora to run the finger along it. He licked his finger again. Then he covered his mouth with both hands and hurried toward the beam, all but knocking Diverus off his feet.

That left the veiled woman, their two undaya cases, the satchel full of Diverus's instruments and their wardrobe.

Behind the woman, two tall thin men with oddly shallow features beneath their cowls, waited stiffly like servants. She, dressed in an embroidered ocher chemise and green overtunic, pressed a finger to Leodora's sunburned cheek. "Oh, my. She was in the bowl when it happened?"

"Yes," Soter replied with what seemed to Diverus an odd inflection of uncertainty.

"A blessing or a curse then, when she awakens."

Diverus frowned at her air of mystical superiority. "Sometimes it's both, and sometimes not worth anything to anyone," he said, holding her gaze to make her understand that he spoke from experience.

Rather than being intimidated, the woman raised her head. He could feel her considering him.

"Diverus, can we lay her down on one of the cases?" Soter asked. "I can't hold her up any longer."

They lifted her onto the nearest undaya case, where she lay as if napping. Soter collapsed beside her. In setting Leodora down, Diverus noted the veiled woman's gold sandals, her painted toes.

"You're a troupe, are you not," she said, and Soter nodded without looking up. "And what do you do?"

"We tell stories," Diverus replied, still annoyed by her superior airs.

"Well," she said, "it appears you've now *become* a story. At least, to Colemaigne." She pointed to the crowd in the Dragon Bowl, many of them with their arms raised, some jumping up and down, others reciting, others jostling.

Just then another group edged around them in the lane and hurried to the crowded beam.

"Yes, quite a story," the woman muttered. "You are performers. In the manner of Bardsham, no doubt." Soter's brows arched, but he said nothing. "If so, coming here may prove difficult for you—at least I would have said so until today, as there is a law here that bans all such theatre. Did you not know?"

"What?" Soter looked up at her. "That can't be! This was the greatest venue—"

"Not since Bardsham's *final* performance have any been allowed here. He was the last. Disorder followed so close upon his heel that the one became tied to the other. He got off this span, but we could not. So either you don't travel this spiral of the Great Bridge very often, or you were last here with him."

"How are those two things of necessity mutually exclusive?" asked Soter, and Diverus thought, *He's angered by her, too.*

Overlooking Leodora, the woman replied, "I very much doubt they're different at all." She raised her face, and through the veil Diverus caught a glimpse of her features: austere, handsome, and hard, though her eyes betrayed some tenderness. "She needs somewhere to rest, and I expect you do, as well. Please come with me, bring her with you, and my men will carry your puppets."

Soter's brow furrowed. "How do you—"

"A long story, dear sir, which I'll willingly relate to you later—after you've settled in."

"Settled in?" Diverus and Soter exchanged a look.

"I own a theatre. Like so much of Colemaigne, it was long ago blighted. Yet this very day and, I suspect, with thanks to this girl, it has been resurrected. If there's to be a performance, you will of course make your debut there."

"Who are you, madam?" Soter asked, clearly troubled. Diverus likewise could not identify the cause of his own ire.

"For the moment, your benefactress. Please, bring her." She turned with a dramatic flourish and led the way back along the cramped lane. Her servants stepped aside to let her pass.

Soter and Diverus lifted Leodora from the black case. She was indeed as limp as if dead. Diverus wrapped his arms around her legs and led the way.

As they shuffled clumsily past, the servants melted into the shadows of a doorway, standing strangely still. Soter slowed to stare at them until Diverus almost almost pulled Leodora out of his grip. Ahead, the woman had rounded a corner and disappear-ed.

Hastily, they hobbled after her.

Soter said to Diverus, "How long did you sleep when it happened to you?"

"I don't know," Diverus replied over his shoulder. "I was

asleep before, and never did awaken till after. I don't know how long was the time between. Hours, I thought, but it *might* have been days. I was very confounded."

"Mmmm." Soter huffed along a moment before asking more quietly, "What was the thing you found in the bowl?"

Diverus glanced back. "A pendant, on a chain. It was beside her, in her hand. It might be what they gave her, the gods." As he spoke he was recalling all the containers strewn in the bowl on Vijganar when he'd awakened, and the madness they had seemed to induce in those who handled them. Of course the scrambling magpies in that Dragon Bowl so long ago might well have been mad already. He kept the woman in sight and tried not to worry that Leodora might never be herself again.

The woman led them to a wider avenue that angled away from the seawall lane and into the center of Colemaigne. Odd spade-shaped trees grew in pots along the center of the avenue. The area bustled with life. There were carts and strollers, and outdoor tables; but the throng had gathered loosely in the avenue in front of certain buildings. They stared up, gestured, as if at holy shrines.

All the buildings were well appointed—not just the ones at which people gawked. The façades looked freshly polished, orna-mented with colorful bright new awnings, umbrellas, and penn-ants. Some had half-round balconies above the shops, of which every variety was represented—markets, tailors, boot makers, drapers, cafés and more within the short distance Diverus and Soter walked. The woman soon turned into a narrower street.

They were moving deeper into the core of Colemaigne. Unlike the few spans Diverus had known so far, here the buildings were packed tightly together, with the result that a state of perpetual dusk hung over the street. The tight intersecting alleys looked darker still.

The woman led them toward the end of the street and a building distinct from the others they'd seen. For one thing it was round. And immense. A wide door, barred and locked, faced the street, but the woman walked past this and into the shadows beside the building.

Diverus scanned the walls, which rose up for two stories be-fore opening into what appeared to be a roofed gallery—at least in the front. Farther back, the gallery became a third storey with small windows. As with the buildings on the main thoroughfare, it looked as if it had been painted and polished just this morning. An adjacent blind alley in the rear led into a still-darker space, and that was where the woman directed them. It smelled vaguely foul, the closed-off space no doubt trapping vapors from out of the sewer grates instead of allowing them to disperse. There, at the very back of the circuit, the woman unlocked a chain and flung open a small and insignificant door. She waved them inside. A different smell—like the fusty odor of old clothes—un-folded from the interior, and it was a compelling and welcoming scent, as if the old place had been awaiting them. Despite doubts traded in glances (and those nearly impossible to see in the gloom), they carefully lifted Leodora through the doorway and inside. The two servants arrived soon after and pushed through with the cases and instruments, walking immediately deeper into the darkness while Soter and Diverus gathered their breath and waited for the woman to tell them what to do next.

Diverus's eyes adjusted slowly to the dim bluish light, most of which came through a row of tiny windows and bathed the interior in what seemed like moonlight.

A long broad table occupied the center of the room. At the far end he could just make out the black recess of a hearth large enough to stand in. Open doorways bracketed it on both sides. One of the odd servants who'd carried the undaya cases knelt before the hearth with a bellows and began pumping air at the ashes, which soon glowed.

The woman spoke from behind, startling him. "This is my home," she said. As he turned about, she closed the door through which they'd entered. She stood in front of a full rack of clothing that appeared to run the rest of the room's length and even along the far wall. She said, "Put it on the table, Bois," and Diverus glanced back to see the servant place a small oil lamp on the table beside the undaya case he'd set down there. The lamp was shaped like a slipper with a curled toe.

"Go on, then," said the woman. "I know you both want to explore." The two servants nodded vigorously and without a word went through one of the doors by the hearth.

"Explore?" asked Soter.

"Yes," she replied. She removed her veil and picked up the lamp. "Follow me and we'll put your friend somewhere she can rest, meanwhile." She crossed to the doorway on the far side of the hearth. It led to a flight of steps.

The stairwell proved difficult to navigate with Leodora between them, as they couldn't all three fit on a step together, and Diverus in the lead with her legs had to go up one step and wait for Soter to go up one before moving up another.

"It might be easier if one of you simply slung her over his shoulder," their hostess suggested. She was probably right, but now in the stairwell they could only crab their way up as they'd begun. "Explore," she explained as if Soter had asked again, "because until an hour ago the theatre wall we circled coming in here did not exist. It collapsed years ago, after . . . after the calamity." She turned and stared down past Diverus at Soter as she said it.

Out of the stairwell, she led them a short way down a corridor with more doors on either side. She opened the first one and said, "Put her in here."

It was a small room, hardly larger than the narrow mattress on the floor. The ceiling slanted, a dormer. They lowered Leodora onto the bed, and Soter banged his head as he stepped back. Diverus knelt with her and carefully slipped the pendant out of his pocket, tucking it underneath her.

"The rear of the theatre is full of tiny chambers like this," the woman was saying.

"It's where the players change," Soter stated.

"Where they used to, yes. Your friend may sleep for days, you know. Or never wake up at all."

"Never wake?" asked Diverus, as he stood. The possibility hadn't occurred to him. It was a matter of when, not if.

"In stories, on occasion," she reassured him. "She was touched by gods, and that hasn't happened here in so long that no one's going to recall what is *supposed* to happen."

"*He* should," Soter said as he stepped out of the room. He pointed at Diverus. "He's been touched, himself."

"That is gratifyingly improbable," she answered. "You will both surely be hungry. Let me have something prepared for you. Bois!"

When nothing happened, Soter said, "You sent them off to explore, madam."

"Well, that was ill planned, then."

Footsteps sounded at the far end of the hallway, and a servant entered from one of the side doors there. He came up beside Diverus and stopped, awaiting her orders. While she directed him what to prepare, Diverus got his first close look at her manservant.

He had a hard, chiseled face, and eyes that seemed almost painted on. Bois, sensing the scrutiny, turned his head and Diverus shyly lowered his gaze . . . and saw Bois's hand. The fingers were articulated, each joint hinged, very much like Leodora's shadow puppets.

Soter seemed utterly unaware of the strangeness of Bois. He was too intent upon ensuring that there would be wine to drink with their meal.

Bois shambled past them and clumped down the stairs they'd come up. Staring after him, Diverus missed the next thing the woman said, coming alert only to Soter's reply of "By all means." The two—Soter and the hostess—started off along the corridor. Diverus glanced again at the sleeping Leodora, attempt-ing to convince himself that she was safe and that the oddness of this place, much less of the whole span itself, was not a threat, or at least no more of one than the parade of monsters had been on Hyakiyako. They'd come through that just fine, hadn't they?

He made up his mind that he could leave her, and turned just as Soter and the woman exited through one of the doorways up the hall. Hurrying after them then, he found that the doorway led to a short descending ramp ending in a curtain, which wasn't quite closed. Light spilled through the center seam. He hastened down the ramp and stepped through the curtain into daylight again.

He stood in an open balcony. Drapery hung on each side, ornately decorated with flowers and vines. Cushions to sit on had been strewn about the floor, but Soter and the hostess remained standing at the rail, overlooking the circular theatre. Diverus moved quietly up beside them.

It was magnificent. Below, a broad, bare stage projected out and wide to either side of the balcony. The remaining servant walked about on it, pausing, opening his arms as if declaiming, but never making a sound; then setting off again, he suddenly struck a regal pose, sprang from it, capered, stopped and stood humbly, demure and shy. It was as if he was trying on one character after another before a nonexistent audience.

The theatre was empty. The main floor—deep enough that the stage stood at waist height above it—contained huge semicircular benches layered in amphitheater fashion away from the stage. The curved rear walls comprised a series of niches, of draped private boxes similar to this balcony. Overhead, thatched roofing extended to perhaps the first row of seats.

"It's a wonder," said Soter.

"Indeed, it is," their hostess replied. "A miracle. Only yesterday this and the two balconies to our right were misshapen holes in the wall, the floorboards below were rotted, the drapery in tatters. The interior walls across there with the boxes for patrons—those had all fallen in, a heap of crumbled stucco and stone. No glassine upon any of it at all. The thatch of that roof was black and rotten, a home for vermin, and had been thus for more than a decade."

"This is because of Leodora, all this change?" asked Diverus. "But you can't even *see* the Dragon Bowl from here."

"Nevertheless, look about you and marvel," she replied.

"And what is *he* doing?" Soter asked her, with a nod to the stage.

"Glaise is remembering. Reenacting. Once, we had a company, and they played to a thousand people in a night. Do *you* remember?" she asked carefully, looking sidewise at Soter, and he tensed, his face pinched as at some unpleasant recollection.

"I . . . of course I do!"

"I thought perhaps the gods had snatched away your past, Soter, as happened to so many others."

He twitched when she said his name and responded in kind. "No, not the gods, Orinda. No *gods* came for me."

A brief smile crossed her lips at the mention of her name. Diverus eyed them both warily, attempting to fathom the meaning interlacing the words. "He died, you know, right after."

Soter rubbed his hand along his jaw. "I recall he was ill. He kept it from us but even so, I knew. Bardsham saw it first, the way he winced when he stood. He was a grand actor but sometimes in the pain, he would forget, his expression failed him, or else it was too excruciating to mask."

She nodded solemnly. "It spared him having to endure the ruin of the theatre for so long. That would have destroyed him just as certainly, but it would have worn him to nothing first." She slid her arm along the railing and covered Soter's hand with her own. How did you lose the tips of these fingers?"

"Storyfish bit 'em off," he quickly replied; it was the same response he'd given Diverus when he'd asked.

"Of course," answered Orinda, and Diverus could tell she didn't believe him. "That child, then—she's Bardsham's daughter." When he didn't reply, she said, "How fitting that she should repair our span."

"She is her mother in spirit."

"And will she bring destruction upon us, too? That *was* the gift you left Colemaigne."

Although Soter didn't move, it was as if his body twisted tight before Diverus's eyes. He said finally, "They don't know about her."

"If they learn of her here, history will rerun its course."

Squirming even more, Soter shifted the subject. "I must tell you, I've hardly a real recollection of you, Orinda. No solid memory beyond . . ."

"You would have dealt with *him*," she answered, taking no offense. "I was busy with our troupe. What would the play have been, I wonder. It was the end of—*Cardenio*, yes, they were rehearsing *Cardenio*. Never performed it. It's lost to the ages, along with its author."

"I'm sorry for both. But surely now you can revive the troupe?"

"Revive. What an appropriate word. I would have to. Revive them, that is."

"What, they've all died?"

She leaned farther over the glistering balcony. "You don't know, do you? You've no idea what happened here."

Soter looked fearful. "Apparently not," he answered.

Orinda glanced back at Diverus, who could only express his own puzzlement. As if to him, she replied, "What they did to punish us for harboring Bardsham. The horror they wrought. Not just the buildings suffered. You understand?"

Diverus, without knowing details, comprehended the enor-mity she implied. He'd seen enough pain dispensed in his short life. He nodded, and the woman brushed his cheek tenderly.

She continued to focus upon Diverus as she asked, "Did they ever catch you, Soter?"

Beyond her fall of hair, Diverus could see Soter's awful face, the eyes looking inward, at what horrible memory he couldn't imagine. Softly, Soter replied, "They found us."

She rubbed the tips of his foreshortened fingers. "I thought as much. No one ever heard of Bardsham again, anywhere."

Soter tilted back his head and sighed. "But you, your husband—Colemaigne never harbored us. We'd no idea that trouble came here. We thought you'd been spared. We'd moved on, after all, far away. A different spiral. That's what a traveling troupe *does*."

"It was what we maintained, as well, but that wasn't what they wanted to hear. What they wished to believe. When your captors have an answer in mind, it doesn't always matter that you tell them the truth. Truth counts for nothing."

"I . . . no, I suppose not."

"Innocence was not one of our choices."

"So it would be better if we left, then."

"Left?" she asked incredulously. She dropped her hand from his and turned. "If that girl has a mote of the talent her father had, she must perform for us. Here. This theatre—this *span*—needs its stories back."

"She's better than him," said Diverus. Soter glared at him. "Well, *you* told her she was."

The woman regarded them both in apparent disbelief, until Soter with strange reluctance said, "It's true."

Diverus found himself watching the figure on the stage. Suddenly he put the performance together with what she had said. "Was Glaise a member of your troupe?" he asked. When both Soter and the woman regarded him in surprise, he added nervously, "I mean, he's not human, is he? Neither of them. They're—"

"*Pinottos*. Both of them, yes." The admission appeared to pain her. At her back Soter fumed with anger as though Diverus had committed the most terrible violation of etiquette. As if the answer had slammed the door on discussion, Orinda stated, "Your meal will be ready by now," and walked back through the curtain.

Soter scowled and, shaking his head, went after her, calling, "Orinda, please!"

Left alone on the balcony, Diverus muttered, "No one tells me anything, and then they blame me for it when I have to guess." Finally he decided that he wanted something to eat, too, and parted the curtains again.

The mute *pinotto* continued to perform for the emptiness.

Leodora awoke. The space around her was dark and sounded fearfully close; for a moment she imagined she was inside one of the undaya cases, transformed into a puppet, locked in with the Coral Man. She reached up with both hands and swept them back and forth through the air. Her fingertips touched nothing and she realized she was in a larger space, a room. The sound of it might have been dull and tight, but it was not a puppet case.

Something was poking at the ribs of her right side. She reached under herself, fingers digging, snaring a length of fine chain. As she tugged at it, the chain made a slithery sound, uncurling against something else metal that was vaguely oval, its surface a symmetrical raised design. Her fingertips couldn't identify what the design was, but it was nothing she owned, nothing she knew. It forced her to try to remember where she'd been last before awakening here.

She had walked—yes, that was right—walked out onto the decrepit dragon beam of Colemaigne. She'd done it on a dare, as a taunt to Diverus. She must have gone into the bowl itself, but squeezing her memory brought forth only a view of inverted buildings that might have been a reflection in a rain puddle, some odd music that tinkled like glass breaking, a few other disjunct and incoherent images, a few swirls of clarity in a fog bank of forgetfulness and beyond that, nothing. She might be anywhere save in the belly of a ship, for the room wasn't rocking in the slightest. That wasn't much, but it was *some* small knowledge. Diverus and Soter must surely be near.

"How do I choose?" she heard herself ask. The words seem-ed to die as they left her mouth. She said it aloud again to hear her voice, dry and muffled against the close walls: "How do I choose?"

In the darkness beside her, a different voice answered, "That *is* a challenge without more information about the choices proposed."

Leodora sat up. The voice spoke from so near that the speaker must have been right at the edge of the bed. Her eyes strained the darkness for any hint of a shape, a body, a face. Finally she let go the pendant chain and reached out. Her splayed fingers found nothing.

She wondered for a moment if she might be hearing the voice of the Coral Man. She had heard it, she thought, in dreams, though they seemed so removed now that she couldn't be certain he'd ever spoken, nor could she recall now anything he had said—just the sound of it, like humming. This voice didn't resonate in her head. It was separate from her, the voice of someone else, even if that someone else proved to be a phantom.

"How do I . . . get more information?" she asked.

"You could simply get up and leave the room," the voice suggested.

"Will that work?"

"If it's not as dark as a crow in a mine everywhere else."

"*Is* it that dark everywhere else?"

"Oh, my, yes. Just now it is. It's night outside, and cloudy, and moonless, so there's no cast light, either."

"You've been outside."

The voice didn't answer.

"How do you know what it's like outside if you haven't been outside?" she asked, slightly peeved by its reticence.

"It's just something I know."

"Who are you, then?"

"I? I can't say."

"Why not?"

"No self-awareness," the voice explained.

She could not help laughing. "That's absurd."

The voice said nothing, and she was sure she had offended the person behind it. "You can speak to me, but you don't know that you exist? You're a figment, then. I must have made you up. Otherwise how can you talk to me and have no self-awareness?"

"I'm a counselor. You ask. I counsel."

"A ghost counsel. You're certainly not the one who visits me in my *sleep*." Upon the last word she lunged and waved both hands in the air this time, all around. She touched nothing until she strained so far that her fingers brushed a wall. No one was there. She realized that she would have sensed movement, heard a rustling if the other had moved. She'd heard nothing. It really *was* a ghost.

Now that she'd touched one wall, she rose. She sensed the slope of the ceiling just before her head brushed it. Close to the wall, everything smelled musty. She slid her palms down the slope to the vertical wall and along it, around a corner and on, until her hands brushed against a door. It rattled slightly and she snatched her hands back, afraid to make noise. Then with care she touched it again, patting as lightly as a butterfly, down until she felt against her wrist a cold bar, the handle. It was small, and she felt all around it, trying to picture what she was feeling, an image in her head of the mechanism. The bar was on a spring, and a pin projected from it that she could pull on to slide it back. Slowly she drew it back; the door swung toward her as on well-oiled hinges.

She glanced outside. Like the room, it proved to be featureless, dark, but some distance away on her left, a hint of illumination—no more than a dull glow—suggested an opening. She stuck her head back into the room and whispered, "Will you come with me?" but the voice of the counselor didn't answer. "Can you hear?" she asked, to no avail. He had apparently evaporated, and she shook her head as if to rid herself of the notion that it had been anything other than imaginary, her befuddled mind's creation after the . . . the events.

Out of the room again she moved toward the wan light, her hands out and to the sides. Her fingers brushed against walls on each side as she shuffled cautiously along. It was a narrow hallway. As she went, her balance seemed to tip, the light ahead wanting to tilt. She turned, pressing both palms to one wall, to a rough, solid coolness that anchored her and stabilized the hall. She hung her head and breathed deep lungfuls of air. She realized what must have happened in the Dragon Bowl.

Like Diverus she had no memory of it, but that didn't shake her belief; rather, it reinforced it. Sounds, smells, where she'd gone or what had come to her—these things lingered in the back of her mind, tantalizingly unreachable. She knew no more of them than of where she was at this moment. Had she been transported? Could she even now be in Edgeworld? Instinct maintained that she wasn't, although she could hardly express why.

She needed to find Diverus. She thought that if she insisted he try to remember Edgeworld, anything he might recall would help her to recollect her own experience—assuming that they were in the same place.

Pressed to the wall, she shuffled along. The nearer she got to the light, the more details she saw in the corridor: other doors, sconces for lamps, and finally an oval of lighter color where the wall had been patched but not painted.

The light shone through a split curtain. Behind it lay a short ramp that ended in a second, heavier drape below. She crept down the ramp to the drapery. With two fingers, she eased one side of it open, revealing a balcony railing that overlooked a large theatre space.

She could see tiers of curved benches beneath a distant wall lined with similar small enclosed balconies. The source of the light remained out of view below the balcony, but it threw shadows that moved, accompanied by soft footfalls and a creak of floorboards.

She pushed her head through the curtain and discovered that hers was one of three balconies projecting from the back wall of a stage, each with elaborately wrought moldings. High above the balconies, a large thatched roof covered the stage area, held up by a framework that must have been attached from above. A higher, larger box-like balcony projected out beneath it.

On the stage below, two figures dressed identically in brown vests and trousers strode the boards. They faced each other and gestured as if in a pantomime of declaiming, of demanding. Transfixed, she watched the curious performance. After a while one of them gestured as if putting on shoes while the other mimed the act of writing on a small tablet. "It's 'The Tale of the Two Brothers'!" She thought she said this only to herself, but the twins halted their enactment and turned to look up at her. They didn't move after that. They seemed to be waiting for a response from her.

"I know your story," she called down.

One of the two took a few steps toward her, gesturing excitedly for her to come down to the stage.

She raised her hands. "How?" she asked.

He pointed a finger around the rear of the stage, through the balconies, directing her back into the hall and beyond the room from where she'd emerged, then effected jagged movements signifying stairs. She nodded that she understood and then retraced her steps back into the dark corridor, where she felt her way along the wall. As he'd indicated, stairs began but a short distance beyond her room.

From then on she navigated by instinct, approximating the location of the stage and feeling her away in search of an entrance. She touched a heavy curtain and, pushing it aside, entered a dark area to one side of the stage, hidden from the audience, but with part of the stage itself visible.

The two figures had stopped their pantomime and awaited her, still as statues. Leodora walked out onto the stage. Four of the lights along the front of it had been lit. Past them she could see the empty theatre space that threw back echoes of her footsteps.

Drawing nearer, she found that *statues* was not an unreasonable comparison to the two men. They were like clockwork creatures that had wound down. Bodies motionless, they watched her approach. Their eyes were alive, though shallowly set; but their mouths were painted on, their chins defined by vertical lines as though separately inserted and hinged. So, too, their fingers had three distinct joints.

Looking from one to the other, she asked, "Am I still in Edgeworld?"

The two faced each other, their expressions changing to show confusion, their painted mouths pursing. Then together they turned back to her and shook their heads. "I'm in Colemaigne, then?"

This time they nodded without prior consultation.

"So my companions, they're here, too? In this theatre?"

One figure nodded; the other pressed his hands together and placed them against his cheek, closing his eyes.

"Yes, I understand," she said with relief. It was night. They were asleep. Everything would be fine. Until they awoke, she was in no position to learn what had happened to her, so she might as well explore on her own.

The two inhuman men waited for her to say something.

"I know the story you were performing. I perform it, too. I'm a shadow artist." One of them pressed his thumbs to his fingertips and moved his hands up and down independently as if raising and lowering something. "That's right—puppets on rods, that's how I tell stories." He placed one hand to his own chest and the other on his twin's shoulder. Again, she understood his intent as clearly as if he had spoken. "I could—if you want—recite it while you perform. If that's not presumptuous of me."

His eyes widened and without warning he clasped and hugged her. When he let go, she said, "Well. I didn't expect *that*." He pretended to be shy then, lowering his head. She laughed at his clowning, and he brightened again. His twin shook his head as if disapproving, but glanced her way to see if she was watching. It was all part of their repartee.

"So," she said, "I will go sit over there beside the lights and tell the story as if to the audience behind me, and you'll perform it for them."

They both nodded their accord and shook hands with each other. She walked to the front of the stage, and they strode off into the wings to await her beginning. She sat cross-legged and for a moment gazed up at the roof, which was like an awning overhead. *This is as strange as the parade of monsters,* she thought, *or the Ondiont snake.* The thoughts wanted to drift her into daydream, but she banished them, flexed her spine, and placed her palms on the floor. She inhaled deeply and began.

≈ The Tale of the Two Brothers ≈

There once were two brothers named Baloyd and Suald. They had lived on the span called Kakotara their whole uneventful lives. Both of them had married by arrangement. Their brides had been betrothed to them when they were children. Their father was a respectable weaver, and their mother raised colorful, exotic birds, many of which were purchased for the court of Kakotara. Because of this neither of the brothers worked nor needed to. The two endured not the slightest hardship despite their combined sloth, and often discussed money, but solely as the object of various schemes to avoid employment while they continued to feed from the parental trough.

One night when Baloyd and Suald were wandering the streets of the span in search of a rumored card game, they happened to pass by the entrance to the dragon beam. At the end of the spiraling walkway, the hexagonal bowl hovered in the air on hidden supports. Suald noticed how it glowed in the moonlight and pointed this out to his brother. They stopped and stood there, watching it.

No one else was near. The Dragon Bowl on Kakotara had then been dormant for more years than the two brothers had lived, and no one paid it much attention anymore except during festivals, when unanswered libations were poured upon the tiles.

Suald stopped. He said, "Does the *hex* seem brighter than it should?" He called it *hex* because that was the way of that span.

Baloyd, the less thoughtful of the two, had little interest in puzzles. "We should find that game house if we want to gamble," he urged. He walked ahead, hoping his brother would follow. Instead, Suald stepped onto the beam and began strolling out along its curve. Baloyd knew full well that once his brother had fixed upon an idea there was no use arguing him off it, so he turned around and followed.

Suald had already completed the first loop of the dragon beam's spiral. He came up directly across from Baloyd, nearly close enough that they could have stretched and touched fingertips. He asked casually, "If you could make the *hex* light up anytime you wanted, what would you ask for?"

"It's supposed to be bad manners to make demands of the gods," his brother replied.

"Gulldroppings. This thing hasn't ignited in thirty years. How does anybody know what you can do to the gods, or what they care about? Or if they even exist beyond stories? Has anybody you know of ever tried to get what they want off a *hex*?"

"Probably not." He said nothing further until he'd caught up with Suald, who waited for him at the entrance to the bowl. "I guess I don't need money, I don't need another wife. Wouldn't want to be king—that's too much work. Guess I'd like to be quick. Then I could take anything I needed anytime and get away without having to pay if I didn't want to. You know, dash down to Balrog Harbor and steal a keg right from under the noses of those greedy trolls. Be worth it for all the times they've bled me for money. But hey, we're knights of the *elbow*, let's go find that game—"

"It *is* too bright," Suald said thoughtfully.

Baloyd finally considered the Dragon Bowl at the center of the spiraling arm. The tiles were luminescent, and not from reflected moonlight. They glowed still brighter as he looked on.

"I think something's going to happen."

"You'd better say what *you* want, then, since it was your idea," Baloyd goaded.

"Well, I surely don't want speed. Too specific, see. What I want—" and he raised his voice until he was shouting at the sky "—is a way to have whatever I want *later*. That way I don't ask for anything particular now, and I get lots more whenever I want!" He grinned at his brother. "Pretty clever, heh?"

"I think *we're* starting to glow, too."

Suald held his hands up. Sparks danced around his fingertips. His hair stood on end, and sparks whirled around his head. The light came from nowhere and everywhere.

Baloyd began to laugh, his giddiness sharpened by fear. Whatever would happen next, they had chosen to demand, and there was no going back, no reneging. The gods had heard them and would either honor their desires or destroy them. He shouted, "Come on, give me speed!" and his brother responded, "Give me everything I want!"

The light turned thick; the world beyond it vanished. The air pressed them and they moved back to back to withstand the pressure. There was a twistedness to the energy, as if they were about to be wrung from head to foot. The air darkened and squealed mechanically; it stank of rotten eggs, of sulfurous pits. The bowl shook so hard that they both fell. They lay screaming, their bravado forgotten, scared witless now, arms over their heads as certain death mashed them.

Then everything stopped.

Neither brother moved.

The terrible shrieking, as though metal were shredding metal, dwindled like a juggernaut rolling off across the sea. The whoosh of waves against the breakers below reemerged as the predominant—the only—sound.

Baloyd opened his eyes.

The night was dark, but along the horizon a faint strip of dawn-light showed. Hours must have passed, although he had no sense of the lost time. Remnants of sour mist hung in the air, already dissipating in the breeze off the ocean. From a distance footsteps came running, and cries of "It came on!" "I saw it!" and "What'd it leave?" rode the air.

The approach of a crowd galvanized the two young men. They sat up and took stock of their surroundings. They were whole, undamaged. Whatever had happened and whatever had arrived—whether it filled their requirements or not—by right it was theirs. They got up quickly. The people rushing along the dragon beam drew up. Across the gap separating them from the platform at the center, they gaped, crestfallen. As a group they had shared in a hope, a promise, dashed now that others had got there ahead of them. The two brothers crossed to the middle of the platform.

Four objects lay on the tiles of the bowl: two unsightly red, bulbous-toed shoes; and a small black metal stylus lying atop a clay tablet.

By instinct the two brothers chose their prizes. Baloyd took the shoes; Suald collected the stylus and tablet. Then they walked onto the beam and followed it back to where the others hovered. If the crowd still held a glimmer of hope that the two might share the treasure, Suald's arrogance banished it. He forced them back along the path with nothing more than a cold sneer.

On Brink Lane he turned his back on them as if daring anyone to try and take him. Baloyd followed, but with frequent glances over his shoulder to make sure no one pursued them. Brink Lane traced the westward curve of the span, and soon the crowd was out of sight around a bend. Suald kept walking. He turned up a narrow side street leading back into the forest of stucco houses and shops, all still dark with sleep. He pushed open an iron gate and entered a courtyard with a small fountain, bordered on three sides by houses. There he finally stopped. "All right, what have you got?"

Baloyd held the shoes up by their laces. They had high necks and spongy red circles at ankle height. The soles were curiously furrowed.

"Well, they're *some*thing. Why don't you put them on."

There was a great deal Baloyd thought of saying: how his brother always created situations and then left him to resolve them; how, since the whole idea of challenging the gods had been Suald's idea, he should be the one to test the Edgeworld gifts—he should be the one to blow up or ignite or melt. But Baloyd said nothing. A lifetime of habit overruled him.

He sat against the lip of the fountain and put on the shoes. He had to loosen the laces to get his feet in and afterward left them undone. He'd never seen laces before; he had no idea what they were for.

Standing, testing, he discovered that the shoes fit him quite well. He walked around the fountain. Nothing happened. When he'd come full circle, he pointed at his brother's gifts and said, "What about yours, then?"

Suald held the stylus and tablet away from his body as if, should they come to life, he might fling them away. For a moment he held them above the fountain, and Baloyd almost snatched them away for fear he was going to drop them into the water.

Suald pushed his thumb into the surface of the tablet. His

nail left a gouge in it.

"Why don't you write something instead?" Baloyd suggested.

"I don't see *you* running any races."

"I put the shoes on. I walked around. Nothing happened. They're just shoes."

"Try running."

Baloyd sprinted up and down in place. "They don't work."

"What do you think I should write?"

"Write that you'd like some breakfast. I'm hungry."

"Naturally." He licked the tip of the stylus and inscribed the words a king's breakfast. Nothing happened. He frowned. "I don't think this thing works, either. Look, why don't you try naming a destination—somewhere you want to go."

"I don't have anyplace in mind."

"Yes, and no wonder you're not going anywhere. Pick someplace—go to the end of the span. Go to Nourey Gate or something." He stared sternly at the tablet, then wrote above the already inscribed words, Give me.

Baloyd replied, "Fine. Nourey Ga—" He never finished the word—at least not within his brother's hearing.

Suald was reading his own writing when a wind threw him off-balance. He slipped on the cobblestones, caught his foot against something in the dark, and sprawled upon a row of metal dishes. He crushed eggs and pomegranates, figs and relishes, sweet breads and popovers. His elbow flipped a creamer, splattering him with goat's milk.

Covered in the food he'd requested, he started to laugh. He couldn't help himself; it was all too ridiculously glorious.

From one of the buildings bordering the courtyard, someone shouted, "Shut up, yer drunken swine!" which only caused Suald to laugh even harder.

The wind whipped up again. Dust sprayed him. Loose grapes rolled past him.

The wind's screech became a shout—a whoop of unrestrained pleasure—and there stood Baloyd, his hair pushed out behind him like a sheaf of reeds. For an instant he was still, and then he began jumping up and down. "Suald! I did it. I've been to Nourey Gate and back again!"

Suald pushed himself up onto his knees and took stock of the damage to his clothes. "Of course you have," he replied.

"No, really. In seconds. I don't even know what streets I took. They whizzed by so fast, all a blur until I got to the gate. I thought my clothes would catch fire. Then I said, 'I want to go back,' and it started all over again." The shoes practically glowed. He saw the food laid out upon the ground, squatted down, and picked a deviled egg that had survived the maelstrom. He popped it into his mouth whole. "Oh, this is good," he said with a full mouth. "Have you tried one?"

Suald cocked an eyebrow. "*Several,* thanks to you." He wiped the smeared food off his shirt. It should have been a joke—it had been until Baloyd returned, and he couldn't say just why he found his brother's beaming presence so galling. "So you ran the length of Kakotara."

"I did. And you ordered breakfast. We got what we asked for. The gods gave us just what we wanted."

"I shall try to remember to thank them later." He licked jelly from the back of his hand.

"Oh, come on, you can't be angry! Not *now*!"

"I happen to be covered in food."

"Well, then, ask for a bath. Ask for clean clothes. You can, don't you see? You can have *anything*!"

A shutter banged open above them and a burly fellow in a sleeping gown leaned out and bellowed, "I told you bastards to shut up, and I meant it! If you don't, I'll come down there and hammer you into the stones."

Baloyd leapt back. "Oh, you think so, do you? What will you do if I come up there"—he stood suddenly behind the man; taking him by the shoulders he whispered—"and push you out." The terrified fellow flew from his window and slammed into the stones beside Suald. Baloyd was there just as swiftly.

The man howled in pain. He clutched his head and rolled back and forth. Blood oozed from his nose and mouth.

Baloyd took his brother's arm. "Maybe you should clean up somewhere else," he suggested.

Suald looked at his brother as if seeing him for the first time. "No," he said, and took out the clay tablet. With his thumb he smoothed his previous request.

"That's right, you can fix him, can't you?"

"You're damned right I can." Suald carved letters with the stylus then lowered the tablet and admired his handiwork.

There beside the fountain a huge wharf rat lay trembling and bloody, dying atop a torn nightshirt. Suald grinned.

Baloyd's brow knitted, and he gave his brother a worried glance. "That wasn't what I meant."

"No?" smirked Suald. "Well, it was what *I* meant. What's one rat more or less in the world?"

Somewhere in the darkness above, a woman called out, "Harky? Harky, where've you gone?"

Suald took his brother by the elbow and dragged him out the gate and away.

Thus began the reign of the two brothers on Kakotara. They did not keep their gifts secret for long. Suald performed a few tricks for his wife, Seru, conjuring whatever she named by writing the words on the tablet. She asked for jewels, then necklaces and bracelets. She asked for fantastic, legendary birds that would impress his mother, and they appeared as well. If she didn't like what came, Suald found that he could send the thing away as easily. As their house filled with squawking and cooing, as a rain of droppings began to decorate everything, he made her choose one bird from the batch and then erased all the others as if they'd never existed. She chose a blue-and-violet one that snapped at anyone who passed near it and shrieked for no good reason.

Seru saw the greater possibilities of this magical clay. She demanded a palanquin fitted with gold trimmings and pink silk cushions. Suald exercised his gift again, and the magic spread into the street. Even as he opened the front door to reveal the prize, Suald's neighbors were gathering to behold the resplendent enclosed litter. Four powerful men stood beside it as she had requested. They were barely human, with faces devoid of expression, of curiosity, of thought. They responded only to Suald's commands. The gathering audience regarded him with wonder and fear: Only lord mayors, princes, and kings had palanquins.

He was both annoyed and thrilled by their awe; but soon he was writing one thing after another. Items popped up left and right—here a table, there a suit of clothes, and of course gold. Someone told him he was greater than the *hex* itself, which he liked, and he strutted on that awhile; but he soon grew weary of it all. Every citizen who went off with something told three others, who told others, until the street had become the object of a pilgrimage from all across the span. Petitioners waved their hands, and some waved scraps of fishskin parchment on which they'd written a list of their desires. Most of these requests disgusted Suald in their simplicity, their foolishness; here he was offering them the unimaginable, and they all trembled at the thought of asking for a bag of rice or a small pot to replace one that had broken last month. Only a few people asked wisely—for sustained health, for cures for their afflictions, for wisdom in the future. Suald quickly ceased to follow their requests; his tired hand wrote automatically. Let them waste his gift. He would not offer it again.

While he wrote, he watched Baloyd.

Every now and again during the great wish fulfillment, his younger brother put in brief appearances. He zigged and zagged, zoomed to the top of the highest tower, vanished for ten minutes to return with hot food from a vendor's cart two spans distant. He carried his own wife, Betinela, on a tour of the entire span from end to end, from point to point, wherever she asked to go. He whisked her in to visit Seru, who gave her a handful of the thousand necklaces and jewels that now lay scattered about the house. Baloyd gave barely a glance to the cornucopia flowing from the clay tablet, as if none of it mattered to him. Instead, he ventured into the crowd, befriending children and taking them off for races through the streets. Sometimes they returned almost before they had left, the children not really grasping the speed with which Baloyd could carry them to their own homes around the next corner. Wherever they went, upon returning, the wide-eyed children invariably cried out, "Do it again," or "Go farther!" Baloyd obliged them, every one.

Betinela frowned at her husband's disregard of his brother's treasure. Placating her, Seru remarked, "At least he seems to be having *fun*."

Suald overheard the remark, and it set his mind darkly. He smoothed over the tablet and pocketed it. "That's all for today," he announced. Hundreds of expectant supplicants moaned, cried out that it wasn't fair, insisted he perform at least *their* miracle. The ranks closed around him, and a few faces looked capable of taking the tablet from him. He marked those faces. "Very well," he said, as if giving in to their demands. Then, pulling out the tablet again, he scribbled the words send them all home into the clay.

The crowd responded as if he had suddenly vanished. As

if some scent rode upon the air, they raised their heads, turned away from Suald, and shuffled off. Suald smirked at his own cleverness: Later he would make them forget that he had this power at all.

He went inside.

Seru pursued him. "Darling, what's wrong, why did you do that?"

He turned on her. "I heard what you told Betinela. You find my brother so amusing—well, go stay with him!"

"What?"

"You find his gift so much fun, while mine is sheer tedium, then take up with him. I'm sure his own wife won't mind another in the house."

She gaped at him until understanding flowed into her expression. "My gods, you're jealous of him. He's enjoying his gift and you can't stand it. You have the whole world in your pocket and it isn't enough for you." Her laugh was a slap in his face.

Suald glared at an unoccupied corner of the room and muttered, "Ridiculous."

"What festers here? If you think they're such a source of entertainment, then why not use the tablet to get your own shoes?"

"Because I want *his*."

After a moment she shrugged and replied, "Well, then take them. What stops you? You caused fig trees to grow on the main boulevards of all the spans you could think of; how much trouble is it to take two shoes?" She said this as if it were nothing, but she walked quickly away from him to the perch of her blue-and-violet bird, which clacked its beak at her and let loose a piercing screech.

He gripped the tablet in his pocket, finally withdrawing it, staring at it, holding it up as if testing its weight. In his other hand he fingered the tip of the stylus. Askance he saw his wife's lips curl with contempt, but when he looked straight at her, she seemed to be petting the obnoxious bird, not even paying attention to him.

He licked the tip of the stylus while watching her. Her gaze shifted. She followed the arc of the stylus from his side to his mouth and down. She didn't see him at all; only the stylus. Only the tablet. In her focus he read with utter certainty that she would kill him for it—for things she wanted but would never dare ask him to provide. He knew where her tastes ran to the perverse, and where his presence would be unwelcome. She would kill him when he slept, or poison the figs he ate at breakfast so that he would die too quickly to be able to write an antidote. Even if she didn't kill him outright, she would find a way to get her hands upon the tablet. She would write him out of existence the moment he closed his eyes.

He could trust her no longer.

Baloyd arrived late in the afternoon. He was barefoot and carried his magical shoes before him. He seemed confused by his circumstances.

Suald met him at the door.

"I want to . . . to give you these," Baloyd said, and held the red shoes at arm's length. His eyes welled with tears. A kind of bottomless terror gnawed at him, the more terrible for being impossible to understand. But his wife understood.

Betinela had been with him when he suddenly expressed the urge to visit his brother. She'd followed him easily, for he hadn't used the shoes and had lumbered stupidly through the streets as if not quite sure of his location. She knew her husband and all his faults: He was not a man given to acts of unconditional generosity. She glared at Suald as he accepted the shoes.

He smiled as innocently as he knew how.

"And where's Seru?" she asked him.

"Away," he replied quickly.

She looked past him at the bird on its perch, at the jewelry scattered through the room, at everything that denied his statement, finally following his gaze down to a yellowish smear on the floor where he'd crushed a very large cockroach. She chose not to contradict him.

Baloyd wept openly, his brain twisting with frustration.

"Your brother loves you so," said Betinela, "to give up this wondrous gift that had pleased him so much, at the peak of his enjoyment. I never realized he felt so tenderly toward you."

Suald's eyelids half closed. "We've always been closer than people thought." He carried the clumsy-looking shoes outside, where he sat and put them on before she could try and make him give them back. His brother shambled after him as if tied to a line.

The shoes were too big for Suald's feet, but otherwise more comfortable than they looked. It was the first time he'd put them on, and he fumbled with the laces, finally tying them around his ankles to keep them out of the way.

As he started to take out the tablet, Betinela asked, "So where will you go then? You've always been smarter than your brother, Suald, so I assume you'll use the shoes for something greater than entertaining children?"

He looked at her from under his brows, agitated by the accusation that edged her every word. Didn't she appreciate the power he held right here in his hand? No, of course she didn't. None of them did. He could obliterate them and they wouldn't know. He was sick of their small minds, sick of the greedy, petty span of Kakotara.

"I'll tell you, and then I'll bid you both farewell. I'm going to travel the whole length and breadth of Shadowbridge as no one has ever done before. I'll see everything, and when I return I'll be the greatest explorer who ever lived, because I can do it all in the blink of an eye. I'll reign among the gods."

"Fine." She moved aside. Her look mocked him. "Go on then. Travel the whole world."

"You doubt that I can? See, then. I shall travel the *whole world*." Upon those words he launched headlong so fast that figs from the trees he'd created rained after him.

The instant he was gone, the spell he'd cast upon his brother broke and the clouds of confusion lifted. Baloyd's eyes widened, first with the shock of recognition, then with the boil of anger. He opened his mouth and shouted at the sky. He flung curses at Suald and plunged back into the deserted house. Sounds of shattering and squawking and screams of rage echoed up and down the street, drawing a crowd. People looked at Betinela for an explanation. Some wanted to know where Suald was, because they had more things to ask for. She said nothing, but stepped quickly aside as a glass lamp flew through the doorway and struck a man in the back. The crowd scrambled out of the way.

When Baloyd emerged with Seru's blue-and-violet-plumed bird dangling from his fist, the crowd scurried farther away, ready to flee. He'd wrung its neck. He dropped the dead bird, turned from them, and shuffled off, barefoot, exhausted, helpless. The neighbors waited until he was gone, then crept into the shambles to sift for treasure.

At home he sat, saying nothing, glowering. His wife chided him. "You could have been a god to those people. If it weren't for your brother, you might have had all the treasures yourself. You could have granted anyone any wish they asked. If he ever comes back . . ." She didn't finish the thought.

The children he'd entertained with rides returned the next morning, but when Baloyd proved unable to perform further feats of speed, they left him. A few of his neighbors came inquiring after Suald, but their inquiries provoked only rage, and they soon stopped coming. Baloyd plunged with suicidal vigor back into his dissolute life—gambling, drinking, and whoring—in a vain attempt to drown out the words his wife had set in motion, that, like a perpetual mechanism, swirled around and around his brain: *I could have been a god. I could have been a god.* He rarely went home, and when he did it was only to pass out until he awoke to go out again. Betinela left him. He had no idea when it happened, whether he'd been home or not, whether weeks had passed without her and he had simply failed to notice.

One hot afternoon while he lay unconscious, shouts from outside woke him. A crowd had gathered before his door. They called his name. As he arose in the shadows he winced and waited for his head to stop pounding. Then, scratching himself, he peered at them from the second-floor window. He supposed he'd done something offensive while drunk—throttled a favorite cat or kicked a child. They might have been there to hang him, although they weren't hammering down the door as he would have expected. They were agitated all right, but not angry. And they weren't going away. He descended the stairs uncertainly and opened the door.

They took hold of him and hauled him through the streets to Brink Lane. He thought of a man he'd pushed out of a window, but that had been so long ago. Maybe Suald's spell had lifted—maybe he wasn't a rat anymore, maybe someone had seen what had happened, maybe he was dreaming, maybe he was mad.

Through the twists and turns of alleys they hauled him. The sun stabbed at his eyes. His head throbbed with each propelled step. He began to think that if they killed him, it could only be a blessing. As they neared the dragon beam, he saw that even more people lined the spiral walkway all the way to the *hex*. Had something else been sent down from the Edgeworld gods—something more for him? What if it was an avatar sent to demand back the gifts? What would he say? He didn't know where they were now.

The crowd accompanying him stopped at the edge, but pushed him onto the beam. There was no going back, no escaping. He didn't try.

As he wound the beam, the people ahead moved aside to give him room. He came to the end, and the crowd, almost reverently, parted.

There, in the center of the platform, stood a terrifying scarecrow. Its clothes were rags. Long tangled weeds constituted the hair. It had a face like a desiccated fish—the mouth a wide, howling oval, the dark leathery skin pitted and taut and tanned. Despite its upright position, anyone could see that it wasn't alive. For one thing, it had no eyes in its ragged sockets.

Finally he noticed its feet.

In complete disparity with the rest of the tattered thing, the big, clumsy shoes on its feet were brightly polished and red as blood. Far redder than when he had given them up. He looked at the dried-out and ravaged face again, and finally recognized the features of his brother.

Baloyd realized what had happened. Whenever *he* had chosen a destination, the shoes had not stopped until it had been reached. Suald had chosen the compass of the entire world: He had run across infinity. He had run himself to death.

His horrifying appearance kept everyone a comfortable distance away from Suald. When Baloyd touched him, the body collapsed like a heap of twigs. He caught it as it fell and laid it down. Then he untied the shoes and took them off his brother's corpse. Bones sprinkled out of them—dust and small bits—all that remained of Suald's feet. He upended the shoes to pour out the rest, then sat and, removing his slippers, put the shoes on again. People stared at him, many with distaste. He didn't care. His brother had stolen the shoes from him, and he wasn't about to let anyone else get the chance. They were his.

He left the slippers there on the hex.

The husk of his brother weighed little. Without assistance Baloyd carried the raggedy body along the spiral of the dragon beam, and bits of it crumbled as he walked, sprinkling over the wall and into the sea. The crowd backed away, some with revulsion, others in wonder. With each step the blood hammered in his head. In the pulse his wife's voice chided him over and over and over again: *You could have been a god. You could have been a* god.

When he stepped from the beam onto Brink Lane, something plopped from the pocket of his brother's trousers. The unblemished clay tablet lay at his feet. He turned the corpse to rummage through the other pockets until he found the stylus. It was dark and sharp, ready for use.

He set down Suald, then picked up the clay. In his other hand he held the stylus. What should he write? He could bring Suald back to life, and Seru as well from whatever hell she'd been cast into. With the tablet he might do anything at all.

People dared to come near him. They asked, "What's wrong, Baloyd? Why have you stopped?"

He considered their eager faces. The pathetic, simple fools. "Nothing's wrong," he said. "Everything is very right, and it's going to be better than right." He inscribed the tablet. Then he lowered the stylus.

Halfway.

That was as far as he got before the transformation took place.

A reddish-brown dust swirled up from the street, spinning a web around his legs. Reddish brown color spread from his fingertips over his palms and up his arms, too. Like a living sheath the color encased his torso, his neck, his head. In a moment he ceased to be human, or alive.

The people on the street dropped to their knees and bowed down in veneration. They chanted his name, "Ba-*loyd*," each time they bowed. Some of the nearest ones reached out and touched him. Their display brought others who, unmoved by the desire to venerate, came close enough to inspect the rough stone figure that had been Baloyd. Beside him they found his brother's corpse and, lying beside it where it had fallen, the clay tablet. On the tablet they read the words he'd written: Make them worship me like a god.

"And so was Baloyd worshipped for many, many years," said Leodora, "until the last of those people who'd been present that day had died. By then, the sandstone form of him had been worn down and scoured by wind and salt. The tablet proved useless to those who'd found it. A few tried writing upon it with sticks and knives to no effect. The stylus had been transformed into stone along with Baloyd.

"Thus we're reminded that the gods are capricious, and that it's unwise ever to make demands of them when instead we should be thankful for what we *do* have."

She faced the twin actors. Throughout the recitation her attention had been focused upon them, upon their movements and gestures—how one jumped behind the other and back again to represent speeding across the span of Kakotara; how one would appear to write on an invisible tablet and the other would become the thing he'd called into being, the birds, the carriers of the conjured palanquin, the fig trees. At the end as she spoke, one of them lay upon the stage with arms bent and fingers curled, as skeletal as he could be, while the other had wrapped his arms about himself and bowed his head, and had slowly sunk down to his knees as his sandstone shape was worn away.

The applause that followed her recitation surprised her, and she jumped away from the edge of the stage even as she peered into the depths of the theatre. The two wooden men arose as one and faced the sound. They leaned forward at the waist as if they might stretch themselves toward it.

From out of the dark recesses a figure flowed toward the stage—tall and slender. Drawing nearer the light, it took shape as a woman in a green embroidered brocade nightgown. She was smiling broadly as she approached. "That is the first performance upon that stage in more than a dozen years," she said. "I had given up hoping there would ever be another." She rounded the front of it and came up the steps at the side. "You gave them the story so well, it was as if they *became* your puppets." She drew up before Leodora and added "You are certainly your father's daughter. No one could doubt it."

Leodora blinked up at her. "You knew my father?" she asked.

"He played here. On this very stage, a rare occasion. Because of the size of the theatre, we stretched a great screen across the front of it and mounted a lens between that and the screen in his booth so that the shadows were cast in giant proportion—quite the extraordinary contrivance that was, but we drew from four spans for the audience. Can you imagine?

Four spans! They traveled that far to see the incomparable Bardsham. They knew he was only here for a short run before sailing off to another spiral, another world. He was covering Shadowbridge then, and every span on every spiral would come to know him by rumor, by legend. That was his goal, you see, which he proclaimed with enormous pride and, well, not a little hubris." Her expression softened as if to say, *It was a forgivable fault*, but Leodora wasn't concerned with her father's ego.

"And my mother?" she asked. "Did you know her, too?"

The woman's express delight buckled. Her gaze clouded, and it was clear she was recalling something troubling. "You could be her sister." She turned sharply to the two players. "Glaise, Bois, go off with you now. It's near morning and will be light soon. Our guests will want their breakfast."

They clapped their hands and bowed, then arm in arm they marched off in matched step.

Watching them depart, she continued, "My husband ran the theatre then. It was, well, just as you see it now. A wondrous place. Magic flowed from here and out across those rows, those benches, all the way up into those boxes every single night."

She focused beyond Leodora on nothing that was there, and Leodora knew that she was peering into her past. "Having Bardsham pick our theatre for his venue. It was—we thought we had realized our dream."

The melancholy bound up in her words prompted Leodora to ask, "He didn't perform well?"

"Bardsham? Oh, my dear, he was a genius. The shadows came to life. They danced, they strutted, even flew . . . It was so grand, so smooth, so elegant that you forgot there was an agency at work behind them." She stared at Leodora. "Soter wants to convince me you are his equal."

She blushed, suddenly shy. "I don't know. I never saw him perform."

"Of course not. You were a fat little thing when your mother . . . when they left here."

Leodora's eyes went wide. "I was—I was here?"

The woman made a stiff, uncomfortable smile. It was clear that she wasn't certain where the boundaries lay. The more they talked, the more she set sail in uncharted waters. Whether or not Soter had instructed her not to speak of some things, Leodora could tell that she was cracking open a subject that hadn't seen light.

She closed her hand on the woman's wrist and said, "I want to know everything," leaving no room for obfuscation or pretense. She said, "But first tell me who you are."

"Ah, I've been unforgivably obscure. My name is Orinda."

Leodora gaped.

"I was once a player here, much like Bois and Glaise, save that I was never made of wood—although neither were they, once. But if I explain all that to you now, I'll lose the thread of it, and it's so difficult anymore to hold on to such threads. The spirals are unwinding for me, and each turn seems farther than the one preceding it. Mr. Burbage's . . . I'm sure I'm making no sense to you."

Leodora shook her head. "Truly, I lost your thread at your name."

"Orinda." She laughed lightly.

"Yes, I heard that much. There's a puppet of that name in my collection. She comes from a story I know, that Soter taught me."

"Oh. I should like to hear *that* story. I hope she's not a villain. I was a traveling player once, and I've never heard my name in a tale. But as to what I was saying before, the proprietor of the theatre, Mr. Burbage, fell in love with me and I with him and I became his wife, and together we ran this—or, to be precise I should say its predecessor—and, oh my, we were in love. I always called him Mr. Burbage because that's what we'd called him when we were all players, not because he wanted formality, and it became more intimate in some way I can't explain, that I did. We were in love, I think, every single day we were together. He took ill right before your father . . ." She looked about herself, at the walls, roof, tapestries, as if to assure herself that they were real. "Right before we fell into ruin."

"Bardsham was connected to that?"

"The members of the high court held us accountable for the blighting of Colemaigne after he left, and they banned all subsequent performances. Of course, we'd suffered as much if not more than any in the blight. The theatre was transformed into a ruin, so it almost mattered not at all. There would have been no further performances. No walls, no stage, just rot and crumbling masonry. Nothing held together, nor could we make it hold. Their ban only meant we wouldn't rebuild, but it proved the end of Mr. Burbage. He might have rallied from his illness, but he had no reason to. Oh, if I could only have shown him the state of things now—and Bardsham's daughter here, performing, I'm sure he would have held on. But if it hadn't saved him, I wouldn't have wanted him to suffer interminably, so perhaps it's better. We can't know these things, can we?"

"It makes you wish that the tablet in the story really existed," Leodora replied. "The blighting—how did it happen?"

Orinda made a face that said *It's not important* and replied, "Bardsham had gone. He and his troupe had sailed on . . . It's all long past."

"Yes, but what was the cause, and how did our arrival repair it?"

"You have no recollection, then. You walked into the Dragon Bowl and the gods paid us a visit. The first time in decades. You're the cause, you've freed us from a terrible curse."

The dragon beam—she remembered walking out along it to tease Diverus—and the bowl with enough tiles remaining to suggest a pattern, but nothing beyond that. "I don't understand," she said. "I don't even recall asking anyone to heal your span—I wouldn't have known to, would I?"

Orinda smiled tolerantly, as she might have at a slow child. "It's nothing to do with what you asked, only with the fact that the gods, when they touched you, answered."

Leodora digested that, then said, "But it doesn't—"

"Oh, my girl, please, no more questions for now. A terrible thing happened in the past and you righted it. You're going to be very popular in Colemaigne, you and your troupe, as I'm certain the ban on performances will be lifted now with you here—you, the cause of our healing—and, oh, imagine the hundreds who will fill our little theatre." She took Leodora by the arm and turned her. "They'll be clamoring at the gates, no doubt, once the sun's up. But you will need to eat, I think. You must be famished, and with all that must be done there might not be another meal today. For now you should come with me." Orinda turned to leave the stage.

"There's a ghost in my room," said Leodora.

Orinda stopped. "What?" she asked.

"A ghost. A voice. He spoke to me, but he wasn't there. It's not a very big room, and I reached all the way to the wall and there wasn't anyone present, but I heard him. He knew it was dark outside, and he knew all about the theatre."

Orinda clasped both her hands. "Mr. Burbage, when he . . . He wanted to be close to the theatre, so at the end he took to sleeping in the balconies of the stage, right across from your room. Do you think it could be Mr. Burbage who spoke to you?"

"He said he was a counselor."

"We'll go to your room and see. If it is my dear one, he will speak to me, surely he will."

They climbed the stairs to her room. It lay dark still, closed off from the light of dawn, but it was possible now to distinguish the bed from the floor, the small armoire from the wall.

"Hello," said Leodora. She knelt on the bed. "Are you still with me?" She half expected silence, but then the same voice as before drawled, "It's not as if I can go off on my own."

"There," she told Orinda. "You hear him?"

"I do. However, it's not Mr. Burbage, unless his voice has changed."

"Are you Mr. Burbage?" Leodora asked the room.

"That would be impossible," came the reply. It seemed to issue from the bed itself, right beside her. Orinda pressed up close behind her.

"Why?" asked the proprietress.

"He has passed from this world and into Edgeworld."

"Into it?"

"Why, yes. What else was he to do? But you are not my mistress, and I answer you from courtesy only, as she openly regards you as a friend."

"Oh," said Orinda, stepping back. Leodora pushed her hands through the bedsheets.

"Speak to me now!" she said. "I'm right on top of you, why can't I find you?" She swept her hands through the covers, finding only the pendant with its chain, on which she was kneeling. She lifted it into the air.

"Thus you resolve the matter without resorting to assistance," said the pendant.

"You?" Dangling it by its chain, she clambered off the bed and out the door past her hostess. In the hallway with the light coming through the distant curtains, she could make out the shape of the pendant, a smoothly crafted leonine face with golden eyes. "Speak now," she said. "Tell me who sent you?"

"Sent me?" the lion head asked. "Why, no one sent me,

you chose me."

Orinda said, "It's a Brazen Head. Oh, my goodness, I've never seen one before."

"A what?" Leodora asked.

"A Brazen Head. There are so many of them in legends."

"There are legends?"

Before Orinda could respond, the pendant chimed, "Indeed. There's a most famous one in a play. It belonged to a man named Bacon. It only spoke while he slept, and it said 'Time was,' and 'Time is,' and 'Time's past.' No one knows what it meant, but everyone suspects it was important."

"What *did* it mean? What does it mean to say *time is*."

"The nature of Brazen Heads," explained the lion, "is that they speak in riddles or at least in ways that are obscure. It's not our choice, you understand. It's simply how we're made."

Leodora pursed her lips. "That's like Meersh's argument that he isn't bad, he's simply consigned to try all the bad ideas he comes across."

"I suppose it is, after a fashion," the head agreed.

"I don't believe *him*, either," she told it.

The pendant and she considered each other, scant inches apart. Then the lion's tongue unfurled as it yawned, revealing ivory teeth, and it blinked slowly several times. "Time is that which ends," it said. Then it closed its eyes and fell silent, a piece of jewelry once again.

Leodora sighed. "If this is what I chose to bring back, I'm not hopeful of my acquaintance with the gods."

"Oh, but," Orinda said, "we now know that Mr. Burbage is in Edgeworld. It means a *great* deal to me to know that."

"I suppose it wasn't something we could have learned on our own." She still wasn't sure that anything the head uttered could be relied upon. "It seems to have gone to sleep, as if we wore it out." She sniffed the air, alert suddenly to a warm scent.

Orinda nodded. "You smell the breakfast cooking, too, don't you?"

By way of answer, Leodora's stomach gurgled.

"Come along, my dear. After we eat, we can ponder all the questions in the universe without being taken by them, as Mr. Burbage used to say." Orinda clasped her hand and led her toward the stairs.

Leodora pocketed the pendant and let her hostess lead her, but she wasn't giving up on discovering how this span had been blighted. Deep inside she knew that the plague visited upon this place had something to do with her.

Upon another spiral, on the distant span of Vijganar, something unnatural came flowing along Kalian Esplanade. In the late-night darkness a darker mass moved, topped by five smooth, pale, hairless heads. The mass or its constituents made no sound, yet thrust along the esplanade without benefit of any torchbearer to guide them. Those who plied that trade saw the approaching anomaly and changed course instinctively to avoid it, which abrupt shift caused their clients to take notice of the five heads sailing past, sunken eyes glistening, watchful, like birds of prey. Some people drew up, backed to the sea-wall, to let the thing by. Bearers and clients were united in their unease, and if anyone spoke, it was to whisper. "Archivists," said some, thinking that the legendary Library had sent its agents to capture some piece of knowledge, a scholarly scroll perhaps. As no one had ever laid eyes upon the rumored archivists, it was a reasonable opinion, though less explicable was why a cluster of library archivists should elicit discomfort if not outright terror, for there were many others brushed against by the flowing mass who instinctively made small gestures to ward off evil before hurrying on their way, all too grateful to be going in the opposite direction.

The place called Lotus Hall, while still open for business, was nearly dormant this late, inhabited by a few regulars who would have sat there no matter what entertainment was proffered. At the moment that entertainment comprised a man spinning four ducks that balanced perfectly poised on the tips of their beaks upon polished clamshells. No one paid him or his trained fowl the slightest attention, although the ducks were working very hard and occasionally let fly a disgruntled *quack*.

The proprietor Nuberne was feeling the pinch since the remarkable Jax had gone. The puppeteer had brought in standing-room crowds, the best he'd ever seen. He suspected that his wife Rolend had hastened the puppeteer's departure with her unbridled overtures, and things had not been pleasant between them since.

He was standing in his small kitchen off the hall when the sounds of the performance ceased. Even the small, innocuous noises of snoring drunks and cautious conversations stopped.

As his head turned, the hair on the back of his neck stiffened and he threw off a shiver in response to the uncanny silence.

The hall, seen through the doorway, became darker than the kitchen, where two low cooking fires tossed trembling shadows as well as heat. Even the wall sconces and the chandelier candles seemed to have guttered and gone out. From the center of this deeper darkness five pale heads gained in size every moment, until he could make out the glassy eyes within the sunken orbits, eager and hungry in their focus upon him. Not until they hovered just beyond the doorway did he make out the folds and darts of their black cloaks. This was the effect they strove for, of course, and though he recognized the manipulation, he could not overcome its dread intent. Later as he clung to his wife's stiff fingers, he would insist it couldn't be real, any of it, because the archivists were a myth. Everyone knew it.

Packed closely together, the five hovered at the doorway as one of them spoke. "You are the proprietor?" The bloodless lips had hardly moved. All eyes still feasted upon him.

Nuberne tried to reply, swallowed, cleared his throat, and managed a raspy, "I am."

"We are interested in a performer who seems not to be performing this night."

He tried to make sense of that. "You're wanting me to hire him?"

The five exchanged looks. "No. What would make you think that?"

"I don't understand then."

At that point his wife Rolend approached from wherever she'd been in the depths of the hall. "What's happened here, Nuberne?" she called as she scanned the wide-eyed stragglers, the nonperforming ducks. "Why has the whole place gone—oh!" Finally, she had seen the swarm of figures before the doorway. The five pallid heads turned in unison to regard her.

"Beg—beg pardon," she said. She eased around them and through the doorway, taking a worried step back into the kitchen.

"Quite all right," said one of the five. "We were inquiring after an artist who performs here, by the name of 'Jax.'"

"Jax," repeated Nuberne. "You're mistaken then. He's not performing here anymore. He shoved off a while ago. But what would the Library want—"

"Yet you have notices pasted up. We saw them all along the esplanade."

Rolend faced him. "Don't you tell them anything, don't you help them."

"Ro, shut up," Nuberne said, more out of fear than anger.

"They don't mean him any good," she argued.

"Ro!" He reached for her even as she stiffened as if poked in the back. She stared at him wide-eyed and managed to utter his name once, faintly, before the color drained from her face and the eyes looking upon Nuberne went blank and flat, the color of her now hardened flesh, the color of the long skeletal hand that was clamped around the back of her neck. The fingers slid away; something glittered in the palm for an instant before it vanished in the black folds behind her. Where the hand brushed her hair, gray grains sprinkled loose. It might have been the hand of any one of them.

Nuberne touched her stone-cold wrist and recoiled in horror.

"Quite all right," the one repeated. "We *don't* mean him any good, that is true. It is also none of your concern. You will tell us where he is, this Jax."

Nuberne's face twisted up but he could not stop looking at her, his wife, dead. "I don't know. He moved on," he said.

"The notices s—"

"I *left* 'em up. I was trading on his fame is all! He filled the place, every night, the best storyteller since—"

"Bardsham. Yes, yes, we know."

"Bring her back," he pleaded.

"Ah, I regret, you credit us with too much power," hissed the one. "Where is Jax now? Or wish you to follow her?"

"Jax . . . Jax moved on. To another span, him and his troupe." He was weeping, trembling with shock. His legs could not hold him up and he grabbed for the edge of a table.

"Another span. North or south?"

"I don't know. North, I think. He'd come from the south."

"North it is then. Tell us one more thing. He goes about disguised?"

His hands on the tabletop curled into fists of impotent anger and he lowered his head to them, closed his eyes. "Masked." He choked the word.

"Of course," said the one.

When he raised his head, Nuberne found the doorway

empty and everyone in the hall, even the hapless performer and his terrified ducks, staring now at the ossified figure that had been Rolend. He sank down to the floor then, and his wail filled the hall with agony.

"The girl touched by the gods," proclaimed Orinda. "That is what we'll put on the banner, and surely you'll fill the theatre."

Across the long table covered now in emptied bowls and cups, Soter sat with his arms crossed and head bowed as if dozing after the meal. Without moving, he said, "You'll still be wanting to call yourself Jax." Though he didn't raise his head, he opened one eye to watch Leodora's reaction. She straightened as if she'd been jabbed, and her eyes blazed. Before she could respond, he interjected, "I'm not saying you should go masked anymore."

"Then why should I hide my name?"

His gaze rolled to Orinda, and he dipped his chin as if to say *You explain it to her.* Glaise and Bois—their places absent of dishes—looked to their mistress, too.

Then to everyone's surprise Diverus spoke up. "Performance name," he said.

Soter raised his head. "That's so," he agreed, but in a tone conveying his bemusement.

Diverus added, "It's all I have."

Bois responded to his dejection by patting him on the shoulder. Orinda asked, "What do you mean, it's all you have, Diverus?"

He answered, "That's what—my name *is* my performance name. Nobody knew my true name. *I* didn't know it."

Leodora interjected, "You told me Eskie gave you your name long before you'd discovered what your gift was."

"That's so, but it doesn't make it my proper name, it's just what they called me in the paidika when they wanted me to do something, instead of saying *Boy* all the time."

"Ah, performance," Soter replied. "I see what you mean now. Not the same thing as we was thinking, though you somehow arrived at the right word anyway. Sometimes, boy . . . Diverus, you startle me."

If Diverus caught the jibe, he showed no reaction. "I don't mean to," he said.

"Is that what you told your last owner before you ran off—

I don't mean to cause you trouble?"

"Stop it, Soter," Leodora said.

"You doubted him the same," he protested back.

"I was asking him to clarify, not belittling him."

Soter made no reply, but finally shrugged off the criticism.

Softly, Diverus asked her, "Why don't you ask your new counselor?"

"Ask it what?"

"About the name, what name you should use."

She had laid the polished pendant aside while she ate, for all of them to see, but it hadn't said a word nor even opened its eyes the whole time. Taking hold of the chain, she raised it in front of her, then turned the head so that it faced her. She wanted to ask it about the blight of Colemaigne, not about her name.

Soter pushed back his chair. "That's right. Don't listen to old Soter's advice, but by all means get the contraption's opinion. You *will* let me know what it says, won't you, Lea." He gave a polite nod to Orinda and the wooden men, and then marched off into the depths of the theatre.

An uncomfortable silence ensued during which Leodora stared after him, Diverus stared at her, and Orinda looked at everything else.

Then the Brazen Head opened its eyes. "In answer to your principal question," it said, "you *can* only continue to call yourself Jax."

"I didn't ask."

"You didn't *speak* it, which is not the same thing."

"Why must she call herself Jax?" Orinda asked. "She needs the reason."

"It is the name the world knows. In time it will surpass that of Bardsham."

"Please, don't patronize me," Leodora protested.

The lion looked as if it might just close its eyes again out of spite, but then it said, "Didn't Bardsham's name surpass that of Meersh?"

"But Meersh—"

"Meersh, Leodora, is as old as these spans and recognized by all of them." And with that it did close its eyes, a plain and simple pendant once more.

"It sounded a little angry to me," said Diverus.

"Testy," Orinda observed.

Leodora sighed, "Wonderful. One Soter wasn't enough."

For an instant after she said that she saw the face of the other one again—the "Soter" from Edgeworld—before both image and memory collapsed, leaving her with a vague and disconnected sense of there being two realities in attendance, but one invisible and forever out of reach.

Carefully, Orinda told her, "I know you have differences with Soter, and I shouldn't want to wade into the middle of that, but I must concur with him and with your remarkable adviser here. You have created a magical persona in Jax, and it is that which will be whispered and remembered. It also frees you to be yourself when you choose, to leave Jax on the stage, in the booth. In the boxes with the puppets." The two wooden men nodded in agreement.

Leodora nearly confessed to her hostess that there was already someone in the boxes with the puppets—someone who manifested in her dreams to disturbing effect, as if a ghost watched her wherever she went, never revealing himself nor his desires concerning what she did. And yet it seemed this ghost waited for some particular event.

When she glanced down again, the pendant had opened its eyes anew. "Tophet," it said. She had no idea what question she had asked this time, but the lion was already inanimate again.

Despite the quirky nature of her brazen counselor, later that morning Leodora wore the pendant as she and Diverus walked the crooked lanes of Colemaigne. It hung between her breasts, an insentient piece of brass.

Many of the lanes folded back upon themselves, cramped and dark. Already twice she had elected a narrow route out of a piazza only to find that they were returned to the starting point as if by magic. And twice, on the much wider, brighter boulevards decorated with fig trees, the two of them had come upon Bois (or was it Glaise?) pasting up posters announcing the premiere performance tonight of The Girl Who Healed Colemaigne! This was the title conferred on her by Orinda and Soter after much debate, playing upon the obvious transformation of the span. The posters drew small crowds even as he was hanging them, and she was thankful that her image wasn't on them.

The resurrected buildings lining the boulevard were perfect, glistening edifices, untouched by time, unworn and brightly colored, and the line of them was easily traceable across the span. Only the blighted buildings had been repaired, looking newer now than the rest. The guild of craftsmen Soter had mentioned were indeed wizards if these were what their creations looked like when new. The pigments inside the sugar shells glowed as if with an inner light, an illusion created by the refracting layers of confection. People clustered before new buildings, chattering, admiring. In one courtyard she came upon a flock of children licking the side of a tall house while others scooted up a tree to break off the orange marzipan leaves and drop them to their friends below. It was strange, otherworldly, and perfectly natural. Everywhere stood statues, and all seemed to be the work of the same sculptor, who captured citizens of Colemaigne in life-like poses. These looked older, too, not part of the regeneration.

"Would they know any stories?" Diverus asked her as they stood watching the children. He had grown tired from all the walking in circles—endlessly it seemed to him. While she had slept and rejuvenated after her encounter with Edgeworld, he had slept fitfully if at all and would on this occasion have preferred to stay behind. He had also begun to worry that they would not be able to find their way back through the maze of alleys and lanes they had traversed. *He* was certainly lost.

"I'm sure they know some," she replied. "But Colemaigne's an ancient span. There has to be someplace where people gather and *tell* their tales. It's been that way on every span, and even on Bouyan, on an island where nothing ever happens. The villagers had a house for storytelling."

"What if it's at the far end, your gathering place?" His tone clearly conveyed his opinion that they should stop looking for now.

"It's possible, I suppose, though I can't believe there's only one such place on a span this long."

"But it was damaged, and performance forbidden for years."

"That's true. Such places may not be easy to find. Maybe I should scale one of the towers. Maybe I could see something from up there."

"You've done that before, then. I remember you saying—" He broke off before he added *right before you were snared by the gods.*

"Before you joined us," she said.

He speculated, "What if the stories here all lie in the upside-down city?" and was surprised when she clutched his arm, bringing him to a stop. "What is it?" he asked, glancing around, expecting there was something to behold.

"You saw that, too?"

He nodded. "When we went to carry you off the dragon beam. There were buildings in the shadows under the span, hanging from the span. I thought it was a reflection until I realized it didn't match the span above at all."

"I remember it—one of the few things I *do* remember. Just for a moment, and then the sky was flashing and I looked up and . . . then I woke up in that room."

"A man came out of one of those houses. He was blue and he was walking upside down. He should have fallen into the sea but he didn't. He came to the edge and he waved to me. And then he was gone." Suddenly he wasn't tired any longer, but strangely roused by the memory.

"How can we get there, do you suppose?"

Diverus thought for a moment. "Well, although it's on the wrong side, there is the opening where the goods from the ship were hauled up. Remember how they were hauled out of sight under the street?"

"Where we climbed the *stairs,*" she exclaimed. "We need to go back there, Diverus."

"You think that's a way in?" he asked.

"We have to see. It could be it's the only way in."

Finding their way back to the point of their arrival proved easy. They had only to follow the trail of gleaming resurrected buildings. The line of renewal led back to the square where Leodora and Diverus had arrived. Even that had been transformed. The fountain where Soter had sat had been repointed, the stone animal figures in the center had been polished, their details freshly chiseled. Leodora could count the feathers on the roc, the scales on the dragon. It was a fabulous fountain now, and behind it lay a garden full of blossoms, purple and white. People lazed in the garden, sprawled here and there, some entwined, as if drugged into a stupor. Now and then one person picked a blossom and fed it to his partner, which seemed to be all the energy he could muster before collapsing again with a vague and dreamy smile. The street, which previously had been full of broken and uneven stones, was smooth, the square-hewn blocks so perfectly fitted that they seemed a single surface.

Leodora looked over the wall at the pulley arms jutting from the stone below. One of the platforms on which goods were hauled up from the harbor hung there unattended. The platform had been pulled up, apparently hours before, because there was no ship below now. Baskets and bolts of cloth swung there in the mild breeze.

"Everyone seems to have taken the day off," Diverus said.

"This is the Colemaigne of legend that Soter described, much more so than what we encountered when we arrived."

"Then maybe it's a holy day."

"If it is, we're the cause." She stepped up on the wall.

"Lea," he gasped, "what are you doing?"

"I'm going to jump to that platform, so that I can go into the undercity."

"But if you miss—I can't even bear to look down there!"

"Yes, but I can. I scale bridge towers, remember?"

"You—you shouldn't do this alone. And you've already risked . . . You just recovered from the Dragon Bowl, from Edgeworld. That's enough, isn't it? Besides, there's bound to be a way into there from someplace up here—people aren't spending their whole *lives* down there!"

"Why? They did on Vijganar, didn't they?"

"Please," he begged.

"I'll be fine, Diverus, I'm not going to miss the platform. There's barely a hand's width between the wall and it. It's hardly a jump at all." With that, as casually as if she were strolling along the boulevard, she stepped off the wall and dropped.

She landed on a bolt of cloth and fell forward onto her hands and knees. The pendant swung and slapped against her, and the platform bounced slightly off the wall but otherwise hung steady.

Where she lay, she was looking directly into an opening, with a pulley arm above her, and the ropes bearing the platform all running to a winch set back far enough to allow for the unloading of the goods. She realized that if she had taken one step to the side before jumping, she would have struck the pulley and possibly missed the platform altogether. Her stomach clenched. She would not point this out to Diverus.

Lifting one of the baskets, she found it to be as heavy as if it were filled with wet sand. She heaved it into the opening and, using its weight as a fulcrum, hauled herself up and in beside it.

The area beneath the span receded into darkness. What light did play through the opening showed nearby containers and amphorae, baskets and crates all neatly stacked. It looked familiar: the cargo from the boat that had brought her here.

"Lea!" called Diverus, and she stuck her head out to show him that she was fine. He laughed in relief.

"I think this might go all the way across the span, Diverus," she called up. "I'm going to follow it. Don't wait for me here, go back to the theatre. I'll find my way out."

"But I'm not sure where the theatre *is*."

"Go to the far side of the span and walk down the sea-lane, same as we did before, past the Dragon Bowl. Just don't walk out onto the beam."

Disregarding her levity, he replied, "I'm not happy about this."

"You could come down here with me."

"No," he said, "I couldn't. I can't."

"Well, I can't come back up now that I'm here. So you have to go on top and me underneath."

"You're crazy, Leodora, do you know that?" He shook his head at her and then withdrew.

"All too well," she said to herself.

When he didn't reappear, she ducked back inside, but his final statement stayed with her. He was right, she *had* taken ridiculous risks, although she hadn't seen them as such at the time. She hadn't expected the hexagonal bowl to ignite, to do . . . whatever it had done to her. She glanced down at the pendant, fingering the edges of it. Whatever had been done, she could hardly reverse it now. She was who she was. Jumping down here, though, had been no risk at all, for someone used to scaling bridge towers. Diverus would just have to understand.

She turned her attention to the space ahead.

The underspan had a low ceiling, and while the floor was not a natural formation, it otherwise reminded her eerily of

Fishkill Cavern where she'd first met the Coral Man. It was the sound of the place, she realized as she headed deeper in. It was the way her footsteps echoed as in a great cave.

Her eyes grew used to the dimness. There must have been hundreds of containers, perhaps thousands if they continued into the darkness. It was as though ships had been coming here since the beginning of time, their cargo hauled up but never passed along.

She soon came upon the first set of steps leading back to the surface, their zigzag shape like a fracture in the darkness.

She went up them bent low, her hands on the steps above, as if ready to fling herself off at the first sign of trouble from above. Nearing the top, she raised one hand and patted it against the shape of a trapdoor. Her fingers closed around a metal ring dangling from it. As the underspan reminded her of Fishkill Cavern, the trapdoor was all too unpleasantly reminiscent of her boathouse on Bouyan, and an irrational terror seized her that if she lifted that trap, she would be back there with her uncle looming over the opening, waiting for her. For a moment as she crouched in the darkness, she had the wild notion that she had never left the boathouse and that all the adventure between there and here had been an illusion, and now she must return to the cold horror, relive it all. This terror so pressed on and compacted her that she flung open the trap in defiance of it.

It wasn't the boathouse, of course. She was in someone's kitchen—there was a wooden block, and on it knives, pots, and empty red-glass bottles. The place looked gray and disused, although that might have been a trick of the light coming through the smudged, distorting glass of the windows. Before anyone came into view, she lowered the trap and retreated down the steps, but then sat at the bottom of them until she could see in the darkness again.

The house above might have been one of those that had been blighted until yesterday. That would explain its sense of emptiness, of stillness. She didn't know if people had continued to live in the blighted places. Orinda had continued living in the back of the theatre, but did that constitute reliable evidence?

In the murk around her she now could make out jagged edges of more scattered stairways up to the surface.

She got up and continued walking. She passed a few small barrows and a larger cart. The cart, half-unloaded, had lengths of rope dangling off it, conveying a sense that all work had simply stopped. That seemed to be what had happened. Perhaps it was because of the rejuvenation of the span, or maybe this was just a day of rest. She thought of the people lying about among the flowers above—a day with no obligations, no work to be done. It sounded terribly inviting if utterly alien to her.

She walked deeper into the space and shortly came upon another stairway to the surface. Beside this one stood one of the stone statues, like those she'd seen along the refurbished boulevard. Someone had opted not to carry this one to the surface, although it looked to her perfectly formed. It was the figure of a man. Even in the poor light she could see how well-defined were the folds of his tunic, how the sculptor had dramatically captured every detail of him. She couldn't imagine why anyone would choose to leave it down here in the dark.

Off in the distance, someone laughed. She listened, and tried to determine where it had come from, but the sound bounced off a hundred surfaces, circling her. She guessed at an approximate direction and started walking, cautiously. She walked past a thick pillar, an unlit lantern hanging from it.

She realized that she was seeing a wan light in the deep distance, one that flickered from behind stacked crates and boxes. She passed by more statuary, figures in crouched poses, looking as if they were in the middle of lifting something, and another pillar hung with another unused lantern, and more small carts. The light from outside, where she'd entered, shrank and shrank until it was like the glow of a distant star. The reflected light ahead looked brighter. She felt her way past amphorae and woven baskets toward a murmur of voices.

Someone cried out, "I serve you with a *writ*!" and she stopped dead. Whatever she expected next, it wasn't the groan of dismay that followed. A woman's voice exclaimed, "That's wonderful. Now I can sue for damages!" Hands clapped. Whoever it was sounded gleefully malicious, but no one else said a thing in reply. Instead there came a clicking sound and the words, "A nine!" and Leodora quite suddenly knew what was going on.

The remaining distance she walked with less concern, then around the stacked boxes that served as a wall enclosing the game. Indeed, it was definitely a game.

Five players—two women and three men—sat in a circle

upon wicker chests and boxes. One sat on a leather drum. In the center they'd set up an equally makeshift playing surface—a large flat cloth that was covered in symbols, lines, squares, and two piles of cards. The light came from lanterns hung from the arms of two more statues placed on opposite sides of the game. The players all held cards, and when she appeared they turned as one to see her. At first they gaped, but then they smiled to her. "Fresh meat," said one of the women. She stood. "Find her a seat."

"You composing poetry now, Meg?" asked the skinny man across from her.

"Could if I wanted," she answered, then to Leodora, "Come in, come in. We need another player, you've no idea—someone whose tricks we don't know yet."

"Hang on, now, my dear," said another of the men. "She could be here for supplies. You here for supplies, girl?"

"No," replied Leodora.

"Lost, then?"

"Not exactly. That is, I know how I got here."

The second woman laughed, revealing a mouthful of crooked teeth. "If you know that, then you're ahead of most of us. Come and sit." She tugged at the wide wicker case she perched on, dragging it to the side to give Leodora a place to perch beside her. "Tight quarters but still room enough, heh?" Leodora circled them and sat on the end of the case. "I'm Garna," said the woman. "That's Meg, then Pelorie, Hamen, and Chork."

"Leodora."

"Now, there's a name. Brave name," said Chork.

"How would you know that?" asked Hamen. He had a flushed, dissolute face, but friendly. "You don't even go up to the surface anymore."

Chork was wall-eyed and she shifted her gaze from one eye to the other, trying to determine which to look at. He said meanwhile, "Never mind how—I just know it from the sound. So tell us, do you know how to play?"

She looked at the cloth, the four dice, the game pieces, which looked to be whatever had been lying about—a cork, two pebbles, a striated shell, and a heavy ring set with a green stone. "This is what I think it is?"

"It is if what you're thinking is *Lawyer's poker*. We don't have a judge. You need a minimum of six to play with a judge.

So we been taking turns as needed. It's not the same, though, is it?"

Leodora didn't want to disappoint them. "I can try," she said. She had never played the game and knew of it only as referenced in one of the stories of Meersh.

"Well, then, toss in your cards," instructed Pelorie. "We'll deal a new game." He raked the cards into a heap and began to shuffle them.

Off in the distance someone called, "Coo-ee! Lignor Alley!"

"Damn," said Hamen. He got up, groaning, stretching his stocky frame. "I'll be right back then." He lifted the lantern behind him from the statue's arm and walked off. His voice echoed back: "What's it want?"

"Lingonberry wine!" came the reply.

Chork scratched his ear. "I'm sure there's some left that *we* haven't drunk." The others chuckled.

"Maybe one or two bottles were overlooked," added Meg.

As if in response, Pelorie set down the cards, lifted a bottle, uncorked it, and drank. He passed it on to Garna, but placed the cork on the board. "This'll serve as your piece, Leodora."

She nodded.

He said, "So, what is it you're doing down here, then? Nobody ever comes down here."

"I saw it when we arrived. We came on a ship and they had mostly cargo, so when we climbed up I saw the goods hauled in."

"That was us all right," agreed Garna. She handed her the bottle. "But how'd you figure to come visiting? Lots of people go up them steps—or used to. They don't usually come swinging in here on a rope."

"I'm a storyteller. I thought—"

"Oh, what kinds of stories?" Meg asked.

"Shadowplays."

"A puppeteer?"

She nodded.

"You'll want to take that drink *today*," urged Chork.

Leodora took a pull from the bottle. The liquor was sharp and sweet at the same time, and her eyes teared.

"Lemons," said Meg, as if answering a question, and Leodora nodded vigorously. She passed the bottle to Chork, who leaned forward to take it.

"You came here to perform," he said, "only to find out they's banned all such here for years and years now. That's a shame."

"No. I'm performing. Tonight."

"Naw! Where? Not on *this* span!"

"At the theatre?" she offered.

"What theatre would dare?"

She didn't recall that anyone had named it in her presence. All she could say was, "Mr. Burbage's?"

"The Terrestre. That old ruin? You can play there all you like, but all you're going to have for an audience is a lot of rubble and some rats. And even so they'll arrest you for it, see if they don't."

"He's right," Garna agreed. "The ban's a very serious thing."

"Not anymore, apparently," called Hamen. He walked up with his lantern and handed a sheet of yellow parchment to Meg. "Proprietress at Lignor give me this just now. Someone's passing 'em out up there."

Leodora knew what it was without reading it.

"The girl who saved Colemaigne?" Meg recited. The group looked from her to Leodora, who tried to smile at the same time as she would happily have climbed inside the wicker container on which she sat.

"Oy, but this calls her Jax. The redoubtable Jax. Not Leodora."

She started to explain but Hamen replied first. "Stage name, like." She met his amused gaze and bobbed her head.

"That's fine and all, but how'd she save Colemaigne? Did it need saving? We didn't hear anything about it."

"We wouldn't, now, would we?" Pelorie answered. "Anybody been up there so far today? I bet Hamen's come the closest with that paper."

"What day *is* it?"

"Who knows?"

"Celebration day, by the looks. So how did you save us, exactly?"

Leodora wrapped her arms about herself. "I don't really know, exactly. All I did was walk out on the dragon beam."

"What? That thing hasn't fallen off yet?"

"Garna, hush," Hamen said. "Go on."

"That's all—all I know. I seem to have gone to Edgeworld,

but I've no memory of it. When I woke up, the span had been put right. The theatre—"

"Terrestre."

"—the Terrestre's whole again, like it's brand new. The blighted buildings, they're fixed up. Repaired. I saw them on my way here. Children were licking them."

"I used to do that," said Chork, "when I was tiny."

"Well, tie me to the gods' gofe," Pelorie said in wonder. Then he glanced over his shoulder. "Hang on, though. How come *they* didn't change?"

The players eyed the statues suspiciously.

"Why didn't you change them back?" Garna asked her.

"I didn't—I don't know what that means," she said, and then all at once she did. "Those were people?"

"Once," Pelorie replied.

Chork focused one eye on her. "When the blight swept through, they were standing in its path. Down here."

"That one's me dad," Meg said, pointing to the one on which Hamen had hung his lantern.

"I'm sorry."

"Long time ago, that. I'm used to him this way now."

Garna asked again, "Why didn't they change back? The buildings but not the people—what's the point of that?"

"I don't know." She fingered the pendant nervously. "What is the point?"

The pendant opened its eyes. Meg gasped and Pelorie fell off his seat.

"The point," said the pendant, "is that a building can go forward in an inert state but life cannot. Once stopped it stays stopped."

"Time is that which ends," Leodora recited.

The pendant said, "Ah-ha," then closed its eyes and was silent again.

"What the mummichog was that?" Pelorie climbed back onto his seat.

"Orinda calls it a Brazen Head."

"Who? The Orinda that lives in the Terrestre?"

Meg and Hamen exchanged glances. "I'm thinking we might want to go up on the surface tonight," she said.

"Take in a play maybe, like?" Hamen looked at Leodora. "What do you think of that?"

"You live down here all the time?" she asked.

He shrugged. "It's akin to being a miner. We have our shifts, live mostly in the dark. We go home, some of us do."

Distantly someone called, "Coo-ee, Arbady Lane!"

Meg got up. "Hold my place," she said, as though someone new might sweep in and take it. She walked off into the darkness.

"Does that happen all the time?" asked Leodora.

Pelorie replied, "Nah. Most like in the morning. Sometimes we'll go a whole shift without a call. Not often, mind you, but it's happened." He took another drink from the circulating bottle, then asked, "So what are you doing down here, 'redoubtable'? You only said that you weren't lost."

"I'm looking for stories."

"The kind you can play out with your shadows?"

She nodded. "I like to hear how stories are told. Every span's a little different. Your characters might have a different name than elsewhere, or the tale reach a different outcome. Maybe they don't cut off their toes to make the magic slippers fit."

"I know that story!" Chork proclaimed.

"Of course you do," she went on, "and I like to hear how you learned it, what names everyone in it has, how it's changed, how it's become part of this span and not of any other. Then when I perform, I'll get it right for here. I mean, I could tell them in a general way and everyone would be pleased, but I would really rather tell them in the way they belong here."

"Never realized it was so complicated," said Garna.

"I'd a'thought you just telled 'em," Chork added, then loosely waved his hand. "Of course, it's been so long since there was a story here, we can't remember. But it's what I'd do."

"And that's why *you* unload ships and *she* performs stories," Garna told him.

"Well, thankee for nothing," Chork replied.

"I don't want to cause a squabble," Leodora said.

"Oh, you're not causing anything. He's like that all the time."

Pelorie added, "To everybody."

Chork looked at the two of them and started to laugh.

"I know a story," Pelorie offered. "Fella off a boat told me it last week. You want to hear?"

"All right."

"But then you have to be our judge, just so we can play a

real hand of Lawyers' Poker. That's my price."

"That seems fair."

"Well, good, then." He leaned back against the statue behind him and closed his eyes.

Leodora quietly asked Garna, "What's he doing?"

"Waiting for Meg."

"Oh."

"Meantime, I'll show you the rules of the game so you'll know how to play it." Garna reached across the cloth and grabbed the deck of cards.

By the time Meg returned, they'd gone through half the deck, and Leodora had seen enough to understand and act her part. She urged them to play first and tell the story after, and that's what they did.

The game—or so Meg claimed—went much faster than usual now that they had a real judge. They shouted at one another, bickered, threatened. As a group they cheered when she threw one of the dice, picked a card from the judge's pile, and handed down a sentence upon Chork that took him out of the game until Garna handed him a card that claimed he had tunneled from jail and into a brothel. "At least," he said, "I'll be happy in my retirement."

"Too bad the whores can't say the same," answered Garna.

In the end the play all came down to a lawsuit between Garna and Hamen. They argued their positions and then the judge had to rule. Leodora threw the dice and read the first card, which was called the amicus curiae. It meant she had to consult with the players who'd been kicked out of the game and get their answers. They talked and then outshouted each other, but without any agreed position. Chork and Meg wanted Garna to lose, while Pelorie opposed Hamen on the argument that someone simply should. She threw the dice again, and the card that came up was called bona vacantia, and stated that the properties owned by the remaining parties had to be divided equally between them. As she ruled, Garna stood up, outraged, bellowing furiously, and Leodora considered diving for safety under the cloth, at which point Garna, unable to maintain her façade of fury any longer, collapsed in laughter. Pelorie decreed, "Thus we know that law laughs in your face while it picks your pocket."

"Just like real life then, is it?" said Meg.

"But now," he said, "our judge has earned her reward. Eh, Pelorie?"

Pelorie patted the cards into a neat stack. He drew the top one and held it up. "Ad arbitrium," he read. "At your will, Leodora."

"You still talking lawyerish, then?" Chork said.

"All right, fold up the game cloth," Garna directed. "I want to hear this story, too."

They passed the bottle around another time. It finished empty, and Pelorie set it aside. "Well, then," he said, "I got this off a navigator. He carried it here from another spiral, so it's not one of ours nor known hereabouts."

"Fresh, then, is it," said Chork.

They all settled back comfortably. Pelorie stood and leaned back beside the statue.

≈ The Navigator's Tale ≈

"There was a girl," said Pelorie, "who lived on an island. It was one of those backwater places where the vermes breed in the salty shallows and one day is like any other. Almost nobody ever escapes from islands like that. This girl, though, she had the desire, you know, the dream. She wanted to leave the island and see the world." He gestured at Leodora.

She said, "That's a real dream, all right."

"Oh, yes. But the villagers, now, they would have none of it. 'You're of us, you stay with us!' is what they said to her. They gave her tasks to wear her down and wear her out, forced her to do the work of three, and fed her just enough to keep her alive. She was a slave, a prisoner, and her own family sided against her. That life was good enough for them, it should have been good enough for her. The village tried to break her will. That's what they intended. It was a fishing village, so life was hard anyway, but it could always be made harder. The family, they treated her like a slave for her pride. No matter what they did, though, she clung to her dream of escape.

"These folk had trained generations of kraken—trained the tentacled beasts to carry the fishermen about upon their backs. Only the men were allowed to ride them. This idea became the law of the gods, and violation of it brought dire consequences."

By now Leodora had become uneasy with the story, but

she didn't interrupt.

"One day while the men were off fishing, the girl escaped from her captors. On foot she traveled perhaps halfway round the island before she gave up. Continuing would only take her all the way around to where she'd started. Soon she saw that there was no escape, no friend willing to defy the whole village and sail her away—any such a friend would have had to stay away ever after, too. She came to realize that her life was doomed, her fate inescapable. She could only circle the island and come back to where she'd begun. And then they would treat her even worse than before.

"She turned and started back.

"It was then that she encountered a mystical kraken. It surfaced out of nowhere, stuck its head up out of the water and called to her. Called her name.

"It told her it had heard her anguish and had come to take her far away. All she had to do for this to happen was climb upon its back.

"You can imagine that she didn't hesitate a single moment. She threw off her clothes and waded out to the beast, which lifted her in its tentacles and settled her upon its back, to ride as the fishermen did. The beast carried her out into the deep, but soon she realized that it wasn't going where she wanted at all—it was headed straight for where the village men fished. She cried out for it to stop but it didn't seem to understand. She beat upon it, but it didn't flinch nor change its course. It was a kraken and this was what it did. The beast swam right through the fishing grounds, letting all the men see her, naked upon its back. They gave chase, driving her and the kraken back toward shore, toward the village. There was a spit of land there that projected like a finger into the sea, and the women—who by now had discovered her escape—came out and saw her. They shouted at her, called her a witch: the witch that conjured monsters.

"Seeing her displaying herself so wantonly, the women picked up stones and hurled them at her. They pelted her, pelted the kraken. The women shrieked at her like a flock of birds. And finally one stone struck the beast a mortal blow. Ribbons of black ink billowed out of it, turning the sea to darkness. It floundered and started to sink. Rolling its great eye toward her, it said, 'Forgive me, forgive me, I've failed you.'

"In some other story, the beast might have transformed

into her lover, or into an enchanted prince, or someone else special. But in this story, it was as it appeared, and it died. Then the girl was struck in the head and slid into the water beside it."

Leodora could not conceal her horror at the specifics of the story. "Did . . . did the navigator tell you what became of her?"

"Oh, yes. The villagers drowned her in that black water, tore her body to pieces, and fed her to the fish, to the barbed and poisonous vermes. In one sense you could say the beast had not lied, for it did take her away from there. She *did* find escape."

Meg, watching Leodora's reaction, remarked, "It's not a very pleasant tale."

"That's true, I suppose," Pelorie agreed. "This fellow, though, he swore it really happened on an island not three spirals from here. He'd got it off some crippled-up fishmonger who came from that island and had seen it all happen. He claimed he wanted folks to know what fate awaits you when you aren't satisfied with what you have."

"More like it's a tale to keep you from ever hoping for anything," said Garna. "It'd be like telling me I'm never leaving *this* place."

"But you aren't leaving, are you?" said Chork.

"Not the point of it. If I wished to, I could, anytime, same as you or them. I choose not to, but it's what I choose. Now, women stoning their own child—that's just cruel for no good reason. That's a place where the rules have defeated the common sense of folks."

"If they ever had any," said Meg.

"Rules is like tradition," argued Chork. "You do what your family's done for every generation since the world began. You don't have no more choice than that girl. None of us does. What would we do different, anyhow. What would you know how to do?"

A long silence followed his question.

"It was just a story," Pelorie apologized. "For Leodora, is all."

She made herself smile, and thanked him for telling it. She didn't try to explain that his tale was strewn with real elements of her and her mother's lives, mixed together by a demented fishmonger who couldn't tell them apart anymore. The story was out on its own now, a version of her released by her uncle or whomever, and whether or not it was an utter lie seemed of less importance than the conclusions being drawn from it, conclusions that said life was defeat, hopeless and pointless. The thing she knew absolutely was that she would never perform it anywhere.

"As Garna chooses," she said, "so must I, and I have to choose to go back up now. Thank you, Pelorie, for a tale. I've a performance to prepare for, and I hope you'll all attend. Do you know if there's an entrance to the Terrestre?"

The others glanced at Hamen, and she followed their gaze.

"Not in it, but next to it," he said. "I'll take you." He stood, a little unsteady on his feet.

"Oh, be careful with him, Leodora," said Meg. "He's drunk enough I'm not sure where he'll lead you."

He waved off the criticism. "I could find my way through the underworld in the dark."

"Blindfolded," added Chork.

"We could test him," Pelorie suggested.

"Test your own selves, spit-frogs," he answered. "Come on, Leodora. *I'll* get you back safely."

She started to follow him, but then remembered the reason she had come down here in the first place, before the game and players had distracted her. "I've a question before I go. Can any of you tell me, is there an entrance from this level to the inverted city?"

"To what?" asked Garna.

"I don't really know its name, or if it has one. I saw it from Colemaigne's dragon beam. The houses pointed toward the water, and I think it must have been below this."

All of them gaped at her. Chork leaned toward her and quietly said, "You actually *saw* it? You didn't just hear of it? Have the notion of it planted in your head by somebody?"

"No, I saw it. And—"

"She *saw* the Pons Asinorum," Meg said in wonder as she eyed the other players. "When is the last time anyone ever saw it?"

Pelorie replied, "Drunks in the blighted lanes say they see it all the time. Drag themselves to a rail to spew up, and there'll be someone looking up at 'em as if the water had moved up close and they were seeing themselves, but it's not themselves nor like themselves, it's someone dark and shadowy, blue or black with fire for eyes. And who believes what a drunk sees?"

"Then is there anyone whose opinion is trusted?"

Pelorie shook his head. "Been twenty years or more, I think."

"Longer than the blighting itself even."

Pelorie reconsidered Leodora. "You saw it, though, you swear."

"She's been noticed by the gods. 'The girl who saved Colemaigne,' isn't it?"

"Don't know as I'd much like to be noticed. Nobody who is ever seems to come to a good end."

"Capricious, that's what everyone calls them—*the capricious gods.*"

"Me, I think we've been blessed by your visit," Hamen told her.

"But then again, you only been here two days," Chork added.

"I hope—" Garna began, but hesitated.

"You hope what?" asked Leodora.

"I hope they take only a passing interest, those gods." She gave Leodora a worried smile.

Hamen said, "Enough of this jabber. Come on, I'll lead you back to the theatre." He lifted a light from a stone figure and walked past Leodora. She acknowledged the group with one final nod, then set off after him.

Meg stood watching until the darkness had swallowed the lantern light. Then she said, "I think we'd best see this performance tonight."

"Because there might not be another?" mused Chork.

"Exactly."

Hamen led her past dozens and dozens of small stairways, past embedded foundations of whole buildings that evoked a walk through a maze, past kegs and barrels, crates and clay jars and cloth sacks, and past dusty, stony upright corpses. In one place they passed an overturned boat that was a little too reminiscent of her uncle's ruined esquif, and she made haste to close the distance to walk beside Hamen, secure in the lantern's pool of light.

"I'm going to dally once I've taken you up," he said to her. "I want to see your performance. The others, too, they'll most likely come along once they talk themselves into it. The idea that something might happen and they'd miss it will play on 'em till they have to see, too."

She nodded but said nothing.

"Pelorie's tale—I saw how you reacted. That was all about you, wasn't it?"

She eyed him askance. "It seemed to be," she admitted. "Everything he said, I kept thinking—hoping—the next wouldn't be more of it, more of me, and then it was. And where it wasn't, it was as if someone had replaced the missing stones in the mosaic with a different color of stone, was all. But the picture—"

"You'll not be performing it, then."

"Not ever, I think."

"Makes you wonder a bit. I mean, how many of the stories you tell do you suppose used to be about somebody—somebody real, once upon a time. And then the story took over—some of the stones, like you say, got replaced with different ones, made-up ones—and the real person and their story went different ways altogether. Separate ways, like. I mean, do any of us ever perform our own stories," he asked, "save for the one time?"

She shook her head, both in answer and in surprise at the depth of his comments and question. "I don't know," she said.

"No, nor does anyone, I expect. You can't know your story when you're part of it. And until you die, you're always in the middle of it, aren't you."

"I never looked at it that way, Hamen."

"Well." He gazed down, as if embarrassed by his own sudden metaphysical opinions. "Besides, what you want to know about is the Pons Asinorum."

"I do."

"Well, then, I hope somebody above can help you, because I can't. I've never seen it, nor really believed in it, nor have the others. Just stories to us." He chuckled then. "All just stories."

When they'd walked a little farther, he spoke up again. "I was thinking, you know, I said that the group of us all live in the dark here, and, well, so do you, don't you? I mean, with your puppets and all, you're in the dark, you know, a lot. People don't see you, just see what you offer 'em."

"That's so," she agreed.

"Yeah, well. Same with us."

"You seem to think a great deal, Hamen."

"Don't know about *a great deal.* No more nor you, I expect. But if the Pons Asinorum exists, I think it'd be good if you found it."

"Why?"

"Can't say, quite. I'd have to think about it some." Then he grinned to himself, and she laughed.

"One more thing—what are vermes?" she asked. "Some kind of fish?"

"A terrible fish. Can climb up on land and pull down an ox, tear it to shreds. That'd be one of those stones of another color in your mosaic you were talkin' about."

"It would, yes," she replied, and wondered where that element had been added to the story. What isle or span did the notion of vermes hail from?

Before long they approached a great curving wall of stone. "The Terrestre," Hamen pointed out. "That's its foundation. The prima pietra's around here somewhere, got Burbage's name etched on't." Around the far side of the wall they came to another flight of steps, and Hamen delivered her to the surface. The steps led to a narrow gated portico across the alley from the rear of the theatre. It smelled of a rusty wetness. She unlatched the metal gate and stepped out. Overhead, the sky was going dark, with the first stars twinkling.

Hamen followed her into the theatre. Diverus, seated at the long table where they'd eaten earlier, leapt up at her appearance. "Lea!" he cried, which brought Soter and the others. By then Diverus had wrapped his arms around her with such obvious relief that she blushed.

Soter pulled Diverus back and said to her sternly, "You age me every single day, child, you don't know how much."

So nonplussed was she by their reaction that she didn't try to explain. Instead she turned and introduced Hamen. Orinda said, "I believe I recognize you, good sir."

"And you, madam," he replied. "You're of my district. It's my services you call on from time to time when you want something brought up from the cellar, you know?"

Her expression brightened. "*Coo-ee*? That's you? You will stay and sup with us then, before the theatre opens for business?"

"I should be most happy to attend your company. Thank you."

"It's nothing," she said. "You've returned to us our savior, it's the least we can do."

Leodora blushed again at being called their savior. As the others turned about, she grabbed Glaise by the sleeve. "I've had an idea for the performance tonight," she told him. "I want to know what you and Bois think of it, because it involves you both."

Bois came over, and the three of them walked off toward the stage, leaving Hamen in the company of the other three.

The kitsune watched as the long-snouted tanuki took a black stone between his middle and index fingers and snapped it onto the *gō* board. "Atari," said the tanuki, and its black eyes gazed meaningfully at the cadaverous figure on the opposite side of the *gō ban*. Two others, nearly identical to the seated player, stood motionlessly behind him as they had throughout the game. Torches burned on either side of them. They stood as still as moonlight.

The player of white stones pursed his thin lips and then raised his hands in a gesture of capitulation. The tanuki nodded respectfully that his opponent had recognized defeat. His whiskers twitched.

The seated figure arose, tall and gaunt. One of its companions said with dismay, "You lost."

The white stone player ignored the observation, but turned to the kitsune and said, "Now I've played your game and it's time you told me about these storytellers."

"You lost?" the second figure repeated.

The player turned coldly about. "Yes. I lost. The stars still burn in the sky, last I checked."

The kitsune looked overhead. "They do," he agreed. "As to the storytellers, what can I say? They came, they watched a game unfold, we told them a story—a very good one I might add—and then they joined us for the parade. Would you like to join us for the parade?"

The bald player's lips drew back over his long teeth. His sunken eyes smoldered, as if he thought he was being toyed with. "What I want to know—was one of them called Bardsham?"

"Well," said the kitsune. "What would your Bardsham look like? I have never seen him, and I had always fancied that he died long ago, for surely he hasn't performed anywhere I've heard of, and our kind do hear things."

"Unusual things," the tanuki chimed in. "It's past sunset," he told the fox.

"Yes, I know," replied the kitsune. "Gentlemen, you've indulged us, and we appreciate it, but we know nothing of whether your Bardsham dwelled among the storytellers. But then we only encountered two of the troupe, and as I understand these things, most troupes of players contain four or more. How many were in your Bardsham's troupe?"

"Three," the player stated.

"Four," his companion corrected. Their eyes locked. "There was the dwarf. Grumyfin or some such name."

"Four, then," said the player to the kitsune. "It doesn't matter. Whoever they are, we must find them all. It's most urgent that we do."

The kitsune adjusted his kimono. "I am sorry, but there you have it. We met two, and who can say if they were, either of them, the one you seek. And anyway they haven't come again."

"I dislike being taken advantage of," the player said, and his words dripped with threat.

"We did not swear to have your answers, only to have *some* answers, of which none seems to belong to you."

"You—"

"We. Must be leaving now," explained the kitsune. "The parade does not wait. If you care to return to the park tomorrow, I'm certain you can learn more, though not more certain of its benefit."

The player stared at his hands, flexed his fingers. One palm glistened as if coated with blue glass. Suddenly he reached for the fox's arm. His hand closed upon empty air. The kitsune had vanished and only the tanuki remained, with bared fangs and bristling fur. "Unusual," he snarled. "Not alive, and not dead enough." The player lunged at him, but the tanuki flipped the *gō ban* into the air, and the stones covering its surface peppered the trio, forcing them to stumble back. When they lowered their arms, the tanuki still stood there, observing them. "*Most* unusual," he said. Where the white and black *gō ishi* had struck their faces, the flesh was pocked and gray. "You're not at all nice. We shall not help you further." Then, like the kitsune, he vanished. It was as if the wall drank him up. The torches guttered and went out, leaving the trio of agents in darkness lit only by the stars and the twin moons.

"I hate conversing with the supernatural," complained the player.

"You lost the game, Scratta."

"If you remind me of that once more, I'll strip the rest of the glamour from you and you can remain fixed right here for pigeons to spatter. Now." He paused to regain his composure. "We will return to the ship. Possibly the others had better luck."

"If not, what then?"

"Tomorrow night we'll hunt the venues, find out where they performed. They had to have performed *somewhere*."

"Why not simply go north to the next span? We're close behind them now."

"I see," he said, and then asked the third one, "Is that what you want to do, too?"

The third glanced nervously between his two companions. Prudently he ventured, "They must have moved on, so why continue looking here? It would *seem* reasonable."

"Fine. Then that is what we shall do. If you're right," said Scratta to the second, "we save time. If you're wrong . . . well, every ship needs an anchor." He turned and strode off.

The others followed. "You can't intimidate the supernatural," said one.

The other replied, "We should know, and better than any."

"So then, when we catch up to this troupe, what if the teller, this performer, is the supposed-to-be-dead Bardsham?"

"Then he's doomed."

"And what if he's not Bardsham?"

"Then he's doomed."

"Oh, good. I like simplicity."

"Indeed. Complications are for stories."

The Terrestre was only half filled, but the audience included the governor of the span, who wanted to see for himself what creature had coerced the gods into healing Colemaigne.

Soter complained about the way the stage was set. He had put the puppeteer's booth front and center, but while he ate and chatted with Hamen, Leodora and the two woodmen had moved it to one side, leaving most of the stage open. He was further dismayed when she told him that she didn't want him narrating the first story as he often did. She would do it herself.

He replied, "Merely because you're revealing that you're a girl, now you want to change the process? Will you be performing the introduction as you manage the puppets, too?"

She told him, "I won't *be* managing puppets for this performance."

Diverus joined her in the booth. She explained to him what she was going to do, and his ritual began. He sat on the floor and spread his instruments in a circle around him. There were new ones she hadn't seen before: Orinda had shown him the Terrestre's instrument collection, and he had selected various items, including a snaky horn that seemed more designed for processionals than accompaniment. Now he closed his eyes and lowered his head. His hands reached out and took hold of one of these novel instruments from the Terrestre, a theorbo. It looked like a lute but with an extended neck and second pegbox. He lay it across his lap and then reached again, adding three small percussion instruments to his choices. One was a clapper. The other two, she couldn't fathom. Then he sighed and leaned back. His eyes fluttered open and he stared, bemused by what he'd picked, despite which confusion he told her, "I'm ready."

Orinda strode out from the curtains and welcomed the crowd. Most of them knew her. Some, like the governor, had known her husband. They applauded her, and cheered her announcement that theatre was coming back to Colemaigne. She gestured to the governor in his box, and the audience stood to give him an ovation for dismissing the ban. He bowed, then gestured broadly for all of them to sit, so that the performance might begin.

It had seemed only fitting to Leodora that the first story re-cited should be "The Tale of the Two Brothers." Bois and Glaise strode out upon the boards, took their bows, and then, as she recited from within the booth, pantomimed the tale as they had done with her earlier. Accompanied by Diverus's score, their movements seemed more fluid and precise. The graceful music carried them along, and punctuated each step deeper into cruelty and greed.

Soter stood beside Hamen in one of the stage balconies. He was edgy and complained unhappily about this unprecedented change in how they did things, until Orinda entered the balcony. She moved between the two men and said, "Your Jax does us great honor by letting them perform the first story. They've waited so long. Mr. Burbage would be elated." He knew from her tone that she believed he'd had a hand in the decision and he did not attempt to dissuade her, but allowed her to kiss him on the cheek.

When she leaned over the rail to watch, Hamen edged close beside him again and said, "Don't worry it, your secret's safe with me." He winked.

Soter replied, "Why am I not comforted, knowing that?" If Hamen heard him, he gave no indication.

The recitation of "The Two Brothers" ended. The two figures, wrapped about each other, seemed to have melted together into the great worn sandstone lump that Baloyd had become. They held their positions as Leodora emerged from the booth. For effect she wore her trademark mask, black silk stitched with a diamond pattern, covering the top of her head to just above the tip of her nose. But now her thick red braid swung behind her, and the loose-sleeved red bodice she wore removed all doubt as to her sex.

The audience uttered not a sound, as though uncertain if the play was finished, or what their role was supposed to be in response.

Then the governor stood and began to clap enthusiastically, and like a lead bird drawing its flock into the air, his applause brought the rest of the audience to its feet. The din of approval surged until the half-empty theatre shook with clapping and calls of "Jax!" Leodora swept off the black mask as she bowed. The footlights flashed over her copper hair. As had happened on Hyakiyako, the audience shouted louder. Those nearest the front of the stage reached toward her, tried to touch her feet. She knelt and squeezed their hands, gestured Bois and Glaise up beside her, and although they were known to everyone in the pit, the hands reached for them as well. They met her gaze, eyes full of wonder, but no more than her own. The charge from this audience crackled through her, made her heart pound, her brain spark. She arose, took one more bow, and then retreated behind the booth again. Diverus stared at her as if in wonder, and she said, "Oh, Diverus, come out," and took him by the hand. At the last moment, she seized upon an idea and drew her domino mask over his head, tying it quickly behind him. He carried the theorbo in one hand, following along as if in a daze. She told him to bow and remove his mask, too, and he did as she ordered, if uncertainly.

The noise must have spread through the streets and alleys, because more people were pushing through the doors, as if they'd been waiting for the signal the applause represented. They entered and marched up the aisles. Even when the ovation died down, more people continued to enter.

Bois and Glaise ran to the side of the stage and began dragging the sections of the booth out into the center. First came the giant screen and, behind it, the tall lens that would enlarge her puppets so that even those at the back could see. Once that was set up, Diverus hauled his instruments behind it and then helped Leodora move the cases from the booth, which the two wooden men would carry. The poles and screens weighed next to nothing. Meanwhile the audience milled about, chattering, imbibing.

From the balcony, Hamen spotted his comrades seated together in one of the front rows. He thanked Orinda for her kindnesses, and she invited him to sample them another night. Soter scowled at the exchange. Hamen saw the look and winked at him again, then walked down into the theatre as Leodora came up the stairs and joined them in the box. Though she'd only known him briefly, Soter noticed that she watched Hamen's departure sadly.

She said, "They're setting up the lens you described – the same one Bardsham used."

"Glaise found it," said Orinda. "I'd hoped he would."

"And what other surprises are in store," Soter asked sharply. "Will we be setting someone on *fire* perhaps?"

"Why are you so contrary?" Orinda asked.

Soter glanced between them, and then insisted, "I'm not contrary. We do things a certain way. Suddenly you're taking charge and changing the performance without even asking if I think it's a good idea."

"Afraid you're obsolete and we don't need you anymore?" Leodora asked.

"To tell you the truth, yes."

Leodora closed her eyes and shook her head. "Oh, Soter. How can you believe that?"

"Not *believe*," he said, "it's not that obvious and clear. But you certainly don't need me to teach you anything anymore, and now you don't need me even to narrate the occasional tales that have always been mine rather than yours to recite."

"*One* story, Soter."

"Not for long. Jax is Leodora now. Your voice could be the one that tells *all* the tales and they'll listen in rapture. There's no longer a reason to divide the task with me. You are the consummate storyteller, how can anybody deny it? You could narrate and perform and never so much as open your eyes. In any case, my fear is *my* burden, not yours, and I will settle with it on my own terms. Now, what do we do next?"

"Another story. I was thinking it's about time we do a Meersh play."

"I think if you perform any of Meersh now, you'll have a riot on your hands. They might pull the walls down, this crowd. It's filling up out there like a tower in a flood."

"If they tear it down, I'll simply walk the dragon beam again," she replied.

"Don't even joke about that."

Orinda had been peering around the balcony curtain. She stepped back again. "It looks as if the whole span has come out."

"What *are* you charging them?" Soter asked.

"A penny."

"But how can you expect to pay us from that?"

"She doesn't," Leodora said. "We're taking a smaller cut, too."

Before he could object, Orinda explained, "It's the first chance they've had to see puppets in more years than some of them have been alive—you said it yourself, this crowd is dazzled. Look at all the children out there. I can't greedily squeeze their families. You want them to return again and again, yes? To tell everyone, here and on other spans. We want other theatres to reopen, to compete with us, which will make the quality of the performances that much better. And if none of that should come to pass, then let them have this event to remember." She parted the curtain again. "Oh, I hope Mr. Burbage can see this where he's gone. It's what he always loved, the sound, the energy."

Soter found himself strung between wanting to complain about the misappropriation of still more of his power and wanting to give Orinda the impression that he was in complete accord with her. The result was that he said nothing.

Diverus entered the balcony. "What are we going to do next?" he asked. "The theatre's mayhem." Leodora told him about Meersh, and he smiled. "Well, *I* want to see one even if nobody else does. You and Soter have gone on and on about Meersh stories ever since you found me."

"They'll certainly have their money's worth," said Soter, without any vitriol. "But I'm narrating this."

Leodora laughed. "Of course you are."

"Good. I'm glad you're listening."

Out of the corner of his eye he saw Orinda cover her mouth so as not to laugh, too.

"Now," said Soter. "Which tale of Meersh do you propose we tell them?"

"I don't want to do one of the long ones. So I was thinking of 'Meersh and the Sun God' or 'How Meersh Tried to Become Immortal,'" she replied.

"'Sun God.'" He stared at her critically. "You wouldn't be," he asked, "proposing this tale because of your horrid Coral Man that we should have dumped overboard before we got here."

He watched her dwell a moment upon the implications before she shook her head. "There's no ulterior motive, Soter," she assured him. "Now, Diverus needs to pick out his instruments. We've kept them waiting as long as we can." The two of them left the balcony, Diverus glancing back as always, as if trying to comprehend the meaning of everything around him after the fact. Soter took a step after them, but Orinda touched his shoulder. He turned.

"She loves you, you old fool," Orinda told him. "You both fight jealously for every knuckle's distance of territory, but do you suppose she learned that on her own?"

"I—"

"Shush!" She put her fingers to his lips. "I'll not listen to your explanation. It's not for me anyway to know it. Tell the walls if you're looking to persuade something. Not me." She slid her hand to his shoulder blade then and impelled him to leave.

Below, in the booth once more, Leodora selected her puppets while Diverus chose his instruments—the theorbo again, and a duduk. She had the feeling the theorbo, with its more resonant bass strings, was going to become a permanent addition to his repertoire.

Once he had his choices she perched upon her seat, raised her hand to the lantern, and slid a blue filter in front of the side facing the screen. Then, slowly, she raised the black curtain and the theatre was bathed in a blue glow. The hidden lens in front of the booth redoubled the strength of the light, and even over the top of the booth she could see the glow, like the most intense moonlight striking sapphire.

The audience shrieked with joy. Some whistled or yelled, but their noise soon fell to a murmur and then the silence of anticipation.

From the case beside her, Leodora lifted out the figure of Meersh. Her hands nearly trembled upon the rods controlling him. Here was the figure Soter had once used to represent her father, the puppet most closely tied to him, the one who like Bardsham had acted on impulse and stolen a million hearts as he did.

She raised him to the screen. They all knew that profile, even if they'd never seen him before—the beaky nose, the wicked smile that knew your secrets, the wide and mischievous eyes: the consummate trickster.

Applause and more shouts greeted his appearance.

Soter, standing on the far side of the booth, just beside the larger screen, began an introductory speech. "You know this story already, many of you, because once upon a time the immortal Bardsham told every tale of Meersh the Bedeviler, and told them so well that we have them still. Here, tonight, the old Bedeviler returns to us, now in the hands of the formidable Jax." Some of them repeated the name. Someone shouted it.

Soter continued: "As you know, Meersh had *many* adventures, and not all of them turned out for the best. Meersh, helpless in the face of his own desires, paid a price for his every pleasure."

≈ The Tale of Meersh and the Sun God ≈

Back in the early times, when only a single strand of spans graced Shadowbridge, Meersh the Bedeviler took a wife named

Akonadi and settled upon Taprobane. Akonadi was a remarkable huntress who could stand in a boat, throw her spear, and skewer a whole school of fish at once. Meersh had married her out of lust, as he did everything, but especially because she kept him well fed. The old saying goes, "When you want to eat, marry a huntress." And when you want trouble, marry Meersh.

Now, even in the earliest times, Meersh had difficulty staying in one place for very long. This is why he's known far and wide across Shadowbridge. And even though she looked after him so well, did our Akonadi, he could not resist his peripatetic urges. Thus he went traveling while she remained on Taprobane, hunting and keeping house.

Meersh stayed away a long time, and Akonadi pined for him. She prayed to Edgeworld that he be returned safely to her, for even when they were furious with Meersh, women loved him, and Akonadi loved him the deepest of all, for most of his follies were still to come. Nevertheless, after many months had passed, she began to pray that *somebody* be delivered to her, whether it was Meersh or not. If any gods were paying her the slightest attention, they offered her no sign.

One day while she was fishing, she sailed farther out than ever before and came to an unfamiliar shoreline, an island she'd never visited. Its shore was rocky, precipitous, and hazardous. Before the sheer cliff face, many stones jutted out of the sea like teeth or tines. One in particular had been worn by the waves into a familiar shape. Upright in the shallows, it looked like Meersh himself. The play of shadow and light chiseled the stone into his recognizable visage, an illusion to be sure, but illusion, she decided, was better than nothing, and she took the rope from her spear and tied it around the shapely pillar. She tugged on the rope and, mighty warrior that she was, dislodged the stone. It tilted farther and farther until it wrenched loose. The rope pulled but she held it and, with the figure in tow behind her, steered a course for home. The wonder is that the weight of the stone didn't pull her boat under, but by now you might have guessed that there was something unnatural in it all.

She tied up her boat at the base of her span, and then hauled in the stone figure. As it bobbed to the surface and rolled, Akonadi saw that the swirling waters around the island had endowed the figure with another prominent feature of her husband's, and she was careful not to damage this as she dragged the stone up the many steps to her house. Neighbors saw her and clambered down the steps to help her with it. If they thought anything odd about the stone, they said nothing. They helped her carry it through her house and into her garden, where she stood it upright and let it dry in the sun. In the daylight in her garden, the stone looked less like Meersh, save for that smooth phallus that the water had shaped and polished, an object of ceaseless arousal. That was *very* like him.

That night, every time she walked past the garden, she found herself glancing at the stone figure. The twin moons cast their light so that once again the facets of it resembled her husband.

Finally, Akonadi's longing broke free, flooding her thoughts, drowning her senses in need. She rushed to the stone, embraced it, kissed its cold hard lips, its face. She hiked up her skirt, wrapped her legs around it, and slowly, steadily, with immense pleasure, impaled herself upon its most prominent feature. She rode the stone figure for hours. Consciousness fell away and wonderful sensation consumed her. When at last she stepped into the dirt again, her legs would barely hold her up. It was as if her spirit had flown to some other place and returned. She stumbled off to bed, leaving the stone figure glistening in the moonlight. The essence of Akonadi was absorbed into it, permeated it, ran like divine blood through it.

Sated, Akonadi slept soundly. In the morning when she awoke, she was astonished to find that the gray stone figure lay beside her in her bed.

She sat up and scrabbled back the way a crab scurries across a beach. The stone rolled over. Its features were more distinct than before, the face real. A piece of the stone figure seemed to tear loose from the body. It stretched toward her—an arm. Fingers uncurled, invited her. Tentatively, she gave it her hand, and the stone man drew her to him, lifting her up on top of him. She impaled herself once more and began again the previous night's lascivious ritual. How long it went on, Akonadi didn't know or care. She succumbed to sensation, lost all thought, all awareness, and only later came to her senses lying beside the stone, now warmed like flesh by the sunlight, and she drifted away to sleep.

For weeks after that Akonadi and the stone man lived in bliss. Each day it seemed he was more alive. He attended to her every need, obeyed her every request, strong but always looking to her satisfaction. The only desire he did not satisfy was her eagerness for conversation. His mouth remained no more than an imperfection in the stone. He said nothing.

Some time later, word arrived from the neighboring span of Valdemir that a great convocation was going to take place to elect sun and moon gods. The span of Valdemir, then newly formed, did not have any, and in those early times Edgeworld was not so cleft from us as it is now—a span could elect its own gods.

The news meant little to Akonadi, but it traveled along the spiral and reached Meersh wherever he was, and he came running home, for the idea had come to him in a besotted epiphany that he might be able to have himself elected a god.

Entering the house at night, he discovered the great stone pillar lying in his place and feigned outrage. "I'm gone a few months and this is how you replace me?"

Akonadi answered, "Husband, you've been gone a year and more."

He brushed aside her defense. "All the same, you replaced me! And with a brute. I'm not at all pleased."

"You weren't at all *here*," she countered, growing angry. "For all I knew, you had found someone else and weren't coming back."

Meersh's penis stood up and said to him, "She's right, you know, and hardly far off the mark. Best you'd be contrite."

Meersh, who had in fact dallied with too many to count, changed tack. "Well, I'm back for now so we must all get along, mustn't we? What is this hard fellow's name?"

"I don't know. He never speaks." She refrained from telling him how the stone man had come to life, but Penis whispered, "Look at the size of *that*!" Meersh knew what Penis was looking at.

"You probably just don't know how to talk to him," he said. "I have traveled so widely that I know how to speak to anybody. If you'd but asked I would have shown you."

She marveled at his ability to deny his absence while proclaiming his skill, and only shook her head at the hopelessness of arguing with one for whom reality had no permanent shape.

Meersh unloaded his pack. As always it was full of games, and he drew these out and set them aside—boards and playing pieces, markers of various sorts. From the bottom of it he produced three multicolored, polished pebbles no bigger than his thumb. He held one to his ear and nodded to himself. He pressed that pebble to the stone figure's face where its mouth should have been. Around the pebble a gap formed, spreading to either side of it. Abruptly, the stone man gave a sucking sound, drawing his first breath, the pebble disappeared into the gap, and Meersh snatched his fingers back before they vanished, too. "There, it's really very simple," he said.

"It's really very simple," parroted the rock man. His voice creaked and clacked – the sound of stone grinding on stone.

Then Meersh took the two remaining stones and pressed them with his thumbs into the hollows where the Stone Man's eyes might have been. When he drew his thumbs away, the stones remained, like bright irises embedded in the deep sockets. The pebbles shifted as the stone figure looked from Meersh to Akonadi.

To her, Meersh said, "I know where you found *him*. There's enchantment in those isles. I've seen it before." He addressed the Stone Man then. "Hereafter, you can speak, and I'm going to make use of your newfound talent."

"What do you mean, husband?" Akonadi asked.

"On Valdemir they need a sun god, and I need someone who will nominate me. It's never a good idea to nominate yourself. It looks suspicious." He patted the stone man's shoulder.

"And why should he do that for you?" she asked.

"Because he's in my debt. I've given him a voice and much improved his eyesight. Once I'm sun god, who knows what I might do for him? And for you, as well, wife. I'm sure I'll be a benign sun god." And he wandered off, contemplating how he would transform Taprobane once he had become a god, and how he would sleep when he wanted to and eat what he wanted to, and no one could gainsay him.

The Stone Man waited until Meersh was out of earshot, then said, "I will do this for him because I am in his debt, but I can tell you, no good will come of it."

"None ever does," she said, and was about to turn away when he touched her, a delicate touch for one so huge and seemingly brutish.

He whispered her name then, and the sound came from deep within him. It was thick with all that he felt, that until then he had not been able to express. All he said was "Akonadi," but the syllables thrummed with the desire all women want to hear when their lover speaks their name, and she embraced him and remained there.

The Stone Man learned his lines. He knew what Meersh wanted and didn't care. To him such cupidity meant nothing.

At the palace of Valdemir there were hundreds of petitioners on hand in the great hall. Most stood in a circle around the few seats, which had been taken early; most stood with their backs to the center, as if they were interested in the architecture of the palace. It was impressive: Glass panels decorated the walls and ceiling of the hall. The eastern side, lined with slender columns, was fashioned as an open balcony overlooking the ocean.

Beyond the crowd something sparkled brightly, and Meersh, magpie-like, was drawn to it. He cozened his way through the crowd. He misdirected some, and wheedled others, slipping through the gaps that appeared as people turned, until finally he could see it.

There in the center hung the robe of the sun god. It so dazzled Meersh's eyes that they teared immediately. Penis complained, "That's so bright it could blind a one-eyed mouse!"

Others beside him shielded their faces from its glare. Thus he understood why almost everyone had turned their backs to the center. Far easier to look upon was the robe of the moon, hanging like an afterimage beside it. Meersh saw those robes and knew he had to wear one of them.

Behind him, the Stone Man followed without a word. For his imposing figure the crowd parted immediately. He stood behind Meersh and with his pebble eyes looked upon the robe as if it gave off no light at all. Penis was laughing gleefully at the prospect of becoming a godhead, until the Stone Man's pebble eyes fixed upon him, and then, unnerved, Penis shrank away.

The governor of Valdemir entered with a small retinue. He surveyed the crowd carefully as he strode before them to a marble rostrum. The chatter grew as he stepped up, and he waved his arms, calling out, "Friends. Neighbors. Please!" The conversations quieted. "I'm glad you have all come." He glanced at an adviser, who nodded solemnly. "It's as Edgeworld predicted—so large a body, a group, and somewhere in the midst of you our sun god. It comes to me now—"

Before he could finish, the Stone Man had stepped forward and said, "I would like to nominate my good friend, Meersh, who is certainly worthy of the title." His voice, raised to a bellow, rumbled about the room. "He is widely traveled across these many spirals. He is widely known."

"That's a true statement," someone interjected. "Widely known, and as widely *sought*!"

The crowd roared. Penis scolded Meersh, "You should have let me write this."

Unfazed, the Stone Man continued, "Of all those here, he has seen the sun from more places, more mornings of the world."

"And more often hanging from a windowsill!" called another member of the crowd. The laughter that followed drowned out everything the Stone Man tried to say. He was treated to slaps on the back, and even the governor and his staff joined in the merriment. Meersh clucked his tongue at outraged Penis. *He* had anticipated it all. In fact it was as he'd intended.

With the Stone Man drawing all attention, Meersh walked straight to the sun god's robe. No one could look at it and none paid him the least mind as he shamelessly snatched the robe and placed it upon his shoulders. He strutted about, enjoying the sense of self-importance it conveyed. Let them laugh, he didn't care. He was going to be divine.

Nobody realized what he had done immediately . . . until he burst into flames. "Aah!" he shouted, and ran in a circle. The nearest of the crowd lurched back from him. "Aah!" he shrieked, and then charged straight at the balcony. "Aah!" he screamed as he flung off the robe and leapt over the railing. "Aahhhhh!" The cry descended through octaves as he plunged from sight and into the sea.

Here Leodora turned the lamp from bright day to cool blue evening and eased the glittering glass-encrusted robe from the screen. She rested while the audience laughed and shouted and applauded. For many it was the first interlude they'd ever seen and they fell silent at the blue glow, where an experienced audience would have known to stretch their legs, to stroll about. The silence told her that they expected her to continue.

She worked quickly to make the changes in the puppet of Meersh, prepared her new props, then craned her neck and gave Diverus a nod.

A note of music took to the air behind her. She lifted Meersh to the bottom of the screen and let him show up just slightly, had him rise and fall, rise and fall, as if floating upon waves. Watching the screen from outside, Soter cleared his throat and continued the tale.

Many hours later, Meersh drew himself out of the ocean. His body was blackly charred; his hair stuck out like burned twigs. Most of his clothing had disintegrated. He had little hope of recouping his loss and would have been better served by slinking away, but Meersh never chose what would best serve him, only what appealed to his appetites.

He climbed the steps up the span to the balcony. His penis, burned as badly as the rest of him, muttered, "You should have asked me, I'd have *told* you not to touch that robe."

Meersh's doubtful response was drowned beneath a great cheer from overhead. A light pulsed from within the palace, its beams shooting out between the rails like a mist, spurring him to climb faster.

At the top he stepped through the rail to discover there in the hall a huge figure wrapped in the robe of the sun god, the robe that should have been his. The incandescence of it had flowed into the figure, whose shaved head glowed now like copper rather than stone. It was only when the figure turned to face him, and he saw the bright pebble eyes, that he recognized what had happened.

"Ah, friend Meersh," the Stone Man said, his cheeks burnished and smooth. The crowd around him began to laugh at the burned, wild visage Meersh presented, but the Stone Man ignored their caterwauling as he came forward. "You survived, and that's good. I was going to come resurrect you if you hadn't, for you do fall under the aegis of the Sun, whether you know it or not."

"I what?"

"I have to look out for you . . . or, rather, *we* do." He turned and gestured back to the robe of the Moon, and who should be wearing it but Akonadi.

"What is this?" asked Meersh, although he'd already

gleaned the answer.

"Oh, dear," said Penis. "I could have told you this was bound to happen while you gallivanted about on the other spans. But would you listen?"

"You?" Meersh snarled at it. "You're the one led me all about from one debauch to the next."

"Akonadi has consented to be the Moon," said the sun god. "I could think of no huntress as skilled."

"I . . . how could you? You'd take my *wife*?"

"I'm surprised you remember that she is for all the attention you've paid her."

Meersh glanced about, taking the time to work himself into a state of outrage. He would gain from these events yet. "So *that's* how it is. Well, if you're taking Akonadi with you, then I should be recompensed. It's only fair."

The sun god considered him a moment. "All right. Anything you like that I may give you."

"One thing," Meersh said, and he reached into the glowing robe, grabbing hold of the smooth copper phallus on the front of the sun god. "I'll have this."

The sun god didn't even flinch. His pebble eyes bored into Meersh, who sensed that they saw all of his plan, and every bit of his scheming soul. "As you wish," said the god.

"Wait!" cried Penis, the very last sound he made before he was encased. Meersh stared at himself, erect and polished. "Now we're even."

The sun god chuckled. "Very well, Meersh."

Meersh slapped his new member. "*This* one will do as I say and not taunt me." The Sun, the governor, and the crowd roared with laughter and taunts of "a suit of armor for his little knight."

The Sun and Moon stepped hand in hand to the balcony, then opened wide their arms and blended with the evening. The shimmer of their robes hung afterward in the sky as a swath of stars.

Meersh went home. He left behind him a trail of charred bits. He was only mildly dejected by the loss of Akonadi. He had wanted her as he wanted everything he saw, and the wanting had more sway than the having. His spirits were further buoyed by the wine he'd stolen from the banquet in the sun god's honor. On the way across the spans he strutted proudly to show off his phallus. "Hard as a rock and twice as shiny!" he proclaimed to any women foolish enough to venture near.

Later, seated on his bed, he admired it between drinks of wine. "Now," he said to himself, "at least I won't have to put up with the taunts of that evil Penis anymore!" He blew out the candle and settled back to sleep.

A moment after that the candle rekindled as if by magic. The top of the copper sheath rose up like a tiny helmet. Penis peeked around cautiously and, finding Meersh deep in slumber, it slipped free of him and scurried off, tittering, in search of more trouble.

". . . in search of more trouble," Soter solemnly finished. Leodora turned the lamp to the solid side and the great, lensed screen went dark.

The house had fallen completely silent once more, but this time it lasted for only a moment.

The applause exploded, almost solid in its force. The stage and booth poles shook, jolting Diverus from his trance. He dropped the chimes he'd played and hunched against the rear corner.

As Soter had often described it—as it had happened so often for Bardsham—the audience began to chant not the puppeteer's name, nor even Meersh's, but rather: "Pe-nis! Pe-nis!" Even though Soter had recounted it to her dozens of times, Leodora found herself howling with joy at the daft sound of it. She stood to take her bow again, but found that she couldn't move. A ghost hovered in the booth beside her, hearing the same cacophony from the audience; his hand rested with hers around the rods that controlled the puppet of Meersh. She could not see him clearly but only in the periphery, at the very edge of the visible, where she could just assemble an impression of his sparkling eyes, bright with pleasure, expressing such pride that her breath caught and the heat foretelling tears burned her cheeks. He had stood there—in the very spot—basked in this very afterglow of the performance. She retained no memory of his face, knowing it only from Soter's descriptions, yet she'd no doubt who was smiling upon her.

She managed to whisper: "Father."

A hand touched her opposite shoulder. She turned to find Diverus there, and in that instant the sound of the crowd, which had submerged below the strangeness, came roaring over her again.

The ghost of Bardsham was gone.

"Diverus," she said.

He took a step back. "The audience. Soter."

The words meant nothing. She couldn't focus on that. She turned to the open undaya case into which she placed each puppet after its use, grabbed the ribbons at both ends of the top boxes, and lifted them away.

"Lea, what is the matter?" Diverus asked.

"Him. You saw him. You must have." She handed the boxes to him, stacking them on his arms.

"Saw who?"

She tugged up the false bottom, holding her breath in anticipation . . . but his question penetrated. "You didn't see?"

Diverus studied her face, back and forth from eye to eye. Then he peered past her, into the box, and her own gaze traveled after his, into the recess where the powdery gray Coral Man lay, silent, calcified. Lifeless.

"I thought—" She broke off. Now the tears came and she couldn't explain why or what had happened. She wrapped her arms around Diverus, buried her face against his neck. His hands pressed tight to her back to hold her. He asked for no explanation. He let her weep.

The crowd thundered so loudly that the theatre shook with their calls for "Jax!"

When Soter stuck his head in and saw them, he yelled, "Are you two insane—get out here!"

Diverus looked across at him, a face Soter had never seen before, one that was cold and protective and challenging. He understood then the nature of the embrace, if not its cause. Then he realized the Coral Man had been exposed and he reeled back. Whatever had happened, he could not venture in to find out its nature. He fled into the protective confines of his role, in which he had only to face the far less intimidating ire of an audience about to be disappointed in its demands. He waved his hands and hoped he could control them.

Chapter 6
Pons Asinorum

Diverus awoke far too early. The theatre and its environs lay so dark and silent that the only thing he could hear, lying in the small room, was the distant chatter of morning birds in the fig trees along the boulevard. He rose onto his knees, pushed the unlatched shutters apart, and leaned out the window for a better look.

The boulevard lay off to the right, around the curve of the theatre's white stucco wall and just out of sight. His view was of the smooth wall of a neighboring building, purplish in the predawn light, with a single, dark window directly across from his own, its pane made of round colored quarrels of yellow and red. He wondered if the quarrels would taste sweet if licked.

It had been three days since Jax's premiere performance on Colemaigne, and it seemed to him that life had become a perpetual bustle ever since that name had roared up into the sky. That first evening had provided a modicum of what once had been a nightly occurrence here. Word had spread quickly, and ever since there had been a line outside the entrance to the theatre. Sometimes it wound past the fig trees and as far along the boulevard as anyone could see; as a result, Orinda had insisted they perform both matinees and evening shows the next day and the next. Although Leodora had complied, even repeating the same tales at each performance—which he'd never seen her do before—it was clear to Diverus that she was reluctant to remain in the booth once she'd set down the last puppets. For her the space was haunted. She said nothing, but she didn't have to. He knew her routine too well, and knew when she'd deviated from it.

Now at each performance audiences flooded the theatre, clogged the aisles—and praise the gods there'd not been a fire or some other incident, because no one would have reached the exit alive.

The first night had been the maddest celebration he'd ever witnessed, far more frenetic and dizzy than anything that had ever happened in the paidika. Upon emerging from the booth, Leodora was immediately surrounded by a crowd that rushed the stage to get near her, to touch her, to shout her name. They sang toasts to Meersh and his penis, to Jax and her skills, and it had gone on almost until the sun came up. Leodora had finally thrown off the effects of whatever had happened to her in the booth and joined in the celebration, drinking and cheering with the crowd. Soter, well lubricated much earlier, even went so far as to embrace Diverus, calling him "my dear boy!" as if he were some long-lost nephew. That familiarity evaporated the following day as if it had never been, but the next audience was already hammering at the doors for the upcoming performance and there was no time for reflection. For the matinee they had to stretch awnings over the stage from the highest projecting balcony, out past the thatch, to keep the sun from ruining the shadows, and then they unleashed Jax on another penny-paying crowd. Orinda might have been charging nearly nothing in those first days, but even so they were making more money with each performance than they had on Vijganar or Hyakiyako.

It seemed to him that they'd been doing nothing but preparing for or recovering from performances, and if anything the crowds were getting larger.

Diverus ought to have been asleep; nor did he particularly want to be awake, but now that he was, he couldn't help but brood over what had happened that first night in the booth, what was haunting his only friend. What had Leodora seen? She would not say, but he knew, or thought he knew. The Coral Man, who haunted her dreams, had appeared to her, beside her. She'd called the apparition "Father" and then she had done the thing that truly terrified him. She had begun to cry. In an instant she had transformed from the enigma he all but worshipped into a child, a simple girl devastated by loss and loneliness, and while he had no words to explain himself, his heart ached with love for her the more because of it. His goddess was human, and she had turned to him for comfort. Even Soter, the cursed old bastard—even he had seen that. But the question—the real question—was what had *she* seen and what did it signify? The phantom hadn't reappeared since, but that proved nothing, did it? Standing behind her the first night, he hadn't detected any apparition in the booth. The statue in the bottom of the puppet case was just rock. Soter was terrified of it. She was haunted by it. Yet Diverus, who'd slept in the booth on top of the very case, had experienced nothing. His dreams . . . his dreams contained apparitions of another nature altogether.

Diverus drew back from the window and sat cross-legged on his bed.

The sphinx came to him in his dreams. Most of the time he didn't recollect the dream itself, but awoke with the image of her lingering in his mind, receding even as he recognized the desolate surroundings of his waking life and knew that she had come again. A few times it had been one of Bogrevil's milk-eyed afrits instead, descending from the cracked ceiling of the paidika to suck the life from him. But those dreams he remembered vividly. Those dreams jolted him awake. They weren't real. The afrits weren't real, but recalled.

He folded his arms and considered. Supposing that the sphinx *was* his mother, transformed or reborn in another world he could only access through dream—was it possible that the Coral Man was Leodora's father, also transformed, and that Bardsham also visited her in her dreams? It was as reasonable a speculation as any, although it didn't explain why the same ghost would terrorize Soter. Why should Soter fear Bardsham?

The old man thought Diverus hardly more than an idiot, and that was fine by him. He'd learned to play that role in the paidika. Soter had no idea that he was listening and watching, nor that he'd overheard enough drunken rants and whispered gibbering to know that Bardsham's ghost or something very like it was stalking Soter from span to span now. It had put him to flight twice. How long, Diverus wondered, would they stay here before the specter beset Soter again? It would be more difficult to convince Leodora to leave the Terrestre. The span of Colemaigne treated her like a treasure returned. Remembering the ovations, Diverus smiled, but as quickly frowned and shook his head.

Already his mind had wandered off the topic, which was whether or not the ghost of Bardsham traveled with them, and whether or not it emerged from that piece of cold chalky coral. He knew, as with everything else, that no one was going to enlighten him on the matter. Nobody had yet informed him what the Coral Man was doing in the box in the first place. If he wanted to know, he must find out himself. The notion of ghosts didn't frighten him. Compared with afrits, a human phantom was positively welcome.

He rose up, dressed, and then crept from his chamber and along the darkened hall.

The middle balcony had its own stairs to the back of the stage, something he had learned the second day, and he slid around the rear curtain, through the small doorway to the side, and down the darkened stairwell. It had a fusty smell to it. Cautiously, although he knew nobody was about, he eased open the door in the back wall of the stage and stepped out. Closing it again, he walked quickly, head down as if that would help obscure him, into the puppet booth.

The cases were as Leodora had left them, open upon their respective collapsible biers, the case on the left draped with the discarded puppets she'd used in last night's performance, with more piled inside. She wasn't lingering long enough anymore even to put them all away.

At the top of the pile was the hook-nosed figure of Meersh. Diverus took hold of Meersh's rods and lifted the puppet from the box. Then, clutching the two main rods in one hand, he raised the one that pushed Penis up from the body of the puppet. Penis was still sheathed in the yellow-dyed skin she placed on it to signify the transformation courtesy of the sun god. The larger body of the puppet was draped in a translucent gray membrane to reflect that it had been scorched. He thought of Meersh launching himself over the balcony and into the sea, and for an instant relived the memory of his mother's corpse sliding down the chute, down past the foul layers of habitation beneath Vijganar and into the dark swirling waters around the piers. Such a small splash, instantly erased and untraceable. From that height, the water flow had created the illusion that it was the bridge that moved upon the water.

He set the puppet down and stepped away from the box.

The confined booth was stuffy. Behind the undaya cases, his instruments—shawm, theorbo, sarangi, piba—lay strewn around the pillow on which he sat as he played. He glanced up at the thatched roof far overhead, at the striped awning still unfurled against midday sunlight, at the wan light bleeding in. He let his eyelids lower halfway and tried to listen, to sense with his body what might hover around him, but apprehended no presence other than his own in there. No Coral Man, no Bardsham's ghost. He didn't want to deny Leodora what she'd seen, but he couldn't make it manifest for him. Why couldn't he experience what she had? That would unite them further, wouldn't it?

Stepping back beside his instruments, he reviewed how she had turned to him, her eyes welling with tears, her hair swinging like a great skein of rope behind her as she reached out for him, and he opened his arms to her, embraced her. Once more he smelled her as she pressed against him, and this time he let it stir him, and closed his eyes and fell into the memory and the sweet smell and the slick, sweaty feel of her. Gods, he loved the smell of her. For how long, he couldn't say, but eventually he became aware that he was standing with his arms curved, his hands pressed against a back that wasn't there, and he lowered his arms and sighed long and heavily.

He trudged to the rear of the booth and pushed his hands through the gap in the curtains beside the corner pole, emerging on stage. One of the wooden men, standing at center stage, jumped with mute surprise at the sight of him.

"Sorry, I didn't mean to startle you," Diverus said, and the wooden man pantomimed fluttering his hand as if to express that his heart was racing. Did they have hearts now that they were wood? He didn't know. Bois or Glaise—Diverus couldn't tell them apart, though Leodora seemed able to. Then the other one entered from the back of the stage and came up beside his partner. They shook hands as if they'd been formally introduced by someone, then both faced Diverus expectantly.

He thought it strange that he could understand them so well.

"Do you believe in ghosts?" he asked.

They looked at each other, then back at him. In unison, they gravely nodded.

"Have you ever seen one in this theatre? I mean, a real one, not part of some play."

One of them shook his head immediately. The other gazed toward the ceiling while tapping one finger against his chin before he, too, shook his head. He then spread his hands in query.

"Leodora thinks she saw one in the booth, the first night we performed." One of them pointed at the puppet booth. "Yes, in there. I just wondered if the theatre was known to be haunted. Orinda, the way she speaks of her husband, I thought maybe . . ."

Again they shook their heads, with obvious sadness this time.

"Well, there's my answer, then. Good morning, gentlemen."

They bowed and he started to leave, but stopped after a few steps.

"I know. I've one other question. Are you acquainted with an upside-down span?"

This time they nodded in the affirmative.

"Is there a way there? Can you take me?"

They gestured back and forth at each other then, finally reaching some agreement, stepped up beside him, each with an arm slung over his shoulders, and impelled him to come along with them. They climbed down off the stage and walked up the center aisle of the theatre, then down the ramp to the main doors, which were barred. One touched a finger to his lips and the other charily lifted the bar and opened one of the doors.

Outside, a few dozen people sat or lay dozing in the dark street. Diverus and the woodmen stepped quietly among them. Posters pasted on the wall, already ragged and torn, proclaimed Jax! in great squid-ink black letters. Diverus supposed that was all anyone needed to say now. Her name had become a promise of a cornucopia of delights.

From the small street the trio strode up the boulevard only a few blocks before turning and entering a street Diverus hadn't been on before. It made a wide curve, and he supposed it must direct them around the far side of the theatre and back toward the sea-lane that ran past the Dragon Bowl.

In the distance ahead, above the rooftops, the top of the bridge tower across the southern end of Colemaigne was cast golden by the early sunlight, its pennants flying languidly, dotting a parapet above an arcaded passageway that ran like the top of a wall the full width of the span.

The curving street did at last empty into the lane that ran along the sea edge of the span. This was the opposite end from where they'd arrived, though, with the Dragon Bowl a distant feature back the other way, a cup riding on the horizon.

The whole of the lane glistened in the light of dawn, the surfaces of the buildings reflecting like polished glass. The tower leg ahead was cylindrical, rising into a fluted turret on that end of the tower face. Unlike the few bridge towers he had encountered so far, the wall of this one one appeared to be fully habitable across its length. Three rows of round windows lined it, interrupted in the middle by the archway of a great gate. Some of the windows were bright from lights flickering in the chambers within; the rounded bulwarks of attached and window-lined bastions jutted from it at regular intervals—perhaps ten of them across the breadth of Colemaigne.

The tower leg sank out of sight below the railing. Diverus, wedged between his guides, couldn't lean over the edge to see what lay below. He was being guided toward a small portcullis in the leg.

Along the front of the tower wall ran a wide avenue, still in deep shadow. Beneath the lowest tier of windows in the tower stood carts and makeshift stalls. The street itself was littered with confetti and streamers as if a parade had passed by earlier. Neither of the woodmen seemed to take any notice. They crossed it briskly.

The portcullis turned out to house a gate that opened on well-oiled hinges. Inside the tower leg, dank and dark, stairs spiraled down along a central shaft, and Diverus followed his companions in their descent beneath the surface of Colemaigne.

The pillar did not offer any windows or landings along the way. The light, what there was of it, came up the open shaft from the water far below, while the way to the top, so far as he could tell from leaning his head back, receded into darkness. There must have been doors to the various levels of habitation, but those likewise all must have been closed.

The trio spiraled to the bottom. There the exit was barred with another iron gate, and this one seemed to be locked, reminding Diverus all too uncomfortably of the paidika. While the woodmen fiddled with the latch, he circled the open well to the water in the middle. If the tower leg extended all the way to the seabed below, as it surely must, then there had to be holes or cracks in the stone, letting in the dark water.

Finally, the gate creaked open, and he looked up to see one of the woodmen lifting the lock aside. He followed them out onto a wide shelf that girdled the columnar leg. One peered over the edge. The other struck a pose and indicated that

Diverus should look above.

He turned as the two of them glanced at each other with obvious consternation.

Overhead was a huge transverse arch, its ribs chalky with calciferous stalactites. It curved to the center of the span, where more support pillars jutted down. Beyond them another arch reached to the far side. Even at its lowest point the ceiling was high enough for small sailing vessels to pass, but it was nowhere near the height of the span, and there was no undercity there, no levels of desperate, squalid habitation as he had known beneath Vijganar. The thicker structure didn't allow for them. Diverus said, "There's nothing at all."

The woodmen circled the tower leg, scanning the arch. They completed their circuit, then dejectedly came over to him and patted his shoulders.

"So," he said, "there *was* an inverted span up there once?"

In unison the two shrugged.

"You never actually saw it yourselves, did you?"

One shook his head. The other pressed fingers to thumbs repeatedly.

"Talk. You heard people talk of it."

The nearest woodman touched one finger to his nose and smiled, opening his hands as if to say they'd meant no harm. For all they knew, after all, it might have been here.

Diverus started to say that he had actually seen the place, then decided against it. What could they possibly add to what he already knew? He'd asked them if they had heard of it, and they had. There was nothing more they could tell him.

Disheartened, the two woodmen plodded back to the gate. Diverus ushered them along and then closed the gate after them, choosing to remain behind by himself. They reached through the bars for him, but he said, "No, I'll be fine. You tell them at the Terrestre where I am. I'll be along in a while."

He watched them climb out of sight, unable to explain to them why he felt compelled to linger when there was nothing to see. He couldn't have explained it to himself.

He sat on the shadowed side of the ledge, removed his sandals, and dangled his feet into the water, sloshing them back and forth and peering into the wavelets. Sunlight reflected through the depths below him revealed shaggy moss on the bridge support. Thick tendrils of it waved lazily back and forth in green-gold depths full of tiny darting fish. He tried to imagine a fathomless world where the light never reached. A kingdom in the depths. He'd conjured it once with childish ignorance, a place where his discarded mother was reborn; he wondered now what sort of creature *could* thrive in such darkness. Not someone he knew—not someone close. Rather, someone transformed beyond his knowing.

The undulating light upon the water and the moss below proved hypnotic in combination and his eyelids lowered. The little fish suddenly zipped away in all directions, and ripples hinted at a coalescing shape in the depths. The light grazed the side of something pale that slid into the shadows again. It should have jolted him alert but instead his eyes grew heavier, his head lolled, and he folded onto his side, dozing but also, as though in some lucid dream-state, aware of a shape climbing smoothly out of the water beside him. He heard small splashes, followed by a wet and supple emergence. Try as he might, he could not open his eyes, although—as if his eyelids had turned to glass—he saw at the rim of his vision a shape of milky skin, of round moon-like eyes. In his dream he instinctively recoiled from the horror that had once sucked in his thoughts, his memories, and would have absorbed his life, given more time. The afrit. He remembered Bogrevil, or was it Eskie, explaining that the creatures dwelling in the giant hookahs were water demons, repelled by light, forever rapacious, seeking an easy sup, so naturally they would hang about piers in the hope of finding the occasional dozing watchman . . . or the fool musician who'd already been sampled and had about him the scent, the taste, of one already opened to them. It explained to him why he'd stayed behind: He'd been under the influence of the creature even before he saw it. Easy prey. And now he could not fend it off, the remnants of his conscious self urging his entranced body to resist but held motionless. He thought how Leodora didn't know where he was. No one knew, nor could help.

The pale shape edged close. It touched his cheek with gelid fingers, then crawled upon him. He strained and strained and in the end managed to open his eyes, or at least his dream-self did. He was staring into a face that was no afrit at all, but something entirely unfamiliar. The skin was bone white, and the eyes as fully black as marbles. Hair that wasn't hair hung about its face in wet, knotted strands of green and brown, parting about shell-like ears, and dripping upon him. Long sharp fingers that could have flayed his cheeks tenderly combed them. Soft slits in her throat waved open and closed. He felt her breasts pressing into him.

She smiled, her thin lips drawing back from a row of short bony fish teeth. "Sing for me," he heard her say, and the music emerged out of him as it had out of the multicolored cat—and in that instant, he remembered: the gods, an open pavilion with fountains and pools like no place he'd ever seen because it was no place he'd ever seen; it was Edgeworld, and beside one pool lay a cat he'd been drawn to, one he'd touched and stroked, and which had stood up, stretching its back to produce the purest, most exquisite sound. Someone had proclaimed, "The choice is made!" though he didn't understand what that meant at all, but the cat had licked him, and opened its jaws wide as if yawning, except that the mouth had grown and grown until it surrounded him or he shrank into it, tumbled down into darkness, into deeper depths of memory than he'd ever known before.

The light above receded. Somewhere in the mossy depths below lay her home, his mother, and she, with the unraveling winding sheet waving above her like a ribbon, would come looking for him, would rise up to take him from the living world of spans and bridges, spirals and magic and the confusion of what they all expected of him, whom the gods had shaped and fed to a cat. Farewell to them, farewell to the music. Farewell to Leodora. His mouth formed her name. The sound swam, an eel, through the waters. From high above came a distant reply. He cast his eyes toward the surface and through the green moss he saw her—pale skin, red hair ablaze, Leodora in the beams of sunlight above, and he knew he didn't want to leave her. Not yet, not before she understood what she meant to him. Why couldn't she recognize that? It wasn't so much.

Far below lay the kingdom of the afterlife and if he turned back now, he would never arrive. *Choose*, demanded the situation, like the voice in Edgeworld. "Choose," said the apparition of his mother far below in her streaming shroud.

Why must it be either one or the other? He objected to the options even as he sensed that he remained on Colemaigne, embraced by a dream that even now was retreating—never his mother at all. That was a layer of meaning drawn out of him, not one imposed by the creature. She wasn't stealing his soul; instead she was sharing, stirring his memories into her own.

She had his and he had hers now, hints of it anyway, like flecks of sunlight scattered across the water's surface.

The image of Leodora blurred into striations, into colors woven through the green and the gold beams of light, the fish playing around her, all glittering. Then his real eyelids, which had been closed all along, parted, and the glittering light became the fierce brightness of the sun blazing upon his face.

He was lying on the pier, on his back, and the sun had toured the sky until it was warming him where he slept. He could think Leodora's name but not make his lips obey enough to say it. He told his body to sit up and it refused. The most he accomplished was to turn his head enough to see the stones beside him. She was not there, the sea creature, but a puddle of water and strands of seaweed beside him assured him that she'd been no dream.

With enormous effort, he finally rolled over, dragging his legs out of the water. For how long she had embraced him he couldn't be sure, but the sun had moved up to midmorning position, so an hour or more at least. "Why," he protested to no one, "does it have to be *me* they come for?"

After a while, unsteadily, he was able to get up.

The puddle of water became a wide wet stripe leading to the gate into the bridge support, which now hung open. She had not gone back into the water.

He picked up his sandals as he tottered beside the moist trail. It narrowed and then, as he entered, the stripe separated into wet uneven ovals. He closed the gate behind him. Wet footprints with discernible toes climbed the stairs ahead of him, but shrank as they ascended until they were just smudges, vanishing altogether by the time he'd made it halfway up the spiral. Her feet had dried. He gave up then. He sat and rested.

The climb the rest of the way back to the surface seemed to take all morning.

The name of the street that ran along the tower was now visible, sunlight splashing across the carved plaque and the nearly redundant designation of Towerside Thoroughfare.

People moved about up and down its length. None of them appeared to be either a sea creature or naked. More likely she, whatever she was, had climbed to one of the levels above. He wondered how long she could endure out of the water, or if she transformed utterly, becoming a land creature when it suited her, and if she did, then how many others of her kind had he met without knowing? How many might have passed through the paidika? He shook his head, dismissing the matter. There was no way he could resolve it.

Music echoed off the buildings, tugging at him. He smelled food cooking and instinctively followed the scent. Though he might have been disoriented and uncertain from his encounter, he was ravenously hungry.

Shortly he came to a stand selling sweet buns, and he bought three. He'd eaten the first one by the time he paid. The others he ate as he continued walking. They were filled with some kind of fruit in a thick paste. He'd never tasted its like, and he determined to go back and buy more of them for everyone in the theatre—but not until he'd taken it all in.

He didn't know what else to call it other than a fair, but it looked to have come together haphazardly. Citizens stood in clusters in front of various booths, most of which were nothing more than a few poles with a simple curtain across the front if they were closed, swept aside if they were doing business.

In short order he saw a jeweler—a horned faun—selling bracelets and necklaces, many of which dangled from its leathery wrists; next a chandler peddling bulbous orange candles—according to a sign, they would miraculously replenish by day to be burned again by night; then a huge, ogreish seller of knives, and next to him a duo performing sword swallowing to the delight of a small crowd. Farther on, a woman with vestigial wings was juggling painted balls while balancing barefoot on a rope a few feet off the ground. These performers must have gathered as word got out that the ban had been lifted. Had they been waiting in their houses for a dozen years, practicing in secret, or were they newly arrived off a neighboring span, perhaps Sacbé, which after all lay just on the far side of the great tower gateway?

That central gateway was framed by figures carved in high relief, one male and one female. Seeing them, he stopped, turned, and approached. On the left was a winged male figure with arms pointing skyward above it, in the act of bursting from the pedestal base. It was an exciting, active figure, but he paid it hardly any mind after the first glance, because of the effigy to the right of the archway—a female figure with long unjointed arms that ended in sharp sinuous fingers. A wild halo of seaweed hair on which small shells and starfish balanced surrounded her face, which was not entirely human. The eyes, wide and as perfectly round as her breasts, were like the eyes of an afrit, blank and terrible, although he knew they were black. Her mouth smiled in fierce and irrefutable invitation. *Sing for me*! Her command echoed in his mind. The lower half of her body, emerging from the elaborate plinth as out of a fountain, appeared to metamorphose from flesh to scales. Her sex—the lowest part of her showing above the lip of the plinth—was masked by a ribbed shell. He raised his eyes to the circular windows dotting the whole length of the wall and wondered if such creatures lived behind each.

As he stood gawking, a stilt walker abruptly materialized out of the dark gateway before him, wearing loose bright blue-and-green skirts almost to the ground, scarves and clinking bracelets seemingly awhirl. Affixed to the walker's head was a grotesque and oversized laughing mask. Long, thickly woven strands of dark hair surrounded that face of japery. Then, in an impressive feat as he walked past, the walker somehow doubled over on the stilts and reached down to hand Diverus a coin. It was copper and bore a face like that of the stilt-walker's mask on one side. He flipped it over, and a similarly distorted face snarled at him from the other side. Glancing up again, he watched the stilt walker pivot on one leg and then seemingly—at least from Diverus's perspective—continue along while walking backward, with the cruel face from the back of the coin now facing forward.

He watched transfixed as the giant figure strode nimbly around every impediment; meanwhile the laughing face jeered back at him like a taunt, a clown's jape. Encountering a group of people, the walker bent over again, parallel to the ground, and flung out more coins, then righted up, pivoted, placing the snarling face in the back once more. It strode on. Diverus could no longer be certain which was front and which back.

He pocketed the curious coin but chose not to follow. He'd been teased and tricked enough for one morning.

Later then, as he waited in line to purchase more of the sweet pastries for everyone in the theatre, he gasped with the sudden realization that for the first time in his life he was alone and free in the world. He was with no one and no one knew where he was. He could have turned right then gone up inside that tower wall and hunted for the merwoman who'd beguiled him, or fled through that broad gate and into worlds unknown, abandoning Leodora and Soter (who, he was certain, would have been delighted). He stared at the central gate, and knew he never would. He never would abandon Leodora. She had given him this freedom. The merwoman, if she was real, had revealed to him how ready he'd been to embrace a death he'd been yearning for secretly since the moment his mother sank from view beneath the underworld of Vijganar.

A threshold had been crossed—one he hadn't known he'd been skirting far longer than he'd been "Diverus"—and it was all because of her.

His human goddess.

"Diverus, you terrify me!"

"I didn't mean to. They were supposed to tell you where I was. Bois and Glaise." Diverus had given out the treats he'd brought back. Soter had glowered at him, but Soter always glowered. Sober, he seemed to have no other expression these days. Then again, it was Leodora who chided him.

They'd gone into the booth, and she was setting up for the next performance. She chided him because his absence meant she couldn't be in the booth. She could no longer endure the space by herself. Alone.

He answered her charge by pointing out, "You go off all the time. You mount span towers and overlook the bridge. You told me so. You hunt up stories. Why shouldn't I be free to go off, too, if I want? I mean, I could have run off and not come back. I'm free to do that now, too." He spoke the words of defiance as if surprised by them.

She set down the rod puppet of the fisherman Chilingana, a figure from the second story she would perform today. "You know, you're absolutely right. Don't listen to me. I was worried, but Bois did explain they'd left you down at the waterside. It just—when you didn't come back . . . well, I don't know what I thought. That maybe you'd found the inverted span, that something had come out of the water and swallowed you, that you'd decided not to come back at all. All of those things, I guess. And how could I sit in here without you? If you'd never come back, we'd never have known what happened." She drew a breath, dismissing her careworn expression. "All the same, you're right. I suppose I cause Soter such terror every time I go off."

"So now you appreciate how Soter feels?" he teased.

"Let's not presume *too* much. I still mean to climb towers if I'm so inclined."

"This one will prove a strange journey. It's inhabited. It's like a great wide palace dividing the two spans."

She was intrigued. "Did you have any luck finding it, the Pons Asinorum?"

"The what?"

"That's what it's called, according to the porters down below—the inverted span is known as Pons Asinorum. The Fool's Bridge. Did you see it again?"

"No." He sighed, then muttered, "Fool's Bridge, that's what it is all right. Bois and Glaise told me they knew where it was, but it turned out what they really meant was that they'd *heard* about it being there, or heard of it being seen from there. Or something. But there's not even space for an underspan down there—no one's living there like on Vijganar. It was just arches to let boats pass through. I don't see how the Pons . . ."

"Asinorum."

"I don't see how it could ever have appeared there. Besides, we saw it in the middle of the span, you and I, where the Dragon Bowl hangs."

"I think it doesn't appear in just one place," she answered. "It seems to come and go."

"Come and go," he repeated as if that had some other meaning. Then he brightened. "You probably will want to see the street fair. Where I purchased the buns, there's a fair, with all kinds of performers. Fortune-telling and sword swallowing and the like. A lot of them are different, not exactly human. It must be a good place to find more stories, with all those creatures."

"We should go this afternoon, then. You can take me there."

"I would like to, Leodora," he said, and tensed up. She heard the peculiar notes in his words, too, and stared at him curiously. He blushed under her scrutiny, and abruptly concentrated on arranging his instruments in order, an act that both of them knew to be superfluous: When she told him what story she was performing, he would grab the appropriate instrument regardless of what lay nearest.

She gently placed her hand on his shoulder. He turned to

her much too fast. His features were twisted in misery. Before she could ask what was wrong, he took her face in his hands and kissed her. His lips crushed hers, his whole body trembling behind the kiss as if even the energy he needed to stand up was pouring from his lips. Then he let go, wrenching himself away as if to escape some intense force—let go and dove out of the booth, kicking the theorbo, which spun like a compass needle, coming to rest with the neck aimed at her.

She brought her fingers to her lips, and stared at the blackness of the booth. "Oh, gods," she whispered but couldn't move.

They didn't go to the fair. When the sun dipped below the theatre's walls, Orinda let in the sizable crowd for the early performance. It was the last show in which she would charge a mere penny, and word had spread.

Until the time of the performance, Diverus could not be found anywhere. Soter strode about behind the stage, loudly complaining that he'd never trusted "the thankless boy" and that they should be glad he'd run off. Leodora was too lost in her own distress to object, leaving Soter to enumerate Diverus's various offenses: laziness, disrespect, thievery, and, worst of all, bad musicianship. Orinda, at the gate with Bois collecting the entrance fees, heard none of it, and Glaise—who could say nothing in anyone's defense anyway—ignored him.

Then Orinda returned and it was time to begin, and Leodora, ignoring the shouts and cheers, sullenly walked into the empty booth, while Soter continued quietly to denigrate the absent Diverus until Orinda said, "Hush!" with sufficient authority to shut him up.

It was at that point that Hamen and Meg appeared in the wings. They dragged between them a barely conscious and groaning Diverus. Dark purple stained his shirtfront.

Soter took one look at him and pronounced, "By the gods, the rascal's *drunk.*"

Orinda remarked, "Of course *you'd* recognize that." Soter twitched at her tone and held his tongue. To the two porters, she said, "Here, set him down."

"Very sorry about this, madam," replied Hamen, "but we didn't discover him until Melangia Street wanted lingonberry wine, and there he was, having hacked open a cask and drunk most of it hisself."

"What he isn't wearing, that is," Meg added. "Good thing Hamen recognized him. Most thieves get tossed off the span, we catch 'em, and I doubt too many survive the plummet."

"We'll pay for the wine, of course," Orinda said, and she offered them a handful of coins.

"We'll give it to Chork. It's his territory."

"We're about to begin a performance. Would you both care to stay?" she asked.

"Looks like you've got a full house already," Hamen said.

"We do, but I have a private box that can't be entered save from the back, and you're welcome to that. It gives a very good view of the screen."

They accepted her invitation with the rationalization that no one would miss them for an hour or two; but before Orinda led them away, she turned to Soter and said, "Get him to the booth so we can start."

"He can't play like this."

"Not from back here, no."

Soter snorted contempt, but withered under her steady gaze and dragged Diverus onto the stage. The crowd thought this was part of the show and hooted at them. Diverus stumbled free of him and lurched off to career in a circle until Soter could catch hold of him again, by which point the crowd was roaring. Soter cursed as he shoved Diverus through the opening, and Leodora, where she sat between the puppet cases, swiveled around. She watched Soter deposit his besotted burden with obvious contempt. Diverus collapsed in a heap amid his instruments.

"He's in his cups," Soter carped, "*and* at the start of a performance, too."

"So then, he's adopted you as a role model."

"You sound just like Orinda," Soter answered. "Does everyone hold so low an opinion of me?"

"Just the ones who know you." She said it almost as an afterthought, because her attention was on Diverus. She knelt beside him and helped him sit up. His head drooped, but he looked up at her with bleary eyes. She said his name. He focused on her briefly, then let his eyes roll and closed his eyelids.

"Lemme go," he slurred. "Just lemme go."

"I can't. You have to play now, you have to accompany me."

He shook his head.

"Lea, he can't—"

"Would you please shut up and get out of here? Go announce us. Do your job instead of weighing in on everyone else's!" She stared daggers at Soter until he left. Then she ministered to Diverus as best she could. She cupped his cheek, then picked out the shawm and placed it in his lap. "Here, I think you should use this."

"No, I . . ." He shook his head again. "I can't anymore. She tore it out of me, wanted my song."

"Who did?"

"The wraith. Water-wraith."

"What water-wraith?"

He tried to answer. She watched his mouth working to shape words. Finally he lowered his head in defeat. Only a few hours ago he'd been teasing her, asserting his newfound independence. Now he couldn't even explain what had happened to him.

From outside came Soter's call to order: "Hear-ye all! Welcome to the Terrestre, returned like your span itself from the ash pit of the gods!" The crowd cheered.

Leodora left Diverus and returned to her seat before the screen. The puppets for the first tale were laid out there—the thief, the vizier, the princess, the emperor, and the dragons.

Overhead, dusk was darkening the sky. She lifted the flap on the screen, to which she'd already pinned the frame of a palace; she reached up with her other hand to turn the lantern on her cue. Peripherally she looked at Diverus, hunched over, motionless.

Soter finished his introduction, asking them to enjoy to the fullest the artfulness of Jax. Applause and whistling followed, the crowd rowdy and eager. She turned the lantern slowly to light the screen in the blue of evening.

From behind her, the eerie tenor of the shawm rose, tremulous, out of the booth, snaking up and around the theatre like a lasso looped about them, drawing them tightly into its spell. As the last note of the introduction faded away, there wasn't a sound from the audience.

Leodora relaxed, let go of the lantern, and began the tale

of the Druid's Egg.

The Druid's Egg was followed by the tale of "How Chilingana Brought Death into the World," although here in Colemaigne his name was Sparrowgrass and he shared certain ignoble traits with Meersh, and sometimes even replaced Meersh in stories. All of this Leodora had learned from Orinda.

At the end of the performance she stepped past Diverus and went out to take her bows. He, still in his trance, set down the wooden fish drum he'd played at the end in imitation of the rattling of Death's bones, and then lay upon his side between the santur and the drums. When she returned, she found him softly snoring, which struck her both as amusing and oddly endearing, reminding her of the gulf of unvoiced emotion between them. She didn't disturb him. The puppets lay strewn about, but there would be a second performance tonight and she would put things in order later. She had a few hours now, and at the moment what she wanted most was to speak to the one entity that must tell her what she wished to know. She left Diverus asleep on the floor.

She went to her tiny room and scooped up the Brazen Head.

Before she could ask it anything, Bois was at her door and gesturing furiously. Someone, it seemed, had come calling for her specifically. When she asked who, he made as if to stroke a huge plume coming off the top of his head, which she finally translated as someone of importance, at least in their own opinion, and from guessed at the identity of the visitor: the governor of Colemaigne. She was wanted downstairs.

"All right," she said, "but in a minute."

Bois nodded and went off.

When he'd gone, she dashed up the hall and through one of the balcony doorways, making sure no one saw her.

At the bottom of the ramp, before parting the curtains, she crouched low and waddled onto the balcony. It lay in shadow, the only light coming from the sconces around the theatre below.

Sitting cross-legged on the floor, she held the pendant up by its chain. Its eyes were already open, staring back at her.

She said, "You heard my question already, did you?"

"A shout can wake even the dead," the lion replied.

"Don't misdirect me with one of your riddles. Tell me true. How do I find Pons Asinorum?"

"Symmetry is the answer," it replied as though that explained everything.

"How so?"

"Looks to and fro, inside and outside, true and false. At once forward, at once backward."

"What looks to and fro?"

"Why, what you seek. That was your request."

"Why is it you can never just say *Go see Vorparal the Vintner and he'll have your answer?* Why is every answer a challenge?"

The lion yawned.

"Don't you dare go to sleep on me, you. I picked you and you *have* to counsel me."

"Just so. Then be warned that the thing that unites also divides."

"No clearer, beast."

"Reflection. You stand on but one side, existing twice, and frame the most important question." Then, infuriatingly, the lion paused, waiting for her prompt.

She withheld it as long as she could; clearly the lion could outwait her. With a loud sigh, she said, "All right, what would the most important question *be*, then?"

Smiling, the lion answered: "From the other side, can you see yourself before your reflection?"

"Before?"

"From the other side, does the mother see the daughter?"

Leodora shook her head. "I don't understand. Do you mean does my reflection see me? Or something else entirely? Who's the mother?"

"It's a question of time. Time—"

"—is that which ends," she interjected angrily. "Yes, I know!"

The lion's brow lowered. "Not what I was going to say at all." His eyes closed, and he was inanimate once again.

"What were you going to say? Tell me!"

She shook the chain, but the lion didn't wake. She had a petulant urge to fling it at the wall, to smash it. But destroying it was hardly the way to get what she wanted. It would gain her nothing.

"I'm sorry," she told it. "I didn't mean to be impolite. Really." But of course she had; she'd responded as she would have with Soter and his evasive answers. Unlike him, the pendant didn't have to abide her rudeness.

She understood that it had told her the truth in its fashion; it was up to her to decipher what it had said. The head would argue, of course, that it wasn't being perversely elusive, it had to answer that way, just as she was compelled to prove her cleverness.

When she'd coaxed and cajoled further to no avail, she gave up and put the pendant back around her neck. Maybe it would wake again before she took it off for the next performance. For now the governor of Colemaigne awaited an audience with the redoubtable Jax and had been kept waiting long enough.

The huge table at the rear of the theatre lay buried beneath silver trays, copper tureens, bottles, earthenware mugs, wicker platters, and assorted cutlery, all lit by a circle of tall candles and outside that circle another formed of servants. It was obvious the governor had brought his celebration with him. He sat at the far end of the feast. When Leodora entered the room, he looked to Orinda and asked, "Is it she?" and Orinda replied, "Yes," and he rose, beaming, as if Leodora in her gray tunic were royalty herself. He wore a powdered wig cascading in ringlets, and an embroidered salmon-colored coat with silver buttons down the front.

"I marvel," he said, "I marvel. The hands that work the rods."

Leodora flushed and lowered her eyes, embarrassed and thrilled, but he wasn't having any of her modesty. He came around the table and extended both his hands to take hers. His fingers flashed with a dozen rings. She obediently held hers out to him. He cupped them on his palms and then busied himself studying them; brushed his hands across her palms, felt her wrists, peered at her short nails. "Clearly, the hands of a young woman, so you are no ancient, accomplished crone in disguise. I can feel the strength here in the wrists, but truly the calluses at your fingertips offer the only definite clue to your craft."

Orinda, looking amused, explained, "M'lord is a student of hands."

Beside Orinda, Soter guessed, "Palmistry, is it?"

"Not at all," replied the governor, keeping Leodora's

hands clasped in his. "Palmistry is absurd, mere physiognomy focused upon the hands. The idea that how you are shaped reveals your deep nature is ridiculous. Should we say that if you'd been born without hands you cannot live because you lack a lifeline or heartline to chart? Of course not.

"No, this is the art of observation. I look, I touch, I discover. It tells me what you do but it cannot tell me how well you do it, do you see? Your skill, that is not apparent beyond a certain equipoise, a balance to both hands. No, to know your skill I would have to see the performances themselves, which as it happens I've done now thrice. Your gifts, m'lady, are extraordinary and were I not chaste in my vows I would certainly chase you." He chuckled at his own word play.

"Erm, thank you," she said uncertainly.

He released her hands to roll up the sleeve of his coat so that he could reach across the mounds of food for a pastry that had caught his eye. "The burning question addressed to both of us is always, *How is it done?* Your craft looks like magic to we who lack the talent, exactly as my conjecture from observation of your hands might look like magic to those who don't observe." He waved his treat in the air. "Of course no one sees the hours of practice, trial, and error that go into the final performance, hey? They see only the culmination. The rest can but be inferred . . . can be nothing else, just as all of our citizens hear my judgments but cannot discern to what extent I have anguished over them, weighed discourse and debate to arrive at my answer."

Behind him Orinda was covering a smile. His servants were looking mildly embarrassed, too. Leodora intuited that, whatever the topic, he invariably brought the focus back to himself. She took a seat.

"The interdict on performance must have been a terrible burden, then," she said.

"Ah, before my time, that, and enacted by a body of jurists in any case. Mind you, I was on hand to witness the blighting itself."

"You saw it?"

His eyes looked inward for a moment, and he shuddered at the memory. "I was standing in the doorway of my house, no farther from Tophet than you are from the end of the room right now. I remember him huge and bright."

Tophet—it was a word the pendant had spoken. So it was

a name. "Who was he?"

"A fiend. Tophet the Destroyer, the god who drinks life. He came here from the other side of the world—at least that's what my father said. From a part of Shadowbridge where death reigns. He has drained the life from whole chains of spans, fed upon their lives."

"Bright," she repeated. The image of him conjured by the governor was nothing like bright.

"Oh, yes," said the governor. "So bright that you couldn't look at his face, couldn't make out his features at all, as if his face was a great shining mask of metal lit by the sun. And the blight, now, that unfolded in front of me. It literally spread along the street right before my doorway. The stones crumbling, the figs on the trees shriveling up, the people . . ." He closed his eyes. "Had I stepped out into the street for a better look, I would have been turned to stone along with them. That is how those distant spans had died before us, so I was told. He simply willed it and it was so."

Leodora thought of Meg, pointing to the statue behind her: *That's me dad.* She imagined him, below the street, oblivious to the events above, to the decay sweeping inexorably toward him. Did he realize at the last moment? She doubted it. His petrified pose was of someone reaching to take hold of something. Life had changed that fast. It did, after all, didn't it? Outside of stories. Stories always painted the bigger pictures, showed the terrible transformation approaching so that the audience, watching, listening, knew what was coming and had time to fear it. It was more compelling that way, more horrible, really. People in her audiences had been known to stand up and cry out warnings to characters—to the little thief in the Griffin's Egg tale, to the vagabond who spent the night with the woman known as the Fatal Bride. They knew more than the characters, embedded in the story like insects in amber, always at least a few steps ahead.

She realized that she had been sitting in silence too long. She said to the governor, "It must have been very hard for you, then, to *reverse* the ban."

"Indeed. The memory of that day haunts me still. But Tophet never returned. Neither he nor any of his ghoulish Agents has been seen here since that day. Nor is the cause of his wrath present among us any longer." He traded a look with Orinda.

It took her a moment to realize that he was referring to her father.

"Still, yes, difficult," he said. "I had to wrestle with the question of what was best for us all. All of Colemaigne. I felt we'd hidden in the grayness of fear long enough." He beamed at her again. "And now that I've witnessed your art, I know I chose right. So please, no more darkening the night with reflections of the Destroyer. Come, sit, and tell me how many stories you know. That is the *real* secret everyone wants to hear."

For the second show Leodora and Glaise propped Diverus into a sitting position, handed him the shawm, and hoped for the best. He moaned and complained in a sloomy way, but was too slurry-witted to do more. With his head down, his eyes closed, he muttered her name, but she had already taken her position beneath the lantern and Soter was already making introductions to the audience, and she didn't hear him. He barely heard himself. He sagged in defeat, his bones seemingly going soft. He had time for one final coherent thought—*This is how Soter goes through life*—before the tale was announced: "The Dream of Fortune." Immediately his comprehension of his surroundings evaporated. Then the spirit invaded him. He acquiesced—not that he could have fought against it, which would have been like fighting against an undertow. He let it have his arms to raise, his lips to shape around the reed. It was as if he were observing himself from outside his own body, as though the source of his skill wanted nothing to do with him in his disgraceful, besotted state.

Then he blinked and the sensation of separateness collapsed. He became bound to the song, living but a fraction of a second ahead of it, his fingers guided to the holes of the shawm as if born to it, flowing eerie trills to shiver the bones. Music filled his mind to the exclusion of everything else. He became forged of music.

When it ended, the tale, he collapsed in a gray slumber, insensate, out of which he arose only when the succeeding tale was announced. His conscious self didn't even hear his name, but his body took over, reached for the hourglass drum, which he could flex with his knees as he played.

Somewhere in the middle of that tale he began to sober up.

An edge of self-awareness flowed through the movements as he drummed, as he picked up a *guiro* and scraped a stick along it to imitate the clacking of bones. *I am Diverus,* he repeated in his head. *I am Diverus, and Leodora . . .* but he couldn't finish, wasn't even sure what it was he had intended to say. No, he wasn't all that sober after all. Besides, he had no idea what she thought of him now, and it didn't matter, not really. When he'd slept some, he would leave. If he was lucky, he would wake up in the middle of the night and nobody would miss him until he had gone far enough that he could begin as someone else, someone with no past, no name. He yearned to be the idiot that the gods had unmade, the simple creature that only felt things in a dumb way and didn't have to think them.

When the performance ended he sank down again, aware as at a distance of applause, of cheers and shouts. They were happening somewhere else to someone else. He drifted into unconsciousness beneath the roar of waves pouring over him. *Back into the water,* came the thought. Let it pull him under for good and let sea creatures feast on him, turn him into a new coral man.

He considered it a fitting end, imagining himself as the creature in the case, down below the puppets, and like the case his mind grew dark and silent.

It was while Bois and Glaise were carrying Diverus up the steps to his room that the copper coin fell from his pocket, bounced on the step, and came to rest on Leodora's bare foot.

In the light of the lamp she carried, she couldn't tell what it was, just something shiny. "Wait a moment," she called to the woodmen. She bent down and picked up the coin. Holding it up to the light, she muttered to them, "Go ahead, sorry, it fell from his clothes." The distorted face on the coin seemed to be leering at her. She was certain she'd never seen it before.

Up the stairs then while she held the coin between thumb and forefinger, she'd almost caught up with Bois and Glaise when idly she turned the coin to see the other side, the second face.

She stopped.

The two woodmen reached the hallway, where they waited for Leodora to catch up to them with the light. When she didn't arrive, they turned, but Leodora barely noticed them. She was hearing the lion as clearly as if it had just then awakened, saying to her: *At once forward, at once backward*. She flipped the coin over and over. "To and fro," she whispered.

When she looked up, Bois and Glaise at each end of the drooping body of Diverus faced each other like mirror images, almost identical in stance, in shape. But, she thought, nothing like the coin. It couldn't be that obvious and simple—the coin wasn't pointing the way to them. In any case, they had tried to show Diverus the Pons Asinorum and failed. They wanted to help but had admitted that they didn't know how. They knew only the stories that everyone else had heard. Yet viewed another way, perhaps they hadn't failed at all—not at their true task, which had been hidden even from them.

She sprang up the steps and then led the way to Diverus's room. The two men placed him upon his pallet. Leodora held up the lamp and showed them the coin. "Have you ever seen this?" she asked. They shook their heads with looks of regret. "It's all right, don't apologize. Now you go on, I'll attend to him."

Bois crossed his arms over his chest and looked farcically affectionate.

"You're wrong," she insisted. "It's nothing like that."

Glaise rolled his eyes as if to say he didn't believe her, either, and followed Bois out.

"I'm simply going to wait here," she said to no one.

She stood over him, the lamp held waist-high. Her hand holding the coin shadowed his face, and she lowered it. He winced as if the brighter light penetrated his sleep, but she didn't move to shield him again. His black hair was tousled and matted, his face shiny with sweat. Drink made him look feverish. Shortly, he began to snore.

She knelt to brush back his hair, and her hand touched his cheek. He needed to shave soon, or else grow out the hair on his jaw and chin. He couldn't remain in this median state between boy and man anymore. The paidika had cultivated the child in him, but that life was behind him forever. No one owned him now. His shirt, unlaced, showed his naked breastbone, the hollow of his belly almost to his navel, the rhythm of his breathing. He was, she thought, very like the puppet of the little thief who stole the Druid's Egg and defeated the wizard. And won the princess.

A sharpness cut within her, and her nostrils flared. She

knew what that tender sensation meant. Her heart suddenly had an edge. Each beat tore it loose. Each scored her. She put her hand to her throat. It slid down and grasped the pendant. Where was the counseling for this?

She could not remain here or the pain would swell until it drove her to action. Looking at him in that moment, all she wanted was to lie beside him, with him.

She got up and backed away from her desire.

At the doorway, she pressed to the wall. Would there ever be a time when they could express such feelings, either of them? What sort of troupe would they be, then? She had no idea; she knew only that now wasn't that time. Both of them were confused. Confusion had driven Diverus to drink. If only he had said . . . but the kiss had said it for him, hadn't it?

She thought suddenly that she understood him more clearly. He was afraid of rejection, afraid that his were the *only* feelings in play, and so to avoid that pain he'd drowned his sensibility with drink rather than court that rejection. "Oh, Diverus," she whispered. He didn't stir. She fled the room.

In the hall she stood against the wall awhile, eyes closed, hand over the sleeping pendant. In all the time she had lived on Bouyan, she'd never felt anything like this for Tastion, although he had wanted her to if only to make her more pliable to his desires.

Finally she slid down into a sitting position with her heels tucked close. The lamp rattled against the floor as she set it down, and she stared at it as if unable to recall what it was doing there. What she was doing here.

She must have dozed, because she came awake at the sound of a floorboard creaking in front of her, opened her eyes to see two legs that sprang past even as she raised her head. It was Diverus running.

"Wait!" she called and hobbled after him. Her left leg had fallen asleep and she pounded on her thigh to awaken the muscles as she half stumbled down the stairs behind him. "Diverus!" she yelled, fearing as she did that she would awaken the whole of the Terrestre and the street outside as well. But when he threw open the door, gray of early dawn surrounded him, and Diverus remained in the doorway. She caught up and saw why.

Soter, wearing a green shawl, stood outside, blocking his way.

Diverus retreated inside, his head down, as if sure it had been a trap they'd planned for him. Soter, at his heels, considered the two of them and asked, "What are you playing at, hey?"

Glum Diverus didn't answer. Leodora said, "What are *you* doing awake this early? I thought after all the celebrating you did last night, you'd be sleeping forever."

Soter didn't want to change the subject but felt compelled to defend himself. "In the first place, for all the celebrating, I in fact did very little. That goatish governor talked incessantly and on every imaginable topic, and damned if he didn't repeatedly ensnare Orinda with his prattle. It was all I could do to keep him from running his hands under her clothes right in front of us. Other than that, you wouldn't notice, but I sleep very little these nights. Very little. Seems to be my nature, unlike *some* drunken louts." He stared accusingly at Diverus. "And now before you elude me altogether, I will ask once more. What are you two about?"

"We're off to look at something with two heads," she told him, and Diverus glanced at her from under his brows, an uncertain look that she attended with her own. The silent exchange did not go unnoticed by Soter.

"Listen to me, Leodora. You won't like what I'm going to say, but then you never do. Do not tangle yourself up with this boy, do you understand? No good ever comes of these affairs."

"Like Leandra and Bardsham?" she said.

"Exactly like—" He clamped his lips so tightly that the color drained from them. "That's not at all what I meant."

"Of course not, seeing as I'm the 'no good' that came of that *particular* affair."

"I'm trying to warn you about something."

"Then you've done your job. I'm warned. Just as I have been by everything you've taught me. And one day, you are going to stop giving me warnings and tell me the truth about what lies behind them. Clearly that's not today." She pushed herself around both of them. "We'll be back later. Come on, Diverus." At least the boy had the decency to avert his eyes from Soter as he made his more tentative exit behind her.

Soter didn't watch them go. He didn't have to. He already knew what was developing between them, even if they still didn't admit to it. From the moment the gods had deposited her in that Dragon Bowl, Diverus all but mooned over her, and her quick defense now only proved to Soter that there was partiality on her side of it as well. It was their secret that wasn't a secret to anyone with eyes. He suspected that even Orinda had worked out why Diverus had been brought home drunk.

Fine, then, let them have their secret for the moment. Let them gambol about Colemaigne, collecting stories and kissing in alleys while he worried for their safety. He hadn't told them the truth, either, about why he wasn't besotted, why he hardly slept; but to explain his fear to them he would have had to tell them everything, including more about that *no good* union of Bardsham and her mother. There was no piece of it he could tell and not be forced into revealing all. That was Leodora, cut from the same cloth as her mother—not about to let anything go without an answer.

What they were up to could keep for now. He would find a way to address the problem of Diverus later—hire someone to get rid of him if no other methods worked. More pressing now was the very real need to come up with an excuse for leaving Colemaigne before history repeated itself, which it would surely do if, as Orinda and the governor claimed, they were drawing an audience now from four spans in either direction. Word was spreading here faster than it had on the other spans, faster even than it had in Bardsham's time. Soon her name would stretch the length of this spiral, and only the gods knew how far that was, how many spans. Sooner or later, word would reach the one person who mustn't hear of her. He feared that had already happened, and that death was on its way even now. *You'll be found,* the Coral Man had told him in his dream on Hyakiyako as a tentacle gripped his arm, and he suspected that statement would come back to haunt him wherever they went, no matter how many times he put them in a boat and sailed to another strand of spans, until he'd sailed them around the world and back again. It wouldn't matter. It was Fate the Coral Man had warned of. Inescapable Fate.

He looked at the fading mark on his wrist, the round red suction scar that told him it had been no dream, no illusion. It was a reminder to ensure that he didn't change his mind.

Soter hardly dared drink more than a cup anymore, certain that if he did that damned coral monster would return to gloat as it twisted his entrails with terror. If it was

Bardsham's shade, then that shade was far crueler than its corporeal self had ever been. He mustn't lose control, because if he did that Destroyer would strike again. Destroyer—it certainly suited. Soter's whole life and livelihood had been destroyed.

He glanced out the door. "If he finds you, you'll wish those fishing folk in Tenikemac had drowned you," he said to the long-gone Leodora. "And so will I."

From there, Soter wandered through the darkened theatre like a lost man, along the halls and then out onto the stage, where he strode boldly into the booth. He lifted the puppets out of one undaya case, pulled up the false bottom, and stood the case on end. Then he dragged Leodora's stool before it and sat down.

"Go on, then," he told the Coral Man. "Come out, emerge, manifest right here. Stride out of your box and scare me. Threaten me with doom." The figure did nothing, lifeless, all but faceless. Soter finally let go of his lingering terror. "No, I thought not, not when I'm watching, you can't. You know you can't scare me now, not compared with the fate that looms out there across the water. Why, you bastard? Why did she have to inherit your skill? Why could she not have been clumsy and stupid? Want me to admit that I thought I could minimize the attention she would get? Fine, I admit it. And it's not even enough that she's skillful, she has to be the favorite of the gods. Does *nobody* want her to live a long life? They'll come, you fool, the same as they did for you and that red-haired witch of yours. And this time, he'll obliterate this span, turn it into one of his sterile palaces, and she'll end up joining her mother in whatever abyss she's been consigned to. So come on, burst into being again and terrorize me, if you've anything left at all."

The Coral Man didn't move. It was as lifeless as rock, and nothing took shape in the darkness of the booth. Soter got up. "I'll go and sleep now, I think. Come and invade there, if you like, show up when I'm helpless to resist you. I'm tired of the burden of guilt. I'm tired of being responsible for your absence, and for the witch, too. It was *me* you should have confided in. Who'd been with you longer? Who *cared* for you? If you'd just given her up . . ."

There was no more to say. He could not make history revise itself. And anyway, the coral figure wasn't going to do anything, was it? He'd jettisoned Leandra's ghost on Bouyan, and now he would deny this one, too, its assaults upon him. The threats it had leveled in the past would not have a hold any longer. It was a piece of detritus, a shape fashioned by dead sea creatures. If anything of Bardsham lingered beneath that crusted surface, it didn't matter. Bardsham wasn't the danger to him. Bardsham had done his damage already, long ago, to himself, to them all.

"And you stop haunting your daughter at night, too," he added. "It's enough that you inveigled your way into her life just so you could travel the spans one more time on her back. Leave the living alone, you chalky wretch. You hear me? Leave us alone!"

The figure stood as if at attention as Soter exited the booth. He glanced at it once more, then drew the cloth closed and stormed into the wings.

At first Diverus walked slightly ahead, and neither of them spoke nor knew if the other's thoughts tracked anywhere near their own.

He strode from narrow lane to narrower alley, his movements sharp, turns brusque, as if daring her to keep up, as if angrily urging her to go her own way, to let him be. It soon became obvious to him that he would not break into a run and try to get away, nor would she fall back or fail to match his every turn; and so he slowed enough to let her catch up. Yet even when she drew beside him, he continued to walk along as if unaware of her presence until, peripherally, he saw her reach toward him—he thought—to stop him. Instead, she held between her thumb and forefinger a copper coin identical to the one he had . . . or was it his? Now he turned to face her.

"You dropped this," she said.

He stared at her, anger beneath the gaze. "You stole it while I slept?"

"No," she replied firmly, "it fell from your trousers as Glaise and Bois carried you to your room last night. I wasn't about to return it to your pants myself while you were asleep."

As he reached for it, she closed her other hand over his. He gave an instinctive twitch in response to her touch, but took hold of the coin, and she opened her fingers beneath his and thereby pressed his hand between her two. He didn't try to pull away. In truth, he didn't want to. He came to a stop with her.

"Where did you get it?" she asked.

"The fair. The street fair I started to tell you about, where I thought you'd find more stories. Leodora, I—"

"Shh," she hushed him. "Don't speak it. I know what's there between us, the same as you do, but if we say it, either of us, then it becomes something we have to confront and act upon, and I don't know, Diverus, I don't know if I'm ready to compound the journey I'm already on with that one as well. I don't want to risk it."

He swallowed.

"It isn't because it's you, it isn't that you're unworthy or anything else that Soter might intimate. It's because I'm not certain of me."

"And if you were certain?"

"Then . . . we would have to see," she answered.

They stood a long while, gazing into each other's eyes, joined with their hands wrapped around the coin, in an alley lined with empty urns, debris, and rotting vegetables. She could not tell him that her fear arose more than anything from the Brazen Head's warning, *the thing that unites also divides*; that to speak aloud what was between them would set in motion some unpredictable destructive force that might sever them forever, an idea she could not bear. So in superstitious fashion she protected herself by not voicing anything.

Finally, she slid her hands away, and he lowered his. He said, softly, "I'll show you where I got it." They struck out then side by side.

The fair was assembling when they arrived, but they smelled it before they'd even reached Towerside Thoroughfare. Once again someone was cooking the sweet buns that Diverus had purchased, and because it was impossible to pass by the booth and not want one, they bought their breakfast before moving on.

As Diverus had described, the bridge tower was itself an inhabited structure with rows of windows, ledges, and small balconies across the breadth of the span. At the enormous gateway in its middle he drew up. "This is where he came from, the stilt walker who gave me the coin. Out of there." He pointed into the dark tunnel between the two figures.

"Then I suppose it's where we're going," she replied.

They walked beneath the gate, Diverus keeping his eye on the huge relief of the water creature that seemed to be rippling up the side of the tower. As they crossed into shadow, the spiked bottom of the barbican became visible in its niche overhead. The floor of the tunnel was wet as well as dark; the grooves between the paving stones glistened with puddled water, the surface sloping on either side of the middle to wide channels at both edges, which appeared half filled with brackish standing water. The smell clogging the tunnel air suggested that sewage from the tower must drain somewhere close by—perhaps behind the various square grilles set in the wall at street level.

Past a pile of what appeared to be panels, poles, and uprights from dismantled stalls, two small fires clouded the air with a greasy haze. Dry sea grass lay in loose patches on the ground as if someone had bedded for the night here in the tunnel. Jars and boxes were piled up against the tunnel sides. Diverus drew Leodora's attention to a huge figure leaning against one such pile of red earthenware shards. "There," he said, "that's the one gave me the coin."

They walked up to the cowled stilt figure, which appeared to be napping against the wall. The hood was pulled so low that the grotesque masks matching the coin faces could not be seen beneath it. In all likelihood the walker had removed them to nap, but if so, its face in the depths of the cowl wasn't visible, either.

"Hello?" Leodora said. "Can you help us?" The figure remained utterly still. She extended her hand to Diverus for the coin. He flipped it to her. As it reached the apex of its arc, a gloved hand shot out from the loose folds of cloth and caught the coin. The stilt figure shifted away from the wall and hauled itself upright, so tall that its head appeared to brush the tunnel roof. The scarves draping it danced as in a breeze, as if to bewitch.

The stilt walker lifted the coin close to the cowl. "One of mine," it said, the voice sonorous but rough, reminding Leodora of the voice of Shumyzin and Diverus of the paidika gate on Vijganar. "What is it I can do for you? Is it a story you're looking for?"

How did it know that about her? "I'm looking for the Pons Asinorum. I think you might be able to help me."

"No secrets from the storyteller. She wants to know it all." When the walker laughed, she was surprised the stones didn't shake apart. The black gloved hand emerged from the layers of cloth again, and the angular figure bent over her. It held something. She reached up to accept it. "I hope," said the stilt figure, "you are as fearless as you seem."

She felt a cold thing placed in her palm, and brought it down to eye level. It was a dark stone phial about the length of her smallest finger, but thicker around with two tiny pierced flanges through which a cord ran. The phial might have been malachite; she couldn't be certain in that dim and uneven glow. One end of it was corked. Beneath it in her palm lay the copper coin.

"One drop upon a dark reflection," said the figure. "No more. And take care that you hold your destination in mind."

"A dark reflection?"

"No more," repeated the figure, and it canted over to the side and returned to leaning against the wall.

"Wait a moment," she said. "That's no better than my fool of a counselor. I don't know what you mean—whose dark reflection?"

Diverus took hold of some of the walker's blue-and-green skirt material and tugged.

"Hey!" came a cry from farther along the tunnel. "Stop that!"

They turned from the stilt figure. A tall, lithe woman dressed in a dark leotard was approaching them. She balanced something on the top of her head, which proved to be a mask. Another mask dangled from the strap in her hand. It was the stilt figure's laughing face. "You won't get an answer out of him," she told them, "not without *me* in there."

"What do you mean?" Leodora asked.

"I mean, without me he doesn't walk, much less talk," said the woman. She was a head taller than Leodora. Cropped blond hair framed her face. She had a broad smile and a gap between her front teeth. "Clererca," she said. "A big puppet is all I am, really." She gestured to the stilt figure. "It's not going to do anything for you unless I'm in there among those scarves."

"But—"

"Say, *you* look familiar," she said to Diverus, then squinted more carefully at Leodora. "By the doors of Janus, you're the puppeteer. I saw your first night's show. The very first performance of Jax."

"That's right."

She clutched Leodora's hand. "You don't know how

grateful I am—we all are—for what you've done. Any of us who wanted to perform—we've been exiled to Sacbé for years. You've made it possible for us to have lives again in Colemaigne, to have a livelihood."

Leodora blushed. "Clererca," she said.

"That's right."

"Forgive me, but you say this figure is just your giant puppet."

"In a sense."

"He's not alive."

"Good grief, no. Not until I get inside him. Here, I'll show you." She ran around behind the figure and climbed the stacked pottery shards. "I have to set him down carefully, where there's a ladder or something I can use." She pulled up the back of the loose costume. "Has to be high enough to let me stand, you see." The figure shivered as Clererca slithered through the back of the costume, her head finally poking out beneath the dark cowl. She pushed the cowl back and drew the scowling mask down over her face. The other she hung on the back of her head. Then with both hands she pushed off hard from the wall and came upright. "There we are." She waved her hands, which were separate from and much shorter than the dangling arms of the figure. She shoved her hands down into the sleeves, and a moment later the stilt figure's arms waved about in front of it. Each hand held a coin. The figure seemed to bow and extend its arm to Leodora. The fingers parted and a copper coin dropped into her palm.

"What's he called?" Leodora asked.

"Cardeo, because he lives on the threshold of things."

"He certainly does that."

The figure of Cardeo spun about on one leg and now presented the laughing face.

"How do you walk backward that way?" asked Diverus.

"Practice," she answered. "A lot of practice. I'm sure the great Jax knows what I mean." Cardeo strode off in the direction of Towerside. "You be sure to find me when you come out into the thoroughfare. Let me introduce you," she called back. "They'll *all* want to meet 'the girl who healed Colemaigne.'"

Diverus walked up beside Leodora. "I don't understand. She wasn't in the puppet. She . . . how did it talk to us? How did it *move*?"

"Edgeworld," Leodora said.

The word set alight his memory—the memory pulled free by the wraith. "I remember now. Something happened, I didn't tell you, I didn't get to—but I—"

"Remember what, Diverus?"

"Fountains jetting out of all kinds of colorful pools. And rainbows rippling on the surfaces of them as if oil had been poured upon the waters." His eyes closed. "The pavement was smooth beneath my feet, too, and the light, the sky, it was molten gold." He looked at her.

"Where was this?" she asked.

"In Edgeworld. I can remember Edgeworld now."

The incredulity on her face caused him to grab her hand and drag her out from beneath the arch. In the street he turned her and pointed at the sea creature statue carved on the wall above. "One of those came out of the water. Bois and Glaise led me down to it, trying to show me the upside-down place. And they didn't, it wasn't there, but I stayed behind. And that came out of the water . . . It *did* something to me, and all of a sudden I could remember being in Edgeworld. Everything was so queer there. Golden. And this woman spoke to me, guided me about, told me to choose my prize. I can see her hands, long, purple nails curving from her fingers. Her face was hidden, hidden under a mask, or it *was* a mask with nothing under it. I'm not sure."

She searched through her own memory for something that matched his descriptions, but nothing did, not even a hint. She gently shook her head, recalling nothing.

Insistently he went on, "There was a cat. A huge cat. It perched on the edge of one of the pools. It had fur so long that it looked like quills, and all different colors flowed across it, the same as the pool. I remember that I went to it. The mask woman said *Choose*, and I chose it."

"And when you stroked it, the air filled with music," said Leodora in awe.

"That's right, that's why I went to it. People were stroking it and the music drew me. You saw it, too."

She squinted, staring hard into memory. "I can—I can almost see it, where I was. Not bright like yours. It was dark. Different. I can't—it won't let me see it. But I remember that cat, and someone stroked it and music came out of its mouth, and then they all tried to sing, to harmonize with it. I can almost see them, but they're gray like shadows. And there's someone talking to me."

"Telling you to choose."

"Yes." Her eyelids fluttered. "Oh, it's just right *there*," she said, frustration in her voice. "I can almost reach out and clutch it."

"It was a woman. She told you to pick."

"No, a man. A man spoke to me."

"She was, that is—the mask she wore was my mother's face."

"Like someone you knew," she agreed. "I think they trick us that way. The gods can look like anyone they want. They can be anything." She looked at the green-and-black phial in her palm. "We think we're acting upon our own whims and choices, but we're not. We're guided, ushered through the unseen pattern, some labyrinth or maze—like the world has all its spirals, we've each got our own." She pondered. "Our memories of Edgeworld could be called dark reflections, but you can't pour a potion on a memory. That can't be what it means."

He apprehended where her thoughts had led her, and he looked around as if expecting the answer to present itself. From the booth at the mouth of the tunnel, a large man in a sleeveless tunic emerged, carrying a bucket. He walked to where the gutter began and tipped the bucket, pouring gray and soapy water into it.

"The water," said Diverus, and he left Leodora and went back into the tunnel. Up the street the stilt walker was gesturing in her direction, but she turned to follow Diverus.

He stood at the side, overlooking the drainage channel there. The water, with bits of debris floating in it, looked black and greasy. When she came up beside him and peered down into it, she could make out both their faces, like flowing apparitions. "Can there be a darker reflection than this?" he asked.

"Water in shadows."

"Or at night," he added.

"Should we wait for night?"

"I don't know. If it was night, would we see our reflections in the water?"

"Not without a torch or a lamp. So then, maybe this is what it meant?" She smiled at him. "Only one way to find out, I suppose." She made to pull the cork from the phial.

"Only a drop, Cardeo said," he reminded her.

"I know." She tilted the phial ever so slightly. A thick drop of glowing blue liquid formed on the lip of it. The drop clung tenaciously as she held the container outstretched over the water.

"Jax!" called a voice, and she glanced up to see the stilt walker approaching along the thoroughfare and surrounded by dozens of people.

Diverus watched the blue drop let loose of the phial and start to fall. He recalled the other thing the figure had warned. "Leodora," he asked, drawing her attention back to the business at hand. "Where are we going?"

"Pons Asinorum," she answered as the drop hit the smooth surface in the drain.

"Jax," Clererca called, but her voice wavered strangely, as if the tunnel distorted it. Diverus's hand found hers and gripped her tight as the blackness in the water turned bright and spread with impossible speed between the paving stones, then across them from every direction, congealing into a great oval, like a mirror. From the opposite side of the oval, oriented upside down to them, two faces looked back—ebony dark and with burning red eyes. Leodora thought of the Brazen Head's riddles, of reflections and of which side one stood upon, and she said, "I want to be on the other side." Still holding his hand, she placed one foot into the reflection. Diverus yelped as her weight fell through the reflection and tugged him in after her.

They stumbled as if they'd been running. She fell to her knees but stood up again immediately, compelled by fear. She faced a cherubic little man and a tall woman. Their eyes blazed like flames, and their skin was a dull blue. Their hair was black, shot through with oily blue streaks like reflections upon the wings of a raven. Their ears curved to points at the top, and their noses were long and sharp. The man babbled something that sounded like "Kadnari muus kelado pwee."

She shook her head that she didn't understand and happened to look up, which must have been down, for there far above/beneath her was a surface of luridly bronzed water. Vertigo rushed over her and she clawed at the air, certain she was about to fall away. Diverus tugged free of her hand and dropped to hands and knees on the metallic street above/below. She knew she must fall. No one could be upside down like this and not fall.

And then the world wheeled about her, the water was flowing overhead, spreading into a burnished liquid sky, and Diverus was kneeling by her feet.

On every span she'd entered there had been a moment of disorientation, of a membrane pierced, where everything was alien and incomprehensible, and invariably that moment yielded to sudden acclimation, to the strange made normal as the newly penetrated world enfolded and welcomed her. This was more expansive a transition than any other in that the world itself had turned to give her balance.

The round-faced man grinned. "By your expression I see you've adjusted. That's capital. And your friend—I can't tell you how rare it is to have *two* travelers at once."

"Or really any travelers at all," the woman added.

"*And* of their own volition."

"Hush!"

"Where *have* we come?" Leodora asked, looking beyond the couple at the intensely colored buildings, which bore a striking resemblance to those of Colemaigne.

"Where, she asks," he said to the woman, who laughed mellifluently and answered, "Nowhere and everywhere. Where you are depends on where you've been. We are the Pons Asinorum you sought because that's the name Colemaigne maintains in its thoughts. But we are known far and wide, as Nazar, as Breasail, as Yggdrasil and TirNaNog and a thousand more besides."

"How can that be?"

"We're the world of the timeless, of desire and elusion."

"It looks very much like Colemaigne. The buildings, I mean."

"Yes, but that's also because of how you arrived. Enter from, say, Palipon, and we are an island world full of cells, although ours are open, the inverse of a prison."

Leodora pondered that. Diverus shook his head in incomprehension. "What's Palipon?" he asked.

"Would it help," asked the woman, "if I told you that your upright world is connected everywhere below the surface by us, through us?"

"Connected to what?" said Leodora.

"To everything else, everywhere." Both of them grinned,

and while their demeanor was outwardly gracious and jolly, beneath it lurked the slightest hint of something not quite as generous, as if some darker truth was not being shared.

"But you are our guests," said the man, "and you must stay. Feast, relax, and please yourselves in our company. Everyone will want to meet you, storyteller."

Her hosts turned. Leodora glanced again at Diverus. With his head, he gestured at her hand. She surreptitiously showed him the corked phial still clutched there and then slipped it into her tunic.

"I don't know if we should," she said. "We have a performance—"

The woman turned back to her. "Oh, but you cannot *refuse*. You're questing for stories and we have them, the oldest, the most arcane, the least retold, the original, the consigned-to-oblivion."

Over his shoulder, the man said, "We connect everything. We *are* story." He looked back. "It's why we've become your preoccupation. The omphalos of your obsession."

"What you *need*," the woman emphasized as she followed the man.

"What I need," Leodora repeated. Her voice seemed to come from someone else's mouth.

Diverus urgently said her name, but it barely penetrated. They, these people, had the world's stories. Many times over the years on Bouyan she had expressed a desire to Soter to travel to the mythical Library of Shadowbridge, there to retrieve all the stories that had ever been; but now she needn't bother. She could learn every one of them here.

Diverus clutched her arm. She stared at his hand and blinked away her disorientation.

"Diverus," she said. "Surely we can stay a few hours, hear a few stories before we have to go back. It's only morning, after all."

"I don't trust them," he said, but smiled pleasantly when the woman looked back. "I don't trust *here*. What sort of world can transmute the way they claim?"

She peered once more at the oceanic sky. "One that isn't real," she replied, "but let's find out more first, before we decide. Please? If they have all the stories . . ."

He could not deny her that possibility. He knew how much that mattered, but mistrusted the place all the more that they knew just what to say to ensnare her.

Shortly they left the broad bright street of orange, red, and yellow houses for narrower crooked lanes of more subdued and empurpled tones. The street surface remained oddly metallic, with a sheen running through bands of color as if from various alloyed minerals. People greeted them as they passed, and then fell in after them. Diverus, glancing back, found the way clogged with dozens and dozens of inhabitants.

"Does it ever rain?" asked Diverus, watching the liquid sky.

"Of course," the man remarked. "It falls up from the ground most nights."

They arrived before a decrepit hovel. The stone walls were cracked, the thatchwork bald in places. Sitting on a stool before the hut was a small fellow with hair and beard of silver. He had a table before him and, on it, a copper pot that he held inverted over some kind of spindle allowing him to rotate the pot, as he tapped at it with a tiny hammer. At their approach, he set the hammer down.

They drew up before him. "My lord," said the man to the tinker.

"Yes, Archimago?" the old fellow replied.

"Our guests." He gestured to Leodora and Diverus.

The tinker, hunched with age, stood stiffly, then shuffled forward with his hand out. "My lady," he said to Leodora. "An honor to meet you. And you, sir." Diverus gave an irresolute bow.

To Archimago the tinker said, "There's going to be a feast, then, isn't there?"

"Well, of course, of course."

"Ah, and what's it to be?"

"Boar," replied the woman.

"Oh. Lovely. Brought back from—"

"Yes. From a hunt."

"Brodamante, you fill me with rapture," he told her, and she made a deep and formal bow, her red eyes focused on Diverus as if she was demonstrating to him that *this* was how one bowed.

She straightened, then asked Leodora, "Is there anything you would like to ask of our king?"

Leodora's brow knitted. "Do you mean him?"

"Indeed."

"Oh. Well. How did . . . how did—"

"How did you come to be king?" Diverus asked.

The tinker pressed his hands together. "That is a story. It was time for a new king and as I am sure you know, the old king sends out an army of advisers to find a successor. They have so many questions to ask, a list of them, and they go absolutely everywhere asking them. And it's finally a matter of who gives the best answers.

"Well, I was here, right here at this table in fact, and was mending Miggins's kettle, which had a hole in it because he had gone and cut himself and they'd needed a pot to catch the blood in, and wouldn't you know they picked one that reacted badly to his blood, and it cracked open and so he bled all over the floor anyhow, and now his kettle was in need of mending to boot. And so while I'm staring at it, up comes this fellow in green pantaloons and waistcoat, and he says to me, 'What do you know?' And I tell him, 'I don't know anything at all for certain. Not a thing.' And it just happens that was the best answer anyone gave them, and they proclaimed me king. That very same morning. I wasn't even allowed to finish fixing Miggins's kettle."

"That's mad," Diverus responded.

"'Tis," agreed Brodamante. "But it makes him the *best* king. As he knows nothing, he can but listen and decide, unprejudiced by strongly held opinions."

"But what if his advisers lie to him?" asked Leodora.

The blue people looked puzzled. "Why would they do such a thing?" Brodamante said.

"Greed?" she suggested.

"What an uncommon idea."

"Yes, unlikely," Archimago concurred thoughtfully. "We would have to cut off their heads. For a time anyway."

The old king shook his own head heavily. "Oh, I would hope never to have to decide such a matter as that. Life and death, what business is that of kings? No, no. I have my pots to fix. Much more important. You can't have a feast without pots. Can't eat without them."

"I suppose not," Leodora agreed.

"Of course not." And he settled back on the stump beside his table again. "I'll have to get this one repaired then."

Archimago's eyes shifted from the king to the guests. He pressed his hands together and said, "There, now you've met the king, we ought to . . ." He stopped as he turned about and found the lane choked with citizens as far as they could see. "Oh, dear. Should have known. We'll never get through there again."

Leodora looked back the way they'd come, and just for an instant way off in the background beyond the long and tightly packed crowd, she thought she saw a parade go marching by. She couldn't be certain—not at that distance—but she thought it looked like the parade of monsters from Hyakiyako.

Archimago, apparently seeing no distant parade, said, "They'll be wedged in for hours while they try to turn about and go home. Here, you two, follow me this way instead."

He led them past the old king, who was so intent upon his pot repair that he didn't seem to notice. Archimago opened a low door into the hovel. They had to crouch to enter. Straightening up on the far side, they found themselves in a large blue-tiled room as big as a palace, complete with a great sunken pool in the middle of it. Squares of lapis formed a band around the lip of the pool. To their left and past the pool, three rows of blue stone columns, nine columns in all, polished and smooth, held up a ceiling that was easily two stories above them. Beyond the columns lay an open courtyard where a fire was burning in a pit. The columns obscured most of it, but the smell coming from there made them salivate. To the right stood four more columns flanking an entryway.

Leodora turned just as Brodamante closed the small door, the interior side of which was bronze with decorations and shapes hammered into it. It had a large middle panel containing a cross-legged figure with long, thorny horns growing from its head.

Diverus commented, "This can't be the inside of his hut."

"Who claimed it was?" asked Archimago. "You are correct, not the inside of the hut but it *is* where we're feasting over that boar they're roasting right now. It will take the rest of the citizenry quite a while to get here from where we left them, as they can't take this shortcut. It's not allowed them."

"What is a boar?" asked Leodora.

"A very tasty meat, which comes from much farther away than you have. Brodamante hunted it herself." He strode over to the pool. "I think you should have a soak before the festivities. We would be most disrespectful hosts if we didn't allow you that."

"How," asked Diverus, "can you have a king that knows nothing?"

Brodamante replied, "Because he has the great wisdom to recognize that he does know nothing, and so, knowing nothing, he listens carefully to all persuasions before ever rendering a judgment. 'Tis the wisdom of innocence."

"I still don't see how, if he's that innocent, there's anything to stop someone trying to bribe or otherwise persuade his decision in their favor."

Brodamante and Archimago traded horrified glances. He said, "You have the most barbaric ideas I think we've ever heard, young man. Where do you come from? I want to stay away from there."

"Are such acts common in Colemaigne?" asked Brodamante.

"We wouldn't know. We're travelers."

"Well, of course," Archimago said, as if that settled things, but he shivered as though at the horror of the notion of cheating, and the blue-black hair seemed to curl upon his brow as if alive. "Now, please, we have attendants who will assist you, and you must avail yourselves of our every service while you are guests here."

"Yes," said Leodora, "and we do appreciate this, but we also have a performance late this day—"

"Oh, but we won't keep you all *that* long. In fact all of Epama Epam will turn out for your performance . . . once you've bathed."

Leodora was certain the name of Epama Epam hadn't been among those Brodamante had named earlier, and she wondered if that was a different span or still another name for this place that was no place and every place at the same time. She had no chance to ponder it, however, as a cluster of four more of the blue, red-eyed creatures came running from behind the columns. The four wore diaphanous skirts that glittered with stars of gold, and all were naked from the waist up—two males and two females. Each had four arms.

"We leave you in most capable hands," said Archimago, and he laughed as if at a joke. Then he and Brodamante walked into the forest of columns from which the servants had come.

Leodora's attendants took her by the hands and shoulders and directed her to the opposite side of the pool. Then they disrobed her. She tried to stop them, but it was futile. One set of hands removed her belt while another unwrapped her tunic, fingers tugging on its hidden ties as if intimately familiar with it. The second attendant knelt and removed her boots and trousers while the first folded up the tunic and set it aside. When they turned away, she looped the phial around her neck again. In short order she stood naked save for it and the pendant. When one blue hand reached for the Brazen Head, she slapped it aside, and neither attendant tried that again.

Her attendants led her to the water. There were semicircular steps below her, three of them. She put one foot in, discovering that the water was warm and also somehow oily, buoyant. She drew her foot out, and threads of blue ran between her toes. On each side of her the four-armed female attendants smiled warmly, but their eyes were fierce, eager, urgent. They moved onto the first step with her and gently compelled her deeper, down the next step, the hems of their skirts now immersed.

Across the pool Diverus was likewise naked and no less uncomfortable. He and his two attendants all but mirrored every move. On the second step, he stared back at her with wide eyes, his body lean and, she saw, aroused. The look in his eyes was of hunger, yearning, and fear, as though the emotions he felt shocked him. Those beside him looked at her with hunger alone. They were waiting for something to happen, and all that expectation focused on her. She puzzled as to why.

The Brazen Head spoke up suddenly, the voice such a shock that she nearly stumbled and fell in. "The waters of desire!" it proclaimed. "Of eternity, if you desire that, though I could not recommend it."

"I didn't ask."

"You did, but you didn't notice. It is no normal pool they wish you to enter."

The women beside her hissed and said, "Shush!" to the lion.

She stood in the pool to her thighs now, on the third step, and the attendants beside her, their skirts darkening from white to blue. "What if I go in?"

"Then what you desire will consume you. It is the opinion of those around you that you most desire your companion as he does you. Most travelers here arrive alone and are persuaded to stay, by a maiden or a gallant, by beauty or by indulgence upon which they are fixed. But you have brought your own."

"And the traveler swims in the pool," she said, "to what end?"

Behind her the girls urged, "Go on. You must. Don't listen to that."

"Bliss," the lion replied, "at a price."

"Go," said the attendants. "Swim."

Even as she hesitated, Diverus stepped into the water.

"Your friend is in. You must join him," urged the attendants.

"Why must I?"

Diverus swam into the center of the pool. His head went under, and when it came up it was blue, stained somehow by the water. He treaded water as if lost and unsure where to go, turning in a circle until he spied her. Then he swam straight to her. She held her place on the final step even though she was revealed, naked before him. He drew up below the step. His eyes burned into her. "Oh, Lea, I love you," he said.

"Go to him. Take him," the girls urged. "He wants you. You're his desire, all he can see. You feel the same, you know you do."

The tug of that desire almost drew her off the edge of the step but, tottering, she pulled away from it and fell back, with a splash, onto the second step. The two attendants stood over her. "You can't, you mustn't! He wants you. You want him."

She looked at Diverus, at the passion in his gaze. For her and nothing else. It was love without conditions or limits, and to resist it cut her like a searing blade. All the desire that had twisted inside him and driven him to flee from her, all that he'd held in check, denied, or confessed to himself alone—all of that blazed in his eyes. If she entered the pool with him it would bind them both. With all the passion of a thousand lovers from all the stories she knew, they would be the kitsune and the emperor, Akonadi and the Stone Man, the thief and the princess—the love that lived in dreams, in all of the stories. She would have all of that and more, an eternity of it, and she had only to surrender, let the color of bliss inundate her. Diverus already bathed in it, and she wanted that no less than he.

She could not bear the look in his eyes. It brought tears to her own. She closed them and answered through clenched teeth, "My greatest desire is not to remain here forever!"

The women gasped. "No one refuses," they cried. "No one can."

"Enough!"

The word echoed through the hall, off the columns and balconies. Even the water seemed to shiver. The hands let go of her. Leodora opened her eyes.

A figure emerged from the entryway and strode to the head of the pool. Light thrown off the pool danced across his fine red robe, so that it shimmered as if knit of liquid. His features, also subject to the rippling, were so transformed that she didn't immediately recognize him. Even without the reflected light he had changed completely. His hair had twisted into small spires like points on a crown, like the tips of his ears. His pale gray beard now hung in a row of skinny stalactites, which were mirrored in the smaller spikes that jutted up from his brows. No longer a ragged, simple tinker, he looked like a sea god, majestic, decisive, and terrible.

The attendants, both hers and those of Diverus, retreated from the pool as the king stepped to the head of it. "It's rare we have guests," he said. "But far, far rarer is the one who has the will to rove free among us. We know your traveling name and your profession, but tell me, lady, who *are* you?"

"My name is Leodora. My mother was Leandra. My father gave himself the name of Bardsham."

The king's eyes lowered and he smiled. "We know that name."

"So you knew me only as Jax."

"Just so."

"How? Was my coming foretold?"

"Not foretold. Inevitable." He swept his arm across the pool. The long sleeve of his robe seemed to flutter like a sail after the arm. "You may bathe now in comfort and contentment. No magic of ours will be thrust upon your will in there. It is become a pool of healing."

She glanced at Diverus, still moon-eyed below her. "What of my friend?"

"Your . . . lover is released as well, although the water has rather swiftly drawn his desire to the surface." He stepped out upon the water and walked to stand over Diverus. "He is susceptible. Has he perhaps encountered spirits of the water before now?"

"Afrits," she said. "On another span on another spiral."

"Oh, more recently than that, I think." He knelt upon the water as upon a sheet of glass and brushed one slender hand across Diverus's eyes. Eyelids fluttering, Diverus turned away from Leodora and focused on the king above him.

"Ah, yes, and he's been to Edgeworld."

The king of Epama Epam tilted his head and looked past Diverus then, into the distance past the rows of columns. "No conflation of such piquant rarity is possible. This can be no mere matter of destiny." He rose, and Diverus leaned back his head to follow him. The king gave a flick of his wrist, and Diverus went floating deeper into the pool.

"What does that mean?" she asked.

"That we surely have something you need, and our quest now will be to discover it together while you're here."

Leodora started to climb from the water, but the king held out a hand to stop her. "No. Swim in soothing waters. Your Diverus is unsorcelled now, although neither you nor I can suppress his true feelings that have emerged. After a time the attendants will bring you robes, and then the feast will go on. Whatever there is to unearth, it shall be found in time." He walked then across the pool as across a solid surface, stepping up onto the lapis stripe and then out between the columns.

When he had vanished from sight, she stood on the last step and clutched the pendant. "Counselor?" she called to it softly.

"Truth was spoken," said the lion. "Economical truth." It went back to sleep.

She glanced around at the attendants, who remained well back, no longer pushy, standing cowed instead, as though she might charge out of the pool and hit them. She could not say why exactly she believed the king, but she did. She turned from them and dove into the blue depths and was not consumed.

Applause filled the Terrestre, but it was not so enthusiastic as in the past—at least, that was how Soter heard it. He got up stiffly from the stool in front of the curtained screen, and turned to Bois. "You did very well. Very well, indeed." Bois put down the lute and bowed his head. He gestured at the exit from the booth. "No," Soter told him. "They mustn't see me. They have to think Jax is still working the puppets, and they've seen her, some of them." Bois tilted back his chin as if to say he understood.

Soter stepped into a front corner of the booth, where he

drew back the cloth along the side of one upright and surreptitiously peered out at the dispersing audience. Glaise and Orinda ushered them up the aisles.

Soter stretched, and his spine popped and creaked, and he groaned. "This is too hard on an old man like me," he told Bois, who shook his head in denial. "We can go out now, I think."

Orinda met them on the stage. "You did it perfectly—both of you."

"I'm sure we were adequate at best," Soter remarked.

"Far better than adequate, you foolish old man. She learned everything from you, which means you've as much skill as she."

He snorted, but Orinda would not let him refuse the compliment.

"She's more talented than any of us," she said, "probably all of us put together, but her skill comes from a man who spends half his time arguing with her over what he thinks is best and the other half pretending he has nothing to do with who she is at all. You'd do well, Soter, to inhabit one of those roles and dispense with the other."

He wrapped one hand about his lower face and gave a small grunt that was part scoff and part chortle. Then he remarked, "All the same, what are we to do?"

She placed a hand on his arm. "We are going to hope they return shortly. If not, we're going to put on the show tomorrow as we did this one. In the meantime, we cast our nets farther. Bois and Glaise will cover the whole of the span and go on to the next if need be." The woodmen nodded their enthusiasm and made to set off.

Soter said, "You'll want to contact Hamen and those underspan dwellers. They seem to hear of everything."

"That's a very good idea."

"Well . . . he seemed a decent enough fellow." He clasped his head in his hands. "I don't understand, Orinda. She's much too careful, too clever. If she went off to gather stories, she wouldn't forget the evening performance."

"Of course you're right. So we have to assume something important or terrible has kept them away, and probably against their will."

"Tophet's Agents . . . ," he muttered.

"Oh, surely not. Bardsham is long dead. What could Tophet want with her? Or with you?"

"She's his daughter. And no one knows for certain that Bardsham died. No one witnessed his death, no one hereabouts. What if Tophet doesn't know any more than we do as to the fate of Bardsham? Then he might think—"

"If that were true, Colemaigne would right now lie in ruin. We'd be dead and stone, every one of us, exactly as the governor described. That monster doesn't spirit people away. He punishes them without mercy and sups on their marrow." Her gaze slid side-to-side watching him, as if she looked for some sign of concurrence in his eyes. "Furthermore, outside of here, how could he recognize them? If he believed Bardsham were on the loose, he would be looking for a man he knows, not a young woman and her beau."

"Her beau?"

"Oh, dear, do you think I'm blind to love that runs as deep as that?"

"Nonsense."

She laughed gently, but with a teasing edge. "You know it as well as I. It's why you object to him so. You think to guard her even from her own feelings. It's time to stop doing that and let her feel. If you want to keep her affections, Soter, you have to let her take wing."

He stared into her eyes and his own grew hot. Orinda knew too much of him, nearly the truth of him; but he knew the rest and could never admit it to her. He nodded heavily and swallowed the anguish of tenderness. "I'm sure you're right about Tophet. But then there is *no* explanation, is there?"

"None as yet, my dear. None as yet." She linked her arm in his. "Come with me now. We should eat something before you exhaust yourself."

He let her lead him through the wings and the hallways. He felt quite suddenly a thousand years old and as helpless as a newborn. Where in all the world had his Leodora gone?

"I believe a story is in order," said the king.

Leodora, feeling warm and sleepy from the food and drink she had shared with them, drew her legs beneath her and smoothed the dark purple robe she wore. She asked, "And who's to tell it, sir?" then waved her hands about. "I have no puppets here."

A few of the dozen feasters smiled. They were all clustered

close around the fire.

The king tugged on the sharp tip of his nose and became for the moment contemplative. Then his eyes brightened and he told her, "Hold your hands out thus." He spread his hands before him with the palms up.

Leodora imitated him. He arose and stepped to the fire pit, where he reached down into the embers. When he turned back to her, his hands seemed to be ablaze. He cupped them and blew into them, a visible breath as if the air had chilled about him. Opening the palms side by side as if reading them, he blew sharply once more and strode up to her. Then, leaning down, he parted his hands across hers; six flames tumbled onto her palms. The flames were colored greenish blue and didn't burn her hands at all. She moved her palms back and forth, and the fires slid upon them. She glanced up from the magical flames. "What do I do?" she asked.

"Now," said the king, "you pick a story and hold the image of the characters in your mind. Try it. Pick any."

She brought her face closer to her hand and concentrated. The most obvious character to imagine was Meersh, and immediately one of the flames swirled and grew, forming into a tall, gangly body in worn loose trousers and a vest, his nose hooked and crooked, his chin sharp, his eyes sharper, and his orange hair a tangle around his head. He looked at himself as if surprised to be there, then at his audience. He stepped to the edge of her hand and stuck his tongue out at them.

The members of the feast roared with laughter, even Diverus. Here was Meersh as only she could realize him.

With a delighted smile she gazed at the king again, and the figure unraveled and shrank to a green flame.

"There you have what will pass, I think, for puppets. Let us begin the storytelling."

She traded a glance with Diverus and was about to ask them if they would equip him with musical instruments to accompany her, but some instinct prevented her from mentioning his gift. She gave him a smile of reassurance instead. Then she focused on the flames, and settled upon one of the stories she had been performing on Colemaigne. The flame that had been Meersh coiled and shaped into the form of a man wearing a tattered cap, a striped shirt, and loose trousers that fell just below his knees. She looked up at her strange audience and began.

≈ The Dream of a Fortune ≈

There once was a poor man who had no hope. His name is recorded as Loctrean, and he lived in an old, dilapidated house in the span of Guhnavra, which lay on a spiral far from here. He lived with his father and mother and sister.

His father was a dreamer, a teller of tales who was very popular at the local tavern because he always had a story and enough coin to buy his audience a round, and if they disbelieved his adventures, the free drink bought their complaisance.

The father claimed to have been a sailor on board the ship of the mythical Captain Sindebad, to have walked in exotic lands, seen impossible monsters, and sailed to the very edge of Shadowbridge and back. "Believe me," he would assure his audiences, "there is an edge of the world."

At home he told the same tales to his children, filling their heads with dazzling images, breathtaking adventures, and promises that one day they would all be terribly rich; but when he was off fishing, their mother would say, "The truth is, your father hasn't been anywhere at all. The only place *he's* sailed is inside his head." The children would have preferred not to know this, but they were children and at the mercy of the adults. Loctrean in particular wanted his father to be the adventurer of those wonderful stories.

His life might have gone on like that forever, except that one evening his father didn't return from the day's fishing, and no one knew at first what had befallen him. Eventually, other sailors found his father's boat and dragged it into the cracked and broken courtyard of the house. The keel had been shattered, a hole punched in it as if upon a sharp point of rock, and the sailors left it overturned there. Of his father they had found no sign. Loctrean overheard the superstitious sailors whispering that the gods had struck down his father for all the lies he'd told, and Loctrean burst upon them, shouting, "He didn't lie! He did travel far, he *did* have adventures!" But despite his defense, he was ashamed, though whether for himself or for his father, he didn't know.

It wasn't long after that before his mother succumbed to a wasting disease, a lingering, slow, and expensive disease. Paying for her medicine cost the family nearly everything they had. Before she died, she clutched her son close and whispered that she'd lied about his father because she was jealous. "He never took me on a single one of his adventures," she said, "even though I wanted to go. He hurt me, but he didn't lie to you." Now, she said, she was embarking on her own adventure at last. Then she closed her eyes and died.

In short order, then, he lost both of his parents and found himself suddenly an orphan with a sister to care for.

Loctrean inherited his father's house and the fishing boat, which is to say he inherited debt. The house fell into further disrepair. He couldn't afford so much as to replace the wine-colored awning over the door, which was too threadbare to keep even light rain from spilling through.

His father's boat remained in the courtyard. Its smashed planks grew so rotten that it would never be seaworthy again. He felt like that boat, as if a hole had been punched through him, never to be healed.

He could not repair the boat in order to fish, which was all he knew how to do, nor could he afford to buy a new one. There were a few fishing crews on the span but none of them would hire him as they believed he was the same as his father, a dreamer who would be a danger to the others who sailed with him. Even the kindest of them explained to him that they couldn't take a such a risk.

The only good news came when his sister married a neighboring grocer. The grocer made just enough money for the two of them and had nothing left over to help with the debts their father had left, but at least his sister was looked after, and Loctrean took solace in that.

He accepted that he was going to lose his father's house and there was nothing he could do about it. He determined that he must sell the property for whatever he could get, pay off all the debts, and use whatever was left over to start again somewhere else.

The night he made this decision, however, Loctrean's father appeared to him in a dream. "You must close up the house," said the vision, "but not sell it. Then travel to the span of Perla. There you will find your fortune."

"So it's true, you are dead," Loctrean said sadly.

"I drowned. It wasn't any fun."

"And how is Mother?" he asked.

"No longer in pain," his father's shade replied. "You were a good son to her. A good brother to your sister, too."

"Thank you," he said, and a longing to embrace the man welled up inside him. He wanted to reach out and hug his father, but in the dream he seemed unable to do anything but stand and observe.

"Never mind all that," his father admonished him. "Just wake up and go!" With that the dream ended, and Loctrean awoke.

Well, he thought, *I suppose it's no worse an idea than what I was going to do. I wish, though, I'd asked him to tell me one of his stories. That would have been nice.*

As instructed, Loctrean closed up the house, and with his remaining coins he set out for Perla.

Perla was an ancient town built upon a broad peninsula of land that jutted off the side of a span far removed from Guhnavra. It wasn't even on the shore; to get to it, a boat had to sail up a dark and forbidding river. Perla had a reputation as a dark place, surrounded by marshes and swamps, ghostly lights, and thieves who preyed upon the spans above. The air was tinged with the stink of sulfur long before the city came into view. Loctrean couldn't help but wonder why his father was sending him there of all places, or even how his father might have been familiar with it. Still, he could not imagine refusing to obey the wishes of his father's shade, and he booked passage on a ship that took him as far as the nearest spiral; there he had to sign on as a crew member to make the remainder of the journey. The captain of that ship worked him hard, too. He learned to tack and wear, to sound depths, and even to bake biscuits for the crew. There was no job aboard ship that he didn't learn before they had reached the mouth of the Black River.

The smell of the noxious city arrived long before they caught sight of it. Upon both sides of the river, strange lights danced in the mists. Some of the crew cowered at the sight of them, but Loctrean was unimpressed. He'd heard of far scarier things at his father's knee than bobbing lights in the fog. Besides, his father's ghost had told him to go to Perla, and so he remained confident that no harm would come to him on the journey. There was a reason he was here, and he must find it.

Once the boat arrived and tied up at the wharf, Loctrean took his leave.

Of course he didn't know what to do now that he had arrived. His father had not been specific at all about what to do once he got to Perla, only that he should go.

He walked the whole length of the city, and as anyone who's been there can attest, it's a long, narrow place, trapped between the swamps and woods on the one side and great hulking piers of the spiral on the other. Loctrean walked to the far outskirts of Perla without discovering anything. He was penniless and hungry, and had no idea what to look for or where to look for it.

A rain began to fall. First there was a drizzle, and then the skies opened up and a torrent poured down as if upon him alone.

An ancient, domed fane stood at the edge of the city there, on the last street before the city wall. Multiple rows of columns lined the front of the old temple, all of them gouged and pocked from centuries of bitter sulfurous rain. Loctrean hid beneath the roof that the columns supported, and while there he looked inside. The interior was dark and quiet and cool, filled with still more slender columns like a forest thick with trees. Small rugs were strewn everywhere. No rain dripped there. In fact, dust hung in the air. No one was praying or attending. He couldn't fathom to what deity the fane had been built in the first place—all icons and statues seemed to have been removed, or stolen—but it was dry and offered protection from the rain. He found a secluded alcove, curled up, and went to sleep. He hoped his father would show up again and tell him what to do.

Instead, while penniless Loctrean slept, a group of thieves crept into the fane. They had been coming there nightly for weeks. Each night they chiseled and loosened the mortar around a stone that, once removed, would give them access to a usurer's shop that abutted the old temple wall. The moneylender was a true fiend but known to be enormously wealthy. The thieves intended to kill him and rob him of his obscene fortune. The previous night they had succeeded in removing the large stone on which they'd been working for weeks, lifting it from the wall of the fane. Now they worked even more cautiously but urgently to remove the smaller bricks from the wall of the adjoining house. What they failed to take into account was the usurer's penchant for staying up late into the night to count his fortune. He had blacked all the windows where he kept the money so that no one could see inside. To the thieves it appeared that he'd retired for the night.

Thus the evil usurer, sitting in the very room they

intended to plunder, was alerted to their intrusion. He blew out his candle and waited.

At last, the thieves removed enough smaller bricks in his wall to allow one man to slide through. Triumphantly, their leader insisted he should have the first look, and he stuck his head into the hole, only to find a cackling madman awaiting him, brandishing a scimitar.

When his feet frantically kicked out, his friends hauled the thief back into the temple only to discover that his head had been lopped off. Even as they stared in horror, the alarm was sounded. The usurer had rushed into the street and bellowed for the police. The thieves dropped the corpse of their leader and fled.

Poor Loctrean awoke to their commotion. He stumbled from his alcove just as the authorities arrived.

"Here's one!" shouted a deputy, and the police fell upon him and beat him senseless. Of the gang they found only the headless body.

They dragged Loctrean to the jail and threw him inside. He lay battered and bleeding upon his cot that night, and thought, *This is not what I came here for.*

The following day he was hauled before the chief magistrate. Bloody and bruised, he could only insist that he knew nothing of any robbery beyond what they themselves knew. The usurer of course demanded his execution on the spot, but that only infuriated the magistrate and swayed him toward more leniency than he might otherwise have shown his suspect.

"Were I a thief," Loctrean put forth, "would I have *waited* to be captured, sir? Did you capture any others of this gang waiting in the dark? Any who still had their heads, I mean. Why would I have lingered?"

The magistrate sensed that he was hearing the truth. "What were you doing there, then?" he asked. "No one has worshipped in that temple for years."

So Loctrean explained his situation, his poverty, and how his father's ghost had appeared in a dream and advised him to seek his fortune here.

"You mean to say you sailed all the way from Guhnavra because of a dream? You're crazy, do you know that? Acting upon such things. Why, I myself was visited just the other night in my dreams by a woman who told me she knew of a house where a great treasure lay buried."

"Did you find the house?" asked Loctrean.

The magistrate sighed. "You haven't been paying attention, have you? The woman and her treasure aren't *real*. In the first place, such a house doesn't even exist in Perla. It looks nothing like houses here. It was a square-topped place, with an old purple-striped awning and a rotted boat in one corner of the courtyard and a dried-up, broken old fountain in another. Crumbling old place, the sort of thing one sees only in dreams. Furthermore, and even more ludicrous, she insisted that the hidden treasure had come from the legendary Captain Sindebad. Well, I mean, *really*. It's a fairy tale, isn't it? Something recalled from my childhood no doubt and brought back by some turnips or bad beer."

Excitedly, Loctrean asked, "This treasure, where was it hidden?"

"How should I know that? I woke up, didn't I? You have understood nothing I've said. This isn't . . . oh, never mind." The magistrate saw that the matter was hopeless. He had a simpleton here who could neither have robbed the usurer nor compre-hended that the world did not operate via magical dreams.

"Listen, the best thing you can do, fellow, is go home and stop attending to these fantasies. Learn a trade. Establish yourself." He took out a small purse and placed two coins on the table. "Here," he said, "because we beat you and I'm certain you're innocent. Naïve, gullible, but innocent. Go home, my friend."

Loctrean thanked the magistrate and limped stiffly out of the police barracks.

He used the coins to buy part of his passage home on the same ship that had brought him. As before it wasn't enough, but the crew were happy to have him because his cooking had proved better than anyone else's. All the same, they taunted him. "Didn't find that treasure after all?" they asked. "No magic beans, no djinn in a bottle floating in that foul river just waiting for you?" He hardly paid them any mind, because he was fearful that something might have happened to his house meanwhile. However, it awaited him as he had left it, save for a few more rodents as tenants in the growing holes of its walls. The awning had finally split in two and hung down in shreds.

Loctrean entered the house and began searching

everywhere. The woman in the magistrate's dream—surely it was his mother—had said that the treasure was buried, and he pulled up every stone in every room only to find dirt or sand or mice beneath. Exhausted, he went out and collapsed in the courtyard against the boat.

From there he found himself staring directly at the fountain pedestal. Hadn't the magistrate made mention of the fountain?

He got up, and even as he did, the stones beneath the fountain cracked, and it tilted slowly to one side.

Loctrean climbed over the retaining wall and into the dustbowl that had once been a shallow pond. He grabbed the canted pedestal and began wrenching it back and forth until it came away completely.

Pushing it aside, he stared into a dry hole where, presumably, water had once upon a time been channeled. He knelt and then lay amid the rubble and reached his arm down into the hole. His fingers touched the sides of a cloth bag. He caught hold of it and dragged it up onto the stones. It was heavy and thick, the neck tied with a cord. The outer layer of cloth had frayed, but there were at least two more layers beneath that one. He heard the coins before he saw them. When they spilled out, they were so big that he couldn't circle his fingers around them. They had strange writing on them, and faces of some other span's gods or emperors stamped onto one side. Loctrean had never seen any coins like them. One bag, he thought, must be worth a fortune. He lay on the tiles again and reached into the hole, and his fingers touched a second bag. He drew it out, and this one contained gems: rubies and sapphires, diamonds and emeralds. It was a fortune for a king.

Kneeling there in the dust he praised his father for telling the truth, even though no one had ever believed him. He *had* sailed with the mythical Sindebad. Here was the proof.

That night Loctrean had another dream. In it his father apologized for not telling him about the fortune years earlier. "I kept it hidden," he said, "because I wanted you and your sister to grow up unspoiled by riches, to know what it was like to have to work, to earn your way, the way almost everyone must. I wasn't supposed to have an accident."

After that, Loctrean saw both his parents from time to time in his dreams. His mother would tell him some incredible tale of the afterlife—how grapes grew as big as her head or animals talked—and his father would explain, "She's lying. It's nothing like that at all here, let me tell you."

Loctrean paid off his debts. He had the house refurbished from top to bottom, and hung a bright new awning over the door. He bought a fleet of fishing boats, but left his father's decrepit craft in a corner of the yard as a shrine. He showered his sister and her husband with gifts and ensured that they would never want for anything.

Eventually he sailed back to Perla on the very same ship, which he now owned. He cooked for the crew because by now he liked doing that. In Perla he gave the dismayed magistrate a generous sum in thanks for showing him compassion, adding, "Had I not listened to you, I wouldn't have found my fortune."

When finally he married, he doted on his wife, keeping her and their children happy every day—mostly by telling them fantastic stories of the glorious adventures of their grandfather, who had sailed to the ends of the world and faced every peril imaginable. And if the children didn't believe him . . . well, it hardly mattered, after all.

Leodora sat back and the shapes of the flames on her palms unwound from the figures of a family and back into dancing green fire once more.

Diverus watched the gathered feasters press fingertips together in front of them and hum as they bowed to her, their faces lit with delight, their red eyes glowing with rapturous wonder.

The king of Epama Epam said, "Ah, that was quite . . . exquisite." He waved one hand over hers, and the flames evaporated. "Your reputation is well earned, storyteller."

"Thank you," she said. "And your puppets are the most unusual I've ever seen."

"Yes, but what else would you expect from the world that threads all worlds?"

She laughed at that, then tilted back her head as she stretch-ed. Overhead, the ocean sky had grown darker and the sparkling upon its surface turned to stars. "We've missed our perform-ance," she said, mostly to herself, so that Diverus barely heard it. Her brow knitted as if puzzled by the indifference with which she acknowledged this.

"Surely you can afford one or two," said the king.

"You don't know Soter," Diverus replied. He hid his concern, stretching as if he had just awakened.

"Perhaps not, but now as you say you've missed the performance, you might as well settle in and enjoy our company. The night in Epama is nascent, and there are too many stories you still want to hear. That I know for certain."

She nodded in a dreamy way. "You *do* owe me some in return." To Diverus she added, "We can't very well leave without the stories, can we? If we've sacrificed a performance, we deserve our reward."

"There, it's settled then." The king grinned. He called for wine.

Diverus scanned the faces about them, all of the sharp features crinkled with friendship, smiles split wide to display teeth as white a clouds on a clear day. Nowhere was there a member of the court not expressing unbridled joy or radiating pleasure. It enticed, caressed, soothed, and he could not help immersing in it as in the pool where he'd swum. Yet beneath the camaraderie lay something undisclosed, something he was sure he would recognize were he only able to clear his head and distance himself from them enough to deliberate. It was a disquiet he could not even express to Leodora. Something essential was being stifled.

She, like a cat, stretched out before the fire, her eyelids heavy, her smile soft and smug. She took the tall-stemmed glass of wine when it was handed to her, sipped, and then said, "Tell me stories, then. Lots and lots of stories."

"Aeternalis," promised the king. The alien word reverberated through the columns; and despite being on his guard, Diverus sank back and gave himself up to their stories.

"She's dead," Soter bemoaned. He clutched his head in both hands. His ring of hair stood up in tufts and swirls, making him look mad. He sat on a wide settee painted so as to seem feathered, a prop he'd dragged from one of the Terrestre's storage rooms to a spot beside the puppet booth. "It's from a play," Orinda had told him, "about a young queen who is sent to her doom by a jealous adviser."

"I would prefer to find no irony in that," he'd replied.

Beside the settee stood two small blue faience amphorae, most of their former contents now residing inside Soter.

"Everything I did to protect her . . . all for naught. Lost."

Orinda sat facing him. In the light from the lamps at the front of the stage she appeared both regal and grave in her long robe and gold sandals. She had been forced to cancel that night's performance because of his unraveling. She didn't begrudge him the crumbling of his will. He was right to worry.

In the week since Leodora's disappearance, the audiences had fallen off appreciably, and she suspected that word had spread that the great Jax had vanished and left her troupe to cover for her. A night or two without a performance would not harm anything—the citizenry was too desperate for stories now—but if it continued much longer than that, who knew what would happen, or if the theatre could open again.

"What about the street performer?" she asked. "Surely that was a clue."

"The stilt-walker?" He pushed his hands over the top of his head, his chin almost against his breastbone, and looked at her through his brows. One of Hamen's people had stumbled upon the stilt-walker at a street fair two days earlier. "She claims only that she spoke to the two of them, but that when she went out to tell everyone in the street that the famous Jax was among them, Leodora didn't follow her. She went back into that tunnel."

"The one to Sacbé."

"And they just disappeared there. Never came out."

"But surely that means they're *on* Sacbé."

"So one would surmise, yet nobody there that Hamen's folk spoke to ever saw her or Diverus emerge at the other end." His eyes closed. "No one. Whatever happened to her, I tell you it hap-pened in that tunnel. In darkness. Has to have." He grabbed for his cup of wine. "Gods, I am *cursed*!" Then he slumped sideways on the divan.

"That's not so, Soter."

He came alert angrily. "It isn't? The gods paired me with Bardsham, didn't they? I was doing all right on my own. I could spot a mark half a span away, size him up before he set eyes on me. I could tell how much his purse would have and reel him right in. Practically had to stop him from handing it to me, every coin."

"You were a thief?"

"Thief? I was an artist. I could convince princes to offer me the jewels right out of their crowns."

"How?"

"By promising them more. *Always* more." He drained the cup. "Everybody always wants more." He lifted the nearest blue amphora and tipped it. When nothing came out, he grabbed the one beside it, which also proved to be empty. He glowered sullenly a moment, but then pointed at them and gave a mad laugh. "You see? My point exactly, isn't it?"

Bois was standing across the stage. Orinda gestured toward the empty jars, and he nodded and scurried off.

Soter watched it all, his head tilted.

"So, you were doing well when Bardsham found you," Orinda prompted.

"Oh, *better* than well." He broke off speaking, his brow furrowed. When he focused on her again, it was with a suspicious look. "I'm wondering, as you've never said, there's something I'm curious about."

"What would that be?"

"Why is it that, if everyone else who crossed the bastard Chaos's path was turned to stone, your two actors were only turned to wood and got to keep their lives?"

The question seemed to catch her entirely off guard, and a look of fear crossed her face before she regained her composure, forming a brittle smile as she tried to laugh away the question. "Why," she said, "distance, I'm sure. Some fluke, some accident of his attentiveness."

"Oh, no, I don't think that's likely, now, is it?" He sat up, suddenly quite sober in his actions and his gaze. "Distance had nothing to do with it. People under the span were turned, too. Leodora saw them. There aren't any others like your two anywhere hereabouts, are there? Tell me, do *they* wonder how it is they survived, Orinda?"

"What is wrong with you, Soter?"

"I'm cursed by the gods, just as I said. Here I was thinking from the moment you took us in that you and I might share a bed one night, that we two might find one another's company . . . amicable. But my dearest Orinda, there's a nagging question no one has ever answered."

She cleared her throat. "What's that?" she asked, her voice barely louder than a whisper.

"Who told Tophet the Destroyer where we had gone? The Agents did come after us, to Remorva and then straight on to Emeldora. I wonder, as I always have, who set them after us in the first place? A lot of spans out there, a lot of spirals unfolding across the sea. Scattered islands, too. We were lying low, and then hardly showing ourselves. But they reached Emeldora not four nights after we did. No happenstance that."

"It must be," she offered, "that they asked along the piers, asked the boatmen, who would have identified a group such as yours."

"Boatmen along the pier would have had no cause to lie to them. But the Agents *never* came looking after Bardsham's little girl. Didn't know she existed. Wharf rats would have given her up, no reason not to. If they'd been asked. If there'd been a *need* to ask them. Someone who cared about the girl, though, might not have mentioned her, even to save two members of her own troupe."

"Soter—"

He held up his hand to silence her. He was wincing, as if pained. When he opened his eyes again, he didn't look at her but off in the distance at some memory. He displayed his hand with its missing fingertips. "He could be very persuasive."

Orinda glanced away from him. She said, "The Agents were going to kill them. Both of them."

"I've no doubt of it," Soter replied. "The wonder is, really, that once you'd told them what they wanted, Tophet didn't kill 'em anyway." A crash followed upon his words, from the rear of the theatre. Bois stood there, his expression an admixture of horror and outrage. The faience amphora he'd been carrying lay shattered on the floor, broken blue glass and wine like pooling blood. He turned on his heel and vanished into the wings.

Orinda cried, "No, wait, Bois!" as she climbed to her feet. She gave Soter one final helpless glance before hurrying after the wooden man.

Soter sank into a heap on the settee. There was no triumph in the learning of Orinda's complicity. His own overshadowed it completely.

"Cursed," he repeated. "As if it matters anymore."

Late into the night the storytelling unfolded. For every story Leodora told, she heard a dozen new ones from the people of Epama Epam. She learned of the Green Snake's terrible revenge, of the Milkbird that fed the starving, of the Armless Maiden and her hands of silver, of so many more stories that

Diverus lost count and the details bled together. Each one seemed to carry her farther away from the desire to leave this wonderful place. In return she told them the story of the Fatal Bride and then how Meersh had lost his toes. As with human audiences, these people championed Penis at the end of it, while the flames danced merrily across her palms. Eventually she admitted that she was surfeited with stories and one more would make her explode. Be-sides she was exhausted, and she begged them let her rest awhile.

The king commented that they had not yet determined what story she needed to hear, and that it was possible they might have to give her every story they knew in order to find it. It could take a long, long time.

Without hesitation, Leodora answered, "Then I'll stay here until the discovery is made."

This shocked Diverus. It was impossible she could feel that way.

The king took Leodora by the hand and led her and Diverus back into the forest of columns, turning to the side in the midst of them, emerging in front of a row of cerulean curtains. He parted the curtain directly before them. Behind it was a small chamber, the floor of it a thickly padded mat covered in blankets and pillows. A brazier to the side burned with a sweet, intoxicating incense.

"Here," said the king, "you and your consort may retire at *any* time."

"I'm not her consort," protested Diverus.

"As you say," the king agreed, though his tone suggested anything but agreement.

"Why do you think I'm her consort?"

Leodora tugged at his arm. "Diverus," she entreated.

"You must remember, I've seen your true self, revealed by the waters of our pool. You could not take your eyes from her. She was everything in your sight, she was your world, your intoxication. You displayed love of the greatest depth. Whether you wish to acknowledge it or not is of no consequence to me, but it ought to be of appreciable interest to you."

"Your pool was a trick, a magic."

"A magic that plucked upon your heartstrings. Not all tricks are necessarily lies."

Leodora curled up on the bed and pulled a pillow to her belly. "Diverus can pluck the heartstrings, too," she mumbled.

"Certainly yours," the king said. "Now rest awhile, and we'll continue."

Leodora only murmured, but Diverus met the king's genial red gaze defiantly. "What has to be done to learn the reason why we were directed here?"

"I assure you, it's a story you need, but I cannot tell you which one."

"Cannot or will not?"

The king smiled tolerantly. "Perhaps, when she awakes," he said, "we can take steps to identify it. I know, young man, that you think me scheming against you both. Please don't deny it. I knew it when first I met you, and the episode of the pool supports your suspicions. I cannot deny what took place. We have our scripts to live by as you have yours. Ours is a retreat from the world, and we must by nature try to draw visitors in. We thrive upon them. Had you both welcomed the nepenthe offered by our waters, we would not now be speaking thus, and you would be contented, happy, and at peace forever."

"But at the cost of our will?"

"Which you would not have missed." The king smiled. "Sleep now. You can doubt me more ably once you've rested." He stepped back and let the curtain fall.

Leodora was already soundly asleep. Diverus knelt, then lay down at her side. The brass pendant was draped across the pillow she clutched. He stared at it, wondering what it might tell him, and whether it would respond to questions that he wanted answered.

He sighed. Without awaking, Leodora reached over and put her arm over him. In her embrace, Diverus lay beside her but could not fall asleep. Her touch galvanized him. He stared instead at the pendant and resisted the desire to clutch her to him, sleep, and wake in the darkness of early morning, to make love. It was what her "consort" would do.

Had she entered the pool with him, even now he would be living out that desire, but it would all be a lie, and he didn't want her if it was a lie. It seemed to be the nature of this place—this Pons Asinorum or Epama Epam or whatever they called it—that every truth encompassed an untruth. Misdirection defined their nature, and what should he have expected of a world where the sea became the sky, flowing forever overhead? He needed one reliable answer—to know the nature of the cached lie under-pinning all that had been explained. It would not come from the king or his people. They would act according to their script, just as the king had intimated—which Diverus took as another truth cloaking another lie. Leodora had fallen under the spell of stories and would petition to remain until the essential story had been told, assuming there was one. How long might they keep her here, promising to find the essential tale, trying another and another like sweets offered from a tray, each sapping her will a little more, until everything of her former life was forgotten and remaining here was all she would ever want? He knew this because what he had felt in the pool was not only to bind to her but to live here with her everlastingly, and while that spell no longer bound him, its memory served as sufficient tocsin. Having been under their sorcery and then released seemed to provide him a kind of immunity, although that might be only temporary. He might go to sleep now and wake up as dazzled as she. He wished desperately to leave before that happened; but she would not go with him, and if he left her behind he would surely never see her again. She would never go.

She rolled onto her back, and the pendant slithered up the pillow, coming level with his eyes. As it did, its own golden eyes opened and contemplated him. He realized that Leodora could not have roused it.

He sat up. "Will you answer me?" he whispered.

"Naturally," it told him. "So long as you are in her dreams." Then it became inanimate again.

With great care, he knelt and worked the necklace and the Brazen Head over her face and up above her hair, but he needed to lift her head to release it altogether.

Slowly, he slipped his fingers into the tangled fall of her hair, edging them beneath the back of her head. Ever so slightly, he raised her head up. She murmured his name, and both of her arms circled his neck. At the moment he drew the pendant free of her hair, her lips met his. She kissed him deeply. He tasted the wine on her breath and the tip of her tongue. She let go of him and sank back. Her eyes had opened a little, and now rolled up as her eyelids closed. She moaned softly, body shifting, and then lay still, her arms and legs pushed apart as if open to him. He ached to continue, to follow her desire—if only he could trust that it was hers. Instead, he made himself roll away, with his back to her, and then lay still, the Brazen Head clutched in one hand. He waited while her breathing settled, softened, became slow and regular. Then he rose and crept out beneath the blue curtain. He peered in each direction. There was no one to be seen anywhere among the columns. He scurried across the cold stone floor and ducked behind the nearest pillar.

The liquid sky above was still dark and shot with stars. Firelight flickered from the distant feast and from torches beside the still pool of nepenthe.

Diverus stole from column to column until he had reached the far side, near the tiny door where they had entered. No one was about there, either. He crouched against a column in the last row and held up the pendant so that the brass head dangled before him.

"All right," he said. "Tell me."

The eyes opened. "Your deepest desire is to know if she loves you."

"I would hear of that, yes, but not now. Not—"

"I couldn't tell it to you anyway," the head interjected.

That brought him up short. "What do you mean?"

"She loves stories. All else must needs occupy a second place."

"I don't care," he answered, and for that moment he believed it. "I want to know how to get her away from here. I want to know what this place is about and how to find out why we came."

"Time," it replied. "Time is no more."

"I don't understand you. How is time no more? Here? Everywhere?"

"Here *is* everywhere. Your eyes play you as false here as does your heart. The rising and setting of suns and moons is illusory. You cannot trust what you know. What you sense. What you want."

"I realize that," he answered impatiently. "Why do you think I'm holding you? Why do you think we're talking?"

The lion's muzzle flexed as if perturbed, as if it might shut its eyes again.

"*Please,*" he implored. "What's being withheld? How do we get away from here?"

"She needs one story for the final battle to come, but be assured they will not serve it up to you."

"And how long until this battle?"

"Forever, if you remain here. This world is its own spell, enchantment concretized. They don't lie as you think of it, they merely act from the quintessence of that artifice."

He thought about that, about the pool, about her. It seemed a fine distinction that carried the same result. "If we're safe from the battle here, then why shouldn't we stay?"

"However long she remains, it won't matter. Her enemy will devour steadily everything else, encroaching span by span, until all but this interstitial world is lost, and no one who leaves it will return. Then you become prisoners of nonexistence."

"How do *we* leave here, then?" he asked. "How do I convince her to go?"

The lion gave him a look as if it thought him imperceptive. "You seek escape from the wrong source, from inside the spell. Use your own formidable powers, Orfeo, if you want to rewrite the script." Then it closed its eyes and was silent.

The name it had spoken shook him to the bone. He slid from his crouch and as he sat, the chain of the necklace slipped through his fingers and the pendant clattered to the stones, and with it the second object, which he'd taken off her accidentally, the two cords intertwined. It lay in his lap but he was oblivious.

In all the time that had passed, he'd not heard that name—not since before she had been wrapped in her winding sheet and cast into the water, a corpse that had taken his identity with her, snatching away the self she had gifted him with but that he could not hold on to.

His true name had returned.

A tickle about her neck woke Leodora, fingers in her hair. She opened her eyes and Diverus's bottomless black ones were right beside her, watching as if he could not see enough of her, as if even as she slept he had watched; and she was reminded of a time she had done the same beside him.

She could not be certain what it meant, his closeness. Was it in the aftermath of some welcomed intimacy? But no, she still wore the purple robe from the feast.

The feast.

Her mind tumbled with a riot of images drawn from all the stories she'd heard last night: the clever Green Snake swallowing its larger adversary, the boar, with jaws that hinged impossibly wide; the melancholy maiden who sacrificed her hands to save her father and nearly lost her whole body as well; the girl whose feet were snagged by a seemingly innocuous loaf of bread that dragged her down into an infernal underworld; the king who turned all that he loved into cold metal; the conniving girl who drowned her elder sister to gain her sister's privilege only to have the sister's ghost return and denounce her through the strings of a harp. These and more clamored for her attention, too many to contemplate but still not enough, never enough. Stories filled her and she hungered for more. Here they had them all.

"Are we starting again?" she asked.

"Yes," he replied.

As she sat up, his fingers threaded through her hair, and her pendant slid into the front of her robe; its chain caught around the back of her neck. His hand withdrew.

"I'm going to perform with you this time," he said. "Accompany you. I want to."

"It's my turn to tell them another then?"

"Your turn," he agreed. Then after hesitating as though making up his mind, he added, "We'll miss another day's performances if we linger." His eyes, almost sly, watched her.

"It's only another day." She would have missed a week, a month, if it meant more stories from these dark creatures.

He nodded slowly, as if she had confirmed something for him. "You'll tell them to let me play this time, yes?" he requested.

"If you wish." She rose and stepped over him, out the curtain and toward her passion.

Fire still burned in the feast pit beyond the columns and she started toward them without thought, drawn by what they promised. She looked at her palms, already imagining the flames dancing there, taking shape. They would want a story. Which one should she tell them? One they hadn't told her. Turning back, she asked which he thought would be the best.

"Tell them of how the zmeu stole the sun and moon."

"Isn't that one they told me?"

"It won't matter," he promised, and she tried to understand that.

When she reached the fire, it was as if the feast had never stopped. All the people were still there. The king rose to greet her, and her attendants scampered out from behind the columns to assist her as if she were old and frail and had forgotten her way. Diverus, in his green robe, shrugged off the hands of his attendants and sat next to her. He stared at her solemnly until she remembered his request and to the king said, "He's going to accompany me for the next story."

The king arched one brow. "Oh. You have another one to tell us?"

"Yes."

"How does he accompany you?"

"On musical instruments."

The king leaned around her. The coils of his hair were sharp as knives. "He seems to have arrived without them," he said, and the feasters laughed.

"I'd hoped you would be able to provide me with something appropriate," Diverus responded. "You seem to be a musical people."

The feasters laughed again, and the king nodded. "You've read us well enough, young consort. What would you play upon?"

"Oh, a harp would be nice. Anything else you might have. I'm very partial to the shawm as well."

"Multitalented, are you?" He gestured to the attendants to go retrieve what Diverus had asked for. "This should make for a very interesting telling then. Tell me, what story will you play out?" he asked Leodora.

"It's—"

"We can't reveal that," Diverus interjected. "It's more effective if it's a surprise."

She caught something in his voice, but she couldn't say what it was—some lilt she felt she ought to have known, which she might have identified if her head weren't spinning with stories. She lifted a goblet of wine and sipped while she waited for the next thing to happen.

The attendants returned with a small four-stringed harp and a lacquered shawm. The king turned from the fire with flames upon his palms again.

Diverus tucked the shawm in his belt and picked up the harp. She paused to watch him, recalling how remarkable his music was. It seemed to be an ancient memory.

He brushed one hand across the strings. His eyes closed and he began to pluck a dancing tune, a reel. It began slowly, softly, but his fingers moved faster and faster. The nearest feasters leapt to their feet and began to dance. They wore expressions of surprise, as if the desire to dance belonged to their feet, which hadn't told their brain. They pranced and stepped, skipped and swung about, spinning in time with a music that seemed to have taken possession of them. The king, although he restrained himself from joining them, couldn't keep from performing a small jig in place. Like his citizens, he seemed amazed, and his red eyes narrowed as he stared at Diverus, as if he had begun to identify what was happening. Leodora wondered when her story was supposed to start.

Then all at once Diverus lifted his hands from the harp. The dancers swayed, stumbled. A few of them collapsed. Those farther away were laughing, thinking the whole thing a delightful jape.

Diverus inhaled deeply. His eyes opened. He looked at her and smiled as he set down the harp, picked up the shawm. Pressing the reed to his lips, he stared sharply at the king.

The song that emerged from the shawm was the very essence of grief. More painful than anything she had ever heard him play in the paidika where he had caused patrons to burst spontaneously into tears, it personified loss and longing, the threnody of an empty soul.

This time even the king collapsed beneath its weight. The flames on his hands hissed and turned to smoke. She looked around in wonder as people dropped to their knees and began to wail, to clutch at their bosoms, to claw at the stones.

Then at the highest note, Diverus broke off playing again. He drew the reed from between his lips, and surveyed them.

"Diverus, what are you doing?" she asked.

"I'm bidding them good-bye" was his reply. "Aren't I?" he asked the king.

The king pressed a hand to his breastbone, reached the other, trembling, toward them. "I—I—" he tried to say.

"Release her from the spell of this world of yours, or I'll play all of this tune and no one of you will survive it."

The king shook his head and Diverus put the reed to his mouth again. He raised the shawm like a weapon, taking aim. He played one simple verse and one of the four-armed attendants who'd pushed him into the pool fell dead beside the king, tumbling into the fire.

Diverus lowered the shawm. He stared at the king with dis-gust. "I know it's your world that enchants, not you. You merely act your parts, as you said, expressions of the enchantment. But you *can* shield the spell, as you did for me. You have that power, don't you." When the king said nothing, he threateningly lifted the shawm again.

"Wait!" cried the king.

Diverus waited.

"You have only to depart and it will pass, she'll come to herself again. We mean no harm, we only worship her skill. She is as a goddess to us."

"And to me, as well," Diverus said. He kept the shawm as he reached out and took her hand. "Come with me," he said.

The king called, "Tell me, please, who you are."

Diverus glanced over his shoulder. "My mother named me Orfeo," he replied.

The king's molten eyes enlarged with recognition. "We know this name," he said to the others, "don't we?" The citizens traded looks, uncertain.

"Perhaps one day you'll enlighten me," replied Diverus. "Meanwhile, allow me to play for you."

The king bowed his head and stepped aside.

Leodora witnessed all of this as if watching a play in some strange language, understanding and yet unmoved, untouched by the events and portrayals. She let him lead her from the feast, into the grove of columns and to the heart of them where it was always dark. He let go of her hand and took the goblet from her other. He poured its contents on the stones and smashed the goblet. "Here," he said, and handed her the shawm.

From around his neck he removed a cord, on its end a small phial. She tilted her head. The green-and-black phial seemed familiar. Reflexively, she touched the chain of her pendant.

He tipped it and a drop fell from it into the wine covering the floor. After capping it again, he reached toward her with it. "I'm sorry, I took this while you slept."

She lowered her head as he slipped the cord over it, although uncertain why he was apologizing to her. At her feet, the wine rippled and seemed to reflect a different place.

"Come," he said, and held his hand to her as he stepped into the liquid. She reached out but handed him the shawm. When he tugged, she let go and he fell into the wine as if into a hole.

"Diverus?" she called, and leaned over the dark pool. "Diverus." It was dark below. As dark as a prison cell. She remembered Brodamante saying that from Palipon this world would look different. As she stepped into the pool of darkness, she wondered how.

Stumbling, she came up immediately against a wall of rough stone.

When she turned around, a creature with huge dark eyes, a long snout, and a woman's body clothed in rags was crouched in the corner opposite, watching her. A wig made of skinny black beads hung off her head, around her prominent ears.

The creature rose. She tried to speak, showing small sharp incisors and larger teeth at the sides of her mouth, top and bottom. Her words were strange, raspy, a language full of clicks and odd breaths. Leodora understood none of it. But when the creature stepped forward, her ankle rattled, and Leodora realized that she was wearing metal cuffs and a chain.

Behind her, a small barred window revealed a row of flat-roofed buildings with trellised windows some distance away and bluish with twilight. This wasn't where she'd intended to come at all. The woman said something urgent.

Leodora turned to leave, but no passage remained behind her. Instead she faced another stone wall, a dirt floor, and a small, thick door banded with metal. She was locked in a cell in a place she'd never been before, and Diverus wasn't there.

Part 4: Lord Tophet's Bane

Chapter 7
Reflections

Diverus stood beside the broad wooden table on which they ate their meals at the Terrestre. The empty room lay dark save for one dim candle amid the debris of dirty cutlery, plates, and cups strewn across the table. It looked as if no one had cleaned up in days. He couldn't recall it having looked nearly so squalid the day before. No light came through the windows, which told him that it was night here. He said, "Leodora," and turned around, expecting to find her there. She should have been right behind him, but he was alone.

He realized there was a background din as of a large shouting crowd, and within it he made out cries of "Jax!" She must have manifested on the stage instead of here with him. Hastily he threaded his way through the wings, past ropes, past bags full of sand, dangling screens, and props of all sorts. The crowd's impatience was palpable—they weren't cheering her, they were demanding she present herself or start the show. From the shadows behind the curtains he peered past the rear of the puppet booth at a theatre half filled with noisy, drunken miscreants. The various broken vegetables lying on the stage testified to their unruliness. By contrast, in one of the private boxes above the rabble, four faces watched the mêlée, unflustered by the clamor of the crowd, looking as if they could have waited forever for the show to begin. It was like watching four corpses propped up in chairs.

In the shadows of the wings opposite, movement caught Diverus's eye. Someone was working his way behind the backdrop, around the back of the stage; a moment later Glaise appeared with his arms outstretched. He crushed Diverus to him.

"Yes, Glaise, I'm glad to see you, too," Diverus said. "Have you seen Leodora? Where's Soter?"

Glaise pointed enthusiastically at the booth, and Diverus plunged forward, but fumbled with the drapery at the rear corner until he found a slit and stepped through. "Lea," he cried, but she wasn't there, either. He thought he was alone, but then saw that Soter crouched on the floor beside the trestles supporting the undaya cases.

"Diverus!" Soter shouted. As fast as he could, the old man scrambled to his feet and embraced him. "Oh, lad, where have you been? The two of you had us convinced you were dead for sure. We looked everywhere, even turned out Hamen and those people from the underspan, but nobody could *find* you." His expression tightened. "Where is she? We can't let her perform tonight. We've got to get her away from here immediately. You don't know what you've blundered into, coming back now."

Overwhelmed and confused, Diverus answered, "I thought she was in here. I mean, I hoped. The calls for Jax—I thought . . ." Agitatedly casting about the tiny chamber, he said, "I don't know where she is."

"Well, we have to stop her from taking the stage, you understand?"

"No, I don't. Find her *and* hide her?"

Soter put his hands over his face. "Oh, gods, this was inevitable, wasn't it? The moment we climbed those steps from Bouyan and set foot on Ningle I knew, I knew it must come to this." He turned to the front of the booth and cautiously parted the screen to peer out. Audience members called again for Jax.

Behind Diverus two wooden hands pulled open the cloth of the booth, and Orinda stepped in past them. Glaise ducked in after her.

"Diverus, oh, my dear," she said, and hugged him. "Where have you been? Where's Leodora?"

"Oh, gods," Soter murmured at whatever he saw.

"Why is everyone so giddy?" asked Diverus. "I'm sorry about missing the performance, but we found a way to reach the Pons Asinorum and once there Leodora wanted to hear all the stories she could, and they enchanted her, and me, but we got away. At least I thought we did. We didn't mean to miss the performance, but they were going to keep us there forever." They stared at him dumbly and finally he said, "What is it? You all act as if you thought you'd never see me again."

Glaise stood with a hand raised to his mouth. Orinda answered finally, "You've been gone for weeks, both of you."

He blinked. "It was only the one night. A night and part of a day."

She shook her head. "Not *here*, it wasn't." Placing a hand on his shoulder, she added, "We sought you for *weeks*, Diverus, even onto adjoining spans. Bois is still gone looking, and Hamen and his people."

Without turning, Soter said, "He doesn't understand that they've found us, Orinda. If she comes back now . . ."

"Where is she, Diverus?"

"I don't know. She was right behind me," he said.

"She's not here?" asked Soter.

"I fear she isn't. Maybe I can find the stilt-walker again, get another phial to open the dark waters—"

"No, no, that's *good*, don't you see?" Soter said. "She's in the world of the Pons Asinorum. They can't track her there. They'll never find her."

"I should go after her."

"That's for later, later you'll get her, once we're away," Soter proclaimed. He was scheming then, his eyes sharp but looking askance, as if calculating the details. "At the moment we have a final performance to give. We'll trip them up."

"But, Soter—" Orinda objected.

"The situation's changed, Orinda. With him here we can have a performance. He has the power to quiet them all. Don't you? You can put them all to sleep if we want. Merge their dreams with the stories. Right?" When Diverus didn't answer, Soter grabbed him by the shoulders. "You would do anything for her, wouldn't you?"

"Soter—"

"Yes, I would," Diverus answered with no hesitation.

"You love her." Diverus hesitated to respond and Soter shook his head. "It's all right. We both do, don't we? That's the thing that draws us and the thing that's divided you and me. Divided me inside myself." To Orinda, he said, "You're going to get away. You take Glaise, and Bois if you can find him, and get far away from here. We'll perform, we'll keep them riveted. They won't even notice your departure, and after, if he can lull them to sleep, we'll slip out and come after you, too."

"But Leodora—" Diverus began.

"You don't want her to be here right now," Soter said. "She's better off where she is, and you can go fetch her once we've escaped."

"Soter, you can't!" Orinda insisted.

"Can't I? We've been here before, Orinda. Or rather, you have. Glaise has. What do you suppose those creatures will do to him this time to get you to tell them what they want to know? If we were to flee and leave you here, you would pay the price again. Worse even than before."

She looked from him to Diverus with a sickened expression. "You're insane, Soter."

"Probably." He grinned and it made him look the part. "Now, you have to do one last thing. You have to introduce us. Introduce us like there's nothing wrong at all, and then take Glaise and go and hide. Go down below with Hamen's folk. Hide out until they've gone or *we* come find you."

She held her ground another moment, but finally acquiesced, pushing Glaise to turn him about and following him out the back of the booth.

Soter handed Diverus the mijwiz. "You like playing this double-pipe thing, don't you?"

"I am partial to it."

"Good. Good. Because tonight you're playing for your life. All our lives."

The principal problem was, the cell was utterly dry. The rough dirt floor had seen no water in a very long time. Near the prisoner, straw had been strewn about, not much of it but enough to absorb any and all moisture. Nowhere was there a container, a cup, even a slop bucket. The chain attached to her ankles allowed the prisoner to cross past the window as far as the opposite corner to relieve herself, and the noisome stink of the straw told Leodora that it hadn't been changed in a long time. The small window prohibited the flow of enough air to overcome the smell.

"I need water," Leodora explained.

The prisoner tried to communicate with her, babbling excitedly and incoherently for so long that Leodora thought the confinement had driven her insane. She had no experience of a place where the world didn't transmute naturally and the language become comprehensible. Finally, the long-snouted woman seemed to realize that nothing she said was making any difference, and she stopped. She tilted her head and stared at Leodora as if seeing her for the first time; this caused the black beads of her wig to clack and chitter. She gave her head a small toss and the beads shook again. She had human eyes beneath her prominent animal brows but the shape of the face was more like that of the kitsune, except for a surface of iridescent scales shaped like those of the Ondiont snake. In the silence, Leodora pointed to herself and said, "Leodora," then repeated it.

The prisoner placed her fingers on her chest and said, "Yemoja a Iunu." Her snout twitched. She seemed to be trying to smile.

"All right," Leodora replied. "Yemoja?" Then she pointed to the room, the door, out the small window. "Where?" she asked. "Where is this?"

The creature nodded in understanding. "Palipon," she growled.

"Oh." Leodora sank down then. Palipon: the prison isle. Its name, it seemed, transcended language barriers. It was the place where Gousier had sent the woman who'd tried to kidnap her when she was small. Nobody banished to Palipon was ever seen again. Nobody ever came back. Legend made it the original home of Death before Chilingana had called him forth by dreaming the spans. Whether or not that was true, she wasn't about to be trapped here.

Standing again, she went to the window. The light was fading fast, though she could still make out the flat-roofed buildings. They stood on a rise on the far side of a deep gorge. The drop from here to the bottom of the gorge appeared to be sheer—at least, with her face pressed against the bars she could see no obstruction below the window. She couldn't see them, but imagined there must be hundreds of windows like this one overlooking the dry, craggy drop. She stepped back with a sigh.

Yemoja spoke to her again, a series of growls and clicks. Leodora could only shake her head in incomprehension. She said, "The least I can do is try to get you unchained before the light's gone." She took a step toward her and Yemoja backed against the wall. "It's all right," Leodora said cautiously. She raised her hands to show them empty, then knelt. She had to press her lips tight and hold her breath to get close. Yemoja's whole body was begrimed, but her slender ankles were worse. The cuffs around them looked to have rubbed them raw, leaving them blackened, maybe putrid. Leodora's eyes began to tear up and she wiped at them with the back of her hands, then clutched at the cuff all but blindly. The cuff was hinged, the lock a small box exhibiting an odd cross-shaped keyhole. She grabbed hold of it and tried to pull the halves of the cuff apart, but finally sighed and gave up. There would be no removing it without a key.

She withdrew then to the window and breathed the night air until her eyes stopped stinging. She shook her head in exasperation, then withdrew again to the corner beside the door. There was nothing to do now. She needed both darkness *and* a pool of standing liquid. The darkness was here but she wasn't going to get the other until someone brought Yemoja something to drink, and she surmised that nobody would be coming tonight. Whatever meals were served, they had been consumed well before this.

"I need to get out of here," she said. A solution occurred to her then. She stood up and began pounding her fists against the door. "Obviously," she explained as though Yemoja would understand, "no one can reach the door, so anyone pounding on it is impossible. I just hope somebody can hear."

As if in response to that, someone shouted. Then other voices joined in, and the cacophony of yelling prisoners drowned out her pounding completely. To her discouragement, nobody came to see what the noise was about. Nobody cared. "And why should they? No one here can go anywhere anyway. If that gorge circles this place completely, then no one can escape very far." She did give up then, and glumly returned to her corner.

Across the small cell, Yemoja was being reduced to a shadow within a shadow as the last of the light faded.

Leodora drew her knees up and rested her forehead against them. "I have to get out of here," she said. "Right now, Soter will be yelling at Diverus because he came back without me, and so another performance was missed. Did I tell you we'd gone to the world between all worlds? That's what it is for all its formal names. It's full of sorcery, too, and hurled at you from every direction—everything that seems benign on the surface will trick you. I was caught there. Snared. I didn't even notice, because I wanted something and that's what that place does, it finds what you want and it entices you with it, giving you a little, and then more and more, until everything else you've ever been has been swallowed up in desire. They had stories, all the stories, and I wanted them. I wanted them so much, and if Diverus hadn't pulled me from there, I would never have left. Diverus . . . enchanted them with his own power. He has power, and a true name. I know his true name now. Orfeo."

Yemoja looked up sharply at that and repeated, "Orfeo."

"You know that name? I wish I could understand you. You probably have stories, too, from wherever you're from, stories I've never heard before, and I would like to hear them. I'm greedy, you see. I want them all, all the stories, because my father gathered them before me and I want to . . ." Her throat clutched and her eyes burned hot. She had to wait awhile to go on. "I never even knew him, but we're alike on this. And we both need someone to watch out for us, too. The only escape route from here is back through that world between worlds. Pons Asinorum. Fool's Bridge. It's a good name for it. But now I won't have Diverus to shield me. I wonder if they'll trick me again? Of course, I have to find that out, don't I? There's no choice. I have to go back."

Leodora prattled on of nothing and everything, the way Yemoja had when she'd arrived. She babbled, soothed by the sound of her own voice, not telling a story this time, just talking about anything. Eventually the talking lulled her to sleep, where the Coral Man appeared to her in a dream as he had on so many nights; but this time his figure appeared less well formed. She recognized that as his song floated across the oceans, his body was wasting away, and she perceived a glowing knot in his chest, something orange and pulsing.

During the last story performance Soter had Diverus packing the puppets in the cases—all but the few he was using, and those he handed off one by one. The booth, they would have to abandon. "Perhaps we'll come back for it later," he told Diverus, "but leaving it standing might give us time to get away." What they were getting away from remained unspecified, but Diverus didn't argue.

Soter presented a Meersh story and the audience howled at the trickster's foolishness. Then, in the midst of their laughter, Soter swung about and gestured for him to pick up the piba and play something. "Don't put them to sleep. Make it lively," Soter whispered. "See if you can send them all on their way.

Diverus nodded and closed his eyes. He plucked the first note and then his mind went blank.

When he next opened his eyes, Soter was patting him on the shoulder and saying, "Excellent. That was *just* what we needed." He turned from Diverus and lifted the lantern from its hook, but didn't blow it out as Leodora always did. He set it down beside a bottle of oil, and Diverus thought, *What an odd time to fill the lamp.* The undaya cases stood on the floor beside him, fastened and ready. Soter said, "We need to make certain Orinda's gone. Will you go and look? If she's still here, then you force her out. The same with those woodmen. Get 'em out, lad. Be sure they're all gone—it would be too terrible if they remained. Then you come back, we'll take the cases and go. All right?"

"Where?"

"For now, down under Colemaigne with those carters. We'll get a boat. Has to be a way down somewhere."

"I know a way. Through the leg of a tower, at the end of the span."

"Good, good. All right, you go. Stay to the shadows, though, out the back and don't let a soul out there see you."

"There's someone out there? I thought you said—"

"Please, Diverus. *Go.*"

Even as he pushed through the black fabric out the back of the booth, Diverus knew Soter was getting rid of him. He crept into the wings, and then scoured the back hallway behind the scrims and backdrops, finding no one, as he'd expected. Dutifully, he climbed the stairs and searched the rooms on the second floor, too. He entered Orinda's L-shaped room, which he'd never seen before. It was full of costumes and wigs, makeup and props, but deathly still. The Terrestre was empty.

Finally, he picked a ramp to one of the curtained balconies, walked down it, and with great care parted the drapes. He peered out. The pit and all the benches stood deserted. Whatever he had played on the gourd-shaped piba, it had driven the crowd away. Music contained stories, too, he thought. It could take people out of themselves the way stories did. It could transport listeners to rapture or to tears. It could . . . he shuddered then with the memory of what he'd done in order to rescue Leodora. He wanted to tell her what he realized about songs and stories now—how he grasped the power they both shared, how he needed to say to her *I love you* because he'd done something so terrible that the reason couldn't go unspoken between them any longer. But mostly he wanted to hold her, to tangle his fingers in her hair. To say to her . . .

Movement caught his eye, so subtle at first that he wasn't sure he'd seen it. Then out of the darkest recesses at the back of the theatre, something flowed: four pale gray ovals, hovering above the floor, moving in unison like the segmented body of a snake. They slid down the steps and only as they neared the footlights did he make out that the ovals were faces – the faces he'd seen in the theatre box. Cold, implacable, as unfeeling as stone, the pale heads streamed forward. It wasn't until they were rising up to the stage that he could see the bodies beneath the heads, bodies swathed in black, and he knew without a doubt that they were what Soter feared, they were the cause of his sending Orinda away, and of sending him, too. Even this far away and hidden, Diverus felt the terror of them. They threw it off like hoarfrost.

They moved across the stage and easily into the booth, one after the other, as if they could see where the slit in the material was, which he never could. The blackness of the booth absorbed them, but then he could see the tops of their heads as they collected in the middle of it.

The booth erupted in flames. "Soter," he cried, but even then realized that Soter could not be inside the booth any longer. The four sides went up as one, trapping the quartet. They whirled within the flames. They stretched their hands into the air as if imploring the gods to save them, and then one of them plunged back out, his body ablaze. He ran straight off the edge of the stage and into the pit. No one else emerged, and after a few moments the stage itself caught fire. Sparks rose in the updraft, and Diverus feared that the thatched roof was going to ignite, too. He dropped the curtain and ran back into the hall.

Soter had to be somewhere nearby. Somewhere in the theatre with the puppet cases. He would never have let them burn.

Diverus bounded down the stairs to the first floor. Even as he reached it, Soter was climbing up the steps from the trap room beneath the stage. He'd made at least one trip already, leaving one of the cases by the door. Seeing Diverus, he gestured with his head to the large hemp bag beside the table. "Our clothes, and your instruments, Diverus," he said. "Can't do without our musician."

Diverus ran across the room and grabbed the nearest undaya case. He slung its strap over his shoulder and grabbed the bag, and then stepped aside to let Soter lead the way. "I doubt Orinda will be able to forgive us," Soter said grimly as he reached for the door. "The gods won't resurrect it for her this time." He flung back the door and stopped, filling the doorway. Diverus peered past his shoulder.

Outside, a pale bald head seemed to float in the darkness. It said, "No gods will resurrect *you*, either." Then it flowed nearer, driving Soter back.

The black-clad figure closed the door without turning. A short cape covered his shoulders, over a longer black cloak that swept the floor. His dead, unblinking eyes dismissed Diverus with a single glance before fixing on his target again. "Well, well," he said, a sly voice, "if it isn't the man who sells his friends. I never thought to see you again. How is that elf—what's his name?"

"Grumelpyn."

"Grumelpyn. Can he walk now? He couldn't when we left him." The Agent moved farther into the room, and a vertical band of light from the fire on stage ran up him. One black eye gleamed in its deep socket like a star in the night sky. "So, tell me." He raised his hand, and Diverus glimpsed what looked like a blue-violet jewel pressed against his palm. "Where is the storyteller calls himself Jax?" The bright eye looked at Diverus again. "We had doubts, you know, as to the identity of this Jax. Surely, we said, the comparison to Bardsham was made up from ignorance—for who has seen Bardsham perform recently enough to say? I had convinced myself that was so. After all, I am the authority on Bardsham's health. But now I've discovered you . . . and if you are here, then so must he be, too."

"No, he's not. You lot killed him."

"Oh, you know that for a fact, do you? I don't recall you were there that day." A slow smile of memory spread on his face. "But as it happens, so we did. However, Lord Tophet, whom we serve, has concluded there was a child left behind, hidden from us intentionally, and look, here *you* are, giving that idea credence."

"What—" Soter cleared his throat. "What difference could a child make to your master?"

"The lord is of the opinion that a child of Bardsham's might pose a threat to him."

"How, for the gods' sake? Bardsham was no threat to him in the first place!"

"The how is not a matter I involve myself with. So I shall ask you once and only once more. Where is Jax?"

Soter looked back at Diverus and in the same instant swung the undaya case at the Agent. "Run!" he yelled. The Agent must have anticipated the attack. He sidestepped the case and slammed both hands upon it. The case pulled Soter off-balance, and he stumbled into the Agent. The hand bearing the jewel grabbed hold of Soter's wrist. He screamed in agony. Diverus hadn't moved, hadn't run. Soter collapsed to his knees, but the Agent held on, and held his wrist up. "Stop it!" Diverus yelled. "Let him go!" The Agent considered him.

"Well?" he said. "Tell me what I know already."

"If you know, then why do I need to tell you?"

Soter, pooled on the floor, made whining sounds.

The Agent smiled but there was no humor in it. He released his hold and Soter's arm dropped. Soter curled around it, moaning in agony. "So Bardsham did have a son, heh? *He* was a small man, too, you know."

"What do you want?"

"You. I want you to come with me now."

"Why should I do that? Why shouldn't I run as he said?"

"Oh, dear. Didn't you explain it to him, old man?" The Agent prodded Soter with the toe of his boot. "There is nowhere to run *to*, boy. He should have told you that at the very least." Diverus sensed movement behind him. He turned, to be astonished by what he saw. The four Agents he'd seen cast ablaze stood there. Their bodies smoked, so charred and blackened that he couldn't tell how much of their costumes remained, how much was blackened skin, but their gray faces, smeared with soot, were the same, as humorless, hard, and smooth as marble. "Quick," the Agent commanded.

The four surrounded Diverus so swiftly that he barely saw.

"You will accompany us now. We want those cases and that bag as well, all of it." The Agent turned, opened the door and walked outside.

They took hold of Diverus, and despite their condition, their touch was ice. He went with them without a struggle. Glancing down as he passed, he saw that Soter's forearm had turned as gray as dead coral. Soter looked up at him through tears and, trembling, gasped, "I'm sorry."

Diverus knelt to touch him, but the charred Agents kept

him from quite reaching Soter. He said, "It's all right," though he knew it wasn't. It was his doom he was going to. At least, he thought, he would save Leodora from that fate—the thing they called Tophet.

Leodora awoke to a squeal of metal above her head: the hinges of the door as it swung open. She shoved herself up on one elbow, having stretched out onto her side during the night, but the door kept opening and she pressed against the wall, her head turned, eyes squeezed shut against the impact. Then the squeal stopped. She opened one eye.

Through the gap between door and wall, she watched a tall man step into the room. He carried a board horizontally and passed almost immediately out of her line of sight. He murmured something to the prisoner that sounded almost tender; then he laughed and Leodora knew it hadn't been tender at all. Yemoja snarled. The man said something else. When he went out, his hands were empty. He left the door ajar.

Leodora eased out from behind it. The guard had placed the board in the middle of the room. On it were a bowl and cup, and a lump of bread, and although the morning light coming in was gray and wan, she could tell that both bowl and cup contained liquid. The important thing was, the cell was dark. Yemoja said something to her, making no move toward the meal. She seemed to be indicating that Leodora should eat—a remarkable gesture given their circumstances.

Instead, Leodora went to the crack of the door and eased it back. It creaked again, and she ground her teeth at the noise. But nobody came to investigate.

Cautiously, she stuck her head out the door. She looked to the right down a long and dark corridor of rough stone walls and floor and a low ceiling. At the far end of it, two men were pushing barrows. Lanterns swung from the handles of the barrows. The first man took a wooden shovel and entered a cell. A moment later he came out with a pile of straw balanced on the shovel, which he threw into the barrow. Then he shuffled closer along the hall. The second barrow contained a large mound of straw already, and that was being tossed in to replace the old. Between her and the barrows but nearer to her stood a board full of pegs against the far wall. On the pegs hung what she guessed were rings of keys.

She looked in the other direction, where the corridor was perhaps a third as long before reaching a dead end. A cart stood in the darkness, so close that in two steps she could have touched it. It contained stacked boards like the one in Yemoja's cell, all of them balanced upon the bowls of the morning meal.

Shortly, the tall guard emerged from the next cell along, and she drew her head back in. She pressed to the wall and listened to the sound of him coming back to the cart, then wheeling it farther up the corridor. It scraped and rumbled along, and then stopped. Keys jingled and another door creaked open. She glanced out. He had gone. The men at the other end were moving slowly, steadily closer.

She counted until the guard reappeared. He pulled another board off the cart and walked across the corridor to the next cell, spent a moment fumbling the keys, and then went in.

The instant he did she was away. She walked briskly down the hall, pulled the purple robe tight around her, and kept close to the wall. With every step she expected someone to yell, but nobody saw her. Nobody paid her the slightest attention. She passed a narrow doorway into a stairwell, but kept going until she reached the board on which the keyrings hung.

There had to be dozens of them. She scanned them for a key to match the lock on Yemoja's ankle. It was easy to spot, replicated as it was at least a dozen times over. Duplicates, so that multiple jailers could work in multiple cells at once. It didn't matter if all the locks were the same, not if you were chained to one.

She lifted one set of them and pressed it against her robe to keep it from jingling. She turned around. The guard with the food cart was picking up another board. He glanced toward her, paused, and raised his head. She pressed hard to the wall and slid along it. Reaching the stairwell, she stepped into it, then stood and counted to ten before carefully peering into the hall again. The tall guard was carrying another meal into another cell. He hadn't seen her after all in the corridor's gloom. She ran back to Yemoja's cell.

She knelt before Yemoja. It took only a moment to fit the key into the slots and open the cuffs on both ankles. Yemoja babbled something and Leodora hushed her, then listened. Nobody came to the door. All the noises in the hall were from far away.

She realized she'd been holding her breath, and sighed.

"All right, now," she said. "Just wait a moment." Then she took the cup from the board and carried it to the corner where she'd slept. The sun was rising outside and the cell was already too light. She needed darkness. There was only one way to get it.

Turning, she reached to Yemoja to take her hand. Yemoja complied, and Leodora drew her to the corner. She poured some of the contents of the cup onto the floor, and it was immediately absorbed in the dirt. "That won't work," she muttered. She got the bowl and set it on the floor at their feet. It was too small, too contained, to qualify as a pool of water. She glanced back at the board. It was certainly larger. It would have to do.

She carried the board to the wall and set it beside the bowl. Then she took out the phial. "Now comes the hard part," she said, and picking up the bowl she gave it to Yemoja, then gestured to indicate how she wanted it poured out onto the board. The long-snouted creature whuffed but said nothing, and finally nodded.

Leodora looked back out the door. She watched the guard lift another board from his cart and walk into a cell. It was now or never, she supposed. She grabbed the door and dragged it open.

It squealed on rusty hinges, the sound seeming to fill the whole prison. She dragged it back until it cast the corner in darkness. "Now," she said and dipped her head at the board. Yemoja poured out the contents of the bowl. It was a dark, watery soup and it floated on the board long enough for Leodora to spill a drop from the phial into it. Distantly, she heard someone yell, but she stayed focused on the rainbow colors swirling across the water, expanding as it ran off the board and onto the floor.

Taking hold of Yemoja's hand, she watched for the dark liquid to form shapes. After a moment, she could see people distantly, black hair and blue skin. "There!" she cried and leapt into the pool with Yemoja following.

They sprawled onto a hard dirt floor and she thought, *It didn't work!*

A pair of sandaled feet strode up to them. Expecting the guard, Leodora raised her head to find the king of Epama Epam standing over her and holding a silver chalice.

"This is quite unorthodox," he commented.

"Perhaps so," said a female voice behind her, "but she rescued *me*."

The king gasped, and Leodora realized that the voice belonged to Yemoja, which she now understood as if they spoke the same language. She got to her knees and glanced back. The woman had turned greenish black, and her eyes burned orange. She was tearing off the rags that clothed her.

"Goddess," said the startled king.

"Oceanus," she replied.

The surroundings bemused Leodora. Everywhere, the walls were old and made of rough stone, the ground was dirt, and it seemed as if everybody on this street lived in flat-roofed houses like those she'd seen through the bars of the cell. "This can't be right," she said, but no one was listening.

"This girl's been here before," the king was saying querulously. "She disrupted everything, refused to enter the pool of true desire, refused to accept the offer of our eternity, and what's more, her companion—who also escaped, I might add—caused the deaths of *two* of us in making his exit."

"Really?" The goddess's orange eyes considered Leodora anew. "Good for you," she said. "He really is a bastard, you know."

"Goddess—"

"Oh, shut up about your petty issues. Would you care to hear instead how mortals caught *me*, trapped *me*, and put *me* in a prison where the guard clutched at me every morning? A dry, dusty prison without any moisture? Without any way out and none of you knew where I was nor came to my aid? Prison, where I wasted away for more than a year, subsisting on the tiniest cups of liquid that hardly deserved to be called water? Living in my own filth in a space the size of one of your glorious pots?"

"We couldn't have known."

"Indeed not. *She* rescued me from there. So you will afford her every courtesy, help her with everything she needs from now until eternity, and you will not so much as grumble or try any slyness at all."

"Goddess," he importuned.

Yemoja touched her shoulder. "Leodora. Oh, yes, I know you, and I know why you're here. So does he. Epama has something you need, a story you must hear before you can leave. It was why you were sent to us in the first place by another demigod." She shot the king a severe look, and he hunched up like a child. "Oceanus ought to have told you that story before, but he's an inveterate trickster and a liar by nature and would withhold what you require until you're driven mad by the need and then give it to you as if the whole matter is your fault."

"I'm insulted," said the king.

"I doubt that's possible," she replied.

Leodora dusted herself off. "I have to go back to Colemaigne. They'll think I've died by now."

Yemoja shook her head. "You must take what he has for you. You dare not refuse it."

"Can I . . . can I go back first and then return for it?"

The goddess considered Oceanus. He shrugged. "It would seem you can do whatever you like."

"Indeed, she can, but she is best advised not to refuse this gift here and now."

Leodora considered this and finally nodded. "All right, then. A little longer. I would like my clothes returned to me, too." She turned to the goddess. "Thank you."

Yemoja laughed. "You save my life and thank me. You're too good for your own world, child. Come. Let's swim and feast and hear what he has to tell you. Then you can return to your Colemaigne equipped to face whatever it is."

They walked down what seemed a dusty corridor identical to the one in the prison where she'd stolen the key to free Yemoja, but the door at the far end of it opened once again upon the many-pillared palace with the deep blue pool and she knew that, no matter the outward shape of this place, this was its core, the center of a maze she was learning how to thread.

Many hours later, alone in the dark of that same dirt corridor and dressed in a freshly laundered tunic, she poured a goblet of Oceanus's best wine upon a metal platter and a drop from the phial into the wine. She held in her mind the image of her booth in the Terrestre, and this time stepped through without any misdirection. Her destination, however, was transformed beyond anything she might have anticipated.

She stepped down onto the stage of the theatre . . . and nearly fell through it into the trap room. Half of the floor, including the part where the puppet booth had stood, was gone, burned away, and the edges around the gaping hole were charred and blistered. The back wall and two of the balconies had been destroyed, leaving one of the doors to the wings standing inside a frame without a wall around it. Gone, too, was one of the uprights supporting the roof, and most of the thatch overhead, which now leaned precariously to the side. Given the damage she could see, it was a wonder the whole place hadn't burned down. The stink of smoke still tainted the air although the fires were long cold. The remaining floor of the stage had buckled. Boards had popped up or split, probably from a combination of intense heat fought with buckets of water. Standing puddles remained under the last two rear balconies, causing her to think somewhat incongruously that the stage must not be level.

She looked down into the trap room below, full of unidentifiable debris. She saw no bodies, no sign anyone had been on hand when the fire began. The blaze had done its worst damage where the booth had stood and she couldn't escape conclusion that it had begun *in* the booth—the lantern, perhaps, falling off its hook, spilling oil and flames all in a moment. Had it already happened before Diverus came back? It must have, else the embers would still be glowing. After all, it had been only a day since they'd parted company. Surely he was near.

After circling the hole, she walked to the rear and around the surviving door into the back wing. The various screens there had been raised high to avoid the fire, a move that had probably saved them. She walked through the crossover hall to the side of the theater left intact. The floor creaked underfoot. The heat had warped the boards.

The opposite wings, redolent with smoke, looked to have been saved. She turned to climb the stairs at the back, and there stood Orinda at the top. They saw each other in the same moment.

"Oh, thank Edgeworld for hearing my prayers!" cried Orinda. She flew down the stairs as on wings and clutched Leodora to her, saying, "You're alive after all," by which time she had burst into tears. "We thought you would never find your way back. Diverus didn't know how to go after you."

"He couldn't. He gave me the phial. But what happened? How did the fire—"

"There's much you need to hear, and none of it good, I'm afraid. The fire is the least of it. Come with me, he needs to see you."

"Who?"

"Soter. He hoped you would return in time. I think his

conscience would never be clear if anything had happened to you."

"A lot *has* happened to me, but his conscience wasn't involved. It wasn't his doing. Why do you say—what do you mean *in time*?"

They came to one of the rear rooms in the hallway, one she hadn't seen before. It was, by comparison with the small chamber she had occupied, opulent. There were racks of costumes, a shelf lined with wigs, with shoes and boots, with makeup and mirrors. Bois and Glaise stood at the back of it, looking worried until they set eyes on her. Then both of them beamed with rapture and jumped to her. She hugged them, but even as she did she was turning to see what lay around the corner of the room that they had been guarding.

He lay on the bed. The top of his head faced her, his thin hair pushed up by the pillow, and even from that view she recognized him.

Soter rested with his eyes closed and his breathing shallow.

"Oh, no," she said, though she'd had sufficient warning to guess. "The fire?" she asked.

"No, dear heart," Orinda replied. "He started the fire—in the hope of escaping."

"Escaping. I don't understand."

"Who is that?" Soter asked. His voice creaked like dried-out leather.

"It's me," answered Leodora. She pushed around Orinda to circle the side of the bed.

Soter's feeble gaze followed her. Tears ran from his eyes. "Oh, you're all right then."

She sat on the edge and reached to take his hand. She noticed only then that his arm, lying straight by his side atop the covers, was as chalky white as the Coral Man.

"I don't understand," she said again. "How did this happen in a few days? Where's Diverus?"

"It's not been a few days," Orinda explained. "Before Diverus returned, a month passed. We'd exhausted every effort to find you. Bois and Glaise traveled to other spans, we'd interviewed the stilt walker you spoke to and the tunnel seigneur as well, who swore you'd never crossed from here to Sacbé. Hamen and Pelorie and the rest all scoured the piers to learn if a ship had sailed you away. There wasn't a trace."

"There wouldn't have been. We didn't tell anyone, we didn't know we were going. But a month, you say?"

"Diverus responded the same—only a day to you," Soter rasped, "an eternity to us."

She looked from him to Orinda. "Where *is* Diverus?"

"My dear," he said wearily, "you have to listen to me now."

"First, tell me what's happened to Diverus?"

"They took him."

"Who did?"

"Soter." Orinda said his name anxiously.

"Orinda, my time is short now whether I speak or not. Better that she know everything than wonder ever after." His rheumy eyes met hers. "The truth was kept from you for your own good as well as mine."

"By you," she said.

He answered, "If you'd never wanted off that damnable isle—if your uncle hadn't cooked up such absurd plans—if you'd taken up with Tastion and married and had babies and become part of the village . . . but I should have known that wouldn't happen. Not with your family history. I cursed Gousier for all this, but maybe it had to be. You would never live inside anybody's proscriptions."

"No, I wouldn't, but—"

"Give us a drink then, and I'll tell you what you need to know, everything of Bardsham and Leandra. And Diverus."

There was a tray on the floor with a clay pitcher. She poured him a cup of wine. When he didn't take it from her, she realized he couldn't move the stony arm. She reached under his head and pulled him up enough to drink from the cup. As he tilted up, the cover slid down and she saw that the paleness of stone colored his chest, blending back to flesh just beneath the collarbone. *The most important thing*, Shumyzin had tried to tell her, so long ago atop the tower of another span that it seemed like a memory of a dream. The sun that gave him life had been pushed aside before he could finish. And here it was, the demigod's petrifaction a harbinger of this moment in time, like an echo thrown ahead of the sound that made it.

Soter drank and then pressed his head back. Seeing the look of despair and recognition in her eyes, he wheezed, "Hardly any of me left, is there? Another day in your Pons Asinorum, you'd have missed me altogether." He smiled, as if acknowledging that his approaching death were mere japery. "Now listen," he said, "and afterward you can hate me as you see fit."

≈ Soter's Tale ≈

"I hated your mother, Leodora. I hated her and did all I could to be rid of her. That's the truth and now there's no point in keeping it from you. I'm your friend, whatever you may think. I've always looked out for you. Always, child. More'n your uncle ever did or would have done. But I shared his odium for his sister.

"I'd had Bardsham to myself for so many years, you see. There were hundreds if not thousands of indiscretions, assignations, and peccadilloes in that time, on every span probably. Bardsham and women . . . you wouldn't have thought it to look at him, scarred and rawboned as he was, but he had such charisma, such presence, that when he spoke to you, it was like the gods were gifting you with his attention. Like you were the only one in the world who caught his eye."

Leodora swallowed. She said, "You were in love with him, weren't you?"

Instead of answering directly, he replied, "He always came back to me. Asked his dearest companion to dust him off, dry him out, and protect him from the woman who'd mistaken a dalliance for a proposal. As it was with that woman on Vijganar who'd have left her husband for Jax, and you not even encouraging her—that's how it was all the time with your father. In love with him? Hardly scratches the surface of it. Nobody gave a toss about Soter except him. Nobody else scraped the dirt off and saw the pathetic wretch below. He loved me and I loved him, though neither of us spoke such words. That's just how it was.

"Until she came along.

"Whatever his power, Leandra gave it right back. He wanted his little affair. She turned him down. He plied her with gifts, jewelry, costumes. He tried to seduce and tempt her. She said no, and sent the things back untouched. His performances began to flag. Audiences noticed when he cut back to two tales, and then one, and they actually stopped coming. Stopped paying. They thought it was ego. Mooncalf that she'd made him, he didn't even notice. I'd never seen him like that.

Nobody'd ever shaken him up, not in all the years we'd traveled. He was like your emperor in that kitsune story you like so much.

"Leandra had been nicely accommodated by somebody. She didn't need gifts to get along. She had come to the show and found what Bardsham did to be exquisite, that's what she said and the way she said it I knew she felt the same as me. She'd come back again and again. And she'd seen him beguiling the barmaids and the patronesses. She knew what he was like—more Meersh than little thief. And she had that about her, too. Cut from the same cloth, they were, neither one conforming nor acknowledging anyone's rules. She knew better than to give her heart to him or he'd be after the next conquest before she could roll over. Turned out she was a skilled dancer. She'd trained, that lithe and supple beauty, with that flame hair you inherited. So I made her a proposition and hired her on as a dancer to entertain between acts, because I couldn't think of another way to fix it so he'd go back to work. I hoped at close quarters they would discover they hated each other and we could move on. Though I didn't get my wish, he did start performing again then. He had a reason to now—every performance became a love letter to Leandra. The audiences came back, filled the halls and theatres again. Soon enough I knew how it was going to be. The Red Witch and the World's Greatest Puppeteer. He never looked at another woman again. I think he stopped seeing 'em. Stopped seeing me, as well. Didn't need me now to protect him from himself. I was just another member of the troupe, with Tahman and Grumelpyn. Well, I bore it, didn't I? And nobody so much as asked if I could.

"That was our sea change as a troupe. We moved on, and one day Leandra was pregnant and the dancing between acts stopped once it became obvious. I thought a baby would keep her away, in the wings, and I'd have him back. A little. Was that so much to ask for? He doted on you, though you don't recall, and he coaxed your mother into working herself into shape again for the dancing. Fuller hips but no one complained about those. She danced barefoot between tales, she took to doing some of the voices in them, and to the world we must have seemed the happiest family on all of Shadowbridge. The troupe what had everything.

"Your mother never stopped trying to get rid of me. Anything went wrong, any place didn't have our lodging ready, she went after me for it. Only fair, I guess, since I did the same with regard to her, trying to make him see her for the petty, jealous creature I thought her. She'd been a kept whore when we found her, hadn't she? I could always remind her of that, and make her twist with anger. Our war, hers and mine, because we both loved him. Ain't that laughable. I think it was the two of us drove him into his cups most of the time. Him and Tahman and that elf, they'd sit and drink and watch the two of us go at it like *we* was the married couple. Like it was a show we put on for them."

"But what happened?" asked Leodora. "What happened in Colemaigne?"

"The story changed is what. We'd come to this very theatre and the crowds were huge. Your father's ego, it must have been as big as the sun resting on the horizon. Gods, but he was revered.

"And then one night I noticed a couple of creatures in one of the boxes out there, watching us. They were hairless, humorless things, like you'd get if you bred the moons Saphon and Gyjio together. Orinda and Burbage conveyed the hearsay that they was archivists from the Library itself, and didn't that inflate your father's ego still more. Nobody knew then or knows now what the rumored archivists look like. They was queer things, and that was certain. And it made a good story imagining Bardsham's reputation had brought them—that we had no doubt of. They carried with them a glorious jewel they called Tophet's Eye. It's the *sort* of thing you'd call a spectacular jewel . . . at least one that had brought bad luck, Tophet being a far-flung name for the god of Chaos and sometimes for where he dwells, a place no one had ever seen."

She asked, "Why don't I know the stories of him?"

He winced as if pain stabbed into him. "You don't know the tales because I kept those from you. I replaced Chaos in every story with some other god or demigod's name. I didn't want you to know that name ever. It was never to be spoken on Bouyan. Your grandfather, your uncle and aunt, I was shielding them, too. What they didn't know, they couldn't ask after. It seemed then the only way to be safe."

She nodded with understanding, and he went on.

"Third night there was five of them in that box, all of 'em as pale and cold as marble, and by then the chatter that the Library was come to canonize Bardsham was irrepressible, all over Colemaigne. After our performance they appeared backstage, immediately approached Bardsham, and announced they represented a great and powerful lord on another spiral who would pay an unimaginable sum for us to come and give an exclusive performance for him. The entire troupe had to agree—they were quite specific about that. Well, we'd done the like before, and for far less coin than this secretive lord was offering. It was too good to be true and I said as much. Of course, Leandra and I were fighting, so if I said it was a bad idea, she was bound to say it was brilliant and we must leave at once. Bardsham, drunk on booze and himself, didn't need coaxing anyways. At that point his vanity was as wide as the Adamantine Ocean. I'm sorry, child, and that's the whole truth of him.

"He was for it and that was that. Now, you, a baby, weren't going to make no voyage like that. Or maybe it was your mother having a premonition of what waited for us. She already had a nurse looking after you—Bois's sister, I think it was. You stayed here with her and Orinda. We sailed willingly off the edge of the world.

"I suppose we sailed for a week or more. Went right past spirals and beneath who knows how many spans, and soon we were far outside anyplace we knew or had ever heard of. Mostly those Agents kept to themselves, but more than once I saw one of them with that blue jewel, holding it up as if trying to peer through it to see Leandra where she sat. Then one morning we woke up and the ocean was a darker color as if it was full of wine, and the look of those places we sailed beneath was dark and silent, 'cept for the birds perched about, watching us. It was like we'd sailed into another world or into the past, to the places in that tale of Chilingana's you tell, before any people had come. Whole spirals seemingly awaiting their tenants, that's how it looked. Then finally we hit this sargasso of dead calm, a whole surface of violet and black weeds that should have tangled us all up but didn't somehow. My misgivings had grown all the while, as had Grumelpyn's, although our hosts had given us no cause to worry. They'd fed us well and let us be, and more importantly they kept Bardsham merrily lubricated. Tahman, too, when he wasn't seasick. Always smiling they were, those hairless things, but not a drop of humor in it. Too late then even if everyone else had agreed with me and been willing to turn back. We didn't know it but we had passed into some other place.

"We reached our destination that day. It was a great curving span near the end of a spiral. The span and the whole spiral as far as we could see in either direction was gray and dead. Not a soul in view save where we anchored, and then they were like our hosts, cold and somber. Pale as skulls. The span itself was in worse shape even than Ningle, as if neglected for centuries. The Dragon Bowl of it had broken apart, and the beam and one little curved slice of that bowl just hung there in the air.

"They hauled the cases up for us, onto the surface of the span, and save for a coterie of staff, there was nobody about, just hundreds of statues in various positions, many of them crumbling, old like the buildings. His palace though was low and long and gleaming, and it ran half the length of the span. More dour, pale servants greeted us, led us to our rooms, left us.

"By then even Bardsham was voicing the opinion that this was a mistake and not worth the money we were promised. He proposed we give our performance, collect our treasure, and leave as quickly as possible. We persuaded ourselves that he was but a demented recluse who chose to live on a dead span, cut off from most of the world. But in order to pretend that, we had to deny everything we saw, everything we heard. We had to pretend not to see that the birds flying past were not a kind of bird we knew. Most of all we had to overlook that the creatures waiting on us weren't terrified out of their wits. To do otherwise was to admit that we were terrified out of ours.

"We set up the booth in a great hall of the palace. That night Bardsham performed Chilingana's tales, and the Fatal Bride, and finally 'How Meersh Lost His Toes.' Our host was delighted by the stories. He sat across the hall from us, in an enormous carved throne with an odd drapery hanging before it that kept him in the shadows. When he emerged, one of his attendants always stood before him, bearing a pole on the end of which was a huge mask—of hammered gold, and bigger and broader than a human face, with a serene expression. So we never glimpsed his true face, even as he proclaimed the first performances captivating. I stared at his hands. They appeared to be the same color and substance as that jewel the Agents had carried with them. His fingers, long and slender, looked to have extra joints.

After the first stories, Tophet insisted on having his own personal musician play along with Tahman. It was an old blind man who sawed with a bow upon some wretched stringed instrument with a long neck and one peg in it. He surprised us with the quality of his playing—provided that we liked the one song he knew. The blind accompanist played while your mother danced between the tales, over and over and over, slow, fast, whatever was called for, but always the same damned tune. I've only heard it once since then: the first time you had Diverus play for me. You remember? *That* was why I raged at him. It was the most vile thing I could have heard. Right then I thought Tophet must have sent him after me. That's not true of course—I know that now, but how had he latched onto that of all the music in the world? I still don't know.

"Anyways, we played for this hidden madman. The world is full of eccentric kings, lords, and emperors. It's they who populate all your stories, after all. We told ourselves he was just a bit more demented than most. His span was all but a ruin, a municipality of ghosts. Who wouldn't be mad after living there? Then one of his staff, who was helping us, let it slip that he was *called* Lord Tophet. The jewel was named after him. Grumelpyn, who heard it first, told the rest of us, 'He styles himself the god of Chaos.' Bardsham said so long as he paid, we weren't going to care. We kept reminding ourselves that another performance or two and we were off back to Colemaigne and much richer for it, and he could think whatever he liked. We still ignorantly believed we had some say in the matter.

"The second morning I was sitting outside his palace when two of his entourage approached to tell me that their lordship wanted to speak with me. I assumed—I hoped—it was about settling up, as I took care of that sort of thing. They led me to his private chambers. Quite lavish, they were. Polished and shiny, marble and smooth reddish wood everywhere, and not a hint of decay. His lordship was still abed, and as with the throne, a gauze surrounded the bed, obscuring him from view, casting him in shadows. The servant with the mask on a pole stood beside the bed. By then I was convinced that he was deformed in some manner, cruelly shaped by nature or a curse. He was in the middle of eating his breakfast, and I wondered why he'd felt compelled to bring me in before he was finished.

"The moment I arrived he remarked to me, 'I know you

despise that whore who travels with you.' And whatever I had ever thought about Leandra, it took me a moment to understand that he meant her. His voice . . . it was like a hive of furious bees. I squinted, sorting out what he was saying, the words from the sound.

"'Whore,' I repeated, as though I didn't know the meaning of the word.

"He clarified by saying, 'The common dancer. I wish for her to remain behind when you leave, which you may do now at any time. As I'm informed of your hatred for her, I thought it best to apply to you. Arrange to leave her behind. I don't care how it's done. Give her to me, take your fortune, and depart.'

"I babbled something about how she was Bardsham's wife, but that relationship didn't matter to him, either, nor should it matter to me if I hated her to the degree he knew I did.

"I listened to him and gods forgive me I thought about it. I blamed her for our being there. That much was easy to justify, but not enough to warrant what he asked. Bardsham would have killed me on the spot if I'd suggested it. I was about to try to explain this to the madman—for now it was clear that he was truly insane—when the door to his chamber opened and two of those gruesome Agents came in. Between them, they were dragging Tahman. He'd been thrashed and beaten, his shirt shredded, sopping blood. His mouth was swollen up, his face bruised. He saw me and his eyes pleaded and hoped. He tried to say something, and I saw that some of his teeth had been knocked or pulled out. Before a word of explanation was spoken, I knew what had occurred, and under my breath I cursed the stupid bastard.

"Lord Tophet announced, 'Your drummer is a thief. He attempted to steal from me earlier this morning. I promise you untold wealth and you respond by sending a thief into my private chambers to rob me.'

"'We didn't send him,' I said. 'We didn't know.'

"'Oh, but you *knew* he's a thief.'

"I said, Yes, of course we'd known about that forever, and then added, 'But we didn't suspect him to be so infinitely stupid as to attempt to rob you.' Until that moment, I believe Tahman thought I was there to rescue him, to bargain for his freedom.

"'Yes, that is accurate, I think,' said Tophet, and he parted the curtain and stepped out to confront Tahman.

"The servant with the pole and mask didn't move to cover

him this time, and I saw him clearly. Cloaked in a green robe, he was, his hair long and black. The face—it was the face of Chaos. It's almost indescribable. Horrible. Not because of any deformity or scars like I'd thought, but because it was hundreds or thousands of faces all flowing through each other at once. Faces of agony, of terror, of more pain than can be withstood by any of us. Tahman screamed at the sight of him, because that slithery face was intent upon him alone. The lord rolled back one sleeve, revealing more of that gleaming purple arm. 'There is a single punishment for theft in my world,' he explained, and then he grabbed hold of Tahman's wrists. Tahman twisted, kicking out, but was held in place by the two Agents while the color drained from him and the grayness rose up his arms, his whipped torso, his neck, his face. It must have taken mere seconds but it seemed I stood watching that unspeakable progression for hours, and at the end of it Tahman's face slid across Tophet's writhing features and was sucked into the worming mass, and Tahman the thief, the fool, was an eyeless thing of stone like the hundreds we'd encountered upon our arrival. Not statues at all, they were the former citizens of that span—whatever it had been before Tophet claimed it. His body seemed to swell with vigor as he turned to me. 'One less division of the spoils now,' he declared. 'Two, once you give her up.' He cast off the robe and his attendants came flocking to fit him with costume and wig for the day, but beneath it was that horror of a visage ever in motion until the mask moved up between us again.

"He gestured my dismissal. 'Now I will have your boat prepared,' he said. 'We'll see you off in the morning. I expect you will explain to your comrades why this one is unable to play. Should they need further prompting, I'll stand him in the dining hall for all to see. He makes your job that much simpler, yes? This could happen to any or all of you—for me it would be simpler to execute—but I've no wish to deprive the world of its Bardsham just yet.'

"I took from his words that he *wanted* this story performed. He wanted the world to know he existed: Tophet the Destroyer, the god of Chaos, did not reside in Edgeworld, but rather walked the spans of Shadowbridge with all of us.

"The Agents who'd brought in Tahman took hold of me and dragged me away.

"None of this could I keep from your father or the troupe.

Tophet didn't really grasp the bond at the center of a theatrical troupe, even when they war with each other.

"Unbeknownst to me, he'd already met with your father and your mother. Your father, he'd entertained late into the night, and as was Bardsham's custom he'd hobnobbed with his lordship, who had wanted to hear only one thing: What stories did Bardsham know of people who'd sold their souls? He'd asked him to list them all, every story he'd ever heard like that, and your father of course obliged. He saw no harm in it. And as he knew literally hundreds of such tales, it meant he got to continue enjoying Tophet's cellars while he rattled off every one. In the end, it seemed that Tophet had been satisfied with that recitation, and had sent him to bed.

"We were more surprised to find he'd also made overtures to your mother. She'd rebuffed him, no surprise there, but she'd known that wouldn't be the end of it—she had too much experience of men who thought themselves powerful and desirable. She just didn't know where it was going to come out next. And do you know what she did?"

Soter leaned forward though it cost him in pain. "Your mother told us to go, the three of us, to leave her behind. She wanted to save you. To save him. I think she knew what was coming if we didn't comply. As is said of the gods, the best you can hope for is that they don't take notice of you. This one had fixed on her, and that was that. Your mother . . .

"Bardsham, he wouldn't hear of it. 'Are they providing us a ship?' he asked and I said they were, Tophet claimed it was being readied. 'Well, then, we'll take it,' he said. 'Not tomorrow at his lordship's convenience, but tonight, after our performance.' He told Grumelpyn to find out where it was moored, but to be careful not to end up like Tahman.

"And that's what we did. Bardsham gave one of the best performances of his life, like he was in the grandest hall, in front of the very gods of Edgeworld themselves for an audience. It was so fine that Tophet had to toast him, hail him a genius and all that. For once your father's excesses and ego came in handy. He matched that monster drink for drink—he'd taken his measure the night before while babbling away—and he drank him into oblivion. When Tophet finally collapsed and had to be carried to bed, Bardsham retired, too, unsteady on his pins and having to be helped to his room. Of course he wasn't half so drunk as he feigned, but it convinced the staff, which was what we wanted. Grumelpyn had mapped the palace for an escape route to the quay below. Nothing was secured—they weren't used to having to guard things. No one stole from Tophet. We found our boat, loaded with bags of silver. Bardsham dumped most of that into the harbor to lighten our load. We were away and gone within half an hour.

"Then it was sailing halfway round the world and us not knowing where we was going for most of it. We'd stop on a span and ask where we were, use the silver we'd kept to provision the ship and buy anyone's silence—at least we hoped as much—and then we sailed on. I suppose it should have come as no surprise, but we *were* surprised to encounter a few people on those nearer spirals who'd fled the spans that Tophet had taken over. Whether they recognized the silver coins, or maybe just our furtiveness, I don't know. They told us he'd been moving across the face of Shadowbridge slowly, for centuries, like a plague, a great devouring juggernaut. A sucking louse in no hurry to kill what it lives off. No one knew where to run to next. Maybe they prayed he would just go away.

"We sailed on and never saw pursuit, but they'd no idea which way we'd gone and neither did we, and they thought we would be drafting deeper, slowed by the weight of our abandoned fortune.

"Eventually we reached familiar waters, the Adamantine Ocean and a span we'd played on, and from there we were able to make our way back to Colemaigne, coming into Sacbé, one span below it, at night, in case the Agents were there ahead of us. They didn't know about you. We collected you right away along with what belongings we had, bid Orinda farewell, and sailed on to a span called Remorva, way down the far end of another spiral, well away from our usual circuit. We hid there for weeks. There was no sign of anyone coming. We thought maybe we were safe. Just to make sure, though, we put two more spirals between us and Remorva before we tried performing again, settling in Emeldora. That copper-faced kingdom had never seen our like before. They had pantomime but no tradition of puppets, and Bardsham was a wonder to 'em. Leandra, though, stayed hidden. She didn't dance any longer, and Bardsham performed simple, unembellished stories, the way Peeds had taught them to him when he was a boy. That's what he called himself there, too: Peeds. It was a small place. You couldn't have packed but a dozen people into it. Two weeks we were there and no hint anyone was hunting us. It looked like we'd rid ourselves of them.

"Then one night while Bardsham was performing 'The Armless Maiden,' I went outside and they grabbed me. Tugged a bag over my head and when they removed it, I was on board a boat and in front of me was one of those hairless gobshites holding up a gold mask on a pole. This one didn't look serene, either. It was a mask of rage, of fury, and I knew who was sitting in the shadows behind it.

"'We had a bargain,' his voice buzzed at me, 'and I'm going *well* out of my way to allow you to fulfill your part of it.' He suddenly closed the distance between us and took hold of two of my fingers. It didn't last but a moment, but I cannot describe how much it hurt, the two fingertips turning to stone in his gelid grip. Pain sliced right into my bones, all up my arm like you'd run a blade to split my marrow. I thought I must have screamed so loud the sky cracked. What this feels like now, creeping up me like a vine, is nothing compared with that pain from him directly. He pushed the fingertips he'd taken onto the floor and leaned past the mask, so close that I could see every wriggling snake of his face, all the shifting hollows around his eyes. 'You'll get her for me this time,' he said. They'd already come to Colemaigne and destroyed half the span looking for us, though we didn't know that then. He'd drunk up half the lives there, finally settling on Burbage's theatre. But Burbage was dying from something else already and so Tophet's threats didn't move him. Instead he had his Agents torture those two decent fellows standing at the end of my bed. Bois and Glaise. You know what he did to them. He could have destroyed the whole span, but gods are chimerical, who knows what—"

"He's not a god," Leodora scorned.

"Oh, Leodora, you don't *know*, you haven't faced him."

"What god chases a mortal woman across the world?"

"In stories, girl—"

"*Only* in stories, Soter. Nowhere else." She drew a deep breath. "What happened, then? What did she do? Did she give herself up?"

Soter tried to look her in the eye, to hold ground one final time against her ever-challenging sureness, but he finally lowered his gaze. Blanched tendrils crawled like worms up his neck as she awaited his answer. He squeezed his eyes against the pain. Tears leaked from the corners.

"No," he said at last, then gasped a breath. "*I* gave Leandra up. Out of my own terror. I'm a coward, Leodora. I gave her to them. I betrayed everyone. I made up a story, led her outside, and they took her. She looked at me . . . like she'd foreseen it all and had already accepted it. She forgave me, saying just one word. Your name. That was worse—infinitely worse—than if she'd spat on me."

"My father?"

"Asleep after his performance. Exhausted. By the time he came around, they were long gone, and there was Agents left behind to keep him from ever trying to leave Emeldora again. Two of them with another boat. He knew I'd been the one, sold him out. I couldn't work up enough bile to lie to him. He made me swear to protect you, keep you away from them, keep you off the spans. Whatever happened, you were my responsibility from now on. Then we hatched a plan that used poor Grumelpyn as a decoy. We couldn't tell him. Sent him down to our own little ship with one of the undaya cases. It was empty, but he didn't know it. He was to make ready to sail back to Remorva. Of course those Agents went right after him. They must have tortured him awfully—Scratta said as much—but we'd told him nothing so he couldn't tell them anything they wanted to know and I suppose they kept at him and at him, and meanwhile Bardsham had stolen their boat and gone after your mother. I never saw him again.

"Someone, a mangy fellow, recognized the undaya case quayside and brought it to me. The boat was gone, he said. I paid him and gave him some money to give Grumelpyn but for all I know he kept it or drank it and never even looked for Grumelpyn. For all I knew there *was* no Grumelpyn anymore anyway. I didn't dare look for him myself. I had to look after you. If anything had happened to me, there was no one. I hid on Emeldora with you a full month before I bought a boat and sailed to Ningle. I knew that if either of them lived, your parents would know to find you on Bouyan. I buried my guilt, what I'd done, and it would have stayed buried but for your ambition and that damned coral ghoul Tastion found."

"The Coral Man—"

"It's your father, girl! Come back to haunt me, to plague me for all I did to him. To *her*!" He sobbed, and when he inhaled, his chest crackled and the tendrils slid into his jaw. "Oh, gods, it's coming for me."

Leodora pushed him back against the pillows. "Soter, the Coral Man isn't Bardsham," she said. "He's not my father."

He focused on her again. "What do you mean? Of course he is!"

"No. That's your *story*, that you've told me now. The truth is, he's part of a different story, one that I've now been given to know. But you have to tell me, where is Diverus?"

He shook his head, a gesture of pain and denial. "Gone. The Agents took him. Came for you and found him. He's like your mother—he gave himself to them to save you, told them he was Jax."

She clenched her jaw and doubled over as if in pain. "Did they . . . did they do the same to him?"

"No," he said. "Took him is all. They won't harm him till they're in front of Tophet. They acted as if they expected to find Bardsham in the booth."

"How could they think that? They killed Bardsham."

"I don't know, Leodora. Maybe because they saw me. But they'd found out about Leandra's child. They think Diverus is him. Is you. That's why it was 'Jax' all the time, why it had to be. You understand?"

"Where are the cases?"

"They took those, took his instruments. Took everything."

"Then the Coral Man's on his way." He stared at her without comprehension. "You and I," she said, "we've become part of his story. It's like Shadowbridge itself, Soter —yours, mine, Bardsham's, Tophet's, Orinda's—all these stories, they're all coiled together, braided."

"No, he came to me," he insisted. "He *haunted* me! Look what he did to my arm!" He lifted it to show her the sucker mark where the Coral Man had grabbed him, but the mark was gone.

She shook her head slowly, sadly. "Was your guilt haunted you, that you'd tried to bury on Bouyan. When you returned to the tales to give them to me, I think you made it manifest. You haunted yourself, Soter, all along. Back on the island, as well. It was never my mother's ghost. Nor my father's. They were never there."

Miserably, he looked up from his arm and stared at her. Then he began to cry, keening for the burden he'd carried for so long, which had made him mistreat Diverus and lie to her, and had twisted his every decency into an act to divert her, keeping her safe but at the price of her very freedom. He sobbed, and the anguish seemed to speed the effects of the jewel's poison. The veins in his neck went powdery white. Suddenly he took one ragged breath. He looked at her with eyes that knew the time had come. "Forgive me, sweet child," he said.

"Soter, no." She fell across him. "You taught me *everything*," she whispered to him.

"I—I did," he sighed. He made a small dry sound, and it was as though the venom surged up into the last of him. She felt the change and drew upright. The face below her was as blank and dead as Shumyzin's at the top of a tower so long ago that it felt like years. Upon the bed lay a lifeless statue.

The Brazen Head opened its eyes and softly iterated, "Time is that which ends."

She sat alone on top of the southern tower of Colemaigne. This one sported no statues, just the pennants seen from the street, hanging listless now. A storm had passed, its clouds scudding away across the sea in a single line, leaving her bathed in late-afternoon sunlight, all too reminiscent of Vijganar where they had all been alive. She knew she should go, but could not compel herself. Her thoughts churned through everything she'd shared with Soter—starting with all the tales she'd learned to perform, the people and traditions she'd defied on Bouyan; the gods and demigods who'd intervened along the way, and the avatars and tricksters she'd encountered; ending with the quiet musician she'd rescued from a randomly chosen paidika, who had now sacrificed himself for her. Closing her eyes, she could see Soter as he held up the figure of Meersh in his hut, dazzling her with the revelation of who her father had been and what powers might be hers if she applied herself. From then on, it was a jumble of events, disconnected and disparate, that had brought her here, and Diverus—what *was* Diverus, no simple musician. Did she love him? She wanted to but couldn't trust the authenticity of her own feelings any longer. What did she know of love, after all? Her most reliable examples were all from stories, which were the least reliable sources.

Soter, who claimed to have loved her most, had feuded with her at every turn, had lied to her, tried to rein her in. None of it felt like love. Dymphana, she supposed, was the better model, but a surrogate one, and yoked to a bastard upon whom that tender word could not find purchase.

And Tastion? Did what he had claimed to feel even suggest anything like love?

As for Diverus, Soter had known Diverus loved her. He'd needed no pool of true desire to reach that conclusion. He'd recognized what he was jealous of. He had seen Diverus look at her the way Bardsham had looked at her mother and had done everything he could to stamp out that passion before it caught fire. Soter had known so much and hidden so much more. In the end, he'd been protecting her from her own heart. Now that was over, the shield gone.

She sat, gazing out to sea, and grief grew tangled in the complexities. She could have awakened the Brazen Head and asked for advice again, but she had no desire for riddles now, no interest in clever puzzles, and anyway she wanted no one's advice anymore.

Soter had always been. Like Meersh he was a permanent fixture in the world, dependably grouchy, as adamant as she was recalcitrant. She'd no concept of what a world without him was like, but one thing she did know: She would be damned before she gave up Diverus, too. The gods could hang themselves if they thought she would sit by and allow it. As she'd said to Soter, while they thought they were forging their own story, they had all become characters in a different one, one that belonged to a seemingly lifeless husk, which Soter in his terror had mistaken for Bardsham's body and ghost. They were like bees carrying pollen from one place to another, from an island, across spirals, to its proper destination, although it might well be to Death that she was delivering hers. Bees acted out of their own needs, never realizing that flowers would bloom as a result. Were the patterns of the world as capricious as the gods or merely inscrutable? There was a question for the Brazen Head to answer sometime. Some other time.

Now it was time to go.

She got up, and even as she did, one lone straggling gray cloud let loose a few drops of rain on her.

Then out of the turret at the end of the bridge a figure emerged, and Leodora was astonished to recognize Orinda in a violet mourning gown.

Soter's body lay on a cot in the costume room of the theatre. No one knew what to do with him now. The theatre itself was closed until further notice. Somebody would have to send to Sacbé for wood to repair the stage and the galleries – Colemaigne had none. Probably it would fall to Bois and Glaise to mend the damaged stage.

Orinda took in the view as she approached, her face encased in a violet veil. Only her eyes showed above it, and Leodora realized it was her poise that had identified her. "I have never been up here before," she said. "I wasn't aware it was accessible. You can see everything, can't you?"

"You can see a great deal."

"Sometimes a different perspective helps."

"How did you – "

"Glaise followed you. I think he was worried you might do yourself harm. I knew better, but still I didn't want you to go." She hesitated before adding, "We'd hoped you might stay on with us."

"You know I can't do that."

"Of course. Your puppets are gone."

Leodora asked, "Did you love him?"

The eyes widened, stung and unprepared. Orinda raised a trembling hand to her mouth, hidden though it was. Her eyes looked inward awhile before she spoke. "I suppose I must have. He whinged a good deal, and was unnecessarily harsh to you, but he always brought me in mind of Mr. Burbage, and of the best times ever this theatre knew. And now you go, too, and that will be the last ember. The fire dies and I've no energy to kindle it afresh. Gods come to the rescue just so many times, I think."

"Love makes no sense."

"Nor ever has, dear. The theatre is full of examples."

"He named that puppet after you, didn't he? There was no figure in any stories with the name Orinda."

Above the veil, Orinda's eyes teared and she squeezed them closed until she had fought back the urge to give in to sorrow. "Where do you go now?" she asked.

"Back through the Pons Asinorum one last time. From there to . . . wherever it is Diverus has been taken. I'm not certain where that is, but I know now who lies at the far end of it."

"Nothing other than uncertainty is certain in this world," Orinda proclaimed. She reached out and grasped Leodora's arm. "Return to us," she said in words laced with fear. As she had already given an answer to that, Leodora said nothing and, when Orinda let go, she stood her ground. Orinda turned and walked quickly back into the turret. Above the crenellations, she gave one last look out across the ocean, then descended.

The sun hugged the horizon now, and the puddles on the rampart were dark enough for her needs. She straddled one and took out the stone phial from the recesses of her tunic. As she let one drop fall, the Brazen Head animated. It watched the drop splash into the puddle and the reaction ripple out to the edges.

"You're wondering why you have to pass through Epama Epam like a gateway each time," said the Brazen Head.

"I was, that is, yes."

"Well, you *don't* have to, you know. You can go where you want to go directly from here or anywhere so long as that fluid holds out."

"Then why wouldn't I?" she asked.

"Direct doorways open both ways, and what lies there can then come here. The continuum of Epama serves as a buffer."

"Oh. You might have said earlier," she scolded it.

"You might have asked." It closed its eyes. It might not have been Soter, she thought, but the Brazen Head shared enough of his elliptical traits that she would never forget how he'd vexed her.

She stepped forward and sank as if into the great broad tower.

It was night and the sea-lane of Epama Epam was deserted. No one awaited her arrival this time. No one was celebrating her return. She supposed that by the perverse rules of this place, as she was neither a traveler to be tricked nor someone to whom they now owed anything, she was of no interest to them—not so much unwelcome as dismissed. Physically, at least it looked like Colemaigne again rather than the dusty prisons of Palipon.

Nevertheless, she'd no intention of staying long. She walked the street in search of a puddle of water, but could find no moisture on the stones. She went to the houses lining the lane and knocked on doors, but there were no answers. No one was about and no lights shone anywhere. It was as if everyone had gone someplace else. She recalled glimpsing the monstrous parade from Hyakiyako and wondered if all manner of unnatural things sooner or later must thread through here. By whatever name, it connected to everything else. The goddess had called it the world mountain, although Leodora could see nothing anywhere in Epama Epam that qualified as a mountain.

She finally abandoned the houses, crossed the lane to the railing, and peered over.

Below, stars twinkled back at her from a black tapestry of sky. The effect was not so unnerving as it had been in the day. Night made it seem a reflection as if an impossible liquid sky didn't lie above. "A dark reflection," said the Brazen Head.

She glanced at it but it had already gone back to sleep—or had she only heard its voice in her mind? How far away the undersky lay she couldn't be sure. Darkness made it appear as a void: It might be terribly close or else have no bottom, no dimension. She climbed over the railing, and stood on the narrow ledge of hard, glistening street. The darkness below did not reflect her. Faint stars floated there.

She drew out the phial on its cord, uncorked it, and poured a single drop into the night sky. Then she stood craned over the rail, expecting . . . something. The drop, she concluded, must be falling forever. After all, it wasn't *really* a reflection, was it? She resolved to go back to the houses, maybe break into one to get what she needed. She didn't like the idea much.

Then as she was about to climb over the rail to safety, the stars below rippled.

She craned her head back and stared.

A pure darkness unwound from directly beneath her. Swiftly it devoured or blotted out the stars. Nothing showed in it, nothing but emptiness: She had not yet fixed upon any destination. She didn't know the destination, didn't know how far along the journey the Agents might be, didn't know where Tophet might dwell. Nothing in Soter's confession had told her where the Destroyer might be now. How much more of Shadowbridge might he have devoured while she grew up on her little island? How many years remained before he banqueted in the long house of Tenikemac?

Meanwhile, the darkness below spread, absorbing all. She could not wait.

Taking a deep breath, she stepped off the ledge and into the sky that was no longer sky. As to a destination, she said only, "Diverus." She held him in her thoughts, his face in the darkness ahead, remembering him with his eyes closed as he played some tune that had absorbed him, his fingers delicate upon the shawm. Down and down she fell, knowing all the while that down was up, that everything about this journey was inverted. With no surface below drawing her to it, she seemed to hover, immersed now in the blackness that had pushed the stars aside. And then she passed through a gossamer surface she could not see.

Her feet touched something solid. Instinctively, she bent her knees to absorb the compression of landing, even though it was gentle. She settled in a crouch like a tumbler, coiled to spring and roll if need be, but there was no need.

Rising, she found herself inside a small room with a low and solid ceiling through which she must have passed despite no evidence of it. An empty pad lay on the floor for a bed, and upon it were shackles. A prisoner's cell, then.

Light spilled in from a small porthole in the wall, and that combined with a vague sense of rocking motion told her she was on board a ship.

The view through the porthole was of a shifting gray fog behind which towered sheer walls, so high that she couldn't see the crest from there.

In turning, she kicked something that clittered across the floor. She picked it up—a flat reed set in a jagged cylinder of wood. She turned it in her hands, not recognizing it immediately. The reed had been scraped unevenly, and the whole piece had obviously broken off something larger. She realized then that she held part of the shawm that Diverus played. It looked as if someone had stepped on it.

She glanced at the bed again, imagining him shackled there. The mouthpiece of the shawm had drawn her, even though Diverus was no longer here. She had arrived too late to spirit him away mid-voyage.

With great care she opened the door and entered a corridor leading past other small rooms and out into a galley strewn with clay pots and jugs, bottles and cups. Curiously none of these objects looked used. The bottles, full of wine, were corked and wax-sealed; the pots were dusty. A door on the far side of the galley led her up onto the deck of the ship.

The rails and masts were lacquered black. At the stern, red bulbous lanterns hung like two extinguished eyes off a wing-shaped taffrail. The place she had just emerged from was a foredeck house. A ladder ran up the side of it. She climbed high enough to look across the top. A curious waist-high cylinder protruded from the center of the foredeck, looking something like a capstan, but at a location that made no sense to her.

She climbed the rest of the way up and went to it. Recessed in the top was an elaborately etched brass plate. She traced a finger across the black lines in it, which fanned out from a second, smaller pocket in the lower half of the plate. Other, curving lines intersected the rays, and at the top of the circle was a kind of gnomon on a swiveling needle. The small niche at the bottom was empty, but seemed intended to hold some object smaller than her palm. She rubbed her finger on the projecting gnomon, then pushed at it. The ship abruptly canted, and she pulled her hand back. The ship settled against the jetty again, and its lines went slack. Whatever this was, the device exercised control over the ship. She left it and walked to the prow.

The ship had sailed into a channel of some sort. High walls loomed everywhere, curving out of sight in both directions, suggesting that they'd sailed into a giant's labyrinth. The ship was moored at the end of a jetty, one of three that lay like huge fingers upon the surface of the water. Two additional boats were tied up at the others, and the three jetties led to a single pier running along another stretch of wall. She could just make out the zigzag of steps leading up, up into fog.

She reached into her tunic, clutched the Brazen Head. "Where are we?" she asked.

The head yawned, showing its fangs. "At an end," it replied, as cryptic as ever.

"Might you unravel that?"

"All spirals," it told her, "come to an end. This is one such. Called Calcaria once upon a time, but no longer."

"The end of a spiral," she said in wonderment. Soter had told her that all the spirals on Shadowbridge began or ended in a helical span, which was why they were called spirals in the first place, but she had never reached one before. Spirals stretched far across the oceans before coming to an end. She imagined the nautiloid shape enclosing her, and wondered where the ship had entered the maze and how far she might be from where she'd begun.

"You are halfway across the infinite," the head told her as if she'd asked it aloud.

"Where is Diverus?"

The lion's brow creased. Its gold eyes shifted away from her. "He is above. A soul in torment. Another displaced." The eyes rolled back to her again. "Act wisely and take care to be Jax." It became still again.

She held it a moment longer to be certain it had finished riddling. She gnawed awhile on what that was supposed to mean, and finally reached into her tunic and pulled out her domino mask. Wrapping it around her face and the top of her head, she tied it firmly in back, tucked her hair into her cowl, and pulled the cowl up. She didn't know why the pendant thought it important, but she knew better than to disregard its advice.

She left the foredeck, then stepped up over the rail and down a plank to the jetty. Even from directly below, the end of the span seemed to rise up forever. All the same and however far, that was where she was going.

If the span that had once been Calcaria looked like anything at all, it looked like the first glimpse she'd had of Colemaigne, but in far worse condition. Here a powdery shale covered the surface and billowed with each step she took. Buildings, however they'd once stood, had decomposed into gritty heaps that made it seem she walked through an antediluvian graveyard of enormous creatures, their bulk decayed and deformed into mounds over skulls and ribs and long, broken limbs. And everywhere beside these grotesque heaps stood the statues. She knew too well how these statues had come to be, and what they really represented—the populace of the span caught forever in a final moment of terror, of trying to escape. The citizens of this span had been creatures reminiscent of Yemoja but with longer, thinner snouts, inhuman round eyes, and crested foreheads. Weaving through their various silent poses, she mourned not merely their obliteration but the eradication of their collective story of themselves, a world of tales that would now never be heard.

The only sound on that windless span was her feet crunching through the ruins. Unlike Colemaigne, nowhere here did any pristine structures remain, and no living creatures lurked among the groves of the pale dead.

Then, somewhere in the middle of the span, she turned a corner and stopped, amazed.

There, as if grown from the debris surrounding it, stood a stepped ziggurat of the same grayish white hue, except that this shape gleamed. Its curved edges were smooth and hard. Against the gloomy backdrop of fog the structure seemed an illusion, a place where the lowering clouds had congealed. Barely visible from here, a bluish dome capped its heights.

A great rectangular arch had been cut out of the lowest step of the ziggurat, an entrance so large it could have accommodated the Agents' abandoned ship in the harbor.

In no doubt of her destination, Leodora walked to the ziggurat.

No torches or lamps were visible, but the walls themselves gave off a glow, a phosphorescence that she'd seen before in sea creatures at night. The entrance became a ramp. She had no choice but to ascend, though her legs were already tired from the climb onto the span. She found it odd that the ramp took her up without any access to lower levels, of which there surely had to be at least three or four. Instead it rose steadily until she reached a landing that opened upon a chamber so vast she couldn't see the far side of it. Ahead, light poured down from the blue dome she'd seen. It made her feel that she was moving through water. She thought of Oceanus and his pool of the true heart, but this was nothing so benign.

Furniture and objects lay scattered everywhere—benches, rugs, draperies, hookahs, filigreed trays and stands, painted amphorae, faience bottles, and real statuary—a treasure hoard taken from spans too numerous to count, the final remains of whole worlds devoured and destroyed in Tophet's passing.

Far back, and directly under the blue dome if the color was any indication, stood a dais shrouded by gauzy curtains that seemed to pulse with the glow of the dome. There was movement behind the thin fabric. What lay there she couldn't tell; she started toward it.

Almost immediately, on her left there was movement, rhythmic and flowing. Various furnishings stood between her and a clear view of the source, a tall rectangular shape.

At first she didn't know what she was seeing. Then as understanding dawned on her, she gasped, and quickly wove her way around the various piled treasures and toward the object. The impossible object.

Her first impression had been that the thing was a tall mirror. Its frame strangely carved, it stood on a pedestal of granite. Reflected or held somehow in its surface was a room virtually identical to this one, filled with similar treasures, but not quite the same ones nor in the same place.

Amongst the treasures wandered an image of *herself.*

The image wore a gossamer white gown that left her taut but scarred belly exposed. A jewel-studded collar circled her throat, but the jewels could hardly compete with her flaming red hair. Coming right up to it, Leodora saw that this near twin "reflection" was barefoot and wore bangles with tiny bells around her ankles. A heavy belt of garnets pulled the skirt low on her hips. The image in the glass did not match her own movements at all. It was weaving, dancing around the room to some tune she could not hear. She stood directly in front of it, and the image looked straight at her—but its focus was past her, as if the dancer scanned some distant landscape. But then as if something had caught her eye, she slowed in her dance and sashayed through the piles of treasure, coming right up to the glass until they stood face-to-face. They might have been watching each other had the other's forlorn gaze only found her.

Leodora felt as if she were peering into the future, perhaps ten years from now if those years served to take a heavy toll on her, deadened her features, killed her spirit. But by then she had noted the many differences between them and knew the truth.

"Mother," she whispered. The word cracked, spilling anguish.

For one horrible instant it seemed the image had heard her. The green eyes stared straight into her eyes. She pressed her hand to the glass as if she might reach through it, but Leandra's eyes did not see the hand, or her. She recalled the man who had come upon her lying on the beach of Bouyan and cried out "Witch!" in the misapprehension that Leandra had returned. She understood now that in a sense Leandra had. "I can see you," she told the image. "I can—"

"She doesn't hear you," said a voice behind her. Even as she started to turn, two of Tophet's Agents snaked through the piled treasures and grabbed her by the arms. A third, the one who'd spoken, circled around and eyed her menacingly. "What manner of creature strays into Chaos's realm?" he asked.

Her heartbeat pounded and for an instant reason left her, she felt undone. Then it was as if all the terror fell away: These creatures had taken Diverus, and a surge of anger doused her fear. She answered him: "One who resents being misrepresented by fools."

The Agent massaged his chin with thumb and forefinger. The one gripping her left arm asked, "What's she mean, Scratta?"

"What we already know—that the old man lied to us, and we've set about torturing the wrong captive."

Her heart sank. "Torturing?"

"What else are we to do when the boy can't provide Tophet with any stories other than his own? And it's a paltry thing at best, one for the weepers—a mother turned into a mermaid, the boy abandoned and sold into slavery, into supper for some demented afrits. I expect by now he's confided how he was rescued, but it's evident he's withholding, he really doesn't *know* any of the stories and so couldn't have used them to escape his fate."

"He's only a musician," she said.

Scratta smiled flatly. For a moment his eyes looked away from her, looked at some internal discomfort, and she suspected he was in trouble for having kidnapped the wrong person. Then he focused again upon her. "The god is not going to be pleased. Although *your* presence may ameliorate." He pointed at the curtained dais beyond. "Take Jax to him now."

"What? This one's Jax, too?"

Scratta almost tried to explain, then sighed. "Yes, this one's Jax, too. Take her to his lordship."

The two dragged her past Scratta. From behind he called, "Wait!" Then he stepped up to her and yanked back the hood. Her red braid tumbled out. Scratta sucked in his breath. "Oh," he said. "Is it possible?" "You're no clever *boy*, but you are Jax, the masked storyteller. I do see. You had no choice but to hide your real self, not from us but from all of them. Why, on some spans, they'd have thrown you off the side if they knew." He tucked the braid back and pulled her hood up again, nodded for them to continue.

They dragged her among the treasure trove to the dais. Closer, she saw that what she'd taken to be more statuary was in fact a line of the round-eyed and long-snouted natives, lushly appareled in a rainbow of surcoats and coathardies, both males and females adorned with heavy wigs. They watched her dragged past them, never moving, their expressions an admixture of silent horror and supplication—but what were they begging her to do? Free them, or cause no trouble and give in? At least, she thought, the god hadn't killed *all* of them, though they had been transformed like the Agents into something other than their original substance. They might have been standing there like that since the day Tophet arrived and took away their span.

Behind the curtains, beneath the blue glow, the treasures had been pushed back, leaving a broad uncluttered space in the center.

A three-sided puppeteer's screen had been set up before them, the white square of its center burning like a blind rectangular eye. In front of it, hanging from chains, was Diverus. His body, as naked as when he'd entered Oceanus's pool, ran with sweat, and he was babbling, his tormented words falling over themselves as if he couldn't keep up with what he had to say even though it was nonsense.

An Agent stood just behind him beside a brazier. He held a set of tongs from which something long and paper-thin dangled. She twisted in the grip of her captors as she recognized that it was skin.

The Agents hauled her around the end of the semi-circle. More of the natives in their forced finery stood there as if watching a play. Some of them wept silently, their terror palpable. At the midpoint of the group, upon a high-backed throne, sat a figure in a dark robe that might have been green under other light. To the side of him a naked and ice-pale bald female held up a pole that was like a gibbet. From the crosspiece at the top of the pole hung a golden oval mask portraying a sun god's cherubic face. It was at least five times the size of a human face, a sun disk. The attendant herself was either blind or else had eyes that were utterly black and reflected nothing. From behind the enormous mask, a voice that buzzed like a hive of hornets said, "What is this, Scratta?"

"Lord," answered Scratta. "I believe I have solved the puzzle of Jax."

Behind the mask, Tophet drummed long fingertips on the arm of the throne. The fingers were shiny, and of the same blue as the dome overhead. "That is good," Tophet replied, "because this one has passed the point of making any sense, and all we can do is finish stripping the surface off him for the mere pleasure of doing it, not in order to learn anything further." Another pause. "So what is the puzzle's solution, hmm?"

"Lord, *this* is Jax." Scratta turned, and the two behind him dragged Leodora forward.

"Well. Is that right?"

She didn't realize he was asking her until Scratta raised a hand as if to cuff her. "Answer him."

"Yes," she said. "I'm Jax. The one you're torturing is my musician and I would like him back intact, if it wouldn't be too much trouble."

The laughter began low, as inhuman as his speech, like metal grinding against metal, ending finally in the words, "A female puppeteer. That's unheard of, isn't it?"

"Lord, *we* have never encountered one to bring before you. Storytellers, yes, but not a puppeteer, much less one compared to—" He faltered.

Tophet seemed not to notice. "But how did she escape your attention, Scratta?"

"Lord?" Scratta asked, the word rimed with fear.

"She must have come here on your boat along with this useless creature. How did she elude all of you?"

"I don't know, Lord. We saw no sign of her."

"Perhaps your eyes are going in your dotage, hmm? I may have to consider that it's time you were freed from your position, Scratta."

From the way he stiffened, Leodora could tell that *freed* in this instance didn't mean anything as pleasant as it sounded. "I shouldn't care to leave your service, my Lord Chaos."

"Mmmm," Tophet answered equivocally. "So the real Jax has come to rescue a musician. I'm impressed you didn't flee. Most are disinclined when they receive my invitation."

"I suppose that's why you lie and promise them great wealth?"

"Who have you been talking to?"

She shrugged. "I was told you were looking for a storyteller and that you pay handsomely for a good performance."

Tophet shifted upon his throne. "Where would you have heard such a thing?"

"From . . . oh, what was that name?" She seemed to be asking Scratta, who gave her an anxious look. "Oh, yes, now I recall. Bardsham."

The entire group became a diorama in blue. For a stretch of moments, no one moved. Only Diverus made a sound, whimpering, half out of his mind. She desperately wanted to go to him, but knew they would both die if she did. She had to stand her ground and play this out.

The buzzing voice of the Lord of Chaos slashed the air, dismissing her claim: "Bardsham is long dead. He told you nothing."

"Yet your Agents here sought that name in seeking me. How is it they were thus confused?"

"It was your *skill* that confused the masses. *They* compared you to him, in fact thought you had to be him. Of course I—we—knew better. Bardsham was thrown off the mid-tower of a span just like this one, long ago. A great height, wasn't it, Scratta?"

"Thrown?" she asked. "Not turned into stone like all the others? Was it because he *knew* the story? The story you fear?"

Chaos rose up. "I fear nothing! And why am I explaining myself to this puppeteer?" he shouted. "Scratta?"

"If I may," Leodora interjected, then waited for the tension to dampen. "The story you requested as a proof from him" — she pointed to Diverus— "he couldn't provide you with it."

"Your musician. You said."

"Whereas I am a collector of stories from across all of Shadowbridge. And I happen to know the one with which you're obsessed. The one that got Bardsham killed, because he knew it, too, and surely would have spread it everywhere. Just as I intend to do once I leave here."

Behind the hanging mask, Tophet hissed. "You ensure with your words that you'll *never* leave here. You surely must understand that."

Instead of answering, Leodora gestured at the stacked undaya cases. "You've kindly provided me my puppets, too, so I will give you a tale to hold you rapt and you will give us safe passage come morning."

Tophet the Destroyer chuckled. "I've seen hundreds of your kind, and most of them you'll find strewn among my possessions—the ones we haven't left behind. You are brazen for someone so young and untested. You had best hope your talents match your presumption. Even then—"

"Lord." Scratta filled that single syllable with all his misgivings.

"Yes," Tophet answered and likewise in a syllable dismissed those doubts. "I'll have her shadowplay now. What is your concern in it? You failed even to collect the right individual, tricked by an old sot."

Scratta bowed his head. He looked at Leodora from beneath his brow. His lips stretched in what might have been a retributive smirk. "Yes, Lord," he answered softly.

Leodora didn't move.

"Well?" Tophet asked.

"My musician?" she said.

"One of you get him down."

"I'll need water for his wounds. Wine for him to drink."

"Brazen," he said again, and she unconsciously wrapped one hand around her pendant to keep it from speaking up.

"I don't *have* to perform. We might instead take a meal with all your friends, Lord Tophet."

His fingers squeezed the arms of the throne. "Do you appreciate at all to whom you speak in this manner?"

"I'm aware of your opinion," she said.

Another pause followed, and then he sighed. "You remind me of someone, girl, who defied me even though she drowned in fear. Why don't you remove that mask and show us your face?"

"Perhaps after my performance, and you can show me yours."

Diverus, lowered from the chains, collapsed on the floor. They had torn three strips the length of his back. She could hardly keep from screaming at the sight of what they'd done to him. He babbled softly with foam and vomit on his lips.

"I doubt he'll play you any tunes today," Scratta said to her.

"Maybe not, but he won't suffer any further because of me."

The pale Agent shook his head slowly. "The day is long from over, storyteller."

"You're wrong," she argued. "The day's nearly done." She carefully took hold of Diverus. His eyes fluttered open and focused on her a moment. He breathed her name and she shushed him. If Scratta heard the name, he didn't respond. She held him to her, raised him to his feet, and then supported him while they shambled around the broad puppet screen.

An attendant delivered a goblet, a bowl of water, and a cloth. Leodora directed him to place them on the performer's stool under the burning lantern that cast the silk screen in glaring light—too much light. She eased Diverus against the stool, where he stood leaning, his legs trembling but holding him up. She walked back into view of Tophet and his terrified audience, and struggled to remove the lid from the larger puppet case. Then she pulled it around the side of the screen. The second one she lifted as it was and carried out of sight. She stood the case on end directly in back of the lantern, where it threw a long shadow across the polished floor.

She took the bowl from the stool, rolled the cloth in it and then washed his face and mouth, soaked the cloth again and squeezed some of the water over Diverus's back. He cried out, then hung his head and muttered, "I'm sorry, I'm sorry." Again she hushed him. Then she turned away with the bowl and crouched down and poured the rest of the water in the stripe of shadow cast by the puppet case. A few moments longer she knelt there, her back to Diverus.

She set aside the bowl and stood. Beside her, the other puppet case lay open. Glancing down, she found that the figure of Meersh lay on top of the pile. She picked it up and carried it to Diverus.

"Hold this," she told him. Then gingerly she wrapped her arms around his waist and guided him to the standing case.

Either he realized or saw what she intended and tried to struggle. "No, Leodora, no," but she covered his mouth with her hand.

"Epama Epam," she said. "Go into the pool. The goddess will help you. She's called Yemoja."

"No. I have to—"

"Do it, Diverus, you'll die if you don't. You're dying right now. And someone has to look after Meersh." She lifted him, and he hadn't enough strength to defy her.

She pressed her lips to his, tasting his sweat, his pain like cold fire. "Good-bye, my love," she whispered in his ear, and then let go.

The moment he was gone, she pulled the case aside and laid it down. There was only a shiny puddle of water on the floor, a many-colored oil sliding snake-like upon its surface.

She opened the second case. The flat-piled puppets waited for her to bring them to life. She crossed to the larger case.

"What is wrong, storyteller?" called Tophet the Destroyer. "Can't get your musician to play?" Then, "Where is my story?"

"It's here," she answered. From the larger case, she took out the puppets and set them aside, then reached in and tugged the ribbon, lifting the lid on the secret compartment.

A hiss of surprise escaped her. She took a step back.

In his cavity in the case, the Coral Man had turned to dust.

Kneeling beside the open case, she sorted through the puppets but kept staring at the powdered coral. In the middle of it something black sparkled in the lantern light. She turned from the puppets and dusted the thing off. It wasn't very big, a knobbly fused lump like a clump of beach sand that had been struck and transformed by lightning. She smiled grimly. Her last lingering doubts about the Coral Man had been banished.

Rising, she carried a piece of setting with her to the stool.

"I want my story!" yelled Tophet like an angry child.

"Here, then," she replied, and she hooked the flat strip of scenery onto the screen. It cast the shadow of a rough surface, representing a span, any span, all spans.

"This tale," she announced, "took place long ago and far away in the season of the monsoon on a span called Dyauspitar."

There was a commotion on the far side of the screen.

"Dyauspitar sat low, a curl hovering just over shallow marshy water. Gnarled and twisted trees grew on either side of it in incalculable numbers, and the people harvested the wood for their every need. The buildings were made of strips of this wood woven with great skill, houses like giant baskets that could flex and bend against the terrible winds that came with the season of monsoons."

While she spoke, she lifted up a handful of the dust and threw it at the screen. It burst like a cloud into the air, and as it floated between the lantern and the screen it created an illusion of soft rain. Then she took the goblet of wine and flung the contents across the screen, and the sky burst crimson.

"Stop!" cried Tophet. "Stop it now!"

She only lifted another handful of dust and flung it into the air above herself. Then she grabbed the strap of the large undaya case and hauled it, empty of puppets, around the screen in front of the throne.

"You will not tell that story!" commanded Chaos.

"Why?" she asked. "It's the one you've asked to hear, time and again. From every single storyteller you kidnapped and killed—all of these petrified forms surrounding us—you anticipated that story, the only one that ever concerned you. Bardsham with his tales of Meersh, of girls who gave up their arms for their fathers, of brothers who fought over magical gifts out of a Dragon Bowl—you didn't really care about any of those. There was only the one, and nobody knew it. But you put them to death anyway, just in case. As someone said to me not so long ago, how many stories we keep is the secret everyone wants to know."

She tipped the box and poured the dust of the Coral Man across the floor, into a large ring. Setting it down, she stepped into the ring and sat down, cross-legged.

Tophet was on his feet, and the blind attendant had somehow lost her sense of things, had forgotten him. His true face glared at her over the golden mask. As Soter had described, it was a gruesome war of faces, a horrible roiling, writhing coil of slaughtered features.

"Dyauspitar was home to a priesthood," she continued, "dedicated to the god Dyaus, who had once been a celebrated sky-god, until a collective of demigods struck him down for his excesses and drove him into the sea. That span, according to legend, was built along the spine of Dyaus, which kept the waters shallow there. The truth is, the ousted god embraced his submarine exile and gave himself a new name: Oceanus.

"I doubt you knew that, but it hardly matters, for this tale doesn't concern him anyway."

"You will stop now, storyteller."

She stared at his terrible face and replied, "I think I will *begin* now." She pushed back the cowl, caught the thong in her hair, and unwound it. Then she clutched the mask and dragged it from her face.

At the sight of her, Tophet sat down upon his throne again. "The child." His voice cracked. Then more loudly: "I don't have to stay for this."

"Well, you can't leave now. You've breathed in my dust, and you'll stay put for the story that you've ensured no one could know." She gathered another handful of coral dust.

"Leandra," he tried to say, but the dust stole his speech.

The name cut Leodora and angrily she flung more dust at him, but when she spoke, her voice was calm and controlled. "On Dyauspitar when a child reached the end of his childhood, he endured a ritual of passage where his soul was removed for three days from his body and for three days he lay dead while his soul entered an animal selected by a class of priests known as enchanters. And when the spirit of the boy was put back in his body, it was mixed with that animal spirit and he was a man. This was the ritual of manhood and it had gone on since Dyaus fell. It was so perilous that the priests who could perform it were few.

"Our story concerns one of them, whose name was Auuenau. He'd come to the order early, an orphan, and his training had begun well before he was ready to pass through that ritual. He was better versed in mysteries of the enchanters than most of his elders. He knew, for instance, that one member of his brotherhood guarded a cache of scrolls containing the secrets of Dyaus, which had been found floating upon the water after he fell. In them were secrets of life and death and eternity. Had the archivists of the fabled Library of Shadowbridge known of its existence, they would have taken the cache from Dyauspitar to protect the world. Even the gods of Edgeworld would never have bestowed such knowledge upon any mortal, else risk the destruction of the world.

"Auuenau coveted the hidden knowledge, and for years he collected hints, clues, and inadvertent comments that knit together to lead him to the scrolls. They were concealed in a rough stone kist in the order's ossuary.

"He was careful to present his interest in the ossuary as an expression of reverence. He tended to the bones of his forebears. One by one, however, he removed the scrolls, replacing each with a blank, until he had them all. He hid them in the cistern inside his house.

"The house was filled with seashells and coral and desiccated sea creatures that he'd collected, some shells so large that it took two hands to lift them. He shared the small house with an apprentice under his tutelage, and out of fear of discovery he had to limit his examination of the scrolls to the times when the apprentice was absent. Thus he read with the intention of memorizing every detail of every spell and ritual. In those texts he found the source of the enchanters' power to remove the soul at puberty. The grander shape of the simple rituals he had learned was explicated, and soon enough he had the means to expand upon the limited powers granted the enchanters—to cleave body and soul completely, potentially achieving true immortality. No one can say what might have happened if he had accomplished this as he intended, unhindered. Unnoticed.

"On Dyauspitar when the monsoon arrived, everyone retreated to their houses and remained inside until the storm abated. It was called the Month of Cold Rice. To go outside during the monsoon was to risk disappearing forever. Although ropes were strung from end to end, and looped around bollards down the main avenues, these were no guarantees against the screaming winds and the crashing waves. Let go for even a moment and you would be blown into the trees or over their tops and out to sea. Only a fool ventured out during the monsoon. As the storm began, Auuenau sent his apprentice out on a fabricated mission to the far end of the span, from which he could not possibly return before its full force struck. Thus safely isolated by the storm, Auuenau assumed he could achieve what he'd read in the scrolls.

"To begin he had to score a specific and intricate pattern into the woven floor of his house. Drawing it first with a stick of charcoal, he discovered that it took up almost the entire space. He had to tear up his bedding, and shove aside tables and cushions. His collection of shells and dead sea creatures he piled up in the corners. Then began the task of carving the pattern he'd drawn, using a mallet and small chisel. This proved to be exhausting. It took him days to chisel out its symmetrical curves and whorls. All the while the storm pushed the walls and roof so that the house seemed to breathe in and out like a living sea creature itself, with curved window eyes and slatted ribs.

"At last he completed it. He rested, he couldn't say how long, for the monsoon made everything dark, everything the same, so that night and day melted together. But finally he stuffed the scrolls into the front of his tunic and began to walk the pattern. At various points he was to stop and recite certain text. Most of it was in arcane languages he did not know the meaning of, forcing him carefully to sound out the words, the phrases. What the scrolls failed to mention was how enervating each recitation was, as if at each stage some part of him was siphoned off. He found that he could not go any farther than the first two stops upon the pattern that first day. Having arrived at the second branch, he had to retreat, his legs barely holding him up as he backed carefully along the line he'd walked, and out again. Then, in the corner, he collapsed, sleeping as if dead.

"Hours later, perhaps the next day, when he awoke, he entered again, finding that he could pass the points where he had already recited from the scrolls. He entered deeper into the pattern, making it through the third and fourth stages before he had to withdraw again and rest.

"The storm never let up. It shrieked and shook the house, and the walls and roof continued to flex. By the time he entered the fifth stage, the outer darkness seemed to have entered the house and penetrated him as well. He could feel the blood in his veins going gray, then black. It seemed he'd been walking this pattern for eternity. There were places along it, so the scrolls claimed, where a wrong step could suck him into nonexistence, into some other world, or turn him inside out. He couldn't remember how many times he'd backed out and come back in, how many times he'd passed out from exhaustion, nor when he'd last eaten. The swirling pattern of spirals was no larger than this room, this hut, yet it seemed to have expanded to the size of Shadowbridge itself. As he cleared the tenth and final stage and dizzily walked toward the center, he sensed a second self beside him, an umbra in his shape walking at his shoulder. Precariously he stepped, balanced on one leg, and then set the other foot down in the center of the pattern.

"He had arrived.

"Auuenau glanced sidelong at the dark self sharing the center with him. It hadn't gone away, but turned and looked back at him with blackness for eyes, and in the blackness stars sparkled.

"He stood, waiting for something explosive—for the fabric of space to tear apart, for the gods to unveil themselves and embrace him, for the sense of cleaving, for anything to tell him that the transformation had occurred. There was nothing. He dangled in the wedge between wholeness and split. The thing hadn't happened but hung on the brink. Exhausted, he fumbled for the final scroll again, peeled it apart, and read. What had he forgotten? Nothing. He was sure of it. He scanned the text, his vision blurring. He rubbed his eyes, stretched the scroll out again. And there, amid the warnings of dire consequences awaiting he who failed to follow the path to the end, *there* was the final opaque phrase that had to be recited from the center of the pattern. He laughed at his simple foolishness. Then he read the lines, whatever they meant, in whatever language it was.

"The darkness closed in from all sides. It circled the

pattern, pressed down from above. The shade beside him began to spin. He watched tendrils drawn out of him, pulled into the whirling thing, which grew smaller as it spun faster. Warmth left him, beginning in the core of him and withdrawing to his extremities. Behind it came a sharp chill, like the touch of marble. When the last warmth left him, the tendrils vanished and the spinning form compressed still further, until it was a small flickering thing, hard, burnished and knurled. He reached out to close his hand around it . . . at which point the door to his house flew open.

"The head of his order stood there, clinging to the sides of the door, and clinging to him was Auuenau's apprentice. The apprentice let go one hand and pointed. 'See?' he cried.

"Auuenau, standing with an unfurled scroll in one hand and the pearl of his soul gripped in the other, could only shout, 'No!' Even as he said this, the room changed. The chaos of the monsoon was pulled through the doorway and into the pattern. It sucked the hapless priest and apprentice with it, whirled them like dolls around the pattern and straight at him. He watched them scream as the forces of the storm and of the magic he'd unleashed tore them apart, shredding skin from bones and grinding the bones to dust. He howled and the dust of their deaths poured into his open mouth, down inside him. What was cold as marble became as jagged as fishhooks within. The floor beneath him was disintegrating. The pattern itself turned to blue crystal, flowing out from him. Still he clung to the twisted pearl that was his separate soul. The scrolls had made it clear that he could not leave the pattern so long as he held on to it, yet he dared not let it go with disaster unfolding about him. He stretched his arm across the pattern, and the only thing he could reach was a nautilus shell in the heap of those he'd collected. He dropped the pearl that was his soul into the shell, listened to it rattle through the chambers and into the center.

"He found that he could move then and walked quickly back around the pattern. He tucked the shell into his robe. The other scrolls blew and tumbled about the room. He dashed to grab them as he balanced on the path, but they were being torn apart, too, and he managed only to snatch shreds. The knowledge contained within them was lost forever. Even had he wanted to, Auuenau could not now undo what he'd set in motion, which his apprentice had disordered; but he did not want to undo it. His very substance had by then become Chaos, and what was happening around him was his doing.

"He exited the crystalline pattern and from the doorway watched as it began to unthread, the scored boards torn loose and drawn down into the center. Then the floor outside the vortex broke apart, whirling around it. Shards of crystal gashed him, embedded in his flesh. The woven walls of the building shredded and fell in, every moment the great whirlpool growing, expanding as if unappeasable. Auuenau remained in the avenue for only a moment before the storm seized him and yanked him off his feet. Instinctively he clutched a guide-rope, but in doing so he let go of the final scroll, and it flitted away on the wind.

"The surface of the span of Dyauspitar cracked beneath him and collapsed into the maw of the whirlpool. Like the dark form that had arisen beside him, that core seemed shot with stars.

"He dragged himself along the rope, and the darkness circled after him. The rope came suddenly unmoored and flung him into the air, all the way to the opposite side of the span. He struck the rail, doubled over it, but hung on. Below lay a skiff, anchored and storm-tossed. As the span shook apart, he leapt over the rail and down into it. It was half full of water and he fell, but he untied the lines and with a long pole pushed away. The edge of the span split behind him and the wind threw flinders at him. Between the piers the water swirled, capturing the collapsing fragments in its force, sucking them in, and like a fire fueled by new wood, the whirlpool expanded across the water.

"Auuenau tried to pole his skiff away, but he couldn't. The thing had caught him, and helplessly he began to whirl around it, faster and faster, riding the crest but certain to follow everything else down into the star-shot blackness of eternity in the maw of the pool.

"He comprehended suddenly what would satisfy it. As he clung with one hand to the side of the skiff, he tore the small shell out of his robe as if tearing out his own heart. He stared at the striped nautilus and understood that he and the whirlpool were of one substance now, one purpose shared. It was his shadow self, rapacious and unappeasable unless he gave it the one thing it wanted. He lifted the shell, and the pearl rattled inside it. He grinned sickly, and that was the first moment when he felt the faces of those he'd absorbed moving across his own—the features of the monk and his apprentice.

"He tossed the shell over the side and into the mouth of the maelstrom. He didn't even watch it vanish, but set down the pole and lay back to let events play out.

"The whirlpool drank his soul, and at once it shrank beneath him.

"Within moments Auuenau's skiff was circling a patch of foam, of nothing, of water indistinguishable from any other. Of the span of Dyauspitar all that remained was the ridge of rock that had supported it, the spine of Dyaus. The rest, all of his brethren, all of the people, were gone, absorbed, the fuel that fed his immortality, their faces moving, intertwining like eels.

"He, the embodiment of Chaos, began to laugh. He looked at his hands, his arms, his skin transformed into something harder than flesh.

"Light rain sprayed over him, but the winds had ceased their howl and sun-speckled clouds floated overhead. Even the storm had been sucked down into the horror of the force he'd unleashed. Lying back in the skiff, he let the currents of the ocean take him wherever they would. He was deathless and fearsome now. He needed a new name for his new self, and by the time he reached another spiral, he had one, extracted from ancient legends in a language he didn't know. It was, he believed, the name of a god: Tophet the Destroyer, the Lord of Chaos. Thus Auuenau became Chaos, and no one the wiser save for another god whose span he'd destroyed."

She reached into the dust and picked up the gnarled burnished pearl in her fist.

Casually, she added, "If you like I could repeat the whole tale for you with puppets," she said. "It's always better with puppets."

When he said nothing, she gathered herself up and walked to the throne. No one tried to stop her. No one moved at all. The golden mask hung before her, his last protection.

"When you had Bardsham's puppet cases brought here—you didn't know that, did you? That these are his?—when you did that, you brought the very thing you feared, not just the story of it. Your tale, like the whirlpool in it, has spun full circle. After all, you never were truly a god."

She went around the mask. He sat defiantly, but his head was tilted away as if in fear of her. His robe had fallen open, and she saw that his body was covered in spurs and sharp splinters of bone that had pushed out of his skin. She stepped up to the end of the throne, between his knees. He reached out suddenly, triumphantly, and grabbed her wrist. She winced, stiffening at the frigid pain that burned to her marrow. But then suddenly the flow reversed and a charge ran out of her fist and into him.

His fingers leapt free of her and he bucked violently with a great cracking gasp.

She opened her palm and the knobby black pearl was gone.

Tophet's head began to vibrate from side to side faster and faster until she couldn't distinguish the awful features anymore, the millions of faces blurring into a smudge upon the air. The blur flung off sparks that spun through the room. She recalled the story the Ondiont snake had told her of the bride of Death, who had captured souls like tiny lights; and of the brothers who were turned to rock with a final wish to be worshipped; of the thousand stories of people who wished for something before they understood the price of it.

The sparks flicked and vanished, flicked and vanished, around her, past her, through her. They pitted the gold mask behind her where they hit it until it became as thin as mesh. And when the last one burst forth and died, the body of Tophet stopped moving. His indurate form had become a dried husk, a gaping mummified thing without a face.

She stepped back from the corpse and brushed against the huge mask. It fell, slipping past her shoulders as she turned to see the figure of the attendant stumble and release the pole on which it hung. The mask bent when it hit, and slid across the floor like a leaf skimming a pond. The pole clattered after it. The blind attendant caught her balance against Scratta. Grinning, he in turn rocked to and fro and then fell, shattering when he hit the floor. All around Leodora, the Agents of Chaos had become stone that within moments had begun to crumble away. The force that had knit them together was gone.

Her hand where Tophet had grabbed her was burned white as if covered with powder, but it hadn't turned to stone. She looked at the people around her, the survivors of this span, who were too fearful yet to believe that the Destroyer was really gone. She stepped down from the throne and walked away, out from under the dome, and by the time she'd left the curtained dais behind, she was running, weaving back through his trove of treasures until she reached the mirror. In dread she approached it, hopeful that the magic behind this, too, had been banished; her heart swelled when she discovered it had not, and that her mother still agitatedly filled the frame.

"Why didn't she go?" she asked as she touched the pendant.

The Brazen Head awoke. "His magic was cast in the glass, independent of him, as with the dome. Magic needs magic to be undone."

"How do I set her free? I can't leave her this way."

"What is she?"

"My mother."

"But if I say your mother is long dead, then what does she become?"

"I don't know. A reflection."

"A reflection," he repeated. And he fell silent again.

She stared around her, turning in a circle. Finally she looked up through the blue dome and shouted, "You knew all along! All of you! Shumyzin! Cardeo!" Her voice echoed through the vast chamber and came back to her unanswered. The most important questions were the ones they never asked.

She gripped the phial. It had to be nearly empty. The drop that had rescued Diverus had taken forever to spill from it. She couldn't pour the last drops on the upright mirror and couldn't tilt the mirror on its stony base. Instead she held out her hand and tipped the phial over her palm. Two drops splashed out.

For a moment she hesitated. The air filled with distant cries of "Jax!" as if the crowds from the Terrestre were clamoring for more; but she knew it was the survivors of Calcaria, freed and seeking after their savior.

"Good-bye, Mother," she said, then she wiped her hand over the glass, smearing the oily drops across the reflection from top to bottom. She stepped back as the image in the mirror rippled and faded. The mirror turned black as a void.

"Diverus!" Leodora called. She reached into and then stepped through the darkness.

Part 5: The Puppets Of Bardsham

Chapter 8
Epilogue

There is a span on Shadowbridge called Calcaria that claims it possesses Bardsham's original puppets. The span is terribly ancient, so old that its Dragon Bowl has long since fallen into the sea, and most of the span is composed of uninhabited ruins. The puppets, however, are on display in a museum that is a great towering ziggurat of a structure like no other on the span, and which lends credence to the story they tell there of how the span fell into ruin. The people of that span—tall, slender creatures with prominent snouts and eyes like black marbles—tell a story about how they were once tormented, tortured, and held captive by a fiendish god named Chaos, and how the ghost of Bardsham's wife came out of a mirror and destroyed him with a story, leaving the puppets behind as a tribute to those who'd suffered under his yoke. The mirror from which she emerged is a dull and unpolished surface that no longer reflects anything at all, save in a lower corner, where a single handprint seems to have melted into the glass. It is also on display there, beside a pocked and damaged mask that the Calcarians claim to have been the face of Chaos.

This local tale would be dismissed as pure fantasy were it not for the puppets themselves: Bardsham is not known to have performed on spirals anywhere near Calcaria, and in truth most of the other nearby spans are dead ruins, too, peopled only by statues, the cause of their abandonment likewise attributed to the same shattered god. The puppets, however, are quite real. Detractors of the story point out that there's no puppet of Meersh in the collection, and we all know that Meersh was

Bardsham's signature figure. Of course, the people have an explanation for that, too: that Bardsham took his puppet with him when Chaos had him thrown off the span into the sea—if indeed that's what happened to Bardsham.

It's a perplexing story to be sure.

On the other side of the world, far across the Adamantine Ocean, the spans sing stories of a girl puppeteer, who followed in Bardsham's footsteps but was even greater than he. Some say she was his daughter, and others that she was a goddess who healed the span of Colemaigne. What happened to her is not known. At the height of her powers, she stopped performing and disappeared. Many there are who believe she and Bardsham were so skillful that the gods of Edgeworld whisked them away and they live now as immortals for the entertainment of the eternals. Stories of her—of a puppeteer called Jax, who grew up on an island and brought Colemaigne back to life—are now performed far and wide in pantomimes and puppet shows, recitations and comedies. No one really knows any of it for certain, but then, not all mysteries are explained.

About the Author

GREGORY FROST is an Asimov's Readers' Award-winning author whose work runs the full fantasy gamut. His novels and stories have been finalists for the World Fantasy, Stoker, Nebula, Hugo, James Tiptree, International Horror Guild and Theodore Sturgeon awards. His latest works include The RHYMER trilogy (Baen Books https://www.baen.com), which Jonathan Maberry proclaimed as "the best fantasy series currently running!"; the short story collection BEYOND HERE BE MONSTERS (Fairwood Press https://fairwoodpress.com); and the horror novel, THE SECRET HOUSE (JournalStone https://journalstone.com/). Author John Kessel's review of The Secret House concludes: "I can't imagine a novel published this year more deserving of awards attention."

About Book View Café

Book View Café is a professional authors' publishing cooperative offering DRM-free ebooks in multiple formats to readers around the world. With authors in a variety of genres including mystery, romance, fantasy, and science fiction, Book View Café has something for everyone.

Book View Café is good for readers because you can enjoy high-quality DRM-free ebooks from your favorite authors at a reasonable price.

Book View Café is good for writers because 90% of the profit goes directly to the book's author.

Book View Café authors include *New York Times* and *USA Today* bestsellers, Nebula, Hugo, National Reader's Choice, and Philip K. Dick Award winners, World Fantasy and Rita Award nominees, and winners and nominees of many other publishing awards.

BOOK VIEW CAFE

www.bookviewcafe.com

www.ingramcontent.com/pod-product-compliance
Lightning Source LLC
Chambersburg PA
CBHW032036050726
47590CB00001B/13

* 9 7 8 1 6 3 6 3 2 4 2 3 4 *